Acclaim for Gary Worthington's *India Treasures*:

Finalist for Book of the Year (Historical Fiction).

—ForeWord Magazine

"*India Treasures* is an order of magnitude better than most of the fiction we see for review.

"It has all the essentials, characterization, plot, locale, and first rank writing.

"Worthington creates an authentic ambience of time and place in India ancient and modern. He offers us a cast of believable flesh and blood characters who face realistic problems. He sets his scenes with authority and a grasp of detail.

"In short he has put together a very good book that is exciting even to our jaded taste."

—Rowse Reviews

"An engaging and entertaining sequence of eight dynamic novellas about Rajasthan and Northern India across the length of human history, all connected by a modern-day treasure hunt.

"Incorporating crucial events of Indian history seamlessly into the story, India Treasures brings the reader before the wisdom of the Buddha, the canvas of a medieval artist, the throne of the Sultan of Delhi, and many more wondrous places.

"An utterly absorbing historical. Highly recommended."

— The Bookwatch, Midwest Book Review

"This book is spellbinding and thought-provoking entertainment."

—Tacoma News Tribune

"I am truly impressed. The book is enticing, informative, gripping, descriptive without bogging down, fluid, and very stimulating. I will recommend it to everyone traveling to India."

—Step ´

God:
.nd
of Hindu
Institution

D1367542

India
Fortunes

INDIA FORTUNES: A NOVEL OF RAJASTHAN AND NORTHERN INDIA THROUGH PAST CENTURIES

Copyright © 2003 by Gary Worthington

Cover art, maps, illustrations, and book design by Gary Worthington

Published by TimeBridges Publishers LLC
1001 Cooper Point Road SW, Suite 140-#176
Olympia, WA 98502

On the World Wide Web:
http://www.TimeBridgesPublishers.com

ISBN 0-9707662-1-1 Hardcover
ISBN 0-9707662-3-8 Trade paperback

Library of Congress Control Number 2003093911

First U.S. edition

Printed and bound in the United States of America

Printed on recycled paper

03040506 10 9 8 7 6 5 4 3 2 1

India Fortunes

A Novel of Rajasthan and Northern India through Past Centuries

Gary Worthington

TimeBridges Publishers
Olympia, Washington

Also by Gary Worthington:

India Treasures: An Epic Novel of Rajasthan and Northern India through the Ages (TimeBridges, 2001).
Published in South Asia as *The Mangarh Chronicles* (Penguin India, 2002)

Dedication

For Sandra, my wife, my true love, and my fellow traveler on our journeys, who has inspired me and supported me in so many ways, and who has edited my drafts, enthusiastically promoted our books, and patiently helped keep me on task throughout the lengthy projects.

For my Dad, William M. Worthington, who showed me how to work hard, persevere, live up to my responsibilities, and try to do things myself before asking someone else to do them, and from whom I learned not to discard the old just because a newer version becomes available. He has read a lot of books in his life.

For my Mom, Meryl E. Woosley Worthington, who showed me how a truly generous, spiritual, and loving soul lives and works, even though her earthly life was far too short. It was she who introduced me to the joys of local public libraries.

Preface

I've been immensely pleased by the enthusiastic comments from so many readers of *India Treasures*, most of whom I would never have corresponded with had it not been for the book. Reviewers, too, both in America and abroad, have been kind in their judgments. These responses and the many emails asking if the sequel is available have provided strong motivation to keep me working on the final polishing of *India Fortunes*.

I originally wrote drafts of both novels as one long project. But the body of writing became so huge that I divided it into two books, the first one published as *India Treasures*, and as *The Mangarh Chronicles* in South Asia.

Although it is not essential to read *India Treasures/Mangarh Chronicles* first, that novel depicts events happening prior to those of the book you're holding. I wrote each book to be self-contained, but each does enhance the understanding of the events and characters in the other.

Each novel is intended to be enjoyed as a whole; however, the eight individual stories of each book are mostly complete in themselves, so they can be read separately as time permits.

A Character List and a Glossary, both with pronunciation guides, are at the end of the book to help readers unfamiliar with Indian names and words. In the Notes near the end of the book, I discuss the extent to which the characters and events in each story are fictional or real.

My Web site at GaryWorthington.com has additional background information, including some personal tips on traveling in India, and various links.

I'm greatly interested in your comments regarding the book. Please contact me by email through the address posted on my Web site, or else write in care of the publisher at the address on the copyright page. Above all, enjoy your reading!

Gary Worthington

Olympia, Washington
October 1986—July 2003

Contents

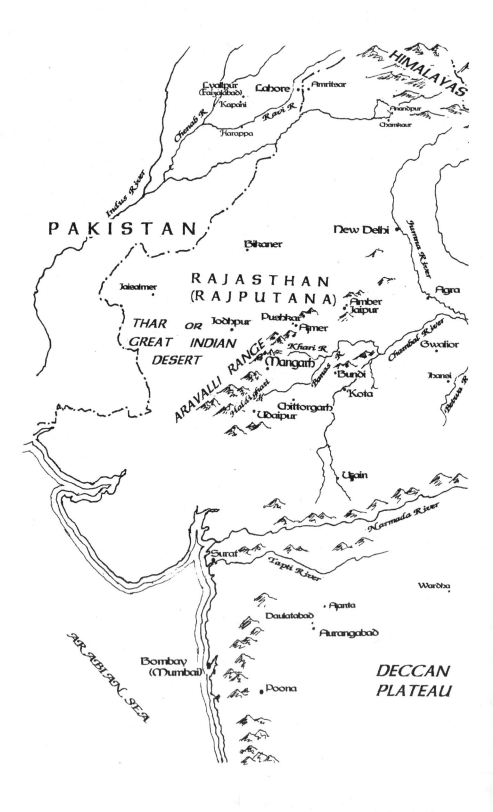

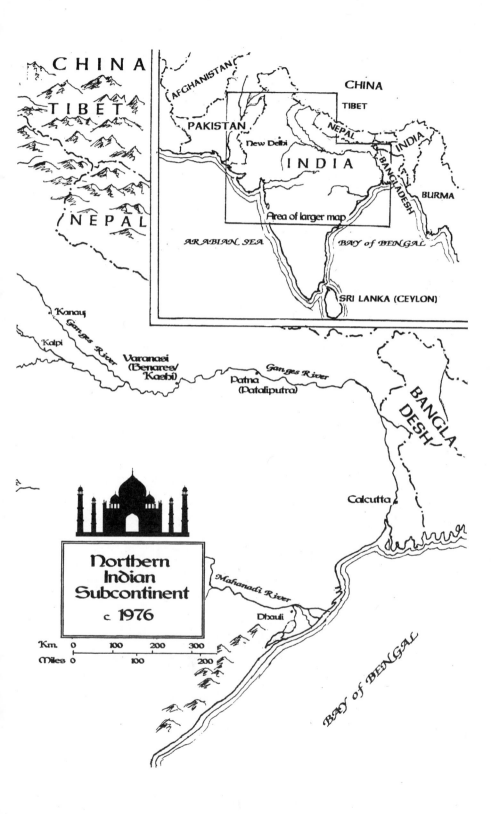

CHINA

TIBET

NEPAL

AFGHANISTAN

PAKISTAN

CHINA

TIBET

NEPAL

New Delhi

INDIA

INDIA

BANGLADESH

BURMA

Area of larger map

ARABIAN SEA

BAY of BENGAL

SRI LANKA (CEYLON)

Kanauj

Ganges River

Kalpi

Varanasi
(Benares/
Kashi)

Ganges River

Patna
(Pataliputra)

BANGLA-
DESH

Calcutta

Northern
Indian
Subcontinent
c 1976

Mahanadi River

Dhauli

BAY of BENGAL

Km. 0   100   200   300

Miles 0   100   200

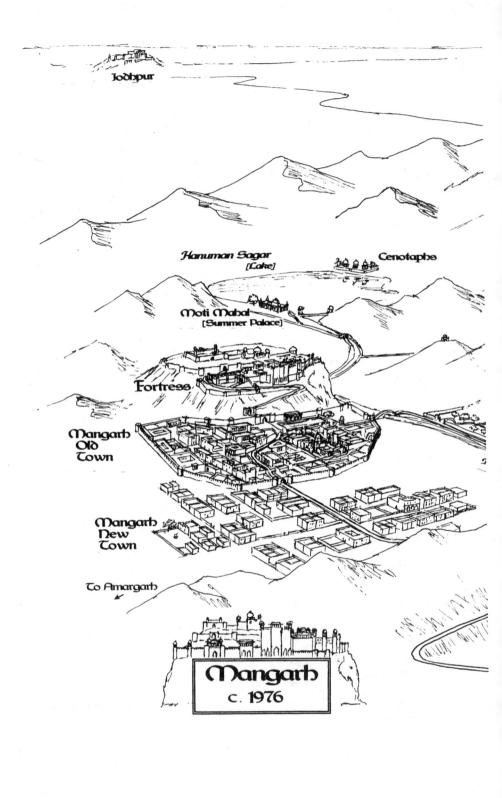

Jodhpur

Hanuman Sagar
[Lake]

Cenotaphs

Moti Mahal
[Summer Palace]

Fortress

Mangarh
Old
Town

Mangarh
New
Town

To Amargarh

Mangarh
c. 1976

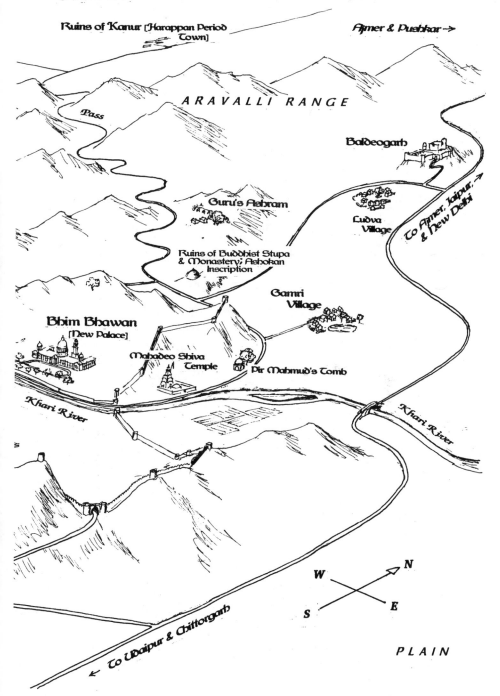

In the Previous Book

India Treasures, *and this sequel companion* **India Fortunes,** *portray key historical persons and events in the nation's religious, cultural, and political evolution. Novellas set in earlier historical periods are linked by a treasure hunt in the mid-1970s through the immense fortress of Mangarh and archaeological sites by government tax raiders, during Prime Minister Indira Gandhi's suspension of civil liberties.*

In **India Treasures**, *Vijay Singh, the capable and conscientious leader of the searchers, battles the corrupt political boss Dev Batra, who imprisons Maharaja Lakshman Singh of Mangarh and preys on the Maharaja's daughter, the lovely princess Kaushalya. Vijay fears that in Mangarh his secret may be exposed: he is masquerading as a member of the high Rajput caste, but in fact he is an Untouchable from a nearby village.*

During the search, Vijay is captivated by the beautiful and talented princess Kaushalya, an unwilling target of the tax raid. At the same time, Vijay is increasingly drawn to the lovely and competent Shanta Das, a member of his search team, but she is an Untouchable, and hence not an appropriate romantic interest for a Rajput such as Vijay claims to be.

Vijay succeeds in finding a huge, hidden trove that is part of the legendary Mangarh Treasure. But he realizes afterwards that the treasure's most famous gems, including a world famous diamond, have not been found. As the book ends, the Maharaja of Mangarh remains unjustly imprisoned, and India's suspension of civil liberties continues in effect.

India Treasures includes these novellas set in earlier historical periods:

In "Three Peoples," two children of the Indus Valley civilization are seized as slaves during the Aryan invasions of 1500 B.C.E.

In "A Merchant of Kashi," a caravan merchant's life is changed after meeting the Buddha and being lost in the Great Indian Desert, c. 506 B.C.E.

In "Elephant Driver," a farm boy becomes a spy for the great Emperor Ashoka and rides an elephant in a war that changes history, c. 260 B.C.E.

In "The Art of Love," a medieval artists paints what will become a celebrated mural masterpiece, c. 488 C.E.

In "Bride's Choice," a lovely princess defies her powerful father for the famous enemy king whom she loves, c. 1191.

In "The Price of Nobility," a wealthy Muslim disciple of a great Sufi saint is persecuted by the hostile Sultan of Delhi, c. 1320.

In "Saffron Robes," the Raja of Mangarh matches wits with the mighty Mughal Emperor Akbar at the famous siege of Chittorgarh in 1567.

Part One
The Treasure of Mangarh

1

Kaushalya Kumari hated to make the phone call, but she at last concluded it was unavoidable. She rose from the cushioned platform swing that hung from the ceiling of her apartments in the Bhim Bhawan palace and padded barefoot to her desk. The princess had been out in the hills earlier, so she still wore the traditional Rajput ankle length skirt, though she had removed the *odhni* from her head, and the long, veil-like scarf now lay on her shoulders. Gopi, her elderly maid and companion, sat nearby in a wicker chair, absorbed in sketching a flock of parrots in flight from the *neem* tree outside the tall windows.

Kaushalya picked up the telephone, carried it almost to the end of its long cord, and stood gazing at the view over the balcony to the sparse *khejri* trees on the hillside. She sighed, set the phone on the deep window sill, and dialed the operator for a trunk call. After first trying the Ashok Hotel in New Delhi, she located Dev Batra at his farm in Rajasthan. "Princess, how good to hear from you," said Batra through the noise on the line.

She tried to swallow her distaste. "I assume your recovery from the bee stings is progressing satisfactorily, Batraji?"

He chuckled, obviously pleased she had been forced not only to phone him but to inquire about his health. "Quite well. Over a hundred stings, Kaushalyaji! Can you believe it? But I should be back to normal soon."

Too bad, she thought. She said, "Now that our treasure has been found, I assume my father will be promptly released from Tihar Jail?"

"Of course, Kaushalyaji. Why not?"

She held her breath. "You'll truly set him free now?"

"I see no further reason to hold His Highness. After he apologizes to the Prime Minister, naturally, but I'm sure he'll be willing to do that."

Oh, God, she thought. Her father would never, ever, apologize to that woman.

"Kaushalyaji, why are you so quiet?"

"You—the government—has what it wants now that the treasure is found.

Surely an apology to the Prime Minister isn't really necessary, Batraji."

"Oh, yes. Her son would never agree otherwise. Sanjay has said so every time I've asked him."

I bet you've asked him a lot, she thought. "That may be a problem," she said. "My father is stubborn. If anything, he'd want Indiraji to apologize to *him*."

"Then it appears you'll have to talk with your father, won't you?"

"Since when has lack of an apology been a legal reason to hold someone in prison?"

Batra gave a harsh laugh. "The Emergency's still in effect, or didn't you remember? Besides, there was that big arsenal we found. It looks to me like your father might have been a serious danger to state security."

"You know those weapons were legal when they were imported in 1947! And there's no evidence whatsoever they were intended for use against the government."

"But the whole matter certainly looks suspicious, doesn't it? With the press censored so heavily, any publicity about those arms might make it appear quite dangerous to release your father."

She tried to swallow her anger. "We all know he's not dangerous. Especially with his health so bad. Can—can you talk with Sanjay? Maybe get him to make an exception?"

There was silence. Then: "Possibly. However, I'm still most uncomfortable from my bee stings, you know. Anyway, it would cheer me immensely if you could come visit me, to take my mind off the pain...."

She clenched her teeth. "I'll think about that."

"Good. Another thing, Kaushalyaji. Now that your treasure's been found, you have a great deal of wealth at your disposal. Maybe you could use some of it to speed up your father's release. I wouldn't be interested in it myself, of course, but I might convince others in positions of influence to support your father's cause."

He was certainly not being subtle. "Batraji, you know the government has tied up everything until the amount of tax we owe has been determined."

"Of course. But now that you know that you'll definitely be coming into *crores* of rupees sometime within the next few years, you should be more free to make use of the assets you do have control over."

She gritted her teeth. "You must know from the tax investigation that we have almost nothing left in liquid assets, Batraji. Until the government releases the items from the treasure to us, we're in a tight bind. We can hardly even pay our servants. Maybe you could help speed the process of determining the tax owed."

Silence for a few moments. "I'll consider doing that. Meanwhile, I do have contacts with buyers who are selling art objects abroad. There is now quite a market in America and Japan and Europe for items salvaged from old buildings in India. I think if some of the buildings in your fortress were, uh, partially dismantled, the profits from selling things such as carved doors and windows and all those marble elephants might be quite impressive."

She was so shocked that for a few moments she wasn't sure she'd heard right. "That fortress is our heritage! It's not only an historic monument, it's a masterpiece of architecture! We'd never, ever, agree to anything that harms the buildings!"

He was apparently taken aback at her vehemence, as it was several seconds before he resumed. "Well, maybe I got a bit carried away, Princess. But as you know, the government's now claiming ownership of the fort. Maybe I could get the claims dropped if you ah....reconsidered selling part of it off."

She was too furious to think of anything to say.

"Anyway," he resumed, "if you came up with some funds to contribute to the cause of getting your father released, it could speed things up considerably. Especially since you seem to be reluctant to meet my other suggestions."

Her fingers hurt from gripping the phone. She shifted it to her other hand. "I'll have to think about it all."

"Don't think too long, Kaushalyaji. Almost no people jailed in the Emergency are getting released, you know."

Two days later, Kaushalya and her brother Mahendra, with Gopi in the rear seat of the jeep, drove to New Delhi to visit their father. In the outskirts of the city, Kaushalya averted her eyes from a big signboard declaring in English: **Courage and Clarity of Vision, Thy Name is Indira Gandhi.** With the State of Emergency continuing, messages to the citizenry were appearing on the busier avenues in New Delhi. Each one was an added annoyance to Kaushalya.

After so many frightening hours as a passenger with her daredevil brother at the wheel of his jeep, she was relieved to arrive intact at Mangarh House. Amar, the elderly *chowkidar,* swung open the gate, and they entered the oasis of the tree shaded gardens surrounding the big bungalow. She stepped from the jeep to greet Amar, who stood with his palms pressed together and his head lowered. "So good to see you," she said.

"Welcome, Princess. You had a good journey from Mangarh?"

She laughed, glancing toward Mahendra, who was entering the house, followed by Gopi. "Let's just say I survived. My brother drives quite aggressively, you know."

Amar suddenly turned his head and shouted, "No!" He glanced back to Kaushalya. "Pardon, Princess!" He snatched his long bamboo staff and hurried to chase a large, white, humpbacked cow back out to the street.

He closed the gate and returned to Kaushalya. "That cow! She's always hanging around outside, just waiting for a chance to come in and eat all the flowers."

Kaushalya grinned. "Well, I'm sure our garden's safe with you protecting it. I'd better go get cleaned up."

Inside the house, she spoke to Mahendra and they agreed to meet later at the jail for the visit. After checking the cook regarding meals, she went to her own rooms and took a refreshing bath and a brief nap. Then she drove herself and Gopi in the Maharaja's old Jaguar sedan.

Facing one of the main thoroughfares, a big white billboard with red letters stated: **The emergency provides us a new opportunity to go ahead with our economic tasks. Smt Indira Gandhi, Prime Minister.**

"How can we go ahead with our economic tasks if most of us are in jail?" asked Kaushalya tartly.

"It's disgraceful to treat His Highness as if he were a criminal!" said

Gopi. "Who could have thought such a thing would ever happen?"

They saw that Mahendra was already waiting outside the main gate to Tihar. Gopi remained in the car as Kaushalya walked to her brother. "There are more of those disgusting signs every day," she said, not caring if she were overheard by the nearby guard.

Mahendra tightened his lips and nodded. They ducked their heads as, one at a time, they stepped through the small door inset in the larger steel one. Inside the building, at least the filling out of forms went faster, now that the staff recognized the two as regular visitors.

When Maharaja Lakshman Singh was escorted into the visiting room, Kaushalya thought he looked terrible. His thick mustache had gone all gray, and it gave the impression of drooping listlessly. His frame, once so impressive at his original six-foot-two height, had shrunk visibly.

"So they found some treasure in the fortress," her father said.

Kaushalya couldn't resist: "Daddyji, why didn't you tell us about it? Maybe we could have done something."

"What would you have done? Told the income tax raiders about it?"

"Not without your permission, of course, Daddyji. But it could have saved everyone a lot of trouble, and maybe even have gotten you out of here sooner."

He shook his head. "It wouldn't have gotten me released. You know that."

"Still, Father," asked Mahendra, "why did you feel you had to keep the treasure so secret?"

Lakshman Singh coughed several times, hard. When he had recovered enough, he said, "I didn't want this corrupt government to get control of it. For at least three centuries, every Maharaja of Mangarh has preserved that wealth, as a sacred trust for the people of the state. I didn't want to be the one to lose it."

"Bad as the government is, Father," said Mahendra, "I don't think it'll keep control of the treasure forever. Once the taxes and penalties are paid, we can keep the rest."

"Maybe. But the Indian government promised me certain things in exchange when I gave up my throne and turned over the assets belonging to my state. You know I was to receive a pension for life, to keep my title of Maharaja, to keep certain privileges. It was even in the Indian Constitution! And look what that woman did! Do you blame me for not trusting this government with our remaining wealth?"

Mahendra and Kaushalya glanced at each other. She said, "I do understand, Daddyji."

Lakshman Singh added, "And see what they've done with my fortress! Claiming ownership now! That fort is clearly mine under the agreement merging Mangarh with Rajasthan." The agitation brought on another round of coughing.

"Daddyji," Kaushalya asked, "have you seen a doctor lately?"

"I did just last week. He gave me some antibiotics." He was overcome by another coughing fit.

Kaushalya and her brother again looked at each other. She looked back to her father with pain in her eyes. "Are you able to stay warm enough at night with the extra blankets we brought?" she asked.

"Oh, yes. When the room gets cold—" he coughed several times "—I just pull the blankets and durries over my head."

"Father," said Mahendra, "we haven't given up on getting you out soon."

Lakshman Singh shrugged. "I've quite resigned myself now. I have so many friends in here." He grinned feebly. "I spend much more time with them now than when I was on the outside."

"That still can't make up for it," said Kaushalya.

Their father bent over again in a fit of coughing. When he had recovered enough to talk, he said, hoarsely, "You must be relieved that the income tax people are leaving you alone, now that they have found the treasure in the fort."

"Yes," said Mahendra, "we're delighted to be rid of them. What a nuisance that was, having them poking their noses into every corner of our lives."

As they left the jail, Kaushalya said to her brother, "I can't believe he's still in there after all this time. That cough's going to kill him!"

"I know," Mahendra said. "Unfortunately, I don't put much faith in the legal system at the moment."

"What other choices do we have? Everyone who protests too loudly gets arrested himself."

Mahendra did not respond at first. Eventually he said, "I don't know for sure. But maybe it's time to do some serious negotiating with the people who are running our country. Give them at least something of what they're after."

She thought of Dev Batra's continually trying to seduce her. She'd been careful to keep that from her brother. She eyed him curiously. "What more can we give them? Other than an apology from Daddyji, which he'd never do. The treasure has already been found."

Mahendra scowled. "I thought of something that might even be better than an apology. But it's too early to talk about it. I'll let you know when I've worked out more details."

"You won't do anything Father would disapprove of?"

He looked away. "Let's not talk about it right now. It's chancy, anyway."

2

New Delhi, 10 January 1976

Anil Ghosali ambled into Vijay Singh's office, seated himself, and took out his S-curved pipe. He lit it and began smoking. All without a word.

Vijay was not as annoyed as he would have been previously. With his reputation enhanced by his success in the raid at Mangarh, he was now considerably less worried about Ghosali's rivalry for the upcoming promotion to Assistant Director of Inspection. He rang the bell for *chai*. He had just invested in a new china teapot with a matching set of cups and saucers, mainly so he could offer better hospitality to visitors.

Ghosali stared at Vijay through the thick lensed eyeglasses. "You must be quite pleased," he said, "to have been the one to find the famous treasure."

Vijay shrugged and said carefully, "We all found it. Naturally it's gratifying to have come up with the idea. But you and all the other officers tried hard, too. I was just lucky enough to be the one to get the inspiration."

Ghosali smiled tightly. "Very modest of you to put it that way. You remember," he said, laying his pipe on the desk, "when we visited the gem dealer in Mangarh? You asked about a number of well known items of jewelry that were assumed to be part of the hoard."

So that's it, thought Vijay. He's realized it too. The most famous of the Mangarh gems were not with the treasure. "Naturally, I remember," he said. "Those still haven't been found, of course. So I assume they were probably sold or broken up into smaller pieces long ago."

Ghosali again smiled. "You have evidence that the stones were cut up?"

"No, it's only the most likely assumption. You know something to the contrary?" He wondered what Ghosali was leading up to.

Ghosali shook his head no. "Yet, it seems our job was only partially done."

Vijay shrugged. "Maybe. But that's not really for us to say, is it?" The tea arrived, and Vijay momentarily busied himself with clearing a space for Ghosali's cup and saucer on the desk.

Ghosali took a sip of the *chai*. "I also made certain inquiries and cultivated sources of information while I was in Mangarh. There are tales of huge quantities of gold in the treasure. However, only the one small chest of ingots was found."

"To most people, that *is* a huge quantity," said Vijay dryly. "Look, even if there was originally more gold, it was probably sold long ago."

"Perhaps. Still, there are higher authorities who might be interested in the information. Dev Batra, perhaps, and through him, Sanjay Gandhi."

Vijay tried not to show his irritation. "Don't tell me you're thinking of stirring things up by mentioning it to them?"

Ghosali raised an eyebrow. "Isn't it our duty?"

Ghosali was obviously still angling for the promotion, Vijay realized. He was sympathetic to Ghosali's wanting the increased salary to help pay for the dowries upon the marriages of five daughters. But Vijay wanted it, too, to help fund the school and other improvements he was donating to help the lower castes of his village. Plus, of course, there would be the recognition of his abilities and the increased prestige and responsibilities.

Vijay said, "Our superiors seem happy. It was the largest find ever in a tax raid. And the Mangarh royal family's been harassed so much already. Why not leave well enough alone?"

Ghosali again smiled. He leaned toward Vijay and lowered his voice. "I rather thought you'd say that. Your hero image would be a bit tarnished if it became known that the job was only half done, wouldn't it? And it was obvious to everyone that you fancy the beautiful princess. Some conflicting interests there, wouldn't you say?"

Vijay's tea cup shook in his hand, and he carefully set it down. "I think it's ridiculous to say the job's half done, just because a few gemstones weren't found with the treasure. And you're extremely mistaken implying I might have interests that would impede my work. I never had any kind of personal relationship with Kaushalya Kumari. That would be highly improper with the target of a raid. And it assumes she had some attraction to me, which is absurd, given the differences in social status if nothing else. Besides, I went directly against her concerns when I led everyone to the hiding place, even after the search had been called off. She was quite upset at me."

Ghosali looked him in the eye. "Yes, I think your self-interest in promoting your career won out over any personal feelings for the princess. And royalty is indeed a lot higher class of Rajput than you are, isn't it?" He rose. "Still, maybe you've had some regrets about her that are coloring your views on whether or not to raise the issue of the missing gems. Besides," Ghosali smiled knowingly, "I wonder if you had any *other* potential conflicts." He stared a few moments at Vijay, pushed aside the door curtain, and left.

Vijay felt tied into knots. Ghosali had read him so accurately on every point. And how much did Ghosali really know or suspect about the "other potential conflicts"?

The Brahmin almost certainly couldn't know about Vijay's recent discovery that Maharaja Lakshman Singh had paid for his education, making it possible for Vijay to escape the poverty of his youth. The fact hadn't stopped Vijay from vigorously searching for and finding the Maharaja's treasure, but it still didn't look good to be so significantly indebted to the target of a raid.

And Vijay definitely did not want to return to Mangarh for another search. There was too much risk of someone discovering and exposing the fact that he'd been born a Bhangi, an Untouchable. Ever since he started university he'd pretended to be a Rajput to avoid the humiliations of being labeled as an outcaste. While the fear of discovery probably wouldn't qualify formally as a "conflict of interest," it certainly diminished any incentive to resume the tax raid.

Minutes later, a knock came at the open door. He looked up to see Shanta Das and immediately his spirits lifted. She displayed her usual pleasant smile. Although recently she had taken to wearing the *shalwar kameez* to the office, today she was dressed in her green sari, the one that he always thought went so well with her dark coloring.

He waved her to a chair, and sent for tea for both of them. She handed him a red-bound book. "I thought this might interest you."

He read the title, *Indian Memories: The Reminiscences of a Civil Servant.* The author was a Stanley Powis.

"I happened upon it quite by chance in a used bookshop," said Shanta. "I noticed on the dust jacket it mentioned the author had served in a number of Indian states during the British Raj, including as the Political Agent in Mangarh."

He and Shanta had talked previously about the missing jewelry, and Vijay instantly grasped where she was headed. "We should have thought of this approach before—and researched what visitors to Mangarh might have written about seeing or hearing of the famous treasure. Hundreds of Englishmen, women too, of course, wrote their memoirs after they returned home."

"Right. You'll be interested in reading the place I marked."

He turned to where the slip of paper was inserted. And read:

> *I was sworn to secrecy, so I cannot reveal the name of the ruler involved, or, of course, even what state it happened in. But I was greatly privileged to be shown a fabulous treasure held by one of the Maharajas. It was truly stunning. The Maharaja made cer-*

tain I saw the pride of his collection, an immense diamond, which surely must be one of the largest in the world. Also a huge emerald, used as a turban ornament. And a necklace of several strands of unusually large, matched pearls. There were wooden boxes holding miniature paintings, many of them depicting scenes from the early history of His Highness' own state.

The ruler also showed me a sword of fine workmanship, which he considered to be the legendary Bhavani sword of the famous Maratha King Shivaji. The weapon was reputed to be inhabited by a powerful goddess, so it was worshiped regularly by the Maharaja's family. However, for reasons the ruler did not go into, family tradition held that the sword's existence must be kept secret from the larger world. He could show it to me, he said, only because I was already sworn to secrecy and he trusted me to keep my word.

Aside from the giant diamond, I think what struck me the most was the large number of chests filled with gold bars. I had not expected so many could exist anywhere outside of a Swiss bank or America's Fort Knox.

The location housing the treasure was fairly obvious, but the trove was well guarded by soldiers personally loyal to the Maharaja, and hence not accessible to anyone other than His Highness and those few persons he chose to honor with a viewing.

Vijay's excitement grew. "That has to be it!"

The peon delivered the tea, and they both sipped at it. Shanta said, "I thought at first that the treasure Powis mentions could have been the one in Jaipur, or Bundi, or one of the other states where the rulers were reputed to have big hidden troves. But I don't think so now. I read the whole book, and in a separate chapter it's clear that Powis had a close friendship with Maharaja Lakshman Singh, right up until Independence in 1947."

Vijay read the passage again, and asked, "Would you call the location of the treasure we found 'fairly obvious,' as Powis' says?"

She laughed. "Hardly. We'd never have found it if you hadn't had that sudden inspiration. But we know that at one time, the wealth must have been stored in the treasury at the top of the fort. Maybe that's where Powis saw it."

"Hmm. We didn't find *any* of the jewelry items he mentions. We didn't find the miniature paintings. And most of the gold we found was in coins—there was only one box of ingots."

She said, "The gold bars and the paintings could have been sold. Like the gems."

Vijay gave a nod. "I suppose. We'll probably never know." He started to hand the book to her, then hesitated and looked at it again. "That's an interesting part about the Bhavani sword of Shivaji. According to legend, Shivaji's sword was supposed to have miraculous powers. Some persons attributed his success in battles to his possessing it."

"You never saw any sign of the sword at Mangarh, did you?"

He shook his head. "No, there wasn't a hint of it."

"Lots of people would consider finding that weapon even more exciting than finding the treasure."

"Yes, and I'm sure some Hindu fundamentalists would be glad to use it to rally their people." He returned the book to her and smiled. "Fascinating."

She smiled back. "Isn't it, though." She finished her tea and rose to leave.

He opened his mouth to ask her to stay, then realized he didn't have a good excuse to keep her there. She stood for a moment, her warm eyes meeting his, as if waiting for him to say something more.

"I appreciate your showing that to me," he said, awkwardly.

"I had a feeling you'd be interested." She nodded goodbye, and left.

His office seemed quiet and empty now, the files on his desk not very interesting. He needed to make a telephone call to one of the inspectors, but when he picked up the phone, he wasn't in the mood to talk about work matters.

He replaced the receiver, rose and stood at the window, not really looking at the neighboring office building across the narrow open area with its row of trees. It was ironic, he thought, and regrettable for him, that Shanta came from an Untouchable family of leather workers in Agra. Their converting to casteless Buddhism didn't really change that. His posing as a Rajput had ironically put his apparent caste so far above hers that it seemed out of the question to consider her as a possible wife.

Pursuing Shanta Das would be just as unrealistic as courting Kaushalya Kumari. The lovely Rajput princess was so far above *him* in status and wealth as to be unreachable. And his masquerade would quickly be exposed when her family made the mandatory inquiries into his background.

He sighed and returned to his desk, again frustrated by knowing he was almost certainly destined to spend his life unmarried, in a society that valued family above all else.

3

The next morning, when a man with a gun came to the office to take him away, Vijay felt he had little choice but to go. The tall, broad figure appeared abruptly at the doorway, and Vijay looked up from the file on his desk to see Dev Batra's bushy haired, glowering henchman. The office boy stood behind the visitor, wide-eyed and no doubt worried he'd be blamed for not screening the visitor and warning Vijay.

With no preliminaries, Sen announced in his cold voice, "Batra *sahib* invites you to visit him at his farmhouse."

Vijay quickly shifted his attention from the contents of the file. "At his farmhouse?"

Silence.

He had always assumed that Dev Batra employed Sen, at least in part, to intimidate people. "Right now?"

Silence.

Vijay tried not to show annoyance at Batra's presumption that he should just drop whatever he was doing and leave, much less go somewhere far out in the countryside. "I am in fact quite busy," he told Sen. "But naturally I'd like to comply with Batraji's request. Where is this farm house?"

"An hour from here, in Rajasthan." Sen put his hands on his hips, and the tail of his white shirt bulged from the pistol concealed at his waist. The gun made Vijay vaguely uneasy, even though it wasn't a cause of worry for him personally.

Vijay gritted his teeth. One hour probably meant a of couple hours each way. He'd be working late tonight to make up for it. "I see. Well, I'll need a few minutes to finish some matters, then I'll be pleased to accept Batraji's invitation."

Sen stood silently glaring at him. Vijay gestured toward a chair. "Sit if you wish. Would you like some *chai*?" Sen scowled and continued to stand.

Vijay shrugged mentally and took a sip of his own tea. He made a couple of notes, stuck them in the folder, and bound it with the brown string.

At last he stood. He tugged on the lapels of his navy blue sport coat to smooth them and fingered the knot of his necktie to ensure it was centered. Sen abruptly turned and left. Vijay followed him down and out into the sunshine, to where Dev Batra's white Mercedes with the government license plate was parked. It blocked the narrow street, and the drivers of other vehicles were leaning on their horns even more continuously than usual.

Sen opened the rear door, and Vijay entered and sank into the deep, leather covered cushions. Sen slammed the door, got in himself and started the engine. He ignored the angry honks from the other cars, except to force them to reverse so he could leave. Once free of the congestion, he drove the car as if it were a weapon, shooting down the streets bordering the offices and shops of Connaught Circus, taking the corners fast.

The weather was pleasantly sunny, not uncommon in midwinter in northern India. As long as he had to go anyway, it was a good day, Vijay thought, for getting out of the office and visiting the countryside.

He remembered riding in the Mercedes with Batra five months ago in Mangarh, how the leather smelled so new. The odor wasn't so strong now, and there was another faint smell, unpleasant, like maybe someone had recently vomited.

At the next traffic circle, a huge sign urged, Support Prime Minister's 20-Point Programme. A green Delhi Transport Corporation bus sped by, spewing dark exhaust, the sign on its side exhorting in capital letters: WORK MORE, TALK LESS. How, Vijay wondered, could anyone possibly think propaganda like that did any good?

Despite the background odor, the car was by far the most comfortable he'd ever been in. He realized everyone who saw him in it would assume he was a VIP, so he decided he might as well enjoy the brief moment of imitation status. There was absolutely no chance he'd ever have a car like this to use in his own right. He drew himself erect, but at the same time he squirmed back into the cushions, striving to appear relaxed yet distinguished.

They drove past the edge of a residential colony, and far overhead danced at least a couple of dozen kites of various shapes and colors, flown from the rooftops by people of all ages. It was the beginning of the main season when enthusiasts flew kites with crushed glass glued to the strings and tried to cut their opponents' lines.

On the national highway they passed Palam Airport, and the number of buildings thinned out. Sen overtook heavily laden lorries and crowded buses, swerving around them quickly. Like every other car driver, he expected anything other than a truck or bus to get out of his way or perish: farm tractors, bullock carts, motor scooters.

They continued through undulating terrain, then the land flattened for the remainder of the distance to Rajasthan. An occasional farmer worked in his field, and women walked alongside the road bearing bundles of firewood or baskets of produce on their head. Camels began to appear, most of them pulling carts and driven by farmers.

Vijay had plenty of time to think about what Dev Batra might want. To express appreciation to Vijay for saving his life and finding the Mangarh Treasure? Quite possibly.

Vijay still could not completely comprehend the extent of the publicity resulting from the discovery. After interviewing him, the *Times of India* ran a front page story headlined, "Tax Raid Finds Maharaja's Fabulous Fortune." The *Hindustan Times* printed a piece titled, "Huge Hoard of Gold and Gems Discovered by Income Tax Officer." The *Indian Express* ran a more conservative piece titled "How the Mangarh Treasure was Found."

He wondered if Dev Batra had somehow found out that the most valuable, best known Mangarh gems were still missing. If so, maybe Batra also wanted to question him about those.

Well into Rajasthan, they turned east off the main highway and onto a dusty, unpaved road between yellow mustard fields. Sen had to slow to minimize the bouncing and jarring of the car from the potholes.

Near the road were occasional areas where cow dung patties, spread out on rock ledges, were drying as fuel for cooking fires. Other dung cakes were piled into cylindrical stacks. Off to the right, on a knoll, was a small fortress, its towers crumbling into ruins. The car entered a village of mud brick buildings, some with roofs of thatch, and others of rough, hand made tiles. The community was larger than Vijay's own home village near Mangarh, and Sen slowed even more to thread through the congested little bazaar in the center. Under a huge *pipal* tree, vegetable vendors sold their produce from handcarts, and a cloth seller had piles of fabric encroaching onto the dirt street.

At the far edge of the village stood a small, whitewashed temple in a compound. Then came a new masonry wall with broken glass embedded in the top, bordering the dusty road and stretching into the distance. After a few hundred meters, the car arrived at an ornate gateway of wrought iron.

A khaki-uniformed guard with a rifle slung from his back ran to swing the gate open, and the Mercedes sped up a long, curving drive of crushed rock toward a two-story building still under construction. Numerous concrete balconies protruded from each side, and the door and window openings were surmounted with arched overhangs. Workmen wearing *dhotis* and turbans perched in various parts of the bamboo scaffolding covering much of the facade.

It was an imposing mansion, but to Vijay, it didn't look quite right. The three-story overhang above the main doorway seemed too high for the scale of the building, and the structure as a whole was off-balance, with too many windows crowded onto the wing to the right.

When the car stopped, Batra's other assistant, the shorter, slender Gulab, appeared and opened the door for Vijay. Gulab wore his usual ingratiating smile, counterbalancing Sen's habitual dourness. "Welcome, sir," he said in his high pitched voice. "So wonderful to see you again. Batra *sahib* is expecting you." The smile appeared even broader than usual, possibly due to his gratitude at Vijay's saving his boss' life and hence Gulab's position. He led Vijay around to the back of the house, to a large covered patio area that appeared more finished than the rest.

There, Dev Batra, dressed in his usual white *khadi*, lay propped up on a bed, talking on a telephone, a cigarette dangling from a corner of his mouth. His face and hands were still puffy and oddly mottled from the bee stings he'd received at Mangarh. He waved Vijay to a nearby chair of wrought iron.

On the other side of Batra sat a tall, attractive woman with a high forehead and arched nose, probably in her late 20s, wearing a red and yellow *shalwar kameez*. A lit cigarette in an ashtray and an open magazine with color photos lay beside her on a small iron table. She was examining Vijay with obvious interest, as women often do with handsome men.

Gulab gestured toward a bar and asked, "What would you like to drink, sir? Batra *sahib* has everything. Vodka, Scotch, sherry, ales. All imported, of course."

Vijay would have preferred a soft drink or a *lassi*, but he always tried to be an amiable guest. "Scotch would be fine. Can you mix in plenty of Thums Up?"

"Of course, sir," said Gulab, showing no reaction to Vijay's defilement of fine imported liquor with a domestic cola. He moved to the bar and selected a couple of bottles.

The woman nodded at Vijay, adjusted the fall of her *dupatta* over her shoulders, picked up her magazine, and began rapidly turning pages. It looked like one featuring film stars. Batra was speaking on the telephone in English: "I tell you I talked with the Prime Minister only this morning. Indiraji wants it done now! Well, see to it then. Report to me when it's completed."

An older woman padded out, bearing a tray of refreshments: tiny sandwiches, dishes of roasted cashews and peanuts. Vijay took a cucumber and tomato sandwich.

Batra hung up the phone and turned his attention to Vijay. "Welcome to my farm, Singhji!" He glanced toward the younger woman and said, in a tone that seemed designed to impress her, "You've probably seen Income Tax Officer Singh on television! He just found the famous Mangarh Treasure, you know. Not only that, he's the man who saved my life!"

The woman showed renewed interest in Vijay as Batra went on, "Urvashi is an actress. You may have seen her in some perfume adverts. I'm helping her a bit with her career. She's also working with Sanjay on his family planning campaign. Anyway, how do you like my farm? I would show you around, but as you can see, I'm not quite fully recovered. Gulab will do the honors."

"How are you feeling, sir?" Vijay tried to put a tone of concern in his voice.

Batra waved a hand. "Much better. More than a hundred bee stings! Can you believe that? I would have died if I hadn't been taken to hospital. Of course, if it hadn't been for you, I would have been killed first by the fall anyway. It's a long way to the rocks below that fortress wall." He met Vijay's eyes. "I won't forget you saved me."

Vijay shrugged the matter away and took the drink from Gulab. "I'm glad to have helped, sir. But anyone would have done the same."

Batra said firmly, "I won't forget it. Or that you personally found the treasure. In addition to your men finding those hidden weapons." He grinned. "My bosses were delighted."

Vijay gave an embarrassed grin. "I'm glad we earned our pay."

Batra's face clouded. "If I'd listened to that bloody Ghosali, the treasure would never have been found. He's got a lot of explaining to do. I intend to bring him here and tell him that."

Vijay failed to think of an appropriate response.

Batra continued, "You'll have to excuse me now. I need to make another phone call. Gulab, show Mr. Singh around. We'll talk more when you're done with the tour."

"I'll go, too," said Urvashi, standing quickly.

Vijay finished the sandwich, and glass in hand, followed the assistant. Despite Gulab's ever-present grin, Vijay had always had an uneasy feeling about the man. It was as if the smile were pasted on to conceal whatever was going on in Gulab's mind. And anyone who worked for Dev Batra probably had few scruples about following orders, legal or not.

Inside the house were seven bedrooms, each with its own bathroom and its own balcony. Batra naturally had a big suite of his own. There, finely carved wooden window frames leaned against the walls near the unfinished, gaping openings. "These look old," Vijay remarked.

"Batraji had them taken from a *haveli* in Shekhavati. These doors also. He is starting a business shipping such items to America and elsewhere, but these are for this house."

Vijay kept his expression blank. Old buildings with character should be preserved and restored, not looted of valuable parts to sell to foreigners.

"That Batraji. He has so many schemes going," said Urvashi. "I prefer," she added firmly, "to concentrate on one activity at a time, and work hard on it."

"Like the family planning campaign?" asked Vijay.

"Exactly. What could be more important to our nation? We simply *must* bring our population under control, or we cannot make progress in other areas. Sanjay is showing great leadership in this area. It's high time someone did!"

Vijay carefully replied, "It's certainly an issue of major importance. Is there any particular aspect you're focusing on?"

She smiled devilishly at him. "*Nasbandhi.*"

Unused to the mention of such topics by a woman, Vijay swallowed. "Uh, vasectomies?"

"Definitely! My goal is to work with Sanjay to motivate every man with two children to ensure he has no more. The vasectomy operation is such a simple and inexpensive procedure, yet it has such profound implications for our nation!"

Vijay hesitated, then nodded. "I see your point."

"And I assure you, I intend to make progress on the matter. I'm not accustomed to allowing obstacles in my way." She stepped toward him, beaming. "With Sanjay's support, there will be no stopping me."

He backed away and took a deep breath. "I wish you well with it." He motioned to Gulab to continue the tour. They entered what would become the huge living room, with wide doors opening onto the patio. Beyond, outdoors, a giant hole had been excavated for a swimming pool.

"This room will have a disco and a bar,' said Gulab. "The basement will have both, also."

"What fun!" said Urvashi. "I love discos." She said to Vijay, "You must come back here when it's all completed, and we'll dance."

He had never so much as stepped into a disco. His mouth dry, he replied, "I'll hope to do that one day."

On an upstairs balcony they looked out over the flat fields. A bulldozer was scraping an extremely long, straight area. "What's being done there?" Vijay asked, more to get his mind off Urvashi and discos than out of genuine curiosity.

Gulab's smile broadened. "The airstrip, sir."

Vijay mulled this over. "Batraji has an *airplane*?"

"No, sir. Not yet. But some of his guests will."

Gulab took a huge knife from a pocket, pressed a button, and the blade sprang into position. Vijay had never seen such a large pocket knife before; it must be intended as a weapon, or at the very least to impress people. Gulab bent and speared a big spider that was sitting in a corner. He cast the spider over the railing, wiped the tip of the blade on his shirt tail, closed the knife and returned it to his pocket.

Urvashi, ignoring Gulab's activity, said, "I was up flying with Sanjay only last week. From the air, you can easily see just how much of Delhi is turning into slums. Our capital should be a showplace! But so many people are leaving their villages and coming to the city. All the more reason to quickly get our population under control."

"One can't blame people for coming to look for jobs," Vijay said. "But I agree, it's unfortunate that the cities are growing so much faster than services can be provided."

Urvashi beamed her smile at him again. "Exactly right! Maybe, Mr. Singh, you can work with us in our crusade!"

Vijay tried to be tactful as he replied, "I do wish I had more time to volunteer on important charitable work. Unfortunately, my job takes most of my time and energies at the moment."

Urvashi's smile vanished. She gave an abrupt nod. Vijay looked out over the view again, at the farmland, wondering if he should mention his efforts to help out in his home village. But she was already moving toward the stairway.

They returned to the ground floor, and Gulab escorted them back to where Dev Batra lay on the bed. At first Vijay thought Batra was asleep, but as they approached his eyes popped open. "How do you like my farmhouse, Singhji?"

"Very impressive, Batraji. It seems to have most everything."

"I hope so. I lost all our family's assets at Partition, you know. We were big landowners in the Punjab. I loved our farm. All my life I've wanted another. At last I'm able to restore us to our rightful wealth."

"An impressive success story, sir."

Batra peered at him, soberly. "I know you don't like me, Singhji. Don't bother denying it. There are two types of people in this world: predators and prey. I long ago decided which I'd rather be. But I owe you. Don't hesitate to call on me."

Vijay was trying to think of an appropriate response to an awkward situation, but Batra's attention turned toward the direction of the main gateway, and Vijay heard vehicles arriving. Sen hurried into view. "Swamiji is here, sir!"

Batra's eyes brightened. He sat upright, his energy seemingly renewed, although he remained seated.

Around the corner of the mansion appeared a rotund, orange robed figure, whom Vijay instantly recognized as the famous Swami Surya. The chubby cheeked holy man, moving fast despite his weight, was trailed by a couple of other men in orange, as well as a man and woman in white robes who appeared to be European.

"Batraji!" said the swami as he drew near. "I came to see if I can help you with some healing energies!" He halted and held up a hand. "No, don't get up, no need to touch my feet. You shouldn't strain yourself. And I see that lovely socialite Urvashi is here, too! I'm doubly pleased."

Urvashi hurried to touch the swami's feet.

Batra was smiling broadly. He settled back to the bed, but he remained seated upright. "What an honor, Swamiji! I thought you were in Europe."

"I came back when I heard of your mishap. But how *are* you, Batraji? I sense your aura is subdued."

"Yes, Swamiji, but I'm improving every day. And I can feel your healing powers at work already!"

"Excellent! I'm so relieved." The swami gestured toward the house. "Quite a little bungalow you're building! I'm most impressed."

Batra's smile widened. "Are you? I'm so glad!"

"Oh, yes. And are you building the airstrip you promised?"

"Certainly, Swamiji! It's under construction this very moment."

"It will be long enough for the Learjet to land?"

Urvashi squealed, "You have your own jet?"

Swami Surya grinned at her. "It's only leased, not bought. My good industrialist friend, Mr. Shrikanth, offers it for my use." He shrugged, spread his hands wide, and asked loudly with a broad smile, "What am I to do? I don't care about luxuries myself, of course. But my followers keep showering me with them, and I want to make all my people happy, so I act as if I enjoy these trinkets."

He looked back to Batra and said casually, "I must admit the jet is convenient when I visit my followers abroad, but those customs men at Delhi and Bombay can be so annoying, always wanting their payoffs." His tone became more serious: "As I've mentioned before, Batraji, I prefer to avoid them. The airstrip will be long enough to land here?"

Batra frowned. "We've solved that problem, I think, Swamiji. I'm extending the runway through some neighboring fields. The farmers are, uh, objecting and talking of taking it to court, but they'll change their minds fast. I'll see to that."

The swami grinned. "I'm sure you can be quite persuasive, Batraji. However, if you have difficulty, merely send Urvashi to unnerve them."

The woman laughed gaily. "Swamiji! You're always such a card."

The swami at last appeared to notice Vijay. "You have another guest,

Batraji."

"Yes, Swamiji. This is the man who saved my life. Income tax officer Vijay Singh. He also found the Mangarh Treasure, you know."

The swami's eyes bore into Vijay. "I'm deeply indebted to you, then! Batraji is one of my foremost disciples."

Vijay touched the swami's pudgy, sandaled feet and straightened.

The swami waved an empty hand in the air. Ash materialized on his palm, and the swami presented the holy particles to the surprised Vijay.

Swami Surya moved on to precipitate more *vibhuti* for Urvashi, who received it with her beaming smile.

Vijay gazed at the ashes in amazement. He rubbed them gently between his fingers, feeling the grittiness. He'd heard of such feats being performed by holy men, but he'd never before experienced it.

Batra said, "That is only a small example of Swamiji's miracles. He's made photos of himself appear, and gold rings, and even this Rolex watch for me!" He held up his swollen arm to display the timepiece. "All out of the air!"

"Astonishing," Vijay said, impressed despite his ambivalence about the holy man.

"Now then," said Batra to Vijay, "I must take advantage of the great honor of Swamiji's visit by consulting him for an astrological reading. Would you like to stay awhile and enjoy the country air of your home state, or should I have Sen take you back?"

"I really should be getting back, sir. I left some unfinished business on my desk."

"Then goodbye for now."

"Uh, one last thing, please, Batraji."

"Yes?"

Vijay glanced quickly at the swami, who had seated himself and was watching the exchange. "Now that we have the treasure, is there any further reason to hold the Maharaja of Mangarh in jail? Couldn't he be released?"

At first Batra was silent. Then he said wearily, but firmly, "There are other reasons to hold him. The Emergency, if nothing else."

Vijay decided to press the matter. "May I know the particular reasons, sir?"

Batra scowled. "I don't see it's your business to know. But since I owe you, I'll tell you. Indiraji doesn't like Lakshman Singh. He insulted her and her father Nehru too many times, or so she thinks. Sanjay *sahib* doesn't like him because his mother doesn't like him, and because he opposed one of Sanjay's pet projects. If His Highness were released, he'd probably just criticize the Emergency and end up right back in jail."

Vijay hesitated; he had to be careful not to arouse Batra's suspicions. Batra couldn't possibly know of the discovery that the Maharaja had anonymously paid for all of Vijay's schooling. It was probably a conflict of interest for Vijay to try to intervene, even though the raid as such was over. But he wouldn't be able to live with himself if he didn't make the effort. "Sir, with all respect, those don't seem like legal reasons to hold His Highness. Most people would say he's been punished enough by being in jail for months already, not to mention by our raids and the big tax penalties he'll end up paying."

Batra stared at him, and Vijay hoped he hadn't gone too far. He willed himself to remain calm. Batra said, "It's not your call, Singh. Not entirely mine, either, for that matter. I frankly don't see why you're so interested."

Vijay's mouth had gone dry, and he wet his lips. "I like to see fairness done, sir. It must be a real hardship for any elderly person, much less an ex-ruler, to be in jail in the winter."

Batra continued to examine Vijay with obvious puzzlement. Then he shrugged. "That's life, Singhji. Sometimes the stars are in our favor, and sometimes they aren't." He grinned and added, "Anyway, I rather enjoy having something to hold over his daughter. I still hope to get that pretty princess into my bed."

After that comment, Vijay didn't trust himself to speak. Urvashi was staring wide-eyed at Batra, a slight smile curling the corners of her mouth. If she was annoyed, she didn't let it show. The swami laughed. "Batraji, you are such a rascal! And with Urvashi here, too. What am I to do with you?"

Batra laughed also. "Maybe your presence will reform me, Swamiji."

"I hope not!" said Urvashi, her smile broader now and her eyes lively. "You're wonderful just as you are, Batraji!"

There was silence.

"I really must go," Vijay said, his voice flat. He went through the motions of courteously taking his leave.

Back in New Delhi, Sen stopped the Mercedes outside the office building. He opened the door, and Vijay stepped out. "Wait," said Sen. He opened the boot and withdrew two boxes, wrapped in white paper. "Gifts from Batra *sahib*." He handed them to Vijay.

Vijay reflexively took the boxes, heavy for their size. He opened his mouth to object. Sen was already climbing back into the car. "Wait!" Vijay called.

The Mercedes shot off. Vijay looked down at the parcels, each of which felt and looked like it probably contained a bottle of liquor.

He walked to the building entry and saw Anil Ghosali standing in the shadows at the bottom of the stairway. Ghosali stared through his heavy eyeglasses and asked, speaking in the English normally used in the office, "That was Batraji's government car, was it not, Singhji?"

"Yes. He wanted to see me." Vijay almost added more of an explanation, then he decided it was none of Ghosali's business.

The Brahmin no doubt was still looking for information he could use against Vijay in maneuvering for the promotion to Assistant Director, though it now seemed more likely the upcoming position would be Vijay's. Ghosali had strenuously argued against searching in the spot where the treasure was finally located. Had his view prevailed, the riches would never have been found. The fact that he'd been proven so wrong made him look rather foolish. No doubt it had hurt Ghosali's chances for the promotion, which he'd felt was his right as the longest serving of the income tax officers in the Delhi office.

Ghosali glanced down at the boxes and opened his mouth, apparently intending to ask about them, but Vijay moved past and hurried up the stairs.

Back at his desk, he called Ranjit Singh in. "I need a witness." He gestured toward the gifts. "These are from Dev Batra."

The tall Sikh raised an eyebrow and nodded. Vijay unwrapped the paper on one, then took his letter opener and slit the tape securing the top flaps. He withdrew a bottle of Chivas Regal Scotch.

"It's no doubt genuine," said Ranjit. "Considering who it came from."

"I'm sure it is. He's fond of imported things."

"I assume Batra doesn't know you're not fond of liquor."

He shook his head. "Probably not. I did drink some Scotch at his farmhouse, so I suppose he thinks I like it." Out of curiosity, he was opening the other box. He partially withdrew the bottle and saw it was identical to the first.

"Are you going to keep them?"

"I shouldn't. Even though he didn't give it as a bribe, I don't want to be indebted, no matter how small, to someone like him. It could also look bad if anyone ever heard of it."

"So what will you do?"

Vijay thought for a moment. "Batra has a suite at the Ashok Hotel. I could take the bottles back there, with a note saying I appreciate the thought but explaining why I can't keep them."

Ranjit grinned. "He might be insulted if you returned them. Besides, even though they're probably worth a few days of our wages, it's not like he gave you a television set or expensive jewelry. No one could seriously think you'd be corrupted by two bottles."

Vijay smiled back. "I suppose I could just give them to someone who would truly appreciate them."

"Anyone in mind?" Ranjit's grin broadened.

"I thought of you, but you prefer rum in your cola, instead."

Ranjit assumed a look of hurt. "I don't have *that* much of a preference!"

"Oh, all right. They're yours. I should mention them to our Deputy Director, though, so it's clear we aren't trying to hide anything."

Ranjit nodded. "Probably a good idea. So how was your visit to Mr. Batra's farmhouse?"

"Interesting. His farmhouse is more like a palace. And while I was there, Swami Surya arrived."

"The celebrity himself! What did you think of the famous holy man?"

"I'm not sure. He certainly doesn't lead an ascetic's lifestyle. He even has the use of a private jet, though he wasn't flying it that day. But he materialized *vibhuti* out of thin air, right in front of my eyes!"

Ranjit looked at him oddly. "Did he, now. And you were impressed by that, I see."

"I think you might have been, too."

"Possibly. Do you think that certifies him as genuine holy man and miracle worker?"

"It's probably not enough by itself, but it does make one wonder, doesn't it?"

He had barely gotten back into his work, when a young income tax inspector newly assigned to Delhi came in. A.S. Nimbalkar—he preferred to be known as "A.S."—was from Poona. He was one of the most overtly religious people in the office, always displaying the vermillion mark on his forehead from his early morning temple visits. Nimbalkar dressed in *khadi* and a vest while most of the others in the office wore European business attire. Rumor had it that he was a member of the fundamentalist Hindu RSS organization, the Rashtriya Swayamsevak Sangh. "Sir," he said, "I wanted to ask you a question about your time in Mangarh."

"Of course." Vijay gestured toward a chair. "Join me in some tea?"

"With pleasure, sir."

Vijay pressed the bell. "Now then, what did you want to know?"

"You may know I come from Maharashtra. I am a member of an association called the Shivaji Restoration Society. Our purpose is to promote King Shivaji's importance as a national hero, to hold him up to all Hindus as a name to rally around. My personal quest is to find the famous weapon of Shivaji, the Bhavani sword."

Vijay thought of the mention of the sword in the book Shanta had shown him; it was quite a coincidence to have it come up again so soon. "Yes, I've heard of it."

"Sir, the Goddess Bhavani appeared personally to Shivaji and presented him with the weapon. Whenever the King called upon her after that, her powers in the sword made him invincible. However," Nimbalkar paused for emphasis, "the sword has been missing for around three hundred years. Many persons thought it was held by the royal family of Satara, but experts now think their sword is merely another one that may have been owned by Shivaji. Anyway," he said, "the owners will not let the sword out of their possession, so its usefulness to our cause is minimal."

Vijay nodded and waited.

Nimbalkar's eyes brightened. "Imagine—if the true weapon were found, how powerful a symbol it would be! I envision huge processions crossing India, with the sword carried in a chariot at the forefront. It would revitalize our religion." He lowered his voice. "There are many sacred sites, you know, where Muslims have destroyed temples existing for thousands of years and built their mosques instead. The birthplace of Lord Rama is only one of them. I can see us marching to these places, following the sword, which would be held high by our leaders. Such a huge number of us could easily evict the Muslim trespassers and tear down their mosques, and then restore the temples."

Vijay shifted in his chair. "What you propose, A.S., seems, uh, like it could stir up considerable unrest. And from what I remember of my readings about Shivaji, he made a point of never destroying mosques."

Nimbalkar's eyes widened. "Could that be true, sir?"

"Yes."

"But—but our leaders never told us that!"

Vijay shrugged.

Nimbalkar looked pained.

The tea came, and Vijay cleared a spot for his visitor's cup. "Anyway," he said, "tell me, what does this have to do with our raid in Mangarh?"

Nimbalkar's eyes again lit. "Sorry, sir, I was getting to that. In my research, only this week I came across a reference to the possible existence of the Bhavani sword in Mangarh. Given your extensive search there for hidden assets, I thought perhaps you might have come across it."

Vijay shook his head no. "I remember an old sword or two in the strong room, and some in displays on the walls of the old fort. But I saw nothing that would lead me to think the Bhavani sword was still there, if it ever was."

"The Mangarh royal family might want to keep its existence secret, sir. Maybe the family wants to keep control of such a powerful goddess all for themselves."

Vijay again shifted in his chair. "Well, as you may know, the Maharaja of Mangarh himself is jailed at this moment, so it would be difficult to ask him." He took a sip of his tea before reluctantly adding, "I remember a mention of the sword in a book Shanta Das showed me. But the event described in the book probably occurred thirty or forty years ago, and it didn't say where it was."

Nimbalkar frowned. "I was thinking, sir, about contacting other members of the royal family. But they might be reluctant to talk to me."

"I suppose they might at that. Look, I think you're better off looking elsewhere. I highly doubt the sword is in Mangarh now. We'd almost certainly have seen some evidence of it."

The young man's disappointment was obvious. "Do you expect to go to Mangarh again for an additional search, sir?"

Vijay suppressed his unease at the thought. "That's highly unlikely."

Nimbalkar rose. "I see, sir. Well, I'm grateful for your time."

At his desk the next day, Vijay ordered his first *chai* of the morning and had scarcely finished it when Ranjit entered. "Watch closely," the Sikh said. "*Very* closely."

He showed his open palm to Vijay. "Nothing there, right?" He waved the hand in the air, and held it out to Vijay.

A tiny mound of ash lay in the center. He said to the astonished Vijay, "Hold out your own hand." Vijay did so, and Ranjit dumped the ash into it.

Ranjit grinned. "It's always good to start the day with a miracle or two, don't you think? You can come for my *darshan* any time you want."

He left.

After a moment, Vijay followed. Ranjit halted in the hallway and, still grinning, turned to face him. "All right, how did you do it?" Vijay asked.

"I was quite interested in magic in my younger years, so I learned some tricks. You can hide the ash in a false thumb tip, but it's simpler to just use the fold of skin between your thumb and forefinger. Most people could probably do it if they learned how and practiced it some."

Vijay thought for a moment. "But what about materializing a watch or a piece of jewelry? You can't hide those in your hand."

"Was the swami wearing a robe?"

"Yes."

"Did it have loose sleeves?"

"I think so."

Ranjit smiled and shrugged. "It just takes more practice."

Vijay shook his head and went back to his office, thinking about Swami Surya. Maybe the swami really *could* perform miracles like materializing the ash and other things from the air. On the other hand, if he was using trickery, did that mean everything about him was fake? Not necessarily. His teachings as a whole might still be valid.

Vijay decided he'd better get back to work. He returned his attention to the open file on his desk and started reading about a wealthy Delhi television factory owner who was suspected of concealing considerable assets in his home.

4

With the tax raid over, and unable to think of any immediate way to help her father, Kaushalya decided the time was good to retreat to her guru's ashram in the hills. She had been forced to postpone the visit due to the tax raid and her father's imprisonment.

It was a bright winter day when she and Gopi set out in the old blue Bentley with the family's elderly driver, Bhajan Lal, at the wheel. Since numerous local people would almost certainly catch sight of them, both wore the traditional clothing with the *odhnis* draped over their heads. The road first paralleled the bank of the Khari River past the large compound of the temple of Mahadeo, its golden tipped tower bright in the sun. Then came a set of Persian wheels, their chains of buckets raising water from the river to irrigate fields of *jowar* and mustard. The road turned away from the river and passed the domed tomb of the medieval Muslim saint, *pir* Mahmud, shaded by a huge mango tree. Then the car ascended into the hills, the roadway following a tributary with tumbled boulders lining the watercourse.

The car passed the hemispheric mound of the ancient Ashokan *stupa* and the adjacent crumbled ruins of the Buddhist monastery, then continued higher and at last reached the hillside site of the ashram of Guru Dharmananda. Peter Willis, the guru's slender, dark bearded American secretary, met Kaushalya when the car deposited her and Gopi. "It's so wonderful to have you here at last, Princess! Your cottage is waiting for you. It's not much compared to what you're used to, but you already know that. Let me help you with your luggage." English was normally spoken at the ashram, both because of the large number of foreign visitors and disciples, and because the guru spoke it fluently, having been trained as a medical doctor in the U.K. Willis took Kaushalya's suitcase in one hand and Gopi's in the other.

The air felt and smelled fresher here compared to the dusty dryness of the plains below. They followed Peter past several tree-shaded, whitewashed cottages to one that was slightly larger than the rest, and showed her inside. Designed with European or American visitors in mind, it was simply but attractively decorated with a fiber rug and with locally woven blankets on the beds. "You probably remember there's only cold water in the bathroom, but morning and evening you can get buckets of hot water on request," he said.

He turned to leave. "Guruji will see you whenever you wish before evening meditations. We're close to capacity this week, almost eighty people." He looked at her pointedly. "We did tell the other disciples who you are, and that you want to be treated no differently from anyone else."

Kaushalya felt a twinge of annoyance at the thought that her presence had been mentioned to everyone, but then she realized maybe it was for the better. Word would have spread anyway, and this way it was clear she didn't want to appear to be anyone special.

While Gopi unpacked the relatively few items they'd brought, Kaushalya went to the Guru's bungalow. She slipped off her sandals on the veranda and stepped inside. Peter, seated at the desk in the front room, gestured toward the inner doorway. "Guruji's expecting you, Princess."

Guru Dharmananda sat on cushions before his own low writing desk. She thought his white robe, belted tightly at his slender waist, went well with his light skin and greying hair. Smiling warmly, he rose when Kaushalya entered. She started to bend to touch his feet, but he put out a hand to stop her. "We know that's not needed, don't we, Kaushi? It's wonderful to have you here again, at last! Please sit."

He returned to his seat, and she lowered herself to the cushions facing him. "It's such a relief to have that tax raid over, Guruji, so I can be here, instead."

"Have you been able to see your father recently?"

"Three days ago." She lowered her eyes. "He has a terrible cough. And he doesn't look good." She raised her eyes to the guru's, and saw his soften at the sight of the pain in her own. "If only there were something I could do."

"I wish I could help him, also," said the guru, fingering his neatly trimmed beard. "As you know, some things simply have to be endured. It appears this is one of them. It can be hard to accept that."

She nodded. "I suppose. Still, I keep trying to think of a way to get him released."

Guru Dharmananda said after a silence, "Is the government still trying to take the fortress from your family?"

"I haven't heard of any change. It seems so unlikely they'd succeed, though. I'm hoping it's just a maneuver to put more pressure on us."

"I suppose it will be some time before the amount of tax due on the treasure is resolved."

"It will probably be months. Possibly years." She couldn't resist: "Now that the treasure has been found in the fort, without violating any confidences, can you tell me if my father told you where it was hidden?"

The guru thought for a moment. "No, he never told me the whereabouts of the treasure in the *garh*. But then, there was no reason for him to."

"I know he truly loves me, but he's never really confided in me," said Kaushalya. "Nor in my brother. He always seems to enjoy keeping concerns to himself, and making decisions without explaining them. I suppose that comes from ruling his own state for so long."

"He has his friends among one or two of the other ex-rulers," said the guru. "But I think he's seldom truly confided in them, either. He has sometimes used me for that purpose. I've been honored to have his trust."

"I'm sure he's felt the honor is his, to have you to come to."

As usual, the residents and visitors gathered in the afternoon on mats under the huge banyan tree for the guru's talk and discussion. Guru Dharmananda sat on a slightly elevated platform near the central part of the tree.

The guru began: "You already have the answers to most questions within you. Listen to your innermost being. The meditations here will help you quiet your mind and get in touch with your true spiritual core, the part of God that is within you and that forms your essential self. But you can call upon this inner wisdom at any time. It is not necessary to be in meditation. Simply ask yourself, any time you face a question or decision, 'What should I do?' Or, another way of stating it is, 'What is right?' The first thought that comes to you is almost always the best. It may not be the answer you think you want, but it likely will be the right one.

"It's necessary to add a caution, though," said the guru. "What I've told you applies to people who are basically healthy psychologically, and to those who have had a fairly sound moral upbringing. It obviously doesn't apply to a Hitler. It's unlikely to work for someone who was in such a bad family situation as a child, or was so badly abused, that he never learned right from wrong, or to someone seriously in need of intensive therapy. And now," he looked about the group, "are there questions you'd like to ask of me?"

"Guruji," said a young Indian man speaking quickly, "are you not being inconsistent at this moment? Why should we ask you questions, if we already know the answers inside us?"

There was laughter among those seated. "I was hoping you'd ask that very question," said the guru. He was smiling broadly. "But maybe you have just fallen into your own trap, so to speak. By your reasoning, the answer to the question you yourself just asked should be within you. So I'll ask you to answer it."

The young man grinned good naturedly; the guru often turned questions back upon the person asking. He thought for a moment before responding, "One of the reasons we come here is to learn techniques to help us in life. When you invited us to ask you questions, it was partly in case we still want to know more details about the method itself that you just taught. Though the method seems simple, it is a new approach for some of us, so it's natural we may want clarifications or more information."

The guru nodded, still smiling. "See—you've learned it already. You've answered your own question. If everyone else follows suit, I'll soon be out of business."

There was more laughter, although some of it seemed automatic, as if the disciples were uncertain as to whether the guru was serious.

"Asking questions of your inner self really does work," a white haired lady with a German accent said. "I have been using it for years."

"Then why are you here?" a young, blond American girl asked her, a shy smile softening any chance of offense. "If you already have the answers inside and can call upon them at will?"

"Because," she said calmly, "I want to get better at implementing what I know."

Kaushalya spoke. "I certainly have the same difficulty. Most of the time I do know what's right. It's doing it that can be difficult." She was aware of curious looks, especially from the non-Indian visitors. She knew many Westerners were fascinated by royalty. Even though the attendees had been asked to treat her no differently than anyone else, that curiosity was still there.

"I think everyone here is in that situation," said the German woman.

"So how," asked the guru, "can we get better at living the way our inner voices tell us we should live?"

No one replied immediately, so Kaushalya spoke again. "One way is through meditation and prayer. These spiritual practices will help us stay in tune with our inner self, and they'll also act as daily reminders of what's important in life, and therefore of the way we should be living."

The discussion continued another ten minutes before the guru brought it to a close. As Kaushalya was walking back to her cottage, the American girl approached. "You speak English like someone from the U.S.," she said. "How did you become so fluent?"

Kaushalya smiled at the implied compliment. "I did go to English medium schools here. But I also have a masters degree from the University of Washington in art history. I spent almost three years in America."

The girl raised an eyebrow. "How did you like our country?"

"I found a lot to like. Women have so much freedom there! It was hard in many ways to come back here and adjust again to all the rules. But I missed my family and friends when I was there, and it was sometimes hard to eat vegetarian." She asked the inevitable question in turn: "How are you liking India?"

"Oh, I love it! Everyone is so friendly, always inviting me to their homes. And I'm fascinated by the culture." The girl turned off the path, toward the small women's dormitory. "See you later!"

Kaushalya continued to her cottage. After a brief rest, she and Gopi went for a walk on the grounds. Farther up the hillside, they stood for a moment at the entrance to the small prehistoric cave where *rishis* had dwelled thousands of years previously. They then passed the chambers carved into the rocky hillside by Buddhist and Jain monks in ancient times as living quarters, now with padlocked, heavy wooden doors to prevent access due to the dangers of cave-ins. Then, from the trail that looped through the forest, they looked out over the ashram buildings in their peaceful wooded setting.

She thought of the many legends about these hills. Lord Rama and his brother Lakshmana, from whom Kaushalya's Rajput clan was descended, were said to have hunted and chased away demons in these very forests. And there was something about walking here that was more conducive to thinking clearly.

She thought about her father, first of all. "There must be *something* I can do to get Daddyji out," she said.

Gopi glanced at her but said nothing, realizing there was nothing to be said.

"Even visiting the Prime Minister herself didn't work," said Kaushalya bitterly. "It's obvious she has Daddyji exactly where she wants him. My pointing out how she must have felt when the British kept her own father in jail didn't seem to affect her."

Gopi gave a nod. "His Highness knows you're doing everything you can."

Kaushalya sighed. "I suppose."

"Even talking to that terrible man."

After a time, Kaushalya replied simply, "Yes."

She turned her thoughts to the question of what to do with the treasure that had been found, when it was ultimately released by the government. She had definite ideas about how to use it for the benefit of the people of Mangarh, but at this time implementing it all seemed a dream for the far future.

They walked farther along the path. She thought about how most other young women her age were married by now and many, probably most, even had children. That, too, seemed far off for her, especially with her father in jail. And until she had her doctorate, she refused to consider any of the previous expressions of interest, virtually all of which had come on behalf of sons from other princely families. She thought about some of the potentially eligible men she knew. Of the various sons of royal families, she saw obvious faults with most of them: too obsessed with partying; or womanizing; or arrogance; or lack of ambition; or lack of concern for bettering society. Pratap Singh, graduate student and son of the Raja of Shantipur, was an exception, but she considered him mainly as a good friend who shared interests such as social reforms and environmental causes.

The image of Vijay Singh came to her. Older than most of the rest, but handsome, considerate, intelligent.

She abruptly was annoyed with herself. Why did he even occur to her? Aside from the fact that he had been the one who led the searchers to the treasure, he wasn't of the appropriate social class. Though she tried not to be overly influenced by other people's views, her father and brother and everyone else would consider him totally out of the question.

She forced him, as well as the others, from her mind.

5

Three months later, New Delhi, March 1976

Dilip Prasad had taken another position, and Vijay had a new boss whom he didn't much like. A week after Trilok Mishra's arrival, Vijay returned to the office in mid-morning to find the peon waiting outside his door. "The DD *sahib* wants to see you straight away, sir. He asked for you some time ago."

Vijay had met the new Deputy Director of Inspection only briefly. He wondered if the man ever smiled. Trilok Mishra reminded Vijay of a lizard, with small, cool, heavily lidded eyes set in a round, chinless face.

"I'm sorry I'm late, sir," Vijay said as he entered Mishra's office. "I had a meeting with the investigations people."

Mishra frowned and glanced at his watch. He then stared at Vijay and said, as if he hadn't heard the explanation, "I summoned you, Singh, as I am doing with the other officers under my direction, to tell you my expectations and my philosophy. You are working for me now. And I am working for those above me. If you perform poorly, it reflects upon me. If you perform well, that also reflects upon me. Do you understand what I am saying?"

"Yes, sir. I always strive to do my best." Vijay wondered if there could be some provocation for the statements; he was unaware of any problem with the way he did his job. Quite the contrary. He noticed that the decor in the office was different from what Prasad had previously. The new photo of Indira Gandhi on the wall was huge, much bigger than the standard issue one in his own office.

Mishra said, "I've been told, Singh, that you are an officer of high ability. Before coming here, I heard about your finding that maharaja's treasure in Mangarh. But I want you to know, I form my own opinions. You are starting from zero with me, so to speak. To me, nothing you did before I came has happened. You start afresh."

Vijay tried to maintain an appearance of calm. After the success of the Mangarh raid, he had assumed his promotion to Assistant Director was almost assured. Now, his previous successes apparently counted for little.

Mishra gestured toward the big photo. "Ultimately, we all work for our Prime Minister herself. She has shown great leadership in the proclamation of our current State of Emergency. I have long admired Indiraji as the embodiment of Mother India. I firmly believe the Emergency is setting our nation back on its proper course. Discipline is now reestablished among government servants. Corruption is being rooted out. The railroads are running on time. Even shopkeepers no longer cheat their customers with impunity, now that price tags are required on items.

"And so," he stared at Vijay in emphasis, "I expect those officers under me to give their complete commitment to carrying out whatever orders are given us. Tax evaders rob our government of its rightful income that is needed to carry out its functions for the good of our nation. We must root out tax evaders whenever we are so directed. Do you have any questions of me?"

Vijay hesitated a moment, then said, "No sir. I firmly believe in the importance of the mission of our department, of course."

"Good. By the way, Singh, you may know that large numbers of people are calling at the Prime Minister's home to voice their congratulations on the Emergency and show her their support. I plan on doing so tomorrow afternoon. I encourage others in the department to join me. We may not be privileged to see her in person, but we can leave our good wishes in writing. Ghosali and a couple of others will be coming. It would be a good opportunity for you, also."

Vijay moistened his dry mouth. It would obviously be unwise to say what he really thought. "I, uh, will certainly consider it, sir."

"Good. And now," Mishra paused for emphasis, "I must bring up a delicate matter. I have heard that you are in the habit of, shall we say, taking gifts." He speared Vijay with a disapproving stare. "I will not tolerate that from my officers. I expect my entire staff to be beyond reproach at all times."

A numbness spread through Vijay. Never, ever, had he knowingly done anything improper, and never had he been accused of it. Who could be spreading such a lie?

"I have no definite proof of wrongdoing as yet," said Mishra. "You must hope that I find none."

Was that a hint that some sort of investigation was going on? Mishra was clearly waiting for him to respond.

"I don't know what to say, sir." His voice sounded weak to himself, almost as if he were in fact guilty of something. He tried again: "I go out of my way to ensure my conduct is above reproach, sir. I can't imagine how such an idea could have gotten started!"

Mishra said, "I should hope you are telling the truth. We'll see. You may go."

Vijay hesitated, feeling as if he should say something more. He didn't know what. He rose. "I'll do my best for you, sir." It sounded feeble and incomplete to him.

Mishra gave a nod. Vijay left.

Downstairs, he met Ranjit Singh in the hallway. The Sikh inclined his turbaned head toward Vijay's office, raising an eyebrow in question. Vijay nodded, and they entered and sat.

In a low voice, Ranjit said, "Our new DD told me I'm starting all over from zero with him. I'm supposed to prove myself all over again."

Still in inner turmoil, Vijay said, "It sounds like he's giving us all the same introductory speech."

"He emphasized our duty to please his bosses. I just hope it doesn't get even more political here. The Mangarh raid was bad enough."

Vijay's mind was elsewhere. "For sure." He absently began rotating the teacup on his desk.

"Everyone's been sure you'll be promoted soon, *yaar.* Did he say anything about that?"

Vijay tried to concentrate on what Ranjit was saying; he shook his head. "No. Mishra gave me the clear impression nothing I've done before counts with him."

"Bloody poor luck. You deserve better."

"We all do, I think." The teacup fell off the saucer; fortunately the cup was empty. Vijay returned it to its place.

Ranjit glanced at the door and grimaced. "Did the DD mention going to congratulate the Prime Minister?"

"Yes."

"You're not doing it, I assume?"

Vijay sighed. "No. I try to keep my hypocrisy within limits. Apparently Ghosali is going, though."

"Ghosali! Wouldn't you know it. Anything for an advantage."

"He may actually think the Emergency's good, like Mishra does."

"I suppose he might at that. I just hope it doesn't give him any edge over you."

Vijay nodded, his lips tight. Should he say more? Ranjit could certainly be trusted. "I think I may already be at some disadvantage. Mishra said—he said he'd heard I take gifts. Obviously implying I can be bribed."

"No! How could he think such a thing?"

Vijay cleared his throat. "Apparently someone's spread a rumor."

Ranjit shook his head. "I can't imagine that. Everyone likes you. Except, maybe, Ghosali."

Suddenly Vijay remembered the Scotch, months ago. "The only thing I can think of that might possibly be used—Ghosali saw me leaving Batra's car with the bottles. They were still in the packages, so I suppose he might not even have known for sure what it was."

"Regardless, that Scotch wasn't from someone we were investigating or raiding, it was from a man whose life you saved. Anyway, it was such a small thing, and *I* ended up with it all. Besides, you told Prasad about it."

Vijay swallowed. "Actually, I didn't. He was gone when I went to tell him. After that, as I remember, I got busy and time went by. Finally, I just decided it had been too long, and it probably wasn't really that important."

"Oh. Well, actually it *wasn't* that important. It's just unfortunate someone may have twisted it around and tried to make you look bad." Ranjit met his eyes. "Would you like me to go tell Mishra what happened?"

Vijay hesitated. "That would be awkward for you. And it drags your name into the matter, too. Maybe we should just wait and see if it really becomes necessary. This thing should just blow over."

After a time, Ranjit nodded. "Let me know if you do need me to say anything."

Two days later, the Deputy Director again summoned Vijay. Mishra was frowning, and Vijay became uneasy at the sight of Anil Ghosali already seated.

Mishra said, "Singh, while we were waiting for Indiraji to appear yesterday—which she did, by the way; you missed an inspiring few minutes—Ghosali and I had time to talk. He says he and you visited a gem dealer in Mangarh. That you asked about a number of major stones. A huge diamond, a big ruby, a big emerald, a highly valuable pearl necklace. And Ghosali says none of those pieces were found with the 'treasure.'"

Mishra waited, obviously expecting a response.

Vijay took a deep breath. So Ghosali was indeed trying hard to gain an advantage. "That's true, sir. I've thought about the fact myself that those major gems weren't found. But I have no idea where they are, or if they even still exist in the same form."

Mishra had been watching him intently. Now he turned to Ghosali.

Ghosali said, "That gem dealer, Shri Mahajan, didn't know either. However, he said they hadn't been sold, so far as he knew. And it was his business to know."

"Mahajan said he'd know if they were sold *in India*," Vijay pointed out. "But not necessarily if they were sent abroad and sold there, or if they were cut up into smaller gems and sold."

Mishra tightened his lips. "I also understand there's a rumor of a huge quantity of gold at Mangarh. But there was only the one box of ingots found with the treasure."

"Most people would say that's still a lot of gold," Vijay said. "There's nothing to indicate there's more hidden."

Mishra sighed and shook his head. He said, "Ghosali also mentioned the gems and the gold to Dev Batra. And Batraji now insists we send another search team to try to find them. He thinks it makes him—and us—look foolish if we only did the job part way."

Vijay didn't try to stop himself from saying, "The biggest find in the Income Tax Department's history, and he's suddenly decided it's not enough?"

Mishra said, "We have our orders. You will return to Mangarh. You and Ghosali are in charge again. But Batraji will be there part of the time, too, overseeing things."

Just like the last raid, Vijay thought. It had been a ridiculous arrangement, with neither him nor Ghosali fully in charge of the team of searchers. And Dev Batra, who held no official position in the line of authority, was in ultimate command because he worked for Sanjay Gandhi, who had no official position either, but was the Prime Minister's son.

Vijay thought momentarily about telling them of the fact the gems were mentioned in Stanley Powis' book, along with all the gold bars and the sword, but he decided there was little value in doing so. It would merely raise the question of why he hadn't mentioned the book earlier. And, he had to admit to himself, much of the reason had to do with not making life more difficult for Kaushalya Kumari and her father.

"My superiors want results from this raid," said Mishra. "And that means I do, also. It may be a long shot to find something as small as the gems. So if you don't find them, find something else."

"Sir, we were looking for weeks last time," said Vijay. "The most likely spots were all covered intensively. It's hard to imagine much of significance escaping our notice."

Mishra scowled. "You can always find something, Singh. Do it legally, of course, but the laws are open to considerable, uh, interpretation. Keep in mind that our nation is in the state of Emergency. These tax evaders are undermining our society, not to mention our Prime Minister's great vision."

"Of course, sir," said Ghosali, before Vijay could speak. "We will do everything possible to achieve your aims. I will personally see to it."

6

Mangarh

The sun had barely risen above the low mountains when the raiders' vehicles crested the rise and drove though the tower-flanked gateway of Mangarh's outer defenses. The small city lay spread before them, dominated by the huge fortress on the ridge above, with the profile of the elephant's head on the northerly end of the hill. The battlements and towers and cupolas of the *garh* glowed in the rosy orange early morning light.

"Even though we think we searched every part of that fort, it still seems like there's a mystery to it," said Ranjit, seated with Vijay in the back seat of the jeep driven by Akbar Khan. "It's like there's more to it than anyone can grasp, with so many different sections added over so many centuries, and they're on so many levels, and each part is so complex. I can take one building at a time and eventually understand the layout, but put it all together, and it's too much."

Vijay's stomach was queasy, and he was growing increasingly on edge as they approached the town. On the previous raid, he'd persuaded the only person recognizing him as a Bhangi not to expose him. He might not be so lucky this time. He probably wouldn't lose his job, but the humiliation and embarrassment after all the lies to his coworkers would be unbearable. And a promotion anytime soon would be out of the question.

He forced himself to focus on what Ranjit was saying and tried to speak lightly. "You're almost getting poetic about the fort. That's unusual for you!"

Ranjit shrugged. "I suppose. It's an impressive group of buildings. Not just the size, but the architecture's so elaborate."

Vijay realized that Dev Batra's Mercedes was already out of sight up ahead. He turned to look back and saw that the white Ambassador carrying Anil Ghosali and others still was close behind; then came the bus carrying the remaining income tax personnel.

"I assume we didn't need another search warrant," Ranjit observed, "since

Mangarh Fortress, c. 1976

the previous one's probably still in effect."

"Right," said Vijay. He tried to suppress his anxiety. "Besides," he continued in a tone of irony, "the government's still claiming ownership of the *garh*. So I suppose we can argue that we're searching our own property when we're there. A warrant's only needed to search the newer palace and any other locations."

"Do you think the government can get away with taking the fort from the royal family?" asked Ranjit.

"You know how long matters can get tied up in the courts. And so long as the Emergency's in effect, I'd guess the family will have an even harder time than usual. Eventually, when the Emergency's over, I hope our leaders will be more sensible."

Down on the valley floor, the vehicles entered a newer, middle class residential neighborhood on the outskirts of the town and passed several uniformed children walking to school, then a horse-drawn tonga crowded with still more children. "Go slower now," Vijay directed Akbar Khan. Since Vijay spoke the local dialect, he had been chosen to recruit the two *panch* witnesses, and he kept a lookout now for likely persons. The Ambassador and the bus passed the jeep and continued toward the fort.

"How about them?" asked Ranjit. Two gray haired men, wearing *kurta* pajamas and vests, and almost certainly retired, were conversing outside the gate of a home, enjoying themselves from the looks of their smiles. Vijay quickly glanced about. "Stop here," he told Akbar Khan.

He took the needed forms from his brief case, approached the men, and briefly explained the search and the legal requirement of two impartial, reputable citizen witnesses. The newly recruited observers, a retired engineer and a retired Army brigadier, seemed glad for a change from their usual routines. After quick explanations to their wives, they took the remaining seats in the jeep, and the party continued onward.

A light haze of smoke hung in the air from the wood and dung fueled cooking fires. The road became increasingly crowded with men walking or bicycling on their way to work. The jeep entered the walled old town, and the streets narrowed. Akbar Khan honked the horn continuously as the jeep slowed to ease past several vegetable vendors with their pushcarts. A cow ambled across the roadway, forcing the jeep to stop for a moment. Barefoot women clad in the colorful full skirts and veils typical of the area bent over displays of produce or stopped at the small street side temples to ring the bells and worship.

At last the jeep reached the huge lower gateway of the *garh*, where the massive wood doors, studded with sharp spikes to prevent assault by charging elephants, hung open. The bus had not attempted to climb the access road, so it was parked nearby, empty now except for the driver. Inside the gate, the narrow, cobblestoned roadway made a sharp right turn through another archway flanked by towers, and ascended the side of the hill.

As they neared the top, they passed the tax officers from the bus who were climbing the hill on foot. Several black faced langur monkeys scampered along the top of the wall lining the road. The jeep entered the gateway and stopped in the big main courtyard. The Mercedes and the Ambassador were already parked. Dev Batra, Anil Ghosali, Shanta Das, the other woman tax officer Janaki Desai, and several others from the Delhi office were waiting. Vijay and his party left the jeep and joined them. He saw that a large gang of workmen was already near the gate, awaiting instructions.

The remaining officers, including Nimbalkar and Krishnaswamy, arrived, some appearing out of breath after the climb.

Batra shoved his sunglasses up on his forehead and looked about. "By God," he said. "This time we'll tear the place apart until we're sure we've found *everything*! Anil, go get those workmen started. Vijay, get the other tax agents busy on their areas."

Ghosali strode toward the laborers. Vijay hesitated momentarily. The other tax officers were experienced, and they knew their orders. Having him repeat their instructions seemed superfluous.

Airavata, the huge elephant, was chained in his usual corner of the courtyard, and Batra, as if he'd already forgotten what he'd just told Vijay, said, "That bloody animal! I'll never forget how he soaked me. I'm keeping my distance this time, but I'm waiting for my moment. If he's so smart, I wonder if he's realizing he's as good as dead!"

Airavata was standing motionless, eyeing them. Vijay strongly hoped Batra wouldn't get around to following through on the threat. He thought of how Batra had tormented the elephant on the earlier raid, and how fitting it had seemed when Airavata later got even by drenching Batra with a trunk full of water. But Batra was clever as well as vengeful, and he had Sen and Gulab with him to carry out his wishes.

The timekeeper's gong reverberated across the courtyard, and Vijay looked up to see the turbaned old man in his small porch above the main gate.

Batra glanced at his Rolex. "Only nine minutes off, this time," he said. "I could hardly believe it when I heard he still uses a water clock! And hasn't he heard of Indian Standard Time?"

"Mangarh has been in another world," Vijay said. "Outside time isn't important here."

The sound of a noisy engine came from the approach road, and a tractor drove in through the gate, a blade attached to its front and a power shovel on the back. "Well," said Batra, "we're bringing Mangarh into modern India. Fast."

After the team of searchers began their work again in the old fortress, Vijay had Akbar Khan drive him and Shanta Das down to the newer Bhim Bhawan Palace. The weather was getting hotter, a harbinger of the oven-like temperatures that would gradually build up over the next couple of months. Vijay wore his sunglasses to be less easily recognized.

The tree studded, parklike area surrounding the new palace was quite in contrast to the noise and congestion of the nearby crowded city. The European style palace, with its symmetrical, columned facade and domes, and its clock tower, was also dramatically different from the indigenous architecture of the old fortress and the walled town.

Vijay could not help but think of his experience in the waste removal tunnels beneath the palace on the earlier raid, when he had been so upset by the practical joke played upon him by the Maharaja. He knew the ruler's intention had probably not been to embarrass him personally, but rather the prank had been a relatively harmless way to get back at the tax raiders for the harassment of the royal family. Still, because the incident triggered emotions in Vijay involving his secret background as an Untouchable, he had, to his immediate regret, reacted much more strongly than he would have in normal circumstances.

Without the Maharaja in residence, the pillared veranda was bare of visitors. Shiv, the ancient retainer, met them at the top of the steps and escorted them into the palace office. There, Naresh Singh, the Maharaja's aide de camp, dressed in his usual khaki uniform, rose and invited them to be seated. He knew, of course, about the resumption of the raid, and he sent Shiv to inform Mahendra Singh and Kaushalya Kumari of the visitors.

Naresh Singh's eyes met Vijay's and he nodded with a slight, brief, knowing smile. On the previous raid, the ADC was the one person who had recognized Vijay as a Bhangi from Gamri village. Vijay fleetingly returned the smile and gave a nod of gratitude for keeping the confidence.

The handsome, slightly heavy, prince soon appeared, with his sister. Vijay was again captivated by the princess' beauty. Elegant in a pastel blue *shalwar kameez*, Kaushalya Kumari had a light, wheatish complexion, and the type of well-defined features a sculptor would love.

Vijay forced himself to concentrate on the reason he'd come. "Miss Das," Vijay said, "would you kindly show them the passage in the book."

Shanta opened Stanley Powis' memoir at the marked page and handed the volume to the prince. While Mahendra Singh was reading, Vijay glanced surreptitiously at the princess, then at Shanta Das. They were both so attractive, he found it hard to keep his eyes away from one or the other. He had done considerable fantasizing about the princess, especially during the previous search. He had found it almost impossible to erase her from his mind. Except, that is, when he was near Shanta.

He returned his attention to Mahendra Singh, who shrugged and said, "This may not pertain to Mangarh at all!" The prince gave the book to his sister.

Kaushalya Kumari put on her glasses, read the page, and looked up.

"I've never seen these chests of gold ingots. And we have very few miniature paintings left—only those that you've already seen. If we did have more, I'd know of them. That Maharaja mentioned here by Stanley Powis could have been any of a number of rulers."

Vijay said, "It's clear Powis was the political agent at Mangarh for several years and was quite friendly with your father."

Mahendra Singh said, "That's true. It's common knowledge he was here. But it proves nothing. Even if the items Powis mentioned were in the Mangarh treasury, most of them must have been disposed of years ago."

Vijay started to leave, then halted. "I have to ask out of curiosity. Can you tell me anything about the Bhavani sword that Powis says he saw?"

The two exchanged glances. "If Powis is speaking of a sword in Mangarh, I have no idea what happened to it," said Mahendra Singh slowly. "Years ago, our family worshiped a sword belonging to our ancestors. But it's not in the *puja* room any more. My father would be the only one who might know what happened to it."

Vijay sighed. "I appreciate your time." He had not really expected anything to come of the visit, but there had been little lost in trying.

The princess escorted him and Shanta out. At the top of the steps from the main doorway, Vijay hesitated, looking down to where Akbar Khan was polishing the jeep.

Kaushalya Kumari stood near. Vijay knew his superiors would probably prefer he not say anything about the matter, but he decided he needed to. "Princess," he said in a quiet voice, "you may want to ensure Airavata always has someone with him these days."

Kaushalya Kumari stared at him, first blankly, then with understanding growing in her eyes. She nodded, and said casually, "Yes, I'm concerned about his health. I'll tell Harlal, his mahout. And the guards."

Relieved that she had grasped the situation so quickly, Vijay, with Shanta following, went down the steps. "I'm glad you said something," said Shanta, when they were in the jeep. "I've been worried also."

Vijay smiled tightly. "I had a feeling you'd figure it out."

"Mr. Batra isn't someone who would easily forgive being humiliated."

"No. Even when he deserved it."

The team from New Delhi was again staying in the *dak* bungalow, and that evening after eating, they remained in the dining room under the flickering fluorescent lights. Dev Batra held court at one table, with his two men Sen and Gulab, and with Ghosali and several other tax officers. A.S. Nimbalkar sat on the fringe of the group, looking awed by the privilege of being in such close proximity to such an influential man.

Vijay caught parts of the conversation, in which Batra was extolling the virtues of Swami Surya. "Swamiji predicted I would advance quickly," Batra said. "And that's just what happened."

Ghosali, frowning, said in a voice Vijay could barely hear, "He predicted the same for me. I'm still waiting."

Batra laughed. "Well, he didn't say exactly when, did he?"

"No," admitted Ghosali.

"It helps," Batra said, "to be close to Sanjay. I see him almost every day, of course, and people know that."

Ghosali looked glum, probably at the realization he was unlikely to gain such close access himself.

At Vijay's table were Ranjit, Krishnaswamy, Mrs. Desai, and Shanta. Janaki Desai said to them, "I'm still uncertain as to just how we go about searching this time, when we looked so thoroughly before. It's hard to come up with any new places to look."

Ranjit took a sip of his rum and cola and said, "I think we have to search the old places again, but in a different way. We were looking for large quantities of treasure before. Entire strong rooms full. The gems we're hunting for are so much smaller."

"What about the gold?" Shanta asked. "That would take more space than the gems. It should be harder to conceal."

Vijay absently rotated his Limca bottle around on the table. He said, "That's true, if it's indeed still here." He abruptly realized he had been gazing at Shanta almost to the exclusion of the others, and he quickly glanced around to see if anyone had noticed. If they had, they were tactfully pretending otherwise.

"You think it was sent elsewhere?" asked Krishnaswamy, with his hint of a Tamil accent. "We went over the books so carefully last time. It seems like if the gold or the gems were sold, the transactions would have shown up in the ledgers."

"That's only true if the sales were recorded," said Janaki Desai. "They might not have been written down, to keep them secret from tax people such as us."

"Or," said Vijay, "there may be two sets of books. One for them, and one for us."

Everyone smiled, since keeping two sets of books was indeed such a common practice.

"We didn't find any others," said Krishnaswamy. "And I looked hard."

"It seems," said Shanta, "so easy to store such small items as the gems off the premises for safekeeping. Maybe in a strong box at a bank or other business in town, or even in another city."

Krishnaswamy said, "The deposit boxes in Bombay and Delhi we've looked at belonging to the royal family have had little in them, you remember. Securities, cash, some rings and other jewelry of relatively small value."

"Again," said Vijay, "there may not be any obvious records of them."

"It seems to me," said Ranjit, "this is a real 'needle in a haystack' search." He looked toward Batra. "But I guess we have to keep trying."

7

Kaushalya and Gopi were seated on round cane stools in the mango orchard in front of the Bhim Bhawan Palace. On her watercolor pad, Kaushalya was trying to create an arrangement of the trees, with the barest hint of the domes of the palace in the background.

She at last gave up; the balance of the composition was simply wrong, and she didn't have the energy to concentrate on getting it right. It was too hard to focus on imaginative work when she couldn't get her mind off Daddyji in jail, or the tax raiders up at the fortress and so close nearby in the palace.

"How are you doing, Gopi?" she asked her maid.

Her elderly maid almost always used animals or birds as her subjects, and she was drawing the peacocks parading beneath the trees. The birds were arranged at almost equal spacings over the page, and as if seen from an angle above. They were drawn in realistic detail, although two-dimensional.

Kaushalya said, "Your perspective is similar to the artists who painted Mughal miniatures. Maybe you're a reincarnated painter from that time."

Gopi laughed, pleased at the thought. "Maybe I am!"

Through the trees, they saw a jeep speeding along the approach road to the palace. She assumed it was one of the income tax officers' vehicles, although it could be a Rajput visitor also, since they so commonly drove jeeps. Seeing no reason to linger, she and Gopi gathered up their drawing materials and walked back to the palace. Soon one of the servants summoned Kaushalya to the veranda of her brother's apartments.

She was delighted at the sight of Mahendra's guest. "So good to have you here again, Pratap!" she said to the son of the ex-Maharaja of Shantipur. She'd last seen him in New Delhi, where he was doing graduate studies in botany. "Are you just passing through?"

"Actually, yes," replied the slender, pleasant faced, bespectacled young man. "I'm on my way home. But of course I wanted to see how you and your brother are faring in your problems with the government."

Kaushalya inclined her head. "That's so kind of you. Many of our friends are avoiding us now, you know."

"I gathered that," said Pratap Singh. He shoved his eyeglasses higher on his nose. "I'm sorry."

Mahendra shrugged. "Understandable, under the circumstances. Still..."

A servant approached with drinks for the two princes, and Kaushalya ordered a *nimbu pani*.

Pratap said to her, "Your brother was just telling me about the government claiming title to the fortress. It will never stand up in court. Nevertheless, it could take years to clear up."

"I think that's what the government's counting on."

"Undoubtedly. It's worrisome. If they do it to you, they can do it to anyone. My own family, too. Anyone at all."

They sat in silence, sipping their drinks. Mahendra noticed how Pratap's eyes lingered on Kaushalya, who seemed unaware of the fact.

"I worry a lot about your father," Pratap said, shifting his gaze back to Mahendra.

"We all do," said Mahendra. "But so far we've been totally frustrated in getting him out of jail."

Pratap shook his head. "I wish there were something I could do." He gave a crooked grin. "I miss looking through his telescopes with him. He always took me up to the roof to look at stars and planets whenever I visited. The first time, I must have been only five years old. Yet, he treated me as if I were an adult."

"Some of our best conversations were up on the roof at night, with those telescopes," said Kaushalya. She blinked back tears and looked away, lost in memories.

After a time, Pratap looked about, as if he had suddenly become wary. "Is there any chance of our being overheard here by someone who might report to the government?"

"I don't think so, no," said Kaushalya, her curiosity aroused.

"We're safe at the moment," said Mahendra. "The tax people are all up at the *garh*."

Pratap hauled some folded cyclostyled papers from his pocket. He grinned and said, "I thought you might appreciate seeing these." He handed one to Mahendra, another to Kaushalya.

Both were newsletters criticizing the Emergency. On the one held by Kaushalya was a cartoon depicting Indira Gandhi as a school teacher. Madam stood before a blackboard on which was printed in large letters, "INDIA IS THE WORLD'S LARGEST DEMOCRACY." The PM was pointing to the phrase with a big, spike-studded club and directing her class, "OK, children, repeat after me...."

Kaushalya burst into laughter. "Oh, that's priceless!" She peered at the cartoon again. The style looked familiar. She looked up at Pratap. "You drew this."

He grinned again. "That would be treasonous. How could I do such a thing?"

"Easily, given your sentiments."

Pratap did not deny his involvement.

The ancient manservant Shiv appeared on the veranda and bowed to them. "Highness," he said to Mahendra in the local Rajasthani, "Captain Surmal requests that you come to the fortress. He says it's urgent."

"Oh, hell," muttered Mahendra, setting down his drink and rising. "What now?"

"I'd better come, too," said Kaushalya.

"Do you mind if I join you?" asked Pratap as he refolded the newsletters and returned them to his pocket. "Or if you'd rather, I'll leave."

"We're glad to have you," said Mahendra. "But you must be aware, it could be troublesome for you if the government thinks you're closely associated with us. The tax raiders might jump on your own family next."

"I'll take that risk," said Pratap calmly. "I refuse to let them intimidate me."

"Then please do come," said Mahendra. "You can see in person what we're up against here."

Since Pratap's jeep was conveniently parked outside, he drove them to the old fortress. Indeed, a jeep was the most appropriate type of vehicle for negotiating the steep, cobblestoned switchbacks climbing the rocky hillside to the huge *garh* and palace complex.

As they entered the big main courtyard where Airavata the elephant was eating his fodder, the timekeeper in his little balcony by the gate sounded the gong signaling three o'clock in the afternoon.

Surmal, the Bhil guard captain, quickly led the three to the old public audience hall. Between the delicately carved pillars near a corner of the open-sided pavilion, workmen had just begun using a jackhammer driven by an air compressor to break up the marble floor. Dust from the stone spewed up and drifted across the structure.

"Oh, God," Kaushalya moaned. She stormed over to where Vijay Singh stood in the courtyard with Anil Ghosali. "Stop it!" she screamed, trying to be heard above the racket.

"Yes, stop at once!" Mahendra shouted.

"That floor's three hundred years old!" shrieked Kaushalya.

Vijay fervently wished he could help, but at the moment he lacked the authority. He scowled at Anil Ghosali, who was calmly smoking his pipe.

The jackhammer halted as the operator changed locations. Ghosali removed his pipe from his mouth and said stonily to the newcomers, "Your Highness, and Princess, I have my own orders from Batraji. Our metal detectors show there's something under there."

"Of course there is!" said Kaushalya. The marble dust in the air was irritating her throat, and she cleared it. "The builders used metal pieces to tie the stones together. You can see them all over in the basement levels."

Mahendra said, "You know we're suing the government to challenge the order claiming the fort. Can't you wait until the court decides?"

Ghosali gazed expressionlessly at him. "Regretfully, it's out of my hands, sir."

"So it's Dev Batra's doing?" demanded Mahendra.

"That's correct," said Ghosali. "Before he left for Delhi this morning he gave me specific instructions. He represents the Prime Minister, you know. And he'll be back in two days."

"Bloody hell!" Mahendra said, looking about helplessly. "They never let us alone."

"This is outrageous," said Pratap Singh to Ghosali.

"And who might you be?" asked Ghosali icily.

"My name is Pratap Singh."

"The *Rajkumar* of Shantipur," said Mahendra, "and not without some influence himself."

Ghosali gave a curt nod that somehow managed to be respectful and disdainful at the same time, and turned to look at the workmen.

Kaushalya said loudly, more to Vijay than to Ghosali, "This audience hall was designed by the same architect who built the Taj Mahal! How can you tear it up?!"

Vijay groped for a way to respond. While he tried to marshal his thoughts, he asked, "It was designed by the same man? I always thought no one knew for sure who designed the Taj."

"We can't prove it," said Kaushalya. "But there's a story in our family. That marble is from Makrana. The same as the marble for the Taj—"

The jackhammer started again, drowning her voice.

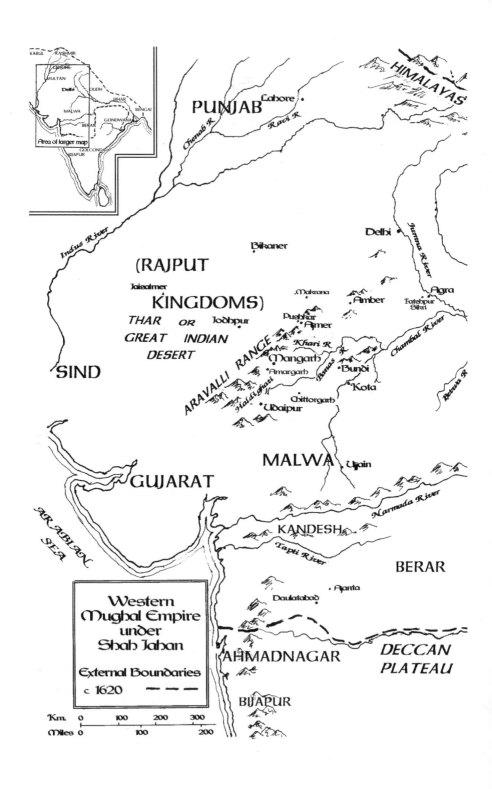

Western
Mughal Empire
under
Shah Jahan

External Boundaries
c. 1620   — — —

Km.   0   100   200   300
Miles 0   100   200

Master Builder

1

Udaipur, Mewar State, in the third year of the reign of Maharana Karan Singh, 1623

The sun had disappeared behind the hills guarding Lake Pichola, and darkness would soon blanket the valley. Mohan Lal, atop the bamboo scaffolding on the addition to the small summer palace, felt the first of the cooling breezes which would disperse the heat of the spring day. In the air was a whiff of mango and orange blossoms from the trees in the adjacent gardens.

Three boat loads of workmen had already left for the landing at Udaipur, visible only a few minutes away. Mohan Lal clambered down a ladder and hurried around the corner at his habitual rapid pace.

His friend Bhagwan Das, head of the sculptors' guild, was squatting on the ground, gathering up favorite hammers and chisels. The sculptor would take them with him to the mainland for the night, not trusting to leave them out of his sight. He glanced up as the chief architect approached. A smile flooded Bhagwan Das's round face in greeting for the stocky, sun-darkened man whom the Maharana had brought in to design and oversee the project.

The sculptor stood in respect and said, "We'll begin carving the cusps on arches in the morning, Master Builder. Are you satisfied with the blocks? They seem sound to me."

Mohan had already inspected the white Makrana marble when the workmen unloaded it from the barges, and he had carefully noted the differing subtle grayish patterns. Even though he trusted Bhagwan Das's judgment, Mohan bustled over to where the blocks had been stored in readiness and strode down the line of stones, as the sculptor hurried to keep up.

"These are all fine pieces. Top quality," Mohan said. He pointed to two of them. "Let's use these in front of the door on each side, where they'll be seen the most."

Bhagwan Das marked the two blocks with charcoal.

"Good work by your men today, as usual," Mohan said. "But you'd better go—your boat's already loaded. You don't want to be stuck on the island with me all night."

The sculptor laughed; it was one of the chief architect's standard jokes, said almost every day to whomever was last to leave the island. Bhagwan Das retrieved his tool bag, hoisted it to his shoulder, and hurried off.

Mohan cast his eyes over the work site one more time, looking for potential problems. He examined the curved stone blocks for the dome. The masons had been rough-fitting them on the ground prior to hoisting them atop the roof.

Satisfied, he turned to watch as the boat moved away, trailing a fan of ripples across the placid surface of the lake toward the landing near the Maharana's palace, where the sun's last glow was fading from the uppermost cupolas. It was a sight Mohan loved; maybe some day he could add a building to the mainland, as well as this one he was completing on the tiny island.

As usual, Mohan himself would spend the night on the island with his son, Chandra Lal, and their servant and cook, Ram Das. The construction of an addition to the island's small guest palace was the center of Mohan's life so long as it remained uncompleted; while he was supervising a project he always lived on the site.

He was about to turn away when he saw another boat, a much larger one, moving rapidly toward the island. The high, canopy-covered stern and the row of oarsmen on each side marked it as a barge from the Maharana's own fleet. But who would be visiting now, with night falling?

Mohan's sober faced, slender nineteen year old son and apprentice, Chandra, joined him. "We have visitors, Father."

"So it seems."

They hurried to the water's edge. As the boat drew near, they were surprised to see seated under the canopy the short, thin figure of the Maharana's chief minister, Dungar Shah. The vessel slid alongside the stone landing. Two boatmen leaped ashore and secured the mooring lines. Dungar Shah, followed by several attendants, stepped from the boat.

Mohan Lal bowed his head and folded his palms in welcome. "An honor, Chief Minister," he said.

Dungar Shah returned the greeting. He peered toward the construction project. "How is your work coming, Master Builder?" His voice gave no hint of the reason for his visit.

"Quite well, Chief Minister. We're ahead of schedule. May I show you around?"

Dungar Shah raised his eyebrows. He was noted for reorganizing the administration of Mewar to operate more efficiently, and he was clearly impressed by the uniqueness of a project progressing faster than expected. The minister replied, "I regret I don't have time to examine your work more closely. But I've no doubt whatsoever it's being completed to perfection."

Dungar Shah motioned for his entourage to remain where they stood, and he beckoned Mohan Lal to come a short distance away. Mohan followed, his curiosity aroused even further. Dungar Shah resumed, "I regret any inconvenience to your work, but His Highness the Maharana will be housing a guest on the island. The visitor will arrive after dark tomorrow. Everything must be ready for him."

The minister saw Mohan's consternation and continued, "I see no reason for your construction to slow. The visitor will occupy only the main wing. You should scarcely be aware of him and his party except when they come and go from the island." After a slight hesitation, he added, "And that will mostly be at night."

Mohan had tensed at the mention of the visitor occupying the older wing. That was where Mohan himself was staying. But the impact on the project itself was more important. He said, "His Highness knows my building mustn't be delayed. I have to return to my Varanasi temple project as soon as possible."

"His Highness is aware of your situation, Master Builder. However, it's vitally important that the presence of this guest be kept secret. The island is ideal for that. In fact, your construction work even provides a good screen. No one should suspect we'd house someone of such high rank under these conditions."

Mohan clenched his teeth. "Who is this guest?"

The minister's eyes slid away. "Maybe you'd best not know. His Majesty has ordered that the guest be afforded strict privacy. He's a noble, a very high noble, who is in an awkward position at the moment."

The guest must be extremely important, Mohan Lal realized, for the Maharana to go to so much trouble. He sighed. "As you wish, Chief Minister."

Mohan ordered his servant, Ram Das, to move their belongings from the three-storied main wing, near the southern shore, to a small pillared pavilion at the edge of the garden. Throughout much of the next day, boats came and went, ferrying servants and workers who cleaned and resupplied the building the guest would occupy. Mohan's men slowed their own work as they watched these activities which were so new to the quiet little island, but there was no direct interference with the construction project.

After darkness, the guest and his entourage of a couple hundred or so arrived quietly in the Maharana's barges. The majority of the party were soldiers armed with swords and shields. "I wonder who he is," said Chandra, as he and his father watched. "With so many men, he's obviously a great lord."

"Any high noble could have that many," replied Mohan Lal.

"But who would come in such secrecy?"

Mohan sighed. "Well, hopefully, he won't stay long. This island's barely large enough for the buildings and gardens, much less a big camp of soldiers."

"Our construction is bound to be hindered."

"You're right. I want you to be my representative to them. Do your best to keep them away from me. And from our workmen."

Chandra frowned at the unusual task given to him, but he nodded. "I understand, Father."

Mohan smiled at the way his son calmly accepted the added responsibility. "I'm sure you'll handle it well."

Chandra, who seldom smiled himself, managed a slight one in response to the praise.

Early the next morning, Chandra's eyes were unusually bright as he hurried back from conferring with one of the mysterious guest's aides. "Father! Our visitor is the Emperor's son—Prince Shah Jahan! He's still in revolt against his father, so he's hiding here from the Emperor's army. I don't understand it. Didn't Shah Jahan almost ruin Mewar several years ago when he conquered the Maharana's father?"

"Yes," said Mohan. "But afterwards, Shah Jahan was quite generous to Maharana Karan. They've been on good terms ever since."

Chandra glanced about. "This does seem a good place to house a guest secretly."

Mohan considered the implications of having the heir-apparent to the Emperor's throne in such close proximity. Mohan himself was too used to dealing with members of the royalty to hold them in awe. Kings and princes frequently sponsored his building projects, and as chief architect he dealt with them from necessity. But princes often made waves that could inundate others near by. He said, "I certainly hope the Emperor's army doesn't attack our island to capture the prince."

Shah Jahan's rebellion had been a frequent topic of conversation. Ironically, the crown prince was thought to be still loyal to his father Jahangir. However, the aging and ill Emperor had fallen almost completely under the influence of his favorite Queen, Noor Jahan. She had turned against the crown prince and convinced the Emperor to send Shah Jahan on a military expedition to far-off Afghanistan, so the prince would not be in a convenient position to assume the throne if Jahangir should die. The outraged Shah Jahan, who had expected since childhood to succeed his father, had set out to thwart those who would deny him his right.

So far, the prince's campaign had failed, and the imperial troops were only a few days behind in their pursuit. "I think the Maharana's risking war by sheltering him," Mohan said to Chandra. "Our safety depends on it being secret, but the Emperor will have spies here. We'd better hope the prince's stay is short."

"Another aspect, Father," said Chandra, his eyes serious. "I'm sure the prince and his men are accustomed to doing as they please. I may find it impossible to keep them from getting in our way."

Mohan gave a wry smile. "You may at that. We'll manage as best we can."

Mohan Lal's new quarters in the stone pavilion of the fragrant garden were ample for his and Chandra's simple needs, so he did not mind giving up the larger building to the prince. Indeed, in the hot weather, long before the pre-monsoon showers, one scarcely needed shelter at all.

Mohan pointedly remained away from the prince's apartments, and he caught only occasional glimpses of the important guest. But on a warm evening the fourth day after Shah Jahan's arrival, as Mohan made a last inspection of the day's work before darkness fell, he became aware of a presence nearby. He turned and saw the richly robed and turbaned crown prince with several courtiers and bodyguards.

"You are the architect," Shah Jahan observed, staring at him with almond-shaped, dark, piercing eyes.

Mohan quickly bowed his head and touched his palm to his forehead. "I am, Your Highness."

Shah Jahan gestured toward the partially finished row of marble arches atop their pillars. "This building is a harmonious balance. At first glance it appears less sophisticated than the work of most architects these days. But to my own eye, your more subdued ornamentation is much lovelier."

Mohan carefully hid his surprise at how knowledgeable the crown prince sounded. In the smooth voice he affected whenever he spoke to persons of high rank he replied, "I'm most pleased that you like it, Your Highness. I try to construct all my buildings to perfection. May I show you around?"

"Yes. I want to see your efforts in detail."

Mohan made a conscious effort to move slowly so as not to leave the prince too far behind. As Shah Jahan stopped to eye the sculptors' work, Mohan Lal examined the prince. Shah Jahan appeared close to Mohan's own age of thirty-five years. He was of medium height and build, with a neatly trimmed short beard framing a sharp featured face marred by smallpox scars, but otherwise quite handsome.

"This reminds me of a pavilion I once visited on the lake at Mangarh," Shah Jahan said, turning to Mohan Lal.

"My father designed the one at Mangarh," Mohan replied with pride. "I was inspired by it when I designed this. And when I did the renovation a few years ago of the rooms where you're now staying."

"I see. The circular room under the main dome is unusual, but I find it pleasing. And I like the inlay work in the marble."

Mohan smiled. "Other builders have mentioned marble inlays favorably, also, Highness."

"Indeed." The prince continued his inspection of the construction site, saying, "I remodeled a small palace in Kabul when I lived there. And I designed gardens in Kashmir for my father. Some day I hope to be able to build again." His eyes shone brightly at Mohan, and his voice took on an eagerness. "Tell me. What problems did you encounter building in the middle of a lake? How did you divert the waters?"

Pleased at the perceptiveness of the questions, Mohan was glad to respond. "This island was already here. I'm sure Your Highness knows the lake is artificial. In the dry season, I had the waters drained while the foundations were sunk. The only remaining difficulty was transporting materials and men."

Shah Jahan slowly nodded. "You've been using boats and barges. I assume the project wasn't big enough to justify building a causeway."

"Correct, Highness. Frankly, I could not have agreed to take on a larger job. I'm occupied with another project at Varanasi, so I'm here a few months at most. I'll be finished well before the rains come." He added as explanation, "When I did the original renovation of your quarters, I agreed with the Maharana that I'd also build any future additions. He insisted on holding me to my promise."

"What is your project in Varanasi?"

In his enthusiasm, it did not occur to Mohan that a Muslim such as the prince might not share his ardor. He replied, "A temple, Your Highness—a great temple to Lord Shiva! It will be the largest in Varanasi. My patron is the Raja of Mangarh."

Shah Jahan was silent for a time before saying, "I know the Raja well. One of our finest commanders." He looked away and added, in a tone of displeasure, "There are already so many temples in Varanasi, are there not?" He abruptly strode away, his entourage quietly following.

Mohan stared after him, then shrugged to himself. One couldn't expect princes, whose every whim had always been indulged, to be either agreeable or polite for long.

The troops pursuing the crown prince had apparently not yet discovered that he was secluded in Udaipur; they were reported to be chasing the main body of Shah Jahan's army southward. In the meantime, when Shah Jahan was not occupied with his host the Maharana, he sometimes sought out Mohan Lal or summoned the architect to a meal. Always the purpose was to discuss architecture, with the prince extracting information from Mohan about construction methods.

"That temple of yours that you are so eager to build in Varanasi," said Shah Jahan at one visit. "Why do your patrons such as Raja Arjuna continue to build more temples when the cities and the countryside are already filled with them?"

They were beneath a large, open sided cloth canopy erected in front of the prince's apartments. The evening was hot, and attendants were briskly waving fans to move the air and discourage the mosquitoes. Several of the prince's attendants and courtiers sat near. Mohan tried not to show his puzzlement at a question with obvious answers. "Your Highness, the temple will honor Lord Shiva, providing him another fine home." He smiled to show he was partly jesting as he added, "Much as a prince or a king might want to build another palace."

Shah Jahan did not smile at the attempt at humor.

Mohan continued, "It's another place for Lord Shiva's people to worship him. And good works confer great merit and good karma upon the project's sponsor. They also are an obvious demonstration to everyone of the sponsor's high standing and wealth. Of course, sometimes building a temple is done in fulfillment of a promise made to a god in exchange for granting a boon."

"When a mosque is built by a follower of Islam," said Shah Jahan dour-faced, "it is an act of charity, providing an added place for worshipers to declare their faith and their submission to Allah."

"That's really not so different from the main purpose for building a temple, Highness."

The prince's eyes were cold. "The difference is that your gods are false. Mere idols. There is only one true God, whose prophet is Muhammad."

Mohan looked away, unsure how to respond. Although some earlier Muslim conquerors and rulers had been quite tolerant of other beliefs, even sponsoring the construction of new temples, some had also ruthlessly destroyed thousands of temples and built mosques on the sites.

"I fear I have earned your displeasure," said the prince to Mohan's surprise. "I had not planned that. I value your friendship and your knowledge of the arts of building."

Mohan looked back to him. "I—I'm honored, Your Highness." Could the prince truly think a friendship was possible between two men of such vastly unequal status, not to mention such different backgrounds and faiths?

"I have been in a foul mood," said the prince, "with my father's army so close to attacking me."

"Quite understandable, Highness."

"I must now tend to other matters," said Shah Jahan in dismissal.

The presence of the prince and his entourage sometimes annoyed Mohan and the artisans. One evening, when Mohan and Chandra were about to take their dinner, they heard splashing and shouting in the direction of the steps at the lake's edge.

They found Shah Jahan and most of his retinue assembled, watching and commenting loudly as a servant hurled pieces of meat into the water. There, a number of giant crocodiles brutally jostled each other for the food.

Chandra's mouth fell open. "I knew there were crocodiles here. But—"

"They're huge!" Mohan exclaimed.

Chandra began to count. "Eight, no, nine of them!" He turned to his father. "After this, I'll bathe in the garden pool, not in the lake."

"The crocodiles have never bothered us before, but now they'll be coming around looking for more meat." Yes, Mohan thought, princes were always a nuisance; the only question was what form the trouble would take.

A few days later, in mid-morning, the sound of a musket shot came from the gardens and echoed about the stone buildings. Mohan's workmen uneasily halted their labors to peer in the direction of the shooting.

Another shot. Then another.

Mohan hurried toward the sound, slowing his pace as he entered the garden, uncertain as to whether there was any danger to himself.

Another shot. At the far left end of the garden, he saw Shah Jahan seated on the ground. Beside him were several servants, reloading matchlocks and handing them to the prince, who would quickly aim and fire at targets at the garden's far end. Shah Jahan took no notice of Mohan Lal, who watched through several firings.

Mohan returned to tell his workmen to resume their jobs. The prince repeated his target practice on two other days, but the workers then paid little attention.

Sometimes, during the working time, Mohan would look up from his supervisory duties to see the prince and a small retinue standing a short distance away, watching. Occasionally, Shah Jahan would approach Mohan to ask a question about the project; he seemed especially interested in the way the masons were rapidly piecing together the small dome crowning the roof. But the greater part of waking hours, Shah Jahan was away on the mainland, presumably hunting or being otherwise entertained by Maharana Karan Singh.

Sometimes Mohan and Chandra would be awakened late at night by the noise of the prince's entourage returning to the island. The men always sounded quite drunk, no doubt from revels in the palace of the Maharana or one of the nobles.

When the first monsoon clouds were darkening the sky, shortly before Mohan Lal himself was to return to Varanasi, word came of the approach of imperial troops pursuing the prince. Shah Jahan quickly gathered his followers to leave.

Mohan's workmen, putting the final touches on the building, stood in their workplaces to watch as the prince's party prepared to board the boats. Mohan himself went to the landing to bid Shah Jahan farewell.

Although moving with haste, the prince seemed in good spirits, well rested after almost four months in Udaipur. He smiled slightly at Mohan and said, "I've had many occasions to observe you, Master Builder. I'm impressed with all aspects of your work."

"It's most kind of you to say so, Your Highness. I wish you well."

"I'll need an architect one day," said Shah Jahan, his face abruptly serious. "I'll send for you."

"I'd be honored, Your Highness."

However, that was unlikely to happen, Mohan silently told himself as he watched the prince's boat depart. Shah Jahan's own future was uncertain. And Mohan would be involved with the giant Varanasi temple for at least ten more years.

He was mildly amused that neither fact appeared to unduly trouble the prince.

2

Varanasi, also known as Kashi and Benares. Eight years later, in the fourth year of the reign of the Mughal Emperor Shah Jahan, 1631

Surrounded by scaffolding, the massive *shikhara* soared high into the clear winter sky. The sound of chisels striking stone drifted downward from the upper reaches of the tower. Normally, a holiday would have been declared in honor of the sponsor's visit, but Raja Arjuna of Mangarh had commanded that the work continue so he could watch the artisans in action.

Accompanied by Soma, the supervising Brahmin priest, Mohan Lal was showing Raja Arjuna and his entourage around the huge structure. When the Raja, now in his mid-thirties, last visited Varanasi five years ago, the temple had been a little more than half completed. Today, viewed from a short distance, the almost finished temple resembled a sacred mountain such as Mount Kailasa, where Lord Shiva was said to dwell. As one moved closer, the intricate carvings revealed themselves, both horizontal and vertical in their arrangements, a representation in miniature of the cosmos.

Mohan hurried to a panel in the plinth, the high, broad stone platform upon which the temple rested. "Look at the joints between these stones, Your Highness," Mohan said. "You can scarcely see the cracks."

A frieze of sculptures depicting scenes from daily life ran entirely around the plinth. The Raja stepped close and bent to examine a procession of howdah bearing elephants and foot soldiers. Mohan said, "This depicts Your Highness' triumphant return to Mangarh from the Deccan, after winning your great victory for the Emperor." Shah Jahan had managed to regain the favor of his now-deceased father and assumed the throne, and as his subordinate ally, Raja Arjuna occasionally led armies to suppress rebellions against the Mughal Empire. The Raja looked closely at the scene for some time, then nodded his head, a smile of approval on his lips. "It's fine work. Almost as if the sculptors were there and actually captured the event."

Followed by his umbrella and flywhisk bearers, as well as a few nobles and several bodyguards, Raja Arjuna moved on to a carving of a guru surrounded by disciples, and then to a scene depicting stone carvers themselves at work with their chisels. But Mohan was eager to show the Raja the remainder of the temple. "This way, please, Your Highness."

He had followed rules of the *Vastu shastras*, the ancient texts specifying the precise proportions of a temple. However, the *shastras* left considerable room for interpretation by the architect, and Mohan Lal had fully utilized his

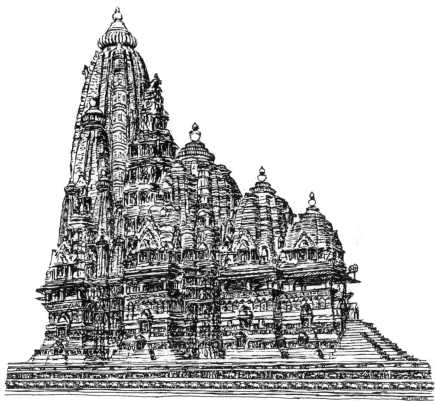

(Dohan Lal's Temple

own creative talents. He ran up the stairway to the terrace of the plinth and strode across the paving stones to the building itself. Here three tall rows of carvings marched around the facade.

Mohan pointed to a sculpture on the middle row. This carving depicted *maithunas*, couples consummating the act of love. "These *maithunas!*" Mohan exclaimed as the Raja caught up to him. "Such grace, such delicacy. Bhagwan Das is a master of his art. We're fortunate we could lure him away from Udaipur to work on your temple, Highness."

Raja Arjuna at first stood some distance from the wall. The carvings were in such deep relief that the figures seemed almost free to escape from the stone blocks from which they had been formed. Given the energetic postures of the subjects, the play of light and shadow made the figures appear alive and moving.

The Raja walked closer to examine a carving that caught his eye. In flowing, bold contours it depicted a standing man and woman locked in a sexual embrace. The woman, wearing only a *mekhala*, the jeweled girdle of earlier centuries, stood with one leg raised high. Her hip jutted out at a jaunty angle, and her pert face wore a delicious smile. The handsome, well-built man, dressed only in a graceful waist cloth, also had a look of pure enjoyment.

Erotic subject matter had long been a decorative motif for temples. Good sculpture, like good poetry, evoked *rasa*—esthetic pleasure. By showing the moment the two bodies reached the highest sensual delight, the sculpture evoked *sringara rasa*, appreciation of the erotic, the theme of much romantic poetry also.

"They're exquisite," said Raja Arjuna. "Comparable to the best at Khajuraho or Mangarh."

Mohan was also curious to see the effect of the carvings on the other visitors present. Several members of the Raja's entourage were intently examining the sculptures. Two of the nobles, one elderly and the other barely old enough for his beard to fill in, were sober-faced, perhaps trying to give the impression of being as cultured and knowledgeable as their Raja. Three of Raja Arjuna's body guards were also looking at the works, but from their bland expressions it was obvious they had little experience of the finer arts.

"These are better than any carved in living memory, Your Highness," Mohan said, loudly enough for all to hear. "Only some masters from long ago can compare." He waved his hand in an arc indicating the surrounding Varanasi area. "It's said that over seventy new temples are being built in Varanasi. But your temple is not only the largest, it's the finest, because of the skill of these sculptors."

"Lord Shiva will be pleased with his new temple, Your Highness," said the priest Soma, his frog-like eyes bulging. "You're acquiring tremendous merit by sponsoring such a magnificent structure."

Mohan tried not to show his dislike for the large-bellied priest. He said to Raja Arjuna, "And each year, Your Highness, many thousands of pilgrims will visit this temple."

The Raja gave a nod in response and moved on to examine the other carvings, going from sculpture to sculpture around the building's base. Though the temple would be dedicated to Shiva, likenesses of dozens of other gods and goddesses graced its surfaces. Under the sculptors' chisels the stones had yielded a multitude of deities, demons, humans, animals, and plants, destined to ornament and inhabit the outer surfaces of the temple for the pleasure of generations upon generations of pilgrims.

"May I show you inside now, Highness?" asked Mohan Lal.

The Raja waved his hand toward the entrance. "Please do, Master Builder."

Mohan escorted him up the steps and into the first of the two *mandaps*. They looked upward into the porch's dome-like ceiling, where the Raja's eyes roved over the intricate ornamentation.

Then they moved into the hall, which resembled a larger version of the outer porch. The Raja stood, slowly moving his gaze about. He smiled. "I can already imagine the dancers entertaining Lord Shiva here," he said, his voice echoing about the hard surfaces.

They slowly entered the womb chamber itself, which would house the *lingam*, the great stone phallus that was Shiva's symbol. If the outer structure of the temple represented a mountain, this darkened inner chamber was a cave carved into the mountain's depths.

The Raja stood for a time, as if imagining the scene after the *lingam* was installed: the priests chanting and burning incense, anointing the God with oil and draping him with flowers, the onlookers crowding in to observe the worship.

Raja Arjuna then turned to Mohan Lal. "I would like to visit the upper levels of the *shikhara*. I assume you have no objection?"

Mohan was surprised, but he said, "My only concern is your safety, Highness. It would be so easy to slip on the scaffolding or the ladders."

"I'll take that chance. Once the scaffolding is removed, I'll never again have the opportunity."

Mohan glanced down at the Raja's feet. Raja Arjuna smiled. "I anticipated the ladders, so I wore riding shoes. They're less likely to slip, since they're designed to stay in place in a stirrup."

So they left the interior, and Mohan led him high up the flimsy-seeming, yet strong, bamboo ladders, to where the sculptors were working to smooth the joints between the carved stones. Mohan was amused to see that Soma, the priest, also felt obligated to climb with the Raja. So far as he knew, the chubby Brahmin had never before been above the plinth level. Two of the Raja's escorting nobles and an attendant also felt that duty required the ascent, but the others suddenly found the sculptures of the lower levels to be so fascinating as to require minute inspection.

Upward they climbed, past stone after stone, all fitted without mortar, but engineered to remain in place for millennia. At the highest level of the scaffolding, sculptor Bhagwan Das set down his chisel and stood on his plank to bow and greet the Raja. "Outstanding work," Raja Arjuna told him. "Many of the masters who carved on earlier temples would be envious."

"You flatter me, Highness."

"Not in the slightest. I'm honored to have such magnificent craftsmanship adorn my gift to Lord Shiva. But tell your men to continue their work so I can watch them."

The stone carvers resumed the delicate chipping away at the stone. The Raja chatted with Bhagwan Das, complimenting him on the *maithunas* and other particular sculptures. Mohan noticed that the priest Soma gripped the bamboo upright tightly, sweat on his face, his eyes appearing to bulge even more than usual. Raja Arjuna, however, seemed little bothered by the height, and indeed stood on the board for a time holding onto nothing whatever. Mohan himself always moved cautiously whenever he climbed the scaffolding, but he respected heights rather than feared them.

After a time, the Raja braced himself on the nearest vertical pole and turned to gaze out over the forested area of lakes and temples of central Varanasi. A short distance away lay the broad, shiny ribbon of the Ganges. Past the base of the temple flowed the small Matsyodari River, which poured into the Varuna River less than a mile to the north. The Varuna then meandered easterly a similar distance before joining the Ganges. The Raja examined the scene for a while, then faced Mohan Lal. "I don't see how the Matsyodari River can reverse course at times. Is the legend really true?"

"It certainly is, Your Highness," Mohan replied. He pointed northerly toward the confluence of the Varuna and the Ganges. "In an unusually heavy monsoon season, the level of the Ganges becomes so high that the waters back up into the Varuna, and then into the Matsyodari." He turned to point in the opposite direction. "The Matsyodari then flows backwards, through those ponds, and falls into the Ganges upstream. This area where we're standing becomes a temporary island."

"Those times are most auspicious, Your Highness," said the priest in his most pompous tone. He still gripped the bamboo as if terrified it might pull free. "You must try to visit on one of those occasions."

"Unfortunately," Mohan Lal said, "it may be many years until the next occurrence. I've seen only one during the building of the temple. The times can't be predicted in advance. And they always happen during the rains, when traveling is difficult."

"Then maybe I'll have to be content with imagining the scene," said Raja Arjuna. He looked at Mohan Lal. "Shall we go back down? I fear our priest doesn't much like it up here."

The Raja spent close to a month in Varanasi, visiting the temple several more times during the period. When he left to return to Mangarh, he assured Mohan Lal he would be back for the temple's consecration, the ceremony at which Lord Shiva would be invited to take up residence.

Construction continued, consisting now mostly of hundreds of finishing details. Mohan was ecstatic over the result; this temple, his own temple, would set a new standard for all future ones.

Early on a spring morning as Mohan Lal stood talking with Bhagwan Das, there came the sounds of many hoofbeats. Both men turned to watch as a troop of cavalry rode onto the site. From their fine horses and glistening helmets Mohan immediately recognized them as soldiers of the imperial army.

The commander dismounted and approached. He appeared to be around thirty years of age, and his mustached, round face bore a sober expression. "You are the Master Builder, Mohan Lal?"

"I am. Please come and sit. Would you honor me by taking some refreshment?"

"Regretfully, that must wait for another time." The man opened a leather pouch, and he extracted and held up a paper bearing a large dark seal. "Orders of the Emperor, may God grant him life eternal, and endorsed by the governor. All new Gentile temples, including those still under construction, must be immediately dismantled."

Mohan stared in dismay at the officer, whose abruptness and lack of courtesy were so surprising in themselves. Uncertain he had heard correctly, Mohan asked, "Did you say...?"

The commander declared, "I have orders to begin dismantling your temple immediately."

A line of a half dozen bullock carts rumbled into view, filled with shabbily dressed men who appeared to be laborers.

Mohan was aware of the other soldiers dismounting. "Let me see that order!" He took the heavy piece of paper and scrutinized it. He had seen the black ink imprint of the imperial seal on other documents. It appeared authentic. He read the flowing Persian calligraphy, the script of official writings. His anger grew as the import sank in. He glowered at the officer. "It's a mistake! It has to be!"

"No mistake. The orders were confirmed by the Emperor's staff. My own superiors were explicit in their orders."

"But this is Lord Shiva's house! You can't destroy the home of the Great God himself."

"Allah has no use for Hindu idol houses."

Mohan realized he had forgotten how intolerant some Muslims could be. "But—" he glanced up at the *shikhara*, then quickly back. "This temple's almost finished! You can't tear it down!"

"You saw for yourself. The Emperor's order specifies *all* new construction, completed or not."

Mohan glanced at Bhagwan Das, whose eyes were wide in disbelief. Mohan said, more loudly, "We've almost fourteen years' work! It cost fifteen *lakhs* of rupees! This can't be."

The commander stood firm, his lips tight.

"The Raja of Mangarh himself endowed this temple," Mohan shouted. "He's one of the Emperor's principal allies!"

The officer stepped forward, his eyes narrowed at being addressed so brashly. "The Raja's not of the Faith. And I told you, the order's been confirmed." He gestured to the foreman of the laborers in the carts, and men clambered to the ground.

"No Emperor has ever ordered such a thing before!" Mohan screamed.

The officer turned away as he said firmly, "His Majesty Shah Jahan is noted for his dedication to the teachings of the Prophet."

Mohan suddenly thought of his brief acquaintanceship with Shah Jahan, eight years ago. "I know the Emperor personally!" he shouted. "He knows of this project. He'd never intentionally order it harmed!"

The officer hesitated for the first time, and turned back toward Mohan. Mohan began to take hope. But then the commander straightened. He spoke less curtly, but said, "There are no exceptions in my orders, sir. You'll have to take it up with the Emperor."

"Then you must wait until I can contact him!"

"My orders don't permit that. However, it may take the workmen several days to bring down such a large structure. You can send word to Agra in the meantime."

"You know it would take too long to get a reply!"

The commander raised an eyebrow and gestured with an open hand. "It can't be helped, sir." He added after a brief pause, "There's a good chance the stones will be used to build a mosque on the site. Maybe you can get the contract for the work."

Mohan gaped at him.

Soma had hurried over, and the priest was listening with a horrified expression. "Sir!" he said, eyes almost popping from their sockets, "This temple is about to become the home for Lord Shiva himself!"

The officer said with scorn, "A heathen idol!"

"Lord Shiva will strike you down!" Soma yelled. "He'll never allow this temple destroyed."

The officer laughed harshly. "Allah will have to decide that." He waved a hand in the direction of the main part of Varanasi. "Yours isn't the only one, you know. Many temples in this area are designated for demolition—seventy-two, I'm told." He turned away, saying to Mohan over his shoulder, "I suggest you order your workmen down from the tower, before we start."

Mohan stood rigid in shock. The priest's mouth hung open. Bhagwan Das was swaying as if he were about to collapse.

The commander directed several of his soldiers into the temple. Mohan Lal tried desperately to think of what to do. A personal appeal to the governor? The Emperor himself was clearly too far away to act quickly enough, as was the Raja of Mangarh. At last he said firmly, "Wait on everything—I'm seeing the governor."

The commander shook his head. "That's your right, sir. But it will do no good. My orders are to begin immediately."

Dazed artisans, holding their tools, begin spilling from the temple's doorway. Mohan Lal looked about for a rod, a pry bar, a chisel—anything to use as a weapon. If all his workers resisted....

He glanced at the soldiers grouped behind the commander. Their hands were on their swords, and they looked ready to act instantly. He swore loudly, and screamed, "You can't! This is an outrage!"

The commander ignored him.

Mohan pulled back his fist and lunged toward the officer. Before Mohan could strike, a soldier called, "Sir!" and drew his sword. He leaped toward Mohan.

Mohan jumped sideways to avoid the sword. The soldier stopped, weapon held high. "You shit eaters!" Mohan screamed. "What kind of a god would want a house of worship destroyed? A god like that is a vandal himself!"

"Enough!" shouted the officer. "He's gone too far. Arrest him!"

Mohan backed away as the soldier moved forward, and another moved to assist.

"Sir!" Mohan heard Chandra call in a voice that sounded both harsh and anxious. "My father's upset. I'll watch him."

"No one curses Allah in my presence," the commander said loudly and bluntly.

The two soldiers had grabbed Mohan, one on each arm. "Of course not, sir," Chandra said. "My father would normally never think of such a thing. But—" Chandra waved toward the temple, in explanation. "And my father does know the Emperor personally. His Majesty would never want him confined."

The commander now hesitated.

"Sir, he's suffering enough," Chandra said in a firm voice.

"Then keep him out of my sight." The officer nodded to his men. "Let the builder go."

Chandra took Mohan firmly by the arm. "Let's leave, Father," he whispered urgently.

Mohan, his eyes blasting anger and hatred, strained to pull free. Chandra gripped him harder. "Father!"

At last, Mohan looked at Chandra. He relaxed his muscles. Then he turned. With a vigorous twist, he slipped from Chandra's grasp and stalked away, his fists clenched like they would never again open.

He stopped, then whirled about. Eyes blazing, he started to move again toward the desecrators of his soul's labor. Some of the soldiers were watching him, and they readied their weapons.

He halted. Struggling with the soldiers would be futile. But he *must* stop this! No builder could tolerate such a monstrous outrage.

Suddenly he remembered the other temples destined for the same fate. The other builders!

He began to walk faster. Seventy other temples were to be destroyed in Varanasi. If he and all the other builders went together to the governor....

He began to run.

3

How quickly the work of fourteen years could be destroyed, Mohan Lal thought a few days later, as he and the other workers numbly stood by the mountain of rubble.

He and a large group of the other master architects and masons had immediately gone to petition the governor to end the madness. But thousands of soldiers now guarded the palace of the nervous official in case the outraged Hindu population should try assaulting it.

Mohan's delegation had been firmly turned back by the officers of the guard and informed that Hindus were barred from the governor's presence for the time being. Short of taking up arms, which would be equally ineffective, the builders could think of no further recourse. Mohan Lal had dispatched a messenger to Mangarh to inform the Raja what was occurring, but it would take days to receive a reply.

Minor riots occurred in several areas of Varanasi, but imperial troops quickly suppressed the protests.

The Emperor's laborers had not gone to the effort of digging up the foundations of Mohan Lal's temple, nor dismantling the plinth. But the upper levels were now a tumbled pile of rock.

The temple had been well built. The commander had expected to destroy it easily, as if his soldiers could merely push on the *shikhara* and topple it. But the demolition crew found they had to start at the very top, proceeding downward layer by layer, prying loose one massive stone at a time, then urging it into a ponderous tumble down the side of the tower, where its glancing fall would knock off pieces of sculpture from the surfaces below.

The foreman had quickly realized that the *mandapas*, the halls and porches of the main level, had been built to last millennia. They would be damaged, but only superficially, by the rocks falling from above. It would take many more days to dismantle these portions if they became buried under a mountain of rubble which would have to be cleared first. So he had part of his crew demolish those sections of the structure, while the rest of the workers, high up on the far side, pried loose the stones of the *shikhara*.

In the end, it had taken less than a week. The Mughal commander, anxious to move on to the next temple, ordered that the crew not even try to tear up the massive plinth, now piled high with tumbled stone. Instead, he settled for merely breaking up the edges with heavy hammers.

Mohan Lal had become a master builder with nothing to build. Indeed, he now had no interest in building—or in anything else.

Chandra and the artisans shared his outrage. The sculptor Bhagwan Das sat in his quarters in deep depression. Some artisans tried to lose themselves in wine or opium or prostitutes; others terrorized their wives and children. Some sought out fights in the poorer sections of the city; others had packed up their belongings and left Varanasi. Still others simply disappeared.

After Mohan had left to petition the governor, Chandra had loudly and continuously expressed his own anger at the workers demolishing the temple. Only being forcibly led off by some of his artisan friends had saved him from arrest. But much of his fury had been released in his lengthy outburst, and now he was merely desultory, continually worried about his father.

During the first hours of the demolition, after returning from the fruitless attempt to see the governor, Mohan Lal had charged around the temple, glaring at the workers, even threatening them with dire consequences when the Emperor learned of their acts. He, too, had finally been restrained by some of his own workmen to prevent the soldiers from escorting him to jail.

Now, formerly so vibrant, he was silent and withdrawn. Chandra worried about his father, who did not even appear to contain a smoldering anger buried somewhere within, waiting to burst into flames. It was as if his very soul had been driven away.

The temperature was increasing every day as the hot season approached, and tempers flared more often among the remaining artisans in their encampment. But Mohan Lal appeared indifferent to the growing discomfort.

Chandra followed on some of the occasions when Mohan would slowly walk the short distance to the waterfront, his shoulders slumped, his face expressionless. The builder would turn to stare above the tree tops at the spires of the older temples which had not been subject to the demolition order. A vacant area of sky marked the former location of his own *shikhara*.

Late one hot morning, a letter of commiseration arrived from Raja Arjuna. Mohan Lal, wearing only a *dhoti*, was seated in the dim interior of the small house they had occupied during construction. Chandra read the missive to his father, who otherwise would probably have ignored it. The Raja urged Mohan Lal to remain in his employ, suggesting that some renovation work might be in order for the Jain temple at Mangarh, and another small wing added to Mangarh's fort.

"Father, you need to accept the Raja's commissions," said Chandra. "He values your work, and Mangarh is a pleasant place."

Mohan was slow to reply. At last, he said, staring at the floor, "I'm not interested."

Chandra took a cloth and wiped the sweat from his own forehead. "Father, if you don't want to work at Mangarh, the Maharana of Mewar will almost certainly welcome your services again at Udaipur."

Eventually, Mohan said, "Maybe, some day."

Chandra narrowed his eyes. He thought about the fact that the other master architects whose temples had been destroyed were now looking for commissions. "Father, I'd like to be working, even if you don't want to."

Mohan raised his head and looked at him. Chandra held his gaze. Eventually, Mohan said, "You're right. I shouldn't keep you from finding work yourself."

Chandra's eyes widened. "Of course, I don't want to work for someone else. I couldn't leave you. Even if you weren't the best master builder anywhere, you're my father. "

Mohan hesitated, then gave a nod and again looked down. Reluctance in his voice, he said, "I'll think harder on the matter."

Chandra let out a sigh. "Hopefully," he said, "there will still be work available when you're ready."

Mohan said nothing for a time, then he nodded.

Chandra thought of the rumor he'd heard that the Emperor intended to build a large tomb for his favorite Queen, who had recently died in childbirth.

A few of the builders had left for Agra, hoping to find work on the project. But he knew better than to mention the tomb to his father, who would want no part of any work sponsored by Emperor Shah Jahan.

On an oven-like summer morning an imperial cavalry officer, accompanied by four mounted soldiers, found Mohan Lal seated on the gray mud bank of the riverfront, watching the Ganges flow slowly by.

The officer dismounted. Quite unlike the officer bearing the previous order from the Emperor, this young man, sweating and dust covered from his journey, courteously extended the folded document toward Mohan. "A command from the Emperor, may God give him the life eternal."

Mohan at first made no move to reach for the letter. Then he took it and slowly opened the thick paper. The message bore the familiar round, black imperial seal, and it commanded him to appear before the Emperor in Agra, on a date one week away, to consult on a building project.

He glared at the officer. The man, short and round faced with the features of the Mongols of the central Asian plains, smiled good-naturedly and said, "Sir, I'm ordered to accompany you, with these soldiers for your protection. I'll requisition transportation for you if you wish."

Mohan cast the paper into the mud. He glowered at the officer. "I'm not going."

"I'm sorry, sir," the man said, not unkindly. "I have my orders."

"I don't care about your orders."

The officer waited patiently.

"If I refuse to go?"

The man looked embarrassed. "Sir, I'm ordered to bring you to Agra. I don't dare come back without you."

Mohan looked beyond at the soldiers for some time. He glanced about, searching for a way to escape. Eventually, his shoulders sagged. "All right. How in the name of God can I fight the Emperor?"

The officer looked away. Atop the bank, his men waited quietly on their horses.

Mohan thrust himself to his feet, turned, and trudged toward his home. The officer wordlessly retrieved the Emperor's order, shook off the muddy water as best he could, remounted his horse and followed Mohan. The four soldiers rode behind.

At his house, Mohan gathered belongings and informed Chandra of the unforeseen and unwanted development. Chandra insisted on accompanying him. Mohan didn't have the strength to care and so did not object.

Ram Das, their elderly servant, readied the old, ox-drawn, two wheeled carriage that had been in the family since Mohan himself was a small child. Mohan said facetiously to Chandra, "I'm entitled to transportation by the Emperor. Shall I ask for the imperial treasury to hire palanquins for us?" But they climbed into the cart. Ram Das would serve as driver and cook.

Chandra acted as his father's intermediary, occasionally conversing with the friendly young escort officer. The journey was miserable, even though they did most of their traveling at night and rested during the stifling oven of the afternoons. On the third day, as the sun was going down and they set out again into the dust and heat in the creaking, jolting cart, Mohan asked, "What does one say to an Emperor who can destroy years of work, then summon the victims as if nothing happened?"

Chandra glanced about to reassure himself that none of the escorting soldiers were within hearing. "Since he's the Emperor, maybe one keeps one's mouth closed."

After a time, Mohan observed, "His grandfather Akbar never destroyed temples. Just the opposite. I heard he actually donated money for some."

"Even Emperor Jahangir never interfered with anyone's temple worship," said Chandra. "I suppose it's just our bad fortune that *this* Emperor is ruling when our project neared completion."

"The stars were definitely against us," said Mohan. "Or I did something terrible in a previous life."

It was the first time Chandra had heard him make such comments since the temple was destroyed. At least, he thought, there's some feeling at last. He said, "I do keep wondering why you're being summoned. Maybe it's something to do with that tomb." He watched his father's face.

Mohan looked away. "I heard about that project. I want nothing to do with it."

"You may have no choice."

On the fifth day, just short of Agra, relieved at last to be near their destination, they took an old, wooden, barge-like ferry across the Yamuna to the river's southern bank, which bore most of the city's populated area. To the right of the road into town, on an open area bordering the river, they saw a vast congregation of people. Large numbers of soldiers lined the road, and over the top of the throng numerous large, brightly colored tents were visible. In the heavy traffic Mohan's carriage slowed to a crawl. Dust hung in the heated air, and hawkers bearing trays and baskets on their heads loudly advertised refreshments as they pushed through the crowds.

Chandra called to the officer of their escort from Varanasi: "Why has the crowd gathered here?"

The man hailed another rider and conversed briefly. He then rode closer to the carriage and informed Chandra, "Sir, the Emperor's holding an *urs*, a memorial service on the anniversary of his favorite Queen's death." With his usual friendly smile, the officer explained, "She was said to have been a beautiful and kindly lady. His Majesty was heartbroken when she died. It's said he still hasn't recovered from the loss, although today marks a year since her death." He added loudly over his shoulder as he moved ahead to clear their path, "This is the site where the Emperor will build her tomb."

4

At mid-morning two days after his arrival in Agra, Mohan stood with other building experts, awaiting the Emperor in the *Diwan-i-Khas*, the Private Audience Hall of the great red sandstone fort. Shah Jahan's public audience in the main audience hall had concluded, so there should not be long to wait.

This smaller hall was a pillared pavilion, elevated on a terrace overlooking the Yamuna River, and Mohan could not resist running a finger across the smooth white marble of the nearest column. Each pillar was enriched with inlays of precious and semiprecious stones, forming tall, slender rectangles on the vertical surfaces and stylized flowers and curving geometric patterns toward the bottoms. The bases of the columns and the edges of the platform floor were adorned with marble relief carvings of flowers in vases and sinuous patterns. Mohan had to reluctantly admit that the Emperor hired expert craftsmen.

The day was already hot, and Mohan shifted position so the wet reed mats covering the otherwise open side of the pavilion would better shield him from the sun. He looked about at the other masters present, who were gathered in a rough semicircle facing the empty, jewel encrusted, cushioned platform throne on its raised dais. In contrast to the rigid protocol of the much larger Public Audience Hall, in this room the men were not assigned positions. However, they still would remain standing in the presence of the Emperor, the "Shadow of God on Earth."

Mohan had met these men yesterday and this morning. They were an impressive group that included an expert builder from Arabia named Qadir Zaman Khan and a Turkish master draftsman named Ustad Isa who lived in Agra. Also present were an expert on dome building, a master stonemason, two other master builders, and a garden designer. Mohan realized that other than Ram Lal the garden designer, he was the only man present who was not a Muslim.

The head of the Emperor's building department, Mukarrimat Khan, an official with a charismatic smile and smooth manner, had informed him yesterday of the nature of the construction project, but Mohan still saw little reason he had to be included in this group. Such a gathering of luminaries in the building field must surely contain enough expertise for the task.

Several guards appeared with swords held ready and took up position on either side of the throne. Then came the attendants with fans and flywhisks. Hidden drums and trumpets sounded, and the Emperor entered and seated himself on the throne. Mohan and the others present did their three *taslims*, bowing to touch the back of the right hand to the thickly carpeted floor, then straightening and touching palm to forehead.

They stood, awaiting the Emperor's pleasure. Mohan at first avoided looking directly at Shah Jahan. But he felt the Emperor's eyes upon him, and Mohan returned the gaze momentarily, then looked away.

Did Shah Jahan remember their talks of eight years ago? Almost certainly. So maybe the Emperor had specifically requested Mohan Lal by name, although one of his staff could also have summoned Mohan because of his reputation as a master builder.

In spite of the antipathy he felt, Mohan examined the Emperor, curious to see how the man had changed over those years. Though the traditional forty days of mourning were long past, the Emperor still wore only white, the color of bereavement. His beard had considerable gray, and he looked sad and worn, much older than his forty years. In yesterday's meeting, Mukarrimat Khan had told Mohan that the gray hair had appeared only in the past months, in Shah Jahan's despair at losing his life's great love.

Mohan Lal felt no sympathy. What twist of *karma* was this, that the one man in the empire who through his actions had won Mohan Lal's undying enmity should now summon him and demand his talents as if nothing had happened!

The Emperor addressed the group in Persian, in a voice that was slow and quiet: "You all know you are here to create a tomb for my departed wife. She was an exceptional woman. She was as kind and generous as she was graceful and beautiful. There will never be another such as...." His voice trailed away. He blinked at the moistness in his eyes. He bowed his head and covered his face with a hand. After several moments, he dropped his hand, raised his head and managed to resume in a stronger voice, "There will never be another such as she. She must have a memorial that is graceful and beautiful like no other."

He sat for a moment, gazing into the past. Then, he said, "Before she died, she told me of a dream in which she saw a beautiful palace and garden, the like of which had never been seen on this earth. I promised her I would build such a place for her to enshrine her mortal remains."

His face still lined with sorrow, he gestured to an attendant, who handed each man a large leather-bound folio. He resumed, "As a basis for beginning, you must be familiar with these buildings I find attractive. But these are merely a start. I want to go beyond them. I want a monument that's unique, as she was unique." The tears again formed in his eyes. He wiped at them. "At the center of a large garden, I imagine a building in white marble, like the tomb of Itmad-ud-Daulah. But that is a much smaller monument than what I will build."

The group stood in an uncomfortable silence while the Emperor was again lost in sadness. Finally, he glanced quickly about the circle and said, "This project, large though it may be, must be completed with all possible haste. I've already ordered preparation of the site to begin. I've also taken steps to ensure a constant supply of white marble from the mines of Makrana. All of you must visit the building site immediately. Then you must each present drawings of your proposals. The best ideas will be made into a model. You'll meet with me again in four days." He rose, and swept from the hall.

Four days, Mohan thought as he watched the Emperor leave.

A deep voice said quietly near his ear, "Very little time for a proposal, especially on a project of this scope."

He turned to see Qadir Zaman Khan, the master builder from Arabia. After a time, Mohan said, "Not much time at all."

Qadir said, "I think I will be very busy the next four days. But this is the type of project I've hoped for. It's been years since my last large tomb." He peered at Mohan. "May I be honored by your company in visiting the site?"

Mohan tried to think of appropriate words to refuse. He had no intention of working on the project, Emperor or no.

He examined Qadir, truly noticing him for the first time, though the two had met earlier that day. He saw an obviously well-fed man of medium height, a few years older than himself, with a handsome face. Qadir's greying beard was in the same style as Shah Jahan's, short and neatly trimmed to follow the contours of his skin. Qadir wore a rich robe of orange brocade, more as if he were a courtier rather than a builder.

The draftsman Ustad Isa joined them. "May I accompany you also?" he inquired. It seemed to Mohan that the manner of the tall, slender, thin-faced man was slightly anxious.

"Our pleasure," said Qadir with an expansive sweep of his hands.

It was too much effort for Mohan to think of a polite way to decline going with the two. And, he decided, much as he wanted to refuse to work on the design at all, antagonizing Shah Jahan right at the beginning could bring difficulties he'd rather avoid. He'd experienced just how much harm the Emperor could inflict.

No, Mohan Lal decided; he would go through the motions of presenting a drawing, then beg the Emperor's staff to be allowed to attend pressing business elsewhere.

Mohan forced a rigid, polite smile. "Shall we go, then?" He moved toward the doorway, and added, "My son's waiting outside. With your permission, he'll come with us."

5

Mohan was surprised to see that in addition to a manservant, Qadir had a gilded palanquin and four bearers waiting—an expensive extravagance. However, after arranging to have the palanquin ready for him later, the builder seemed willing enough to climb into the rear seat of the old carriage. Mohan sat next to Qadir, leaving barely enough room for Chandra to squeeze in. Isa folded his long frame onto the front seat beside Ram Das the driver, but facing the others in the rear. He shoved his small, rolled Muslim's prayer rug into a corner. Qadir shouted for his servant to bring a prayer rug and umbrella; the man climbed in next to the driver.

Qadir smoothed his elegant brocade robe along his legs. "You're new to Agra, I believe," he said to Mohan. "May I inquire as to where you're staying?" He continued to speak in Persian, as had everyone in the meeting with the Emperor.

"We've taken a room near the Akbari Mosque." Reluctantly, he added, "And you?"

"I've a modest house near Nakhkhas," Qadir replied offhandedly. The locale was known as an upper class residential area. He looked at Isa. "And you, sir?"

"I live near the Chowk Bazaar. Quite close to here," Isa replied in his high voice as the wheels drummed over the fort's drawbridge. The area he mentioned was a lower class one.

"I see," said Qadir. "Do you have a design in mind, yet?" he inquired of Isa.

"My specialty is the humble one of merely committing plans to paper," Isa said. "Cross-sections, details, elevations to guide the masons and carpenters. Design isn't my principal area of expertise."

"Nor mine," replied Qadir with a wry smile and a shrug. "My area is construction. I'll submit a design, but I've little doubt the Emperor will quickly reject it."

Chandra looked sharply at him; although superficially Qadir sounded sincere, given his obvious fondness for prestigious trappings Chandra found it difficult to trust the builder's current air of modest self-effacement.

The carriage slowly forced its way between the wandering cows, the food vendors, the burden-laden porters in the noisy bazaar. Qadir looked to Mohan, awaiting a comment. When none came, he said loudly to Mohan, "I haven't spent much time in this land. How does a person who isn't of our faith come to know of our building styles?"

The ride was hot, even with the carriage's canopy shielding them from the late morning sun. Mohan was acutely aware of his discomfort. He noted sweat glistening on the foreheads of the others, too, but they appeared to be less troubled by it than he. With resignation, he replied, "Our Muslim rulers have always relied on local artisans. We in turn have adapted our building methods to their requirements. You know of our *Vastu shastras*, the architectural rules passed down from our ancestors for all kinds of structures, from temples to houses. Many of us have been involved in building mosques. One of our masters even prescribed rules for designing them, since your own faith has no canons."

"Indeed." Qadir waited for Mohan to elaborate further. When Mohan remained silent, Qadir watched the passing scene for a few moments. He then looked down at the folio given him by the Emperor. Though there was little room in the crowded seat, he rested the folio on his lap, opened the cover part way, and began leafing through the renderings.

Isa did the same with his folio.

Mohan did not open his own, and after a time, Chandra asked, "May I, Father?" Mohan looked at him blankly. Chandra indicated the folio and said, "I want to know what buildings the Emperor likes."

Mohan nodded. Chandra took it and began turning the pages. Mohan uninterestedly glimpsed small paintings of buildings he readily recognized:

Humayan's Tomb, Delhi

—The tomb of the Emperor Humayan in Delhi, a massive, oblong, red sandstone structure with white marble accents, crowned by a large central dome of white marble. The outer walls were broken by large, inset, pointed arches.

—The tomb of the Emperor Akbar, at nearby Sikandra, also in red sandstone with marble accents, and with four white minarets on the entrance gate building.

"Excellent renderings," Qadir commented in his rumbling voice.

Mohan said nothing, but Isa responded, "They were done by artists working for the Emperor. Some are my friends. The drawings show the buildings as viewed by an onlooker. Although," he added as if in afterthought, "they'd be of little use in actual construction."

Chandra continued turning the pages. Mohan saw a painting of the smaller but exquisite white marble tomb of the nobleman Itmad-ud-Daulah, with its four corner minarets, located across the river from Agra.

Mohan tired of looking over his son's shoulder. His gaze idly drifted over his other two companions. Qadir had closed his folio, but Isa's long, narrow face was bent over his own, intently perusing each rendering, ignoring the bumping and lurching of the carriage.

The busy road from the Red Fort to the site paralleled the south bank of the river. Between the road and the Yamuna lay the riverfront mansions of wealthy nobles, set in large walled gardens. Mohan absently watched the magnificent dwellings roll by.

The Emperor had selected a huge, level tract of riverfront near the last of these mansions as the site for his wife's tomb. The land had belonged to Maharaja Jai Singh of Amber before Shah Jahan had traded four mansions in exchange. The tents and crowds from the *urs* earlier in the week had disappeared. On this hot day, with the monsoons expected at any time, laborers with elephants and teams of oxen were clearing trees from the eastern edge. A haze of dust hung in the air from their work.

Near the western boundary of the parcel, guarded by soldiers, sat Mumtaz Mahal's temporary tomb, a small square stone structure with a dome. Her earthly remains would reside here for however many years it took to build the huge, permanent sepulcher.

As Qadir stepped from the carriage, his servant hurried with an umbrella to shield him from the sun. Ram Das extricated another umbrella from under a seat and moved to hold it over Mohan Lal.

Small puffs of dust rose with each step as they walked into the property. Mohan stopped, and from the dirt he pulled a curved stick, a scrap of debris left from tree removal.

He continued with the group to the center of the site, the usual location for a major tomb. There everyone halted, examined the views in the various directions. Mohan bent and dug a small hole with the stick.

Qadir said, eyeing the dry, crumbly soil, "It seems stable, at least on the surface."

Mohan cast aside his stick. "So it does."

The party continued to the edge of the bank and looked out over the river. "Structures at the water's edge can be difficult," Qadir observed. "I've never had to concern myself with that problem before. Have you ever built at such a location?" he asked Mohan.

"A couple of times," Mohan said absently. Although the umbrella shielded him from the full intensity of the sun, his court clothes stuck to him from the heat, and he wished he had been able to strip to his *dhoti*. Better yet, he wished he were elsewhere, where he could rest in the shade, and think of nothing. He mentally cursed the Emperor who was in such a rush on this project. What was the hurry when the woman was dead?

When Mohan did not elaborate, Chandra said with unmistakable pride in his voice, "Father's built a small island palace on the lake at Udaipur, and a temple in Varanasi at a site which is sometimes flooded by a river. He's studied all he could about footings and foundations in those types of locations."

Qadir looked at Mohan with what might have been respect or envy or both. Eventually, he asked, "What particular problems do you see on this site?"

Mohan shrugged. He scuffed at the dirt with the pointed toe of his shoe, noting the consistency of the earth. Eventually, he replied, "The obvious. A large building concentrates tremendous weight over a small area of ground. Seepage from the river could cause the structure to sink if the foundation doesn't properly distribute the mass. And a river has amazing force, especially at flood stage. It could undermine the foundation."

He looked first up, then down the river. He peered at the bank, noting the manner in which the water had eroded the various layers of soil. He resumed: "The bend here is such that the currents should be at their weakest when they pass this bank. From that standpoint it's a good place for building."

Qadir slowly nodded.

Isa said, "Of course, the main building would be at the center of the garden, which would place it some distance away from the river itself. Wouldn't the ground be more stable there?"

Mohan shrugged, then stared at him a few moments. Eventually, he said, "No doubt." But Isa's comment had started a train of thought. The Emperor wanted Mohan to submit a design. Well, by God, he would! But he'd place no limits on his imagination. He had no intention of being bound by the Mughals' traditional patterns.

And he did not care in the slightest whether or not Shah Jahan liked it.

Qadir Zaman Khan was silent while they inspected the remainder of the site. Then, he glanced at Mohan and asked, "Shall we continue together to Sikandra to look at *Padshah* Akbar's tomb, since it's one of the buildings we need to be familiar with?"

"An excellent suggestion," said Isa.

Mohan was wiping the sweat from his brow with a piece of white cotton. He glanced at it, saw that it was dirty from the dust in the air—to be expected, of course, at a construction site. After a few seconds' silence, he responded in a half grunt, "Of course."

Again, they all rode in the ancient carriage. The party retraced its route toward the Red Fort. Near the beginning of the bazaars, the *muezzin's* call to the post-noon *zohar* prayers drifted over the noise of the shoppers and other traffic. The driver Ram Das, although Hindu, knew enough to stop the carriage. Qadir and Isa boosted themselves to the ground. Isa carried his small prayer rug under his arm, and Qadir took one from his servant. The Muslims faced toward the west and lay their rugs side by side. They began their rituals of kneeling and touching their foreheads to the carpets, then standing, then kneeling again.

The Hindus in the carriage waited patiently. Mohan himself was not particularly interested in worshiping gods; building temples was—or had been—his own form of making offerings. The Muslim faith had much to offer, he

Gateway, Akbar's Tomb, Sikandra

thought, with its principles of brotherhood and submission to Allah. Why, though, did some Muslims have to be so intolerant of the beliefs of others? The thought of the Emperor's destruction of his temple again infuriated him, creating a wall of anger that virtually obliterated his sense of his surroundings.

Qadir and Isa and the servant returned to their seats in the carriage. Quietly, Ram Das urged the two oxen into motion. The party proceeded through the crowded center of Agra, and then some distance to Sikandra, beyond the city's outskirts.

The tomb of Emperor Akbar dominated a vast walled garden, which was entered through a massive archway in a rectangular gateway building. The portal both protected the items inside from plunder and served to divide the worldly ground outside from the sacred ground within. After stepping from the carriage, Chandra and Qadir and Isa stood, shielding their eyes from the brightness as they gazed upward at the four white marble minarets adorning the red sandstone gateway. Mohan had visited Sikandra twice before, several years ago, and each time he had admired the grace of the portal's soaring towers.

Silently, followed by their bearers, the group walked slowly past the armed guards into the gateway arch. They stood in its shade while several monkeys on the grounds sat watching them as they examined the formal garden, laid out on the traditional plan of the *char bagh*, a giant square divided into quarters, with the mausoleum sited at the exact center. The massive sepulcher was an intriguing conception, sprouting an agglomeration of staggered cupolas from the roof levels.

"I've heard," Chandra said, "that it was originally planned with a large dome on the roof."

Isa and Qadir both glanced at Mohan, who shrugged as his eyes swept the layout of the garden. "So I've been told," he said.

"Why would it need a dome?" Isa asked. "To me, it looks complete as it is."

"No, no," said Qadir with a frown, departing from the charming demeanor he had affected. "A central dome would have added a needed balance."

Akbar's Tomb at Sikandra

Mohan agreed with Qadir, but he said nothing.

"I still think the building is a well executed concept just as it sits." Isa sounded annoyed at Qadir's abrupt disagreement.

The paving stones radiated intense heat as the party closely inspected the mausoleum. Mohan hurried the process as quickly as he could. Although the incised stucco carvings, the painted plaster, and the other details were well executed, he could muster no enthusiasm. It was those slender white minarets on the gate that had imprinted themselves in his mind.

None too soon for him, the group left and returned to Agra, where they ferried across the river. After a brief halt for the Muslims' late afternoon *asar*

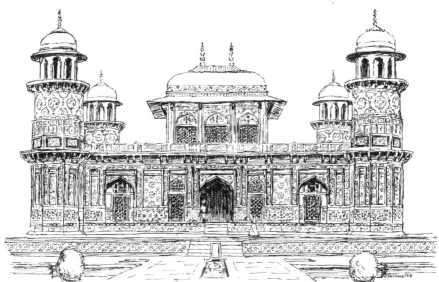

Comb of Itmad-ud-Daulah, Agra

prayers, they arrived at the tomb of Itmad-ud-Daulah, a prime minister under Emperor Jahangir, and the father of Jahangir's chief Queen, Noor Jahan. Like Sikandra, the sepulcher lay in the exact center of a square garden, but both mausoleum and garden were on a far smaller scale.

The party stopped at the gateway to admire the tomb itself from afar. What a lovely little building! thought Mohan, intrigued although he had seen it before. Like a fanciful jewel casket, it glistened dazzlingly white in the sun. On a previous visit to this very mausoleum, some years ago, Mohan had come to realize that a building in pure, white marble called for a different, much more subtle and delicate type of ornamentation than did a building in sandstone or schist.

As he admired the ethereal quality of the sepulcher, he reluctantly admitted the Emperor's idea of building an entire monument in white marble was good. And in spite of the heat, and his antipathy toward Shah Jahan, his mind continued the chain of thoughts which had begun at the site of the Emperor's proposed project.

Exquisite though it was, this particular building was not without flaws. "What do you think of the minarets?" he quietly asked Chandra, referring to the four marble towers, one of which thrust upward from each corner of the square mausoleum.

"They're appropriate for the building," Chandra replied, pleasantly surprised at the question that showed his father was interested. He peered at the towers a moment before continuing, "But they seem a little short, maybe too big around. Not as graceful as the slender ones on the gateway at Sikandra."

Isa said, sounding slightly puzzled, "I have to agree. The building as a whole is too small, and the minarets emphasize the fact." He glanced quickly at Mohan, as if to see how his remark had been received.

Qadir said loudly, "No, no. I disagree. The minarets are Persian in feel.

And hence most appropriate for a Persian nobleman." But he, too, glanced at Mohan's face.

Chandra had seen the looks, and he abruptly realized: These men each viewed his father as the most formidable competitor, and they were trying to discern what approach he would take in his design.

Sounding annoyed at Qadir disagreeing again, Isa said, "I believe their beauty is due more to the materials used, rather than to their own form."

Qadir frowned. "You're quite wrong. Perhaps you're too accustomed to drawing other men's ideas, and it has distorted your judgment."

Isa turned away, scowling.

Mohan was already walking around the outside. Qadir casually followed. Finally Isa did, also.

The party examined the building's exterior carefully, then entered it and toured each of the small rooms opening off the outer walls, rooms which surrounded the larger center chamber containing the burial crypts. "This inlay work is extraordinary," Qadir said at one point. "Such painstaking detail."

"The finest I've seen," Mohan concurred. Qadir was watching him carefully. But Mohan was examining the arrangement of the echoing marble rooms, evaluating their overall effect upon him, their *feel*.

By the time they had left the grounds and taken the ferry back across the river, the sun was low in the sky. Qadir said, "Regrettably, I'll have to leave. I should go to my home so I can begin putting my ideas on paper. It's been a true pleasure touring with you. I look forward to our next meeting."

Isa said perfunctorily, "I likewise. An honor! Until we meet again, then."

"The pleasure has been all ours, to be with such expert colleagues," Mohan replied, summoning the energy for the expected courtesies.

He and Chandra dropped off Isa. They purchased water from a vendor, and Mohan thirstily poured the liquid into his mouth while the carriage continued southeasterly past the Red Fort.

Chandra said, "Qadir and Isa didn't agree on much." He gave a tight smile.

"True."

"I wonder how Qadir can afford to dress so well and maintain his own palanquin."

Eventually, Mohan replied, "He probably had a generous patron on his last job in Arabia."

"Possibly. Anyway, his extravagant tastes are no doubt one reason he wants this project so badly." Chandra looked at Mohan. "Father, did it occur to you that you're knowledgeable in more areas than either of them? Isa can do drafting, and Qadir construction, but neither of them have much experience in conceiving and designing. Especially on a site by the water."

Mohan remained silent.

Chandra said, "I think they're worried about you."

Mohan looked away.

Chandra said, "Qadir and Isa know of your reputation. I think they hoped to learn something by touring the sites with you. Something to give them an advantage in submitting their own designs."

Mohan shrugged. "Then I wish them well."

"Father, the Emperor's wealth is said to be beyond imagining! A project such as this would likely have unlimited funds. It's an opportunity for you to build to complete perfection, and on a scale as never before!"

"My temple approached that."

Chandra frowned and stared at his father. "So it did. The Emperor's action were unforgivable. But that must not blind you to this new opportunity."

"Maybe so," Mohan said, his voice flat. "I'll think on it."

Chandra thought of saying more, but he decided he'd made his point for the moment. After a while, Chandra asked, "Where are we headed now, Father?"

"Back to the site of the Emperor's project. I have some ideas, and I want to see how they might look there."

Chandra raised his eyebrows. "So you have a concept in mind?"

"Possibly."

Puzzled, Chandra stared at his father and said, "I'm glad, Father. But it's getting so late." Already the scent of smoke from cooking fires for evening meals wafted through the air. "Why not wait until morning to revisit the land? If we go there now, the sun will be setting by the time we arrive."

"I know," Mohan said. "That's one reason why I want to be there."

Chandra shrugged. As they approached the less congested area of the great mansions, he said, "I'm still worried about Qadir and Isa."

"Don't be. Let them win with their designs. Then I can get out of Agra as quickly as possible. I doubt the Emperor will look kindly on my own plan in any event."

Chandra let out a sigh of frustration, not caring that his father heard.

6

On the third day of working on the plans, Mukarrimat Khan summoned Mohan Lal. Mohan suspected the reason behind the meeting, but he wasn't entirely sure. The head of the Emperor's building department was as jovial as on the previous occasion of Mohan's conference with him. "I'm grateful you could honor me with your esteemed presence," said Mukarrimat Khan in the flowery Persian of the court. "And I apologize for interrupting your labors."

Mohan Lal was tired from working with little sleep, and his eyes were red from drafting plans by the light of oil lamps. But he gave a bow. "The honor, of course, is entirely mine, sir."

A servant brought iced *sharbat*. Mohan Lal's eyes widened in surprise and pleasure. The *sharbat* was fantastically expensive, as the ice had to be brought by runners all the way from the Himalayas. Normally such an extravagant luxury would not be offered to someone of his status. It tasted deliciously refreshing on such a hot day.

"Now then," said Mukarrimat Khan. "How are your plans progressing?"

Mohan gave a casual shrug. "Well enough, your honor, given that we have so little time. I'm glad to have my son's aid in the drafting."

The official nodded. "Ah yes, a family enterprise. It's indeed fortunate when we have sons to help us. Allah, praise be to him, has seen fit to bless me with two sons of my own."

"Indeed, you're doubly blessed, your honor."

"You realize, of course, that the competition for the design is intense," said Mukarrimat Khan, shifting direction.

"Indeed I do, your honor. The Emperor has summoned the true masters in the field. Myself excluded, naturally."

"You're far too modest! Far too humble. I happen to know you are one of the two or three foremost contenders. Of course, the Emperor—may God grant him the life eternal—will make the final decision. But I flatter myself that he listens to me in matters of this nature, and that I can perhaps even have a decisive influence if the decision is a close one."

Mohan's guess about the purpose of the meeting was confirmed.

"Of course you know, having had such great experience in matters of this nature," said Mukarrimat Khan, "that there can be many obstacles to achieving one's goal in constructing such a huge project—not only the Emperor's initial decision, but the approvals of the various stages of building, the awarding of contracts to the best suppliers, the timely disbursement of funds. It is important to have friends who can smooth the way." Mukarrimat Khan waited with an expectant smile.

"Indeed." Mohan Lal gave a nod.

The Khan's smile broadened. "I would like to be your friend in this process. Someone in a position to ensure that the difficulties are minimized."

"I'm so flattered I'm speechless, your honor."

"Not at all. It's I who am flattered at the opportunity to work with so gifted a builder. However," Mukarrimat Khan abruptly turned sober, "persons in my position have certain problems. I almost hesitate to mention them. But since we are now good friends..."

He made a show of hesitating. Mohan Lal casually gestured for him to continue.

"Well. I find that in order to maintain my position, the very position in which I might be of help to you, it's necessary to expend certain funds. A great amount, unfortunately. I must maintain a home and sufficient servants and trappings appropriate to my station. I must entertain the Emperor's other officials in the style which they expect. I must sometimes pay commissions in order to ensure that building materials arrive at the time they're needed."

"Of course." Mohan gave a nod. "That's to be expected."

Mukarrimat Khan flashed his smile. "I knew you would understand."

"Indeed. I understand fully. You need have no worries on that account."

"Excellent! Well, then. Enough of business. More *sharbat*? Perhaps some mangos? I have some excellent ones brought all the way from the coast, south of Surat."

"I think not, thank you just the same."

Mukarrimat Khan again turned sober. "Oh, I understand! You need to get back to your work. And I am keeping you from it. Please accept my humble apologies. I'm so glad you could come, so we could cement our friendship."

Mohan nodded. "Likewise, your honor. I consider your inviting me to be a rare privilege." He rose and returned to his lodging.

The room Mohan Lal and Chandra rented had a small, roofed veranda, reached by a narrow outside stairway from the street which it overlooked. The two men had been working and sleeping on the veranda to take advantage of the slight breezes. Below on the busy street, people, animals, and carts frequently passed, stirring up dust which drifted in. But that was typical of accommodations in the crowded city. As Mohan approached, he looked up at the covered porch and saw Chandra, seated on the floor, bent over the drawings.

Chandra rubbed his tired eyes as he looked away from where he was inking a line. He took a cloth and wiped sweat from his brow. "What did the Khan want, Father?"

"The usual. A share of the cost of the contracts awarded, if I win the design and happen to supervise the project."

"I assume you agreed."

Mohan shrugged. "I had little choice. I'm sure he'll have the same understanding with the other designers. But I don't suppose I'll be here for the construction, anyway. The Emperor seems likely to choose a Muslim to oversee that work, since its an Islamic tomb."

He sat and examined the drawings they had completed so far. He had devised the concept and had done rough sketches, which he and Chandra were now turning into the preliminary plans to present to the Emperor. It was a serious design, one he felt was completely workable. However, it also had some major features which were unusual enough that he felt the plans stood a likely chance of being rejected by the Emperor.

That was exactly what he hoped would happen. He sighed and began inking the plan for the garden, a key feature in his concept.

They worked the remainder of the day and through the evening. Sometime in the middle of the hot night, when they were too exhausted to continue, they stretched out on the mats and quickly fell asleep.

Chandra was first to awaken in the morning, the morning of the day the plans were to be presented to the Emperor. He went to the water urn, dipped in a cup and splashed some over his face. He dried his hands and sat to begin on the drawing he had been working on.

The paper was not where he had remembered putting it. He looked about the small covered porch. None of the papers was there. Nor were the pens or the ink pots. Or the other drafting tools: the rulers, the compasses, the curves....

Trying not to panic, Chandra looked down at the street, where already people were going back and forth. Could the materials have been stolen by someone passing by? Because of the heat, the wooden doors at the top of the stairway from the street had not been closed; only curtains hung over the opening.

Ram Das, who acted as their watchman at night, was asleep, stretched on his mat across the entry. Chandra shook him awake. "Ram Das! Were you on guard all night?"

The servant rubbed his eyes. "Yes, sir. Only at first light did I allow myself to sleep."

Chandra hurriedly awakened his father and explained what had happened.

"I know it was Qadir!" Chandra said. "Or someone he sent. They must have come after Ram Das fell asleep."

"Why couldn't Isa have done it?" asked Mohan, frowning. "He knows where we're staying, too."

Chandra scowled. "I don't know. I just think...he wouldn't be bold enough."

"Why not anyone who just happened to pass by?" asked Mohan, gesturing at the increasingly crowded street.

"The drawings would be no use to anyone except us. Or someone wanting to gain an advantage over us with the Emperor."

Mohan stared at the street. "That's not necessarily so. The pens and ink could be sold. So could the paper. The culprit might merely have been a thief prowling about in the night."

Chandra said, peering at his father, "I don't believe that's what happened. Neither do you. The timing is too precise."

Mohan sighed and turned to face him. "You're no doubt right. I doubt we'll ever know. We can't accuse someone on the basis of a guess." He thought for a moment. "I wonder if this will excuse me from presenting a plan to the Emperor."

Chandra shot a quick look at his father. "Surely not! The Emperor might possibly give you more time, but he won't summon you all the way here and then let you not show him anything."

Again Mohan sighed. "Of course. Well, I can't see asking for more time. We'd better get some new drafting materials in a hurry. We can produce only some rough sketches, but they'll have to suffice."

The Shadow of God on Earth glanced at the various experts standing before him. He made no reference to, and perhaps did not notice, the fact that more than one of the masters appeared on the verge of exhaustion from working in the heat with little or no sleep for the previous four days.

Although only midmorning, it was stifling in the hall. The male attendants on each side of the Emperor kept the air moving with oxtail flywhisks and pipal leaf shaped fans, but Mohan was too far away to feel the breeze.

Qadir and Isa had exchanged perfunctory greetings with Mohan. Like himself, the two were clearly worn from the ordeal of the past few days, and Mohan could not tell if either of them were trying to conceal a theft.

Shah Jahan said, "I'm ready to receive the proposals each of you has prepared. So that I don't unduly influence anyone with my own opinion, I want an evaluation from each of you as every design is submitted. Be candid, and don't take offense at criticism of your own concepts. Our purpose is to achieve the best possible design, so I want to make full use of the talents of each of you. The final plan may well be some combination of elements from each rendering."

He looked at Mohan Lal. "Master Builder, we will see your design first."

Mohan, who had been paying little attention in his weariness and hostility, gave an almost imperceptible jump upon realizing the Emperor had called upon him. He silently handed his drawings, consisting of four unbound sheets of heavy paper, to the pleasantly smiling Mukarrimat Khan, who passed them up to the Emperor. Shah Jahan first examined the front elevation.

He saw a rough sketch of a building that, with its pointed inset arches, its chamfered corners, and its large central dome, superficially resembled Emperor Humayan's tomb in Delhi. But according to the labeling, this building was entirely in white marble as he had wished. The main structure was both taller and less broad than Humayan's tomb. It sat on a high, wide plinth, and on each corner of that platform stood a towering, slender minaret.

Shah Jahan placed the drawing on the cushion beside him, and he perused the site plan. He saw that the tomb, instead of being placed in the garden's center, was at one edge, by the bank of the river. The Emperor glanced down at Mohan. "Unusual," he commented, but his face gave no hint of either approval or disapproval. He quickly looked at the cross section of the sepulcher, and a sketch of the proposed gate building.

Without comment, he returned the sheets to Mukarrimat Khan, who passed them to Qadir Zaman Khan, who happened to be standing nearest. "What comments from the master builder from Arabia?" the Emperor asked.

Qadir stared for a time at the drawings. At last, he said, "An attractive concept, Your Majesty." He looked at Mohan, and appeared to hesitate. He then held up the drawing so the Emperor could again see it, and he said with the politeness customarily expected at the Emperor's court: "With all due respect to the designer, who has my greatest admiration, I'm concerned about these minarets. They are completely detached from the building. The effect seems to me to make the plan somewhat, uh, fragmented. Not a unified whole. As if the minarets were added as an afterthought, for balance."

He now avoided looking at Mohan.

Shah Jahan had been peering intently at the rendering. "Hmmm," he said. After a time he looked at the dome expert from Persia, Ismail Afandi, and asked for a critique.

"The dome is taller than usual, Your Majesty. The fact that it is elevated on a drum adds to the height. The double-shelled design adds strength. Except for the need to hoist materials higher and build taller scaffolding, I see no major problem in the construction."

"What do you think of the dome's esthetics?" Shah Jahan asked.

The dome expert's face was animated with enthusiasm: "Your Majesty, it's perfect! It's like the giant pearl above the throne of Allah in paradise. The building is so high, it appears to be soaring into the sky!"

It had been the ancient Hindu *Vastu shastras*, which emphasized height, and his own experience with temple *shikharas*, that had led Mohan to design a building so tall and narrow compared to other Muslim tombs.

Ismail was continuing, "The central dome would seem too tall without the minarets, and without the smaller *chhatris*, cupolas, around it which echo the main dome's shape. But with them, it is superbly well balanced."

When polled by Shah Jahan, the others present were divided as to whether or not it was desirable to have the minarets so far detached from the main structure. The Emperor looked at Mohan Lal. "Would the designer care to comment?"

Mohan Lal stood silently for a moment, uncomfortable in the heat, clothing sticky from sweat. He boldly met Shah Jahan's eyes and said, "Your Majesty, my drawing speaks for itself."

The Emperor appeared perplexed. The other builders stood rigidly tense. After a time, Shah Jahan said calmly, "Very well. Any comments on the siting of the tomb and its gardens? The plan is a major departure from the traditional *char bagh*, since the sepulcher is at the garden's edge rather than the center. And there is the matching garden across the river."

Qadir Zaman Khan spoke, his powerful voice filling the room: "Your Majesty, perhaps the traditional layout is not important to one who's not of our Faith. But as Your Majesty knows so well, an earthly garden is a representation of Allah's heaven itself. Any modifications should be considered with skepticism."

Shah Jahan observed, "The main garden is still a *char bagh*, a square.

The only innovation, though it's indeed a major one, is that the sepulcher is outside the square, rather than in its center." He looked at Mohan and directed, "May I have your reasons for such a layout?"

Mohan replied, straining to control his animosity, "This particular site provides a wonderful opportunity if you locate the tomb beside the river. When Your Majesty approaches by boat, the sepulcher will be reflected in the water, like a great white lotus above its pond. It will also be reflected from the opposite approach by land, but there the image will be in the pool at the center of the garden, and in the water channels. Also," —he still struggled to restrain his hostility— "with the building perched high atop the river bank, it will be more visible from Your Majesty's palace here in the fort."

Mohan intentionally did not say that his idea for siting the building on the very edge of the river had come from the traditional placement of Hindu temples by a body of water for purposes of the worshipers' purifying baths. He continued, "And when Your Majesty is enjoying the gardens across the river, you will see the main structure reflected in the pool there. The sight should be especially beautiful in moonlight."

At last, the Emperor said, "Your design gives even more emphasis to the building than placing it in the center of the main garden. It's as if the entire garden is lying in admiration at the foot of the building."

"But, Your Majesty!" said Qadir Zaman Khan. Surprise flickered momentarily in Shah Jahan's eyes at being addressed so abruptly. However, Qadir was rushing onward, and the Emperor let the minor breach of etiquette pass: "This plan means placing the building itself at the edge of the river, in the most unstable location on the site!"

"Hmmm...so it does." Shah Jahan looked again at Mohan Lal. "Master Builder?"

"Your Majesty may recall," Mohan said dryly, "that I've had some experience with buildings adjacent to water bodies. It will increase both the construction time and the cost. But with a proper foundation, there should be no problem."

Shah Jahan again sat in thought before directing, "Let's look at the next rendering."

Designs were considered from five other masters. Mohan thought any of the plans would be suitable, if not particularly inspiring. They were all far more complete and finely executed in their drafting, comparable to those of his own plans that had disappeared.

When the time came for Ustad Isa to submit his own design, he requested, and was granted, the Emperor's permission to speak prior to hearing the reaction from the other builders to his plan. "Your Majesty," Isa said, "I have the honor of being the humble disciple of my *pir*, the venerable Shah Yar Muhammad Chishti." Mohan had listened to the discussions so far resignedly and with minimal interest. At the reference to the famous *sufi* mystic who resided at Agra, he grew curious as to where Isa was heading.

Isa, thin and almost ethereal in his appearance, was saying, "After Your Majesty told us of the departed Queen's dream, in which she saw her own monument, I asked my *pir* to pray so that I might be honored with a vision of that same monument. Your Majesty, I can now say that my *pir*'s prayers were answered!"

The Emperor's face mirrored the astonishment of the others gathered.

"You believe you've seen the same building as my dear wife?" Shah Jahan asked.

Isa's high voice sounded dramatically confident as he replied, "I'm virtually certain, Your Majesty! And this is what I saw."

To Mohan's surprise, the proposal was rendered as a painting in the style of the miniatures popular at court, rather than as architectural drawings. The full color made it a more attractive, eye-catching proposal than the others, especially Mohan's own hurried sketches. Mohan wondered how Isa could have executed it so quickly. Then he realized that as the head of both a draftsman's guild and a family of other draftsmen, Isa would have ample help. And having resided in Agra for some time, Isa had friends in the Emperor's large atelier of artists.

The building was reminiscent of Akbar's tomb at Sikandra. Isa had made full use of his draftsman's skills to carefully detail the numerous small cupolas clustered around the outer walls of the building.

Shah Jahan's brow furrowed with interest as he examined the rendering. To Mohan, it seemed as the Emperor half wanted to believe, and half did not want to believe, that this was the same vision his beloved had seen just before her death. Eventually, Shah Jahan said. "Fascinating." He looked at Isa. "I have the greatest reverence for your esteemed *pir*," he said. "And I'm eternally grateful for his assistance. But I believe it is appropriate to receive comments on this design, as we have on the other proposals."

It seemed to Mohan that the other experts showed even more care than usual in their remarks, probably fearing to offend the famous *sufi* saint, or the Emperor if he should decide to accept the design from Isa's dream.

When the time came for Mohan's critique of Isa's design, he said, "It's an outstanding rendering, Your Majesty. I greatly admire the skill of the esteemed draftsman. However, with all due respect both to him and his saint, the building appears overly ornate to me, with so many cupolas scattered about it. A design that depends more on, uh, grace of line, as well as ornamentation, might be more in keeping with a building to honor a woman of rare beauty."

Shah Jahan sat staring at Mohan for a time. Then, he nodded. "Very well." He turned to Isa. "What response does our master draftsman wish to make?"

Isa said, his voice oddly quavering, "Your Majesty, I carefully duplicated the design that was sent to me in my dream, so I take little personal responsibility for its details. But it seems to me the ornamentation is reminiscent of the adornments worn by a lovely woman. And at the same time, the building has its precedents in the magnificent tomb of Your Majesty's own illustrious grandfather, may Allah have mercy on his soul."

Shah Jahan slowly nodded. "I see." He once more mused over the painting, and then said to Isa, "A most attractively presented proposal."

Qadir Zaman Khan's rendering was considered last. To Mohan, Qadir's design appeared similar to the tomb of Itmad-ud-Daulah, but on a larger scale. The minarets were short and stubby, masculine rather than feminine.

When his turn came to comment, Mohan said, "Your Majesty, this is an intriguing design, as I'd expect from so expert a builder. My only reservation is that to my eye, it seems more a man's tomb than a woman's. It appears low and broad, and therefore a little heavy. I'd prefer some slight modifications so it appears more delicate, lighter. More full of feminine grace."

The Emperor turned to Qadir. "What do you say, as the designer?"

"Your Majesty," said Qadir loudly and forcefully, "I have the utmost respect for my colleague. However, on this particular point I disagree. I feel the delicate inlay work in the marble makes the building feminine in feel, as do the minarets."

Shah Jahan sat silently for a time. Then, he said, "I'll reserve my own comments until tomorrow. I'd like more time to review the designs."

Mohan was leaving with the others, when Mukarrimat Khan approached him and whispered, "The Padshah wishes to speak privately with you."

Mohan approached the Emperor and stood, waiting, as Shah Jahan stared expressionlessly at him. At last, the Emperor picked up what Mohan saw were his own drawings. "This is an intriguing design," said Shah Jahan. "However, I could not help but notice that it has a much less finished look than the plans of the other masters. As if it were drawn hurriedly." His voice became hard: "Explain this."

Mohan looked away. "My original renderings were somehow misplaced, Your Majesty. Regrettably, I had to redraw them in only a few hours this morning."

"Misplaced?"

Mohan returned the Emperor's stare. "Yes, Your Majesty."

"Try to find them. I wish to see your conception at its most complete."

Mohan hesitated momentarily, then again looked away and said, "I'll try, Your Majesty. However, they unfortunately disappeared from my rooms. It seems doubtful I'll be successful at finding them."

"They *disappeared?*"

Mohan looked back to the Emperor. "Yes, Your Majesty."

Shah Jahan's eyes narrowed. "You have no idea what happened to them?"

"No, Your Majesty."

"Could they have been stolen?"

"That, uh, seems the most likely explanation, Your Majesty."

Shah Jahan was silent for a time. Then he said, "You may go."

When Chandra heard from Mohan of Isa's dream design, he shook his head admiringly. "What a masterful scheme. And fully colored, you said. How can anyone compete with that? Especially your plan, when you had only the sketches to submit?"

"It seems to give him a big advantage," Mohan agreed. "Well, so be it, if the Emperor is impressed by the claim."

"Do you think the Emperor believed him?"

"Much as I hate to say it, Shah Jahan does have sound artistic judgment." He sighed. "But the purity of Isa's saint is admired by everyone. Whether the holy man's aura will transfer itself to Ustad Isa remains to be seen."

"You don't seem to care much either way."

"I don't. All I care about now is finding the coolest possible place to sleep." He called to their servant: "Ram Das, get my mat."

Chandra said, "We could go down by the river. Maybe even find some shade at the building site."

"It's too far, and I'm exhausted. I'll settle for our veranda."

The next day, Mohan waited with the other master artisans for the Emperor to call them into his presence. Ustad Isa said quietly, "I had an unusual experience yesterday. Three of the Emperor's agents visited me. They insisted on searching my entire home. But they didn't say why! Fortunately, they didn't find whatever they were looking for, and they eventually left."

"I had the same experience!" said Qadir Zaman Khan, his face bland. "How odd. I wonder what they were after." He looked to Mohan. "Did you have a visit, also?"

Mohan shrugged, "I slept soundly most of the day. If they visited, I didn't know of it."

Mukarrimat Khan then summoned them in to where the Emperor waited.

Shah Jahan told the assembled master artisans, "I've carefully considered each proposal." He looked at Ustad Isa, and continued, "I gave special consideration to the eminent draftsman's rendering, in view of its origin. I have the greatest respect for both Shah Yar Muhammad Chishti and his disciple. I'm certain there are aspects of the vision that can be incorporated into the final design.

"But, by the grace of Allah, I have more than a little knowledge of architectural design myself. I must bring my own judgment into the matter." He held Mohan Lal's drawings up before them. "I prefer this approach. It not only makes use of the natural beauty of the site; it also captures the essence of what I had pictured in my own mind for the monument. It's reminiscent of Padshah Humayan's tomb in Delhi, but in the more pure, more elegant white marble. This building and its dome are also taller, and hence more graceful than Humayan's tomb. The minarets compensate for the mass of the main building. They lighten the overall effect, and add grace and ornamentation. It's beautiful, as my wife was beautiful." Tears formed in his eyes and he stopped. The artisans waited uncomfortably.

He regained control of himself and directed the group: "Build a wooden model on this design. I'll then entertain further refinements. Give attention to the design of the companion buildings—the mosque, entry gates, structures for the support staff, visitors' housing."

The Emperor rose and left.

Qadir Zaman Khan approached Mohan. In a voice slightly louder than Mohan felt necessary, Qadir said, "I congratulate you on your winning design. Even though my own wasn't selected, I assure you the project has my complete enthusiasm."

Mohan gave a noncommittal nod. He began walking toward the door. Qadir hesitated a moment, apparently expecting a more complete response. When none came, he strode away, an enigmatic look on his face.

Ustad Isa approached and said, visibly unhappy, but with a forced smile, "May I congratulate you, Master Builder. I hope to be able to assist with more detailed renderings."

Mohan paused only a moment. "I admire your skills as a draftsman, as does everyone," he said. He resumed walking out, ignoring Isa's puzzled expression.

Chandra said, "Congratulations, Father! You won in spite of Qadir—or Isa—taking your plans."

Mohan shrugged. "A person never truly benefits by stealing from another, even if it is only ideas. What would it have profited Qadir if he had won because of the theft? He would have known that his winning might well be due to his evil deed. The knowledge would have eaten at his soul. And he would ultimately be held accountable by his God."

Chandra frowned. "Well, I suppose that may be true."

"Anyway," said Mohan, "I rather wish he had won after all."

Chandra stared at him for a time. "Regardless of how you feel about the Emperor, Father, aren't you pleased, anyway? This is a major monument, probably the greatest project to be built during Shah Jahan's reign!"

"Maybe," Mohan said dully, in a tone indicating he preferred not to discuss the matter.

"So you still don't care?"

"Not much."

Chandra pressed his lips tight, then asked, "But why did you even submit that design, then?"

Mohan shrugged. "I couldn't very well refuse the Emperor's command. The concept came to me while we were touring the other buildings. Presenting it seemed a way to satisfy His Majesty. Hopefully, he won't prevent me from leaving, now that I've given him a useful plan. Qadir Zaman Khan or any of the other builders can supervise the actual construction. Ustad Isa will be delighted to handle the drafting. The Emperor doesn't need me any more."

"You don't have other commissions, Father. And we need work."

Mohan again shrugged. "I'd go without, rather than work for this Emperor. But another job will turn up eventually, maybe in one of the Rajput states. I think it's time to go there. We'll be farther from the Emperor's reach."

Chandra was silent and motionless for a time. He sighed. "I suppose I should be glad you're willing to do *something*. But I hate to see you dismiss a project as grand as this."

For several days minor changes were made on the wooden model, under the Emperor's supervision and in response to suggestions from members of the group. Shah Jahan continually urged haste, and he made decisions quickly. At last, in a meeting with the exhausted builders, the Emperor nodded his approval. Mohan decided it was time to insist on his own departure; he would talk to Mukarrimat Khan about the matter as soon as the meeting was over.

He could not help but be curious as to who would be named to have overall charge of the project. Almost certainly, it would be one of the Muslims, so he himself should have no cause for concern.

Shah Jahan stepped back from the model and seated himself. He looked around the group. He said, "I'm sure most of you have wondered who will be in overall charge of the construction. The entire project must be done perfectly, since our Holy Law says no changes are permitted on a tomb once work is completed. I myself will closely watch the progress. However, the work will take many years, and I'll often be traveling elsewhere to attend to my affairs.

"Mukarrimat Khan will act as my personal representative in my absence. You'll petition him whenever you need funds or other resources, or when you have other difficulties you need resolved."

The Emperor sat quietly for a moment, before continuing, "I've carefully considered who shall be the head supervisor for the construction work itself. You are all capable men. There will be many other masters in their fields involved in various aspects of the work. But I must choose one from among you whose judgment I trust, especially in case of disagreements in my absence.

"I need a master who knows every aspect of construction, from the preparation of the site through the addition of the last ornament. In this case, the stability of the building's foundation will be especially important, since the site abuts the river."

Shah Jahan's gaze moved slowly around the assembled experts. "Whenever I ask who is the best architect, the best of the master builders, one who is an authority on foundations in addition to all other aspects of construction, many of you are mentioned. But one name keeps arising, again and again. I'm familiar with his buildings myself, and I find them faultless."

Mohan Lal began to feel uneasy in his stomach.

Shah Jahan continued, "I met this builder many years ago myself, and had occasion to talk to him at length. I was impressed even then with his abilities. He's not of my own faith."

Oh *no!* Mohan screamed silently. He was staring at the Emperor, willing Shah Jahan not to say what he feared was coming. Shah Jahan continued, "Although most of the contractors will be Muslim, the majority of guild members hired by the contractors to do the actual construction will be Hindu. It may be beneficial to have one of their own religion as head supervisor. But it is also important that the supervisor be the best I can possibly find."

He looked directly at Mohan, and for the first time a smile came to the Emperor's lips. "I'm convinced that in the esteemed builder, Mohan Lal, I have the best. He is the one I've chosen to supervise my wife's memorial until its completion, however many years that may take."

Mohan was staring at the Emperor, making no effort to cover his dismay. Shah Jahan either did not see the expression or chose to ignore it.

Having made his announcement, the Emperor rose and quickly left.

Mohan endured the congratulations and praise from the others present. Qadir Zaman Khan approached with an obviously forced smile and said, "I congratulate you again, Master Builder. Your position is well deserved. If the Emperor and yourself find it helpful, I'd be both available and honored for major involvement in construction. Perhaps some supervisory role, to lighten your own load?"

Mohan nodded and gave a strained smile in return. "Of course. I'll make such a recommendation to His Majesty. Your experience would be valuable to any building project."

Qadir smiled more broadly at the praise. "How kind of you."

At last, Qadir and the other builders drifted away, and Mohan approached Mukarrimat Khan. "Your honor, I must speak to the Padshah. Alone."

Mukarrimat Khan raised his eyebrows, but kept his usual charming smile. He said, "The Emperor, may God give him the life eternal, normally meets in the Shah Burj with his ministers at this time. But since you're now chief architect, I'll see if he's still available."

Mukarrimat Khan disappeared for some time, then returned to lead Mohan through a series of richly decorated chambers to an octagonal room with large arched windows overlooking the Yamuna river. There, Shah Jahan sat leaning against an embroidered bolster, reading a document while his attendants fanned him.

Mohan did his *taslims*, and the Emperor looked up and asked pleasantly, "What is it, Master Builder?"

Mohan summoned his determination and said, "Your Majesty, I'm greatly honored by your confidence in me. Given Your Majesty's own unusual expertise in architectural matters, I feel doubly exalted to be chosen for a project so close to your heart. But I have serious reservations about my involvement in this work."

Shah Jahan examined him with interest. "Oh? How so?"

"I devoted the last fourteen years of my life to building a temple in Varanasi."

After a moment, the Emperor said, "I recall you were working on such a project when we met in Udaipur."

Mohan Lal sat stonily. Eventually, he said, "I'd almost completed the temple."

At last, comprehension dawned in Shah Jahan's eyes. Eventually, he said, "I think I understand." He sat for some time, his face unreadable. Then, he said, "I didn't know."

Mohan was silent. He knew his anger was evident in his face.

Shah Jahan was staring at him. At last, the Emperor said, "Our jurists have held for centuries that even though existing houses of worship for unbelievers can be retained, no new ones can be built. So I have banned the building of new temples, and I cannot restore yours. However, this tomb is the most important building of my reign. It will be a worthy substitute."

A substitute! Mohan strove to contain the anger which threatened to burst from every pore in his body. "Your Majesty, I beg to be relieved of further obligations on this project."

Shah Jahan bit his bottom lip. He said, "You have another commission?"

Mohan hesitated, but knew he must be truthful. "No, Your Majesty. But I don't feel I can do justice to this job."

Shah Jahan gazed out over the Yamuna, toward the building site. After a time, he looked back at Mohan and said firmly, "This work is vitally important to me. I must insist you supervise it. You are the best master for the project. I regret if it causes you inconvenience."

Mohan stood rigidly. After a time, he said, "Then may I make a request, Your Majesty?"

Shah Jahan, still looking at him, gave a slight nod. "Of course. I'll grant it if I can."

"I ask that my name not be associated with the project. After completing the building, I'd like all references to myself removed from any records related to the construction. Payroll ledgers, materials requisitions, any records anywhere."

Shah Jahan furrowed his brow as he stared at Mohan Lal. He said slowly, "I realize that unlike Muslims, it's traditional among Hindus that artisans' names not appear on their work. But why do you insist your name not even appear in any of the records?"

Mohan said coldly, "I told you about my temple, Your Majesty."

Shah Jahan stared at Mohan. Then, he turned his head and again gazed out the window. He looked at Mohan and opened his mouth. Apparently reconsidering, he closed it, still staring at Mohan.

At last, he said slowly, "I agree to your stipulation."

Mohan nodded. He touched his palm to his forehead, turned, and left.

7

Chandra told Mohan, "I've heard from some of the other builders that Qadir Zaman Khan was furious when the Emperor selected you as chief builder."

They were riding in their carriage to the building site. The monsoon had come at last, and water drummed overhead on the canopy. "I sensed he was unhappy," Mohan replied as he examined a sheaf of plans. Occasional drops of rain drifted in onto the paper, slightly blurring the ink. Normally Mohan would have taken care to avoid getting them wet, but for this particular project he almost invited damage.

"He saw you as his chief competitor, Father. He visited the sites with us because he hoped he could learn something from you to give him an advantage. When that didn't help, he stole your drawings, either to learn what you were planning, or else so you wouldn't have anything worthwhile to show the Emperor."

Mohan did not look up. "Too bad he didn't succeed. He's a capable builder."

"Father!" Chandra shook his head in disgust. After a few moments, he said, "Qadir must need top patronage positions to maintain his way of life. Palanquin bearers and rich clothes are expensive. I wonder if he'll be satisfied with what he was offered."

Mohan glanced at Chandra and said gruffly, "He has an important role overseeing the hoisting and laying of all the stone. He'll receive eight hundred rupees a month for his department. That's more than most of the master artisans. Almost as much as my own allotment. He should get by handsomely."

"I'm sure he wanted the fame that went with the top position, too."

"He's welcome to it!" Mohan half shouted, tossing the plans to his feet. "Look at that," he said, waving toward the falling rain. "The Emperor wants us to begin excavating in this weather! The holes will fill up with water as fast as we can dig them. I don't understand his being in such a hurry. As if waiting two or three months until the rains are over would make a difference on a project this large."

Refusing to be intimidated by his father's anger, Chandra said firmly, "You'll do your best. As always."

Mohan gazed out into the rain. "The building will be uniquely beautiful. And a significant monument. It's too bad the sponsor is so flawed."

"Have you changed your mind about being identified with the project, Father?"

Mohan looked away and did not reply. After a time, he retrieved the plans and again studied them as the carriage splashed along the wet, muddy street.

The Emperor quickly approved Mohan's proposed plan for the substructure, with slight modifications based on suggestions by some of the other masters.

The building would rest on a mammoth foundation of vaults and piers. The piers in turn would sit on numerous circular masonry wells, sunk deep into the earth, joined together, and reinforced by sal wood axles and spokes at intervals along their depth. These wells would place the entire structure firmly on the bedrock and distribute the tremendous weight over a broad area. The outer row of wells would also serve to divert the river waters away from the substructure as a whole.

Shah Jahan ordered excavations to begin immediately. The next day, Mohan Lal sought out Qadir Zaman Khan. "I need a master to act as second-in-command," Mohan said. "Much of my own time will be spent on coordination. Keeping the flow of materials coming. Inspecting the quality of marble shipments. So on. I intend to remain in the background except when I'm needed. I want someone to be on site all the time, actually overseeing the work. He'll be the one everyone regards as the supervisor. You're a highly skilled builder. I want you to have the position. You'll have full authority to act in my behalf, except when I direct otherwise in specific instances."

He saw confusion in Qadir Zaman Khan's face. Mohan added, "I'll pay you an extra two hundred rupees a month."

Qadir appeared to ponder the matter. Soon he smiled. "I accept."

Later at the building site, as Mohan had expected, Chandra came to his tent office. Chandra was drenched from the rain, and he futilely wiped the mud from his feet. "Father, is it true about Qadir Zaman Khan? That's he's your second-in-command?"

"It's true." His eyes met and held those of his son.

"Why him? Not only is he probably the one who stole your plans, he cares only about advancing his own interests. Not about helping you!"

"Of course. But his route for advancing himself is to do the best job possible. He does have experience and talent."

"Aren't you worried he'll try to take over—" Chandra fell silent. His eyes were wide as he stared at his father. "Oh. I think I see." Chandra shook his head. "Well, I hope you have no regrets later." He turned and splashed back through the rains to the excavating crews.

Mohan's eyes followed with a certain smugness. His son was no fool.

The laborers progressed on the excavations, even though the rains made the work miserable and slow. A small city began to grow on the south fringe of the site, housing for the vast army of workers, and bazaars to cater to their needs. Although the town consisted mainly of tents and rude huts at first, gradually more permanent buildings were constructed. The place came to be named Mumtazabad, after the Queen whose death called the town into being.

Mohan took his obligations as chief architect seriously, with Chandra as his main personal assistant, but he let Qadir Zaman Khan handle almost all routine on-site supervision. He had known Qadir was an excellent builder, but Qadir surprised Mohan by his ability to handle the other artisans and contractors with finesse.

However, there was considerable dissatisfaction among the laborers, mostly Hindus, about having to work in the monsoons. They had traditionally labored only indoors in this season due to the impracticality of accomplishing much while building in mud and water. Qadir came to Mohan and said with some embarrassment, "I've been accused of forcing them to work because I have no concern for anyone who's not a follower of the Prophet. They say only a Muslim would make them work in such appalling conditions."

Mohan said, "I'll take care of it."

At daybreak the next morning, when the laborers, virtually all Hindus, grudgingly reported to the site, they saw the chief architect knee deep in water in one of the pits. He was supervising a half dozen Muslims who were filling buckets with muddy soil, passing them up from the pit for emptying by a couple more Muslim workers.

Mohan Lal looked up and saw the crew who stood watching him in bewilderment. He climbed the ladder from the pit and said, "Difficult conditions! But you're doing an excellent job. Even the Emperor says so. He's authorized double wages for every day of work in the rain." Mohan gestured to the workers in the pit. "And he suggested hiring additional help to aid you."

He sloshed back to his tent, ignoring the looks of surprise. When he next looked out at the pit, the Hindu laborers were at work.

Qadir received no further objections from the crews, and neither the Emperor nor anyone on his staff interfered with Mohan's decision to double wages during the monsoons.

As Mohan had expected, Qadir gradually became known as the primary supervisor and arbiter at the building site. Mohan was a higher authority and one who demanded perfection, but who stayed aloof, issuing most orders through Qadir. Indeed, Mohan often was away, dealing with Mukarrimat Khan and other administrators in the Red Fort.

Shah Jahan himself took a direct interest in the construction and frequently visited the site once the rains ended. Mohan Lal treated the Emperor with the expected courtesy, but he responded to Shah Jahan's questions with only the minimum necessary information. He took care to ensure that Qadir Zaman Khan answered many of the Emperor's inquiries and also sometimes showed Shah Jahan around the site. The Emperor either did not notice or did not care that Mohan was working competently and diligently, but with a lack of enthusiasm.

The following summer, when the mammoth foundation had been completed to the last of the waterproofed bricks and the iron reinforcing clamps, Mohan sought a private audience with Shah Jahan. The Emperor was in his octagonal room overlooking the river.

"Your Majesty," Mohan said, "I trust that the project meets with your approval so far."

"I'm quite satisfied," Shah Jahan replied, looking curiously at Mohan Lal.

"Your Majesty is no doubt aware that the supervisor on site is doing a superb job. Qadir Zaman Khan is completely capable."

"So I've seen. You made a good selection in him."

"Then, Your Majesty no doubt sees that I myself am no longer needed. Qadir Zaman Khan is quite capable of supervising all aspects of the project. I therefore humbly request that I be permitted to resign from my position."

Shah Jahan pressed his lips together. He stared at Mohan for a time. Then, he said, "I envision this building as the most magnificent of my reign, perhaps—probably—of any reign. I've pledged unprecedented amounts of funds for it. I would be doing you a disservice if I permitted you to resign. I have no doubt a master architect of your experience and abilities would find other patrons. But you likely would never again find a project of this scope."

Mohan made no reply. Rigidly, his face held under tight control, he touched his palm to his forehead in preparation to leave.

"I'm not finished with you!" Shah Jahan's voice impaled him like a sword. The Emperor's eyes blazed. "I'm quite aware of your distaste for this project. And I know the reasons. No builder can be pleased with the demolition of a major work. But no, Qadir Zaman Khan is *not* going to be my chief architect. *I* choose my chief architect!

"My wife's tomb deserves not merely a good architect, she deserves the best! The best. I happen to know something about architects and building design. I know the best when I see it. The best—that's you."

Mohan stood stunned at the Emperor's outburst.

Shah Jahan said quietly, "*Now* you may go."

8

In the third year of construction, the Emperor returned from a lengthy inspection tour of the kingdom of Bundelkhund where his son Aurangzeb had recently suppressed a rebellion by the vassal ruler. Shah Jahan did not appear pleased at the rate of progress when Mohan and Qadir Zaman Khan showed him around the site.

"The quality of the building appears excellent. But I expected somewhat more to be done by now," the Emperor said, eyeing the almost-completed plinth.

Mohan had heard tales of young Prince Aurangzeb's zeal in devastating Bundelkhund for the Emperor, including looting and destroying virtually every Hindu temple in the kingdom. He was in no mood to make any effort to try to please Shah Jahan.

"You wanted quality," Mohan said bluntly, not looking at the ruler. He did not go on to point out the obvious, that if the rate of construction were forced to increase, quality would likely decline.

Shah Jahan stared sharply at him and said with vexation, "I did, and I do. But my wife now rests in a tomb little better than a serving woman's. She must have a worthy monument as soon as possible."

Mohan met his eyes. "A monument on this scale can't be built in a year." He had not intended to say more, but the words were out before he could stop: "Any more than a temple can!"

He heard the intake of breath from the Emperor's companions, and from Qadir.

There was silence as the Emperor stared at him. Finally, Shah Jahan said, "Everyone leave. Except my chief builder."

Mohan realized he had pushed the Emperor too far, but he was beyond caring. The entourage and Qadir quickly moved off, carefully not glancing at either Shah Jahan or Mohan Lal. "Explain your last remark," Shah Jahan demanded.

Mohan hesitated not a moment. "Your Majesty seems intent on destroying some works of architecture at the same time that he's in haste to build another. A temple can be as much of a work of art as a tomb."

With lips pressed tight, Shah Jahan glared at Mohan. Then: "You refer to

Varanasi, or to Bundelkhund?"

"To both."

Shah Jahan stood stiffly in silence, glowering at Mohan. Eventually, he looked away. "I now think the destruction order was an error," he said so quietly Mohan could barely hear. "I let my own distaste for idol houses and the arguments of the *mullahs* who advise me outweigh the desires of my Hindu subjects." He looked back at Mohan, his face still angry. More loudly, he said, "And my son exceeded my wishes in Bundelkhund. He knows I'm not pleased at his excesses. However," he glared at Mohan, "If you tell anyone I said so, I'll see the remainder of your life is so short you'll not have time to lay another block." Shah Jahan stalked over to where his courtiers and attendants nervously waited and commanded, "We return to the palace."

Countless powerful men would have paid a small fortune to know what Shah Jahan had just told Mohan. Each of Shah Jahan's four sons had their own group of supporters who would love to know the Emperor's current displeasure with Prince Aurangzeb. Conservative as well as liberal religious factions would also be eager to know Shah Jahan's current feelings regarding Hindu places of worship.

But, thought Mohan, if Shah Jahan truly had regrets, let him begin rebuilding the temples he'd destroyed. And he could start with what would have been the grandest one in Varanasi.

In their future relations, both Emperor and architect pretended to forget the exchange. The years passed. The sepulcher grew, a giant sculpture of precisely fitted blocks of the finest white marble from Makrana in Rajputana. The subsidiary structures, mostly of red sandstone from Akbar's nearby abandoned capital of Fatehpur Sikri, also progressed, but at a slower pace: the mosque and its matching companion on the opposite side of the mausoleum, the giant gateway and the subsidiary gates, the garden walls, the arcades for the bazaar.

Mohan had convinced a number of key artisans, including his friend the master sculptor Bhagwan Das, to relocate to Agra to work on the monument. The labor force gradually increased to number twenty thousand workers in all. An earthen ramp stretched far away through central Agra for transporting materials.

Annually, on the anniversary of Mumtaz Mahal's death, an *urs* or memorial service was held on the site, attended by virtually all the nobility, and by the Emperor whenever he was in Agra.

Mohan's relationship with Shah Jahan remained one of courteous distance. As viewed by the contractors doing the construction work, Mohan Lal himself was in some ways like the Emperor: a distant, somewhat unapproachable presence whose word was law, but whose commands were carried out through Qadir Zaman Khan and other intermediaries.

Ustad Isa, as head draftsman, distributed the bulk of the working drawings to the contractors at each stage of construction. The account of Isa's mystical dream vision of a monument had spread as a legend, and many artisans assumed he was in fact the designer of the building, an assumption he took care not to discourage.

On an early morning in the summer of the project's fifth year, Shah Jahan, just returned from a military campaign in the Deccan against the Marathas, again viewed the site with Mohan. The huge platform had long been completed, and the walls of the main building stood to half their planned height.

Mohan pointed out to the Emperor the clever manner in which, to correct for optical illusions, he had designed the platform on which the sepulcher rested to be slightly higher, or convex, above the center of each of the big decorative arches. For the same reason, he had designed the facades of the main structure to incline very slightly inward.

"Intriguing," Shah Jahan said, obviously impressed. The Emperor gazed up at the walls, then turned to watch an approaching team of oxen pulling a cart bearing a large marble block. "The inner brickwork is progressing faster than the marble blocks are being laid," he said. "Can't you speed up the marble laying?"

"As Your Majesty knows," Mohan said, forcing himself to speak patiently, "a road has been specially constructed all the way to the quarries in Raja Jai Singh's territory. An adequate number of bullock carts and elephants have also been requisitioned. The main problem seems to be production at the quarry itself."

The Emperor pressed his lips tightly together for a time. Then, he said with a trace of petulance, "I've ordered Raja Jai Singh to give all possible assistance. And Maluk Shah is paying full price for everything from my treasury. So what's wrong?"

Mohan seethed at the implied criticism. "I've no way to know, Your Majesty," he said, "without going to Makrana."

"Then go! Nothing must interfere with this project. Nothing!" Shah Jahan strode away, the crowd of attendants and courtiers trailing after.

Mohan did his *taslim* to the Emperor's retreating back. "As Your Majesty wishes," he muttered.

Chandra accompanied Mohan on the journey. The graveled road shimmered with waves of heat as the builders headed toward the mines of Makrana, two hundred miles to the west. Their carriage met wagon after wagon, huge and solidly built, hauling the giant white marble blocks. Some of the loads were pulled by teams of twenty or thirty oxen or bullocks, some by elephants.

At one point, they saw a wedding party headed for a village, with the accompanying musicians playing cheerful music. After watching them for several moments, Mohan shook his head and said to Chandra, "I've neglected my obligations as your father. I've sometimes thought of searching for a wife for you, but I never acted on it. Instead, I think constantly about the project."

Chandra's lips curled into an embarrassed smile. "This tomb has kept me busy, also. When would I find time for a wife?"

Mohan looked away. "I missed your mother at the time she died. But then I was so busy on first one building, then another, it's been rare for me to think of family matters."

Chandra shrugged. "No matter. As with you, my work is my life."

Mohan looked to where the wedding party was disappearing into the haze of dust and heat. "We have other duties, too. We shouldn't ignore them. You need a son of your own."

After a time, Chandra said, "One day, Father. Maybe after we've finished this tomb."

At the mines, they saw lines of more carts waiting patiently in the blazing sun for loads to haul. There was no shortage of transportation.

Even in the terrible heat of midday the huge pits at the quarries of Makrana appeared every bit as busy as the construction site at Agra. Mohan watched the squaring of a block as two men worked a saw, while another poured sand and water into the groove. The cut progressed very, very slowly.

He turned to the supervisor, a short, broad, nervous man. "What would it take to increase production even more?" Mohan asked.

"More stone cutters, sir. We'd need more miners."

"Where could I find them?"

Sweat glistened on the supervisor's forehead. He took his time before replying, "That's difficult to say, sir. We've attracted stone cutters from all over the empire for this project."

Mohan had noticed the reluctance to answer. "The Emperor insists on more production," he said. "And he holds you personally responsible. If you can't find more miners, then the ones you have will need to work even harder."

It seemed to Mohan that the man's sweat was due to more than the heat. The supervisor again appeared reluctant to reply. Then, he said, in a low voice, "I've heard there may be cutters still at Amber."

"Working for Raja Jai Singh? He was specifically ordered by the Emperor to lend all possible assistance."

"I find it difficult to say more," the supervisor said quietly. "These mines are in the Raja's territories, you realize."

"Of course," Mohan said, seemingly with sympathy. He could afford to sound understanding now that he had the information he needed.

He and Chandra undertook yet another day's dusty and hot journey in the carriage, to Raja Jai Singh's capital of Amber in its secluded gorge in the hills. Even more than the Pariyatra Rajputs of Mangarh, the Kachhwaha Rajputs of Amber had prospered by their alliance with the Mughal Emperors. The setting was most picturesque, with the big hillside palace mirrored in its scenic lake. Within the palace, they found under construction a stone-pillared public audience hall and richly ornamented halls of mirrors. And on the rocky hill high above the palace, numerous workmen labored on a huge protective fortress which was nearing completion.

Obviously, Raja Jai Singh's construction priorities were not the same as those of the Emperor. Mohan had found his stone cutters. Much as he admired the workmanship of the projects at Amber, he had little choice but to ensure that the artisans were moved to Makrana to cut marble for the tomb of the Queen.

Raja Jai Singh was absent on a tour of his domains, which made a direct confrontation unnecessary. Instead, Mohan returned to Agra and arranged the drafting of a *farman* for the Emperor to send to the Raja, politely reminding the Kachhwaha ruler of his obligation to send all available miners to Makrana.

For a period of many months during the seventh year of the project, the Emperor was far away at Kabul and Lahore. Mohan felt relieved to not have to devote time to Shah Jahan's visits, which had become an almost daily occurrence.

The past year or so the Emperor had seemed to become more moody, more introspective. Perhaps because the project had progressed to where the final form could be easily visualized, he had stopped his continual insistence on haste. He had complimented Mohan on the design of the gate buildings and of the mosque, which, if situated other than as mere adjuncts to the main sepulcher, would have been widely recognized as masterpieces in themselves. Still, for Mohan, the visits were an unwanted distraction from the demanding duties of supervising such a massive undertaking.

As the work progressed, other experts brought outstanding skills to the project. The calligrapher designed the inscriptions from the Qur'an with the letters more dense at the bottom of the big arches than at the top, again to make the effect more pleasing to the eye. The inlayers, mostly Hindus, did exquisite finishing detail on the floral designs of the walls. The marble sculptors, the silversmiths, the goldsmiths, the sandalwood carvers all were perfectionists.

The water engineer carefully hid out of sight in an adjacent garden the giant series of ramps by which bullocks raised water from the river for the fountains and pools. He even ensured the water from each of the many fountains would spray to the same height by cleverly directing the water first to a pressure-equalizing copper pot under each spout.

Occasionally, light-skinned travelers from the kingdoms of the European continent passed through the capital and marveled at the project. When they inquired who had designed the building, they were given varying answers: sometimes Ustad Isa's name, or even Qadir Zaman Khan's. Mohan Lal was seldom mentioned, and his name was never recorded by the travelers in their descriptions of their journeys.

9

In the tenth year after the first excavation for the foundation, the gold covered spire of the finial was hoisted to its position atop the center of the giant dome.

More years of construction remained on the companion buildings of Mumtazabad—the inns, the stables, the bazaars, the housing for the many guards and attendants. But the main sepulcher and its garden were completed. The formal transfer of Mumtaz Mahal's remains to the new crypt would also be the occasion for the dedication ceremony for the huge central building, the focal point of the entire complex.

Shah Jahan toured the site with Mohan and Qadir Zaman Khan several days before the dedication. "Magnificent," the Emperor said in a wondering voice as he stepped from the royal barge to the landing *ghat*. "Absolutely magnificent. The reflection in the water, the way the domes appear to be part of the sky itself...." His face kept turning upward, as if he could barely believe such beauty could exist, as if he expected it to vanish at any moment.

He turned to Mohan and Qadir. "I have large bonuses for each of you, and for the other master artisans. You can collect them any time."

They approached the main building, removed their footwear, and entered. Rich carpets in reds, golds, and blues covered the floors, and the marble lattices in front of the windows filtered and softened and dimmed the harsh sunlight. Musicians played in the large octagonal chamber under the false lower dome, and the echoes reverberated softly, hauntingly around the Emperor. "Excellent acoustics," he remarked to Mohan. The Qur'an would be chanted long hours over Mumtaz Mahal's crypt, and musicians would perform near it at many ceremonies in future years.

Shah Jahan ran his hand over the shining metal of the gem-studded gold screen surrounding the marble coffin replica. He nodded thoughtfully, and said, "The gold is beautiful. But I wonder if this might not be too much of a temptation for thieves? Perhaps a marble screen should be substituted." He entered the screen's doorway, approached the symbolic false sarcophagus and quietly examined the inlay work, the delicate flowers made up of thirty-five types of precious and semiprecious stones set flush with the surfaces of marble, and the calligraphy.

On he went, examining every chamber, every angle on this level, and on the level below, where a duplicate casket lay directly below the one above. Then, on down to the cool, windowless sublevel chambers accessible only from the river side of the building, where the body itself would be interred.

The Emperor exited the mausoleum, and strode out along the main water channel of the garden. He frequently stopped, turned, and gazed at the complex from various viewpoints. "All of it is beautiful when viewed from *any* angle," he said.

"As Your Majesty knows, that was the intent," said Mohan Lal.

At last, Shah Jahan beckoned Mohan to walk alone with him, to the edge of the marble plinth by the river. He looked upward. In a voice that was quiet with awe, he commented, "You were right about the minarets. They add balance and grace. And the height of the dome makes the building appear as if it were about to float upward to heaven."

He faced Mohan Lal, and said, "You've more than justified my faith in you. You've given over ten years to this building, I believe. I hope that by now you've decided I'm a suitable patron after all."

Mohan turned toward the structure, and his eyes roamed over the graceful curves of the arches and domes. "It was a worthwhile use of those years," he said.

The corners of Shah Jahan's lips curled into a rare smile. "Good. It will be several years before all the outbuildings are completed. And I have other projects planned in white marble, both in Agra and Delhi. I'd like you to continue in my employ."

Mohan was now fifty-five years in age. The strain of overseeing such a large project had begun to wear on him, reminding him that his career as a master builder would not last forever. He preferred not to spend his remaining years working for Shah Jahan, a ruler who had built with one hand but had destroyed with the other.

He said merely, "I'm honored at Your Majesty's trust. However, I have been wanting to return to the Rajput states where there are specific projects of interest."

"You still don't want to continue with this? With *this*?" Shah Jahan gestured toward the soaring white edifice, an incredulous look on his face.

"That's correct, Your Majesty. This building and its setting are embodiments of my work. God willing, it will all last many centuries. I see no need to be involved in the details of the outlying structures."

Shah Jahan stared at him and said, "You still are angry with me over the destruction of your temple? Even though I no longer interfere with my subjects' practices?"

Mohan replied, "You also have never offered to rebuild my temple, Your Majesty. Or any others that were destroyed."

The Emperor's eyes narrowed. He said in a low voice, "If I built houses for the idols of unbelievers, it would be an affront to Allah, as well as against our laws. I would infuriate the *mullahs* I respect and whose teachings I follow."

Mohan looked away from Shah Jahan, and away from the building, over the river. "We disagree on major matters, Your Majesty. I think it best that I leave."

Shah Jahan stared at him for a time. Then, he said, "A pity. Under my patronage, your great talent could result in so many more outstanding buildings." He strode to his barge and his waiting nobles.

Mohan Lal and Chandra attended the dedication ceremonies, where the Emperor delivered a eulogy composed by himself in honor of the completed building:

The grace of this beautiful mausoleum of Mumtaz Mahal, who was the ideal woman of her time, cannot be described.

She was the Queen of the world, and this is her final resting place.

Like the Garden of Heaven, this place is fragrant with ambergris and incenses. It is so tender and sacred the nymphs of Paradise clean it with the lids of their eyes.

Its doors and walls are inlaid with jewels; its air is fresh and cool.

The clouds of God's grace always shower on this sacred sepulcher. At this place God accepts the prayers of every person....

So sacred is this place, that if a criminal comes to its shelter, he is pardoned of his offence....

And if a sinner comes to this Tomb, his sins are washed away.

It is a monument of sorrow. Everyone who sees it feels its grief. Even the Sun and the Moon shed their tears upon it....

This building is immortal. Its foundation is strong like the earth itself, and like the unshakable faith of the devout follower of God....

So strong are its doors that perpetuity itself has found safety within it.

It is faultless, without defect or blemish.

The day after the ceremony, Mohan Lal and Chandra left in their old carriage for Udaipur by way of Mangarh. The sculptor Bhagwan Das, although traveling separately, was also returning to the Rajput kingdoms. Raja Arjuna of Mangarh wanted a new audience hall, and Maharana Jagat Singh of Udaipur was proving to be an enthusiastic builder. There would be work to occupy architects and sculptors both.

Shah Jahan could easily have insisted that Mohan Lal and Bhagwan Das remain in Agra, but he did not.

***

The Taj Mahal, ultimately to become virtually a symbol for India as a nation, was at first a destination for pilgrims, a site for religious festivals, and a garden oasis for contemplation and relaxation.

The revenues from thirty villages supported its maintenance and its hundreds of attendants, as well as the two thousand white-robed soldiers who guarded its wealth.

Shah Jahan remained an indefatigable builder, and he soon spent most of his time at Delhi, in the fortress city he had built called Shah Jahanabad. There, he reigned from his fabulous jeweled Peacock Throne.

At age sixty-six he was overthrown by his estranged son, Aurangzeb, who had defeated Shah Jahan's other sons in battle. As Emperor, just as when he was a prince, Aurangzeb destroyed far more Hindu temples than his father would ever have dreamed of ruining.

Until his death seven-and-a-half years later, Shah Jahan was imprisoned by Aurangzeb in the palace of the Red Fort of Agra. There, the deposed Emperor could gaze down the river from his windows at the white domes of the Taj Mahal, and remember his beloved wife. Upon Shah Jahan's death, Aurangzeb ordered the body to be interred in the Taj, to rest for all time alongside the remains of Mumtaz Mahal.

Oddly, the origin of the name "Taj Mahal," usually translated as "Crown Palace" or "Crown of the Palace" is uncertain. Some say it was derived, maybe by an Englishman, from the Queen's name, Mumtaz Mahal, which is roughly translated as "Exalted One of the Palace" or "Chosen One of the Palace." The name Taj Mahal does not appear in the records of Shah Jahan's time, when the building was referred to as the rauza *("tomb") of Mumtaz Mahal or the* rauza-i-munavvara, *the "illumined tomb."*

Magnificent though the Taj Mahal is still, we see it now stripped of much of its wealth, a lady bare of her jewels. The rich carpets no longer cover the floor. The golden screen around the crypt was replaced by one of marble for fear of looters. The sandalwood and ebony and silver doors have long since been stolen. Most of the buildings of adjacent Mumtazabad have left no trace, and the matching "Moonlight Garden" across the river also fell into ruin.

Descendants of many of the original artisans continue to reside in Agra; Ustad Isa's family worked there as draftsmen until emigrating to Pakistan at the time of the Partition of 1947.

Unfortunately, the Taj Mahal is being subjected to constant damage: through air pollution; through theft of stone inlays for sale to visitors by some of the very craftsmen working on restoration; through the effects of much heavier visitor traffic than was ever envisioned; through animal and human detritus; and through the extreme temperature variations of the climate. It remains to be seen whether the efforts of the Indian government and other interested parties will satisfactorily solve these problems.

Still, what remains is marvelous, a work of genius, a testament to the aesthetic tastes of Shah Jahan and to the masterful artisans who executed the Emperor's dream.

Part Two
The Treasure
of Mangarh

Mangarh, 1976

Conversation was impossible with the air tool blasting at the marble. Kaushalya Kumari covered her eyes against seeing the destruction of the audience hall floor. Then, tearful and furious at the same time, she fled through the stone-dust filled pavilion. Mahendra Singh shot a furious look at Ghosali, and stalked after her, followed by Pratap Singh.

Dammit, thought Vijay, fully in sympathy, as his eyes followed them. If we could just find the missing jewelry and gold quickly, all this destruction could stop. He couldn't help wondering if maybe Dev Batra wanted to enrich himself by having the marble slabs removed from the site and selling them. That would be an outrageous sacrilege for such a lovely, historic building.

Ghosali walked off to inspect the operations in another section of the fort.

The workmen paused, and the noise abruptly fell off. Vijay called to their foreman, "No more! We're stopping work on the floor."

The laborers exchanged puzzled looks. Vijay said to the foreman, "These men can go help with the digging at the top of the ridge."

The foreman frowned. "Sir, we were told to pull up the floor."

Vijay wondered for a moment if the man would obey him. He said with all the authority he could put in his voice, "Your orders are changed."

"Shri Ghosali agrees with this?"

"Of course!" At any rate, thought Vijay, Ghosali *would* agree if he wasn't such an ass.

The foreman stared at him a moment, then shrugged. "As you wish." He turned and shouted to the laborers. Without haste, the workmen began gathering up their tools.

Vijay knew he was compromising his position. But it was so clearly foolishness to tear up that floor; it was an unlikely hiding place, out here in the open. And how could the slabs have been moved, when they were permanently fixed in position?

Ghosali would be furious and might get Batra to order the work resumed. But maybe he wouldn't bother; he must realize how outlandish the order had been. And hopefully, by the time Batra heard about the stoppage, it would be too late to do anything.

Akbar Khan was, as usual, conscientiously polishing the jeep when Vijay came to him to be driven to the Bhim Bhawan Palace. On the way down the hill, the jeep passed Airavata with his old mahout and an assistant; it was late afternoon and time for the elephant's daily bath in the river. Airavata should be safer today, anyway, with Batra and his henchman away in Delhi.

At the palace, Vijay asked for Mahendra Singh. When told he was conferring with their guest, Vijay requested to see the princess instead.

She came to the reception room, her head high. But her eyes were reddened and puffy, and it was obvious she had been crying.

"I've stopped the work on the audience hall," he said.

She looked incredulous for an instant, then her body relaxed. She gave a nod, and lowered her eyes. "I'm glad you told me."

It was worth the risk he had taken, he thought, to relieve her mind. He hadn't realized how much pleasure it would give him to make her just a little less unhappy. But he still had his duties to the Income Tax Department. He said, "I need to look more down here. I promise I won't use an air hammer."

She watched him, waiting.

"We've only glanced at your prayer room. I'd like to inspect it more thoroughly."

She gave a sigh of resignation. "Very well. I'll go with you."

Her ever-present maid Gopi followed as Vijay and Kaushalya walked toward the *puja* room. "How long has Ekadantji been your family deity?" asked Vijay.

"At least since the 1500s. He was with my ancestors at Akbar's siege of Chittorgarh. He used to be in the temple in the fortress, but when this palace was built he was installed here. I think my grandfather Bhim Singhji didn't like the inconvenience of going up to the old fort to worship every day. And maybe he felt that if he had a new home, the god deserved one, too."

The family priest, a slender young man in a white *dhoti*, appeared by the door. They removed their footwear in the hallway and entered through the drapes. The room smelled of incense and flowers. Kaushalya folded her hands and stood for a moment, paying her respects. Vijay did likewise. Gopi prostrated herself before the image, then rose and moved to one side.

"Was there anything in particular you wanted to see?" asked Kaushalya in a low voice.

"Not really," said Vijay. "I'll just look around." He turned about and visually examined the walls and the ceiling. All appeared to be seamless plaster, of little interest. The polished floor, too, showed no suspicious irregularities.

He looked at the god. The silver image of Ganesha, about a foot high, draped in a string of fresh marigolds, sat on a stone pedestal. A stick of incense burned in a tiny brass pot in front. He saw no likely hiding places for a concealed strong box.

The pedestal wasn't nearly large enough to cover

Ekadantji

a trap door of a size enough to hide anything substantial, but he decided to be thorough. "Do you mind if we move the image aside for a moment?"

Kaushalya Kumari frowned, glanced at the priest, who looked unhappy, but wagged his head "yes."

The priest and the princess first folded their palms and bowed their heads in deference to the god. Then, they each grasped a side of the statue and carefully raised it from the pedestal base, carried it out of the way, and stood holding it.

"I'm just going to quickly tip the pedestal," Vijay said. It was heavier than it looked, but he was able to ease it onto its side.

The stone floor below was smooth. The pedestal itself was hollowed out, but it was empty. Vijay eased it upright again and stepped aside.

At his nod, Kaushalya and the priest replaced the image, then folded their hands again for a moment in reverence. Vijay joined them, mentally asking the god's forgiveness.

9

Gamri village, near Mangarh

The land was his now.

Vijay had negotiated through a lawyer in Mangarh, keeping his own identity as a former Untouchable from Gamri village secret from the Rajput landowner. Word would spread quickly, of course, but as yet, only his family and the other Bhangis knew he was the one who had purchased the site.

Vijay walked about the half hectare of land, raised slightly above the surrounding farmland just outside the village. With him were his mother, Uncle Surja, Surja's son Govinda, and several Bhangi children.

"I can't believe we'll actually have our own school," said his mother. "And it's all your doing!"

Embarrassed, Vijay said, "You can all help, too, as I've told you. The more labor is donated, the less I'll have to pay for."

"We'll all help, just as we promised. " said Uncle Surja, short and wiry, with his weathered, smallpox scarred face. As usual, he wore a *dhoti* and turban grimy from hard, dusty work. "Did you get any reward money from finding the treasure, to help you pay for the school?"

Vijay laughed uneasily. They knew he'd been leading the income tax officers looking for the legendary treasure, so when word spread that it had been found, they realized he had to be involved. "No. I may get a promotion and more pay, but not yet."

"My boy found the Mangarh Treasure," his mother said with a broad smile, shaking her head. "I just can't believe it."

"Well, some of it, anyway," said Vijay. "I don't know if we'll ever find all of it."

"Still," said Uncle Surja, "who'd ever have thought my own nephew would be the one?"

"We should get some trees planted right away, for shade," said Vijay, trying to change the subject. "Since it will take so long for them to grow. Someone will need to see they're watered regularly, especially at first. And protected from the goats and other animals."

"I'll do that," said Govinda, Vijay's handsome eighteen year old cousin. "At least until I get some work away from the village. Then someone else can take over."

Vijay nodded. He felt guilty again that he hadn't yet been able to do more to help Govinda, who seemed to think Vijay had enough influence to get his cousin an entry-level government job in Delhi.

Vijay had paid for Govinda's school expenses to date. The current secondary school was several miles away. And as a Bhangi, the lowest of the low "Scheduled Castes," Govinda had faced some of the same humiliations Vijay had endured at school years before: ostracism by many of the Rajput and Brahman and Jat boys, being the subject of practical jokes. The same types of insults that had convinced Vijay to leave Mangarh and take on the guise of a member of a much higher caste. Govinda hadn't been at the top of his class, as had Vijay, so he hadn't been the object of as much envy and "revenge," but it had still been an often-unpleasant experience.

This school would change that for lower caste children in the future.

"We'll help water the trees, too, Vijay *sahib*," said Hanwant, the eldest of the children.

"Yes," said another boy, Bhanwar. "And we can take turns guarding the trees from the goats."

Neither of the boys had ever been to school. The new building, and the teacher Vijay hoped to hire, would dramatically change their lives. "We'll build a little fence around each tree to protect them from goats," said Vijay. "But you'll still need to keep an eye on them and make sure the fences stay in good repair."

"Oh, we can do that," Hanwant said.

After leaving the village, Vijay had Akbar Khan drive him farther into the hills for another visit, also unrelated to the search.

Of the various spiritual teachers Vijay was aware of, the one who had truly impressed him was Guru Dharmananda. He remembered the guru's visit to the fortress during the earlier tax raid—how the teacher had so capably mediated on behalf of the princess and her family, deftly convincing Dev Batra to set a much shorter time limit on the raid than Batra had originally intended. And from watching the guru's interaction with the princess, Vijay had the distinct feeling that Dharmananda was a person with great spiritual presence. And that he cared deeply about helping others.

Vijay had phoned in advance, so a young male disciple met him and escorted him past several tree shaded, whitewashed cottages to the Guru's bungalow. He slipped off his *chappals* on the veranda and stepped inside. "Guruji's expecting you, Mr. Singh," said the male secretary, in an American accent.

Guru Dharmananda, in his white robe, sat on cushions before a low writing desk. Smiling warmly, he rose when Vijay entered. Vijay started to bend to touch his feet, but the guru put out a hand to stop him. "That's not needed, Mr. Singh. Please sit."

The guru returned to his own seat, and Vijay lowered himself to the cushions facing him. An attractive young Indian woman entered with a tray of tea and biscuits, set it beside them, and left. "Chai?" asked the guru.

"Yes, please."

The guru removed the cozy from the teapot and poured. "Milk is already in it, and here's sugar to add." The guru smiled. "I grew up drinking tea in my childhood in Kashmir, but I think I truly grew addicted to it during my university time in the U.K. It was so pleasant during those cold, damp winters."

"I've never been abroad, but I can imagine."

"Now, then, what did you wish to see me about?" The guru again smiled. "Not official Income Tax Department business, I hope."

"Oh, no. It's definitely personal." Vijay tried to think of how to start. Embarrassed at his silence, he said at last, his voice suddenly hoarse, "I'm sorry. I don't know where to begin. I'm not used to talking about this."

The guru smiled and said gently, "Take your time. I can assure you, I've heard almost everything, from confessions of murder, to rather uncommon sexual practices, to people dying from cancer. There's a lot of pain in this world, as well as the joys. And a lot of dilemmas."

Vijay nodded. He now found it easier to say, despite his dry mouth, "I've been pretending to be of a different caste from my true one." The guru showed no reaction, other than a calm, accepting expression. Vijay went on, "You're the only one I've told. One man did find out, but he won't tell." He took a sip of the tea. "You could say I've succeeded so far, but I feel it's causing me more and more problems."

He stopped, but the guru was waiting with an encouraging look, so he resumed: "I'm continually afraid of being found out. It would be quite bad for my career. And I'd, uh, I'd like to get married, but how do I go about finding someone? My real caste is at the bottom, as you no doubt gathered, so there are no educated girls. I've pretended to be Rajput. But I don't see how I could find a suitable woman in that class, and I don't know what I'd tell her if I did. And what would her family think when they found out about my background?"

Guru Dharmananda slowly nodded. He fingered his neatly trimmed, graying beard.

"There's more to it than that," said Vijay. "I just don't like living falsely. I like to think of myself as basically an honest person. So how do I reconcile presenting a totally fake face to my friends and my co-workers and everyone else I meet? I occasionally even have to tell an outright lie." Finished, he threw up his hands in a gesture of helplessness.

The guru was watching him closely, with a nonjudgmental expression. "You must have felt you had good reasons," he said, "for rejecting the caste you were born in."

"I thought I did. I still think the reasons were good." Vijay hesitated, then went on: "You must have some idea of how Harijans are treated in rural villages. They can't use the same wells as higher castes. They often can't go into shops. They can't enter many temples. They have to do whatever work they're told to do, almost like slaves. Some upper caste men think they have the right to abuse our women. Many of the upper castes think the Untouchables shouldn't be entitled to an education. I was able to go to school because a donor paid for it. Even though I did well there, I had to sit in the back of the room, and the teachers often refused to call on me. I had to eat by myself. The other boys would beat up on me and hide my books and my slate. And no one would have anything to do with me on the playing field."

He sensed his face had taken on an expression of pain, and he stopped the recitation. "I'm sorry," he said. "I never intended to run on like that. I've never had anyone to talk with about this before."

The guru smiled warmly in understanding. "That's quite all right. It does sound like you had well justified reasons." He looked slightly away and said, "Still, although it's possible to live for many years with behavior that's inconsistent with one's basic values, it will gradually eat away at the soul, until the soul cries out in pain."

Vijay was surprised to feel a wetness in his eyes. He blinked. He cleared his throat and said in a quiet voice, "I think that's been happening."

"Most people who are basically healthy psychologically know within themselves what they should do. Sometimes talking with someone else about the problem helps them come to the realization of the answers, which can sometimes be extremely difficult to face." The guru smiled gently again. "What are your choices?"

Vijay had thought so much about the matter that he didn't hesitate. "Obviously, one option is to continue as I have. It causes me more anxiety as time goes on. I'm probably strong enough to handle it without coming apart. But I'll be lonely in my old age."

The guru gave a nod.

Vijay continued, his voice again hoarse: "I could come out and admit to my friends—mainly people I work with—that I'm really a Dalit." He thought for a few moments about the consequences. "I'd have a hard time doing that. I'm not sure I can. It would mean confessing that I've been lying. And I'm hoping for a promotion. When my superiors found out I've lied, it would probably kill my chances."

"How do you think other people would react?"

Vijay was breathing hard, and his voice came out weak. "I'm not sure. I think some of them would feel betrayed."

"Would they hold it against you that you're really low caste?"

He thought for a time. "Some of them might not care. A couple of them would. I don't know about the others."

"Could you tolerate that?"

Vijay grinned wryly. "I've lived through a lot, growing up as an Untouchable in a village. I think I could tolerate almost anything." He stopped grinning. "That doesn't mean I *want* to. I think it would be hell for me at work, wondering what everyone was thinking about me."

The guru was eyeing him intently. "I don't want to minimize your concern about this. Still, I sense that losing the promotion is your biggest worry."

Vijay took a deep breath. "I suppose so. In a way, everything I've done all my life has been toward getting me a position of influence so I could leave my past behind. And so I could have enough income to help out my people back home. That promotion is the next step. I need the added income to pay for a school in my village."

The guru nodded. "I see why you wouldn't want to jeopardize that."

"Yes."

Guru Dharmananda smiled. "Have you reached any conclusions yet from our talk?"

Vijay thought for a time. "I think I need to reconsider the question *after* I get the promotion. Assuming, of course, that I do get it."

"Since that may be some time away, can you continue to live with your situation?"

Vijay sighed. "I've lived with it for years."

The guru sat quietly for a time, then asked, "Do you engage in any regular spiritual practice?"

"No," admitted Vijay. "I suppose walking comes the closest. I find walking to my office from home, and back, usually helps me clear my mind and gives me a fresh outlook." He smiled self-deprecatingly. "I've tried doing hatha yoga positions, but I have trouble sticking with it."

"You've tried meditation?"

Vijay said slowly, "I've never taken instruction. Maybe I should."

"It can be quite simple, and you should find it helpful when it's not convenient to walk. May I give you a mantra, and get you started?"

"Yes, Guruji. I'd like that."

The guru straightened his back and directed, "Sit upright but comfortably."

Vijay adjusted his position.

"Close your eyes. Breathe in slowly...Breathe out...Good...Now repeat after me these words..."

When Vijay left the ashram, he was amazed how much better he felt. What was it that could change him so much?

Certainly, the guru's presence alone had an impact. But sharing his burdens with another, after so many years of carrying them alone, made a huge difference.

The next day at the fortress, he was strolling past the small private audience hall when he saw A.S. Nimbalkar carefully examining the mandala-like display of swords on one of the walls. He approached and asked, "Still looking for Shivaji's sword?"

Nimbalkar jumped and whirled about, his eyes looking guilty. "Uh, yes, sir. I thought as long as I was here...."

"It's not part of our mission, you know."

"Yes, sir. Sorry. I'll get back to looking for the rest of the treasure."

Dev Batra entered, followed by Gulab and Sen. "Finding anything useful, Singhji?"

"Nothing yet, Batraji."

"Why are you looking at the weapons?"

Vijay hesitated momentarily, then replied, "Inspector Nimbalkar, here, has an interest in them."

"Are any of them valuable? If so, we could take them, along with anything else we find. It would mean the raid isn't a total loss, even if we don't happen to find the gems or gold."

Vijay said, "Nothing of unusual value, sir. Probably only collectors would be interested."

Nimbalkar spoke: "Unless we find the Shivaji sword, sir."

Vijay inwardly damned him.

"What's this?" asked Batra.

Nimbalkar said, "The Bhavani sword of Shivaji was said to be in Mangarh, sir. I'm keeping an eye out for it."

"It belonged to Shivaji himself?"

"Yes, sir. It's the one given to him by Goddess Bhavani, so it's very powerful."

Batra's eyes narrowed. "No doubt it's extremely valuable, then. Worth *lakhs*, I suppose?"

"Almost certainly, sir," said Nimbalkar. "But that's not the point, is it?"

Batra's face was bland. "Of course not. Vijay, let's tell all our people to be on the lookout for this sword."

Vijay suppressed a sigh. "Yes, sir."

Batra ordered Nimbalkar, "Look at every sword in the fort. Go down to the new palace and look there, too." He grinned. "If we found it, that alone could justify the raid!"

Nimbalkar was smiling broadly, his eyes bright. "I'll get right on it, at once, sir!"

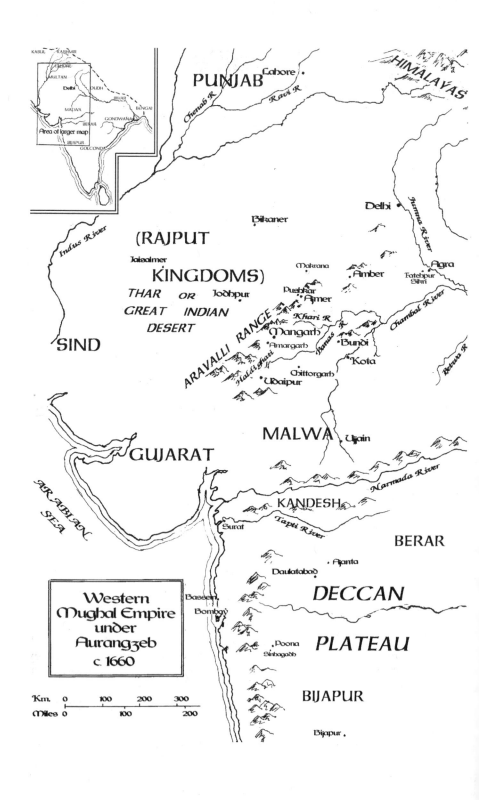

KABUL KASHMIR
LAHORE
MULTAN
Delhi OUDH
BIHAR
MALWA BENGAL
GONDWANA
BERAR
Area of larger map
BIJAPUR
GOLCONDA

PUNJAB Lahore.

HIMALAYAS

Chenab R.

Ravi R.

Delhi.

Jumna River

Bikaner

(RAJPUT

Indus River

Jaisalmer

Makrana
Amber
Agra
Fatehpur
Sikri

KINGDOMS)

THAR OR Jodhpur
GREAT INDIAN
DESERT

Pushkar
Ajmer

Chambal River

Khari R.

SIND

ARAVALLI RANGE

Mangarh

Amargarh
Haldighati
Banas
Bundi
Kota

Betwa R.

Chittorgarh
Udaipur

MALWA Ujain

GUJARAT

Narmada River

KANDESH

ARABIAN SEA

Surat

Tapti River

BERAR

Ajanta

Daulatabad

Baseein

DECCAN

Western
Mughal Empire
under
Aurangzeb
c. 1660

Bombay

Poona
Sinhagadh

PLATEAU

BIJAPUR

Km. 0   100   200   300

Miles 0   100   200

Bijapur.

Shivaji's

Fortunes

1

Poona, the Deccan Plateau, in the fourth year of the reign of the Mughal Emperor Aurangzeb, April 1663

The cooler air of midnight was welcome during this season, the beginning of the hottest weeks of the year. As he reclined against the bolsters in the outer room of his tent, Madho Singh, twenty-two year old second son of the Raja of Mangarh, thrust another *kajoo barfi*, a fudge-like sweetmeat made from ground cashew nuts, into his mouth. "Take more," he urged his cousin and chief lieutenant, Gopal Singh. "They're the best sweets I've discovered yet in the Deccan."

"I'll keep eating the *halva*," Gopal replied. "It reminds me of home."

A short distance away, toward the outskirts of Poona, a dog barked, continuously and insistently. Several dim man-shaped shadows, cast by the light of a dying cooking fire, darted one at a time along the outer wall of the tent. Madho Singh paid no attention; from the carpet beside him, he picked up a completed miniature painting of himself on horseback and handed it to his cousin. "Be sure your hands are clean," Madho said.

Oblivious to Madho's manservant Prem Chand, who started forward with a *lota* of water, Gopal wiped his greasy fingers on his breeches. He then took the painting and held it up, turning it so it caught the glow from the oil lamp.

The painting had been done by an artist Madho had found in Delhi and brought with him to the Deccan. "It's not a particularly good likeness," said Madho, "but look at Nand's use of color."

Gopal Singh shrugged, and returned it to Madho. "Gold and gems I can understand," Gopal said. "But why are you obsessed by paintings? You think about them almost as much as money. Almost as much as food, even."

Both Madho and Gopal loved to eat; they were so heavy and slow moving they gave the impression of being lazy twin brothers. Gopal now walked with a limp from an injury a couple of years before when his horse fell. But they had been champion wrestlers a few years previously, and few men could equal Madho's skill with a sword.

The food and drink, consumed in such large quantities after a day in the enervating heat, was making Madho's normally quick mind sluggish. He took another look at the painting, then set it aside, as he struggled to compose his reply. At last he said, "Paintings are akin to gems." He held his hand near the lamp, so the emeralds and the diamonds on his rings sparkled. "Both paintings and gems are beautiful, both colorful, both small and exquisite. Both valuable." He was thinking particularly of the intricately detailed miniature paintings popular at the Mughal court, which had set the standard now for the past century.

Gopal shoved his turban back and slowly shook his head. "Valuable? Paintings can't compare to gold or jewels or pearls. Or even silver."

Madho gave a long burp, and yawned. "It's a different kind of value. The skill and labor the artist puts into them. Creating beauty where none existed before. And the emotions the painting creates in the viewer."

Gopal belched. He shrugged indifferently.

More dim silhouettes crossed the tent wall, and Madho abruptly noticed them. Several men apparently were heading across the camp toward the mansion of Shaista Khan, viceroy of the Deccan and Madho's ultimate commander. Madho sat up straighter and wondered if he should investigate. But the sentries were keeping watch. Anyway, the Mughal army's Deccan headquarters had such a huge force of soldiers that there was little concern about an attack by the Marathas, especially when their king and leader, Shivaji, was reported to be hundreds of miles away.

Madho leaned back into his bolster and said, "Our present Emperor doesn't have much use for the arts. Aurangzeb's banned music, you know. Painting may be next. A lot of artists will be looking for work. I want them in Mangarh, working for me. That's another reason I need gold and gems. It's as expensive to keep a stable of artists as it is a stable of elephants."

"Also another reason you want to be Raja," said Gopal in a low voice. Only he definitely knew that desire of Madho's, though others must certainly suspect it.

"One reason," replied Madho. It frustrated him that he was only the second son. He would probably be forced to eliminate his older brother, Ajit, in order to rule. He would prefer it weren't necessary, but Ajit just wasn't fit for the throne. Like their father Jagat Singh, Ajit would merely maintain Mangarh, not expand or enrich it. Madho himself, on the other hand, would ensure that the state grew in both prestige and prosperity, maybe in area, too. He might even be compared with his famous great grandfather, Raja Hanuman, revered by generations of future descendants. "In the meantime," Madho said, "it will be easier if I get as rich as possible."

The dog resumed barking. "Damn animal," Gopal muttered. "Why doesn't it shut up?"

"Either that, or someone should put it out of its misery."

Gopal again belched. He said, "Too bad we can't get any of those riches in Surat."

"Yes. It's truly a pity." Madho thought longingly of the wealthy trading port they had visited on their way south to Poona. "All those rich traders, with their mansions full of treasure: Haji Said Beg, Haji Qasim, even Bharji Borah, the wealthiest merchant in the world!"

"And what about those factories belonging to the foreigners?"

"Yes, those, too." It had been frustrating for Madho to ride by these trading posts of the English, the Dutch, the Turks, the Armenians. He said, "All those warehouses full of spices, silver bullion, jewels, gold, ivory, cloth. But with only two hundred horsemen it would have been suicidal to try a raid there."

Gopal said, "Oh, well. Maybe you'll find a way to win the viceroy's favor yet."

"Not unless I get closer to him."

They had now been in Poona two weeks. Through his father's influence at the court of the Mughal Emperor Aurangzeb, Madho had managed to get himself attached to Shaista Khan's army. The viceroy was also an uncle of the Emperor Aurangzeb and the brother of Mumtaz Mahal, the queen whose body lay in the Taj Mahal. If Madho could ingratiate himself into a position of influence with Shaista Khan, the possibilities for taking gifts and bribes from those wanting the Khan's ear would be endless.

Madho said, "Even if I can't get into the Khan's inner council, we might be able to grab some of Shivaji's loot. Those Marathas are the greatest raiders ever. If we could capture one of that mountain rat's caravans, or maybe even the treasury in one of his forts, we'd have enough to last us years. Or," Madho grinned in the darkness, "maybe we could even plunder a rich temple or trading town and blame it on Shivaji."

"So that's why you're learning their tongue!"

Madho laughed. "One reason. I'll also be more useful to the Khan." After hearing of his posting to the Deccan, he had learned Marathi from various tutors. The local language was a rough, practical speech, quite in contrast to the refined Urdu spoken by officers of the Mughal court at Delhi or Agra. "It's also a way to know the Marathas better, so I can predict their moves."

Gopal said, "Now, if you can only figure out a way to pry the Khan loose from his women." So far, Madho's only meeting with Shaista Khan had been to present himself and his gifts upon arriving in Poona. The western Deccan had been quiet, and the Khan spent most of his time relaxing in his harem or drinking with his highest officers, who included Maharaja Jaswant Singh of Jodhpur, but not yet Madho Singh of Mangarh.

The dog stopped barking, suddenly, with a choked off-yelp. Madho thought of the shadows seen dimly on the tent wall. He lay aside his portrait, heaved himself to his feet, and moved to the doorway. There, placing a hand on his dagger, he peered about into the darkness.

A short distance across the garden of widely-spaced mango trees, Shaista Khan's mansion stood outlined against the starry sky. A second floor window glowed dimly from the light of a lamp. "It's odd," Madho said, "how that dog suddenly stopped in mid-bark."

Gopal yawned and again belched. "You're always looking for reasons for everything, even when there aren't any. We're surrounded by sentries."

"I'm looking anyway," Madho said. He padded back into the tent, grabbed his sword and his shield, and slipped his feet into his open-backed shoes. Then he again stepped outside, moved away from the tent, and glanced about the sleeping encampment. He and Gopal and a dozen of their Rajputs were quartered near the troops of the general's bodyguard, who in turn resided next to the wall surrounding the mansion. The house had once belonged to Shivaji's own family; indeed, it had been the Maratha leader's childhood home. But when Shaista Khan had captured Poona three years ago, he'd taken the house for his own use.

Noises carried far in the warm night air, and Madho heard dull clinks, like a knocking together of bricks. The sounds came from the direction of the mansion's kitchen area; as in most large houses, the kitchens were in a courtyard, outside the main dwelling itself.

It was probably just the cooks, Madho told himself. This was the Muslim month of Ramadan. Adherents of that faith fasted all day, taking meals only late at night and early in the morning. The kitchen staff had been keeping unusually late hours, cleaning up after the evening meal and preparing for the breakfast soon to come.

Madho cautiously walked toward the house. He had given a large present to ensure he was assigned a camping place so near the viceroy's mansion in the center of Poona. It meant separating most of his two hundred men from himself, as they were quartered farther out where there was more space, near the encampment of Maharaja Jaswant Singh of Jodhpur on the road leading south to Sinhagadh.

So far, it had not benefitted Madho to be so near the headquarters. But he was in a good location for watching the Khan's movements. Eventually, he would learn something that would profit him.

He was near the wall of the mansion's courtyard now, and he could hear more sounds from the kitchens. Someone was moaning, as if sick. The clinking sounds had ceased. He glanced the length of the wall in one direction, then the other. Where were the guards? Normally, there would be at least a couple in sight, even though the main sentry post was by the front gate.

Madho heard what sounded like a woman's scream from the direction of the Khan's harem. Then came a crash, and more screams.

Fully alert now, Madho drew his sword from its scabbard and ran along the wall. He eased around the corner, where he could see the main gate. In the torchlight were shadowy figures struggling. He halted. From the guards' tents came thudding sounds and occasional yells.

Unbelievable though it was, someone must have managed a stealthy surprise attack on the Mughal headquarters! Madho opened his mouth to shout an alarm.

But he hesitated. He was alone. What if his shouts drew the attackers to himself? Rajput bravery was admirable, but not if it unnecessarily endangered him. And he wasn't wearing his armor.

Should he try to enter the house? If he could somehow aid the general at a crucial moment, it would almost certainly mean a great boost in his prospects for advancement. But no lights showed now in the windows. In the darkness, how would he see whom to aid and whom to slay?

His hand trembled as he clutched his sword. He backed against the trunk of a tree so his bulk would not be outlined against the sky. Another minute passed. Sounds of a struggle came from the outbuilding where the musicians lived, next to the gate.

Suddenly, there came the sounds of the Khan's kettle drums, and then the horns. The band was playing as if the Khan himself had ordered it. Madho was puzzled. Could the band be playing to conceal the sounds of the assault? But the music could not hide the screams still issuing from the harem.

At last, from behind, came the sounds of men running toward the mansion and shouting. The Mughal troops seemed finally to have awakened to the fact that their general was under attack in his own home.

Madho Singh swore to himself and moved from the tree. He must be seen as one of the first to respond to the crisis! He started to run toward the house.

Then he again halted. Sword-wielding men shouting, *"Har, Har, Ma-hadeo!"* rushed out the gate from the mansion. A single torch now burned at the guard post, and Madho saw a short, slender figure, sword in hand, run from the house and stop. The man's metal helmet and chain armor shone in the firelight as he stood calmly, almost casually, and shouted something to the others behind him, waving them on. For several seconds the torchlight clearly illuminated his handsome, bearded face. Over the din of the kettledrums, Madho heard someone shout, *"Jai Shivaji Maharaj!"* "Victory to the Great King Shivaji!" The man at the gate smiled briefly in acknowledgment. Then, he turned swiftly and disappeared into the shadows with the others.

It was Shivaji himself! Madho, unaided, was not about to challenge the famous warrior, whose sword was said to be invested with the spirit of the powerful Goddess Bhavani. If only he had his armor on, and his own men at his side!

Soldiers now ran in all directions in confusion. It appeared too late to render any crucial help inside the mansion. Madho again cursed his loss of the opportunity to be seen heroically rallying the Khan's defense. He rushed back to his tent, where he found Gopal sprawled on the carpet, snoring. "Wake up!" Madho yelled. "Shivaji's attacked!" He tore off his turban, and his man-servant Prem Chand grabbed the steel helmet and shoved it on him.

Gopal jerked and opened his eyes. He sat up, put a hand on each side of his head, and shook it back and forth. "What?" he asked at last.

"Shivaji's here! We might catch him if we hurry. We'll get a huge reward if we do." Madho's servant was helping him into the chain mail.

Gopal dragged himself to his feet. "Shivaji?"

"Yes, you idiot! Help me rouse the men and get them to their horses."

Still groggy, Gopal looked about for his helmet, sword, and buckler, found them, and limped from the tent.

Madho had already disappeared into the darkness. He had a moment of anxiety: what if the Marathas had taken his horses? But he saw the mounts where they had been tethered, and his Rajputs were already assembling, some with torches.

"Highness!" came the voice of Ajay Singh, the youngest of the Rajputs. "Is it true there's been a raid?"

"Yes! Get your battle gear on. Everyone on their horses."

"What about the rest of our men?" asked Gopal as he joined them.

"We'll get them first. We can't challenge Shivaji with so few."

As his small contingent pounded eastward through the narrow streets of Poona, Madho Singh thought about the difficulty of his mission. He didn't know which direction Shivaji was heading. The Maratha King held a number of strong forts in the mountains to the west of Poona, and he controlled most of the territory to the south.

When they reached the encampment of the remainder of his two hundred Rajputs, he was glad to see the men were up and about. Most wore their helmets, and some were already saddling their horses by torchlight. "Mount up!" he shouted. "We're going after Shivaji."

Armor rattled and men swore as they readied themselves. A contingent of the Mughal cavalry bearing torches rode out of camp, heading north, so Madho saw no point in going that direction himself. When all his men were on their horses, Madho led them back through the small town. He reasoned that Shivaji was unlikely to have tried escaping to the east, as he would have had to pass through where the bulk of the Mughal army was camped. So Madho decided to go southwesterly, toward Shivaji's important fort of Sinhagadh.

After leaving Poona, they cantered along the narrow track through the forest of sparse, scrubby trees. The men were limited in speed by the light cast ahead by the torches. As they rode, Madho wondered: What if Shivaji left part of his men to ambush any pursuers? The Maratha King was legendary for his cleverness, which was certainly demonstrated by the fact he'd managed both to get into Shaista Khan's mansion and to escape afterwards.

Madho began riding slower. He realized he and his men made ideal targets, lit by torches. On the other hand, any Marathas waiting in ambush would be in darkness. And given Shivaji's early start, how would they catch him? The Marathas knew their rugged homelands like the necks of their own horses. They traveled fast, and they were toughened, experienced fighters.

Overtaking the raiders in the dark, much less attacking them successfully, would require either a huge stroke of good fortune or some help from the gods. And Madho hadn't spent much time making offerings in the temples lately.

He swore to himself in frustration, then shouted, "Halt!" as he reined in his horse. Then, he ordered, "Back to Poona!" He heard grumbling and muttering from Ajay Singh and Puran Singh, two of the youngest of his men. He said to Gopal, in a voice that the others nearby could overhear, "No point in going on. Shivaji's too far ahead by now."

By the time they reached their encampment, the sky was beginning to lighten in the east. Madho sent his men to rest in their campsites, and he returned to the grounds of the Khan's mansion. A much larger contingent of guards was now posted around the house. Madho lingered near. Although weary from not having slept that night, he was eager for information. He recognized a young Rajput chief, Himmat Singh of Jodhpur, leaving the house.

Even in the dim light, Madho saw that Himmat had shadows under his eyes. He was walking slowly, obviously also tired. Madho greeted him and asked, "What can you tell me about the attack?"

Himmat Singh removed his helmet and shifted his buckler. "The Khan's wounded, but he should recover." His eyes grew wider. "Shivaji attacked the Khan personally! The Khan lost his thumb while drawing his sword. His son was killed, and so were some of his wives!"

"The Marathas killed women? I'd never have thought it."

Himmat shrugged. "It was probably an accident. As soon as the attack started in the *zenana*, someone blew out the lamp. No one could see who was who."

"How did Shivaji get past the guards?"

Himmat shook his head in wonder. "Shivaji and his men apparently came into Poona in the afternoon and claimed to be allies. They told our sentries they were here to go to a wedding."

"Clever!" said Madho in genuine admiration. "Bands of friendly Marathas are always riding in and out of town, so I can see how the guards believed it."

Himmat Singh ran his fingers through his matted hair. "Right. I'm glad I wasn't on duty then."

"But how did they get into the house without causing alarm?"

Himmat turned to stare at the mansion. "It looks like the Marathas waited until midnight, when most of our men were in their tents. Then they surprised the Khan's guards and killed them. It was easy after that to get into the kitchen and kill the cooks. Shivaji lived in the house as a child, you know, so he knows it well. They tore out bricks in an old door between the kitchen and the harem, and got into where the Khan was."

"Ah," said Madho softly. "That must have been the clinking sound I heard."

"What?" Himmat jerked to face him. "You were awake and heard them?"

Madho realized that in his tiredness he'd made a slip. If it became known he could have sounded an alarm and failed to do so, it could be disastrous for him. "I thought I was dreaming it," he said quickly. "I was sound asleep until I heard the commotion afterwards."

Himmat was staring at him curiously. "Well, it probably wouldn't have done any good even if you'd reported it. I think our Khan's going to have a hard time making excuses to the Emperor for last night. A servant did tell the Khan about the noise, but the general was in bed with one of his women. He was furious at being bothered over such a trifle." Himmat shook his head and continued on.

2

South of Surat, eight months later. January 1664

Madho tried to maintain a facade of nonchalance as he led his two hundred Rajputs and their attendants and baggage carts homeward in disgrace. He had barely launched his military endeavors, and already he had earned the Emperor's disfavor. Aurangzeb was furious when he learned of the raid, and he transferred the humiliated Shaista Khan to an undesirable posting in the province of Bengal.

It also became known that Madho Singh was one of the few officers awake at the time of the attack, and that he had done nothing to intervene. He therefore was ordered to return home to Mangarh until the Emperor should again have need of his services.

Shivaji gained immeasurably in prestige as a result of the raid. He was said to possess supernatural powers, especially with the Goddess Bhavani residing in his sword. Men said that no place was safe from Shivaji, no feat impossible for him.

Madho Singh and Gopal and their band first rode across the rugged hills to the coast, then they traveled northward in the direction of the wealthy city of Surat. Though it was the coolest time of the year, the weather was still quite warm this far south.

Madho was finding it increasingly hard to maintain his habitual optimistic outlook. Not only had he blundered militarily, he had also failed to acquire any booty. With himself and his troops detached from the Mughal army, he would receive no more imperial stipends, and that meant that he could no longer pay his men except from his own assets. Acquiring his personal atelier of artists seemed even more unlikely than before.

After a few days' travel along the coast, they saw the tracks in the dusty road of a huge number of horses. The only wheel tracks and human footprints appeared to be newer, on top of the prints of the hooves. Madho halted his men. "That's odd," he said with a frown. He beckoned Nathu Singh, one of the oldest of his Rajputs closer. The dour faced Nathu was probably the cleverest of his men. Madho gestured toward the ground. "What do you think of this?"

Nathu was tall and lean, and he bent far over from his saddle to examine the roadway for a time. Then he rode a few paces ahead, and looked some more. He turned back to Madho. "Enough horses to be a big army. But no baggage carts or camp followers. The prints from those wheels and people walking came later, so the larger group must have been quite a while ago, maybe even yesterday.

"I wonder who it could be," Madho mused. "I'd better find out." At the next village, his party dismounted to rest their horses. They were now in the region where Gujarati was spoken, but Madho found that one of several elders seated in the shade of a huge mango tree spoke Marathi.

"It's Shivaji, your honor!" said the old man, pushing himself to his feet with a cane. "He's leading a big army! At least ten thousand men! They were moving so fast, they only stopped here to water their horses."

"How long ago?"

"Just yesterday morning, sir."

"Do you know where they're headed?"

The old man pointed northward with his cane. "That way, your honor. But no one would say where they were going. Maybe only the King himself knows for sure."

Madho gestured for his servant Prem Chand to give the man some coins. Then he drew Gopal out of earshot. Nathu Singh came closer also to listen. "Shivaji's headed for Surat!" Madho said.

Gopal squinted in the sun as he looked up the road. "That's far from his usual areas. I wouldn't expect it."

"You know he likes to confound everyone by doing the unexpected. Surat's the wealthiest port on the entire coast, and there's no Mughal army anywhere near. You saw how it was—the city's almost undefended. The fort can hold a few people, but there's no wall around the town itself. I'll wager you a hundred rupees that's where Shivaji's headed!"

Gopal shook his head no. "I'm tired of losing wagers to you. But we'd better not go near Surat, then. We're no match for ten thousand Marathas. Especially not under Shivaji."

"Don't be so sure."

Gopal stared at him. "Now I know for certain that you're mad."

Madho saw that Nathu Singh was frowning, clearly skeptical also. Madho chuckled. "I'm in no hurry to return to Mangarh with no victories and no loot. Shivaji could be just the diversion we need."

Gopal's eyes widened. "You'd risk meeting a Maratha army that large?"

"With our carts and servants, we're obviously going much slower than they are. I see no harm in following them."

Gopal eyed him dubiously. "Why take the risk?"

"So we can move fast to take advantage, if an opening presents itself."

Nathu Singh's expression was sour as usual, but he said, "We're far enough behind them, there shouldn't be much danger."

"Well," said Gopal, "We need to keep plenty of distance. They'll have scouts guarding their rear. They better not see us."

A day's ride south of Surat, Madho's band met a family traveling fast in an oxcart. He stopped them and questioned the oldest, a *dhoti*-clad merchant, who knew Marathi.

"What brings you this way? And where is your native place?"

"We're from Surat, your honor," said the pudgy, middle aged Bania. "But we had to flee! Shivaji and a huge army came yesterday and are raiding our city!"

Madho glanced at Gopal and gave a quick nod.

"I was lucky to escape the Marathas with my life!" the merchant was saying. "It was only by disguising myself as a poor bearer that I managed to come this way."

Madho tried to take on a look of sympathy. "Please tell me more."

"Two days ago, your honor, we heard that Shivaji was on his way, with an army of thousands coming to plunder us. Everyone in Surat panicked."

"Understandable," Madho said.

"The wealthiest traders paid the commandant to shelter them in the fortress. The governor of the town fled to the fort, too."

Madho nodded, unsurprised. The governor, Inayet Khan, was notorious for pocketing the money meant to hire soldiers to defend the town.

"Almost everyone else fled northward, across the river," the merchant continued. "But I have no family there, so I decided to come this way. I could not afford a large enough gift to buy protection. Only the foreigners—the English and the French—stayed in their factories and organized to defend themselves. Shivaji's men are looting rich people's houses and burning them. I barely escaped with my life. I've had nothing to eat since leaving."

"My cook will feed you and the others," Madho said. He took Gopal a few steps away and told him, "We've missed Shivaji once. Maybe this time we can catch him, and I can regain the Emperor's favor."

"With only two hundred men? You're truly mad!"

Madho smiled. "Probably. But if we don't get Shivaji, maybe we'll find a way to get rich. Why let the Marathas keep all that gold for themselves?"

Gopal looked at him with incredulity. "You'd loot the city, too? What if word got to the Mughals' new viceroy? And to the Emperor?"

"There's that problem," Madho admitted. "But I smell opportunity. Maybe when we get there we'll see what form it takes. We might even pass ourselves off as the saviors of the city, there to protect it on behalf of the Emperor."

"It will mean the end of us all!"

"See here," said Madho, his eyes abruptly hard. "I have no wish to return to Mangarh in disgrace and in debt. This may be my only chance for years to redeem myself."

As they approached Surat, they saw smoke on the horizon. "Shivaji's still burning the town," Madho said. "We'd better hurry if we want any of it."

"We'd be surrounded by Marathas!" said Gopal. "What if they trap us on this side of the river? How would we get across to head for home again?"

Madho smiled coyly. "They managed to sneak past us in the dark at Poona.

Maybe now we can do it to them. We'll wait until night."

"Rajputs fighting at night? The men will think it's cowardly."

"Shivaji didn't think so," said Madho. "Now everyone admires his cleverness."

"What about the river?" Gopal persisted. "We'll still need to cross it afterwards to get away. Everyone who fled the city probably left his boat on the other side. It's too deep to ford. How would we get across in the dark with thousands of Marathas chasing us?"

Madho was still smiling. "No difficulty. We'll cross before dark. The first time, anyway."

"The *first* time?" Gopal was virtually yelling.

So Madho explained. When he had finished, Gopal shook his head doubtfully. "Those Maratha cavalry are tough fighters. They grew up in rocky hills where it's hard just to survive. They ride fast for days with nothing to eat but what little grain they carry themselves."

"All the more reason to take them by surprise. Even our Rajputs might have a hard time beating them in a fair fight."

In the face of Madho's determination, Gopal at last gave up arguing with his cousin and chief. As they rode, Madho reviewed the layout of the city in his mind. Surat lay about six miles inland from the coast. The central part of town lay on the eastern bank of a north-south bend of the Tapti River, which at high tide allowed all but the largest vessels to approach and anchor at the town wharves. The fortress rose above the river bank, near the customs house and the mansions of some of the rich. Near the fort were the main trading bazaar, the governor's mansion, and *serais* to house traveling caravans and their wares. Residential areas spread outward from this core near the river.

Madho led his party off the main road some miles south of the city, onto a track that branched to the northeast. Shortly before dusk, they arrived at a village on the river a few *kos* upstream from Surat. Madho had one of his officers hire four boats, enough to haul a couple dozen of his Rajputs, without their horses, downstream.

He ordered the remainder of his men ferried across, with all the horses and servants and baggage carts. He split the Rajputs who would cross the river into two groups. One party would take four empty carts and the two dozen now-riderless horses westerly to the ferry landing at the far side of the river from Surat, where they would quietly wait for Madho and the Rajputs accompanying him. The other group would escort the full baggage carts and the servants northward, moving as fast as possible to get away from the area the Maratha army was raiding.

Madho removed his turban and called together Gopal and the others who would enter the city with him. They watched as Madho's stubby fingers rewound his turban into a shorter, wider style. "Do this with your own," he directed his men. "So you'll look more like a Maratha. Those of you with shawls, wrap them across your lower face like so many Maratha horsemen do."

The men laughed as they fumbled in their efforts, but eventually they all achieved a look that Madho thought should be satisfactory in the darkness, at least from a distance. Eager for action they could boast about back in Mangarh, the Rajputs clambered into the watercraft.

The tide was going out, so the boats swiftly took Madho and Gopal and their small party downstream as darkness fell. Only a quarter moon illuminated the smoky town when they landed on the southeast river bank, well to the north of the central part of Surat. "No talking," Madho ordered. "We don't want the Marathas to realize we speak a different tongue." Although some of his men had learned a little Marathi while in Surat, he spoke the most fluently of any.

"We're walking the whole time?" Gopal asked in a high pitched whisper of disbelief.

"Only until we can take some Maratha horses." Madho turned to Devi Singh, and directed him and four other Rajputs to remain behind to guard the boats. His remaining two dozen men lit several torches, and Madho led them into the city boldly, as if they were Marathas searching for plunder.

Much of Surat consisted only of humble mud dwellings. The brick houses of the wealthy were scattered throughout the city, and most of them appeared already targeted by Marathas. Some of the houses were afire, and looting was actively going on in others.

Parties of Marathas rode or walked here and there in the narrow, curving street, many of the raiders laden with their booty. Madho assumed that they no doubt thought only Shivaji's followers could be moving about the city, and they were intent on grabbing wealth for themselves as quickly as possible. Consequently, no one challenged the Rajputs.

In half an hour's time, Madho halted his own group. He said in a low voice to Gopal, "If we can find a small enough party of Marathas, we can relieve them of their burdens. But we'll have to make sure no one gets away. If word spreads of what we're doing, Shivaji could have hundreds of men on us soon. He might trap us against the river before we could get to the boats. I'd rather not try to swim it, especially in the dark."

"We need to be sure we're getting a good haul when we strike," said Gopal in a loud whisper. "Maybe we'd do better to find a house to search ourselves."

"I'd rather let someone else do the searching," Madho replied. "A big house could take us all night, and we might still not find anything worthwhile."

"That's so," agreed Gopal. "Besides, we're supposed to be the Emperor's allies. We wouldn't want the Mughals to hear we were robbing houses along with Shivaji. It's fine for us to take from our enemies, though."

They both knew their men would eventually talk to others, and word would spread. After a time, with little conviction, Madho said, "Right. We'd better not be seen robbing buildings."

They quietly roamed the northern part of the city, working their way toward its center. Almost an hour passed. "I wish we had more men," Madho whispered to Gopal. "It would be easier to ambush a party of Marathas."

"I just wish I had my horse," grumbled Gopal, breathing hard from the exertion. "I've never walked so much in my life."

"Your limp looks worse. Is your leg bothering you?"

"Some, but don't worry about it."

Suddenly Madho halted, at a small mansion on an intersection of a street and an alleyway, near the river. The facade of the narrow three story dwelling abutted the street, and on the alley side a tall wall protected the central courtyard. "I remember this one," Madho told Gopal. "We happened to be passing when the owner came out and got into his palanquin. A rich gem merchant, our guide said. Remember him? A thin, worried-looking little man. Didn't look well-fed like most traders."

"Doesn't seem like anyone's around now," said Gopal.

"No one's looted it, either, from the looks of it," said Madho. They stood eyeing the house for a few moments. "Let's try it," said Madho at last. "If we don't find anything soon, we can move on." He beckoned half of his men forward. "The rest of you wait around back, so it's not obvious we're here. Keep alert in case we have to leave fast."

He and Gopal and a couple of men, one of whom held a torch, mounted the steps of the pillared veranda and examined the massive, ornately carved double doors. Madho gestured to Nathu Singh, who shook the door. "It seems strong," Madho said in a quiet voice.

The sour faced Rajput bent to look at the heavy chain and lock securing them. "Locked from outside, Highness. Maybe that means everyone's gone."

"More likely, there's a watchman or two still inside. They could come and go from the rear door. But an inside courtyard door should be easier to crash. So we'll go over the wall."

Gopal and Nathu Singh and young Ajay Singh followed him down the alley to where the courtyard wall began. "It's too tall to easily climb over," said Madho. "We need something to stand on. Weren't there some *charpoys* thrown out in the street a few houses away?"

"We'll get them," said Nathu. He and Ajay hurried off and soon returned, each carrying a wooden bed frame. They stacked one atop another.

"Stand on them, and lift me," ordered Madho. The rope webbing sagged as the men climbed on. But by bracing themselves against the wall, they were able to gain secure enough footing. The men grunted with Madho's hefty bulk as they hoisted him to where he could examine the top of the wall. "Broken pottery shards embedded all along it," he said. "Give me a coat."

Gopal tossed him a quilted garment, which Madho folded for padding over the sharp fragments. Then, to the relief of the men supporting his feet, he boosted himself to sit on the wall. He shifted his sword to where he could grab it easily, and Gopal passed him a torch. Its flame illuminated the interior court. He looked about carefully, but if there were guards, they remained out of sight. "Come on over," he called to his men. There was a slanting tile roof slightly below, so he dropped heavily to it.

Nathu Singh soon appeared atop the wall and slid down to the roof. He was soon followed by Ajay Singh, who dropped to the soil of the courtyard and then helped Madho down.

Madho looked about at the interior walls of the house. "See which door looks easier," Madho whispered. "Watch out for guards, though, so they don't take us by surprise."

From over the wall came Gopal's call, "Horses coming. I'll tell the others to go hide."

They heard the approaching hooves in the street around front. And voices. It sounded like several animals and their riders. All of them stopped.

Madho whispered to the others, "Put out your torches." He snuffed his own torch on the ground, and hoped the burning odor and the lingering smoke would not be too obvious. At least the smoke in the air from the many burning buildings would help mask the scent. "Help me back up," he whispered. "Then come back yourselves. Don't make any sound."

They boosted him to the low roof, and he carefully climbed over the still-padded wall and dropped heavily to the *charpoys* in the alleyway. The wood creaked as his weight fell into the rope webbing, but nothing broke. Madho clambered to the ground and quietly moved through the darkness to where he could look around the corner to observe the horsemen. He counted ten of them. They had dismounted and were dragging a small man dressed in *dhoti* and shawl who appeared to be their captive. Some of the Marathas wore metal helmets, and most wore quilted coats, but so far as Madho could see in the light of the few torches they held, none of them wore chain mail armor. They had apparently left their shields with the horses.

The Marathas forced their captive to work at the padlock on the double door, and in the torchlight Madho recognized the gem trader to whom the house belonged. The little man's eyes were bulging in fear, and he fumbled in his efforts at the lock.

Finally, one of the Marathas shoved him aside and managed to undo the chain. Soon the Marathas pulled the doors open. The party entered the house, taking their captive with them.

Madho thought furiously. If the Marathas had instilled sufficient fear in the trader, he should promptly show them where at least part of his cache of wealth was hidden. So if Madho stayed, maybe his own reward would not be long in coming. He saw the round dark bulk of Gopal creeping toward him along the wall. "We'll wait," Madho whispered to him. "Keep the men hidden, but ready to attack when I give the word. There are only ten of them, so it should be easy if we take them by surprise." Gopal nodded and slipped away.

Madho heard a brief clashing of metal and then a groan of pain from just inside the house. So there must have been at least one guard .

He steeled himself to wait patiently. Sounds of banging or the scraping of stones soon came from the house, and once in a while the sound of an excited voice. It went on for what seemed a long time, and Madho began to think about leading his men inside to attack the Marathas. But the looters were likely scattered about the house, and if only one of them raised an alarm, the others could put up a strong fight.

Abruptly the Marathas exited the house. In the light of their torches Madho saw that each was heavily burdened: the two men with unsheathed swords guarding the captive had bags slung over their backs; two others, bent half over, struggled with a big wooden chest; another two each carried a smaller box and had bags over their shoulders; the others carried various heavy-looking bags and boxes and urns.

The two men guarding the captive were arguing with each other. One waved an arm toward the house. "We can carry more if we don't have him," Madho heard the captor say in Marathi. Then, the man lifted his sword, stepped back, and quickly thrust it into the trader's stomach. The victim let out a short grunt and slumped to the ground.

Madho whistled to his men as he ran toward the Marathas, his sword gripped in both hands. Numerous rapid footsteps thudded. With a mighty blow, Madho severed the head of the startled Maratha with the drawn sword. The others, outnumbered and burdened with their loot, had little chance to defend themselves. When they all lay still on the street, Madho seized one of the torches before it went out; his men took the others.

"There should be enough horses for all of us now," said Gopal. Madho stooped over the merchant, who moaned with pain, holding his stomach while blood oozed out over his hands.

Madho hesitated. Should he use his own sword to make sure the man did not survive to tell about the Rajputs who came to loot, or should he pretend to offer aid, on the chance of getting more information? Assuming that the merchant traveled enough to know at least some Marathi, he placed his face close to the man's and said, "The Marathas are dead. Can we help you?"

The trader's eyes opened. He whispered, apparently with great effort, "Gems...for Emperor." His breath came in gasps. "Emperor wants—"

Madho thought quickly. "We're from the Emperor's army. I know him personally! Tell me what he wants!"

"Smallest boxes—" croaked the trader. A blankness spread through his eyes. He shuddered and lay still.

Madho looked about. His men were preoccupied with the loot, and even if they had heard the whispering, he doubted their Marathi was good enough to understand what the merchant had said. They already had the large wooden chest opened. In the torchlight, the contents gleamed. "Gold bars, Highness!" Ajay Singh exclaimed.

Another man was rummaging in a bag. "Bracelets, necklaces!" he shouted. "All with gems!"

Puran Singh, youngest of the Rajputs aside from Ajay, was looking into a bag. "Gold coins!" he called.

Madho realized the trader might well have been a major source of supply for gems for the imperial vaults. Aurangzeb's treasury held an unimaginably vast quantity of wealth, and a continual stream of riches flowed into it from throughout the huge empire. He spotted the two small boxes on the ground, and he strode over and took them. "Drag the bodies out of sight, then search the house again," he ordered. "Tear open the walls anywhere you see a shelf in a niche. And look in the well and cisterns. They always hide things there. I'll stay here to guard all this."

A couple of the Rajputs seemed reluctant to leave, but they knew better than to question their prince. Gopal and Nathu Singh and the others moved off, leaving Madho alone for the moment. He examined the small boxes. The locks had already been pried off, no doubt by the Marathas.

He lifted the lid of the first. He unfolded the silk wrappings within. And gasped. He glanced quickly about to reassure himself no one else could see.

Carelessly torn from their smaller wraps by the Marathas was a king's treasury of gems.

A giant ruby gleamed in the light of the flame, larger than any he could have imagined. He knew rubies were fragile, so he carefully rewrapped it so it would be well-cushioned.

Next he lifted out a stone so large he at first wondered if it were real. He held it up to the light.

Oh, my God! he thought. It had to be a diamond.

It dwarfed any he had ever before seen. The irregularities in the surface had been polished, so it was smooth and clear. It felt hard and heavy as he turned it around slowly between his fingers, the torchlight flashing and flaring through it.

A vast fortune in itself!

He was reluctant to put it back in the chest, as if it were a dream that would vanish if let out of his view. But he feared his men would see it. Fumbling in excitement, he rewrapped it.

He glanced toward the house, reassuring himself that his men were still occupied within. Then, one at a time, he held up to the light six giant emeralds. Then he examined a dozen smaller rubies. He rewrapped them for protection.

There were too many smaller diamonds to count, sparkling in the darkness like stars.

He opened the second box. He withdrew a necklace, of five strands of large pearls. It was too dark to see how perfectly they matched, but from the overall appearance he felt sure they must be carefully selected. A true showpiece.

More assorted gems of various sizes, none of them small.

And an emerald, the size of a hen's egg.

He thought about the dying trader's words. There was no doubt these were the jewels intended for the Emperor. And there was no doubt of their incredible value; they were the merchant's last concern even as his soul left its earthly body. That diamond was huge! The ruby, the pearl necklaces....

Madho had become so enthralled as to lose all sense of time. Suddenly, he heard someone coming from the doorway. He swiftly but casually closed both lids.

Gopal appeared. "More in the house!" he said. "Lots of gold, silver bullion, pearls. That's why that Maratha killed the trader—with no one to guard, he could carry more treasure. Even so, there's more than they could have managed. Probably more than *we* can carry!"

"We'll manage," Madho said, boosting himself to his feet. "Put it on their horses. Cut the webbing from *charpoys* to use for ropes. The gold first, then the silver. Do it fast, before anyone comes along and sees us. We'll walk, ourselves, and carry the gems."

Gopal grimaced at the thought of more walking. He gestured to the two small boxes. "Find anything?"

Madho had always before shared his thoughts with Gopal, whom he'd known all his life. But he hesitated to trust *any* man with the knowledge of a find such as this. These two boxes were his future, maybe even the future of the ruling house of Mangarh. Word absolutely must not get to the Emperor or his officials, or they would demand he bring the gems and turn them over.

Maybe he would tell Gopal later. For now, he shook his head and started for the house. "Just some silver coins. I'll save them for an offering to Ekadantji when we're back in Mangarh."

Madho entered the dwelling, carrying the two boxes stacked under his left arm, and his torch in his right hand. By the stairway inside the front door, a guard lay sprawled on his back, blood seeping from his throat. Madho climbed the stairs, and as he'd expected, he found the trader's office. He held his torch high as he glanced around. Here the merchant's wealth was obvious. Rich carpets covered the floor, and finely upholstered cushions and bolsters had been tossed about by the raiders. The doorways and window shutters were intricately carved and inlaid with ivory.

Folios bound in wood lay about on the floor where the searchers had cast them. With his toe, Madho lifted one wooden cover, then another.

Account books.

Disappointed, he strode swiftly through the other rooms of the owner's section of the house.

"Find anything more?" Gopal asked when Madho returned to the front hall.

Madho shook his head. "I suppose it was too much to expect he'd have any illustrated manuscripts. I'd hoped for some paintings."

Gopal cast him an odd look, but said nothing.

They returned to the street, and Madho saw the riches tied to the horses. "Good. Now we'd better get moving. Keep your swords handy in case we have to defend ourselves—we don't want to make the same mistakes the Marathas did. Oh, and bring the rest of the ropes from those *charpoys*."

Madho led them back through the city toward the river. They saw occasional small groups of Marathas down streets and alleys, carrying loot. The Rajputs apparently remained successful at passing as Marathas themselves, as no one challenged them.

Madho let out a sigh of relief when they reached the boats. He ordered Gopal and the greater part of his men to ferry the treasure across the river. Except for the two small boxes, which he placed in a bag gripped tightly by his fist. He wasn't about to let those fabulous items out of his custody.

"You're not crossing the river yourself?" Gopal asked.

"No. Neither are Nathu and ten others. You get the treasure back to our main party and have it loaded in some of the carts. And be quiet—you know how sounds can carry across water at night. Get the carts moving northward. But leave a couple of them, and have a few men bring the boats back here. I'll take these ten and see if we can pull Shivaji's tail a little."

The astonished Gopal asked, "You'd challenge him with a dozen men?"

Madho gave his usual smile. "Fewer to lose that way." In fact, he was worried. But not enough to give up the real possibility of further wealth. He'd thought carefully about whether or not to escape with the fortune he already had, rather than risk his life for more. But if anything, the loot he'd seized whetted his appetite for more. Surat was a rich city, and the Marathas were helping themselves to that wealth. Madho just could not bear to leave so much to them.

Gopal was warning, "You pull a tiger's tail, he'll turn on you fast."

"Only after he figures out what's happening. Look, we have to make sure the Emperor hears we tried our utmost to enforce his authority. That's almost as important as getting more riches." Yet, Madho hesitated. Was it worth risking his life again when he'd already achieved success? Maybe not. But it would likely be years, if ever, before he had such an opportunity again.

He picked out one of the Maratha's horses for himself, a piebald Kathiawari that seemed even tempered. He gave his small party of Rajputs instructions, and they each chose a horse. Nathu Singh divided up the ropes from the *charpoys* and handed pieces to the other Rajputs. While Madho tied the bag of gems securely to his saddle, speaking in Marathi, he told his horse in a calm, reassuring voice, "You have a new master for a short while. I'll be good to you, and you be good to me."

He and Nathu and the other ten men mounted up, and they rode back though the confined, twisting streets toward the center of the city. In ten minutes they overtook a file of eight horsemen, laden with loot, heading toward the outskirts of Surat. Madho looked them over carefully. He had no wish to get into a genuine skirmish with men who were likely to be hard fighters. But these warriors obviously expected no trouble; their shields hung from their horses, and most of the Marathas carried bags or other items in their arms.

Madho signaled his men. They fell in behind the procession, overtook it and moved up, as if passing it. At Madho's shout, each Rajput drew his sword and pounced upon a Maratha.

Madho himself took the leader, who carried a small wooden chest under one arm. The Maratha glanced over at him, curious, just as Madho swung his sword as hard as he could at the man's neck. The eyes bulged in surprise as Madho severed the head and blood spurted from the arteries.

The clanging of metal echoed in the narrow street, combined with a couple of screams, and Madho quickly glanced about to see if any of his men needed help. Young Ajay Singh was clashing with a Maratha, and Madho edged his horse closer and slashed hard at the side of the man's neck. The Maratha's head shuddered from the blow, but the sword didn't penetrate. Madho realized there must be chain mail concealed beneath the cloth hanging from the man's turban. The Maratha was distracted enough that Ajay managed to stab him in the face with the point of his sword, and the man fell from his horse.

Abruptly, the street was quiet. "Everyone all right?" Madho called, breathing heavily.

"Nothing to it," replied Nathu Singh. "They wanted to save their loot more than they wanted to save themselves."

"Listen for a minute," Madho ordered, worried that the sounds of the skirmish might have alerted other Marathas. He heard nothing, so he wiped his sword clean. "Drag their bodies into that ruined house," he said, "so no one finds them before we leave the city."

He noticed Ajay was holding his left arm. Blood seeped though a cut in the youthful Rajput's coat. Madho stepped over to him. "How bad?" he asked.

Ajay shrugged, grimacing. "I'll be all right. I don't think it's deep."

"Bind his arm," Madho told the nearest man. "And keep an eye on him. Make sure he can handle his horse."

"Our brother Ajay never does remember to keep his shield up," said Puran Singh, probably the strongest fighter present.

"He did well," said Madho in admonishment. "He had a tough match."

Madho turned to the loot, and he and the others began sorting through it. Madho started with the wooden chest the leader had carried. It was filled with silver coins. He looked about at his men; they had found more silver, gold, and jewelry, as well as valuable furnishings.

He gave his men a grim grin. "The Emperor should appreciate that we're serving as his police here."

Nathu Singh replied, "We even saved His Majesty the trouble of executing the thieves." A couple of the men laughed.

They again used the newly killed Marathas' mounts as pack animals, securing the bundles with the *charpoy* ropes, and continued on through the city. It was now well after midnight, but the distant sounds of looting still carried in the smoke-laden air.

In a short while, Madho's party came upon several Marathas carrying items out of the doorway of a large house. Madho made as if to ride past, but when his men were opposite the mansion, he signaled. Two of the Rajputs attacked the raiders from horseback, while most of the others drew their swords and leaped to the ground. A couple of Marathas screamed, but this time, none had the chance to draw a sword. Madho's men added more gold and silver to the backs of their pack horses.

He noticed Ajay Singh had remained mounted and was bent over. Madho moved close, saw the blood seeping out from the bandage, and asked quietly, "How do you feel?"

"A bit faint, Highness," said Ajay, his voice weak.

Madho turned and said to the smallest of his men, "Get on the horse with our brother Ajay. Take him back to the boats. Make sure he doesn't fall. Take him across the river if you feel you need to."

"Yes, Highness. Should I bring some of the horses with the loot, too?"

Madho hesitated. He'd like to get the wealth across the river as soon as possible. He sighed to himself. "No, you need to concentrate on getting our brother back. That could be hard if you have other horses to take care of."

He and the rest mounted up and continued through the city. Soon, they met a group of six riders leading a couple of horses packed high with booty. As they passed, in the light of the torches Madho saw the lead Maratha was eyeing the Rajputs with a puzzled expression.

Madho gave the signal, and his men instantly drew their swords and attacked. The head Maratha, apparently already suspicious, sped away. Madho whirled his horse about and started after him, knowing the man must be silenced before he could tell others. Madho heard a couple of his own men's horses pounding behind him. But the Maratha raced through the streets as if shot from a cannon, and after half a minute, Madho realized there was little chance of catching him before he could reach others.

Reluctantly, Madho halted, stopped his two men also, and they rushed back the remainder of their party. "Back to the river, fast!" he ordered.

They quickly took what they could carry of the new loot and galloped toward the river. Near the waterfront, Madho abruptly stopped his party to listen. From behind came the sounds of other horses. Many of them.

Madho again nudged his mount into a gallop. He kept glancing backward, but in the twisting streets the torches of the pursuers could not yet be seen.

As they drew close to the boat landing, Madho called to Nathu Singh, "See if you can draw the Marathas off. But don't get caught!"

Nathu sped onward, and Madho and the remainder quickly dismounted, snuffed out the torches, and led their horses away from the street. They all waited quietly in the dark as a large force of Marathas galloped past.

"Get the boats loaded fast," Madho ordered. His men moved swiftly to obey. It was hard to see in the darkness, but they didn't dare relight the torches.

Madho worried about Nathu, but the man was shrewd, definitely the best choice to act as a decoy. He saw that Ajay was stretched out in one of the boats. "How's he been?" he asked the man who was caring for the youth.

"He's better, now that he's lying down."

Madho gave a nod and turned to supervising the loading.

It would take two trips to ferry both men and treasure across. As the boats departed on the first trip, Madho remained with a few men on the landing, watching for Nathu.

The boats eventually returned, with Gopal in one. The remainder of the treasure was loaded. Madho started to climb into a boat, bag of gems in hand. Then he stopped. "Keep one boat here," he said. "Get the rest of them across the river. And pay all the boatmen plenty to make sure they stay on the other side, so the Marathas can't use them to come after us. Devi Singh and Puran Singh can stay with me." Madho had chosen Devi for his mature judgment and Puran for his unusual strength and fighting ability.

"You're not crossing?" whispered Gopal.

Madho hated to remain so close to danger, especially now that he had much more to lose. But he just couldn't leave Nathu, who'd been a loyal retainer for so many years. He said, "Nathu's still in the city somewhere."

"What if the Marathas come searching and find you? Some of the other men can stay here. But you should get across."

"No. I may need to go look for him."

"The others can do that! You're our prince—you shouldn't risk yourself any more. Especially now that you've got all the riches you wanted."

"Just get in the boat and leave, or you may convince me."

Gopal shook his head and clambered into one of the two remaining boats. It shoved off, and oars creaked as it disappeared into the murky night.

Madho and the two men waited. Their eyes had adjusted enough to see the black forms of each other and the surrounding buildings, but it was too dark to make out details. Madho was conscious of the bag he held. Should he have sent it across with Gopal? Maybe. But it was hard to let such a fabulous fortune out of his control. What if someone opened the bag and saw what it contained? Or even worse, what if it were somehow lost?

Then, as Madho had feared, he heard horses approaching. They stopped on the other side of a warehouse, so he couldn't see exactly how many there were. But between buildings he could see faint illumination from torches. He heard a man speak in Marathi, ordering a search of the area.

He'd heard that resonant, commanding voice before, in Poona.

It was Shivaji himself.

Madho whispered to Devi Singh, "Go make sure the boatman stays out of sight."

"We should get out onto the river, Highness. We can come back after the Marathas leave."

"We wouldn't know if Nathu comes back or not. He might find us gone, and with no boat here, he'd think he had to go back to the crossing upriver. So we wouldn't know if we need to go look for him."

Devi's dark bulk moved toward the boat.

Madho thought quickly. What an opportunity! Was there a possibility of killing or capturing Shivaji?

He didn't know how many men were with the King. Almost certainly it was a larger band than Madho's. And Shivaji was a highly skillful fighter. The only likely possibility was to take them by surprise, but the Marathas had torches and would probably see Madho and his men first.

He felt the bag at his waist. No, better not take a chance on losing such a fabulous fortune, especially when the odds against him were so poor. He peered about the darkness, trying to discern a hiding place. A short wooden wharf extended into the river so boats could load and unload more easily when the tide was low. He whispered to Puran, "Quick—under that dock."

Devi rejoined them, and the three eased down the slippery bank. The tide was in, so cool water was up to their waists, and the suction from mud at the bottom grabbed at their shoes. No sooner were they under, than torchlight shone overhead. Footsteps sounded on the wood planks above. Madho debated about whether to submerge himself more. But he doubted he could get so far underwater as to be invisible, and he might not be able to hold his breath long enough.

He held himself motionless and waited.

The torches moved here and there, at least two or three of them. One shone on the boat. Madho fervently hoped the boatman had managed to hide himself well.

"No one here, Your Majesty," a voice called out.

"I wonder why that boat's still here," the King said. "All the rest went to the other side of the river to get away from us."

"It looks empty," said one of his men.

"Let's move on, then," came Shivaji's reply.

"Should we take the boat in case we need one?" asked the Maratha on the wharf.

Madho stopped breathing. Without the boat, he and his men would have to try to swim across in the dark. They'd have to leave their heavy coats and most of their armor and weapons behind. He'd need to keep his gems secure the whole time.

There was silence. At last, the King answered, "No reason we should need one. We'll be heading south when we leave."

The footsteps moved off the dock onto the land. Then the torches and men rapidly moved away.

Madho waited a few minutes to make sure the searchers had left. The water was feeling colder by the second.

He whispered to Devi Singh, "See that they're really gone. Try not to leave any wet footprints, in case they come back. That mountain rat is clever. He may be trying to trick us into coming out of hiding."

With only a minimal amount of splashing noise, Devi eased himself from the water. He crept up the bank and moved off. Shortly, he came back and whispered loudly, "No one around anywhere close."

"Let's get out of the water," Madho told Puran Singh, who moved partway up the river bank and extended a hand to help Madho clamber out.

They shook off water, then stood dripping. Madho tried to wipe the mud from his shoes at the edge of the bank, so it wouldn't be visible as evidence of his being there.

They waited still longer, uncomfortable in their wet clothing. Madho's quilted coat was heavy with water, and he tried to squeeze as much out as he could, with only a little success.

"Nathu must have run into trouble, Highness," whispered Puran.

"How long are we staying?" asked Devi Singh.

"Until he comes," said Madho. "Or we decide we need to go find him."

"We'd never find him if we went to look," said Puran. "That city's a maze, aside from all the Marathas searching for us."

"That's right," came Nathu's voice from behind them. "You wouldn't have found me. So I won't make you look."

Madho let out a huge sigh. "Get into the boat."

As they crossed the river, Madho worried about the sound of the creaking oars alerting the searchers. At least the Marathas didn't have their own boats, so any pursuit would be delayed. Nathu said in a whisper, "I led those men chasing us farther than I intended. But I didn't want to take a chance on their finding you, Highness, so I tried to make them think we were leaving the city. Then, I had to leave my horse, and it was hard to keep from getting spotted as I made my way back." The boat touched the far shore, and as they climbed onto the bank, Nathu added, "Sorry, Highness. I had to leave most of the loot with the horse. But I brought some of the valuable pieces with me."

Madho grimaced in the dark as he thought with regret about the lost wealth. Then he grunted. "Just so you're back."

Gopal approached, leading Madho's own horse, and said, "At last! The men were all concerned about you."

"Well, I'm here."

"You look a mess, even in the dark."

"Try spending half the night in the river and see how *you* look."

Gopal said quietly, "The men were surprised you'd stayed there so long."

After a time, Madho murmured, "So was I." He tied the bag securely to his saddle, then double-checked the knots as best he could in the darkness. "How's Ajay?" he asked Gopal.

"The bleeding stopped, and he's resting. He should recover."

Madho again grunted. "Good thing it's his left arm. If it ends up stiff, it won't interfere with using his sword. You're carrying him on a stretcher, so he doesn't keep getting jolted by the bumps?"

"Of course."

"Pay the boatmen well to keep quiet about us," ordered Madho. "And send them back upstream to their village so the Marathas won't see them and question them."

As he mounted and set out, he listened to the jubilation of his men, who were having a difficult time being quiet so the sounds wouldn't carry across the river. He felt exhausted, yet exhilarated. He'd been more worried about getting caught by the Marathas than he had let on. But it had been worth the gamble.

At last, he had won his riches. And admiration as a bold, clever warrior.

He would return to Mangarh in triumph, rather than in disgrace. The *charans*, the bards, would sing of him and his courage. And already in his mind's eye he saw the paintings his artists would make depicting his exploits.

3

Agra. 12 May 1666

It was the day of the Mughal Emperor Aurangzeb's fiftieth birthday celebrations—and the day of Shivaji's arrival in the imperial capital of Agra, more than two years after the Surat escapade. Madho and Gopal rode an elephant directly behind that of twenty year old Ram Singh, heir apparent to the throne of Amber, who had the main responsibility for receiving and hosting Shivaji.

The gently swaying howdah was as hot as the inside of an oven. Gopal wiped the sweat from his brow, flicked it over the elephant's side, and exclaimed to Madho, "Who could have foretold that on this day we'd be welcoming Shivaji himself to Agra?"

"I'm eager to meet him at last," Madho said. *And,* he thought, *to bring about his death.*

"Shivaji still looked unbeatable only a year ago," Gopal mused.

"We must give Raja Jai Singh credit," Madho replied. "In only three months, he managed what no other general could do in years."

The sack of Surat had added to Shivaji's already immense reputation. However, the Emperor Aurangzeb, humiliated by the ravaging of his largest and richest port with virtually no resistance, sent his Rajput general Jai Singh, the ruler of Amber, as head of an army to pursue the Maratha King. Jai Singh brilliantly orchestrated a combination of tactics, including besieging the principal Maratha forts, blocking Maratha communications lines, torching Maratha towns and villages, and isolating Shivaji through diplomacy from joining with any potential allies. In particular, the systematic devastation of his homelands and the loss of some principal forts convinced Shivaji to agree to a peace treaty. He gave up the majority of his forts and supposedly became an ally of the Mughal army in the Deccan.

However, Shivaji distrusted Aurangzeb, so he had been most reluctant to travel to Agra to meet the Emperor. Only the solemn oaths of the general Raja Jai Singh himself, guaranteeing Shivaji's safety, had finally convinced him to come. Jai Singh remained in the Deccan, but because of his oath, he directed his eldest son Ram Singh to do everything possible to protect Shivaji in Agra.

For Madho Singh, the Surat adventure had dramatically changed his own fortunes. Emperor Aurangzeb, impressed by how Madho led the tiny force to harass Shivaji at Surat, summoned him to Agra to attend the imperial court and awarded him the rank of a *mansab* of 1,500, commander of 1,500 horses. It was a significant achievement for such a young prince from a minor state.

Madho now suddenly turned to Gopal. "Does everyone still suspect me of poisoning my brother?"

"I'm still asked about that sometimes," replied Gopal. "You must admit his death was convenient, since you'll now inherit the throne."

Madho shook his head sadly. "How can men think so ill of me? I confess I might have had to do something drastic eventually, but I wouldn't have acted until it was necessary. He was my own brother, after all!"

Gopal shrugged. "Everyone knows you're rich enough now to have bribed your brother's cook or servants to administer poison. And that you want even more wealth and power."

Madho raised an eyebrow. "Well, doesn't everyone want that?"

Gopal laughed. "Not everyone is obvious about being greedy."

Madho looked down, scowling. "But I've tried to build my reputation as a valiant warrior. And as a patron of the arts. After all, I used part of the treasure to hire five more artists."

"And you've been showing those portraits of yourself and the scenes of your exploits in Surat to everyone who'll look."

Madho smiled. "Yes, well, I've told my artists to stop painting me for a while. They're doing scenes from the life of Lord Krishna instead."

The welcoming procession was now leaving the congested residential areas and approaching the outskirts of Agra. On the elephant ahead, Ram Singh, his round face dripping with perspiration, called back to Madho, "We should have met Shivaji by now. I wonder if he's had problems. We can't be late for the Emperor's birthday *durbar*."

Madho shrugged; the only reply was the jangling of the elephants' ankle bells. Gopal said in a voice only Madho could hear, "If I were Shivaji, I'd have been insulted to have Ram Singh send a mere clerk to make the arrangements."

"Indeed," said Madho. "Even though Ram Singh didn't hear about Shivaji's arrival until yesterday and had some other duties, it's no excuse. I think the heir to Amber lacks his father's astuteness."

The Mughal court etiquette required that an important visitor such as Shivaji halt one day away from Agra. The Emperor would then send a delegate to greet him and accompany him in a procession through the city. The visitor would be presented to Aurangzeb at an hour determined by the astrologers to be auspicious.

Madho took a quid of *betel* from the silver box beside him and stuffed it in his mouth. His voice muffled from the *paan*, he said, "If I'd been informed in time, I'd have met Shivaji myself. Even a commander of 1,500 has more prestige than a *munshi*. But I don't think Ram Singh trusts me."

"He has a hard job, guaranteeing Shivaji's safety," said Gopal, smiling slyly at Madho.

"So he does." Outside of a select few in the Emperor's employ, only Gopal knew that Madho's duties included more than merely welcoming Shivaji. On secret orders of the Emperor, Madho was to attempt to bring about Shivaji's death at Agra, in a manner that would not directly link Aurangzeb with the deed. The Emperor had never forgiven Shivaji the continual humiliations. The night attack at the viceroy's headquarters and the sack of Surat were the most prominent, but far from the only examples.

And Shivaji's activities had gained him the enmity of other powerful figures. The Emperor's favorite sister Jahanara had been entitled to receive the revenues of Surat. That income was lost for the better part of a year due to Shivaji's raid. In addition, relatives of the former viceroy, Shaista Khan, wanted to punish Shivaji for the night attack at Poona.

Madho was more than a little uneasy that the various plotters had settled on him as the instrument for their revenge. He'd been told it was because he had demonstrated boldness in his Surat raid. But he was astute enough to realize, to his distress, that it was probably also because he was so widely thought to have poisoned his brother, as well as to be greedy for more wealth.

A horseback messenger galloped out of a narrow side street. He reined to a halt by Ram Singh's elephant, dismounted and did his salutation, hurrying to keep up with the moving procession.

Madho strained to overhear as Ram Singh asked, "What is it?"

"Your honor, we've been looking everywhere for you. Munshi Girdhar Lal is wondering why you haven't appeared to greet Shivaji."

"Damn!" said Ram Singh. He spoke to the driver of his elephant to halt the procession. "Where in this forsaken place is the King?" he asked the messenger. "I was supposed to meet him here."

"But, lord, Raja Shivaji is on the road by the Daharara Garden."

"No! That idiot *munshi*! Why didn't he send word?" Ram Singh called to the two Rajput horsemen immediately in front of him, "Go conduct Maharaja Shivaji to this road. We'll turn around and meet him near the Nurganj Garden, by the central market. And no mistakes this time, or we'll all be late for the Emperor's audience!"

The remainder of the procession of eight elephants and the foot and cavalry escort swung about to head toward the central part of the city to intercept Shivaji. The howdah swayed from side to side as Madho's elephant turned in the narrow street. Madho shook his head. "What a fiasco," he said to Gopal. "Shivaji must be furious. And we've lost so much time."

The celebration that day was important. The previous Mughal Emperor, Shah Jahan, who had been deposed by his son Aurangzeb and imprisoned in Agra Fort the past six years, had died last January and been entombed beside his beloved wife in the Taj Mahal. Aurangzeb had ruled from Delhi while his father lived, but within months of Shah Jahan's death, Aurangzeb moved the capital back to Agra. Today's fiftieth birthday *durbar* was the first great celebration sponsored by an Emperor in Agra in years.

The delegation moved through the ever more crowded streets of the city. Citizens, cows, goats, all moved aside to make way for the line of elephants, horses, foot soldiers led by Ram Singh.

At last they saw Shivaji's own procession ahead. As the two parties drew close, the welcoming committee stopped to let the van of the Maratha King's escort pass. A big male elephant came first, carrying Shivaji's flag of orange and red with gold decorations. Then followed an advance guard of a hundred or so Maratha horsemen, their horses trapped in gold and silver. Then a couple hundred infantry, wearing huge Turkish style caps.

Next came a ceremonial domed palanquin, all in silver. Madho eyed the palanquin. He must have one such as this, he thought, when he became Raja of Mangarh.

Shivaji himself now approached, on a horse with splendid silver trappings. Madho examined the King with interest. Short and slender, the Maratha warrior and ruler wore a neatly trimmed beard and mustache. His handsome, fair complexioned face was set in a stern expression, his eyes cool. His small turban slanted backward, and at the top rear it was accented by a jeweled ornament and plume at a rakish angle.

Shivaji's attractive nine year old son, Shambhuji, rode another horse. After the King and his son came his officers, all mounted on horseback. Finally came the heavily loaded

Shivaji

baggage camels, and a hundred or so pairs of pack oxen, and a number of palanquins.

"Shivaji looks furious," whispered Gopal to Madho as they climbed from their howdah.

"Understandably," replied Madho. "And the Emperor will be angry, too, if we don't arrive on time for his ceremonies. Ram Singh bungled everything badly."

Kumar Ram Singh quickly descended from his elephant and hurried to Shivaji, who more slowly dismounted from his horse. The King seemed stiffly reserved, but Ram Singh embraced him enthusiastically and loudly greeted him with the customary, "*Ram, Ram!*"

Ram Singh then tried to smooth over the matter of the lack of ceremony and the confusion. "This has been a terrible mix-up, Your Majesty. It should never have happened, especially not to so great a personage as yourself! I beg you to accept my most humble apologies and not to hold it against His Majesty the Emperor. My father will never forgive me. The Emperor himself would be mortified to learn of our errors."

The Maratha King listened stolidly, staring harshly at Ram Singh. At last he gave a quick nod, as if the matter was beneath his notice. But his demeanor was one of barely controlled anger.

Ram Singh quickly presented Madho Singh and Mukhlis Khan, the Emperor's other representative, to Shivaji. As Madho embraced the King and uttered the traditional, "*Ram, Ram*," he wondered if Shivaji realized he was meeting the very prince whose men had harassed the Marathas raiding Surat. If so, the King made no mention.

"Now, Your Majesty," Ram Singh was saying, "I hope you will honor my humble tent with your presence to take rest and refreshment. Please let me show you the way."

Shivaji eyed the line of eight elephants and asked in his deep, resonant voice, "Why the elephants? It's difficult to travel with them in the congestion of the city."

Ram Singh hesitated, obviously puzzled. "Indeed it is, Your Majesty," he replied at last. "But we wanted to show the honor such a great king as yourself deserves."

Shivaji said, his eyes still cool, "They seem inconvenient inside the town. Why not send them on their own way, so they don't burden us?"

Madho kept his face composed at hearing the curious request. Ram Singh appeared disconcerted. But he said, "Of course, Maharaja. Our elephants are yours to command, as are we ourselves." To Madho and Mukhlis Khan he said, "Let's change to the horses, as our guest wishes."

Ram Singh, Madho, and the nobles who had been on elephants relieved several of the cavalry escort of their horses. As the two princes prepared to mount up, Madho whispered to Ram Singh, "Don't you think perhaps we should head straight to the Emperor's palace? The delay has been so long already."

Ram Singh's face looked strained as he said, "How can I not offer hospitality? Shivaji has traveled several *kos* in the heat. And I must try to calm him after the mix-up on his welcome."

Madho shrugged. "As you wish."

While they rode, Madho wondered about the reason for the switch from elephants to horses. Maybe it was Shivaji's way of showing his anger at the insult of the botched reception. Or perhaps it was the King's way of asserting at least a little control over events which might be giving him an unaccustomed feeling of helplessness. While elephants were fine for show, it was horses that Marathas—like Rajputs—truly loved.

They continued to Ram Singh's encampment in Eunuch Feroza's Garden. In an adjacent portion of the grounds, Ram Singh had erected tents for Shivaji. He escorted the King into the huge red and white *shamiana* and seated him upon a throne of cushions. After the traditional sprinkling with rosewater, attendants started fanning him, servants brought in the drink and food, and musicians began to play. Upon seeing the care taken with these arrangements, the King's face appeared less hardened.

While they sipped *sharbat* and ate melon and various nuts and sweetmeats, Ram Singh questioned Shivaji about the long journey up from the Deccan. Madho watched the Maratha with great interest. In spite of his small stature, Shivaji's bearing was dignified. Now that his anger had lessened, it was clear the King had a certain charm. Shivaji eventually asked, in casual manner, "Is it not the custom for the Emperor to come meet a visiting King?"

No wonder he's so upset! thought Madho. How could he not have been informed of such an important item of etiquette? The Emperor considered vassal kings to be of substantially lower rank than himself and therefore would never come in person to meet them. But clearly, it was indeed almost an insult to send relatively low ranking princes, rather than a raja or high noble to welcome such a well known king.

Ram Singh's face had gone rigid, and it was obvious to Madho he could not think of a tactful answer. He looked to Madho, as if anxious for help.

Madho thought quickly and replied in Marathi, "Normally, Your Majesty, the Emperor would go to great effort to greet such an honored guest as yourself. However, you must know that today is his fiftieth birthday celebration, and there are certain, uh, traditional obligations to which he and the members of his family are required to attend. All the princes of the royal blood, as well as the vassal princes and kings, begged to be allowed the great honor of greeting you. In the end, the only way to settle the matter was to draw lots, and we were the fortunate winners. The others greatly envy us."

Shivaji stared at Madho. Madho held his breath, wondering if the King believed the lie. A smile crossed Shivaji's lips, and he gave a nod. "I see. I'm flattered that so many would hold me in such high esteem, and I feel honored at being given such attention when there is so great an occasion as the Emperor's birthday to divert them."

Madho relaxed. Even if Shivaji saw through the flattery, he would act the part of an agreeable guest.

But Shivaji's next question was equally difficult. He turned to Ram Singh and asked, "Does the *Padshah* plan to use today's *durbar* to appoint me viceroy?"

Madho choked on a piece of melon. Ram Singh's face lost color. His father Jai Singh had been desperate to induce Shivaji to come to Agra as the Emperor wished. Shivaji had been adamantly against the journey, as he distrusted Aurangzeb and did not wish to put himself in a trap. Jai Singh had therefore strongly hinted that the position of viceroy of the Deccan, one of the highest posts in the empire, might be Shivaji's reward for undertaking the journey.

However, it was almost certain that the Emperor had no intention of granting an irritating former enemy such a valuable reward. Ram Singh at last said, "I very much regret, Your Majesty, that the Emperor has not chosen to take me into his confidence on that particular matter. However, I know he holds you in the greatest esteem and will reward you accordingly. But now, we had best be on our way, or he will be wondering at the delay."

Shivaji sat stolidly for a moment. Then he gave a nod, and a slight smile, "Then let us go and meet this Emperor. But first, if you will excuse me for a few moments to prepare myself for the audience."

Everyone rose. Shivaji and his attendants disappeared into the walled-off area, and Madho whispered to Ram Singh, "Shouldn't we ensure the King knows the rules of etiquette at the court today? And shouldn't we tell him the schedule for the birthday program at the *durbar*? It's quite different from the informality he's accustomed to. The Marathi tongue doesn't even have appropriate words of respectful address for use at court, you know."

Ram Singh frowned and looked away in the direction of the Red Fort. "It would take too long. We've already delayed too much. I'll stand directly behind Shivaji and guide him through the ceremonies myself as best I can."

Madho took a last gulp of *sharbat* as he debated whether or not to protest further. The procedures at court were not only strict but complicated. And because of the birthday festivities, the schedule was even more complex than usual. He asked, "Does Shivaji know the Emperor plans to specially honor him today by presenting the robe and elephant and other gifts?"

Ram Singh said with obvious impatience, "I'm sure he was told. He'd be insulted if I repeated what he already knows. He's been upset enough—we'd better leave before he wonders if we're deliberately trying to delay him."

Madho shrugged. He was glad any gaffes at court would be Ram Singh's responsibility, not his own.

Shivaji returned, his face momentarily washed clean of perspiration. Madho noticed the King had added even more jewels to his turban and chest. Everyone went out to where the horses and escorts waited, and the procession resumed, headed toward the Red Fort. This time, Shivaji rode in the palanquin he had brought. It was one of the finest conveyances Madho had ever seen, its cabin all silver, its poles covered in gold plate. Madho ran his eyes over each part of it admiringly. Although slightly small for someone his size, it would otherwise be perfect for himself when he eventually became Raja. He must find a way to acquire it after he had disposed of Shivaji.

At the fort, he watched the Maratha King being carried over the drawbridge across the moat surrounding the seventy-foot high red sandstone walls. Shivaji was looking upward at the battlements, and Madho wondered if the King were impressed by the gigantic scale, so different from the smaller Maratha fortresses which were mostly built on rocky mountaintops and which used the steep approaches as part of their defenses.

If Shivaji was not impressed by the strength of the flatland Red Fort, he should at least be awed by the palaces contained within its walls. Three Emperors—Akbar, Jahangir, and Shah Jahan—had lavished their revenues on the living quarters, audience halls, gardens and supporting facilities. The almost unbelievable luxury greatly appealed to Madho himself.

When the procession approached the *Diwan-i-Am*, the huge marble pillared public audience hall, Madho could tell something had gone awry. Crowds of finely-dressed nobles were streaming away from the hall and from the gigantic red tent which had been erected before it for the festivities. Apparently the Emperor's public ceremonies had concluded. And Shivaji had not been there to be presented.

Madho saw Ram Singh, in the lead, confer with some officials outside the emptying hall. Looking distraught, Ram Singh hurried to Madho and said, "We're too late for the public audience. The Emperor's left for the *Diwan-i-Khas*. We'll have to take Shivaji there."

As Ram Singh explained to the Maratha King that they must go to the smaller audience hall, Madho whispered to Gopal, "I wouldn't like to be in Ram's position. The Emperor must consider Shivaji a war trophy of sorts. I'll wager Aurangzeb had looked forward to putting him on display to show what happens to kings who oppose him."

Gopal, as far too minor a personage to be admitted with the select group of nobles, remained outside while Madho accompanied Ram Singh and Shivaji past the cudgel-bearing guards. Ram Singh sought out Asad Khan, who was coordinating the presentations to the Emperor, and sheepishly explained what had happened.

The hall, which was open to the view over the Jumna River, had been expanded for the occasion by a broad, red velvet tent embroidered with gold. Huge silk carpets covered the marble floor. Jewels glittered throughout the assembly of high nobles, all dressed in their finest. Out of sight, an orchestra was playing softly. To Madho, it seemed that the Emperor had never looked more lordly on his throne. Aurangzeb's low cap-like turban, slanted toward the back of his head, was laden with jewels and wrapped with strands of pearls. With a long nose and pointed beard, his thin face and slanting eyes gave an impression of craftiness even during this birthday *durbar*.

All over the hall heads turned to see who dared to arrive late at such an important occasion. Court rules required that everyone in attendance arrive prior to the Emperor and await his entry. Ram Singh was whispering instructions to Shivaji. The Maratha King's bearing was as erect as ever, but his eyes appeared dazed. A king in his own right, who had never before bowed to another ruler, Shivaji must not only submit to his conqueror, he must also follow rules of etiquette he had barely heard of.

Madho watched as Asad Khan approached the Emperor and whispered in his ear. Aurangzeb's eyes narrowed, and he gave a nod. Asad Khan returned and beckoned Shivaji forward.

Shivaji managed to do the three *taslims* in their proper positions before finally standing before Aurangzeb. The Emperor's expression was unreadable as he received Shivaji's salutation. From the failure to show a more enthusiastic welcome, Madho knew Aurangzeb was furious over Shivaji missing the earlier grand audience, as well as now interrupting the planned order of the proceedings.

Aurangzeb said nothing as Shivaji's gifts of a thousand gold *mohurs* and two thousand rupees as *nazar* were placed before him. Asad Khan next presented Shivaji's young son, Shambhuji, who offered five hundred gold *mohurs* and two thousand rupees as *nazar*.

To Madho, the Maratha King's face appeared both puzzled and angry over the Emperor's lack of warmth as he was led back by Asad Khan to a place in the third row of standing nobles. The other ceremonies of the *durbar* resumed. Shivaji must be outraged, thought Madho, at not being shown more honor and given a place of prominence.

The day's heat was at its peak, and the servants waving fans around the perimeter of the hall made little noticeable difference. Sweat poured off the attending notables, all wearing their heavy robes and turbans and jewels. As the next order of procedure, officials distributed *paan* to all nobles and princes present.

When Shivaji had placed the wad of *paan* in his mouth, he turned to Ram Singh and Madho, who were immediately behind him in the row of commanders of 2,500 and below. The King whispered, "Who are these men I'm with?"

"All are commanders of five thousand," Ram murmured.

"What!" Shivaji exclaimed. "My nine year old son was created a commander of five thousand, and my general Netaji, too! How can I have the same status?" Although Shivaji's whispering was loud enough for those nearby to overhear, Madho thought it likely they didn't understand the Marathi.

"Later, please, Your Majesty!" whispered Ram Singh. "It will take time to explain."

But Shivaji then asked, "And who are these men in front of me?"

Ram Singh whispered, "Directly in front of you is Maharaja Jaswant Singh of Jodhpur."

Shivaji's pent-up frustration at the accumulated insults now exploded, in a voice loud enough to be heard throughout the hall: "Jaswant Singh? My soldiers have seen his back as he ran from us! Why am I to stand behind him? What's the meaning of this?"

All over the room, startled eyes cautiously turned to see who was responsible for this unprecedented breach of etiquette. At least he spoke in Marathi, thought Madho, who stood stiffly with a dignified air, so it would be clear he did not share any blame.

The assembled nobles returned their attention to the Emperor, and Madho wondered to what extent the *Padshah* would show displeasure at such an insult to his dignity. Aurangzeb's face was flushed, but he was obviously pretending to ignore the distraction.

As the next order of business at the *durbar*, the Emperor presented a *khilat*, a robe of honor, to each of the premier nobles: the Mughal princes, the Grand Wazir Ja'far Khan, Maharaja Jaswant Singh.

Madho knew it had been planned for Shivaji to be honored earlier, as part of the even grander ceremony in the larger hall. But when Shivaji hadn't appeared, this item of the business was rescheduled for the end of the day so as not to upset the order of the other events.

Therefore, when the robes had been presented, Shivaji had as yet received nothing. The Maratha King turned and muttered to Ram Singh and Madho, "At home I reign at my own *durbar*! What nonsense is this, to place me here in the mere third row of another ruler's audience?"

Ram Singh appeared frozen, unable to think of a reply, so Madho whispered, "The *Padshah* wishes it to be in dramatic contrast with the great favor he'll show you when he honors you later." It probably wasn't a convincing explanation, thought Madho, but it was the best he could think of on short notice.

He saw that Aurangzeb was glaring at Shivaji. The Emperor tilted his head and commented to an aide, who came and summoned Ram Singh forward. Madho watched as the Emperor and Ram conversed in low tones.

Ram Singh returned, sweat streaming from his face, as he whispered to Shivaji, "The Emperor wants to know what ails you."

Shivaji said, his eyes flashing, "You all know what sort of King I am. Yet you've made me stand here so long with these lesser nobles! I cast off the Emperor's *mansab*."

He turned his back to the throne and began to stride toward the edge of the gathering. Ram Singh tried to grab the King's arm to discourage him, but Shivaji wrenched free and stalked to the side of the hall. He stood there for a moment, and then he sat down, facing the river, behind one of the ornate, double pillars of white marble.

Ram Singh and Madho followed at a decorous pace, well aware that everyone was watching them while pretending not to. "The Emperor doesn't mean to insult you," Ram whispered urgently. "I apologize for not telling you earlier—he means to honor you specially by yourself later, not with these, uh, lesser nobles. Meanwhile, you should stand. No one is supposed to sit in his presence."

Shivaji shook his head, as if not listening. "I know I'm fated to die after this," he said. "Cut off my head *now* if you like. But I refuse to ever go into that King's presence again."

Ram Singh's eye met Madho's. Madho shrugged, no longer able to think of a way to help.

Ram Singh, fear in his eyes, rivers of sweat on his forehead, hastened to speak to Aurangzeb.

Madho saw that the Emperor's face was livid at the frequent interruptions of the decorum. He appeared to consider for a moment, then gave instructions.

Three nobles came to Shivaji's side with a *khilat*, a robe of honor.

"No!" said Shivaji. "I refuse to wear that man's robe after he insulted me."

"But you must!" whispered Ram Singh, desperation in his voice. "No one refuses such an honor."

Shivaji's eyes blazed. "*I* refuse."

Madho said, "Please, Your Majesty, reconsider. The *Padshah* will be gravely insulted. He'll never forgive you if you turn down his robe in front of everyone."

The determination that had enabled Shivaji to rise from a lowly landowner to conqueror of a kingdom now showed; his voice, though quiet, was like the steel of his sword: "He should have considered that before he tried to humiliate me."

Ram Singh's eyes were pleading with Madho to come up with some way to salvage the situation.

Madho gave a slight shake of his head. He whispered to Ram, "It's hopeless now. The best I can think of is to tell the Emperor that the King has been taken ill in the heat."

Ram Singh, dripping with perspiration, hurried to the Emperor with the explanation, in a voice loud enough for those in the front ranks to hear.

"Then take him to his house, so he can rest," Aurangzeb ordered, eyes cold, voice dripping with sarcasm. Again, it was a departure from court etiquette: no one was supposed to leave until the Emperor himself had gone.

Ram Singh returned, appearing unnerved by the debacle, no doubt worried that the Emperor would punish him.

Afterwards, as they were leaving the Red Fort, Madho described the events to Gopal. He glanced around to ensure no one was listening, and added in a quiet voice, "I find I have a certain sympathy for Shivaji. A valiant warrior king should be treated as an honored guest, not subjected to Ram Singh's misjudgments and an insulting place in the audience hall."

"If the Emperor's so angry at him now," said Gopal, "he's unlikely to treat him better in the future."

"On the other hand," said Madho, looking away, "when I bring about his end, the Emperor will be even more satisfied."

"And," said Gopal with a tight smile, "your rewards should be all the greater."

4

The Emperor had arranged a fine mansion for Shivaji's use while in Agra, near Kumar Ram Singh's home, with an attached tent for the hot weather and space for an encampment for the king's troops and entourage. Shivaji was adamant in his refusal to return to the Emperor's presence. However, in response to Ram Singh's urging, he at last reluctantly agreed to allow his son Shambhuji to attend court. Ram Singh informed Aurangzeb that Shivaji was indisposed with a fever. The Emperor therefore presented Shambhuji with the robe of honor that had been intended for the boy's father.

Early the next evening, when the day's heat was lessening, Madho and his entourage entered the encampment in the gardens of Ram Singh's house, where he encountered the Amber prince just arriving. As Ram Singh dismounted from his horse, Madho saw that his eyes were red and set in dark hollows. Ram Singh asked, "Have you heard how some of the nobles are trying to convince the *Padshah* to punish Shivaji?"

"I did hear rumors to that effect," replied Madho. "It worries me."

Ram Singh was perspiring heavily, as was Madho, and a male attendant hurried to wave long handled fans over them. Ram Singh said, "They're trying to convince the Emperor that Shivaji's not even officially a king, that he's merely a large landholder who happens to be an unusually successful bandit. They're apparently saying if Shivaji's insolence is allowed to go unpunished, every petty landlord will feel free to insult the Emperor's person at will!"

Madho shook his head. "This is even more vicious talk than one expects against the Emperor's worst enemies."

Ram Singh's hand tightly gripped the hilt of his sword. "Well, I'm guarding Shivaji with more of my own men. I don't want to take a chance on any assassins getting close."

Madho nodded vigorously in agreement. "That does seem wise under the circumstances." Actually, he was not pleased, as the safeguards would make his own task more difficult. He added, "I thought I would pay a visit to Shivaji today, in a gesture of friendship."

Ram Singh peered at Madho as if unsure of his motive.

Madho said, "The King must be shown that not everyone here is against him."

"Yes, well, I may join you there soon, also."

They parted, and Madho and Gopal remounted their horses. "We need to begin working to gain the King's confidence," whispered Madho to Gopal, who nodded.

At the entrance to Shivaji's gardens, they were recognized by the Maratha King's sentries, and the captain escorted them to the King's tent. Shivaji sat with two male attendants fanning him. Also present were his brother Hiroji Farzand, who resembled Shivaji in looks, his court poet Parmanand, and several of his officers. The King appeared to have recovered his composure. Although rigid in his demeanor, he said with a smile, in his resonant voice, "Welcome, Prince Madho Singhji! Consider my home as if it were your own. Please sit here by me."

Madho smiled, gratified at the honor bestowed him. He presented his gifts, a finely crafted sword from Mangarh, and a painting by one of his artists of the eight-armed Goddess Bhavani, seated cross-legged and wearing a conical headdress. Because of Madho's size, attendants brought an extra cushion and bolster. Gopal sat on floor pillows nearby. Shivaji gestured to attendants, who moved close and began fanning Madho.

After Madho and Shivaji went through the customary exchange of greetings, the King said, his eyes appraising Madho, "I'm pleased to find someone else here who speaks Marathi so well. It helps me feel less sad at being so far away from my homelands."

"I'm flattered at your praise of my poor grasp of your language, Maharaja," Madho replied. "I had time to learn only a little in my brief stay in your land."

Shivaji grinned slyly. "But I understand you had time to kill many of my men at Surat."

Madho bowed his head as if contrite. "Not so many, Your Majesty. I sincerely hope you will not hold it against me. I would now like to make amends "

"Of course I don't hold it against you," Shivaji said. He smiled charmingly. But his eyes seemed guarded as he continued, "I admire you for being so bold and clever. You outwitted me."

Madho smiled back. "You came quite close to catching me, Your Majesty. I was hiding under a river landing at night when you and your men searched that very spot. Even if you didn't discover us, I was worried you'd take our boat."

Shivaji turned his head away and laughed. Looking back to Madho, he said, "You gave many of my men a scare. They were afraid of the devils who lurked in the dark to jump upon them and kill them by surprise. Even after you apparently somehow left the city, they still expected you to reappear."

Madho again smiled, trying to appear humble, but quite pleased at the praise. He waved his hand in modest dismissal. "My exploit was minor compared to so many of your own. I was in Poona when you attacked Shaista Khan, so I have first hand knowledge of your own daring."

Servants brought in *sharbat* and trays of melons and sweetmeats. "*Kajoo barfi!*" Madho exclaimed at seeing the sweet he'd grown so fond of in the

Deccan. Shivaji smiled at seeing his guest's delight.

They all attacked the refreshments, Madho and Gopal with enthusiasm, Shivaji with more restraint. The Maratha ruler said, "I once thought myself clever. But now I'm not so sure. I should never have allowed myself to be convinced to come to Agra. I think the Emperor never intended to make me viceroy. He would have promised anything to get me into his clutches. What's to become of me now?"

Madho caught himself again feeling sympathetic to the King and his plight, and he hurriedly suppressed the thoughts. He must remain detached and carefully observe Shivaji's daily routines, so he could devise a good way to bring about the King's end, preferably without implicating himself.

An attendant was fanning the tray of sweetmeats in a vain attempt to keep the flies away. Madho himself swatted a couple of times at the insects, annoyed that they would compete with him for the food. He tried to think of an appropriate reply to the King, but he was saved from the need to answer by the appearance of Ram Singh.

The Rajput prince, still sweating in the evening heat, was flushed with anger. After exchanging greetings with Shivaji, he waved a paper in his hand and spoke to Madho in Rajasthani: "What is the Emperor doing? He's ordered me to transfer Shivaji to Rad Andaz Khan's house! Do you know anything of this?"

"Nothing whatever!" responded Madho truthfully. Rad Andaz Khan, the officer in charge of Agra Fort and its dungeons, was notorious for carrying out treacherous dealings, sometimes on the Emperor's behalf. Did the transfer meant he himself was no longer trusted to arrange Shivaji's death?

"This is too much," Ram Singh muttered. "It's obvious the Emperor means to dispose of our guest. Well, he'll have to kill me first! Shivaji came here under my father's pledge of safety." He turned to the Maratha King, apologized for speaking in a language the latter might not understand, and said, "You must be very careful now, Maharaja. I think the Emperor feels offended, and I sincerely hope I'm wrong when I say that he may try to have you killed."

Shivaji raised his eyebrows. His tone was calm, but he said, "I trusted your father's word that no harm would come to me. What can I do?"

Ram Singh's eyes darted about in distress. He said, "I'll keep my most trusted guards here to protect you. But please excuse me a moment, Your Majesty, while I discuss this with Madho Singhji." He looked suspiciously at Madho and said to him in Rajasthani, "You're helping host Shivaji at the Emperor's orders. What do you suggest?"

Madho shoved another *kajoo barfi* into his mouth to give himself a moment to think. After swallowing it only half chewed, he calmly advised, "Tell the Emperor how concerned you are. Maybe if you give a security bond for Shivaji's conduct, Aurangzeb will let him stay here in your custody."

Ram Singh stared at Madho, obviously uncertain as to whether or not to trust the advice. But both knew it was essential to keep Shivaji away from Rad Andaz Khan. And time was short.

Ram at last nodded. He said to Shivaji, "Please excuse me, Your Majesty. I must go plead with the Emperor before he retires for the night. And do not worry yourself. My father and I have both pledged our sacred honor and our lives that you will be safe." He backed away, turned, and immediately left for the Red Fort.

Madho reluctantly gave up the refreshment trays. He took his leave from the Maratha King, who cordially invited him to visit again soon.

Once out of hearing, Madho whispered to Gopal, "It would be disastrous if Shivaji's transferred to Rad Andaz Khan's control! I probably couldn't get near Shivaji then, and I couldn't take credit when he meets his end. We have to go to the Red Fort, too, so I can find out what's happening."

They mounted their horses and rode with their Rajput escort swiftly through the congested city. A haze of smoke from cooking fires hung in the evening air, and the odors of the food being prepared made Madho ravenous. But he would have to attend to his business before he could eat.

Once inside the huge fortress, Madho left Gopal and went to a section of the palace housing the office of Falud Khan, commandant of police. He approached one of the Khan's assistants, Mirza Muazzam, almost as rotund as himself, who acted as the contact for many individuals carrying out private instructions under the Emperor's authority.

The two stepped onto a garden terrace, where they could not be overheard. "I must know what is going on," Madho whispered. "Has it been decided that Rad Andaz Khan is to undertake the task originally given me?"

"Oh, no. Not at all," said Mirza Muazzam, his raspy voice hushed. "The Emperor merely wants to make doubly certain that his guest's life is short. It makes no difference to him which of his agents accomplishes that, so long as it is in fact done."

"I see. And the rewards will be the same as we discussed?"

"Of course." The official examined him closely. "You are still willing to do what's required?"

"How can you question it?"

Mirza Muazzam shrugged and turned to look out over the river. "It's not unheard of to become fond of one's intended victim and develop reservations. I merely wanted to make sure."

"I don't allow personal feelings to interfere with my carrying out the Emperor's wishes."

The man's eyes narrowed, and he glanced about. "Remember—although the *Padshah* approves in principle, he knows nothing of the details. It cannot become known that he harmed an important guest to whom he was providing hospitality."

"I understand, naturally." Madho nodded and left.

He returned to where Gopal waited. "I think we're still players in the game," he said quietly. "There's some risk I could later be targeted to take the blame if the accusations against the Emperor become too loud. But the reward they've promised me is big enough I'll take that chance."

Gopal frowned. "All this intrigue makes me uneasy."

Madho laughed lightly. "Me, too. But I won't advance quickly if I don't take chances."

They returned to his own residence, the mansion built by his father for the use of the Mangarh royal family whenever they were in Agra. The small palace was situated in the prime residential area of Agra, overlooking the river between the Red Fort and the Taj Mahal, whose domes Madho could see from his balcony.

There, as the sun set, they dug into the huge meal prepared by Madho's cooks.

Afterwards, Madho went to the outbuilding to see how the work of his atelier was progressing. The six artists, whom he had directed to paint illustrations from the childhood of Lord Krishna as a change from depicting Madho's own adventures, had stopped work for the day. But Nand was still there, organizing his brushes and paints, and in the light of the oil lamp he displayed his work. Madho had always loved the scene where the child God stole the milkmaids' clothes while they were bathing in the river. He looked approvingly on Nand's rendering. "Well done," he said, nodding. "You've managed to give the maids all individual faces."

The next morning, Madho returned to Kumar Ram Singh's camp to await word from the prince on Aurangzeb's response. By now Ram Singh's servants knew enough to provide Madho with plentiful refreshments, so he ate continually as he waited. Anxiety always made him even hungrier than normal.

In an hour or so the Amber prince returned. "Ah," Ram Singh said, seeing Madho surrounded by half-empty *thalis.* "I'm always glad when guests enjoy my hospitality to the utmost."

"I've been treated well in your camp, as usual," Madho responded. "But what is the *Padshah's* response?"

Ram Singh gave a satisfied nod. "The Emperor's agreed to my posting a bond to ensure Shivaji will stay in my custody."

"Excellent," Madho said. "I worried the entire night." For once, he spoke the truth, although his reason for concern was not at all identical to Ram Singh's. Later, he watched with quiet satisfaction as Shivaji came to Kumar Ram Singh's house. There, the King and the prince worshiped before an image of Lord Shiva. The Maratha chief poured water over the idol and gave his solemn oath for his good conduct.

That evening, Madho was taking his weekly turn in attendance on the Emperor when Ram Singh appeared in the small audience hall with the signed security bond. He handed it to Amin Khan, who in turn presented it to the Emperor.

Aurangzeb gazed at the document for several seconds. He looked at Ram Singh and said abruptly, "Now that you have agreed to Shivaji's custody, I have decided to send you to a new post in Kabul. You may take the Maratha Raja with you. You should determine an auspicious day for starting."

Stunned, Madho stopped breathing. He watched Ram Singh's face lose color. The prince stared at the Emperor. "Kabul, Your Majesty?"

"Yes, Kabul. We have need of your talents there."

Ram Singh stood for several seconds, obviously in shock. It was the hottest season of the year, not at all good for an unexpected and long journey to Afghanistan. He at last managed to mumble, "As Your Majesty commands."

This is terrible! thought Madho, alarmed at the thought of Shivaji being taken beyond his reach. It would also be much easier for other agents of the Emperor to assassinate Shivaji away from the protection of the encampment at Agra.

Ram Singh started to back away. Then, he stopped and said, "May it please Your Majesty, no time is more auspicious than this to leave. I most respectfully ask that you give me permission to start immediately."

Madho realized Ram Singh's request to leave so quickly must be aimed at getting Shivaji safely out of Agra as fast as possible, before more specific plans could be laid for the killing.

He was greatly relieved when the Emperor replied, "You will need time to assemble the proper equipment and baggage, and to muster your Rajputs for the march. So select an auspicious hour six or seven days from now and start then."

As he left that hall, Ram Singh's eyes met Madho's. Madho could see that the Amber prince was clearly unhappy, but the Emperor's directions must be obeyed.

The next day, Madho was again visiting Shivaji, when Ram Singh stormed into the tent and greeted the King. Then, he said, "I must speak to Madho Singhji at once, Your Majesty."

Madho went out into the garden with him. Ram Singh said, "Why doesn't the Emperor come right out and say he means to murder Shivaji? I just received word Rad Andaz Khan is to go to Afghanistan also, to lead the vanguard of the army. That treacherous snake will strike as soon as we're away from Agra!"

Madho tried not to show the extent of his own dismay at the added change in events. He said smoothly, "That would anger your father and all the others who want Shivaji kept safe. But it does make one wonder about our Emperor's motives."

"I don't wonder at all. It's obvious Shivaji's intended to die. It will be made to look like he died by an accident on the trip. Or by being shot by rebels in Kabul."

"Maybe it won't be as bad as that," said Madho, rubbing his chin thoughtfully. "You might actually be better able to protect him away from Agra. Just keep him surrounded by your own men, so Rad Andaz Khan can't get at him."

Ram Singh was shaking his head, his face livid. "That devious murderer will find a way. I know he will."

Madho spent a sleepless night trying to devise a satisfactory plan. Then, in the morning, he was further dismayed when word came to him from Mirza Muazzam at the palace to hold off on any action. He hurried to the Red Fort to visit the official. "Why have you asked me to delay?"

The chubby official's face was grim. "It seems Shivaji's plight is generating considerable sympathy. More and more nobles are becoming concerned about the apparent open breach of the Emperor's agreements with him. His Majesty has decided to send a dispatch to Maharaja Jai Singh in the Deccan, inquiring as to exactly what promises were made to Shivaji."

Madho stared at him, trying to discern if the man was holding anything back. "What do you suggest I do, meanwhile?"

The official shrugged, and his eyes shifted away. "Continue to try to gain Shivaji's confidence. Then you'll be well placed when we get instructions to continue."

Madho's stomach was churning as he left. He sensed a possible change in the winds of the intrigue. He was being used as a pawn by the parties who were plotting Shivaji's demise, and he had accepted that role in exchange for the rich reward it would bring.

But what if the plotters now intended not to reward him for doing their work, but rather to use him as a scapegoat?

He had fully understood the Emperor and his associates would deny all knowledge of any plot against Shivaji. However, now that a constituency was developing in support of the Maratha King, the plotters might go even farther. They might openly attach all the blame to Madho and bring him to trial for Shivaji's death.

Madho's agile mind searched desperately for a way out of the dilemma he had uncharacteristically allowed himself to be caught in.

Suddenly, it had become important to him to keep Shivaji alive, rather than dead.

When he told Gopal, he enjoyed the expression on his friend's face. "What?" exclaimed Gopal. "After all the planning, you've changed your mind?"

"Only as to allowing Shivaji to live. We may still profit, you see."

"How could we do that?"

"If I could somehow help Shivaji escape, he might be grateful enough to reward me. He could give me the gold handled palanquin, or even jewels or elephants. The escape would have to be done secretly, and as a fugitive he surely could take very little along."

"Ah, I see," said Gopal, nodding with a grin. "I might have known you'd think of a way to profit from his life, just as from his death."

Madho decided the first step was to gain Shivaji's acceptance of him as a sympathetic ally. So he began calling on Shivaji regularly. The Maratha seemed pleased to have Madho as a visitor to help ease the boredom of his house arrest, and their conversations tended to stretch on for hours. Always Ram Singh or one of his officers was present also. From the manner in which they watched him so closely and listened to every word of his conversations with Shivaji, Madho strongly suspected that they did not trust him alone with the King.

Late one hot day when Madho arrived for a visit, he was surprised to see Shivaji on horseback, riding swiftly around the perimeter of the garden. Several of his men, also on horses, trailed behind him. The King reined to a halt and sat in the saddle, gazing out over the walls when Madho approached him on foot. Shivaji saw Madho, and an odd expression came over his face.

"Welcome, Madho Singhji," he said. Madho was disconcerted by the clear impression that Shivaji was contemplating jumping the low wall with his horse and leaving Agra.

For the first time since the day of the audience with Aurangzeb, Shivaji appeared to have lost control of his composure. The King gestured toward the wall and said angrily, "You do not realize how fortunate you are to be able to come and go freely."

Madho tried to appear calm as he said, "Your Majesty, it's disgraceful how the Emperor's treating you. I would gladly go with you on a ride outside the city if it were allowed."

Shivaji again looked over the wall, his eyes cold. "I would give almost anything to be galloping through my own homelands." He bent and stroked the neck of his horse.

Madho tried desperately to think of arguments that might help deter the Maratha from trying to flee so quickly. Shivaji was eyeing him with a curious expression. Then the King's face softened some. He said, "Don't worry. I won't escape, at least not yet. I've given my word to Ram Singhji, and I wouldn't want him to lose the bond he's pledged."

Madho allowed himself to relax, just a little, although he wasn't sure whether or not to believe Shivaji. Madho knew if he himself were the one confined, he would have fled days ago, oaths or bonds notwithstanding. He assumed an expression of admiration as he gazed at the King and said, "That's most honorable of you, Your Majesty, especially considering that you are in your predicament precisely because the Emperor broke his word to you."

"I don't betray those who are my true friends," said Shivaji, looking at him with a smile, "just as I know they will not betray me."

Now what does he mean by that? Madho wondered as he examined the King's face. Does he suspect that I am not a true friend? Or am I reading too much into his words?

Shivaji had been watching him. The King's smile broadened. "Madho Singhji, the pleasure of your company is so great that it almost makes up for my being confined."

Madho, disconcerted, managed to smile in return and to reply, "The pleasure is truly all mine, Your Majesty."

He was surprised to realize that he meant it. He enjoyed Shivaji's company, and the King had indeed been treated unfairly. The Maratha, after all, was a hero to *lakhs* of people, and he had come as a guest. For the Emperor to deal with him so inhospitably was inexcusable.

But, Madho reminded himself, he must be careful not to become so sympathetic to Shivaji as to interfere with profiting from the King's situation. And above all, he must be careful to not arouse the suspicions of the Emperor or his officials by appearing to support Shivaji.

With Madho and Ram Singh's encouragement, Shivaji began paying large sums of money to various high officials in an attempt to be released. To Madho's great relief, the Maratha succeeded in getting the order to go to Afghanistan withdrawn.

Shivaji then offered Aurangzeb two *crores* of rupees as additional tribute, and promised to be a faithful ally, if the Emperor would allow him to return home. Aurangzeb, however, directed his commandant of police to station a cordon of soldiers around the house and to prevent Shivaji from leaving even for the briefest outing.

Madho was surprised on his visit that day to see, outside the ring of guards, that the Emperor's officers had placed artillery aimed at the gates of Shivaji's garden. Naturally, the additional measures made it more difficult for Madho to pry the Maratha free. Madho spent considerable time thinking about the matter and discussing possibilities with Gopal. The two were not yet able to devise a suitable plan, so in the meantime, Madho continued to visit the King. Always eager to learn from someone he considered clever, Madho encouraged Shivaji to talk of his exploits.

One of the most famous of Shivaji's coups was his assassination of Afzal Khan, the general of the army of Bijapur, Shivaji's strongest rival kingdom in the Deccan. Madho was eager to hear first hand how this was brought about, so on a day when he was alone with the King except for the servants and one of Ram Singh's officers, he brought the conversation around to the incident.

"Is it true," he asked, his words slightly muffled as he sucked on a mango, "that Afzal Khan actually intended to kill you, but you outsmarted him?"

Shivaji smiled and waved a hand in modest dismissal. "It was a small matter. I was at war with Bijapur, you know. Afzal Khan was their general. His army far outnumbered mine. It was imperative that I come up with a strategy that would not allow him to use his superior numbers."

"How did you do it?" Madho asked. "Please tell me, Your Majesty. I've heard only rumors. I'd like to hear first hand."

Shivaji smiled. "Very well." He appeared thoughtful for a moment. Then he said, "You must first understand about Afzal Khan. He was noted for his treachery. He had even murdered a raja who was invited to his tent to surrender under a promise of safety. So I knew he would betray me at the first opportunity. And he had destroyed and looted many of our temples and ruined our idols, so we did not trust him to rule our lands under any circumstances. Nevertheless, I felt the need to have a meeting with him in person, as I knew we could not defeat his armies in battle on the plains."

Madho gave a nod and licked mango juice from his fingers.

"You have stopped eating," said Shivaji with a smile. "Please continue."

Madho reached for another of the *kajoo barfis* that the Maratha always made sure were available on Madho's visits. "As I was saying," Shivaji resumed, "we were to meet for a conference. In spite of his assurances, I heard through spies that he was planning to kill me when we met. I was worried. But the Goddess Bhavani appeared to me in a dream the night before and told me she would protect me.

"So I decided to turn his trap for me into a trap for *him*. It was necessary to lull his suspicions as much as possible. I sent him a message telling him that out of all of my enemies, I feared and admired only him. I told him I would surrender my forts to him if he asked for them."

Madho was so fascinated by the account that he was barely aware of reaching for another mango from the bowl and massaging it to loosen the flesh within. Shivaji was saying, "I prepared a pavilion for our meeting. Along the way to it I hid some of my soldiers in ambush. Under my clothing I wore a coat of chain armor, and under my turban I wore a steel cap. Since he thought I was surrendering to him, it was not proper for me to wear a sword. Instead, I concealed steel tiger's claws in my left hand and a scorpion dagger up my right sleeve."

Madho said, "Very clever, Your Majesty!" He sliced the tip from the mango and began sucking the pulp from the hole he'd made.

Shivaji gave a shrug. "I can tell you, nevertheless I was quite worried. He wore a sword, and in height I came only up to his shoulder. He had a champion swordsman accompanying him. I objected to the swordsman's presence, so the man left the tent. Then, just as Afzal Khan and I embraced, the Khan took me by surprise. He suddenly tightened his hold on me, choking me with his arm around my neck, and he drew his dagger and stabbed me in my side." Shivaji paused, peered at Madho and said, "Please let me know if I am boring you."

Madho's eyes were wide, enthralled by the tale as he paused in sucking his mango. "Oh, far from it, Your Majesty. I'm spellbound!"

Shivaji smiled again and continued, "My chain armor resisted his dagger. I reached around him and tore his bowels open with my claws. With my other hand I thrust the dagger into his side. I wrenched myself free from his grasp and jumped from the platform. He called to his men. They came running. His swordsman struck at me, cutting through my turban so hard he dented my steel cap. Fortunately my own men came to my rescue. They killed the Khan and his men.

"Then, I fired a cannon as a signal to my army. They attacked the enemy camp from all sides and defeated them. We took 65 elephants, 4,000 horses, 1,200 camels, 10 *lakhs* of rupees in jewelry and cash."

Madho said in admiration, thinking of the loot in particular, "A tremendous victory, Your Majesty!" He leaned back, burped in appreciation of the mangos, and again licked his fingers.

Shivaji gave a nod of acknowledgment. "It inspired my people as nothing else before. The bards began to sing my praises. With the help of Goddess Bhavani and the powers she gave my sword, we went on to other conquests, enlarging our territory step by step—until Aurangzeb sent his armies to stop me. And now it appears I am no longer so clever and resourceful. I have allowed the Emperor to get the better of me. But come, my friend, you have stopped eating. Have some of these dates. I'm told they've come all the way from Egypt." He beckoned to a servant: "More refreshment for our honored guest!"

At the mention of Shivaji's magical Bhavani Sword, Madho wondered if Shivaji had brought the weapon with him to Agra. On the one hand, it seemed likely that Shivaji would want the sword available so he could use it regularly in worshiping the Goddess. On the other hand, if Shivaji had been concerned for his safety, he might not want to take a chance on the sword being captured by Aurangzeb's men.

Madho could not resist. He drew a breath and boldly asked, "Your Majesty, I've heard so much about your famous Bhavani Sword. I wonder if I might have the honor of seeing it with my own eyes?"

Shivaji gave his charming smile. "Of course, I'd be pleased to show it to you, my good friend. However, the sword has been purified for worship today and I can not disturb the Goddess at this time. But I'll be glad to have you see the sword on another day."

Madho was mildly disappointed, but at least the sword was with Shivaji here in Agra. He looked forward to seeing it tomorrow, or at least some time in the near future.

However, the next day Shivaji did not mention viewing the sword. Nor the next. Madho would surreptitiously eye the sword Shivaji was wearing at the moment, or the one that was lying on the cushion beside the King whenever he was at leisure. Madho would wonder: is that the one? Like all rulers, Shivaji had a large collection of weapons, and Madho seldom saw him with the same sword twice.

He wondered if Shivaji might keep the sword in the ruler's private *puja* area at all times for worship. He thought of asking to join the King at worship, but he decided that might be too obvious.

Madho's visits to Shivaji continued. They traded tales, Shivaji telling of his exploits, and Madho of those of his Mangarh ancestors: Raja Man Singh fighting on behalf of Prithviraj Chauhan, Raja Hanuman's successful escape from the siege of Chittorgarh. Madho, of course, especially admired the latter due to the cleverness of the ruse to deceive Akbar's men.

Madho noticed as the days and weeks passed that Shivaji's face was growing more lined; his shoulders frequently sagged. Clearly, even though he tried to maintain a facade of calm acceptance the active fighter and ruler did not take well to being under house arrest.

"Please tell me," Shivaji said to Madho one day when he and Gopal were present, but Ram Singh was not. "I consider you my good friend. How can you and Kumar Ram Singhji continue to serve the Emperor?" His face hardened. "I myself am accepting of all faiths. Some of my highest officers are Muslim. I would never destroy one of their mosques. But Aurangzeb is intolerant of anyone who is not of his own faith. He destroys our temples, levies taxes on non-Muslims. He breaks his word to his allies such as myself. Don't you yearn to be able to do as you wish in your own kingdoms, free from his oppression?"

Madho, taken aback, was at first uncertain how to respond. He stared at the carpet as he thought. The important issues to *him* were ample opportunities to acquire both treasure and artists. So long as those opportunities existed, what did it matter who ruled, or whether he was Muslim or Hindu? But at last he looked up at Shivaji and replied, "Your Majesty, we pledged our loyalty to the Emperor. We must of course be true to our salt. Just as you must surely expect loyalty from your own men, whether or not they agree with your actions."

Shivaji examined him for a time. Then he looked away, smiled, and nodded. "Of course. I should not even have asked a question with so obvious an answer. And your Emperor is fortunate to have men of such trust serving him."

Madho and Gopal exchanged quick glances. Was Shivaji sincere, or was he secretly amused by them, discerning that in fact they cared about only whatever advanced their own interests?

Abruptly, Shivaji's fists clenched. "I must get free of here," he said, his voice cold. "That man who calls himself Emperor has no right to keep me."

Madho mumbled words of sympathy. He looked about. Neither Ram Singh nor his officers were present. It was as good an opportunity as Madho was likely to find. "I'm deeply concerned for your welfare," he told Shivaji. "I think you should indeed try harder to get away. Your life is in danger every second you are in Agra."

Shivaji was staring intently at him. "So I fear. But Ram Singhji has taken out that security bond on me." He spread his hands in the air. "What do I do about that? I think he's done his best to help me. If I escape, I would not want him to lose the property he's pledged—or to get into the Emperor's bad graces." The King looked away, frowning.

Madho himself was only mildly concerned about Ram Singh. He saw the Amber prince as seriously lacking in good sense after all the bungling on the day of Shivaji's arrival in Agra. But he had anticipated that Shivaji might be troubled over the matter, so he was prepared to advise, "Try to get the security bond withdrawn, Your Majesty. Then you are free to leave, with my help."

Shivaji's eyes darted back to him. "You've thought of a way?"

Madho said quietly, his eyes meeting the King's, "You must feign a serious illness, Maharaja. And send large gifts of sweetmeats to the Brahmins as offerings for their prayers for your recovery."

Madho went on to explain how the escape would be handled. He saw the interest grow in Shivaji's eyes. Eventually, the King nodded. "Yes. It might be possible."

Madho raised his eyebrows. "You have sufficient funds?"

Shivaji waved a hand, his gold armlet gleaming. "I have enough. Although my own funds ran short, Kumar Ram Singh has advanced me 66,000 rupees in cash. That should be more than sufficient."

Madho gave a nod and allowed himself a smile. "Excellent, Your Majesty."

Shivaji's eyes were intent on his own. "I would like to make a gift to you, as a mark of my friendship, and of my appreciation for your help. What of my possessions do you most admire?"

It was an unusual question; most rulers wanting to honor a man would decide on their own what to bestow. But, Madho thought, Marathas did tend to be more straightforward and plain spoken. Suddenly, though, he realized that Shivaji might have been warned not to trust him, and that the King must be wondering what Madho expected to gain. Madho acted surprised and replied, "Why, I'd like nothing from you but your good esteem, Your Majesty! I want to help because I so greatly admire you. And because you have been treated unfairly. And not the least because I am a Rajput, and I hate seeing a brother warrior caged like an animal." He swallowed, and added, "Also, Your Majesty, because despite your much greater rank and reputation, I have come to cherish you as a friend."

Shivaji smiled warmly at him. "I see. I've also come to treasure you as a friend and brother." He added after a moment, "Maybe you feel you profited enough from me at Surat. Nevertheless, I hope you would accept a gift from me, to help with your artistic patronage."

Madho made a gesture showing that idea of compensation was of no importance. "I'm overwhelmed at your generosity. But your good opinion of me is the highest gift I could ever want." He lowered his voice as he added, "We'll talk again soon, Your Majesty. It might be better if you mention my aid to no one else. Ram Singh can then rightly say he had no knowledge of any efforts to free you, and there will be less chance of one of the Emperor's spies getting word."

Shivaji nodded thoughtfully. "Agreed."

Two days later, Ram Singh called on Madho in the evening. Prem Chand led him to where Madho was relaxing on cushions in his atelier, eating as he watched his artists at work. "Have some mangos and *sharbat*," he offered his visitor. "And see what exquisite work is being done. An entire series on the life of Lord Krishna."

Ram Singh glanced quickly at the paintings that were under way. "Fine work," he said absently. He turned to Madho, and inclined his head to indicate they must speak privately.

Madho heaved himself to his feet and escorted his guest out to the small garden overlooking the river.

"Do you know that Shivaji asked me to cancel the security bond?" Ram Singh asked.

"He mentioned it to me. It might not be a bad idea. How can he escape, since his encampment was surrounded by the Emperor's own troops? The bond seems unnecessary."

"That was Shivaji's reasoning. But I gave the pledge to the Emperor."

"Then the Emperor can release you."

Ram Singh thought for a time, and gave a nod. "I suppose I shouldn't object, after all, it's my own funds that are at risk."

"Quite so."

"All right, since Shivaji seems insistent, I'll talk to the officials in the Red Fort, and tell them the pledge is no longer necessary. But I have my doubts they'll go along with it."

Madho gave a slight smile. "You might increase the size of your gifts to them." Ram Singh raised an eyebrow. "It's worth it to get your bond funds back," Madho pointed out.

Ram Singh nodded, turned, and left.

A few days later, Madho learned that the Emperor had terminated the security obligation.

5

By the end of June the monsoon had come, and whenever other visitors such as Ram Singh were present, it seemed to Madho that Shivaji gave the impression of desultory acceptance of his fate as a prisoner under house arrest.

On a day when the rain was pounding on the tent, Madho commented, "I see fewer servants and warriors at your encampment these days, Your Majesty."

Shivaji peered at him and nodded. "Yes, my men are longing for their homes. I've given permission for some of them to leave."

"They've indeed been away from home a long time."

The King said more quietly, "And if I am able to leave myself one day soon, I'll be less encumbered." He waved his arm to indicate the camp and the area in general, "I find I don't need so many men under these circumstances, anyway."

Madho set aside a half-eaten *kajoo barfi* and said, "I'm still eager to see the sword that the Goddess gives such power to, Your Majesty. Is it possible yet for me to have that honor?"

Shivaji was silent for a few moments, before smiling slightly, and saying, "My good friend, there is no one I would more rather have see it. But recently, Goddess Bhavani appeared to me in the middle of the night, and she told me I must keep the sword concealed. There are those around who would steal it if given an opportunity. So it's unfortunately not readily available to me at the moment, or I would gladly show it to you."

Madho kept his face composed. "I certainly agree, Your Majesty. One can't be too careful." Was Shivaji being truthful? Or did he worry that Madho himself might covet the sword enough to steal it?

"I'm so glad you understand, my good friend. It would wound me if you felt insulted in any way."

Madho took a deep breath. "Of course not, Your Majesty. I fully understand. And now, another matter. You're still considering the plan we talked of earlier?"

"Definitely."

"Then, although it saddens me, it might be best if I visit you less. Then the Emperor's spies will be less likely to suspect that I'm aiding you. And after you do escape, they won't think to blame me.

Shivaji was watching Madho's face. Finally he nodded, and said, "I will miss your visits. But I would truly be saddened if you, my good friend, were implicated in my escape."

Madho stared at Shivaji. He had the impression the Maratha genuinely *did* care about him. He was unused to letting such a consideration enter into his calculations, and he must take care not to let mutual feelings of fondness impair his ability to profit.

The next day, Madho encountered Ram Singh in the Red Fort. The Amber prince looked at him with a frown and said, "Shivaji seems to have taken ill with a fever. I offered to send my own *vaid* to care for him, but he refused. He said he prefers his own physician."

Madho took on a look of concern. "How unfortunate for the King. So many suffer every year when the dampness from the rains comes. Sometimes I fall ill myself."

Ram Singh nodded and looked away. "I usually avoid it, but many of my men suffer."

"No doubt it's even worse when one is far from the comforts of home. I hope the King recovers quickly."

Ram Singh returned his gaze to Madho. "Shivaji's feeling bad enough he even sent away his poet Parmanand. Gave him two elephants and a horse as a gift, and an escort of soldiers."

"Did he, now?" Madho abruptly felt an uneasiness in his gut. Hopefully, Shivaji wouldn't send too much wealth back with the returning men.

Ram Singh shrugged and added, "Shivaji seems to be hoping the Brahmins' prayers will cure him. He's started sending huge baskets of sweetmeats to holy men. So big it takes two bearers to carry the pole the baskets are hung from. The guards posted by the Emperor search them all well before they're allowed out, of course."

So the plan was underway. Did Ram Singh suspect anything? It was hard to tell. "Well," said Madho with a bland expression, "we'll hope the prayers that result will help Shivaji." He decided he'd better pay a visit and find out just what was occurring. He hoped Shivaji would be generous to him when the final escape came. The King could hardly expect to escape with the golden handled palanquin, or any of his other palanquins for that matter. Or his jewels, or elephants, or horses, or camels. Someone would take possession of them. And with the possible exception of Ram Singh, no one had done more to aid Shivaji than Madho.

When Madho visited Shivaji's quarters the following day, he was struck by how few men were about. Only a few servants were in evidence, and less than half as many of Shivaji's personal guards as before. Shivaji's half-brother Hiroji Farzand met him outside the entry to the house. "How is His Majesty's health today?" asked Madho.

Hiroji gave a knowing smile, indicating he was in on the secret. "Shivaji is taking rest. His fever is not so bad at the moment, but he feels weak."

Madho was struck by Hiroji's resemblance to his half-brother. Hiroji looked to be a few years younger than the King and was thinner, with sharper features. But their height was similar and so was the overall structure of their facial bones, and even their smiles.

They entered the house, and Hiroji led him to the curtained-off sleeping balcony, where Shivaji was lying on a cot. Near the King were his son Shambhuji and several servants.

Madho said, "I heard you are ill, Your Majesty. I came with a medication from my own *vaid* in the hope it may help."

Shivaji raised his head. "How kind of you, my good friend." His voice indeed sounded weak compared to before, and he again lowered his head to rest on the pillow.

Servants brought refreshments, and Madho snatched a *kajoo barfi*. He said, "I see that you've sent more of your men away, Your Majesty."

Shivaji said quietly, without raising his head again to look at Madho, "Yes, most miss their homes badly. As do I. But they can leave, while I can't."

Madho looked about, saw that the only persons in earshot were a couple of Shivaji's most trusted servants. He lowered his voice and said, "Hopefully that will soon change, Your Majesty."

He shoved a slice of melon into his mouth. When he'd finished it, he let a servant rinse his hands and added, again in a quiet voice, "I wanted to say, that if there's any way I can make matters easier for you, I'm eager to do so, Your Majesty. When the time comes for you to leave, you may find that you still have elephants or conveyances or whatever that it would be difficult to take. Rather than your simply abandoning them, I wanted to offer my services. I would be glad to quietly remove anything of that nature into safekeeping and hold it until you can retrieve it."

The King turned his head and looked at Madho with dull eyes. "How kind of you. I'm indeed fortunate to have found such a good friend in this alien land. I will definitely keep your offer in mind."

"And now, Your Majesty, I think it's best that I let you rest."

Shivaji nodded almost imperceptibly, and Madho left.

Another week passed. Madho visited again one evening and saw that, as the baskets of sweetmeats Shivaji sent out had now become routine, the Emperor's guards were more lax about searching them.

He began to hear rumors that Shivaji was so sick as to be near death. The time seemed right for the escape effort, and Madho began to wonder why Shivaji was taking so long to act.

Madho wavered over the best course of action for himself. He wanted Shivaji to escape, having grown in spite of himself to like and admire the bold ruler who was also such a clever bandit chief. Still, he wanted the King to reward him handsomely for his help.

To Madho's regret, however, the days passed and Shivaji made no mention of his remaining wealth. Madho decided to take a precaution. One evening while he and Gopal were seated in the veranda of Madho's house, he showed Gopal a document.

"Isn't that Shivaji's seal on it?" asked Gopal.

Madho smiled. "Yes. And this states that in exchange for a loan of funds to him a month ago, Shivaji is granting me all his property in Agra in the event of his death or disappearance."

Gopal's eyes widened. "I never knew you loaned him money."

"I didn't."

"Then why—" Gopal stopped, and he grinned. "This didn't come from Shivaji, did it?"

"Of course not. I had his seal duplicated. It's the only way I can think of that the Emperor's agents would let me keep anything."

Gopal's eyes shone in admiration. "So if you can't profit by the escape one way, you'll profit in another."

"Why not?" Madho gazed out over the river. "We need to be sure we know exactly when Shivaji escapes. Then we can go to his compound immediately afterwards with this." He turned back to Gopal. "Get Nathu Singh to station some of our men to watch Shivaji's house. He's to take charge of the watchers personally. Tell him to let me know any time anything unusual appears to happen."

When Madho could no longer stand the uncertainty, he went again to visit the Maratha King. As he and his entourage rode into the gate, he saw Nathu Singh and two other Rajputs ambling down the street. Hunched over against the light rain that was falling, they looked miserable, and Madho resolved to give them extra pay.

The Emperor's soldiers formed their usual cordon around the encampment. With the security bond canceled, Ram Singh no longer assigned his own officer to watch Shivaji, though he still posted a small contingent of guards to help protect Shivaji from possible assassins.

The rain pattered on the fabric canopy over the balcony. When Madho entered the sleeping area, Shivaji was lying on his bed, his eyes closed. A servant bathed his forehead with a wet cloth, as if the ruler were suffering from a fever. At Madho's greeting, Shivaji opened eyes that looked so dull as to be almost lifeless. He responded in a voice so weak that Madho wondered if the Maratha was in fact seriously ill.

To make it appear to any listeners that Madho himself did not suspect any deception, he expressed deep concern for Shivaji's welfare. Then he said, "I'll not stay long to avoid tiring you, Your Majesty. But I am wondering if you can conclude the matter we discussed earlier."

"Soon, my brother," Shivaji murmured, his eyes opening only momentarily.

"Be sure to send word when the moment comes," Madho urged, "so I can do whatever is needed to help."

"Of course," Shivaji mumbled, seemingly at great effort. "Hopefully in only a few days."

Madho let out an imperceptible sigh of relief. So at last events were coming to a conclusion.

The next day, rain drummed hard on the roof as Madho stood in his atelier peering over the shoulders of his artists at work. The oil lamps had been lit due to the gloom. Gopal suddenly appeared, drenched, and called Madho aside. "I thought you may want to know," he whispered. "Nathu says Shivaji's aides have told the guards the King's so ill that he's not to be disturbed for any reason."

Madho thought a moment, then nodded. "It's the next step in lulling suspicion. But I wonder why Shivaji's starting so early, if he's not going to try to leave for a few more days." What if the King were to advance the date of his departure and slip away, leaving Madho with no possibility of reward whatsoever? He looked at Gopal. "Today's sweetmeats will be sent out shortly. Come—let's go watch, just in case."

The rains had stopped by the time Madho and Gopal and their entourage arrived at the encampment. As they passed through the ring of soldiers posted by the Emperor, Madho saw Nathu and another Rajput standing a short distance down the street. Madho dismounted by the small group of Ram Singh's guards, and he casually chatted with them while he unobtrusively kept an eye on Shivaji's house.

When the usual evening gift of sweetmeats passed out, Madho watched closely as the bearers carried the half dozen large baskets toward the checkpoint established by the Emperor's guards. One of the soldiers perfunctorily checked the first basket, then waved the line of bearers past.

Madho turned and casually asked one of Ram Singh's guards, "Maharaja Shivaji is in his house as usual?"

"Of course. I saw him myself, after the midday meal."

Madho was thinking. After the midday meal. That was quite some time ago. He stared at the line of bearers.

The baskets were passing the outer cordon of soldiers. What if Shivaji were already in one of the containers?

Madho walked swiftly to the house. "I must look in on the Maharaja!" he told the guard at the door, who gave a salute and stepped aside.

Madho entered and approached the balcony. There, under a light gauze covering, was the short, slight figure of Shivaji, apparently sleeping soundly. Madho recognized the King's gold bracelet on an outstretched arm.

He let out a sigh of relief. So he was wrong; Shivaji had not tried to fool him after all, at least not today. But he wished the matter would conclude.

He and Gopal took leave of the guards, and, after reassuring himself that Nathu and the other Rajput were keeping watch, returned home.

All the next day, Shivaji remained in seclusion, apparently with a severe fever. Rain fell off and on, and Madho spent much of the day with his artists. That night, Nathu Singh suddenly appeared, dull eyed and shame faced. "Highness," he said, "Shivaji somehow escaped."

"What! You're sure?"

"Yes, Highness. And the Emperor's police have sealed the entire compound. I couldn't get through to ask exactly what happened, so I thought I'd better let you know right away."

"How could this have happened?" shouted Madho. He shook his head, clenching his teeth. "That Maratha's damned clever!"

Nathu pressed his lips tight and nodded.

"I'm glad he's free at last," Madho said, more calmly. "But he could have kept me informed! And he might have been more generous to those who helped him."

Nathu said nothing, but his wet clothes made him look even more miserable.

Madho frowned. "I need to somehow take custody of Shivaji's property, fast. They sealed the compound, you say?"

"Yes, Highness. Only the police can come and go."

Madho turned away and peered into the darkness, toward Shivaji's house. What to do? He and his men would likely be refused entry. He would almost certainly be suspected of helping Shivaji escape anyway, and going there at this time would heighten the suspicion.

Nathu was waiting, his clothing sopping from so many hours in the rain. Madho turned to him. "Go get yourself dry. And have the men and carts ready to move as soon as I send word."

Less than an hour later, he received a summons to report immediately to Falud Khan, the commandant of the Emperor's police, in the Red Fort. He knew exactly why he'd been sent for. When he arrived, outside the Khan's offices he recognized some of the guards who had been on duty. They sat about with morose expressions.

Ram Singh and a couple of his Rajputs were already in the Khan's office chamber. They stood with stiff postures and drawn expressions before the high noble and several other officials, including Mirza Muazzam. Ram Singh glanced quickly at Madho with a distraught look, then he turned away.

Falud Khan was a tall, austere-faced man, and many found him intimidating even aside from his power as the head of police. His eyes were cold as he asked Madho, "Highness, what do you know of Raja Shivaji in the past day?"

"I haven't seen anything of him today, your honor," said Madho. "I did visit the King yesterday to see about his health. He was sleeping, so I didn't speak with him or stay."

"You're sure he was there?"

The Khan's eyes bored into him. Madho's mouth was dry, and he swallowed. "I took a quick look into his sleeping area. He was on his cot."

"You're positive it was him?"

Madho hesitated a second. "I was sure at the time, your honor. He was under a thin cloth, but I saw the gold bracelet he always wears."

"It appears he has escaped. What do you know of that?"

Madho was ready with his look of astonishment. "Why, nothing, your honor! How could he have gotten past the guards?"

The Khan ignored Madho's question. "Do you know what direction he's headed?"

"Certainly not! I assume he'd head back to his home, but he's hardly foolish enough to take a direct route."

"Your men have been seen watching Shivaji's compound for days. I want to know the reason."

Madho swallowed. "Only to keep me informed as to the state of his health, your honor, and as to what his aides were doing. I did loan His Majesty funds quite some time ago, and I was becoming concerned about repayment."

The Khan stared at him for a time. "You may go. We'll have more questions of you later."

Outside, Madho quietly asked one of the imperial officers who had guarded Shivaji, "How did His Majesty manage to escape? You were all so careful to keep watch on him."

The man shook his head. "Not careful enough. Late in the afternoon

Shivaji's brother-in-law Hiroji Farzand walked from Shivaji's house and asked us not to make any noise. He said the Maharaja was very ill and needed his sleep. Then Farzand and his usual men rode off.

"Hours later, when night was falling and Farzand didn't come back, we grew suspicious. There was no activity around the house. Usually, servants would come and go. So we went in to check. Nobody was there, and the King's bed was empty." The man looked away and fell silent.

Madho shook his head in sympathy. "An understandable mistake. Raja Shivaji was clever."

The soldier looked down at the stone floor. "I'm afraid that won't save us from the Khan's anger now. We'll probably be demoted and sent to someplace like Kabul."

Madho turned and left, his mind working furiously. Was it feasible to ride to Shivaji's compound immediately, show his faked document granting the property, and take control of the elephants and palanquins and the rest?

He let out his breath. No, not so quickly. Not when he was clearly suspected of possibly aiding in the escape. But at least he had prepared the way, by mentioning the "loan" to the Khan.

Madho numbly rode back to his residence, fervently hoping all his efforts hadn't been for nothing. At the house, he strode up and down on his veranda as the moonlight shone on the river, and he tried to think of the best course of action. He knew he had to do *something*, or the opportunity would be lost.

An hour before dawn, he woke his manservant Prem Chand and sent him to summon Gopal and the men and carts. As the sky began to turn light, he and Gopal and their party rode through the light rain to the house where Shivaji had stayed. Even as Madho approached, he saw that soldiers remained on watch outside, but they were men he didn't recognize.

Forged document in hand, he entered the small tent serving as a sentry post, introduced himself to the officer in charge, and asked, "Where are the previous guards?"

The man had quickly risen to his feet in the presence of the Rajput prince. "Replaced, of course, Highness. The Khan was furious they let Raja Shivaji escape."

"And are Raja Shivaji's horses and elephants and palanquins still in the stables? And his weapons and equipment are in the armory?"

"No, they're long gone, Highness. As soon as the escape was discovered last night, Falud Khan sent his agents to impound everything for the Emperor, as unlawful property. It's all safe in the Red Fort now."

Madho stood for several moments, stunned. How could the Emperor's officials have acted so quickly? He reluctantly concluded there were other men in Agra who were as fast thinking as himself.

He turned and stalked back to his horse. "Damn!" He said to Gopal. He tore the faked document in half and crumpled the pieces. "Take these and dispose of them so no one can ever read them."

Gopal's mouth was hanging open as he took the wads of heavy paper. "What happened?"

Madho shook his head in disgust. "Falud Khan ended up with *everything*. That silver palanquin. The elephants. Even the horses, and all those fine trappings. The weapons, too, I'd guess." He looked longingly at the empty stables

and storerooms. "Except for the Bhavani Sword. Shivaji would have taken that with him."

"How could Shivaji leave you with nothing?" Gopal asked indignantly. "After all the help you gave him."

Madho again shook his head. "He was even more clever than I. He's an excellent judge of men. He probably knew I hoped to take advantage of him. He may even have guessed at the beginning that I might try to do away with him."

Madho looked at his comrade and managed a tight grin. "Of course, I quickly became fond of him, even though I never intended to. And even though it interfered with my own interests. I'll miss him, but I'm glad he has his freedom." He boosted himself onto his horse. "Come, let's go eat. Only food will console me now, and I haven't yet had time for a good meal."

The furious Aurangzeb blamed Ram Singh most for Shivaji's escape. He first barred the Amber prince from attendance at court; then he stripped Ram Singh of rank and pay.

Weeks later, a messenger delivered a long, slender cloth-wrapped bundle to Madho. His manservant Prem Chand unwrapped it as he and Gopal curiously watched.

Inside lay a sword. Wrapped around the sword was a piece of heavy paper, folded and sealed with wax. On the wax was an octagonal imprint containing tiny lettering. Having duplicated the same seal only a couple months earlier, Madho instantly recognized it as Shivaji's. He broke the wax and unfolded the paper. On it was written: *"To Rajkumar Madho Singhji of Mangarh. Presented with greatest admiration and respect. Raja Shivaji."*

Puzzled and excited, Madho carefully took the sword into his hands. His instant impression was that it was of the ultimate in workmanship. Oddly, it felt light for its size and quality, yet there was a heft to it as if it were also heavier than normal.

Gopal whispered with evident awe, "Shivaji's rewarded you after all. Could it be the Bhavani Sword?"

Could it be? Was this more than an ordinary weapon?

Madho examined it in detail. The blade was long and beautifully watered, just slightly curved toward the tip. The hilt, inlaid in gold forming an intricate design of vines and leaves, was so small Madho could barely squeeze his own chubby hand into it. Like so many Maratha swords, a curved, horn-shaped spike extended from the hilt in the opposite direction from the blade.

He could not recall seeing it earlier as one of the many swords Shivaji had either worn or had lying by his side. However, inscribed on one side of the blade in Marathi characters was *Raja Shivaji*, so it was obviously one of the King's personal weapons.

Madho turned it over. His breath caught. "Look!" he said.

Gopal bent to peer more closely.

On the other side of the blade was inscribed: *Shri Bhavani.*

Madho tingled with excitement through his very core. *Could it truly be the Bhavani Sword?* Shivaji wouldn't actually be giving away his patron deity, of course. The Goddess could inhabit more than one physical object at a time, just as Lord Shiva inhabited thousands of *lingams* all over India.

He shook his head. It seemed so unlikely a gift. His voice cracking, he said to Gopal, "This can't be the Bhavani Sword. Shivaji would never part with it. The inscription is probably just a charm, or a prayer to the Goddess."

Gopal straightened and stepped back. "But you helped the King at a time when he had few friends," he said. "You gave him the idea which made his escape possible! He knew you were intrigued by the Bhavani Sword. What if he were truly grateful and wanted to honor you? After all, you did try to give him the impression you weren't interested in profiting from the escape. He might have believed you but wanted to reward you anyway!"

Madho held the sword gingerly in both hands, feeling uncharacteristically foolish. "Don't tell anyone about this," he ordered Gopal and Prem Chand. "Not until I'm sure."

Every day Madho took out the sword and examined it. He would run his fingers over the engraving on the hilt and the blade, and wonder: Did the powerful Goddess Bhavani inhabit it?

He felt sure the weapon had an unusual weightiness about it, as if it contained something more than just the steel and the decorative gold. When he took practice swings, it seemed as if the sword acquired a life of its own, with a greater force than what his own body imparted.

Should he place the weapon on an altar and worship it daily? Or was this another example of Shivaji's cleverness? Was the sword merely one from Shivaji's collection of hundreds, one which he might scarcely miss, despite its fine workmanship?

The doubts nagged at Madho, annoying him almost beyond reason. On the one hand, the gift could be a truly great honor. Not only might Madho have been presented with a legendary weapon, he would also be receiving the constant blessings and support of a powerful Goddess.

On the other hand, the gift might well be partly intended to puzzle him with the uncertainty. Madho felt almost certain it was the latter.

But he could never know. He could not simply send a message to Shivaji and ask. Regardless of the reply, the matter would embarrass both parties, especially Madho.

He strongly suspected that Shivaji had shrewdly sized him up, and that the clever King had known exactly what the effect of the gift would be.

Now that the rains had ended, Madho made the journey back to Mangarh. There, he sent a messenger to the Street of Swordsmiths and summoned Chiranji Lal, considered the best sword maker in the region.

In Madho's apartments in the Hanuman Mahal, the wiry, middle aged swordsmith held the weapon in hands that were scarred from numerous incidents at the forge. He examined the sword minutely from one end to the other. "This inscription is a charm, I assume." he murmured. He tested the sword's balance, then stepped to the center of the room and swung the weapon several times. He stopped, examined it again, and Madho was sure there was a slight puzzlement in his eyes.

Chiranji Lal said at last, "It's from Daulatabad in the Deccan, but the watering pattern in the blade is better than most of their work. It's superb. The hilt inlay is the finest quality, though I've seen a couple from there that are comparable."

Madho waited for more, but the swordsmith stood quietly, still peering at the weapon he held. Madho asked, "Is anything unusual about it?"

Chiranji Lal again tested the balance. At last, he shrugged, his eyes still on the sword. "I can't say more, Highness, other than that it's a fine weapon. You already knew that."

Madho pressed further. "You seemed puzzled for a moment by something."

The man again shrugged. "It's nothing. At first, I thought the center of weight was at one point, but now it seems slightly farther down in the blade than I'd originally thought." Madho gazed intently at him. Chiranji Lal gave a mild smile of obvious embarrassment. "It's rare for me to misjudge like that."

"So," said Madho calmly, "the sword's weight shifted when you were holding it?"

The swordsmith stared at him a moment, then looked away. "I had to be mistaken in my first impression. My apologies, Highness."

Since it seemed a good possibility that the Goddess did indeed inhabit the sword, Madho began including it as an object of his private *pujas*. Weapons were often worshiped by Rajputs, and certainly, he decided, this sword of the finest quality was worthy of reverence.

A month later, Madho's father, Raja Jagat Singh of Mangarh, died. Aurangzeb confirmed Madho as the new ruler of Mangarh with the newly created, considerably more prestigious title of "Maharaja" of Mangarh. So Madho was not merely a "king," but a "great king." To accompany the elevated status, Aurangzeb also promoted Madho to the rank of commander of 3,000 horses, with its increase in pay.

Thereafter, the Emperor referred to Madho as Mota Raja, the "Fat King." Madho was pleased, taking it as evidence of Aurangzeb's fondness for him.

Madho immediately doubled his number of artists. Since his enhanced position in the world arrived so soon after he began including the weapon in his worship, he began to feel that, indeed, the sword and the Goddess whose power it embodied might well have strongly influenced the bringing of his good fortune.

Every day when he was in residence at his palace at Mangarh, Maharaja Madho Singh would have himself carried in a palanquin up to the treasury in the oldest part of the fortress. There, the Bhil guards would stand protectively at the entrance while, eyes gleaming, Madho would pay respect to the bulk of his haul from Surat, as well as the wealth stored there by the great Raja Hanuman and other previous rulers.

Over the years, Madho shrewdly increased the revenues from his kingdom, and consequently, his own wealth. When he eventually built a new wing to his palace, named the Madho Mahal after himself, he included storage chambers he personally designed to be well-concealed. He divided his treasure between the various places, so that even if one cache should somehow be looted, the others might still survive.

Every morning in his apartments, Madho Singh would lovingly caress the huge diamond and the other fabulous Surat jewels which he stored in readily accessible secret places. And, at his daily worship of his family deity Ekadantji, he would also worship what he had gradually come to feel certain was, indeed, the true Bhavani Sword.

***

After Shivaji and his son escaped from Agra in the baskets, Shivaji shaved off his beard and mustache and disguised himself as a religious beggar. He took a circuitous route and almost miraculously managed to elude Aurangzeb's vast army of searchers. In twenty-five days of hard, fast travel, he arrived at his home fort of Ramgarh.

In future years, he and his Maratha armies caused no end of trouble for the Emperor Aurangzeb in the Deccan.

Later Indian historians would consider Shivaji the unifier of the Maratha peoples and a premier fighter for the freedom of Hindus from their Muslim rulers. He would be held out as an example of a great Indian patriot and a visionary, willing to risk all for the betterment of his people.

Sadly, many of the modern-day activists and politicians who make reference to Shivaji as a heroic champion of Hinduism ignore the fact that he insisted on respecting all faiths and their places of worship.

Part Three
The Treasure of Mangarh

Mangarh, March 1976

No sword turned up in the search that was a likely candidate for the one belonging to Shivaji. Vijay assigned the disappointed Nimbalkar to help supervise the workers digging in the open areas atop the ridge, adjacent to the oldest parts of the fortress.

The jewelry and the gold, far more important to Vijay's mind, had definitely existed, of that there was no doubt. So where had they gone?

He and Ranjit Singh and Shanta Das were wandering again through the Madho Mahal, built by Maharaja Madho Singh in the late 1600s. They were quite near the area where they had previously found the treasure. A young Bhil guard named Nagario was accompanying them, bearing the rings of keys and keeping an eye on them.

The timekeeper's gong at the main gate rang, signaling the half-hour. Vijay glanced at his watch.

Ranjit laughed his high pitched giggle and said, "Only eight minutes difference this time. Not bad for a water clock that's hundreds of years old."

"It's a wonderful tradition," Shanta said, "What does it really matter if Mangarh's time is a little different from the rest of India?"

Today she wore a *shalwar kameez* outfit, again in green. She was extremely attractive in it, Vijay thought. He realized his eyes had again been lingering on her, and he quickly glanced away. He said, "Maybe it doesn't matter at all. Not really."

They'd mentioned to Ranjit the description of the wealth by Stanley Powis in his memoirs. "Would all the treasure have been kept together, or was part of it somewhere totally different?" mused Shanta.

"There's no way to know," Vijay said. "In Madho Singh's time, I'd guess he kept it all close to him. "From what we've heard of him from the princess, he was greedy enough he would have wanted to be able to dip his hands into the jewelry boxes every day just to gloat over his wealth."

"He was really that greedy?" asked Ranjit.

"Probably. The princess showed Shanta and me a miniature painting of him gazing at the Star of Mangarh diamond. She confessed that Madho Singh oppressed the peasants so much with his taxes that some of them left the state to get away from him."

Ranjit shook his head. "I've nothing against wealth—wouldn't mind getting a little more of it myself. But it's always amused me how tightfisted many of the rich can be. Reminds me of a story about our Sikh Guru, Gobind Singh. A rich man once gave him some diamond bracelets. The Guru immediately threw them into a river, just to show his disciples that they shouldn't get too attached to material things."

Vijay grinned at the notion, and he saw that Shanta smiled, too.

Vijay said jokingly, knowing Ranjit would not take offense, "If the founder of your Khalsa renounced all wealth, then you should gladly do the same."

Ranjit giggled. "I'd be glad to consider the matter, if someone gives it to me first."

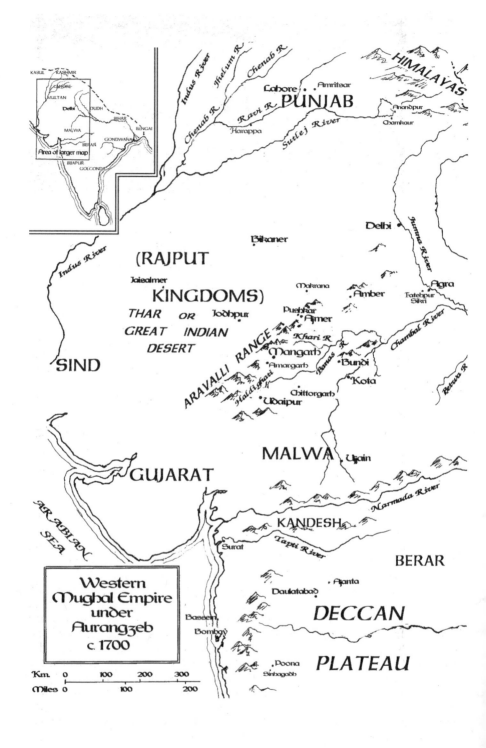

KABUL KASHMIR
LAHORE
MULTAN
Delhi OUDH
BIHAR
MALWA BENGAL
BERAR GONDWANA
Area of larger map
BIJAPUR
GOLCONDA

HIMALAYAS

Indus River
Jhelum R.
Chenab R.
Chenab R.
Ravi R.
Sutlej River

Lahore . Amritsar
PUNJAB
Harappa
Anandpur
Chamkaur

Delhi
Jumna River

Bikaner

(RAJPUT

Indus River

Jaisalmer

KINGDOMS)

THAR OR Jodhpur
GREAT INDIAN
DESERT

Makrana
Pushkar
Amber
Agra
Fatehpur Sikri

Chambal River

Ajmer

Khari R.

SIND

ARAVALLI RANGE

Mangarh
Amargarh
Haldighati
Chittorgarh
Udaipur

Banas R.

Bundi
Kota

Betwa R.

MALWA
Ujjain

GUJARAT

Narmada River

ARABIAN SEA

KANDESH

Surat
Tapti River

BERAR

Western
Mughal Empire
under
Aurangzeb
c. 1700

Baseen
Bombay

Daulatabad
Ajanta

DECCAN

Km. 0   100   200   300
Miles 0   100   200

Poona
Sinhagadh

PLATEAU

Loyalty

1

Ludva Village, Mangarh State, in the thirty-third year of the reign of Maharaja Madho Singh, and the fortieth year of the reign of the Mughal Emperor Aurangzeb, October 1698

The monsoon crop of *bajra* was tall and turning golden, the grain almost ready for harvest. It was late in the day, and except for the two young Jat men, everyone had returned to the village after their work in the fields planting the winter crop of wheat, or sugar cane, or tobacco. Sant watched his big, broadly built friend Kesar buckle on the sword.

"I wish you wouldn't wear that so often," Sant said. "We haven't heard of robbers or tigers around for a long time."

Kesar grunted, not bothering to glance at him. "I feel good wearing it."

"You know a Jat farmer can never be a warrior! People think you're trying to be above your place."

Kesar shot him a look of annoyance. "Let them think what they want." He started along the dusty path that led behind the tiny temple, toward their houses at the edge of the village.

Sant, weary from the day's work, hurried to catch up. Not seeing the partly exposed rock in his path, he tripped, and his gangly body fell face down into the dust. Unhurt except for a minor bruise or two, he picked himself up, straightened his turban, and brushed off his chest and his *dhoti* before Kesar could glance back and notice.

Why was he always so clumsy? Sant wondered. It was one reason he'd been an object of ridicule his entire life. He was reminded of how everyone in the village loved to tell of the event when he and Kesar were out walking one evening. In the moonlight, Sant had seen a stick by the path and bent to pick it up. The "stick" had been a cobra, and Sant was fortunate to have heaved it away fast enough to escape with his life. But whenever people repeated the tale and laughed about it, he almost wished the snake had bitten him to death.

"Look over there," Kesar said, gesturing toward the mango grove by the small temple. A stranger sat tending a cooking fire under the trees. Sant stopped and peered into the shadows at the man. It had been months since anyone had used the temple grounds, as not many travelers passed through Ludva village.

Impatiently, Kesar added, "He's probably just a *sadhu*. Let's get on home."
He continued walking.

Sant again rushed to keep up. He asked, "Shouldn't we see if he needs
anything to eat? We don't get many chances to help a visitor. What if he's
really hungry? And if he's a holy man, he might get angry if we ignore him,
and put a curse on us."

"If he's a holy man, the women have probably already fed him," said
Kesar.

"Then we could just ask for his blessing."

Kesar slowed his pace for a few steps. He said, "That's a good idea. But
let's be quick." He started toward the grove.

"He's not dressed like a *sadhu*," Sant said. Now they could see that the
man was smoking a *hookah*, and he was not wearing the loincloth or the
saffron robe of a wandering mendicant. His clothes, although not elaborate,
were of finer fabric than the coarse homespun the two young farm men were
familiar with. The stocky stranger was not fat, but he gave the impression of
being well fed. It was odd, thought Sant, that an apparently prosperous man
would be here alone, without a single servant in sight. Since occasional bands
of *dacoits* bent on robbery roamed the roads, few people traveled far without
the protection of numbers.

The man drew on the mouthpiece of his water pipe and watched them as
they approached. He smiled genially and called to them in a deep, resonant
voice, "Welcome. Please do me the honor of joining me. May I offer some
tea?" The invitation seemed genuinely friendly, though Sant saw a stout bamboo *lathi*, the pole's ends bound with iron, lying by the bowl of the *hookah*
within easy reach of the man in case of trouble.

"No, we can stay only a moment," said Kesar. He remained standing, so
Sant did, too. "We wondered if we could offer you some food for your evening
meal?"

"That's most hospitable of you," replied the man, who appeared to be
around forty years in age. Round-faced, he wore a short, neatly trimmed beard
that was beginning to turn grey at the sides. "But I have all that I need for
now. I see that you young men must be farmers. Jats, I would guess?"

"That's right," said Sant.

Kesar said, "You could tell that by the way we wind our turbans."

Holding the mouthpiece of the long *hookah* hose in the air, the man
shrugged as if to dismiss the matter as trivial. "True. And in my many travels,
I've acquired a knack for discerning caste. But I knew most farmers in this
area are Jats." He pronounced his words a little different from the manner of
people in the village. "Please, won't you sit a moment? I don't need food, but
I'm quite starved for conversation."

Sant looked at Kesar, who gave a slight shrug and squatted on his haunches.
Sant followed his lead.

"You're from the village up the road, I assume," the man said. He drew
on the mouthpiece of his pipe, and the water gurgled in the bowl at his side.

"That's right," said Sant. "Ludva village."

"It seems a pleasant place."

Kesar said gruffly, "It's not much different from other villages." He was
not at all happy with his lot as a farmer working his father's fields. And like
Sant, Kesar was still unmarried at twenty-two years of age.

Sant said, "We'd be better off if the Maharaja's *kamdar* would not try to get so much rent from us." He glanced at Kesar, and saw a worried look in his friend's eyes.

Kesar shook his head "no" in warning, and hurriedly said, "Of course the *kamdar* has his duty. It's not his fault he has to collect the rent even when our crops are poor."

Sant realized he might have been indiscreet in criticizing the Maharaja. What if the stranger mentioned the conversation to the *kamdar*, who could send his *lathi*-armed men? Ludva lay just inside the northern boundary of Mangarh State, and Maharaja Madho Singh of Mangarh and his agents were not noted for leniency with farmers who objected to the ruler's heavy taxes.

"Where do you come from?" Kesar asked, trying to move to a safer topic.

"Oh, many places," said the man, shifting his gaze to Kesar. He drew on his water pipe. "My wife and my only son were killed by a fever a number of years ago, so I now have no family. These past few years I have been in Mangarh city. I am an artist, and His Highness has been my patron."

Sant and Kesar stared at him in astonishment. Sant asked, "You worked for Maharajaji himself?"

"Indeed. But he has many artists working for him. I was only one. Now it is time for me to move on, to find another patron."

Sant was still gaping at him. "Is it true," he asked, "that our Maharaja has rooms the size of houses all filled with gold and jewels?"

The man smiled again. "I saw no such rooms myself. But His Highness is said to be very wealthy. I once painted a scene of him seated on his private balcony. He wanted it to depict him looking at a huge diamond in his hand. I had the privilege of examining the diamond so that I could paint it accurately. It was larger than any gem I could have imagined."

"He must have paid you handsomely for such a painting, since he is so rich," said Sant.

The man shrugged. "Oh, not so much. He can be quite tight with his wealth. And as I said, I was only one of many artists in the palace."

"Why did you leave?" demanded Kesar. Sant wished his friend would ask the question in a more pleasant manner.

The man seemed to take no offense. He again shrugged, took a puff on his *hookah*, and said, "It was time to move on. His Highness has been off travel-ing much of the time recently, and he no longer needs quite so many artists."

Kesar had been staring with narrowed eyes that clearly showed his skep-ticism. "Where are you going now?"

The man looked Kesar over briefly, as if appraising him. Then he replied, "To Anandpur, in the Punjab. The Guru of the Sikhs is said to be wanting artists and poets, as well as fighting men. He is translating many written works from Persian and Sanskrit into the common tongue of the Punjab. Since I know a number of languages, even if he can't use me as an artist, perhaps I can serve him as a translator for a time."

Kesar demanded, "You said this Guru wants fighting men?"

"Oh, yes. Guru Gobind Rai is reputed to be expecting war with the rajas of the neighboring hill kingdoms. Maybe even war with the Mughal Emperor himself."

"But a Guru is a teacher, not a fighter!" said Kesar, as if having caught the man in a lie.

"This one is a great teacher. He is also a great warrior chief."

Kesar scowled. "You said he would fight the Emperor? That's madness."

The man lifted an eyebrow. "Possibly. But in the hills, a skillfully managed small army can sometimes outmaneuver a larger one. And the Guru is a clever fighter."

Kesar's scowl softened some. "Where is this place?"

"Anandpur? It's at the edge of the foothills of the Himalayan mountains. Part of the Punjab, the land of the Five Rivers."

Kesar asked, his face appearing less hostile now, "Is it far?"

The man shrugged. "Maybe a month's journey, maybe two."

Kesar seemed to deflate. He was quiet a moment. Then he said, "That's a long way."

The man smiled, and again shrugged. "I've been on longer travels."

"You have?" exclaimed Sant. "Please tell us about them."

The man's eyes showed amusement. "It would take considerable time. But your friend appears interested in being a warrior, perhaps?" He addressed Kesar: "I see you wear a sword."

Kesar grunted, his way of saying, "yes."

"He believes he was a Rajput in a prior life," said Sant. "He went to the Street of Swordsmiths in Mangarh and traded a lot of wheat to get the sword. He's also made wooden swords, and he's always wanting me to practice fighting with him."

The stranger was still looking at Kesar. "Then you should come with me," he said. "I would be glad of protection on the journey, and I'm sure the Guru would welcome another warrior in Anandpur."

Kesar looked unbelievingly at the man. "He would?"

"I'm sure of it." The stranger eyed Kesar for a time. Then he said, "But a man such as yourself surely has a wife and a family to care for. I suppose you'd rather not leave them."

Kesar again scowled. "I have no wife. No children."

Sant, eager to impart helpful information to such an esteemed visitor, said, "I'm not married either. There aren't enough Jat women for all the men who want wives."

The man said, "Perfect. Then you should both come." He puffed again on his *hookah.*

"Both?" asked Sant, stunned at the thought.

"Absolutely. You'd have more choices of women there. If you're a Sikh, you can marry some beautiful girl from another caste if there aren't enough Jats."

"How so?" grunted Kesar.

"Because castes are less important to Sikhs. Every Sikh is said to be equal. So you wouldn't have to marry another Jat." He joked, "You could even marry a Brahmin or a Rajputni, if you found one who'd have you." He put the mouthpiece of his *hookah* to his lips.

Kesar's brow was furrowed in deep thought. "How do you know so much about these Sikhs, if you aren't one yourself yet?"

The man shrugged. "I've known some Sikhs, and I asked them many questions. I also once lived in the Punjab for a time."

After a time, Kesar asked, "You'd take us with you?"

The man dipped his head in a nod. "Of course. As I said, I'd welcome your sword for protection from *dacoits*, as well as your company."

Kesar appraised him, still clearly suspicious. "Why don't you already have someone traveling with you? Like a servant?"

"Oh, I did. But the rogue ran off. He must have decided he didn't want to travel so far. And he was afraid of robbers and wild animals. Anyway, I don't mind cooking my own meals, washing my clothes. I've done it before when the need arose. By the way," he paused, and then asked, "is there a customs post ahead on this road?"

Sant felt as if he needed to apologize for the lack. "I regret we don't have one, sir. Not many people cross into Ajmer territory from here."

"I see." The man asked casually, "Are there other paths headed north? Besides the road?"

"Oh, yes," said Sant. "So long as you're on foot, you can take any of the paths between the fields. You won't even know when you cross into Ajmer."

"You want to avoid the customs?" Kesar asked, his suspicions obviously aroused once more.

"Oh, I have nothing to interest them," assured the man. "But why give them a chance to tax my passage? I'd just be giving His Highness' money right back to him, since the tax would come from the pay he gave me. That wouldn't make sense, now would it?"

Kesar scowled as he tried to sort out this ingenious argument. "No, I suppose not." In a moment he asked again, as if he thought the man had been jesting, "You'd really take us with you?"

"Why not? I've already said I'd enjoy company and protection. And who better for companions than two fine, sturdy young men such as yourselves?"

Sant worriedly glanced at Kesar. Was Kesar seriously thinking of leaving? He knew Kesar was unhappy in the village. But Kesar was his only true friend. Life without him was unthinkable. Sant said, "I'm only a farmer. What use could the Guru make of me?" He had scarcely even thought of the possibility of leaving Ludva before.

The stranger shrugged, as if nothing could be simpler. "I'm sure he'd train you as a warrior, too. You look strong and in good health. If you can handle a plow and sickle, no reason you can't learn to handle a sword. Although," he added in a doubtful tone, "I don't think either of you would be eager for warfare if you'd ever actually seen it."

"Why not?" demanded Kesar.

The man smiled grimly. "It's not a pretty sight, seeing dead and injured men and animals. And you might well be killed or maimed yourself."

Sant doubted he wanted to be a warrior. He'd never liked even the mock sword play with Kesar. "I'll have to think about it," he said.

Kesar asked, "What would I have to do to join the Sikhs? Besides going to Anandpur?"

The man smiled and waved the mouthpiece of his *hookah* airily as if dismissing the matter. "You'd have to follow the Sikh's creed. Obey God and the Guru."

Sant said hesitantly, "I think I heard the Sikhs eat with anyone, no matter the caste, even the Untouchables."

The man shrugged, and smiled again. "Is that truly so bad? Anyway, if you're a warrior everyone will respect you regardless."

Kesar demanded, "When do you leave?"

"At first light, after I've bathed."

"So soon?"

The man said nothing.

"I need to think about it," said Kesar.

"Of course."

"If I decide to go with you," said Kesar, obviously deep in thought, "I'll be here before dawn."

The man nodded. "As you wish."

"I'll think about it, too," said Sant, his voice quavering. What if Kesar really went away? He and Kesar were quite different in outlook, but there were no other young men in the village who could be so close a friend.

They left the man contentedly smoking his *hookah*. Kesar was silent, his forehead furrowed in thought as they walked off. After a time, he said, "Something's strange about that fellow. Traveling alone, avoiding the customs post on the main highway."

Sant tried to think of a reply, but Kesar continued, "Still, I see no reason to doubt what he says about the Sikhs' Guru wanting fighters."

"It would be a long way to go," said Sant. "The roads are dangerous, with the bandits and wild animals."

Kesar acted as if he did not hear. "I sometimes think I'll go mad if I spend one more day in these disgusting fields."

"Your family has some of the best fields in the village," said Sant.

Kesar shot him a look of amused disdain. "You'll spend the rest of your life here. Plowing, planting, harvesting. First for your father, then for your brother. And no wife, no sons. Don't you ever want anything of your own?"

Sant thought of beautiful Rukmini, his brother's wife. "Yes. Of course. But here, not somewhere else."

"You'll have to go somewhere else if you want anything different."

Sant felt lost, as if everything he'd known was falling apart. But he reluctantly admitted to himself Kesar was probably right.

2

Sant's emotions were churning as he took dinner with his family in their courtyard. He absently watched the little striped squirrel dashing about in the *neem* tree. Sant was only vaguely aware of his older brother Hukam grumbling about the Maharaja's new rent demands.

Father replied to Hukam in a tone of disgust, "The *kamdar* says Maharajaji must have more money this year for the dowry of his daughter, and for more elephants when he goes to fight for the Emperor."

Sant's mother was still ill with a recurrence of the fever she got every year when the rains came, so she was sleeping on her *charpoy* inside the house. Hukam's lovely young wife Rukmini approached from the kitchen corner of the courtyard with a stack of hot *rotis*. Sant's heart beat faster. He tried not to be obvious as he caressed the girl with a quick glance. Hukam was replying, "Our fat Maharaja is getting even fatter off *us*."

It was rare for anyone to openly criticize their ruler, who was kin to the gods; much more commonly it was the ruler's less divine agents who were blamed. But Maharaja Madho Singh's greed had become legendary.

Rukmini extended the plate of *rotis* to Sant. As he took one, he admired her slender fingers, the smooth skin of her wrist and arm. He was vividly aware of her moving to stand nearby, waiting in case the men needed anything. He tore off a piece of his *roti* and lamented his situation. Why could not *he*, rather than Hukam, have been the elder brother, the one to marry such a divine creature? Sant loved Hukam, but he had also always envied him for being his father's clear favorite, and for his self-assured way of claiming for himself the best of whatever was available, whether food, tools, bed, or bride.

Hukam, not even seeming to notice his beautiful wife, was saying, "Our Maharaja already has so much treasure in his vaults he could support his relatives and his palaces for the rest of his life. Why does he have to rob us of the fruits of our work?"

Their father shrugged. "*Rais hain*—they're the lordly ones. It's their way. Maybe in our next lives we'll be kings ourselves."

Sant fantasized coming to Rukmini's bed on a night so dark she wouldn't know he was not her husband. Or he might even come to her openly, maybe while the rest of the family was out in the fields—

"Brother!" said Hukam. "Kesar is here. Didn't you see him come in?"

"He never sees anything until he falls over it," their father said, shaking his head in disapproval.

His face suddenly hot, Sant jumped to his feet. Kesar, who was standing just inside the gate, greeted Sant's family. Then he beckoned to Sant, turned, and left. Sant followed him into the field behind the house, away from other ears. Kesar said in a low voice, "I decided I'm leaving."

"You're really going with him? That stranger?"

"You know how much I want to be a warrior instead of a farmer. This may be my best chance. Maybe even my *only* chance."

Sant usually didn't try to seriously argue with Kesar. But this time he was almost frantic. "Are you sure you can trust that man? We don't know any more about him than what he's told us."

Kesar hesitated a moment, but then said firmly, "It's worth the risk. If anything does go wrong, I can come back."

Sant tried to grasp that his only friend was truly going to leave.

Kesar grinned at Sant's gloomy expression. "You must come with me."

Sant looked away. "It may be fine for you. I'm not a fighter."

"Look at all the practice you've had with me," said Kesar. "I'm sure the Guru will be glad to have someone with your experience."

Sant said in a barely audible voice, "I couldn't leave our village. And my family. I've never even been to Ajmer."

"Then all the more reason to go. Look, if you come, too, we can help each other if the need arises." Kesar's piercing eyes shone brightly, reflecting the moon. "And we'll become warriors! Not just lowly farmers."

Sant thought of the few times he'd seen the Maharaja's or a thakur's Rajput cavalry, with their fine horses, their elaborate trappings, their fine dress, their poise. He began to see some value in becoming such a man, which previously had been unthinkable, utterly impossible for someone born into a caste of farmers. It would certainly impress his father and his brother. And Rukmini, too, would admire him if he were a warrior.

Kesar watched Sant's change in expression and worked harder on him: "I *need* you with me. You're a brother to me. How could I go myself, if you didn't go?"

Sant wavered, warmed by Kesar's affectionate words.

Kesar added, "Besides, if you don't like it there, you can always come back. You'd return a great hero. You'll have journeyed farther than anyone else in the village. Even Himmat Singh's pilgrimage only took him to Benares."

The thought that everyone in the village, even Hukam, maybe even Father, might envy him was most compelling. "I suppose it could be a good adventure."

"Then you'll come with me?"

"I, uh, suppose I will."

Kesar slapped him hard on the back. "I knew you wouldn't let me down."

Sant felt queasy and light headed. He struggled to comprehend that he had actually committed himself to something so far removed from anything he had previously even conceived.

Kesar said, "You'll need to bring a small water jug and cooking pot, and blanket. And some flour. And that axe you use to cut firewood. It can be your weapon for a while. But one thing—don't tell your family you're leaving."

Sant was trying to remember all the items Kesar mentioned. "Don't tell?" he asked, puzzled as well as distraught. Part of the satisfaction of going could be the look on their faces when he told them what he was doing.

"It would only upset them. They'd probably try to argue with you. This way, they'll just see that you're gone, and they'll have to accept it."

"But they'd be worried when they found me missing!"

"You can send word to them, after we're well away."

That would indeed avoid some heated argument. If his father knew in advance, he would no doubt ridicule the plan, shouting at Sant about how foolish the whole idea was. "I suppose that's the best way," Sant said reluctantly.

"Good. I'll come by here for you when the moon sets—a little while before dawn. You can watch the moon and come outside then."

Kesar started to leave, then stopped and looked at Sant. "Promise me you won't change your mind. And you won't say anything to your family."

"I won't," Sant said, his voice higher pitched than normal.

"Swear it by the Goddess."

"I—I swear."

"Good. I'll meet you in a few hours." Kesar disappeared among the shadows at the edge of the field.

Sant hands trembled as he gathered his traveling items. The axe slipped from his grip and clattered against the plow, and he froze, hoping no one had heard and would come to investigate.

It seemed a long time before Rukmini was done in the kitchen corner of the courtyard, so he could sneak over and take the smallest of the three cooking pots.

He hid the items in the cow shed and spent some time petting and talking with Jasmine the cow, whom he was fond of.

When the family went to bed, he did not dare fall asleep himself for fear he would not awaken in time. He doubted he could sleep even if he had wanted.

It was cold, and he kept rearranging his blanket, trying to get warm. He was in agony over the idea of leaving. His anxiety and the cold made his muscles stiff and tight.

But eventually he fell asleep despite it all.

As he slumbered, a dream came. He was riding a horse, a type of animal he had never so much as touched before: only some of the Rajputs owned horses. But Sant was racing through the hills with a band of other horsemen, all waving gleaming swords. At their head was another horseman, richly dressed, as if he were a king. A golden light seemed to glow about him.

Suddenly, the leader signaled his men to halt, and he reined in his own horse. Sant came to a stop directly behind him. The princely man turned his animal so it was broadside to Sant. He looked into Sant's eyes, and with a smile, he wagged his head in an affirmative nod.

Sant's body stirred in sleep, and he snapped awake. Abruptly, he recalled the dream, vivid in his mind. He had felt wonderful, almost like one of the nobles, riding on the powerful horse, a keen-edged sword gripped in his hand. He tried to recall the face of the king or prince, but the features were hazy in his recollection. The man had said nothing. Still, it was as if the chieftain had spoken to him.

Was it an omen?

He suddenly remembered—he had agreed to travel to Anandpur and become a Sikh, a disciple of their Guru. Could the horseman have been the Guru?

Almost certainly! It was as if the master himself were summoning Sant to come, to be a bold warrior under his command. Glancing out the window, Sant saw that the moon was low, almost touching the distant hills. Soon the women would rise to go relieve themselves in the fields before the sun came up.

As quietly as he could, he rolled from his *charpoy* and put his feet on the floor. Blanket around him for warmth, he moved quietly toward the door. He saw his sleeping family and hesitated.

To leave them! Especially with no warning. His mother was so ill, and she would be especially upset, even though Hukam, not Sant, was her favorite son. But he had promised Kesar. He slipped his feet into his *jutis*, went to the shed and lovingly patted Jasmine on her head. Tears came to his eyes at leaving the cow.

Steeling himself, he grabbed his stash of food and his water and cooking vessels in their cloth bag. Was there something he was forgetting?

Oh, yes, the axe. He grabbed it from the dark corner.

As he left the shed, he glanced at the tree, but the squirrel was likely still asleep. He unlatched the courtyard gate and left, taking care that the gate didn't creak loudly enough to awaken anyone.

He waited only a few minutes before Kesar came, a dark outline now that the moon had disappeared. "I was worried you'd change your mind," his friend whispered.

"I, uh, almost did."

Kesar quietly laughed. "Come."

They hurried to the camping ground.

The sky was beginning to lighten in the east, and there was just enough illumination for them to see that the area beneath the trees was empty. There was no sign, even, of the remains of the stranger's fire. It was as if he had never existed.

"Damn! He didn't wait for us," said Kesar. They stood a few moments. Sant sagged with sudden relief, his dream momentarily forgotten. They wouldn't need to leave after all!

"I wonder if we can catch up to him," said Kesar.

"We'd never find him in the dark," Sant said quickly.

"But we know the direction he went," Kesar said. "And the sun will rise soon."

"If he really wanted us, wouldn't he have waited?" asked Sant weakly.

After a time, Kesar said, his voice resigned, "I suppose that's so. We'd better go back to our beds before we're missed."

Sant eagerly turned toward home.

A voice said from the shadows, "Are you ready for our adventure, my brothers?"

Sant and Kesar whirled around. There stood the stranger from yesterday evening. He carried a bedroll and a bag of possessions over his shoulders, and his *hookah* hung on a cord over his back. "We," Sant stammered, "we thought...."

"That I'd already left? Why would I do that? I had just gone off to answer the call of nature and to bathe. And naturally, I couldn't leave my belongings about for someone to steal."

"Oh, I see," replied Sant dully.

Kesar said, "You didn't even leave the ashes from your fire! Is that usual?"

The man chuckled. "Just an old habit from traveling with armies who wanted to remain hidden from their enemies. I don't even think about it."

Kesar replied, puzzlement still in his voice, "Oh. I see."

"So," said the man. "Shall we leave?"

"Yes," said Kesar.

"Wait," said Sant, his voice high pitched.

"What?" growled Kesar.

Sant wanted to say, "I can't go," but he didn't. Looking at Kesar, he knew he just couldn't back out. Kesar would almost certainly go anyway, and Sant, lonely and regretful, would be constantly wondering what was happening to Kesar, what adventures he was experiencing. "Nothing," said Sant. His voice was hoarse, and he cleared his throat. "I remembered something, but it doesn't matter."

"I wonder," said the man, "have you told your families you were going?"

"No," said Kesar.

"No," said Sant.

"Then maybe we had better not travel the main road. It might be quite upsetting if someone saw you leaving and told your families, and they came chasing after you."

"That's true," said Sant. Whereas last night he had been disappointed at not being able to confound his family by announcing his great intention, now he cringed at the very thought of having to explain his actions to his father or mother, or even to his brother.

"Then please lead the way through the fields," said the man to Kesar. "Oh, and you may call me Bir. May I know your own good names?"

Kesar told him, and they set out. They followed the paths for a time, between the tall fields of *bajra* and the newly planted winter crops. In the trees the awakening birds were beginning to chatter. Sant kept wishing there were some way to both stay behind and yet go on the journey. At the edges of fields they often passed shrines to local deities, and Sant recognized a stone image of the God Bheru, depicted as usual as an archer on horseback.

The sun rose, in the far distance on a low hill they saw the Thakur of Baldeogarh's fortress, bathed in the golden orange light. At some unmarked line they passed into Ajmer territories, and Sant began to see villages and fields he had never before visited. Unlike the area close around Ludva, where the pulley wheels were always supported by wooden uprights, he now also saw some wells with the wheels supported by stone pillars. The colors of the clothing worn by women changed, from bright green and yellow and red, to varying shades of dark red and blue.

Gradually, as he encountered new and different sights, Sant grew more and more intrigued with the trek. He remembered his dream, the thrill of riding a horse and carrying a sword. Maybe the dream actually foretold what awaited him at Anandpur!

By the time they reached the wonders of Ajmer, the provincial capital of the Mughal empire, a city even bigger than Mangarh, he was committed to the journey. In their eagerness to get to Anandpur, they decided not to make the side journey of a few *kos* westward to the famous pilgrimage spot of Pushkar. But Sant saw, high on the hill above Ajmer, the long walls of Taragarh Fort, where the legendary Prithviraja Chauhan had ruled with his bride, the princess Samyogita. At the edge of the city, he saw with wonder the big mosque of Addhai din Ka Jhonpra, its stone arches ornately carved with Arabic calligraphy. And he marveled at the red sandstone Daulat Khana, the palace of the Mughal rulers, built by the great Emperor Akbar.

He was awed by the white marble pleasure pavilions, built by the Mughal Emperor Shah Jahan, reflected in the broad waters of the Anasagar lake. Outside the amazing, huge arched entry to the famous Dargah, he and his companions edged their way though the busy bazaar, where stalls sold rose petals, sweetmeats, incense. Uneasy at the press of so many people, but thrilled at the experience, Sant slipped off his *jutis* and entered the Dargah and prayed for a successful journey at the tomb of the renowned Muslim saint, Khwaja Muin-ud-din Chisti. Inside the Dargah compound he saw the finely carved marble mosques built by the Emperors Akbar and Shah Jahan.

To think that, were it not for Bir and Kesar, today he would be trudging behind the bullocks in the hot sun, working the same fields he had plowed ever since he was big enough to manage the animals!

The party of three was well past Ajmer when a troop of Maharaja Madho Singh's Rajput cavalry passed through Ludva. Their captain questioned the villagers as to whether anyone had seen a lone traveler who was wanted by the Maharaja for unspecified reasons. Some residents claimed to have seen the man, but none could offer definite enough help to claim the reward offered for information leading to him.

The families of Sant and Kesar were distraught about their sons' disappearances, but they feared the Maharaja's soldiers enough that they did not mention their concern or ask for help in finding the missing young men. They assumed that since both friends were gone and had taken supplies with them, the disappearance was planned in advance, and the families were therefore far more puzzled and annoyed than truly worried.

It did not occur to anyone that there could be a connection between the sought-after man and the two young Jats who had vanished from their beds.

3

As they traveled, Bir, who they found possessed a wealth of knowledge on virtually all subjects, told them more about the Sikhs and about Guru Gobind Rai.

The term "Sikh" meant "Disciple," a follower of the "Guru," or "Teacher." The religion had been founded two centuries ago by the first Guru, Nanak. Nanak had preached the brotherhood of both Hindu and Muslim and had taught against idol worship. All men and women, regardless of caste, were equal, and through prayer and meditation all could come to know God.

The persecution of the Sikhs and their Gurus by the Mughal Emperors, recently by Aurangzeb in particular, had made the sect more militant. The current Guru, the tenth in succession, was an outstanding warrior, as well as a spiritual leader who composed his own devotional poetry.

"It's said," Bir told them, "that the Guru once was armed only with a sword and shield when he hunted a tiger that had been killing cattle. The tiger leaped upon him, but the Guru protected himself with the shield and cut the tiger in two with the sword. That's a remarkable accomplishment. I've accompanied Rajput princes on hunts and I've painted some in action. Always they go on elephants or hunt from a hidden platform. Always they use spears or arrows to kill from a distance. Never do they meet a tiger on the ground, face to face."

Sant and Kesar were listening wide-eyed. Bir added, "The Guru used the tiger to illustrate a point. He said the tiger had died like a hero and thus gone to happiness in heaven. It is only cowards who must suffer rebirth after rebirth. Therefore, if a man dies in battle, he should die facing his enemy, not running away." He looked pointedly at them and said, "Assuming, of course, that you have the ill fortune to get into a battle in the first place."

Kesar scowled at the suggestion that fighting was something to be avoided. Sant tried not to think about the possibility of being in a war.

Bir also coached Sant and Kesar in the Punjabi language spoken in Anandpur. It was substantially different from the Rajasthani dialect which Sant and Kesar had spoken in Ludva, so the two men were thankful to have Bir's instruction.

Sant was surprised that Kesar had to struggle more than he to remember the Punjabi words. "How do you learn so fast?" growled Kesar once when they were making camp for the night. Bir had gone off to ask some other travelers about the next day's journey.

Sant's eyes widened. "I never thought about it. It just seems to come easy to me."

Kesar snorted and turned away.

"I'm glad to help you whenever you want," said Sant.

Kesar grunted and strode off.

A week into the journey, they found themselves walking with a party of nine musicians on their way to perform at a large wedding. The men occasionally made music as they walked, with three of them beating drums of varying sizes, one playing small hand cymbals, one shaking *khartals*, and two playing flute-like *poongis*. The final two carried stringed instruments in bags on their backs. The terrain had become flat and uninteresting, and Sant enjoyed the diversion of the music. At dusk, the travelers came upon a camping spot under *neem* trees and halted for the night.

The leader of the musicians, a short, slim, dark complexioned man of unimposing appearance, approached Bir and said, "I've heard a number of bands of *dacoits* operate in this area. You seem like men who could put up a good defense. Would you consider joining with us?"

Bir looked at the other musicians for a moment, then back at the leader. He gave a nod. "Of course."

Sant later commented to Bir, while they were seated away from the other travelers, "If it's true about the *dacoits*, we're lucky to have these others to make our party bigger."

Bir was reassembling the parts of his *hookah*. He frowned. "Perhaps."

Puzzled at the lack of agreement, Sant asked, "Isn't a large party safer than a smaller one?"

"Usually," Bir said. He sat his assembled water pipe on the ground. He stroked his beard as he looked at Sant and asked quietly, "Have you heard of *thugs*?"

"Yes," said Sant. "They're *dacoits* who worship the Goddess Kali by going about in disguise and killing their victims by strangling them."

"First," said Bir, staring at him, "they win the confidence of their victims by appearing harmless."

Sant thought a moment, and said, "Then we shall have to be extra careful to watch out for any other travelers we meet."

After a time, Bir nodded, looked away, and said, "That's right.

"Maybe we should warn the musicians to be careful, too," said Sant.

Bir looked back at him a moment. Then he frowned and said, "I'll take care of that myself."

Kesar returned, seated himself, and began examining the sharpness of his sword edge. Sant told him about Bir's warning of possible *thugs*. Kesar immediately turned to look at the musicians. Then he said to Sant, "Yes, we'd better keep an eye on them."

Sant said with surprise, "No, no, not the musicians. Any travelers who seem harmless—Oh!" He stopped and looked at the men. "I see."

Bir arranged with Kesar and Sant that one of the three of them should be awake at all times at night to keep an eye on their companions. Sant said to Bir, out of hearing of the others, "If you're worried these men might be *thugs*, why are we traveling with them?"

Bir rubbed his beard and glanced toward the musicians. "Would you rather have them ambush us some night when we're all asleep?"

"No, of course not!" Bir looked back to Sant. "This way, we know where they are, and we can watch them closely, just in case." He shrugged with a wry smile. "Anyway, they're probably quite innocent."

The musicians did indeed seem harmless. They were humorous, happy men, who livened the evenings by the campfire with private concerts. Sant decided by the second night that there was no cause whatsoever to be suspicious of them, and he felt foolish for having fallen victim to Bir's and Kesar's wariness. He was more than a little annoyed at having to stay awake a third of each night, thereby losing needed sleep. But Bir continued to insist.

Two more days and nights they all traveled together.

By day, Bir told tales of Guru Gobind Rai as they trudged along, dust rising from the narrow roadway. "He owns an elephant, it is said, which is quite clever. It will go fetch arrows which the Guru has shot from his bow. It will hold the jug of water for washing the Guru's feet and then wipe them with its trunk."

"Will we see it?" Sant asked excitedly.

"Almost certainly," replied Bir. "The Guru would never willingly part with such a valuable creature."

To Sant, it seemed that if the musicians had planned any harm, they would have carried out their plans within the first night or two. It was obviously much more reasonable to watch the roads for truly suspicious travelers, or for ambushes by *dacoits*.

The fourth night, Sant found himself dozing at times on his portion of the watch, which was the last one of the night. He struggled to stay awake, but halfheartedly, no longer seeing any real sense in depriving himself of rest.

He lapsed into sleep just before dawn, and he dreamed of a huge elephant, a once peaceful one that had gone mad, that suddenly attacked him in the night, holding him in place by its foot as it grabbed him from behind, wrapping its trunk around his neck and choking him.

The dream was real enough, and unpleasant enough, that he struggled to waken.

Then he realized the choking was quite genuine.

He gasped, struggling desperately for air. Strong hands firmly gripped his shoulders and his feet, pinning him to the ground.

He was sinking into blackness, straining with all his might against his fate, yet unable to prevent it.

The struggle seemed to go on forever.

Whack!

He heard the sound faintly, as if from another world.

Another *whack*.

A *thump*.

The tightness around his neck eased, but he could only gasp urgently for air.

He was vaguely aware that some sort of commotion was occurring: whacks, thuds, screams. He had no strength to try to discover what was happening.

His neck, his throat hurt horribly, and he still struggled to breathe.

He heard many fast footfalls, diminishing as if men were running away.

Then someone was cradling his head, gently. Bir's voice said something, and Kesar's replied. "Sant!" said Kesar. "Are you all right?" Sant felt his shoulders being shaken.

He tried to reply, but only a croaking moan escaped his injured throat. Still, the sound caused Kesar to say, "He's alive!"

It was light out before Sant had recovered enough to converse, painfully. When he first looked about, he saw four bodies on the ground, scattered as if thrown aside by some demon.

Kesar, who was standing as if still on guard, handed Sant a yellow scarf, with a knot tied on one end. He said bluntly, "This was what they had around your neck."

Sant, leaned his back against a tree and wonderingly fingered the smooth fabric. He swallowed. And cringed at the pain.

"The knot helps them get a better grip," said Bir, who sat nearby on the ground.

Kesar said excitedly, "If Bir hadn't been awake enough to hear them give their cock-crow signal, they would have killed us all! He woke me with his shouts while he used his *lathi* to kill the two who were strangling you. I killed another with my sword, and Bir another one with his *lathi*. The others ran off."

He held his sword proudly for Sant to see. "The first blood! It's no longer a virgin."

Sant gently massaged his tender throat while he tried to think of what to say.

Bir was casually looking off into the distance. Sounding as if the event was an everyday occurrence, he glanced at Sant and said, "I suspected they might have felt they'd won our confidence. So I had my weapons ready, and I listened for their signal. *Thugs* often cry, 'Bring the tobacco' as their signal, or else they make the sound of a cock's crow. This time I heard the cock crow. So I leaped to my feet with my staff in my hands, or they would probably have killed me as well as you."

It was painful for Sant to talk, even more painful to swallow. He managed to ask hoarsely, "Why do they do such a thing?"

Bir again looked away as he replied, "It's a ritual. Their Goddess Kali thirsts for victims as sacrifices. But the killing must be bloodless, and the victims unaware. So they try to make their victims suspect nothing, and they use a knotted handkerchief or a silk cord to strangle. They also," he added dryly, "get an earthly reward by robbing their victims belongings and dividing up the loot."

"They wouldn't have gotten much from *us*," said Sant.

Bir glanced quickly at him. "No, indeed," he agreed, after only an instant's delay.

Later in the morning, when Sant felt up to traveling, Bir led him to the edge of the grove. There, three large oblong holes had been dug.

"They intended one for each of us," said Bir.

Sant rubbed his aching neck. Their bodies would not even have been burned on a funeral pyre! He turned away and vomited. The bile scorched his raw throat.

It seemed to Sant that Kesar was striding more vigorously than before, carrying himself straighter. His hand was more often on his sword.

He's actually glad he had the chance to fight! thought Sant. Neither Kesar nor Bir accused Sant. But why, he wondered, did he have to bungle every-thing? He'd hoped his ineptness had been left behind in Ludva village. As they strode northward the next morning, Sant said hoarsely by way of apology, his eyes on the ground, "I almost got us killed by falling asleep."

There was silence for a time. "Well," said Kesar with surprising lightness, "the only harm was to you."

Bir, his gaze on the road ahead, said, "They would have attacked us soon anyway. And I might have fallen deep asleep myself before long. It was better that it happened when it did." He smiled tightly at Sant. "So in a way, you did us a favor."

It was days before Sant's throat ceased to pain him, and weeks before the purple bruises around his neck completely disappeared.

For the remainder of the journey Bir refused to allow anyone to travel with them. The party did encounter a Sikh, riding proudly on horseback, who was on his way to visit his home village. When Bir mentioned that they were headed to Anandpur, and that Kesar and Sant expected to join the Guru's army, the Sikh eyed the two young men and shook his head. "You may be disappointed. The latest I've heard is that the Guru needs only men with horses. He's just interested in foot soldiers if they've had a lot of fighting experience."

When the Sikh had ridden off, Kesar said angrily to Bir, "How could you have led us this far if the Guru won't even take us!"

Bir replied calmly, "I wouldn't worry."

"But if the Guru only wants men with horses now, why should we even continue?"

Sant, who had been growing ever more apprehensive about the possibility of having to become a soldier, let out his breath in relief.

Bir, however, replied, "I think perhaps we can convince him to take you both anyway."

Kesar said hotly, "We'd better, after risking our lives to get there."

Kesar was sullen the remainder of the day. Sant, while sympathetic toward Kesar's plight, could not help feeling hopeful that they would both be refused by the Guru.

At the next large village, Bir astonished Sant and Kesar by buying three horses, complete with saddles and bridles, from the stables of the Rajput lord who ruled the area.

Bir led a grayish mount to Kesar, and a brown colored one, the smallest of the three, to Sant. "The Guru will certainly accept us if we come with our own horses," Bir told them. "Once you get used to riding, it will increase our traveling speed also. The sooner we reach Anandpur, the sooner we're less likely to fall victim to *thugs* again or to other hazards."

Dazed, Sant held the reins in his hand while he grew aware of the odor of the horse and sensed its muscular strength. "Horses are so costly!" he exclaimed. "Just the wealthy can afford them. And I've seen only Rajputs riding them." The animal stood calmly, swishing its tail back and forth.

Bir shrugged. "No Rajput would sell his favorite steed. These aren't the finest horses from the stables, and the saddles are old and worn. So they didn't cost as much as you might think. I'd saved my earnings from Maharaja Madho Singh. What better use for the gold than three mounts? Guru Gobind Rai has sent out a call for men with horses; he does not care if the men are Rajputs or Bhangis—or Jats."

"You'd give these to us?" Kesar asked, still amazed.

"Not to you personally. To the Guru. But I see no reason why they should not be for your own use so long as you serve the Guru as his soldiers." Bir reached up and fingered the ears of Sant's horse. "See how these point inward and almost touch each other at their tips? He's a Kathiawari. A lot of Rajputs favor them. Or," he gestured toward Kesar's horse, "Marwaris like yours."

Kesar furrowed his brow and stared at Bir. "How does a painter come to know horses so well?"

"I'm far from expert. But I've done considerable traveling in the entourage of my patrons, and on rare occasions I've been loaned a horse for a journey."

Sant began stroking the dark mane of his horse. Bir smiled and said, "I was told his name is Ravana. But that doesn't really fit, given his small size and mild temperament. You may want to call him something else."

Sant grinned broadly at the thought his horse was named after the fierce demon in the great epic, the *Ramayana*. "No, Ravana is fine." He fondled the animal's forehead. While Bir talked with Kesar, Sant spoke to Ravana quietly in what he hoped was a reassuring voice despite his own excitement. The horse eyed him and appeared to accept him calmly, and in a few minutes, Sant felt as if they were friends who understood each other with the same type of rapport he'd shared with Jasmine the cow.

Bir left Kesar and approached Sant again. "I'll show you how to mount up." He demonstrated how to put a foot in the stirrup and boost the other leg over the saddle. Sant failed on the first try, but he summoned more energy and was successful on the next effort.

With only the slightest instruction from Bir, Sant found to his surprise that he could soon direct the animal with ease. The principal difficulty was learning to sit on the saddle without being bounced into the air at every step.

Kesar's gray horse seemed intent on resisting all of his rider's gruff commands. Kesar finally dismounted and cut a slender branch from a nearby *khejari* tree. He stripped the leaves from it, and strode up to his mount.

"What do you intend to do with that?" asked Bir, now seated on his own horse.

"Whip him and make it clear who his new master is," grumbled Kesar.

Bir shook his head no. "That will just make this one more stubborn. Here, try feeding him a lump of *gur* instead."

Kesar took the sugar lump and reluctantly fed it to his horse.

"He needs to see you're a source of things he likes," said Bir. "Then he'll want to please you in the hope of getting more. Eventually he'll fall into the habit of doing what you want without question."

Kesar frowned. He slowly reached up and began stroking his horse's forehead. "That's it," said Bir. "You want him to think of you as his good friend."

Kesar shook his head, muttering, "Friends with a *horse*." But he continued stroking the head, then the mane. He soon mounted his animal again, and the horse slowly obeyed when they started up the road.

The party continued across the Punjab plains, now at a much faster pace. A few days later, the Shivalik hills rose into view, and they reached Anandpur.

4

Anandpur, 6 December 1698

A Sikh commander interviewed the three in Lohgarh, the southernmost of the five forts defending Anandpur, and the one used most for military training. Though the new arrivals were quickly accepted into the army, Bir also arranged a personal audience with the Guru.

The day was sunny and pleasantly warm. Sant's heart pounded and his stomach was queasy as they led their horses to the open sided hall with attached canopy where the Guru held his daily *durbar*. Attendants took the reins of the horses and custody of Bir's staff and Kesar's sword.

Guru Gobind Rai sat on a low, cushioned throne, attended by flywhisk bearers and guards. The Guru was tall, around thirty years in age, and he wore rich robes and a turban with a high jeweled crest. A full beard and mustache framed his handsome, sharp featured face.

Sant felt an instant stab of recognition. Here, he was certain, was the warrior prince he had seen in his dream back in the village. When the three new arrivals were summoned forward, they did their obeisances to the Guru. Upon rising, Bir addressed him in the customary manner of Guru Gobind's followers: "*Sacha Padshah*, True King, we've come to request the privilege of serving in your army." He gestured toward the horses, which stood just outside the canopy. "We offer our three horses to you, and also our weapons."

Guru Gobind gave a nod and a slight smile. Sant thought him the most noble, the most godlike person, he had ever seen. The Guru asked in a voice that, though not loud, carried great power, "Have you had a long journey?"

"From Mangarh, *Sacha Padshah*," said Bir. "We began on foot, but several days ago we acquired our horses and rode the remainder of the way."

The Guru said, "You are obviously strong and in good health, to survive your travels and arrive here still vigorous." He looked to Sant and smiled, asking, "Are you certain, also, that you want to join my army?"

Sant had not expected to be directly addressed by the great man. But the Guru's eyes were kind, and Sant managed to reply, his voice high pitched, "I, uh, yes, True King!"

"I see the makings of an archer in you," said the Guru. "You have the proper build, similar to myself." He then looked to Kesar and said, "And I see a swordsman in you, with your powerful arms and your balanced stride." To Bir, he said, "I'm pleased to accept each of you into my army, though many newcomers find the training to be rigorous."

"We will gladly undergo the training," Bir said. "However, I also have another gift, and I would like to offer my services in an additional capacity." He presented the Guru with a small painting he had done of a tiger hunting scene.

The Guru examined the work and nodded, obviously impressed. "May I know your previous patrons?"

"Most recently," said Bir, "I served the Maharaja of Mangarh. Prior to that, I was at Mewar. And before that, I worked for various rulers in both the Deccan and the Punjab."

Guru Gobind was watching him intently, with eyes now unreadable.

"You've traveled considerably."

"So I have. An artist must go where he can find patrons. But I find I'm tiring of moving so much from place to place, and I would now prefer to be more settled."

"We have poets here," the Guru said after several moments, his eyes still on Bir. "But our previous painter unfortunately has passed on. I'd be delighted for you to serve in that capacity, to depict memorable occasions at our court."

Bir inclined his head. "I'm honored, *Sacha Padshah*."

"While each of you is in my service, I'm pleased to have you use the horses and weapons you brought," said the Guru, his eyes again warm, as he looked directly at Sant, and then at Kesar. "You may leave now. But we'll talk again."

All three again prostrated themselves, and they backed away from the throne.

Afterwards, as they led their horses away, Sant said wonderingly, "He thinks I can be an archer!"

"And he knew right away that I'd be good with a sword," said Kesar, marching confidently beside his mount.

Bir was silent, and Sant said, "The Guru seemed glad to have you as an artist."

Bir looked at Sant blankly for a moment, as if his thoughts were far away. Then, he said, "Yes. Yes, he did seem glad."

"Does that mean you'll spend a lot of time with him, personally?" Kesar asked.

Bir gave a nod. "Yes, I suppose it does. I may get to know him better than most Sikhs."

"Such good fortune!" Sant said. "To be in the True King's presence every day."

Bir glanced at him with a brief smile. "A court artist does have certain privileges."

The next morning, Sant and Kesar began attending the Guru's morning lessons for the faithful. Bir, however, was instead taking up his duties as artist. Kesar shoved his way to a seat near the front of the crowd of several hundred Sikhs. Sant followed and sat by his friend.

To Sant's fascination, the Guru's elephant Parsadi stood beside his master, tirelessly waving a flywhisk back and forth with its trunk. Sant and Kesar still were not fluent enough in Punjabi to understand all the Guru said in the first morning worship sessions. However, with Bir's help, they soon knew by heart the words of the regular morning prayer, the "Japji" of Guru Nanak, the founder of the Sikh faith:

> *There is one God*
> *He is the supreme truth.*
> *He, the creator,*
> *Is without fear and without hate,*
> *He, the omnipresent,*
> *Pervades the universe.*
> *He is not born,*

Nor does He die to be born again.

Before Time itself
There was truth,
When time began to run its course

He was the truth.
Even now, He is the truth.
Evermore shall truth prevail.

Guru Gobind Rai's training regimen for new recruits was rigorous. Kesar took to it with delight and enthusiasm. "Finally, someone is encouraging me to be a fighter!" he told Sant one warm morning, as he wiped the sweat from his forehead. "Finally, I can wear my sword, and no one jokes about it. And I'm with other men who are training to be warriors, too."

"I don't think I'll ever be good at sword fighting," Sant said, his eyes downcast. Despite the padded coat he wore, he ached all over from the bruises inflicted by the blunted practice weapons.

"You'll get better," Kesar said with little conviction in his voice. "Anyway, maybe you'll be good at archery."

Sant brightened some at the thought. The idea of shooting from a distance held far more appeal than competing blow by blow against the strength and skill of another man.

On the first day of instruction in using bows, Kesar, with his powerful arms took delight in being able to draw the string and bend the bow with relative ease. Sant was issued a smaller bow, and with muscles hardened by labor in the fields, he soon grew accustomed to stringing and pulling it.

They began shooting at the targets, bundles of straw tied crudely into the shapes of men. Kesar took aim and let fly with great determination, as if it were his sole purpose in life to demolish the target. His arrows flew with great force, but they frequently missed.

Sant was intrigued by both the bow and the arrows. He frequently ran his fingers appreciatively along the smooth wood of the bow or along the bamboo arrow shafts. They somehow felt warm, as if they were a part of himself, quite unlike the sword he'd been given of hard, cold metal. When he let fly an arrow, it was almost as if a piece of his mind went with it, guiding it to its target. He was delighted to find that he usually came quite close to where he had aimed. With the successes to encourage him, he continued to practice diligently every day, and to improve.

"Why do you keep wearing your archer's thumb ring," Kesar asked one evening, "even when you aren't practicing?"

Sant thought for a moment, then he smiled. "Maybe it's the same reason you wanted to wear your sword, back home in Ludva."

Kesar stared at him, then he gave one of his rare laughs. "You're getting more clever, now that you're away from our village."

Sant felt his face growing warm. It was the first time he could remember Kesar ever coming close to praising him.

He hired a scribe to write a letter to his family back in Ludva village, telling them that he was alive and well, and that he was now a warrior in

Anandpur, with his own horse. He wished he could be there to watch their faces when the letter was read to them.

But it was the Guru's lectures that Sant loved most of all. Far more than Kesar, Sant was enthralled with Guru Gobind Rai's poetry, with the Guru's love for God, his dedication to serving what he saw as God's will, his daily lessons about God and life.

By the end of a few weeks, Sant could understand without assistance when, one fine winter morning, Guru Gobind Rai recited a poem, also by the first Guru, Nanak. Guru Nanak had known how to speak of God to the farmers who composed so many of his followers.

Sant was gazing intently at Guru Gobind Rai. Due to Sant's own farm upbringing, the words struck a most responsive chord in him:

> *As a team of oxen are we driven*
> *By the ploughman, our teacher*
> ....
> *We reap according to our measure*
> *Some for ourselves to keep, some to others give.*
> ....
> *If you would the fruits of salvation cultivate*
> *And let the love of the Lord in your heart germinate,*
> *Your body be as the fallow land*
> *Where in your heart the Farmer sows his seeds*
> *Of righteous action and good deeds,*
> *Then, with the name of God, irrigate.*

As Guru Gobind Rai finished the words, Sant felt the Guru was looking directly at him. A slight smile crossed the Guru's lips as if he sensed how deeply Sant was moved. "May I now have some water to drink," the Guru said.

Several Sikhs were in attendance upon him, seated on both sides. One of them began rising to furnish the water.

But the Guru's eyes were still upon Sant. With no hesitation, Sant leaped to his feet and hurried to where the jugs and pitchers sat in the shade of the Guru's tent. He filled the silver goblet and hastily stepped over and handed it to the Guru. Guru Gobind took it with a smile. His eyes still on Sant, he raised the goblet, poured its contents into his mouth, and returned the container to Sant. Sant deposited the goblet in its place and went back to his seat.

Only when he saw Kesar's look did he realize what he had done. In front of the entire congregation, and in the presence of the great Guru, he, Sant, had the temerity to thrust himself forward in place of those men assigned to serve the True King! His face flushed hot in embarrassment, even though he realized vaguely he had somehow fallen under the Guru's influence. Sant settled himself on the ground and fixed his attention raptly on Guru Gobind for the remainder of the worship service.

Afterwards, Kesar said to him, "Whatever came over you? I could scarcely believe my eyes when I saw you serve the Guru yourself."

Sant said weakly, "I thought he asked me to get the water for him. So I did as he ordered."

Kesar stared at him for a time. Then he shook his head and strolled away.

At the next worship gathering, Sant noticed a shift in emphasis. While the elephant Parsadi waved the flywhisk over him, Guru Gobind began with the peaceful words of Guru Nanak. Then Gobind recited one of his own compositions, a teaching that all men were brothers, that Hindu and Muslim were one:

> *The same are the temple and the mosque;*
> ....
> *For, men are the same all over; the difference is only of*
> *the appearance, the seen.*
> ....
> *From the one fire arise myriads of sparks and then merge*
> *in the same fire again.*
> *From the dust arise myriads of particles, and then blend*
> *with the dust again.*
> *From the sea arise myriads of waves and then fall and*
> *merge in water again.*
> *So also arise all forms, sentient and non-sentient, and*
> *springing from Him are United in Him again.*

Sant listened raptly. Although the images in the poem were not ones of farming, or even of rural life, they were perfectly understandable, dealing with the oneness of all things on the earth.

The Guru next recited another of his own compositions:

> *O Lord, these boons of You I ask,*
> *Let me never shun a righteous task,*
> *Let me be fearless when I go to battle,*
> *Give me faith that victory will be mine,*
> *Give me power to sing Your praise;*
> *When my end comes near,*
> *May I meet death on the battlefield.*

Sant, who had been listening intently, felt faintly disturbed. The Guru seemed to have shifted abruptly from teaching of the unity of all life, all faiths, to teaching that it is glorious to kill and be killed in battle.

Of course, the Guru was raising an army. It was essential to defend the Sikh community against the Muslim Emperor Aurangzeb and against those Hindu rajas who were jealous of the Guru's growing popularity. But Sant had assumed that the call to arms was based solely on necessity. This poem made it sound as if the Guru was actually enthusiastic about the prospect of warfare.

Sant went to that source of all wisdom, Bir, whom he found working on a painting of the Guru mounted on his roan stallion. The artist was completing a depiction of the white hunting falcon with wings spread, perched on the Guru's wrist. Sant watched Bir for a few minutes and then said slowly, "I like the Guru's teachings that there is one God, that he can not be found in the worship of idols such as Hindus do. That he can be found through living a life of prayer and service to him and all men." Sant stopped.

"Go on," encouraged Bir, dipping his brush into one of the small clamshells that held his paint.

"I wonder, though, how he can teach a God of love and peace, and yet be so enthusiastic about urging his Sikhs to kill the enemy in battle."

Bir turned away from the painting, and slowly nodded. "You know my own lack of enthusiasm about fighting." He thought for a moment, still holding the brush. "There has been a change in the Sikhs since the religion was first founded. Guru Nanak taught the importance of devotion, of surrender to God, of worshiping. So does Guru Gobind Rai. But you know that Guru Gobind's own father was beheaded at the Emperor Aurangzeb's orders. Before that, Emperor Jahangir had Guru Arjun put to death by torture. The *Sacha Padshah* believes the Mughal Emperor is a tyrant, and tyrants can only be dealt with by the sword. We are now living in an evil age, when success in the name of righteousness can not be achieved solely through humility and forgiveness. It is also necessary to meet force with force."

Bir returned to the painting. He peered closely at it and painted a tiny streak of gray on the falcon as he continued, "God not only builds. After he has created and sustained for a time, he destroys. Creation and destruction are part of the same process. Guru Nanak, so long ago, had no reason to emphasize God as the Destroyer. But Guru Gobind Rai feels he has such a reason. He and his Sikhs can sometimes act as God's agents in destroying evil. And since so many Jats have joined the Sikhs, the Guru has an ideal race of men to train as his fighters."

Sant sat for a time, thinking. By tradition, all gurus could expect service from their disciples in exchange for the privilege of learning and being in daily contact with an enlightened being. If this particular guru felt it was important for his disciples to learn the martial as well as the spiritual arts, Sant was willing. He said to Bir, "But you yourself are not enthusiastic about fighting."

Bir gazed at Sant. Eventually, he said, "Someone always suffers in war. Usually the more innocent ones suffer most."

"I see," Sant said after a while.

It was customary for the Sikhs to take turns serving the Guru: fanning him to keep him cooler, using the flywhisks to chase annoying insects away whenever the elephant was not doing that service, waiting near to run errands.

One day Sant took his turn with the flywhisk. The Guru was seated in his ornate tent, conducting business. Sant was waving the peacock feather *chowri* slowly back and forth, back and forth.

After a time he noticed a large dark bee in the tent. It first buzzed around randomly, and then it shot straight for the Guru. Startled, and worried that it might sting the True King, Sant swung the flywhisk vigorously toward it.

Realizing he would miss the bee, he leaped forward, half losing his balance. He wrenched himself sideways to avoid falling into the Guru. But at the same instant, as he flung his arms to recapture his balance, he dealt the Guru's turban a solid blow with the flywhisk. Sant landed on his buttocks on the carpet.

Horror stricken, he saw that he had knocked the Guru's turban askew.

A shocked silence fell in the tent. The Guru turned to look at him and smiled. "Sant seems anxious to get my turban off my head," the Guru said lightly as he readjusted the headgear. "Maybe one day I will simply give it to him to wear."

There were several nervous laughs at the jest. The Guru turned back to his business.

Sant, too mortified to even apologize, rose to his feet to resume his duty with the flywhisk. A nudge came on his arm. He turned and saw one of the Guru's chief lieutenants, who beckoned him away.

Outside the tent, the man said to Sant, "Whatever came over you? How could you do such a thing?"

"I, uh, it was an accident. The bee—"

The officer ordered several Sikhs who were standing by, "Give him a good beating. He needs to learn proper behavior when he serves our Guru."

The men led Sant some distance away. They held him firmly by each arm, while one Sikh took a cane and thrashed him several times on the back and buttocks.

Just then, came the voice of the Guru: "Whatever is going on here?"

"*Sacha Padshah*, we were punishing him for his disservice to you," said one of the men.

"But I ordered no punishment. It was an accident, I'm sure. Release him." They let go of Sant. Embarrassed and ashamed, he turned to face the Guru.

Guru Gobind said in a stern voice, his eyes fierce, "This beating should never have happened. I must make a recompense." He eyed Sant. "Do you have a wife?"

"Uh, no, *Sacha Padshah*."

"Not even in your home village?"

"No, True King. My friend Kesar and I hoped when we came here we might get one. I mean, one for each of us!"

The Guru nodded, warmth returning to his eyes. "We must do something about that. Every Sikh should have a wife." He turned away, then stopped and faced Sant again. "In the meantime," he smiled broadly at his jest, "I will think about someday loaning you my turban as you wished."

The Guru continued on his way.

5

Anandpur, two months later, March 1699

After three months of rigorous training, on this spring day Sant and Kesar had the honor of duty as two of the Guru's personal guards. Sant still could scarcely believe, that he, a simple farmer from a village near Mangarh, should have been turned into a warrior and a Sikh, a disciple of Guru Gobind Rai.

The weather was pleasantly sunny without being uncomfortably hot. The wheat was high and green, and the trees sported new leaves. Guru Gobind Rai halted his roan stallion by the edge of a field of lush tobacco. Dressed in a rich robe and turban, the Guru cut a handsome figure with the hunting falcon seated on one hand and bow held in the other. He turned to his escort, which included Sant and Kesar on their own mounts.

"There is no worse plant on the face of the earth," declared the Guru, "than these tobacco crops."

Sant tried not to show his puzzlement. The smoking of the *hookah* had become commonplace among the elders in his own village, and of course Bir took great pleasure from the pipe.

"Have you seen the effects of this plant upon the body?" the Guru demanded loudly. The hunting hawk on his hand stirred, agitated by the strong emotions of its master. Guru Gobind Rai went on to answer his own question: "Tobacco burns the chest. It causes palpitations of the heart and shortness of the breath. It causes a coughing disease of the throat and lungs. It causes many other diseases, and finally ends in death. My Sikhs have no need of it."

Sant glanced at Kesar, whose fierce gaze was fixed intently and with admiration on his hero. The Guru lowered his voice and said more calmly, "Wine is bad. *Bhang*, hemp, destroys one generation. But tobacco destroys all generations." He spurred his horse onward, toward the town of Anandpur.

Kesar and Sant and the rest of the escort followed. The Guru's discourse on the evils of tobacco left behind, the two rode several paces to the rear of the Guru along the banks of the turbulent Sutlej River.

Like a worldly prince, the Guru led his Sikhs regularly in hunting in the hills, believing that the hunt was good training for warriors. Kesar and Sant admired the Guru's horsemanship, his ability to inspire his soldiers. His skill with his bow was extraordinary.

It was this lifestyle, as well as the growing numbers of his followers, that aroused the jealousy of many of the rulers of the small neighboring hill states. These Hindus found a common cause with the Mughal viceroy of the region in trying to bring an end to Guru Gobind Rai. Hence, one reason for the Guru's emphasis on training to defend himself and the Sikh way of life.

Although Sant had become marginally competent in its use, the sword still felt not quite comfortable hanging from his sash. It was as if Sant had merely borrowed it for a time from someone else. The bow, however, fit his hand perfectly, almost begging to be held by him. And Ravana had become an extension of his own body—Sant could now guide the horse without even thinking, by the pressure of his knees and the occasional spoken command.

Sant saw the Guru dismount, hand the reins and the hawk to two attendants, and begin walking along the river bank. Sant, Kesar, and the other guards slid from their horses to walk also, leading the animals by the reins. Sant became aware that a palanquin, escorted by the entourage typical of a wealthy merchant, was approaching from the direction of the town of Anandpur.

The Guru apparently recognized the visitor, for he increased his pace slightly, striding toward the man. When they met, the merchant, a short rotund man dressed in a *dhoti* and shawl, bent to take the dust of the Guru's feet, and then straightened. As customary, he presented Guru Gobind with gifts. Even from a short distance away, Sant saw the diamonds flashing on the two gold bracelets the man offered the Guru.

"What a fortune," Sant whispered to Kesar. He was certain he'd spoken quietly enough not to upset the Guru.

Guru Gobind Rai scarcely looked at the bracelets before he slid one onto his right arm. The other bracelet, he began twirling around a finger. He cast a glance in the direction of Sant, Kesar and the other guards. Then, he casually flung his powerful arm.

The gold bracelet, heavy though it was, sped from the Guru's finger to fall into the tumbling, foaming waters.

Everyone froze, speechless. The merchant's eyes were bulging.

"A pity," Guru Gobind said in a voice that carried to all in his entourage. He looked at the merchant. "May I ask its value?"

The merchant looked as if he had swallowed a snake. He took a deep breath, and said, "Twenty-five thousand rupees, *Sacha Padshah.*"

The Guru said, glancing at his guards, "I'll give five hundred rupees to anyone who recovers it."

Kesar said quickly, "I'll try it, *Sacha Padshah.* But I couldn't see exactly where the bracelet landed."

The Guru removed the other diamond-studded bracelet and threw it into the churning waters. "It landed right about there."

Like everyone else, Kesar and Sant stared, dazed. The merchant stood frozen, his mouth agape.

The Guru, his eyes lively, smiled and addressed those present: "You've all had a lesson on the value of worldly things." He said to the merchant, "Be assured, I accepted your gifts. I have put them to good use. If I had used them merely as ornaments, they would have been of little importance. But now everyone will hear of them. They will become famous as a teaching to other men." He turned away, adding to the merchant, "Would you care to rejoin me after my outing?" He continued his stroll down the path.

After a moment, the merchant climbed back into his palanquin, his face pale.

Sant and the other guards eyed the dangerous looking waters. He and Kesar glanced at each other. Five hundred rupees (a thousand rupees for recovering two?) was a big sum of money. It would pay their families' taxes to the Maharaja of Mangarh for many years.

On the other hand, the Guru had made it clear he considered anyone searching for the bracelets to be overly concerned with material wealth.

Kesar rode after the Guru, but he continued to turn to look back at the waters, until they were no longer within his view. Sant nudged his horse into motion, but he, too, glanced back toward the river as he left, ruing the loss of so much wealth.

On a bright spring morning, Sant was giving Ravana his daily rubdown, when Kesar stomped up to them. "Hurry!" he said loudly. "The True King has summoned us."

Sant lost all thought of his horse. Still carrying the rubdown cloth, he followed Kesar to the Guru's tent. The usual guards and servants were in attendance, and the elephant Parsadi stood by, quietly holding the Guru's umbrella. Several other persons stood before the ruler, including a couple of women.

After Kesar and Sant made their obeisances, they waited. The Guru was smiling at them, his eyes lit with gaiety. "I have two young women here," he said, "who are in need of husbands. Regrettably, they are both widowed, but they are still most worthy. I could not think of anyone suitable as husbands, since they have no dowries. I thought perhaps you could give me some impartial advice on the matter, due to the fact that you apparently have no interest in marriage yourselves, having never seen fit to take wives before coming here."

Dismayed that the Guru had forgotten the promise to look for brides for them, Sant uneasily glanced at Kesar. Did they dare remind the *Sacha Padshah* of the fact?

Kesar seemed paralyzed, staring at one of the women. While struggling to think of a reply to the Guru, Sant now turned his own attention to them. Both stood with their eyes modestly lowered. One was short and somewhat stocky in build, with a pleasant, round face. The other was tall and slender, and quite pretty. She reminded Sant of his brother's wife Rukmini.

"Uh, *Sacha Padshah*," Sant stammered, "if you may remember—" He halted as Kesar's elbow dug him in his ribs. Embarrassed, Sant realized he'd been about to act inappropriately once again, presuming to instruct the great leader about a lapse of memory.

"Yes?" the Guru prompted, his eyes alight. "You were saying?"

"Uh, nothing, True King."

"Come, out with it."

Sant glanced again at Kesar, who was glowering. Well, there was no help for it. The Guru had commanded him to speak. "True King, I beg your forgiveness. You once said you would look for wives for us."

The Guru laughed in delight. "So I did. And I always try to keep my word. I merely wanted to ensure you hadn't changed your minds."

"Oh, no!"

Kesar said, "No indeed, True King." His eyes were fixed on the taller, more comely of the two women.

Sant stole a quick look at the shorter of the two women, who he now realized must be intended for him. Although not as pretty as the other, from her slight smile and her demeanor she certainly appeared as if she would be a pleasant companion.

"Good," said the Guru. "I'm glad I won't have to disappoint these two beautiful young women. He beckoned to Kesar. "Come forward." Kesar did so.

The Guru gestured to the shorter of the women, who was smiling as if embarrassed. "You are to marry each other. Today, if you wish it. I predict you will be blessed with sons. I, myself, will provide the dowry."

Kesar was quiet for several seconds. Then, with a strained smile he said, "As you wish, True King. I am grateful for your generosity."

Sant stared wide-eyed at the remaining, lovely, creature. She stood as tall as he. Had he misunderstood? Surely this beauty was meant for Kesar.

"Sant," said the Guru, "I always like to reward loyalty, devotion, and service. You are a fine example of all these traits. I have selected this woman for you. She already has a small son from her earlier marriage, but I know you will raise him as if he were your own. May you be blessed with many more sons. As with your brother, I'll provide the dowry."

6

Two weeks later. Anandpur, 30 March 1699

It was the morning of the annual Baisakhi festival, celebrating New Year's

Day and the coming of spring. As usual, thousands of Sikhs had arrived, many from far away. This was Sant and Kesar's first opportunity to see the spectacle at Anandpur, and they had come before first light in order to find a seat closer to their leader.

"I wonder why the Guru insisted this time that none of the men should shave their beards or cut their hair," mused Sant as they approached the raised mound where the Guru would speak.

"I heard him say all the great heroes of ancient times wore their hair long," replied Kesar. "He said if God had meant hair to be cut, it wouldn't have been created to grow."

The Guru's richly decorated tent canopy stood before them, sheltering his throne, and behind it was a small enclosure screened off by tall cloth walls. Carpets covered the ground under the *durbar* canopy, and at its rear a flap of cloth concealed the entrance to the screened room.

A multitude of the Guru's followers was assembling, and Sant and Kesar felt the press of the crowds trying to get as near as possible. People talked noisily. The women were in their own groups, separated from the men, and Sant kept glancing toward Sundari, easily visible among the others due to her height.

His bride. He was proud that even among such large numbers, her beauty stood out.

And she was his. He could still scarcely comprehend the fact.

At first, he had been intimidated by her loveliness. How could he ever cope with such beauty? Surely she must think him unworthy of her. Would she haughtily order him around, expecting him to serve her every wish? Would other men try to steal her from him?

But the Guru had chosen wisely. Despite her physical endowments, she was shy and gentle, and she seemed truly devoted to his happiness. The nights together in their tent, as they learned how to pleasure each other, were more gloriously wonderful than he had ever imagined in his fantasies about Rukmini.

And he was charmed by his new little stepson Anand, only two years old, a lively child with big bright eyes and a wide smile.

Sant was immensely grateful to the Guru for such gifts. He knew he would do anything for the Guru now. Lay down his life, if need be. *Anything.* No sacrifice would be too great in the service of such a great king.

"There's Bir, in the very front row," Kesar commented to Sant.

"He probably wants a good view of everything, so he can paint it later," Sant replied.

A hush full over the multitude as Guru Gobind Rai appeared. His famous elephant Parsadi accompanied him, holding the umbrella above the master. Everyone present did their obeisance. When they were again seated and waiting expectantly, Guru Gobind addressed the crowd, his voice thunderous: "Many centuries ago, in a great sacrifice by fire on Mount Abu, the Brahmins created the brave Rajputs to defend our lands. The Rajputs are courageous warriors. But they have failed to keep our lands and our peoples free.

"Today, my beloved Sikhs, I will conduct another sacrifice, to create a new race of warriors. This sacrifice will be one of blood, not of fire. With it I will create a community even braver and bolder than the Rajputs, a community that will liberate our lands from foreign oppression and tyranny!"

Sant and Kesar sat entranced as excitement built within them and within the vast crowd. Clearly this was not to be a typical Baisakhi celebration.

"The task will be most difficult," the Guru continued. "It can succeed only with God's help. That is why this morning I sought God's blessings. I ask you all to repeat after me this call: *Jo bole so nihal, Sat Shri Akal!*"

Enthusiastically, Sant and Kesar and the assembled thousands in unison shouted the Guru's words, "Whoever utters, 'God is true,' will be blessed!"

The Guru launched into a stirring oration in which he reminded his disciples of the dangers to their faith from the unsympathetic Mughal Emperor and the rulers of the various local states. He ran through a list: the humiliations, tortures, destructions of temples, forced conversions by the Muslim oppressors, the execution of his own father Guru Tegh Bahadur.

"But the Hindus do not hold the answer to these threats," he shouted, spreading his hands wide. "They believe in *ahimsa*, in nonviolence. They assume there is no need to oppose tyranny in this life, because the oppressors will be punished in the next life."

The Guru thrust his right arm high into the air, his fist clenched. "No, my Sikhs! We must not depend on Fate to safeguard our rights. We must entrust this duty to ourselves. In this age of Kali, conditions have reached such a stage that we can achieve success only by action. If someone throws a brick at us, we must return it by throwing a stone."

Sant glanced at Kesar and saw the excitement in his friend's eyes.

The Guru lowered his arm. "Goodness alone is no longer enough. We must not only condemn evil, we must fight to destroy it. It is no longer enough to love our neighbors; we must punish the trespassers."

The Guru drew his sword. He held it high, so it gleamed in the sunlight, and he recited a song to it:

> *God subdues enemies, so does the Sword.*
> *Therefore the Sword is God, and God is the Sword.*
> *I bow with love and devotion to the Holy Sword.*
> *Assist me that I may complete this work....*

He lowered the sword, and shouted, "We must destroy the empire of the Great Mughal, and create in its place a new nation. Today, we create a new class of men and women, who are ready to sacrifice all to serve their land."

He paused and again raised his sword. "My Sikhs, every great deed is preceded by an equally great sacrifice. The Holy Sword will create a great nation, but only after the sacrifice of blood."

Guru Gobind's eyes slowly scanned the crowd. There was complete silence. Sant was certain the Guru looked directly at him. He felt a thrill of anticipation, although he was not certain what to expect. Most likely, the Guru would kill a goat for the cause.

Holding his sword high, the Guru shouted, his eyes flashing, "It is time for the great sacrifice! I ask for one of my beloved Sikhs to come forward, to lay down his life by giving his head."

Gasps came from throughout the crowd. Then absolute stillness. The Guru's eyes roamed over the faces. Sant bent his head, pretending to be in prayer, to avoid meeting the fiery gaze.

After what seemed like minutes, the Guru again shouted in a stern voice: "I repeat—I need one of my Sikhs to die by my sword for the sacrifice!"

Still the crowd was silent. Sant glanced quickly at Kesar, who appeared frozen in consternation. Sant fixed his eyes at the back of the man seated before him.

Time dragged.

The Guru shouted even louder than before, "If there is any true Sikh of mine here today, let him give his head as an offering and proof of his faith!"

Sant saw that in the front row even the normally unflappable Bir was looking about with an odd, puzzled, expression. Beyond Kesar, a man stood. "My True King, my head is at your service!" Sant recognized him as Daya Ram, a Khatri from Dalla village near Lahore.

"Come forward," the Guru demanded.

Daya Ram slowly eased through the crowed to the front. There, Guru Gobind Rai took him by the arm, and led him through the canopy and out of sight beyond the curtained doorway of the enclosure.

The crowd was totally quiet. Sant heard a dull thudding sound from within the enclosure, and a sound like a clink.

After what seemed like a very long time, the curtain was thrust back, and the Guru reappeared. Gasps came from the crowd at the sight of the Guru's sword, crimson with blood. Guru Gobind Rai stood by the front of the canopy. He held the dripping sword high. "I ask for another head. Is there another true Sikh who will give his head to me?"

The crowd was again silent.

The Guru repeated the request.

Silence.

The Guru asked again.

On the far side of the crowd, a man stood, and called, "Take my head, Great King!" He pushed his way up front.

"Dharam Rai," someone nearby said quietly, naming him.

The Guru led the man out of sight. Kesar, his eyes glazed with shock, whispered to Sant, "Two men! Has our Guru gone mad?" There were other murmurings in the crowd. Sant, bewildered, had no idea what to think.

The Guru reappeared his sword freshly red. "Is there any other Sikh who will offer me his head? I am in great need of more!"

Low mutters came from various places among the crowd. Sant turned his head slightly and saw people on the outskirts of the crowd edging off. He wished he were not so close to the front, so he could leave also. He glanced quickly again at Kesar, whose eyes met his, then flicked away.

Sant risked a glance at the Guru, and paled. Guru Gobind's bright eyes were looking directly at him. Sant willed himself to shrink into the ground.

A voice came from close behind him in the crowd. "I offer my head, Great King!" Sant felt partial relief. Someone moved past him, brushing against his shoulder. Sant guiltily jerked away as he realized it was the person who had volunteered, on his way to the Guru.

The man disappeared inside with Guru Gobind Rai. "I'm leaving," Sant whispered to Kesar.

"No!" Kesar's hand gripped Sant's wrist with great force. Sant started to attempt to wrest himself free, but he did not want to create a disturbance to draw attention to himself. He settled back to the ground. After a moment, Kesar let go.

All around, other men were leaving.

The Guru reappeared. Sant now felt uncomfortably exposed, with a gap on his right, and another almost directly in front of him, left by men who had fled. He prayed that the Guru would ask for no more heads.

"I need another!" the Guru called loudly. Even his hand gripping the sword was covered with blood.

Would it never end? Sant now wished fervently that he had escaped, regardless of the shame. On the right, a man said, "He'll kill us all!" Half crouched over, he shoved his way toward the rear, turning his back on the Guru.

Seeming not to notice, the Guru repeated the request.

A man stumbled forward. "I give my head, O King!"

Now was definitely the time to leave, Sant decided, as the Guru led the fourth man toward the enclosure. He quickly stood, before Kesar could grab him again, and looked about. At least half the crowd, perhaps more, appeared to be fleeing.

But many stayed. Sant's eyes darted here and there. Two or three men from his training group were seated nearby, showing no sign of leaving. So far, they did not appear to see him standing, poised for flight.

He abruptly remembered his wife, and he shot a glance over the intervening area at her tall figure. She was looking at another area of the crowd, not seeing that he had risen.

Shame overcoming his desire to flee, he resumed his seat. At least she had not seen him ready to desert.

On three sides of his place were gaps. Only Kesar remained by him.

The Guru returned. "I need another!" he shouted loudly over the retreating backs.

Sant sensed Kesar starting to rise, and felt a stab of panic. But this time, another man quickly came forward, and Kesar settled back to the ground, to Sant's great relief. The Guru led the volunteer into the enclosure.

Five heads thus far! Would there be yet another call? And would Kesar this time volunteer? Should Sant, himself, volunteer? It might save Kesar.

Sant felt numb, his head light. By not thinking about it, he did not have to face the decision. If he offered himself next, it would have to be by impulse, for he now knew he did not have the courage to knowingly, with full understanding of his action, offer himself to certain, immediate death.

The Guru returned, his sword still drenched in red. He called to his attendants. They hurried forth. At the Guru's direction, the attendants stripped the cloth from the screen.

There stood the five men who had offered themselves—very much alive, radiantly happy. Each of the five now wore a blue turban and a yellow shirt, short drawers, and swords.

The remaining crowd broke into applause, tentative at first, but quickly becoming thunderous. Sant joined them, feeling great relief both that the test was over and that the five men had not been harmed.

He looked at Kesar. His friend sat with his head lowered, looking glum, staring at the ground.

Sant, too, stopped applauding, as the full realization hit: I thought I'd do anything for our Guru. But I've failed him.

Although he was seated close to the front, Sant still felt overwhelmed with emotions generated by the dramatic test, and he was only dimly aware of what was occurring. The ceremony continued, with the Guru still making full use of the traditional sacredness of the number five.

Sant watched as the Guru initiated a new custom, first stirring sugared water with a dagger, then sprinkling the five men with this nectar or *amrit*: in their eyes, in their hair, and over their bodies.

He gave each of the five men the name of *"Singh,"* or "Lion," a title previously used by the Rajputs. He bestowed the title of *"Panch Pyare"* upon them, the "Five Beloved Ones."

"Now," Guru Gobind said to the five, "I request you to initiate me in the same way I have initiated you. You will be the first of a new brotherhood of Sikhs."

The men appeared stunned. At last, one said, "But we are not worthy. You are our Guru, our spiritual leader, our King! You are God's own representative on earth!"

The Guru smiled benevolently. *"All* who undergo this nectar ceremony will be known as the 'Khalsa,' the 'Pure.' The Khalsa is the Guru, and the Guru is the Khalsa. There is no difference between you and me."

Overcoming their reluctance with difficulty, the five initiated him, in the same manner as he had used. "I now have added the name of Singh to my own, in place of Rai," announced the Guru. "From this moment I will be known as 'Gobind Singh.'"

The Guru addressed his Five Beloved Ones, but in a voice heard by all present: "You are now of one creed, followers of one path. You are the soldiers of God. Today you have taken new birth in the home of the Guru. You are members of the Khalsa brotherhood. Anandpur is your birthplace. Gobind Singh is your father. My wife is your mother.

"In you, all four classes, all castes, have been merged into one. You are all brothers, all equal. No one is superior to the other. Eat from one dish. The independence and defense of our homeland are entrusted to you. From today, your salutation will be, *'Wah Guru Ji ka Khalsa, Wah Guru Ji ki Fateh*: 'The Khalsa is thine, O Lord! So does the victory belong to you!'"

The Guru prescribed five symbols to which all men of the Khalsa would adhere: The "five K's."

First, all men would wear their head hair and beard uncut (*kesh*). This would show that although they were soldiers, they were also saintly, since ascetics traditionally wore their hair long. It would also make Sikhs easily identifiable and prevent them denying their faith when in danger. Combined with a turban the long hair would protect the head from sword and *lathi* blows.

Second, all would carry a comb (*kangha*) to keep the hair neat.

Third, all would wear a pair of short drawers (*kuccha*), a common warrior's uniform allowing freedom of movement.

Fourth, all would wear a steel bangle (*kara*) on the right wrist, a traditional Hindu charm worn before going into battle, and a symbol worn by ascetics to show they were bound to their Guru.

And fifth, all would carry a dagger (*kirpan*), thus lifting them to the status of Rajputs and other warriors.

While all men would have the last name of "Singh," women would have the surname *"Kaur,"* "Lioness" or "Princess." The Sikhs would thus be one family, transcending the castes from which they had originated. The Guru gave a great many other instructions, to which Sant listened still in a daze.

The Khalsa was to hold five beliefs: in God; in the Guru; in the Granth (the sacred Sikh writings); in the Greeting ("the Khalsa is thine O Lord! So does the victory belong to you"); and in the *Japji* or prayer of Guru Nanak. There were five vows. There were five deliverances. There were five rules of conduct for the Sikhs. When the Guru stated the fifth rule, Sant remembered his old lust for his brother's bride Rukmini: "Do not go, even in a dream, to the bed of a woman other than your own wife."

The Guru instructed the Five Beloved Ones to initiate others into the brotherhood of the Khalsa, and the unprecedented ceremony reached completion.

Kesar had not moved the entire time, and his gaze had been fixed on the ground, his shoulders slumped. Sant now touched his arm. "Is something wrong?"

For a time Kesar did not answer. Then he turned his face to Sant. His eyes blazed as he said in fury, "Of course something's wrong. I could have volunteered—been one of the five! I didn't have the courage. I doubted our Guru." He leaped to his feet, and stalked off.

Sant uneasily watched him leave.

Then full realization of his own shame flooded over him.

Only this morning he had vowed that he would do anything for his Guru. *Anything.*

So why had he been so fearful, so untrusting, of this king, who had given him a wife more lovely than the finest spring sunrise?

Shaken, he sat there for a long time.

Eventually, as he finally rose to leave, he realized Bir was still seated.

He slowly approached the artist. Trying to cover his shame, Sant asked, "Was the ceremony a good subject for painting?"

The artist gave him a look that appeared unfocused. It took him a moment to answer, and then he said, "Yes. Quite good. I think we just witnessed a momentous occasion, and I must indeed do some paintings of it."

In the following days, thousands more of the Sikhs, including Sant and Kesar and Bir, came forward to be initiated at Anandpur. Henceforth, Sant would be known as "Sant Singh," Kesar as "Kesar Singh," and Bir as "Bir Singh."

The fact that Guru Gobind Singh had forgiven all those who failed to offer their lives made Sant even more enthusiastic about his leader. Kesar, still obviously angry at himself for failing to show courage during the ceremony, appeared determined to never again allow such a thing to happen.

Sant asked Bir, "Why did you go through the initiation? Surely you didn't need to do so to continue as the Guru's artist?"

Bir shrugged, his face expressionless. "Probably not. However, the Guru is a great leader. Why should I not commit myself fully to following him?"

"But you disagree with his wanting Sikhs to be warlike."

Bir glanced away, then back at Sant. "Perhaps his oration convinced me. Maybe there is no choice now about having to fight to preserve the Brotherhood."

Another matter was bothering Sant. "I haven't seen you smoke your *hookah* in a long time. Have you given it up?"

Bir looked away, gave a nod. "I have. Our Guru disapproves of tobacco."

"And yet, you'd carried it all the way from Mangarh."

Bir shrugged. "I took considerable enjoyment from it. But I did not know better then. And if I continue to use it now, my brother Sikhs would be unhappy with me."

The answers seemed reasonable. Sant wondered briefly why they didn't satisfy him. But he quickly forgot the matter. After all, the reasons were Bir's concern, not his own.

8

More than five years later, Anandpur, 20 December 1704

So desperate was the situation in the besieged town of Anandpur that even the bark of trees was being ground into flour to make bread.

The Mughal army and its allies from among the local Hindu rajas had obstinately maintained the siege for months, in effect imprisoning the Guru and his followers within the walls of the forts. The enemy had cut off the town's water supply, and the Sikhs could replenish food stocks only through costly raids against the enemy's own encampments.

As dawn approached, Sant was cold and damp, and he tried to ignore his hunger and thirst and fatigue. At the small, rear entrance to Anandpur's wall, he and Bir huddled in their blankets, waiting for Kesar and three other Sikhs to return from trying to obtain water outside the city. A single oil lamp flickered, dimly illuminating the area inside the gate. "They're taking a long time," Sant said, worry in his voice.

Bir, who had long ago lost his well-fed appearance, replied, "With the enemy guarding the river so well, it's hard even in the dark to get to it, much less bring water back. But Kesar's proven himself so many times."

Sant drew his blanket around his shoulders against the cold. "Kesar always fights so fiercely and gets so many wounds. It's good they've all healed. Except the newest ones, of course." He closed his tired eyes and thought back over the past few years. Since their initiation into the Khalsa, Sant and Kesar had warred for the Guru against his relentless enemies in nine major battles. "I still don't like fighting," he murmured, "but I won't let down our Guru or our brothers."

"Our Guru is clearly fond of you," Bir said. "And since you're so good as an archer, at least you're usually shooting at the enemy from a distance."

Sant gave a nod. In the current siege, he regularly was assigned to shoot from the town's walls. He looked at Bir, whose sunken eyes were shadowy pits in the dim lamp light. "Despite our hardships, I just don't understand how so many Sikhs can desert our Guru and their brothers," Sant said.

Bir was quiet for a time. At last, he said, his voice hoarse, "This siege is the hardest for all of us. No food. Ammunition almost gone. And water so scarce. If it wasn't for our Guru, I'm quite sure everyone would have given up weeks ago."

Eventually, Sant said, "At least our families are safe." He and Kesar were thankful that their wives had gone to stay in their parents' home villages near the towns of Amritsar and Ambala, taking the children.

"Yes," said Bir. "That lessens the worries some. And for once, the non-fighters aren't the main ones to suffer."

Sant gazed into the light of the lamp and smiled as he pictured his beautiful wife and their son. Although Sundari had not given birth to more children despite his best efforts, he loved both her and her little boy Anand so much that it didn't matter. He thought about how she frequently praised him for his handsomeness, for his abilities with his horse and bow, and for his kindnesses to her and the boy.

He shifted position and readjusted his blanket, trying to get comfortable despite being so stiff from the cold and damp. He wondered again what Kesar and those with him were encountering outside the walls.

And Kesar now had both a son and daughter to be concerned about, besides his wife. Padmini was good natured and hard working, and Sant had seen how she often told Kesar she admired him and his strength, and how Kesar had grown to love her and to try to please her.

"The sky's starting to turn light," Bir said. "They'd better get back soon, or the enemy will see them for certain."

His words were barely spoken when the faint sound of knocking came on the gate, in the pattern of the agreed-upon signal. The Sikhs on guard readied their weapons in case it was an enemy trick. Two of them unbarred the gate and quietly swung it open on well-greased hinges.

Sant saw Kesar and his three companions slip swiftly into the fort, heavily laden with water bags and pots. The guards quickly closed the gate and shoved the bars into place. Surprisingly, as soon as the water containers were deposited on the ground, Kesar and one of his comrades seized hold of the remaining Sikh, Kanaiya Singh, who was small but strong and agile. The fourth Sikh in the party drew his dagger and held it ready.

Sant edged close to Kesar and asked, "What are you doing?"

Kesar's eyes blazed with anger. "This traitor," Kesar gestured contemptuously toward the captive Sikh, "stopped to give water to a wounded Musalman we stumbled over near the river! I wanted to kill him on the spot for aiding the enemy, but the others insisted on bringing him back to be judged by the *Sacha Padshah*."

A growing crowd followed as Kanaiya Singh was escorted to the Guru's *durbar* tent. After the Guru had completed his morning prayers, with an impassive face he heard the charges against Kanaiya Singh by Kesar and the other two Sikhs.

Daylight had now come, and an enemy cannon ball whistled through the air not far outside. The Guru calmly asked Kanaiya Singh, "Are these accusations true?"

"Yes, True King." The small man bowed his head in a humble manner, his eyes gazing at the carpet near the Guru's feet.

"What were your reasons for aiding our enemy?"

Kanaiya Singh raised his eyes. "*Sacha Padshah*, you've taught that we should look upon all men equally. Since I would have given water to one of our own wounded, I also gave it to the Mohammedan."

Nearby, one of the Sikh's big guns boomed in response to the enemy artillery. The Guru nodded, smiled thinly, and said, "You are a most holy man. I order that no Sikh should hold this action against you. You are free to go."

As Sant and his friends walked away, distant musket shots shattered the stillness like fire crackers during a Divali celebration. Kesar, whose face had been glum and angry, shook his head in confusion. "I just don't understand. Kanaiya Singh was aiding the enemy. The very men who have killed so many of our brothers and who've brought us to the edge of destruction."

Sant asked, "You're questioning our True King's judgment?"

Kesar shot him a look of annoyance. "No! I just don't understand it."

Bir had heard the exchanges. "Our Guru was merely emphasizing that the enemy are men such as ourselves," he said. "Our duty to defend our faith and our freedom may force us to fight them to the death, but we should not hate them. They are merely doing their own duty as they see it."

Kesar scowled at Bir and said, "You're playing with words. Our enemy kills us at every chance. He'd destroy all of us and our faith if he could. We must kill all of him if we are to survive!"

Bir rubbed his beard, which had turned mostly gray in the past year. "Perhaps there's another way." He usually knew what was occurring in the Guru's inner circle, and now he quietly told Sant and Kesar, "Our Guru has received many offers of safe conduct from Wazir Khan. The Guru's mother wants him to accept them. She feels there's no choice, since we're almost starved to death anyway. But the Guru hasn't trusted the offers, even though the Hindu rajas have sworn on their idols, and the Musalmen have sworn on the Qur'an. But now," Bir paused for emphasis, "the Guru has decided to see if the Khan can be trusted. He's asked for carts and mules to send out his property first. If the property is allowed through unmolested, then chances are that we will all be allowed through safely also."

That night, both Sant and Kesar were assigned as guards for the "property" the Guru had chosen to send ahead of the evacuation: sacks of broken jugs, old shoes, rags—all wrapped in rich coverings of velvet and silk. The enemy guns had been silent all evening. "Our Guru is certainly clever," Sant commented to Bir, who had come to watch the loading.

Eventually, the artist said, "Clever indeed."

"Do you think the enemy's offer can be trusted?" asked Sant.

Bir rubbed his beard, thoughtfully. "We have to assume so."

Kesar had approached and overheard. He said, "I've seen no evidence the enemy can be believed. Do you know something we don't?"

Bir looked at him in apparent surprise, then quickly composed himself. "Of course not. But if we're to get out of this place alive, we have to assume our enemy's good faith in wanting to end the siege. Otherwise, thirst or hunger will finish us, if the enemy doesn't first."

"That's obvious," said Kesar, turning away.

Bir nodded agreeably. "So it is."

At the Guru's instructions, the Sikhs affixed lighted torches to the horns of the bullocks. The velvet cloths in which many of the packages had been wrapped glowed richly in the illumination, excellent bait if the enemy were planning to loot the caravan.

As the moment approached to leave, Sant thought for a time about Sundari. He pictured her as he had last seen her, with tears in her eyes as she left in the small caravan. He wondered if she were thinking of him at this time. He would give up almost anything, except for his loyalty to the Guru, for a few more minutes with her and Anand before he had to place himself so unprotected in the midst of the enemy.

His stomach was queasy and every part of his body felt vulnerable as he and Kesar slowly rode out the gate of the fort, away from the protective walls. The torchlight made the escorts perfect targets. Sant peered into the darkness, wondering if the next second would bring an arrow in his back or a musket ball in his head. Yet, there should be little to fear so close to the fort. If the enemy were to attack the convoy, they would almost certainly do so some distance away, out of sight of the Anandpur defenders.

The caravan passed through a gap in the barricades built by the besiegers. Sant could see dimly the hundreds of faces of the enemy, calmly watching. He and the small party of Sikhs appeared to stand little chance of escaping if such a huge number of enemy should attack.

On he rode, ever farther away from the security of the fort. He stroked Ravana's mane, comforting the horse, although it was himself who truly needed the comforting.

A shout came from the darkness. Metal flashed in the torchlight as the nearest enemy soldiers drew their weapons and rushed the convoy. "Back to the fort!" screamed the Sikh's leader. Sant tried to whirl his horse about, but in the crush and confusion of the assault he was hemmed in. He could not see Kesar in the mass of bodies and swords, all in near darkness.

He felt a burning sensation on his arm, and a wetness. Somehow, he managed to get Ravana turned and to dash toward the fortress. Guns blasted all around, and any instant he expected to be struck.

Away from the light of the torches, he realized, the darkness made him less of a target. But he also could not see the path to the gate.

Ravana somehow found the gap in the barricade and thundered through, and then Sant could see torchlight from inside the gateway. The doors had been opened to receive him and his companions but were being swung closed.

He and Ravana shot through to safety within.

There, he found Kesar, and a couple of the others from the escort. "Are you all right?" Kesar asked. "You're bleeding."

Sant touched the wound on his arm, felt the oozing blood. "I think so," he replied. "It doesn't seem so bad."

"So much for Wazir Khan's offer of good conduct," said Kesar bitterly. "Lucky for us they were so intent on getting the 'loot' on the bullock carts, or I doubt we'd have gotten away."

Even Bir seemed unusually despondent from the enemy's treachery. Angry Sikh gunners resumed shelling the besiegers, spacing out the shots to conserve scarce powder and ammunition. Sant was glad to find his wound didn't interfere with his using of his bow, and he and the other surviving archers took up their familiar positions on the walls and shot at the occasional enemy foolish enough to present himself as a target.

That afternoon, rumors spread of an apology by the Mughal general, and of a new offer of safe conduct. Kesar said, "I say we spit on his offers! I'd rather fight to the death here than be killed by his ambushes."

Sant checked the bandage on his arm to reassure himself it was not bleeding. He said, "We can't hold out much longer. Maybe it's worth the chance. If we're wrong, we die. But we're probably going to die here anyway." He wandered over to Bir. "What do you think of the new offer?"

The artist pursed his lips, and looked down. Sant saw the hollows around Bir's eyes and the lines in his face. At last, Bir replied, "I think we should take the offer. It's certain death if we remain here. We'll soon be so weak they can easily overwhelm us."

One of the Sikh officers appeared and announced, "The *Sacha Padshah* is summoning all men not needed as lookouts on the walls." Sant and the others hurried to the Guru's tent and were among the first of the warriors to arrive.

When Guru Gobind Singh appeared and took his seat, he was slightly slumped, and his eyes at first appeared dull. He drew himself upright and perused his men. Then he spoke, in a voice loud enough to carry to all, but holding an edge of weariness. "My Sikhs, as you know by now, Wazir Khan has expressed regret for what happened this morning. He sent us an envoy with a letter from the Emperor, swearing on the Qur'an not to harm us if we surrender. The envoy also says the Hindu rajas fighting with him have sworn by the cow and on their idols that they will not harm us. He says those who attacked our convoy have been punished."

The Guru paused, and a few men among the crowd could be heard muttering skeptically. He resumed: "Many of you have advised that you want me to accept the terms. My own dear mother has insisted she must leave, taking my two youngest sons with her. I still have serious doubts about the honor of our enemy, and whether his word can be trusted. But our situation is desperate. And I cannot deny my mother's wishes.

"I have therefore decided, with the greatest reluctance, to leave Anandpur. We will divide into two groups, and we will leave after dark tonight." The Guru sat for a moment, then rose, and walked slowly from sight.

As the Sikhs drifted away from the gathering, Kesar said, "This is madness. Even the Guru thinks so—I could tell. How can the enemy be trusted after what they did to us last night?"

Sant could not help but agree with the feelings. However, he was most reluctant to criticize the Guru's decision, even by implication. "The *Sacha Padshah* has no choice," he said.

"I know. I still don't like it."

"The Mohammedans have sworn on the Qur'an, and the Hindus on the cow and their idols," reminded Sant, without much conviction.

Kesar said in disgust, "They'll tell us anything. What do they care so long as they destroy us?"

Sant and Kesar and Bir left in the party with the Guru himself and his two elder sons. It was rainy and cold that dark night. Four hundred Sikhs escorted the Guru.

Sant was greatly relieved to at last be leaving the place where he had been trapped for so long and endured so much discomfort. But he was quite aware that the danger might not be over. He worried that Ravana was so emaciated from lack of food, and he hoped the journey would not be too rigorous for him. Occasionally, he would stroke the horse's neck and murmur encouragement.

As he rode, his thoughts again turned to Sundari and Anand. He thought of the pleasure he had taken going to his family's two small rooms at the end of each day of military exercises, of how his lovely wife would greet him with such a smile of warmth, of how he had so enjoyed the delicious meals she served him every day, of the delights of her embrace in their bed after Anand had gone to sleep. He thought of the games he played with Anand, of running around in the fields with the handsome, happy little boy, of flying kites off the rooftops in midwinter, of buying sweets at the spring and fall festivals.

Then, a gust of wind would hit and blow the rain into his face, or water would run down his neck, and he would concentrate again on following the dark outlines of the horses and the turbaned riders ahead.

For a time, it seemed that the enemy forces meant to keep their word. The Guru and his Sikhs rode on through the darkness—another *kos*; another two *kos*. Then, suddenly, the night was filled with shouts.

Arrows showered onto the Guru's party, and muskets flashed and boomed. Horses whinnied in protest. Sant found it impossible to distinguish the enemy from his friends in the confusion in the dark and the wet. Swords clattered against shields, and men screamed.

Sant concentrated on staying near the Guru, keeping sight of the dim ghostly patch that was Gobind Singh's white stallion. Eventually he realized the sounds of the fighting were behind them. He and the Guru and several other Sikhs continued to ride swiftly, difficult though it was to discern the path.

When they reached river Sarsa, they halted. Sant was relieved to see in the dimness that Kesar and Bir were still with the party of survivors.

The river was wide and swollen with the runoff from the rains. "We have no choice," the Guru called to his men. "We must swim, or the enemy will have us." Still astride his horse, he plunged into the turbulent waters. Other shadowy figures followed.

Sant bent and said in Ravana's ear, "You can do it!" The horse edged into the river. In the near total darkness, Sant was hit by a wall of icy water climbing up his legs, then up to his waist. Ravana lost his footing, recovered, then lost it again. Somehow, suddenly the horse was climbing the opposite bank. Then, he slipped, and he fell on his flank. "Get up, Ravana!" Sant urged loudly as he hung on tightly, leaning away from the downward side of the animal. Ravana struggled upright, and then he was atop the bank. "Good, good!" Sant said, rubbing the horse's wet head.

A group of dim, mounted figures waited. Others gradually joined them. When it was obvious no others were coming, the Guru counted his men. Of the four hundred who had left with him, a mere forty remained. Surprisingly, they included Daya Singh and the others of the Five Beloved Ones, as well as the Guru's two sons.

Sant was next to Bir, who said quietly, "I lost my bundle of paintings in the river. I know of no others surviving from our Guru's time in Anandpur."

Sant nodded in sympathy, though it was doubtful Bir saw the response in the darkness. He said with sadness, "All your work gone. And now there won't be any paintings of our Guru in court, or hunting, or in battle."

"That's true," said Bir, sounding more bitter than Sant had ever before experienced with him. "I should have divided up the paintings among several people. Then at least some would have survived."

"Maybe you can paint more later," Sant said, "from what you remember. Even though it will be a lot of work."

Bir's outline was barely visible in the rain and dark. Eventually, his voice came above the rushing of the river below. "Of course."

The party again set out. Sant worried about Ravana's ability to continue, especially after the difficulties of the river crossing. But the horse struggled on. The Guru led them on an erratic course through the area, which was familiar to him from hunting and from prior war marches. Dawn came, and the rain turned to a fine mist. They traveled through the day, halting frequently to rest the horses and themselves, and to listen for pursuit.

Often, as they rode, Sant thought again of Sundari and of Anand. Would he live to see them again? In between the numerous wars, his times with his little family had been the happiest of his life.

He talked continually to Ravana, urging him to hold out. The horse was slow, obviously fatigued like his rider, but still he continued.

There was no sign of the enemy. "I think we're free of them," Kesar commented at a rest stop. "The drizzle should help hide us from enemy scouts."

Bir silently scanned the horizon. "So it would seem. There are so many of the enemy, if they knew where we were, they would have cut us off by now." Fatigued like the others, Bir seemed distracted, and Sant was sure the artist must be thinking of the loss of the paintings. Sant tried to think of something consoling to say, but his exhausted mind was unable to summon appropriate words.

The Guru and his forty-odd Sikhs remounted their horses. They rode on, in single file. Bir dropped rearward, to the tail of the column, but Sant was too weary to wonder why.

After a further lengthy time riding, he glanced back. Then he looked around. He called to Kesar, "I don't see Bir. Do you know where he is?"

Kesar looked about, and shook his head. "He was in the rear the last I saw." Sant continued to watch for Bir, worried at the disappearance.

The Guru slowed and rode alongside them. "Our brother Bir Singh. Where is he?"

"He was here only a short time ago, *Sacha Padshah*," replied Kesar. "We've no idea where he's gone."

The Guru stared at them a moment, his face expressionless. Then he said, "I fear our enemy will soon know where we are. We'd better find a good place to fight them off, as soon as possible. Chamkaur village is not far ahead."

Sant and Kesar exchanged puzzled looks. Could the Guru, with his supernatural powers, sense that the enemy was near? "I think we all need to rest in any event," said the Guru as he moved off.

Night was falling, and the men were near dead with exhaustion. The Guru sent two Sikhs to find a place of defense in the village. They soon returned and led the band to a large, two story mud house with a walled compound. There was no sign of the enemy. They put as many of the horses as would fit into the stable, and the rest, including Ravana, they tied to trees in the courtyard.

When they were finished, Sant and Kesar were near the Guru, and Kesar asked, "*Sacha Padshah*, are you certain the enemy will find us? It seems to me that we've lost them."

The Guru said calmly, "Indeed we had. But Bir Singh will tell them where we are."

Sant and Kesar's eyes widened. Sant said, "*Sacha Padshah*, what are you saying?"

The Guru repeated, "Bir will inform the enemy where we are."

Sant said, "But Bir would never betray you! Or us!"

The Guru said, his voice heavy with weariness, "He has been betraying me—and you—ever since he came with you to be in my service. However, I realized it. And he knew that I knew it."

Sant stared at the Guru in disbelief. "But, *Sacha Padshah*! Whom could he have betrayed you to?"

"My enemy, Emperor Aurangzeb, and his viceroy."

Kesar was scowling. He asked, "*Sacha Padshah*, if that's true, why did you let Bir continue to spy on you, if you knew about him?"

The Guru replied, "It is better to know who the spies are within my midst, than to take a chance on having one whose identity is not known to me."

"But how could you know Bir was a—a spy?"

The Guru shrugged. "I knew *Padshah* Aurangzeb would try to plant an informant close to me. Bir Singh was an obvious choice, traveling alone from court to court, knowing so many languages. True, his occupation as an artist was a good excuse for his coming to me. However, I have a knowledge of men and can often see behind the facades they present to the world."

"But why would he do it?" asked Sant, still unwilling to believe.

"Gold," said the Guru. "Artists seldom feel their patrons are generous enough with stipends. The Emperor's government would have paid well for good information."

The Guru moved away, leaving Sant and Kesar to try to cope with the shocking disclosure. Sant, his mind already finding it difficult to function due to his exhaustion, struggled to comprehend the Guru's statement. He could not question the Guru, his spiritual and worldly chief. But it seemed impossible that Bir could betray not only the Guru, but Sant and Kesar and the other Sikhs, too.

Kesar said with obvious anger, "I grew to trust him! When we first met him, I felt something was wrong. But I grew to *trust* him!"

"He saved our lives," murmured Sant, more to himself than to Kesar, "from the *thugs*. And he was always so helpful to us."

Kesar sat, and his shoulders slumped. He shook his head sadly. "Bir has probably helped bring us to our deaths. And our Guru too."

9

Sant and Kesar slept soundly from their exhaustion, except for their short turns at guard duty. As dawn broke, they heard, and saw, the enemy forces approach and move into position. "Oh, no," said Kesar. "They're pulling artillery. Those guns can flatten this house."

"Then we need to escape!"

"There are too many of them. And you can see they've completely surrounded us."

"But we can't let them kill our Guru!"

"We'll fight to our deaths," agreed Kesar. "But we can't possibly defeat so many. The rest must be up to God." They heard one of the Sikhs comment that today was the Guru's thirty-ninth birthday. "Some celebration," said Kesar.

Guru Gobind Singh soon called his men together in a large room opening off the courtyard, except for a few keeping watch on the enemy. His followers crowded around him and spilled out the doorway as he told them, "My Sikhs, we usually deal with our enemies by attacking. Here we have no opportunity for that. There are thousands against us. We can only defend ourselves.

"Do not die the deaths of jackals, my Sikhs, but fight bravely as you have done so far. Avenge the deceit those sinners practiced when they induced you to leave Anandpur!

"The more you strive, the greater shall be your reward. If you fall fighting, you shall meet me as martyrs in heaven. If you conquer, you shall obtain sovereignty, and in either case all mortals will envy you!"

The Guru paused to let his words sink in. Then, he quickly made dispositions of his forty men. The Guru himself and his two sons, as well as Daya Singh, Sant, and Kesar would be on the top floor.

Sant checked on Ravana in the courtyard, then he climbed the stairs to his place near the Guru. There were two windows on one of the walls; he and Kesar had a window to themselves, and the Guru and Daya Singh shared another.

The enemy seemed in no haste to attack. Not long after sunrise, the Mughal commanders sent an envoy to the Guru. Sant and Kesar looked on as the messenger gave an ultimatum to the Guru. He concluded, "You must immediately surrender, renounce your faith, and embrace Islam."

These last words infuriated the Sikhs, but the Guru's eighteen year old son gave the reply: "One more word, and I'll cut your head off and slice you into pieces! How dare you address our leader this way?"

The envoy's face flushed. He turned and stalked out.

It was not long before the enemy foot soldiers advanced, took cover behind fences and trees, and began firing at the windows. A Sikh guarding the walls came to talk with the Guru. "We can stay here and let them shoot us one by one, like rats in our hole," he said. "Or we can defy them by going out in small groups to challenge them, showing them our fearlessness and our willingness to die for our cause."

"As you wish," said the Guru quietly. "You must each choose the manner of your own death. It isn't for me to decide such an individual matter."

The man gave a nod and left. Soon Sant, watching out the upper floor window, saw five Sikhs, swords in their hands, scramble over the wall. The men raced into the midst of the enemy's lines. "*Sat Shri Akal!*" the Sikhs shouted again and again. "God is Truth!" Metal clashed upon metal, and men screamed. It went on for perhaps half a minute. At last, there was a brief moment of quiet, before the enemy started cheering.

Kesar soberly shook his head and said, "They lasted longer than I'd expected."

In small groups, and singly, more Sikhs ran forth to challenge the enemy, with the same results, until twelve more of the Guru's defenders had fallen beneath the weight of scores of Mughal soldiers.

Sant commented to Kesar, "The enemy still haven't used their artillery."

Kesar looked at him with dull eyes. "They want to capture our Guru alive."

Of course, Sant realized. If the enemy should take Guru Gobind, they would drag him in chains to Agra to appear before the Emperor Aurangzeb.

The Guru would almost certainly be tortured and humiliated before his head was severed from his body, as had been the case with his father Guru Tegh Bahadur.

Sant resolved that such a thing would not happen so long as a breath remained to himself.

Daya Singh had overheard, and he said to the Guru, "*Sacha Padshah,* you must find some way to escape. We will stay here to fight. But if you are saved, the seed of our faith will also be saved."

"I will remain here, too," said the Guru firmly. He was looking over their heads behind them. "It is the least I can do, if our friend Bir Singh has chosen to aid us."

Sant whirled around. Bir stood guard duty on the wall, as if he had never left.

Sant, greatly relieved, hurried to him. "I knew it couldn't be true!" Sant exclaimed happily.

Bir looked at him solemnly. "To what are you referring?"

"That—that—" Sant realized he couldn't repeat such an insulting accusation.

In a cold voice, Kesar approached and said it for him: "When you disappeared, our Guru told us it was because you were a spy for the Mughals."

Bir looked out over the wall. He strung an arrow in his bow, sighted, and released it. A cry came from the distance. He looked back at them. "What our Guru said was true."

"I don't believe it," cried Sant. "You'd never have come back here if it were true."

"That's right!" said Kesar, as if the realization had suddenly occurred to him.

"Wrong," said Bir, with a glance at them. "I was an agent for Emperor Aurangzeb. But no longer. I resigned my post in order to return here."

"*After* you betrayed our location?" asked Kesar in a tone of disbelief.

"Regretfully, yes," said Bir, looking out toward the enemy. "It was my duty. Now that I have fulfilled that duty, I am free to help you and my friends defend this place."

Sant and Kesar stared, trying to make sense of the statement. At last Kesar told Bir, "I think maybe I should kill you right now. If you betrayed us before, you may well do it again."

Bir glanced at him and nodded. "I understand your feeling. Kill me if you want. I'll undoubtedly die here anyway."

"No, wait!" said Sant. To Bir, he asked, "Why did you come back, if you're sure of dying?"

Bir looked at him for a moment. Then, he turned back toward the surrounding enemy and said, "I have no family. As you know, my wife died long ago of a fever which had already killed my only son. You and my brother Sikhs are now my family. Over time I came to realize that. But I had already given my word to the Emperor's agents to provide them with all possible useful information about the Guru. I'm sure they did not expect me to return here. But I could not abandon my brothers, even though I'd been obligated to act against their interests." Sant assumed Bir was finished, but the artist added: "I gave our Guru the money which the viceroy's officers paid me. Hopefully, it might prove useful in his escape."

Sant and Kesar were both staring at Bir, unable to comprehend such thinking. After a time, Kesar said, "You're playing with words. You know we're men with no scholarly learning who can't understand."

Bir said calmly, "I understand your not believing me. But the Guru has accepted my reasons. Especially after I reminded him of the time when he approved of the Sikh who gave water to the enemy's wounded as well as our Sikhs' own wounded."

Kesar said, "We're all going to die because of you! Many of us already have."

For the first time since Sant had known him, the artist seemed truly in anguish. Tears came to Bir's eyes. "That's true," he said. "Kill me if you like."

Kesar was drawing his thumb along the blade of his sword. Blood appeared. Kesar looked down, as if surprised that his own weapon would do such a thing to him. Suddenly he swung the sword viciously, hacking out a piece of the wooden window frame. "Damn!" he said. "How could you have done this to us? To our *Sacha Padshah?*"

"I'm not sure myself," Bir answered in a weak voice. "I've been an agent for the Emperor for many years, including when I was at Mangarh. By the time I realized I should quit, it was too late."

After a moment, Kesar snorted in disgust. He said, "I think everything you've said is jackal shit. But our Guru is letting you stay. So I have to go by what he must want."

Bir turned slightly away and wiped at his eyes.

"If you're here to kill enemy," Kesar said, "I'll let you. I'm going to be watching you close, though. If I think you might be betraying us again, I may kill you yet."

Bir did not meet Kesar's gaze. He gave a nod. "As you wish."

Six more Sikhs received permission to go forth against the besiegers. All six quickly fell. Ravana was out of Sant's line of sight, and he wondered how the horse was faring down in the courtyard. But Sant could not leave his post to find out. The horse would now have to take care of himself.

Abruptly an enemy officer appeared atop the wall, dropped over into the courtyard, and began running toward the house. The Guru himself shot one of his gold-tipped arrows. The man let out a yell, grabbed at his chest, and fell backwards to the ground. The head of another of the enemy appeared, and he boosted himself atop the wall. The Guru shot again, and the man tumbled backward, an arrow protruding from an eye.

The Guru's eldest son, Ajit Singh, approached his father and asked permission to advance to fight the enemy. The Guru nodded yes.

Sant turned away to avoid watching father and son embrace for the last time. He saw that Bir had been talking to Daya Singh, who looked disgusted at the close contact with a man he must consider a traitor. Bir appeared to be insisting on something. At last, Daya Singh gave a curt nod, but his expression was clearly one of skepticism.

Bir approached the Guru. "*Sacha Padshah*, I, too, ask your permission to go meet the enemy. It is the least I can do, if your son is going to certain death."

The Guru examined him a moment. Then, he nodded. "So be it."

Kesar whispered disgustedly to Sant, "It has to be a trick. He'll betray us somehow."

Sant did not know what to think.

Bir glanced at Sant, caught his eye a moment. "Farewell," the artist said. "I hope you can somehow forgive me. I've always valued you as a friend. I wouldn't have wanted it ending this way."

Sant struggled to manage a reply, but Bir turned and disappeared down the stairs. Kesar abruptly said, "I'm going too."

"No! You'll die out there!" Sant said.

"If I stay, I'll die in here. I'm going to keep an eye on Bir. If he tries to escape to the enemy, I'll kill him." Kesar abruptly clasped Sant and embraced him, hard. Sant felt the tears come to his eyes as he returned the hug, smelled Kesar's sweat for the last time.

"I haven't always been a good friend," Kesar said, sounding as if it took great effort to say the words.

"What—what do you mean?" asked Sant.

But Kesar had pulled away. He hurried down the steps.

In anguish Sant watched from the window. He saw Ajit Singh, Kesar, Bir, and three other Sikhs rush across the courtyard and boost themselves over the walls.

A shower of arrows came at them. Muskets blasted. The Guru's eldest son stumbled, fell, got up again, and continued. Then he again fell and lay still. The other five ran on, shouting, "*Sat Shri Akal!*" Sant heard the Guru say in prayer, "O God, it is you who sent him, and he has died fighting for his faith. The trust you gave has been restored to you."

Bir was in the lead, almost to where the enemy waited behind a fence. Sant watched in shock and despair as a lance struck the artist square in the stomach. Then an arrow embedded itself in Bir's chest. Several soldiers ran toward him and engaged him with their swords. They soon overwhelmed him and hacked him to the ground.

Sant could scarcely comprehend what his eyes had seen. Bir had always seemed invulnerable.

Kesar was still running, waving his sword high and yelling at full volume as he charged to the enemy positions. An arrow struck his shoulder but did not slow him. He reached the enemy, and several leaped to engage him. He swung his sword wildly. One of the enemy fell, then another. Suddenly Kesar was overpowered by three or four men and borne to the ground. Sant felt each blow as if were his own body that was being hacked and stabbed. The enemy struck at Kesar until there could not possibly be life remaining.

Even having watched, Sant could barely believe it had happened.

Kesar was dead. Kesar, whom he had known and admired all his life. Who had been the only link with his childhood in Ludva village. Who had shared all his experiences from the time they had left Ludva. And who had, with Bir, saved his life from the *thugs*.

Gone now.

Bir, too, was no more. Sant still could not accept that his artist friend had been disloyal. Otherwise Bir would not have returned to help defend the Guru. Surely there was some misunderstanding. Maybe there was a clever ruse of some kind, which Bir would have explained if he had lived.

Numbly, Sant was aware that the Guru's second son, Zorawar Singh, approached his father and asked permission to take five men to avenge his brother's death. The Guru gave his approval and embraced his son, hard.

Sant thought numbly of volunteering. But he lacked the energy to act. He was still too stunned at the deaths of Kesar and Bir. The Guru and his son separated, and Zorawar Singh quickly went down the stairs.

Near the Guru, Sant watched in a daze. The six Sikhs ran across the courtyard, scrambled quickly over the walls, raced toward the enemy. "*Sat Shri Akal!*" they shouted. They fought valiantly, but inevitably, all six died.

Guru Gobind Singh slumped by the window, tears in his eyes. The sun had now set, and darkness was falling. Totally dispirited, Sant looked about. In addition to himself, only four Sikhs remained. And the Guru.

Daya Singh, who had tremendous prestige as the first of the Five Beloved Ones, called Sant and the four other surviving Sikhs into a group, and led them downstairs, out of hearing of Guru Gobind Singh. "The *Sacha Padshah* must escape," he said bluntly.

"Definitely—any way possible," said Sangat Singh. Sant numbly nodded, and the other three murmured agreement. Sangat Singh asked, "But how? Anyway, he refuses to go."

Daya Singh told them a plan. The other Sikhs, except for Sant, looked at each other, considered a moment, and then nodded their agreement. At last Sant, who was still too stunned to think quickly, added his own nod.

"I should also tell you," said Daya Singh, "that it was Bir Singh who suggested the plan to me, before his death."

There was shocked silence. Finally, Sangat Singh said, "Then I wonder if we should trust the scheme. What if it's a trick? Maybe the enemy will be expecting it."

Daya Singh said, "I think not. Bir Singh told me one reason he intended to sacrifice his life was to show the plan was an honest one. If he had meant a trick, he would have either remained here alive, or he would have slipped away to the enemy's side. But we all saw him die in battle."

After a time, Sangat Singh said, "Very well. But I insist on being the one to wear our Guru's plume."

"No," said Daya Singh. "I will be the one."

Sant spoke for the first time since Kesar and Bir had died. He was surprised at how firm his voice was under the circumstances: "I must be the one." The boldness of his next statement, though it was true, astounded himself: "I think I most resemble our Guru in appearance."

The others looked closely at him in the dim light. At last, Sangat Singh said, "Our brother Sant Singh is right. He bears the closest resemblance. He's also our best archer, next to the Guru himself. The honor should be his."

Daya Singh frowned a moment. Then he replied, "When Bir Singh told me the plan, he suggested that Sant Singh, and Kesar Singh if he had lived, should be given the opportunity to escape since they have young children needing them."

Sant again pictured the faces of his beloved and of their little son. But as if from a distance he said firmly, "No. I'll remain here." He knew she would understand.

Daya Singh gave a nod. "Very well." He led the group back upstairs and approached the Guru. "*Sacha Padshah*," he said, "we have all agreed that you must escape. The Mughals must never get your head."

The Guru sat as if he were a sagging, empty water skin. He told them in a flat voice, "I said before, and I repeat: I will remain here. I will not abandon you, or those who have fallen."

Daya Singh could not resist a small, strained smile, although it was obvious he felt the greatest reluctance to dictate to his Guru. "*Sacha Padshah*, we knew you would say that. But you taught us that you and we are one and the same. So now, as at Anandpur five years ago, we five are the Guru, and you are a Khalsa. As the Guru, we are ordering you to escape in the interest of the faith. Three of us will go with you. Two will remain here to fight."

The Guru stared at him. But at last, he said, his voice devoid of feeling, "I see. Perhaps I have taught too well. I accept your decision." He straightened himself slightly. "How then, do we escape?"

Daya Singh said, "There are dead soldiers of the enemy lying about the compound. It's dark now, so we can take their uniforms, which you and the others who leave will wear. You and those who escort you will leave one by one, sneaking out in the darkness. Then everyone who has escaped will meet at an agreed upon place."

"I see," said the Guru, his voice still flat.

Sant now said, "And with your permission, *Sacha Padshah*, I will be honored to remain here and wear your clothing, and shoot your golden arrows. Hopefully, the enemy will see me and will think you are still here."

The Guru was solemnly watching Sant's face. Soon he nodded. He removed his plumed turban and extended it to Sant. "The honor is mine," he said. Smiling, grimly, but for the first time since his sons' deaths, he added, "At last you get to wear my turban."

Sant returned the smile, stiffly but proudly.

The moon went down around midnight. Two hours later, the Guru and the three chosen Sikhs slipped away.

Only Sant Singh and Sangat Singh remained. Sant felt at peace with himself. He was fulfilling his duty, and doing it well. He thought again for a time about his wife, and about Anand. He was leaving them with great regret, but they would be cared for by Sundari's family, and if necessary by other Sikhs. And he would soon be joining Kesar and Bir.

With Sangat Singh's approval, he slipped down the stairs and quickly checked on Ravana. The horse was with the others, and he seemed unharmed. Sant petted him briefly, talked with him, and fed him the last remaining item of food, a small piece of bread. Then Sant hurried back upstairs to his post. He hoped Ravana's new master, whoever he might be, would be kind.

At dawn the Mughals, sensing that few Sikhs could remain, launched an assault on the small makeshift fort. Sant did his best to imitate the Guru's marksmanship. His gold tipped arrows accounted for many of the enemy and convinced the attackers that the Guru was still alive inside.

But the huge enemy force swarmed over the walls, charged the house, and battered in the door. Men raced up the stairs. Sant dropped his bow.

Shouting "*Sat Shri Akal!*" he ran to meet them, swinging his sword.

They surrounded him and quickly cut him down with their blades.

Although badly wounded and dying, Sant was still conscious when the enemy commander ordered that the Guru's head be cut off so it could be sent to the Emperor Aurangzeb.

Sant, beyond caring, felt only the shortest instant of pain before the blackness. Then, he was swept along to the place of light where Kesar and Bir and many others awaited and welcomed him.

The enemy commanders were quite distraught when they learned, hours later, that the head was not that of the Guru. Once more, through the steadfast devotion of his Sikhs, Gobind Singh had escaped.

***

Guru Gobind Singh continued to lead the Sikhs, and eventually he made peace with the new Mughal Emperor, Bahadur Shah, who succeeded Emperor Aurangzeb in 1707. The Guru was stabbed in 1708 by two assassins who were probably hired by a hostile Mughal governor. Guru Gobind survived for a few days before dying of his wounds, and during that time he told his followers that he would be the last of the living Gurus, and that in the future the Sikhs were to consider the Granth, *their holy book, as the Gurus' symbol.*

Although the Sikhs now comprise somewhat less than two percent of the Indian population, they have influence and renown far out of proportion to their numbers. Sikhs have a well deserved reputation for being industrious, and many of them are prosperous farmers in the northwest state of Punjab. They make up a significant proportion of India's armed forces, including the officer ranks. Often, Sikhs own businesses or drive taxis in the larger cities, both in India and abroad, where the men can be easily recognized by their turbans and beards (typically, in urban areas in India, only the Sikhs still wear turbans).

In the decades after Independence, Sikh militants of the Akali Dal party agitated to turn the Sikh majority areas in the Punjab into a separate state of Khalistan. In the 1980s, faced with opposition from the central government, the movement turned to frequent acts of terrorism. Militants took over the Sikhs' famous sacred Golden Temple at Amritsar and used it as a base for terrorist activities, so in 1984 Prime Minister Indira Gandhi sent in the Indian Army in the now infamous "Operation Bluestar" to rout them out. The temple was significantly damaged in the process, and even many moderate Sikhs were outraged by the desecration of such a major holy site. A few months later, Indira Gandhi was assassinated by two of her Sikh bodyguards in retaliation, and this was used as an excuse by some Hindus for a wave of violence in which many Sikh homes were destroyed by mobs and numerous Sikhs were murdered.

Fortunately, in recent years, the relationship of Sikhs to the rest of Indian society has been much calmer.

The thugs, *from whom the word "thug" in English is derived, preyed on travelers in the manner depicted in the story, first gaining their victims' confidence, and then murdering them by strangulation. The practice was eliminated in the 1830s through a bold and concerted campaign led by the British officer, William Sleeman.*

Part Four

The Treasure of Mangarh

11

Mangarh, March 1976

At the topmost level of the Madho Mahal, in the courtyard with its lovely marble water channels, the three tax officers looked out over the town of Mangarh spread below. They had many memories of this courtyard from events in the previous search. Ranjit laughed. "I didn't say Guru Gobind Singh renounced *all* wealth. He just kept it in perspective. He was too busy fighting the Mughals to pay much attention to it."

"You mean unlike our Madho Singh, he didn't fight mainly for loot?" asked Vijay, teasing his friend.

"Certainly not!" said Ranjit, feigning horror at the very thought. "Actually, though, his fighting was a serious matter, you know. Emperor Aurangzeb wanted the Guru's head brought to him on a plate."

Vijay stepped to the low marble railing and looked down to the rocks and the approach road far beneath. This was the spot from which Dev Batra had almost fallen to his death. He turned back to Ranjit and Shanta. "From what I've read, those were violent times when Madho Singh lived," she was saying. "A neighboring ruler who was friendly one day might be an enemy the next. Madho Singh would have wanted much of his wealth close by, in an easily defended place such as this. Well hidden in case he had to flee from his enemies without it. But that was three hundred years ago. It's anyone's guess where the rest of his treasure went in the meantime."

The tax officers, followed by the Bhil guard Nagario, descended to the bottom floor and exited the Madho Mahal; they were now in the courtyard that faced the arched openings in the facade of the private audience hall, with the Hall of Mirrors directly above. On the rear wall of the audience hall, beyond the row of pillars, could be seen displays of weapons: the mandala-like arrangement of swords that Nimbalkar had examined so carefully, a similar array of spears, an arrangement of daggers, and another of old rifles.

Vijay said, "Let's look at the Sheesh Mahal, again, since we're so close."
"Oh, good!" said Shanta. "It's one of my favorite places."

They climbed the stairs, and the Bhil guard unlocked the padlock at the door.

Inside the Hall of Mirrors it was like stepping into another universe. Thousands and thousands of tiny round mirrors and colored pieces of glass embedded in the sculptured plaster walls and ceiling shone like a fantastic display of jewels, or like planets and stars inside some miniature galaxy.

The visitors stood in silence, enraptured, slowly turning to absorb the views in all directions.

"It's all so lovely," whispered Shanta. "I wish I could take it with me when we leave Mangarh."

After a time, Vijay said, "If we hadn't searched so thoroughly here, I'd keep wondering if some of those colored pieces of glass weren't the gems we're looking for."

"It would have been a little too obvious, not quite clever enough," Ranjit said. "Anyway, we examined enough of them carefully to be sure we weren't being fooled by mixing real jewels in with the fakes."

They quietly went back down to the courtyard. "Madho Singh had so much," said Vijay. "In the absence of any evidence the treasure was spent or stolen, I think there should still be more around somewhere. Maybe not in these buildings. But not far away. Within a day's travel by bullock cart, maybe."

"Why so?" asked Ranjit Singh. He felt at his turban, as if to reassure himself that it hadn't slipped while he was looking up at the ceiling.

"It's just a guess. Madho Singh—and his successors—would have wanted the treasure close enough they could keep an eye on it. And if it was transported somewhere else, it seems reasonable that they wouldn't have wanted the movement to attract attention. So they might have moved it at night. That would mean it's not far away."

Ranjit gave his high pitched giggle. "That's as good a theory as any. It's still guessing, though."

Vijay said, "You're right. But I've been putting off examining another place that fits the criteria. I think I'll go there this afternoon. I'm afraid neither of you can go with me this time."

"Ah!" said Ranjit. "You want to keep it all for yourself if you find it!"

Vijay smiled grimly. "I wish that were so. But you can't go because you're Sikh. Shanta can't go because she's...Buddhist." He had started to say Scheduled Caste.

"A Hindu temple?" asked Shanta.

"That's right. This is a strict one. No non-Hindus allowed inside."

"That big Shiva temple?" asked Shanta. "The one to Mahadeo?"

"Yes. It seems a long shot. But some temples have so much wealth of their own, it wouldn't be difficult for them to store a little more."

They returned to the big courtyard.

"I wonder what's wrong with Airavata," said Shanta. The elephant was tossing his fodder about and moving around agitatedly to the extent that his chain would let him.

"Maybe he's gone into musth," Ranjit said. "Male elephants do that occasionally, and they go berserk then."

Airavata raised his trunk and let out an angry sounding blast. They cautiously walked closer.

The elephant's elderly, turbaned mahout, Harlal, appeared from the stables and hurriedly approached the animal, talking all the while. At last the elephant calmed.

The tax officers came closer. The mahout was scratching his ear. "I don't know what's gotten him so upset," the man said in the local dialect. "He doesn't seem to want his food. I don't think he's eaten any at all."

"Could something be wrong with it?" asked Vijay.

"It's what he eats every day." Harlal suddenly frowned. "Before your boss left for Delhi today in his big car, I saw one of his men come out of the part of the stable where the fodder is. I didn't think anything about it. They go everywhere looking for treasure." He bent and picked up some of the dried grass, which he examined closely. "I haven't seen this white powder before." He sniffed. "It smells odd."

Ranjit knelt and took a bit of the powder. "It seems familiar, but I can't quite place it." He stood. "I'm going to go look." He strode toward the stable where the fodder was stored. Vijay followed, but Shanta remained with the mahout and the elephant.

They entered one of the archways of the stone structure and glanced about while their eyes adjusted to the dimness. Then they slowly moved about around the edge of the big fodder pile. Ranjit spied something in a corner, behind a support pillar and a wooden bucket. He bent and picked up a white, smashed cardboard box. He showed it to Vijay. "I thought so. Rat poison."

Vijay saw that there was a stack of the flattened boxes, mostly hidden from casual view. Ranjit said, "I suppose it might well be enough to kill an elephant. You'd normally use just a small amount from a box if you were after rats."

"Damn that man!" said Vijay. "Batra told me he'd get even. I'm just glad it didn't work."

"This time, anyway," said Ranjit.

They returned to where the mahout and Shanta waited with the elephant. Harlal's eyes hardened when Vijay explained the problem and Ranjit showed the box. The mahout gazed at the giant animal and asked, "How can anyone do such a thing?"

Vijay looked at Shanta and saw that her eyes were wide with dismay. "I don't know," he said. "But it's fortunate Airavata was suspicious."

"Can anything be done to your boss?" Harlal asked.

Vijay glanced Ranjit, who was frowning. Ranjit threw up his hands and said, "Even if we complained to the police or someone high in the government, there's no real proof who did it."

Vijay tightened his lips. He shook his head and reluctantly said to Harlal, "I'm sorry. I don't see how we can do anything. I very much wish we could."

After several moments of silence, the mahout said, still watching the elephant, "I'll ensure the fodder is disposed of where it can't do any harm. And I'll keep better watch after this."

Later, Anil Ghosali saw Vijay approach the jeep, where Akbar Khan was waiting. "You are leaving again?"

"Just for a short time."

"On business related to the search, I assume?"

Vijay strove to contain his annoyance as he toyed with telling Ghosali to mind his own concerns. He decided better of it; he needed to at least try to get along since any significant decisions had to be made jointly. "I'm going to make some inquiries at the Mahadeo temple."

"Ah, yes. I've been meaning to visit it myself. For religious purposes, of course. Surely you don't think His Highness would have hidden anything there?"

Vijay shrugged. "Probably not. But it's worth a look. The temple was endowed in part by the ruling family, so there's more than a casual connection."

Ghosali stared at him a moment. Vijay started to climb into the jeep.

"I believe I'll accompany you," said Ghosali. "I'd like to see for myself, out of curiosity. Not that I think anything will come of it."

Vijay hesitated, much preferring to visit the temple alone. But he could think of no argument likely to convince Ghosali not to come. He again shrugged. "As you wish." He put on his sunglasses, and they left.

The golden spired tower of the temple of Mahadeo dominated the riverside area.

Akbar Khan parked the jeep outside the whitewashed walls, and the two tax officers entered the gateway of the huge courtyard. After removing their shoes in the shed, they walked past the big bathing tank, sought out one of the attendants, and eventually were shown to the head priest.

The Brahmin was a short, slender man with gray hair and a thin, reedy voice. He calmly looked up at Vijay after examining the warrant and said in a pleasant tone, "It seems unusual, to say the least, for the Income Tax Department to search a temple."

Vijay tried to conceal his discomfort as he replied, "Historically, sir, this temple had a connection with the rulers of Mangarh. They've made regular donations to it."

"So have thousands of other persons."

"They aren't all suspected of hiding wealth, sir." Vijay added in an attempt at a levity, "At least I hope most of them aren't. And the temple was constructed originally, I believe, with funds provided by a Maharaja of Mangarh."

The priest stared at him a moment. "We're grateful for the support of the rulers. But perhaps under the circumstances I should tell you that your statement is not entirely accurate. The temple was constructed with its own funds, entrusted to the Maharaja for safekeeping."

"Oh?"

"Yes. You won't find any of the Maharaja's treasure here. If anything, *he* still has some of *ours*."

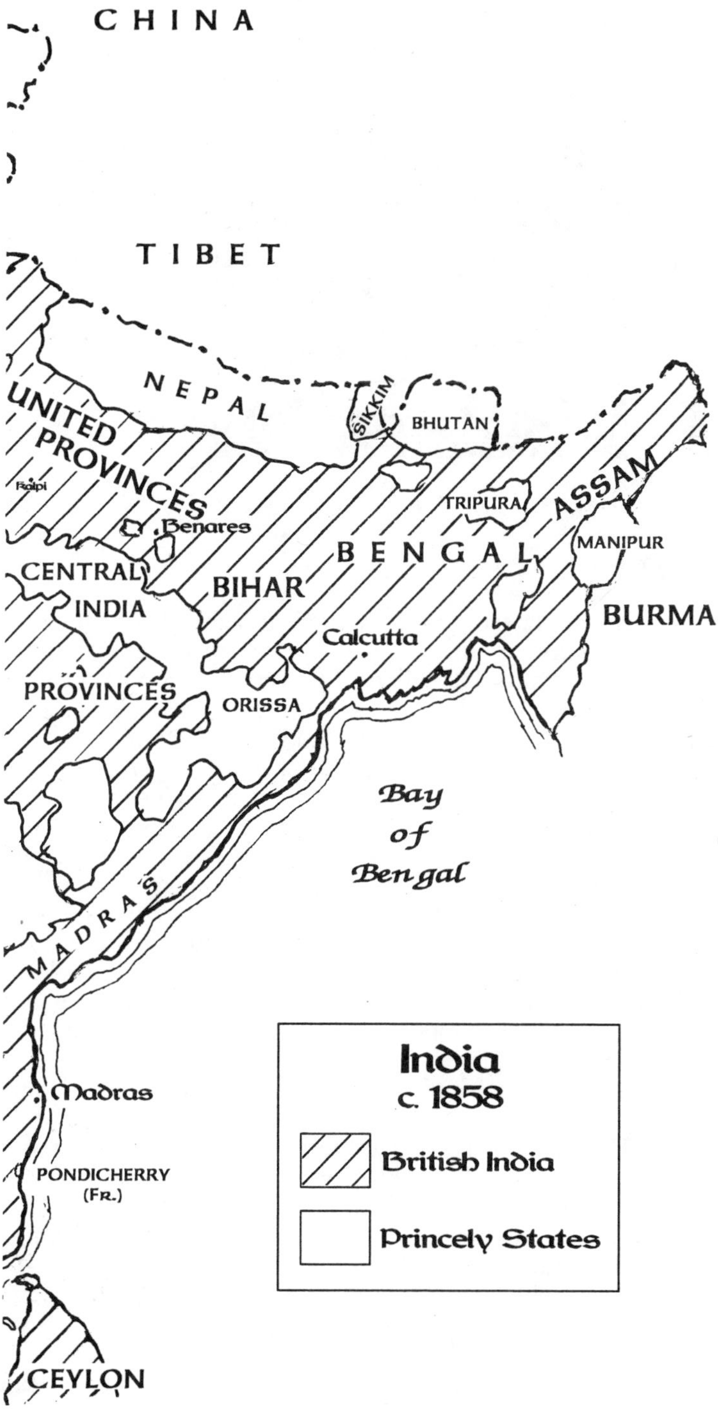

CHINA

TIBET

NEPAL

UNITED
PROVINCES

SIKKIM

BHUTAN

Rajpi

Benares

TRIPURA

ASSAM

MANIPUR

CENTRAL
INDIA

BIHAR

B E N G A L

BURMA

Calcutta

PROVINCES

ORISSA

Bay
of
Bengal

MADRAS

Madras

PONDICHERRY
(FR.)

CEYLON

India
c. 1858

British India

Princely States

Temples to Shiva

1

Jhansi State, 21 March 1858

The Brahmin scholar Natesha, his arms stacked with valuable books to be hidden from the invaders, struggled to quell his anxiety at seeing the emptiness of the temple's courtyard. The sellers of flowers and incense and other items for worship, who customarily set up shop near the entrance, had vanished. "Not a single vendor left," he observed to his friend Maricha.

"They have no one to sell to," replied Maricha, a Brahmin priest who conducted daily worship of the Great God, Lord Shiva. Two decades older than Natesha's forty years, his wide, normally happy face was somber today. After the rebellion against the British began almost a year ago, fewer and fewer pilgrims had come to the temple. Travel was too dangerous, especially since the Pindaris, large bands of looters, had resumed terrorizing the countryside. And now an English army under General Sir Hugh Rose was approaching from the south, eager to avenge the massacre of English soldiers and their families at Jhansi. This morning, it was apparent that even the local worshipers were staying in their homes a few miles to the north in Jhansi city, protected by the town's wall and by Rani Lakshmi Bai's fortress.

Natesha tipped his head back and squinted against the brightness of the sky as he gazed upward at the pointed, pine cone-like towers unique to the Bundelkhund area. He frowned and said to Maricha, "I'm afraid our towers can easily be seen by the British." The soldiers would almost certainly pass on the main road, only half a *kos* away on the other side of the low hill.

"Why should they attack our temple?" asked Maricha. "Aren't they aiming for the Rani and her army?"

Natesha shifted the weight of the books to his right arm. "Yes, but some of the English have enriched themselves by using revenge as an excuse to plunder. They may have heard of how wealthy our temple is."

"I still don't understand why the *Angrezi* want to attack the Queen," said

Maricha. He absently fingered the sacred cord that he, like Natesha, wore diagonally across his bare chest. "You told me she was shocked when the English families were massacred, and she even told the British she was running the city on their behalf."

Natesha nodded. "The British treated her deplorably, but I advised her that they were doing their duty as they saw it, and that she should act with honesty and forthrightness herself." He had often counseled the Rani of Jhansi based on the lessons of the *Bhagavad Gita*, her favorite religious book. Natesha had studied the *Gita* intensively for years, even though it was originally compiled mainly for adherents of Vishnu or Krishna rather than of Shiva.

Maricha furrowed his brow and asked, "You also know the *Angrezi* well—can you explain to me why they are so hostile to the Rani?"

Natesha shook his head. "I only knew the one Englishman I tutored. Major Powis was an honest and fair man who tried hard to understand us. He spent many hours teaching me their language to repay me for instructing him about our own language and our gods. Before he was transferred to Madras, he and his wife often asked me questions about our ways. I think if he were in charge here now, the English wouldn't be attacking."

Maricha's frown deepened. "But what must the *Angrezi* be using as a reason?"

Natesha again shifted the books as he thought about how to answer. For more than two centuries, the British East India Company, with native soldiers composing the majority of its army, had gradually enlarged the territories it controlled until it was the virtual ruler of the subcontinent. When the Maratha Maharaja of Jhansi died, the Company took over the state, refusing to recognize the deceased Maharaja's young adopted son as his heir even though such adoptions were common in India. The Maharaja's capable and popular young widow wanted to rule as regent for their adopted heir, but the British shoved the Rani aside. They then imposed unpopular measures in Jhansi, allowing the butchering of cows and terminating the taxes from villages assigned to support important temples.

In the previous year, the Company's *sepoys* or native soldiers in many areas of northern India rebelled. Among the major causes were fears that the imminent goal of the Englishmen's increasing interference with Indian beliefs and customs was to force all natives to convert to Christianity. In some locales—including Jhansi—the rebelling *sepoys* killed their English officers and even massacred European wives and children.

Natesha replied, "I think many of the British must believe the Rani incited the uprising here to get back her kingdom. Since the Company itself has seized so many states, the *Angrezi* probably assume the Rani thinks the way they do, caring only about grabbing more power. Unfortunately, now that they persist in seeing her as a leader in what they call the 'Mutiny,' the Rani realizes they'll probably execute her if they capture her. So she feels she has little choice but to resist them."

Maricha sadly shook his head. "So much blood is being shed. I hope it's over soon." He tugged up his *dhoti* and continued out of the temple compound, toward his house in the adjacent village.

The sun was hot in the courtyard, and Natesha padded toward the shade of the main building, where the sound of rapid drumbeats came from the pillared hall. He made his obeisance to the big stone sculpture of Shiva's bull

Temple in local Bundela Style

Nandi, then climbed the steep steps and entered the dim interior that was permeated with the odor of incense and flowers. There, his lover Ganga was dancing an episode from the life of Shiva, her ankle bells jangling with her energetic foot movements in time with the drums. In the lamplight, her diamonds and emeralds sparked and flashed, and the white blossoms she wore contrasted with her lustrous dark hair.

Important though his own errand was, Natesha paused to watch, letting himself be lured into the world Ganga was creating. She danced for Lord Shiva, but to Natesha, it was always as if she danced for himself. She had been Natesha's lover for seven years, beginning a year after his wife had died. He had been drawn not only to her beauty, but to her vitality—most obvious in her energetic dances—and to her broad smile and her bright eyes.

Although he was a Brahmin, it was acceptable for him to take a low caste *devadasi* as a mistress, since the dancers were consecrated to the temple. Natesha himself was not one of the *pujaris* like Maricha, who regularly officiated in the rituals. But the temple was wealthy enough to support him and his scholarly efforts, and in the hierarchy he was second only to Soma, the head priest. Three Brahmin boys had been studying the *Vedas* and the *Bhagavad Gita* under Natesha, but he had sent them home to live with their families until the danger from the British was past.

Ganga had been trained in the Kathak tradition, and when she danced, she lived the story she told, expressing her role in rapid, energetic footwork and in elegant movements of her slender hands and neck and her narrow waisted torso. Today she was performing the story of how Lord Shiva's son Ganesha lost his original head and acquired instead the head of an elephant.

Since she performed to entertain the Cosmic Dancer Shiva, Lord of the Dance himself, she must always strive for perfection. Today, however, Natesha sensed that her dance fell short, that she was not involving her soul to the utmost. Her eyes, as they darted about in the pantomime, were dull in a way he'd never before seen, and her movements lacked their normal flowing gracefulness. He was sure it was because, even while she danced, she could not forget the coming of the *Angrezi*.

Natesha had made plans with Ganga to rush to a hiding place in an abandoned shrine in the hills in case the *feringhi* did in fact attack the temple. The past few days he had also carried a number of his beloved manuscripts from his house to the hidden underground treasure chamber of the temple compound, and it was one of the final loads that his arms now held.

The drums beat faster. Round and round Ganga whirled, her hands and feet flashing in the warm glow of the flames, into the climax of this morning's performance. Mahadeva, the Great God, Lord Shiva, watched her through the doorway from the polished dark stone of his *lingam* in the inner sanctum.

Ganga finished. She made her final obeisance toward the *lingam*. Then she backed away, as she had at the conclusion of thousands of performances over the years, performances in which the naked soles of her feet and those of the other *devadasis* had polished the stone slabs of the floor to a high luster.

Now that the God had been entertained, the head priest Soma and his assistant took over, bringing the morning ceremonies to an end. Still breathing hard, her clothing soaked with sweat from exertion, Ganga hurried from the hall. Her anklets jingled, and the diamonds and emeralds sparkled on her nose, her ears, her fingers, her toes. She joined Natesha and gave him her warm smile, though she could not completely hide the worry in her eyes.

They descended to the courtyard. Natesha was uncertain about whether to suggest she go home, or remain at the temple under the protection of the God and the guards. He saw that the sentries by the main gate had not yet barred the entrance, but they were conferring together, obviously troubled. He asked Ganga, "Where will you be, in case we need to leave?"

"I'll wait here for now," said Ganga. "Otherwise, I'll be in the house." They had no other family members to concern themselves over. Natesha had been childless in his marriage, and Ganga had also never conceived. He occasionally considered adopting a boy as his heir, while Ganga wanted to adopt a girl to inherit her profession as a dancer, but neither had yet acted on these desires.

Natesha hesitated a moment, then told her, "I'll be back as soon as I hide these." He shifted his load of books to his other arm and moved off in the direction of the temple kitchens.

The sun was beating fiercely, and Ganga squatted in the shade of the temple's porch. She still wore her jewelry and makeup and her sweaty silk dancing costume. The other two *devadasis* attached to the temple were not present today, since it was Ganga's turn to dance. She wondered briefly if she should go into the village to ensure the others were ready to flee if necessary. But there seemed to be no immediate hurry; she would visit them when she went home to change from her dancing clothes.

In the meantime, she needed to remove her jewelry, which belonged to the temple and must be returned to the strong room after each performance. She started across the courtyard toward the treasury building. The paving stones, exposed to the sun, radiated heat that enveloped her.

Suddenly, a junior priest rushed in through the gate and spoke excitedly to the guards. The guards dropped their *lathis* and rushed to close the massive wooden doors. They had scarcely begun when a horse and rider burst through, followed by other mounted men.

All *feringhis*.

Ganga froze. The *Angrezi*! So soon!

The startled temple guards were drawing their swords. The leader of the invading horsemen, a short, broad man with a red mustache, calmly shot one of the guards with his pistol, then jammed it in his belt and drew his sword.

Ganga tore free from her paralysis. She ran around the corner of the temple, then toward the kitchens, the direction in which Natesha had disappeared. She wished she had removed her anklets so the jingling could not draw attention. The sound of more gunfire, and screams, came from the area of the main gate.

She saw Natesha cautiously poke his head out from a kitchen shed. He saw her and hurried toward her.

"We're too late!" she called. "The *Angrezi* are already here!"

With great effort Natesha suppressed his panic. He stopped, torn as to what to do. At last, he said, "This way! We'll go over the wall in the back." They ran past the kitchens.

They heard rapid hoofbeats and looked back to see several horsemen appear around the side of the temple. The invaders galloped toward Natesha and Ganga, and halted, surrounding them. Natesha knew enough of the English language to understand when an *Angrezi* said, "Look at the jewels on that woman! Can they be real?"

"Why not?" replied another. "This temple's one of the richest in India."

The first *Angrezi* said, "Should we kill them, lieutenant? God, that woman's beautiful for a native—maybe we should take her with us, instead!"

The horseman who answered said, "I don't hold with killing unarmed people. And you know we can't bring anyone along who might spread word of what we're doing."

"The captain will want 'em killed for certain, then, after what happened to his brother last year. And we better not leave witnesses, sir."

The young lieutenant scowled. "Let's get those gems." He changed to heavily accented Hindustani and said to Ganga, "Take off your jewels!"

Ganga stared at him in fright. Although terrified, she managed to say, "They belong to Lord Shiva, *sahib*!"

"Not any more. Hurry, or we'll have to take them from you ourselves!"

Ganga looked to Natesha. "You'd better do it," he said. He hated losing the temple's jewels, but he was terrified Ganga might be harmed.

Reluctantly, she began slowly removing first her earrings, then her nose ring. "Faster!" said one of the *Angrezi*. Another dismounted from his horse and reached for the jewels she had removed. She hesitated, then handed them to him. She began pulling the rings off her fingers, handing each to him as she did so.

Then she bent to remove the rings from her toes. Abruptly, another horseman joined them. Natesha heard him demand brusquely, "What do you have here?"

"Look at these jewels, captain!"

Ganga recognized the newcomer as the red mustached officer who had shot the guard at the temple entrance. The *Angrezi* looked at her, then at Natesha. "Why are you waiting?" he demanded of his men in English, his face flushed and contorted with rage. "Kill them!"

"She's a pretty one, captain," said a soldier. "It would be a shame not to use her first!"

"She's a nigger, you fool!" said the captain.

Although Ganga did not understand the language as did Natesha, the officer's enmity was clear from his voice. She hurriedly pulled the last of the rings from her toes.

But the man galloped close, and his shadow fell over her. Eyes blasting hatred, he raised his sword high.

2

"Captain!" said the lieutenant. "Not a woman, sir!"

"Goddammit, if you're talking about women, my brother's wife was killed! And his daughter, only five years old. All three murdered right here in Jhansi by these black bastards." The horseman swung his sword backward, ready to strike with full force.

"Captain Hatch!" the lieutenant called urgently. "This man's a Brahmin—it's obvious by his sacred thread and that long patch of hair. He may know where the main temple treasure's hidden."

The captain halted, hesitated, his sword still poised. "Bloody hell!" he said.

"Sir," the lieutenant continued, "with the other priests and the guards dead, he may be the only one left who knows where the treasure is."

Natesha, who had been following the exchange, was terrified. Would he be forced to betray his trust to try to save Ganga and himself?

The captain lowered his sword, clearly with reluctance. "You have a point. But now that we have her jewels, the woman's no use. We want no witnesses left since we're blaming the raid on the Pindaris."

A frown came over the lieutenant's face. "Sir, we might use her as a hostage. Threaten to harm her if the Brahmin doesn't help us."

The captain hesitated. Then, he said, "I suppose it's worth a try. We can kill them later."

Natesha, frightened almost beyond feeling, decided it was best to keep his knowledge of the English language hidden for the moment. The captain dismounted. "You, there!" he said to Natesha, in poor Hindustani. "Do you know where the treasure is hidden?"

"Not I, *sahib*," said Natesha. He did know, of course. And the priests had a plan in case someone should try to steal the treasure. But there were far too many *Angrezi* present for the scheme to work.

"You are lying!" The captain seized Ganga by her hair, crushing the white jasmine blossoms as he roughly tipped back her head. She screamed.

The Englishman pressed the edge of his sword to her throat. "I will cut the woman's head off if you do not lead me directly to the treasure."

"I will help, *sahib*," Natesha said in haste. "Only please do not harm her!" He tried to think, struggling against his terror. The captain had said he intended to kill them anyway. But if the moment were postponed as long as possible, the gods might yet intervene.

"No tricks," said the captain. "Or I cut her throat. Understand?"

Natesha swallowed. "I understand, *sahib*."

"Where is the treasure?"

"In the strong room, *sahib*. I will take you there."

"The treasure is all kept there? All of it?"

"All, *sahib*."

Another horseman approached and said in English, "Captain, we seem to have found the treasury. We broke into it. There's some silver bullion there, some coins, some jewels. Not as much as I would have hoped."

"Dammit!" said Hatch. "This temple's supposed to be one of the richest in India. There should be a fortune here."

He pulled harder on Ganga's hair, forcing her head back, drawing a small cry from her. He looked hard at Natesha and said in Hindustani, "I want to know where the real treasure's kept!"

"In the strong room, *sahib*!"

"Is there more than one strong room?"

Natesha hesitated only an instant. "No, *sahib*. Only one."

"Then you are no use to us. We've already found it." He looked down at Ganga and drew his sword along her throat. She again screamed.

"Wait!" shouted Natesha, terrified he was too late.

The officer looked at him. "Well? I haven't cut her deep yet. But I will." He withdrew his sword so Natesha could see the thin line of glistening red.

"Sir," said the lieutenant, speaking in English, "is this necessary? We've found the treasure room. And the longer we're gone, the more likely word may get back to General Rose."

Natesha, terrified, was numbly aware of the scent of smoke now in the air, but he was concentrating on trying to understand the *feringhis'* conversation.

"I'm doing this to save time," said Hatch. "Anyway, the general's order against looting is probably just a formality, in case anyone criticizes him later."

"I'm not so sure, sir. Those orders have been in effect all along. That smoke—" the lieutenant gestured into the air "—must mean our men are burning the village. What if the general investigates?"

"He's punished no one yet for violating those rules," Hatch replied. "Hell, we're blaming it on the Pindaris, anyway. Leave if you want, lieutenant. I'll be glad for your share of the treasure." He returned his attention to Natesha. In Hindustani, he said with obvious impatience, "Your last chance, or I will cut the woman's head off."

"I'll show you, *sahib*!" Natesha did not look at Ganga's face. "If you will please let me lead you, *sahib*."

"I warn you again, no tricks, or she dies."

"I understand, *sahib*."

The captain said in English, "Lieutenant, take the others and search the houses in the village for valuables. Sergeant, you and the corporal stay with me."

The lieutenant hesitated, but finally said, "Right, captain."

Great crashing sounds came from inside the main temple. The captain ignored them and shoved Ganga toward a short man with a broad nose. "Keep hold on her, sergeant." He turned back toward Natesha and demanded in Hindustani, "Take us to the treasury."

"Yes, *sahib*." Natesha tried desperately to think of a course of action as he led the others, not swiftly but not slowly, into the low brick building whose door already had been destroyed. A half dozen horses stood outside, and inside an equal number of *Angrezi* soldiers were searching through broken-open chests and overturned coin storage vessels. Natesha halted abruptly and his eyes widened as he saw the bodies of two attendants lying where they had been shoved aside.

"How much here?" the captain asked another soldier.

"A few thousand rupees, sir, mostly silver. A few thousand more in jewelry."

"Bloody hell! There should be more than that." The captain turned toward Natesha. "Where is the rest?"

Natesha's mouth had gone dry and his voice croaked as he replied, "*Sahib*, this is where the treasure is stored."

The officer's red face appeared ready to burst with fury. He grabbed the long hair of Natesha's topknot and held the sword to his throat. Natesha shrunk from the defilement of the *feringhi's* touch. He felt the sharp edge of the blade. "Brahmin, I know there is more treasure. Where is it?"

Natesha's eyes were bulging as he tried to shrink away from the sword. He opened his mouth to gasp the truth. But before he could reply, the captain said, "It is in the main temple, under the idol, is it not? Most temples have a secret passage behind the idol. Either that, or it is in the well. Come."

He withdrew his sword and roughly shoved Natesha out the door. The soldiers guarding Ganga followed with their captive.

Natesha saw with stunned horror the body of Soma, the chief priest.

Now, Natesha himself was in charge of the temple. He alone held the knowledge of the treasure, and the sole responsibility for safeguarding it.

Under the *pipal* tree in the courtyard a small group of soldiers were examining the well. "Find anything?" the captain called.

"Nothing, sir," replied one. "We sent Taylor down on a rope to probe, but it seems empty."

"Damn!"

"Captain Hatch, sir," asked the man, "shouldn't we be getting back to report that the road's clear? The major will wonder what happened to us. All this smoke may bring them here."

The captain hesitated, then replied, "Right. You round up the rest of the troop. Go find the lieutenant in the village, tell him I said to head back. I'll keep Sergeant Vickery and the corporal here with me. We'll catch up later."

The soldier's eyes shifted away, then back to the captain. "What about the treasure, sir?"

"You can all help carry what we've found so far. We'll divide it up tonight, after dark."

"What if you find more, sir?"

"We'll divide that, too. Dammit, I won't try to cheat you. Get moving!"

"Yes, sir." The men at the well headed toward their horses.

The captain roughly shoved Natesha, who cringed at the contact of his skin with that of the *feringhi*. "Come on, you." They moved toward the main temple. The remaining two soldiers followed, one pushing Ganga. The soldiers stomped up the steps and inside in their boots, forcing the captives along. Natesha and Ganga both gasped as they passed through the dancing hall and saw the inner sanctum.

The great idol, the *lingam* of Lord Shiva himself, lay on its side, broken into several pieces.

Two *feringhi* soldiers passed on their way out. "Nothing here, Captain Hatch, sir," said one. "We used tools from the smithy to smash that heathen idol. And Travis here brought a slab of beef he smeared all over."

"That's right, sir," said the other *Angrezi*. "I did."

Natesha stared at the soldier in horror. Tall and thin, with piercing blue eyes, the man gave a cackling laugh, showing discolored teeth. "They won't be using this temple again for a while."

Natesha felt faint from shock. The mere presence of the *feringhi* defiled the temple. But smashing the *lingam*! And bringing in cow flesh! The acrid contents of his stomach rose into his throat. He swallowed hard several times, desperately straining to control his body. He was glad Ganga could not understand what had been said, although the dark crimson blood smeared on the pillars shouted its presence.

The English captain was laughing. "Good work, Travis. You two go join the troop. I'll let you know if we find any more."

"Very good, sir." The two men clomped out.

The Englishmen herded their captives into the sanctuary. "Now where's the secret passage?" the captain demanded of Natesha.

Natesha hesitated only a moment. "Back here, *sahib*. You must lift this stone." He indicated a large square block in a recess behind the altar.

"Sergeant, keep your gun on them. Kent and I will try to move the rock."

"Yes, sir."

The other man had already grabbed an iron bar apparently left by the soldiers who had just departed. With it, he and the captain levered the stone aside with a grinding screech. A square dark hole appeared, and in it a low, narrow stone stairway. Hatch pulled out a match, struck it. "I'll go down first. I'll call you if there's anything to see."

The soldier called Kent appeared unhappy, but said, "Yes, sir." Hatch slowly disappeared down the steps, his body almost filling the narrow passageway of the staircase.

Some minutes passed. A match flame showed in the darkness below, and the captain's head reappeared. He thrust himself up from the steps. "Not a damn thing," he said in English. "There's a basement under the temple, hardly high enough to crawl about in. It's empty."

"What do we do now, sir?" asked Kent.

The captain gave Natesha a fierce look. He said in Hindustani, "It's empty! You lied!"

"No, *sahib*! I never said the treasure was there. It's all in the strong room."

The captain scowled. At last, he said in English to his men, "Hell, we don't have time for all this. I think the bastard's lying to gain time. Let's just kill them now."

He redrew his sword. He said to Kent, "You hold the nigger and I'll run him through."

Natesha decided he had nothing to lose. He would die, but perhaps he could at least distract them from Ganga. He suppressed his dislike of the defilement and hurled himself at Kent, hoping to knock the *Angrezi* over.

A shot echoed in the marble chamber.

Expecting to feel the bullet, Natesha slammed into the man's chest. He was astonished when the soldier crumpled to the floor, and he himself sprawled awkwardly on top.

The captain screamed, "Dammit, we're being attacked! Take cover!"

Natesha felt no pain from the bullet and wondered why.

Another shot shattered the air. The other English soldier screamed. Natesha looked up, saw the man fall backward.

Natesha turned his head. The British captain, revolver in hand, was behind a pillar, peering around it.

Ganga stood, looking shocked and uncertain. "Get down!" Natesha called to her. He could not comprehend what was happening.

Another man, tall and broad, musket in hand, wearing the red uniform of the *Angrezi*, appeared from the rear. The captain's back was to him. The newcomer pointed his weapon at the captain and said in Hindustani, "Drop your gun and raise your hands, *sahib*, or I must shoot."

The dazed Natesha saw that the newcomer was a native Indian, even though he wore a British uniform. He must be a *sepoy* who had become one of the mutineers.

Captain Hatch stood frozen a moment. Then he dropped his pistol. It bounced and clattered loudly on the stone. The captain slowly turned to face the man. He demanded in English, "What's the meaning of this, *jemadar*? Lower your gun at once."

"I am sorry, captain, I cannot do so. I no longer take orders from the *Angrezi*. Kindly drop your sword also and raise your hands, as I do not wish to shoot you."

The captain's eyes darted about. Then he glared at the man and said loudly, "I have an entire troop of the 14th Light Dragoons with me. If you shoot me, you don't stand a chance. They'll overwhelm you."

"You are mistaken, captain," replied the *sepoy*. "My friends and I watched every man leave except the three who entered the temple. Now you yourself are the only one remaining. Should you decide to try to escape and my gun misses you, my companions are waiting to deal with you."

The officer digested this for some time. Then, he said, "If I don't rejoin my men, they will wonder why. They could be back here any minute."

"I doubt that, captain. But my friends will warn me if indeed they do return. In that case I will have little choice but to kill you."

"Bloody hell," muttered Hatch. Glaring, he drew his sword and threw it forcefully to the floor.

"Now take three steps backward, captain."

Hatch did so. The big soldier eased over, took the weapons, and moved them out of reach of the Englishman. Then he said to Natesha, "Are you all right, Panditji?"

"I—I believe so. Yes, I think we're quite well, now that you are here. We owe you our lives."

The man looked slowly around. Natesha saw that their rescuer's mustache was streaked with gray; he appeared around fifty years or so in age. The man said, "They have defiled the temple terribly."

"Yes," said Natesha. "Indeed." He pulled himself slowly to his feet.

"Can it be cleansed?"

Natesha looked about, sickened. "They have destroyed our image of Lord Shiva, and—and brought in the flesh of a cow. Anyway, the other priests are killed. There is no one but myself to perform the purification. I think probably the temple must be abandoned."

The big man stared at the captain and asked in English, "How could you do such a thing, *sahib*?"

"You ask this? Your uniform is irregular cavalry. Were you at Jhansi?"

The man's gun dipped slightly, then returned to point at the captain's chest. He said, "Yes, *sahib*."

"You bastard! My brother was killed at Jhansi. Lieutenant Richard Hatch. And his wife and little girl. And you ask how we can break your obscene idol, you murdering black bastard!"

The man was quiet a moment. Then he said, "I'm sorry for your brother and his family, *sahib*. I had nothing to do with killing the *Angrezi-log*. I tried to prevent it, to keep the men from mutiny. I told them the *Sirkar* was withdrawing the new Enfield cartridges the troops were worried about using. But they would no longer listen to me."

Natesha knew many native soldiers had been furious over the recent introduction of rifle cartridges which required that the paper end, said to be soaked with a mixture of cow and pig fat, be bitten off before insertion into the gun. Not only was cow flesh abhorrent to Hindus, pig flesh was forbidden to Muslims.

The captain said, "But you obviously mutinied yourself! You who had eaten the company's salt. A *jemadar*! The *Sirkar* honored you with promotion to officer rank, and you deserted it in its time of need."

The huge man appeared as if he were about to break into tears. "I had no choice, *sahib*. They said they would kill me if I didn't join them. My own men! But when they marched for Delhi, I left them."

"Then why are you pointing a rifle at your superior officer, goddammit? Why aren't you offering your services to me instead?"

The man wiped at his eyes. "It is too late for me, *sahib*. I am marked as a mutineer now. There would only be death for me if I turned myself in. So I and my friends were on our way to help Her Highness the Jhansi Rani in defending her city. Anyway," he straightened, "I could not allow you to kill this Brahmin, or the woman."

"You'd fight for the Rani? That traitor?"

The *sepoy* did not reply for a moment. Then he said in a weary voice, "Most Indians do not consider her a traitor. Many believe she is an incarnation of the Goddess Durga, leading her people against the foreign infidels who defile our lands. She is fighting the *Sirkar* most reluctantly. Even when the Company refused to recognize her son's claim to the throne she remained loyal. But she had no choice but to defend herself when the *Sirkar* also blamed her for the revolt in Jhansi even though she had nothing to do with it."

Hatch replied, "Rubbish! I know some of her officers encouraged the revolt that killed my brother and his family." His gaze slid away, then back up at the rebel. "What do you intend to do with me?"

The mutineer hesitated. Then he said in Hindustani, "In spite of what you did to this temple, and what you were about to do to these harmless ones, I cannot kill you when you are defenseless. I think we would have trouble getting into the city with you as our prisoner, now that your army is approaching. So I will let you go—most reluctantly."

The tension in the captain's face lessened.

Ganga spoke, her voice shrill from strain: "You'd just let him go free? After what he's done?" She fingered her throat, where the blood had dried in a long, dark line.

The *jemadar* turned to her; his face appeared tired. He said, "This war is bad. Men are so intent on avenging wrongs to themselves or their race that they lose all reason. Surely this captain should be punished for exceeding his orders. But I'm in no position to bring his actions to the attention of his superiors. Nor can I stoop to killing him while he's my prisoner."

Ganga made no reply. Natesha was thinking about what so much smoke must mean. Did anything at all remain of their village?

The captain appeared to think. His eyes narrowed, and he said in English, "There's a huge stash of treasure here somewhere, *jemadar*. This Brahmin may be the only one left who knows where it is. If you help me find it, half is yours."

The *jemadar* stiffened, his gun still pointed at the captain's chest. He said coldly, "Perhaps I should kill you after all, captain *sahib*. Not only do you defile the temple, you talk of robbing it!"

Hatch' eyes widened. "It was just a suggestion. You no longer have your pension from the Company to look forward to, *jemadar*. I thought you might welcome the chance for a fortune."

"That is one reason I am offering my services to the Rani, captain. Perhaps she may see fit to reward me if I serve her well."

Hatch's brow lowered, and he all but shouted, "More likely, you'll not survive our assault. If you do, the gallows will be your reward, not a pension!"

The *jemadar* shrugged. "My star has fallen. God willing, maybe it can rise again. You better go, captain." He called loudly to his comrades, who still remained hidden: "Let the captain *sahib* pass unharmed. But see that he takes nothing besides his own horse." He waved his gun barrel in the direction of the doorway. "Go, captain."

Hatch cautiously wiped his hand across his forehead, slowly turned, and clumped out, his spurs jingling. Before he disappeared from sight, he cast a final look behind, his eyes spearing Natesha for several moments as if ensuring an accurate memory of the priest who knew the location of the treasure.

"The captain should not have defiled the temple," said the *jemadar* sadly. He looked at Natesha, and at Ganga. Then he said, "These *Angrezi* are not like the officers I used to know. Now they're lusting for revenge. It might be well for you to come with me into the city for safety. If we hurry, we can get inside the walls before nightfall, and before the *Angrezi* block the roads."

Natesha looked about the desecrated temple. He thought about the burning village, about the approaching *feringhi*, and about the other looters who would almost certainly come now. How could he be sure of keeping Ganga safe if they remained here? He himself would hate to have to keep hidden from that murderous captain.

The Rani would not only be glad to give him refuge, she would probably also use his services. "Yes," he replied with resignation, "that may be our best choice now." Thinking of the possibility of encountering yet more British on the way, Natesha asked, "How many men do you have in your party?"

The mutineer stared at him for a moment, before replying, "None, Panditji. I regret having to lie to the *Angrezi*. I'm alone." He straightened just a little when he added, "I am a Brahmin, from village Balaghat, near Cawnpore. My name is Heera Ram."

3

Natesha and Ganga entered the village adjacent to the temple, where a couple of houses still blazed and most of the others smoldered. Heera Ram accompanied them, leading a mottled horse with black mane and tail.

A small, blood-soaked body lay by the side of the lane, and Natesha recognized a ten year old neighbor girl he'd often given sweets to. Dismayed and horrified, he looked quickly at Ganga, who burst into tears and put her face in her hands.

He moved toward her to try to comfort her, when he saw another body, this one a bare chested man with a graying topknot of hair. He halted, stunned. It was Maricha, his good friend whom he'd spoken to so recently—and who had expressed hope that the bloodshed would soon end. Natesha's eyes grew wet.

Someone should care for Maricha's body. But who from that traditional occupation might still be in the area?

Regardless, Natesha and Ganga must hurry to the safety of the city. He averted his gaze, wiped his eyes, and accompanied Ganga, who was still sobbing, to the remains of their house, where smoke lingered in the air. The tile roof had fallen in after the wood supports burned. Only the brick walls now stood, and debris still burned inside. Natesha ducked to look under a corner where a section of roof still hung from the walls. An unsalvageable mound of smoldering pages was all that was left of the books he had not had time to hide.

From the tiny kitchen courtyard they retrieved the few items they could find that were salvageable, including a cooking pot and a brass water jug. Ganga said quietly, "I need to make sure the other dancers escaped."

Natesha nodded. Followed by Heera Ram and his horse, they rushed through side lanes to the small house and saw that the roof was completely collapsed, and debris was still smoldering. Ganga gasped, and then she shrieked. From under the edge of the roof a pair of legs extended, charred so heavily that only the bangles identified them as belonging to one of her dancer friends.

"Come," Natesha said, his voice a croak. He gently took her arm. "There's nothing we can do." She stood a moment, then she came. They followed Heera

Ram and his horse out of the devastated village.

"Who'll dance in the temple now?" Ganga asked Natesha in between sobs. "Only myself?" Tears flowed down her face.

Natesha did not answer for a time. He was still trying to comprehend that his world had been so completely destroyed in so short a time. All he had truly wanted was to live in peace with Ganga and his books and to be part of his temple. Was that so much to ask of the gods?

At last he replied hoarsely, "I think no one will dance here again. With the *lingam* destroyed, and the temple so defiled, all the other priests dead...."

Numb with shock and horror, they followed Jemadar Heera Ram out onto the plain and trudged north toward the city. Soon Heera dismounted, and he and Natesha helped Ganga onto the horse. Heera then led them rapidly along the road.

In only a short distance, the landscape turned barren, cleared of all trees and other vegetation to deny fodder and firewood to the enemy. As they drew farther away from the pillaged temple and village, Natesha began to wonder: How could Mahadeva, the Great God, have allowed the devastation to his own temple, and the killing of the priests and dancers who had devoted their lives to him?

Had someone connected with the temple done something terrible to anger the God? Or, maybe in a previous life Natesha himself had committed evil, and this was his karma working to even the balance on the scales. But why, then, would so many others have been punished, too?

Only a year or so ago, Natesha had thought he was coming to somewhat understand the British and their ways of thinking. He had so many fond memories of Major Powis.

But what could bring the English to commit such horrors as he had experienced today? He could understand the English wanting to punish the particular individuals who had not only killed the British soldiers, but who had also so mindlessly massacred the *feringhi* women and children. But why retaliate against those natives of India who were in no way involved?

And greed for the temple's wealth, he could understand, in a way. But why destroy and deliberately defile a place of worship, a home of the Great God?

The sizzling sun was about to set behind the scrub covered hills as the three refugees, with Natesha now on the horse, came within sight of the city. Strong walls surrounded Jhansi, and its abutting fort dominated the countryside from a low hill. Even from a *kos* away they saw the glint of muskets and cannons atop the walls. Jhansi Fort was not as large as the fortress of Chittorgarh or Gwalior or Mangarh or many others, nor was its ridge so steep or so high. Still, it boasted imposing bastions of reddish tinged local stone, thick walled and tall. On the fort's highest tower, the Rani's orange Maratha flag, limp in the still air, caught the waning rays of sunlight.

Since the British army had not yet arrived, the refugees had no difficulty approaching the city, and they were readily admitted through the southernmost gate. "Come," Natesha said to Heera Ram. "You'll be welcome to stay with us in my friend's home." He led his companions through narrow streets crowded with refugees and soldiers to Halwaipuri, the wealthiest section.

There, he glanced about, uneasy, as they walked through silent lanes lined

Jhansi

with *havelis*, all with their doors tightly closed. "It's so empty here, compared to the rest of the city," Natesha muttered. At his friend's house, he banged on the door and called out, until Shankar, the elderly Brahmin servant appeared.

The man greeting him with folded palms and said, "Panditji, my master has gone to Gwalior for safety. Most of the others here have left also, taking as much of their wealth as they can carry. But I'm too frail for such a journey. Anyway, who would harm such an old man, even if the *feringhi* enter the city?"

After what Natesha had experienced earlier that day, he doubted anyone at all would be safe in such a event. But he said, "Our own village is destroyed, and we're in need of a place to stay."

"How terrible, Panditji!" Shankar deferentially stood aside to let them enter. He said to Heera, "I'll open the courtyard gate for your horse, sir."

By the time Natesha at last bathed and changed into a fresh *dhoti*, night had fallen. He was reluctant to leave Ganga, but it was important he and Heera Ram pay their respects to the Rani.

The Rani of Jhansi's two storied, stucco palace was a short distance northeast of the fort. Since Natesha was known as an adviser to the Rani herself, he and Heera were readily admitted to the lamp-lit *durbar* hall, where elaborately ornamented walls were lined with Rajput miniature paintings and portraits of Maratha warriors. The room was busy with men coming and going, and while Natesha and Heera awaited their audience, they seated themselves on the white silk cushions placed in rows on the red carpeted floor.

Rani Lakshmi Bai had discarded *purdah* some time previously, so the attractive, energetic young ruler sat on her couch in full view. Since the death of her husband she had worn the customary widow's white, but she had defied convention by not shaving her head and by continuing to wear her jewelry. Tonight she wore a pearl necklace and a white sari wrapped modified Maharashtrian style around her legs like trousers, and a white blouse. She appeared weary, but well in command, efficient in dealing with one person after another in rapid succession.

When Natesha's turn came to speak, the Rani looked at him with attentive but tired eyes. He was still distraught over his experiences, but he man-

Fort, c. 1858

aged to take hold of himself enough to say, "Highness, as you know, today the *Angrezi* looted my temple and destroyed my village. I've come with my friend to offer our services."

"You're most welcome here, Panditji," she replied in her low, strong voice. "I greatly regret your losses, though I can certainly use your counsel."

Natesha gave a nod. Although he felt numb and drained, he said, "I'm eager to help however I can, Highness."

"As you know," she said, "I pray every day to Goddess Lakshmi, but in times as troubled as these I need all the help possible." The Rani's reputation as a pious woman had endeared her to her subjects; she habitually rose early each morning for long periods of prayer.

Natesha hesitated, wondering if he should mention his doubts about whether or not he remained in Lord Shiva's favor. But he could still see no reason why he himself might have displeased Mahadeva, and this was no time to bring an additional worry to the Rani. So he next presented Heera Ram: "Highness, this officer saved me from certain death at the hands of the *Angrezi*. He is a Brahmin from village Balaghat near Cawnpore, and he's an experienced soldier who wishes to serve Your Highness now."

Natesha hoped his own influence with the Rani could be used to help repay his rescuer in at least some small way. The Rani was also a Brahmin by birth, and Natesha had anticipated that this fact might help influence her to look favorably upon the *jemadar*.

"I can always use seasoned men," said the Rani, her gaze penetrating Heera Ram as she looked up at his towering height. "What is your specialty?"

Heera Ram stood at attention. "Cavalry, Your Highness," he said in his confident, deep voice. "Twenty-seven years in the irregular cavalry. I was a *jemadar* here in Jhansi cantonment before the troops rebelled. I've also had experience with large guns. For a few years when the army was short of men I was assigned to the Native Foot Artillery."

The Rani's eyes shrewdly examined him. "Have you any experience with sieges?"

Heera replied, "Indeed I have, Your Highness. I was with the native artillery when the *Sirkar* besieged Bharatpur. Also at Kabul."

The Rani turned to Natesha. "So he rescued you from the *Angrezi*, Panditji?"

Natesha's mind had again wandered to the horrors he had witnessed at his temple. But he heard the Rani's question and answered, "Indeed, Highness. I would not be alive now if it were not for him. Nor would my temple dancer friend."

"Then I, too, am indebted to him, for saving such a valued counselor." The Rani looked again at Heera Ram. "What was your part in the revolt against the *Angrezi?*"

Heera Ram said in a voice tinged with sadness, "I wanted to remain true to my salt, Highness. But when the *rissaldar* commanding my troop and all my fellow *sowars* rebelled, I was torn two ways. I took no part in the mutiny and tried to discourage it. Still, when my troop left Jhansi, there was nothing left for me here, so I went with them. Now, I have lost my pension and there is a price on my head. But if you will be so generous as to grant me the privilege, I will be honored to swear my loyalty to you, and I will stay true to my vow to my last breath."

The Rani's face had been unreadable. Now, she said, "I confess I am concerned about my situation, even though my walls are strong and I have more troops than General Rose. The *Angrezi* have often been able to defeat armies much larger than their own. Rose *sahib* in particular has been quite successful in taking cities that are well-defended. If I'm to prevail over him, I need the best advice I can get. My own generals are courageous fighters, but they've had little experience with the British. I want you to come with me on my rounds of my walls in the morning. There you will point out to me where you see weaknesses. Tell me the most likely tactics General Rose will use, and how I might best counter them."

Heera Ram bowed deeply. "I'm most honored, Highness."

The Rani looked at Natesha. "I would be pleased if you would care to come with me also at that time, Panditji."

Natesha, surprised, replied, "As Your Highness wishes. However, I know nothing about military matters. As you well know, my studies have been in quite a different area."

The Rani waved her hand to dismiss the concern. "I don't expect military advice from you, Panditji. But your accompanying me will inspire my fighters. They'll see I'm not neglecting to invoke the help of the gods." Again thoughtful in mood, she returned her attention to Heera Ram. "Such a large man! How is your swordsmanship?"

Heera Ram inclined his head. "I do not want to seem immodest, Your Highness. However, I think few men can equal me, even though I'm over fifty years of age and slightly slower than in my younger years."

The Rani's voice was suddenly quieter, so Natesha had to concentrate to hear: "I have many enemies. Not just the *Angrezi*. I am a Maratha ruling a kingdom formerly belonging to the Rajputs. You know I've had to fight two wars the past few months—attacks against me by a kinsman of my deceased husband, and also by the Rani of Orchha."

She slumped momentarily, as if drained of energy, but she straightened herself, drew a deep breath, and continued, "My bodyguards are mostly Afghan Musalmen I have hired. Although I have no reason to distrust their loyalty, I would like a Brahmin such as yourself close at hand. By your very size you might deter anyone who would try to assassinate me. My guard commander will test your skills. If you satisfy him, you will serve as one of my personal guards, as well as an advisor. You'll have an appropriate rank. Perhaps captain, to start?"

Heera Ram bowed to touch her feet and said earnestly, "I'm deeply honored, Your Highness. I had not hoped for such an exalted position."

The Rani's Prime Minister, Lakshman Rao, stepped forward, indicating the audience was over.

As they walked back to the house, Heera said, "I was afraid the Rani would not trust a man who appeared to have turned against those to whom he'd once sworn loyalty. It was your influence which made her decide to give me another chance. If it had not been for that, there would be no place at all for me in this world."

"The Rani will benefit as well, my good friend. Any ruler would be fortunate to have someone such as you."

That night, the exhausted Natesha and Ganga tried to rest, holding each other in the warm room. But sleep was impossible. They lay, eyes open, possessed by images of what they had seen, still feeling the trauma of the deaths of so many friends and of their own close escapes. Trying to bring at least a little comfort, Natesha stroked Ganga's neck and shoulders and back, so smooth on the surface yet muscular beneath from her dancing. She seemed lost in the experience of her recent horror, as was Natesha whenever his concern was not focused upon her.

What next? he frequently wondered. With everything destroyed—their village, their temple, their friends, their livelihoods, what would they do?

He tried to concentrate on the teachings of the *Bhagavad Gita*, a main focus of his studies recently. The *Gita* taught that one should live with an attitude of detachment, of acceptance of whatever life brought. Until yesterday Natesha had tried to do this, with moderate success, he'd felt. But he now found such detachment impossible. How could one be accepting or detached when his world was abruptly shattered so completely, and when he had experienced such appalling events?

As dawn began to lighten the sky, Natesha observed his customary rituals for the beginning of the new day, albeit in a new location. While Heera Ram's horse looked on, he bathed at the well in the tiny courtyard, pouring water over his head while reciting the Gayatri *mantra* as the sun rose. He then changed into a clean white *dhoti* provided by the servant Shankar.

After obtaining assurance from Ganga that she would be all right in his absence, he walked to the small Shiva temple at the bottom of a stairway in the fort. There, Duleep Ram, the *pujari* who tended the temple and was a prior acquaintance, welcomed him. "How terrible it is!" the short, slight priest said, referring to the assault on Natesha's temple. "I still find it impossible to believe. It's true almost everyone was killed?"

"Almost everyone," Natesha replied quietly. He named the victims he knew of, while Duleep Ram stared at him in shock.

"And the great *lingam* is truly broken?"

"Yes, and cow's blood smeared about."

Duleep Ram stood wide eyed and pale. He looked into the chamber to the *lingam* in his own temple. "We must pray the *Angrezi* don't reach here, also."

"Yes. This temple isn't known for wealth, but the *feringhi* may well mindlessly destroy and defile, even with no gain to themselves."

Duleep Ram was quiet for a time. Then, he said in a voice gone weak, "We must begin today's duties, in any event."

Natesha helped with the rituals of bathing the *lingam* and presenting food to prepare the God for the upcoming day. He felt an urgent need to reaffirm his connection with the Great God, which had been so violently disrupted with the invasion of Natesha's own temple and the destruction of its image.

Still concerned over why Lord Shiva might have allowed the devastation of the temple and its village, Natesha remained alert for a sign the God was displeased. Almost always before, concentrating on the rituals distracted him from other concerns. He normally drew comfort from the familiar routine of the *puja*, and the rhythms of the chants brought calm and relaxation that dissolved any unease that had built up. But now, the shock of what had happened permeated his very being.

By the end of the rituals, he could discern no changes in Mahadeva's attitude toward him. It was Natesha who had difficulty attuning himself to the currents flowing through his world. His conviction grew that, whatever had resulted in the disasters at his temple, it was not his own doing. He still felt in communion with the God's power, and although he could not sense what Lord Shiva's intentions might be, the rituals brought some comfort.

More assured now that the events must somehow be part of the God's plan, Natesha took leave of Duleep Ram and went to the palace to attend the Rani in whatever way he could. Heera Ram's fighting skills had easily satisfied the Rani's guard commander, and Heera began serving duty near the Rani personally as a bodyguard, in addition to being a military advisor.

Not long after Natesha arrived at the Rani's *durbar* hall, a messenger arrived and reported to the Prime Minister, who stepped forward and said, "Highness, General Rose has been observed riding in a circuit of the city this very moment, examining our defenses."

The Rani said, "I must go look at him through my field glasses." She stood, and although Natesha had so often been with her previously, he was struck again with how short she was in height, though she gave the impression of being filled with determination. "It's almost time for my daily round of the walls, anyway."

As requested, Natesha and Heera Ram accompanied her. Also in the Rani's entourage were her army commander, the Rajput Jawahar Singh; her chief gunner, the Afghan mercenary Gulam Ghaus Khan; and a trusted elderly noble, Ram Chandra Deshmukh.

The Rani's tour began at the point where the wall surrounding the city extended southerly from Jhansi Fort itself. The British had not yet cordoned off the city, but their tents were visible to the south. "There appears not to be much activity in their camp so far," observed Jawahar Singh.

"Most likely, sir," Heera said, "they're resting after the long march."

"That may be General Rose," said Jawahar Singh. He indicated a small party of horsemen that had halted beyond arrow and musket range.

An attendant handed the Rani her field glasses, and she peered through them. Jawahar Singh and Gulam Ghaus Khan raised their own binoculars. "A duel of field glasses," said Jawahar Singh. "They're looking back at us with their own." The commanders laughed, and several others in the entourage joined in, though sounding nervous. "That does look like Rose," added Jawahar Singh, "the way everyone defers to him."

Natesha, distressed at the sight of the British so close, turned to examine the city's walls. His recent experience with the English was still only too fresh in his mind. They had overcome the temple guards with such ease, before the gate had been barred against them. It was easy to think of them as some overwhelming evil force.

Still, it appeared to him that Jhansi should be secure behind such massive stone ramparts. Towers flanked each of the ten gates, and most towers held two or more cannons attended by crews who cheered enthusiastically as the Rani approached.

The horsemen out on the plain moved on, and so did the Rani and her entourage. She stopped at a point to the left of the Sainyar Gate on the south wall, away from the hearing of the nearby gun crews. She faced Heera Ram and said, "Tell me frankly. Do you think the *Angrezi* can get into my city?"

Heera Ram said cautiously, "I've been thinking about that, Your Highness." He glanced at the three top commanders, uneasy about replying in their presence.

Seeing his hesitation, the Rani said, "You must freely speak your mind." She stared at him, waiting.

Heera looked again at the parapet, constructed of blocks of solid sandstone like the rest of the bastions and ramparts. The city wall's thickness varied from six to twelve feet, and its height from about eighteen feet to thirty feet. The walls of the fort itself were even more impressive, sixteen to twenty feet thick. He replied, "Highness, walls this solid will be extremely difficult for the *Angrezi* to breach. They can do so if they have big enough guns and they concentrate their fire on one section for a long enough time. Of course, our own artillery must try to silence their batteries to prevent that."

The Rani absorbed this. Gulam Ghaus Khan, her tall, fierce-eyed Afghan artillery commander said bluntly, "But if they bring enough guns, we can't stop them from pounding holes in the wall. Our own artillery can only slow them."

"Yes, sir," said Heera, with a deep nod. "And of course, sir, their sappers could also try to use explosives to blow up a gate, or to undermine a wall."

The Rani stood in thought. Then she asked, "Could their soldiers possibly climb over the walls, without creating a breach?"

Heera fingered an end of his bushy, grey-streaked mustache. He said, "I fear they could, Highness, if there are enough of them, with tall scaling ladders." He gestured toward the parapet. "Highness, one of the lowest sections of the city wall is to the right of this next tower. That would make the area a likely target for the British assault if they do decide to use ladders."

Army commander Jawahar Singh, a stocky, bearded Rajput of perhaps fifty with a perpetually suspicious look, said, "But our own artillery and small arms fire will make it costly for them to get so close."

Heera Ram knew the Rajput general had the Rani's full confidence after recently leading her armies to victories against two separate challengers to her throne. Heera said cautiously, "That's quite true, of course, sir. But I should point out that once the *Angrezi* soldiers begin an attack, they seldom retreat no matter how heavy the cost. They are most determined fighters."

The Rani thought for a time, and then nodded. She continued on, receiving cheers from the crew at the next gun emplacement.

Natesha observed that Heera took his role as a bodyguard seriously, his eyes roaming about, constantly alert for any sign of danger to the Rani.

Later, when Natesha quietly commented on this, Heera replied, "Panditji, it's the Rani who gives her troops their inspiration. And there is no one who could take her place. Without Her Highness to lead us, the resistance to the British in Jhansi would crumble in an hour. It's most important that she remain alive and well."

4

After the round of the walls, Natesha returned to the small temple in the fort for the remainder of his morning. Still filled with worries about the threat from the British, he sat with Duleep Ram while the priest chanted from the *Vedas* and burned incense before the flower-draped *lingam*, petitioning the God's aid in defending the city.

Residents of the city came and went, leaving their offerings, paying their respects to Lord Shiva and offering their own prayers. Ganga, too, came for a time, then she left.

Natesha immersed himself ever more fully in the rituals as the morning progressed, certain of their importance to Jhansi. The gods decided the outcome of battles, granting victory to those whom they favored; men were only fulfilling the roles the gods imposed. But the power of the *mantras* chanted by a priest could, if properly done, procure a god's decision. Surely, Natesha thought, the Great God would be influenced to ultimately bring about what was best for everyone in the city.

It was nevertheless disturbing when he emerged from the darkness of the temple to see the sun bearing down in pitiless heat and the British army moving at last to surround the walls, threatening the very survival of himself and everyone else in Jhansi.

Natesha left the fort itself and headed through the narrow streets of the city toward the library. The mood of the people in the streets was clearly subdued; he saw few smiles, and vendors' cries were less loud, less demanding. When a cavalry troop clattered past, even the cheers were subdued, as if the onlookers had doubts that these men were up to the task of defending the town against the *Angrezi*, rumored to be fearless fighters who never accepted defeat.

The recent rulers of Jhansi, including the Rani herself, had been patrons of learning, and they collected Sanskrit books on religion and philosophy from all over the subcontinent. Natesha had been a constant user of the library, as well as an advisor on desirable books to be acquired.

Today, the manuscripts reposed unused in their wooden cabinets, and the books sat unread on their masonry shelves. Only the assistant librarian, a reticent young Brahmin with a pockmarked face named Rup Prasad was present. He gave Natesha the unsettling news that the head librarian had fled the city.

"He left? Without safeguarding the books?"

Rup Prasad gave a nod.

Natesha had never been fond of the head librarian, who owed his appointment solely to his connections with a previous ruler, and who always appeared satisfied with merely holding his position, having minimal interest in the books themselves. Still, it was difficult to believe that a librarian could be so irresponsible, so lacking in concern for the manuscripts placed in his care, as to abandon them. Too upset for words, Natesha moved about, examining the familiar titles on the cases of *Shastras* and *Puranas*, many of them so rare and important. He noticed the *Surya-vamsham*, an epic poem about the great King Shivaji written in Sanskrit by Shivaji's own court poet Parmanand. And a *Ramayana* from Mangarh, exquisitely illustrated.

What would happen to them if the British took Jhansi? Some *Angrezi* were scholars. However, if a city were pillaged, the looters, in their frenzy of destruction, typically respected nothing. Many of the manuscripts were worth considerable money. But soldiers bent on searching for gold and jewels, or on revenge through destruction, could not be expected to know the value of a rare book.

He turned to Rup Prasad. "Have you made plans to hide the books?"

Rup Prasad threw up his hands in a gesture of futility. "We considered that, Panditji. But what place would be safe from looters? If the *Angrezi* are after valuables, they'll search everywhere for hidden places."

Natesha pressed his lips together. Then he said, "True." He had hidden manuscripts from his own small collection, and two in his custody from this library, in his temple's secret storage vault. But there was no way to take more books there now without encountering the British. And he could think of no way to securely hide, within the city, so many books as remained here.

He sadly shook his head. "We have to pray they stay safe."

When he left the library, he carried the Shivaji epic and the *Ramayana*. He would keep the two manuscripts by his bed for the moment. If he couldn't locate a hiding place he considered safe, he would try his best to bring them along if he needed to escape the city.

After depositing the books in his sleeping room, he went to find Ganga. He knew that the Rani had enlisted many of the city's women in the defense effort. But he was still surprised, when he finally located Ganga, to see her aiding a gun crew by carrying supplies to a gun emplacement atop a tower near the Sainyar Gate on the city's southern wall.

For a few moments he stood in the shade of a house and watched her sweating with exertion as, arms full of bags of some sort, she climbed the steps to the top of the wall. Then he approached her. "Aren't there laborers to do this?" he asked.

She stopped, and gazed at him. "Not enough." She wiped perspiration from her brow. "We all need to do our part to help the Rani." He noticed the hollows under her eyes and the strain lines in her face. No one, he thought, should have to witness the horrors she had seen the past day. She stared at him and said, "You can help, too. All castes can take food and water from a Brahmin."

Natesha gaped at her. He had often been served by other men, or feasted by people who wanted merit or as a traditional part of weddings or other ceremonies. But for a Brahmin scholar to perform that type of work for others! The possibility had never remotely occurred to him.

"The Rani's given you protection," Ganga said. "You should help her, too, besides just prayers and advice. Our very lives depend on how strongly we resist the *Angrezi*."

Natesha thought for a time, then he nodded. There was nothing inherently improper, he realized, in a Brahmin serving others. Indeed, most cooks were Brahmins, since all castes could take cooked food from them. He was not eager for that type of labor. But Ganga stood waiting for his response. He couldn't disappoint her, nor could he let her work alone. He gave her a strained smile. "Very well. I'll help."

She looked at him with warmth and more than a little surprise. "I doubted you'd do it."

"I find it hard myself to believe I agreed."

He was quite aware, as he drew water from a well and hauled the buckets up the stairs, that the men on the gun crew frequently glanced at him and occasionally whispered to themselves. With his long topknot of hair, the Shivaite markings painted on his forehead, the sacred thread across his chest, his pure white *dhoti*, it was quite evident he was a Brahmin of high status.

He could sense the men were favorably impressed by his efforts. But he was not accustomed to physical labor under a hot sun, and he quickly tired. He told Ganga it was time for another *puja*. "But I'll be back."

She wiped the perspiration from her forehead with a square of cloth and gave him a forced smile. "I know you will."

He returned to the Shiva temple in the fort. This time he found it more difficult to establish communion with the God. Although in mind he knew the God's intentions must be sound, he could not convince his tense and worried body that all would be well.

That night, they again lay in each other's arms. It was hot in the house, but Natesha held Ganga close, stroked her forehead. She was rigid as a wood timber, and he wished he could think of some way to wipe the horrors from her mind. "I'm so sorry, my love," he told her, "that all this had to happen."

She was silent for a long time. Then she said, "How could Lord Shiva allow it?"

Natesha shook his head, a slight movement. "I don't know, my love. But he must have had his reasons."

She was again quiet. Natesha stroked her hard shoulders, her back. He had always admired how muscular her body was beneath the soft outer layer of flesh and her smooth skin. Tonight, despite the work of hauling food and supplies, her muscles were rigid, not merely firm.

She said, "I want to train for a place on the gun crew. I've watched them drill. I know I can do it."

He froze in astonishment. "The gun crew? But you're a woman!"

She said, "Our ruler is a woman. Everyone says she may be the rebellion's best general. She even formed a troop of women soldiers. And," Ganga paused for emphasis as she drove home her final argument, "I've heard that even the courtesan Moti Bai has been trained by Gulam Ghaus Khan to fire one of the largest cannons."

"Mightn't it be dangerous?"

"Of course. But many women are sharing the same danger."

He fell silent for a time. "Where would you work?"

"The same tower we helped at today."

Natesha absently returned to rubbing her shoulders. He said, "That's near the Sainyar Gate. Heera Ram says it's the most likely place for the *Angrezi* to attack."

He felt her stiffen. But she said, "Then I'm needed most there."

Natesha's insides went cold in spite of the heat. "What if you're injured? Or killed?"

She shrugged. "Then I'll have helped you and others survive. Anyway, we're all in danger anywhere in the city—especially if the *Angrezi* get inside the walls. We've seen what they do."

Natesha sagged with exhaustion and concern. He wished he could think of a way to protect her.

Shortly after dawn, Ganga appeared on the bastion near the Sainyar Gate. The commander of the gun battery was a short, slight *sepoy* named Munsa Lal who had formerly been a native officer in the East India Company's horse artillery. He stared at her in disbelief when Ganga asked to become a member of the crew. Eventually, his eyes darted away, and he said, "It's much more difficult than it looks. Strength is important in moving the guns. Timing is critical in loading and in firing. It's tiring work."

"I'm a dancer," said Ganga. When he did not seem to grasp her point, Ganga said, "Timing is critical for dance. And strength. Do you think I could dance for hour upon hour if I were a weakling?"

Munsa Lal was silent a moment. He turned to stare out over the plain, where the British were moving about, stirring up a haze of dust. Then, he said, without looking at her, "The *Angrezi* are already setting up their encampments. It's too late to train new people in something so complex."

"I'm fast at learning new things."

Munsa Lal looked about at his men, who were listening intently. One of them called, "Have her dance for us, instead!"

Munsa Lal ignored him and said as quietly as possible, "I think the rest of the crew may be hesitant to have a woman work with them. And the loading and firing procedure must be followed precisely. A woman so beautiful could distract them from their duties."

Ganga said, "I'd guess if I went to the Rani, she'd order them to accept me. If Moti Bai the courtesan can do it, surely I can also."

After a time, the commander sighed, and shook his head. "I thought I had seen everything in thirty years as an artilleryman." He looked her directly in the eye. "I will give you a try."

He turned to the rest of the crew and announced, "We have a new relief man, uh, woman. His eyes bored into Ganga's. "You must learn everything perfectly. Mistakes cause casualties. We're also handling a great deal of powder. The lighted portfires, especially, must be kept away from it! Do you understand?"

"Yes. Only..."

"What?"

"Just what is a portfire, sir?" The men on the crew laughed. Ganga's lips slowly curled into a tight smile.

Munsa Lal strode over and grasped a stick with a cylinder of paper on the end. "This has a saltpetre mixture in it. When lit, you can think of a portfire as a match that burns slowly. With gunpowder all around us, you definitely don't want it to set anything afire with it except at the vent in the cannon. I'll now demonstrate the steps to you."

While the crew stood by smiling to each other, he showed her how the ventsman put his leather-covered thumb on the vent hole near the rear of the gun, while the spongeman cleaned the barrel using a pole with a wet swab on one end. The loader then put the powder charge and the cannon ball into the muzzle. Next, the spongeman reversed his staff and rammed the charge and ball down the bore. "He must use just the right amount of force," said Munsa Lal. The ventsman's next task was to stick a pricker down the vent hole to puncture the bag holding the charge, and then he had to insert a thin tube filled with gunpowder. Finally, Munsa Lal demonstrated how the firer applied the smoldering portfire to the tube to ignite the charge and fire the gun.

"Everyone must cover their ears when the gun fires, or you will quickly go deaf!" he told her. Because the recoil would make the gun jump back, after firing, the crew had to roll it back into position. The commander would then "lay" the gun, re-aiming it at the target, and the procedure would begin again.

"You must watch us now," Munsa Lal said to Ganga. "Eventually, I'll try you in one of the posts." He turned back to the crew. "Take your positions! We must practice the drill, so we all coordinate perfectly. As I've so often told you, rhythm is more important than speed."

The third day after arriving, the British began bombarding the easterly part of the city from a battery on a ridge. The thunder and concussions from the artillery were unnerving to those like Natesha who were unaccustomed to them. The following day, the English batteries to the south of the city began firing on the section where Ganga's gun crew manned its cannons.

Natesha and Ganga were both more terrified than they cared to admit when the British mortar shells and cannon balls howled through the air, smashing into the nearby walls, shaking the earth and blasting sharp rock fragments from the parapets.

Even with his ears covered, Natesha found the firing of the fort's cannons almost intolerably loud, and he tried to be some distance away whenever the guns were booming. Smoke and the odor of burned powder permeated the air. He did not even think of volunteering for the gun crew itself. The idea of becoming, in effect, a soldier, was simply too foreign to his nature and to his concept of his *dharma*. But unwilling to let Ganga assume more risk than himself, he continued to help by carrying supplies and ammunition whenever his other duties permitted.

That it was well into the hot season added to the discomforts. Most workers and members of the gun crews frequently dipped lengths of cloth in water buckets, then wrapped the wet fabric around their heads. Though much of the moisture was replenished by sweat, the cloths dried quickly. The *Angrezi*, most of them from a cool, cloudy land, no doubt suffered even more.

After a day while Ganga merely watched, with her hands pressed firmly over her ears at the critical moments, Munsa Lal tried her as firer. It was probably the simplest of the jobs, but it required care to ensure the burning portfire did not come in contact with anything flammable.

Heera Ram had assumed a concern not only for Rani's protection, but for Ganga and Natesha. Whenever he was not on duty with the Rani, Heera climbed to the top of the bastions on the south wall. With a borrowed telescope, he scanned the English positions, using the task as an excuse to check on his two friends.

He worried about the heavy pounding the position was taking by the British artillery. Already a man on the gun crew had been killed, and three were wounded, one too seriously to tend the gun further.

Apart from his concern for his friends' safety, Heera Ram also looked through his telescope with nostalgia, and a certain longing, at the troops of the enemy he had previously devoted his life to serving. Through his glass, he saw that the soldiers wore a new uniform now of loose blouses and trousers, much more suitable to the intense heat than the old, tight, high collared, heavy jackets. That was good, thought Heera, especially since there was no shade to be found on the plain after the Rani had ordered all the trees cut. The dull colors of the new uniforms also made the men less visible targets than the old red and blue.

As he watched the Englishmen, a strange feeling sometimes came over him. He knew that but for fate—the fate of his being caught up in the mutiny during the previous hot season, he might well be manning one of the British cavalry posts instead of protecting and advising their enemy, the Rani.

Sometimes, as he scanned the English positions, he would find a British artillery officer staring back at him through the man's own field glass. It was always disconcerting for Heera Ram; it was as if he, personally, were being sought out for betraying the Company's trust.

One day during a lull in the artillery barrage, he was on the bastion where Ganga and Natesha worked, watching one of the several cavalry encampments established in a ring around the city. He had noted that the cavalry always maintained itself in a state of alertness, horses saddled and ready to be ridden at a moment's notice. General Sir Hugh Rose was a fine commander, Heera Ram decided. A worthy opponent for the Rani. Suddenly he froze his spyglass.

A British officer stood by the cavalry encampment, scanning the city wall with binoculars. The *Angrezi* lowered the field glasses for a moment, and Heera Ram saw the man's red mustache.

Heera glanced over at the gun crew. Ganga rested under the shade of an awning, waiting until the order was given to resume firing cannon. Natesha sat near her, having just replenished the water buckets used by Raghuvir the spongeman for swabbing out the gun bores. Heera called them over. "Look through the telescope, Panditji," he said, handing it Natesha. "See those horses bunched together this side of those tents? Look just to the left of them."

It took Natesha a few moments to get accustomed to peering through the spyglass, and to find the place Heera referred to. "What do you want me to see?" he asked. Then he froze. "Lord Shiva protect us—is it he?"

"Hatch *sahib*," agreed Heera Ram.

Natesha looked a while longer, then handed the spyglass to Ganga. She soon had spotted Hatch.

"He's looking right at me with his field glasses," gasped Ganga. "I think he sees us!"

"Get down out of sight, slowly," said Heera, who turned his back and now lowered himself to the stone floor behind the parapet wall. Ganga and Natesha did likewise. Heera continued, "He may be uncertain it's you. All

Indians look alike to many *Angrezi*. Especially to the *sahibs* who don't make an effort to know us. I'd still rather he didn't know you were in the city, and where you are."

"You think he'd try to shoot us from so far away?" asked Ganga.

"No. Anyway, he's in the cavalry, not the artillery. But if the British ever get inside the walls, it may be better that Captain Hatch doesn't know where to find you. He'll still want Panditji to lead him to the temple's treasure. He'll also want revenge against me for humiliating him."

For a week the British shelled the fort and the city walls. The Rani's artillery, many of the cannons cast in Jhansi itself, answered them shot for shot.

Sleepless nights became the norm for both besieged and besiegers. The air shrieked as it was rent by flying, hot metal. Buildings and earth shook at the impacts of eighteen pound balls. Men and women screamed as they lost arms or legs or worse. As a section of wall or a tower crumbled, work crews, many of them women, hurried to repair the damage. They used sandbags, timbers, whatever other materials were available. Whenever the enemy destroyed a gun, workmen brought another from the foundry to replace it, and they hauled off the ruined gun to repair or to melt down for recasting.

The afternoon of the fifth day of the siege, as Ganga and Natesha were resting under the awning near the gun, Raghuvir the spongeman, a bandage wrapped around his head and leg, limped over and asked, "Panditji, is it true what we've heard about the Angrezi—that they blow their noses into rags, then put the cloth in their pockets for further use?"

"Yes," answered Natesha. "I've seen it done."

The thin-faced man furrowed his brow in distaste. "They almost always wear their boots and shoes indoors. Even in their holy places."

Natesha nodded. "Yes."

Raghuvir turned to look across the plain at the British tents. "And they use the same brush to clean their teeth week after week, rather than a fresh twig each day?"

Natesha could not help but smile thinly. "Yes, that's true, too."

The spongeman turned back. "And I know for a fact they love eating cow flesh."

Natesha turned sober and nodded. "True again, for most of them."

"Is it true they don't bathe every day, even when there is plenty of water?"

Natesha thought a moment. "I'm sure they must bathe daily when the weather is hot. But when it's cool, no, they don't bathe every day."

Raghuvir again slowly shook his head. "What does it matter if it's cool? Bathing every day is required to keep oneself pure!"

"So *we* believe. The *Angrezi* think otherwise."

Raghuvir drew himself to his full height and peered at Natesha. "But I don't believe that they use paper to clean themselves after shitting. Paper is far too valuable, and any fool would know water works better for washing oneself!"

Natesha glanced at Ganga, and saw that she was staring at him with interest, waiting for the reply. He smiled grimly. "Unbelievable though it is, that, too, is true of them."

The spongeman slowly shook his head. He wiped his perspiring face. "If the *Angrezi* are so foolish as to have such filthy customs, how do they fight so well?"

Natesha thought for a time. "I think it's because, like us, they believe in doing their duty. They are fiercely loyal to their queen and their country, and to their fellow soldiers. And, unfortunately, hate and revenge are also extremely strong urges to action."

Heera Ram worried often about Ganga and Natesha. Their position continued to receive some of the worst pounding. But even if they escaped being killed or wounded by the British shells, the fact that their location was being bombarded so intensely reinforced his belief that the spot would be one of the main targets for the British assault when they tried to enter the city.

So he worried, but he could think of nothing to do. It was obvious Ganga would never willingly leave her post, and Natesha would never leave so long as she remained in danger.

Heera continued to scan the British positions with the telescope. Occasionally he would see Hatch, but he never saw the captain using his own field glasses again. Heera began to feel at least a little less concern for Ganga and Natesha when the British assault came, as it almost certainly would.

Assuming, that is, that the two survived until then.

On the sixth day, Munsa Lal said to Ganga, "Begin acting as relief for the spongeman. You're a dancer, and the post requires the most movement and coordination, as well as endurance. Practice with him so you use the right pressure when ramming."

A part of her wanted to smile at being so fully accepted into the crew, but she was too tired, and the matter was too serious.

Natesha overheard, and his worries grew. The position was the most exposed of all, as the spongeman's duties were entirely performed in front of the muzzle, near the edge of the parapet.

On the ninth day of the siege, a sharpshooter, who had somehow crept close enough to the wall, killed Raghuvir.

The crew stood by, soberly watching, as the spongeman's body was carried away.

Munsa Lal said quietly to Ganga, "Take his place."

By the tenth day, the repair teams had difficulty creating a level platform for the guns on Ganga's tower. The upper portion of the bastion had been battered to a crumpled heap. Half the crew had been seriously wounded or killed. Ganga, always tired and perspiring, and with a gash above her right eye from a flying rock splinter, was now one of the more experienced members.

Every evening, at the same time, the Rani of Jhansi toured the battlements. This tenth night of the bombardment she stopped on the southern bastion. She examined the crumpled section of wall, where women were attempting to reinforce the gap with rubble and sacks of earth. Even as they worked, a British shell howled through the sky and smashed into the repairs, blasting rock and dirt and women alike into the air.

The Rani, lines of pain creasing her forehead, saw Natesha carrying two buckets of water toward the gun crew where Ganga served. "Panditji!" the Rani called. When Natesha stopped, she approached and said, "You shouldn't expose yourself so. I would hate to lose your wise counsel. Your efforts will help most if you are in the fort temple petitioning Lord Shiva."

Natesha stood, weary and perspiring, trying to think of an appropriate response. "Highness," he said at last, "I believe Lord Shiva protects me. Otherwise I wouldn't have survived the raid on my temple."

The Rani soon gave a nod, but she was frowning. She motioned her entourage to move away from her, but she said, "Captain Heera Ram may remain." When the rest of her party was out of hearing, she lowered her voice and asked, "Panditji, is there some reason the British should want to capture you personally?"

Natesha stared at her in astonishment. He glanced at Heera, who appeared equally surprised at the question. Natesha thought of his special knowledge of the temple treasure. Should he mention it to the Rani? Heera's brow was raised, but he was of no help.

Natesha replied quietly, "When the *Angrezi* attacked my temple, Highness, one of the officers realized I might know where Lord Shiva's wealth was hidden. Heera Ram rescued me before the *Angrezi* could force me to show the hiding place."

The Rani gave a curt nod. "That explains it. The *Angrezi* have posted a reward for your capture."

The stunned Natesha asked, "A...a reward, Highness? For me?"

"Yes. One of my spies reported that an *Angrezi* officer is offering a reward of two hundred rupees for you. But only if you're taken alive."

Heera Ram murmured, "It has to be Hatch *sahib*!"

The Rani gave a strained smile. "You'd best be careful, Panditji. Apparently you're more valuable than you realize."

Natesha numbly nodded, and he continued on with his buckets. Rani Lakshmi Bai turned tired eyes to Heera Ram. "Captain, I've heard from my generals earlier. Now I want to know your own opinion of our situation."

Heera thought a moment, and replied cautiously, "Highness, we're told the enemy have about twenty-five hundred men. Five hundred of them are *Angrezi*. That isn't so many compared to Your Highness' own twelve thousand. Every day, they lose more men to the heat and sickness and to our own guns. Their ammunition is also limited. You have destroyed all the fodder and food for many *kos* around. Unless they decide to wait for reinforcements, they need to act soon. Rose *sahib* is famed for moving quickly and decisively. I'd guess the only thing he's waited for is a breach to get his men through. He's close to achieving that by the Sainyar Gate."

The Rani had been watching his face closely. At last, she nodded. "I agree. I'll order everyone to be especially prepared for an attack. What do you think of our chances when they try to take the city?"

Heera Ram hesitated. But he knew she could tell if he was hedging. "Highness, the *Angrezi* are disciplined and they fight like demons. They want revenge for their dead last June. Rose *sahib* is possibly their best general. On the other hand, the morale of our own fighters is high, in spite of losing sixty or seventy men every day to the British artillery and sharpshooters. We must expect extremely heavy losses. And much more damage to the city. But I think we stand a good chance."

The Rani was looking out over the plain. "I'll tell you something my generals know, but few others. It must be kept secret, as I don't want to raise false hopes. I've received a message that my old childhood friend Tatya Tope, the commander of the Peshwa's army, is coming to our aid, with twenty thousand men and heavy guns."

Heera's eyes widened. The Peshwa, Nana Sahib, was the chief ruler of the Marathas and another old friend of the Rani. "That's wonderful, Highness! It will make all the difference."

She turned back to him and said, "*If* he arrives in time." Natesha still stood near, and she said, "Panditji, you must pray for that."

"Of course, Highness."

"We *must* win," the Rani said. "I cannot give up my Jhansi again." She beckoned her entourage closer. As they approached, another incoming round rent the air and tore a chunk from the nearby tower. The Rani did not flinch, although more than one of her officers ducked their heads.

Heera said, "Highness, so much of our high morale is due to you. You warned Panditji against exposing himself to enemy fire. But it's even more important that you yourself remain safe."

Her old *sardar*, Ram Chandra Deshmukh said, "Exactly as I've warned, Highness. If you are lost, so are we all."

The Rani replied quietly with her favorite quote from the *Bhagavad Gita*: "If killed in battle we enter heaven. If victorious we rule the earth." She turned away. Her voice came decisively, "When my time comes, it will come no matter where I am. I've noticed General Rose does not hesitate to expose himself."

5

All the next day the shelling by the British continued, the most intense bombardment of the siege. As casualties and damage mounted in the walled city and the fort, tensions also grew. Soldiers and civilians alike knew they could expect little mercy from the avenging British, who almost certainly would launch their assault soon.

Late in the day, a lookout with field glasses in the highest tower of the fort gave a call. Soon the Rani was on the tower with her own binoculars. Heera Ram, on duty beside her, saw her face break into a broad smile. "I knew he would come in time!" she said. She turned and spoke to her advisors: "Most of you know I sent for help from the Peshwa's army, under Tatya Tope. It appears he's now arrived in the area, with twenty thousand men and many large guns."

"We're saved!" said Jawahar Singh. "With our numbers almost tripled, I see no way for Rose *sahib* to prevail."

"Exactly," the Rani replied to her commander. She glowed with enthusiasm, the strain lines abruptly gone from her forehead. After a moment, she added to no one in particular, "We played together as children—he, and the Peshwa, and myself. I learned to ride and to use a sword with them."

Even Heera revised his estimate of the situation. Twenty thousand men made all the difference.

Word spread almost instantly through the city, and around the entire circumference of the walls the men of the batteries cheered. A festival mood took over the fort and the town. Informal bands began to play, the odors of spices drifted through the air as the women began cooking food for the victory feast. At sunset, the Jhansi defenders saw a huge bonfire glowing on a hill near the Betwa River: the signal to the inhabitants of the city that Tatya Tope's army had come to lift the siege.

The British on the surrounding plain appeared in turmoil. Eventually, a number of their units moved off to the east, toward the Betwa. The Rani ordered her own artillery to increase its rate of fire on the remaining British.

With darkness falling, it was impossible to see what was occurring a few *kos* away near the river. After midnight came the sounds of occasional periods of gunfire. The defenders of Jhansi could only assume the sounds were those of Tatya Tope driving away the enemy.

The lack of knowledge of exactly what was occurring caused a certain anxiety even with the jubilant mood of celebration. "Highness, shouldn't we send Tatya Tope some assistance?" Heera Ram asked at one point. "A cavalry troop could at least bring back word of how the battle is going."

"I've been wondering that very thing," the Rani replied. "However, Rose *sahib* has left at least half his force outside the walls. They would attack any cavalry I send." She turned to her other advisors. "What do you think?"

"Your Highness," said Gulam Ghaus Khan, "Tatya Tope has far more men than we do. His artillery is more mobile. Those of our men who can get through the British lines alive are not likely to be much help once they get to him. Better we wait. We can deal better with the *Angrezi* surrounding the city when Tatya Tope returns to join forces with us."

"I agree, Highness," said Jawahar Singh, who had been eyeing Heera Ram with a skeptical stare. "Tatya Tope must outnumber Rose *sahib* by almost ten to one, even more now that General Rose has split his forces. The Peshwa's army should easily defeat him without our help."

Jawahar Singh's tactical ability had been proven previously when he led the Rani's armies against the enemies who would have seized her throne. After a moment the Rani nodded. "So be it."

Heera Ram felt an uneasiness in his gut; too often he had seen certain victories turn into routs. But the decision was not his to make.

All night they waited, wondered what was happening off in the darkness, where gunfire continued off and on throughout the night.

The sounds of the guns persisted even after sunrise, but the battle was too far away for the besieged to see what was occurring. The Rani and her advisors grew ever more concerned; by now the British should certainly have been defeated.

Still no word came of Tatya Tope's victory. Time dragged as the heat of the day intensified. Annoyingly, the British who remained outside the walls continued to shell the city with their artillery. Their presence also prevented scouts from leaving the town to discover what was occurring on the battlefield by the Betwa.

In late morning, a vast haze of smoke rose into the air over the forests near the river. "The woods are afire," said Jawahar Singh, lowering his field glasses. "Whatever can be happening?"

"Sir," said Heera Ram hesitantly, "if Tatya Tope had to retreat, his men might set fire to the woods to conceal their withdrawal from the British."

The army commander, after his customary suspicious stare at Heera, shook his head. "It's inconceivable he should have to retreat from so few *feringhi.*"

The sun moved beyond the zenith. Still no word.

At last a straggling line of horsemen appeared in the distance. As they approached the lines of the British who had maintained the siege, great cheers arose from the encampments on the plain. The arrivals were *feringhi.*

A worried hush fell over Jhansi city.

Then a message from Tatya Tope was smuggled in to the Rani. Incredibly, he had been defeated by a force one-twentieth the size of his own. Tatya was now retreating to the northeast, toward the distant fortress of Kalpi.

The Rani looked up from reading the message, a dazed look on her face. She said tonelessly, "He tells me his army was mostly raw recruits, and they were armed only with matchlocks. Rose outmaneuvered them at every step and kept charging to keep them on the defensive. Eventually most of Tatya Tope's men gave up and ran away. He says he also had to abandon his artillery—which the British must have taken by now to use against us."

Her generals eyed one another. Jawahar Singh said, "We must keep them out of the city. It comes down to that. We must hold out until they give up, or until more relief comes for us from the Peshwa. The *Angrezi* are losing men every day to heat and sickness. The heat is bad for our own people, but for the *feringhi* who are not born here it must be deadly. Eventually they will have to leave if they cannot take the city."

The Rani sat staring at the wall for a time. Then she said, "It's not that simple." She rose to her feet. "Come."

Puzzled, they followed her down the steps and over to the rectangular stone tank that held the fort's water supply. Two armed guards stood watch. "Remove the cover," the Rani ordered.

The guards called for help, and several men came running. They struggled to fold back the huge tarpaulin on its timber supports.

"Allah protect us!" gasped Gulam Ghaus Khan.

The tank was almost empty.

"I've kept this secret from most of you in order to maintain morale," said the Rani. "But now that Tatya Tope has failed us, you need to know our situation."

The British artillery bombardment intensified, and the spirits of the people of Jhansi collapsed. A hot wind blew all day across the plain, sucking moisture from everything alive.

Natesha went to check on the library. He was sickened to discover most of it a smoking shambles. Whether by accident or not, the British artillery had found the building, and the red hot cannon balls smashing through the roof had set the structure ablaze. The fire now seemed to have died down after destroying at least half of the building.

Rup Prasad was nowhere around. Natesha cautiously moved about the undamaged portion of the structure, and with delight he extracted a rare commentary on the *Vishnu Purana*. He was trying to decide if he could carry more, when a messenger with a summons from the Rani located him. The book in his arms, he left the ruined library to hurry to her.

Natesha had never seen the Rani so dispirited. She sat slumped on her couch in her *durbar* hall, the roof and walls of which had several gaping holes from the artillery bombardments. The chandeliers had been shattered and shards of glass littered the floor.

"The *Angrezi* will try to break into the city at any moment," the Rani told him. "You must pray for us as never before, Panditji."

Natesha nodded. "I'll do so at once, Highness."

She seemed reluctant to dismiss him. "Why," she asked, "has everything gone against me?"

"Surely not everything, Highness."

Her eyes suddenly blazed. "Right from the start! First, my husband died. Then, the British refused to acknowledge my son as his heir, even though I remained loyal to them. After that, the rebels mutinied here and forced me to give them aid, turning the British completely against me. Then, my neighbors attacked me and tried to take my Jhansi. After that, my old friend Tatya Tope failed to lift the siege. And now, finally, our water is almost gone.

"Panditji, fate has thwarted me at every step! Did I do something in a previous life to deserve this? Or were the stars simply against me on the date I was born?"

The Rani's anguished eyes were fixed on him as he groped for words of solace. At last he said, "We must all do as our *dharma* requires. That is what is truly important. We simply do our best. No one can ask more. If the gods will it, you will ultimately achieve success." He knew his words were inadequate, but he could think of nothing better.

At last, the Rani nodded, dismissing him.

6

Jhansi, three days later. 3 April 1858

The British artillery battered the walls, exploded a magazine in the fort, and killed chief gunner Gulam Ghaus Khan as well as numerous others. And the guns had pounded a breach too large to be repaired in the wall by the Sainyar Gate.

An assault would come at any moment. People tried to escape from the northern gates of the city, but the British rifles shot many, and the *Angrezi* cavalry mowed down others.

After nightfall, Ganga and Natesha slept restlessly on *charpoys* by the wall near the cannons. They were abruptly wakened in the darkness of early morning by the sentry on duty at the battery: "The *Angrezi* are moving. We're to be ready for the attack."

They rose and hurried up the steps and over the now uneven surface of the bastion's upper level. The moon bathed the area in light. They saw numerous dark figures in motion a couple hundred yards away on the plain, and they heard distant muffled sounds of voices and of footsteps. Moonlight gleamed on hundreds of bayonets.

The gun crew took up its positions. So far, none of the enemy had been seen near the foot of the walls. Munsa Lal quickly spun the elevation screw on first cannon, then the other, lowering the aim on both guns as much as possible.

They heard three gunshots far off to the west, on the other side of Jhansi Fort. Suddenly a line of shadowy figures was racing across the plain towards the city.

Bugles sounded and muskets blasted all along the wall. "Fire!" Munsa Lal yelled at his crew. The cannons boomed.

Natesha saw men fall on the plain, but in the moonlight it was difficult to distinguish the precise effect of the guns.

Munsa Lal could lower the elevation of the guns no more, and most of the figures running to the wall now were too close, underneath the range of fire. The commander drew his sword, grabbed a waiting musket, and ordered his crew to do likewise. Ganga seized a musket and stood ready. Natesha, too, took a gun.

They heard furious fighting to the right, and they could see that the *Angrezi* troops were at the base of the wall in that direction, hoisting scaling ladders and fighting to get through the big breach in the wall. The defenders along the top of the parapet were firing muskets, hurling down rocks, trying everything to prevent the *feringhi* from ascending the ladders or forcing the gap.

The fighting at the wall went on for minutes while Natesha and Ganga waited in anxiety. "Shouldn't we leave here?" Natesha shouted to her. "There's no more we can do."

She shook her head. "Not yet."

Suddenly the *Angrezi* were over the wall and through the breach. They spilled down the stairs and ramps into the city street below. Ganga aimed her musket into their midst and pulled the trigger. In the dim light she could not see if she hit anyone. But a musket ball whizzed past her head, smacked into the wall, and sent plaster dust flying.

"You've drawn their attention!" said Natesha. "We need to move out of sight."

"There's nowhere to go now!" Ganga replied. They sheltered themselves as best they could in a corner at the base of the wall. Ganga still held the musket. She reloaded it as she had been taught by the gun crew.

Even though the wall was breached, the defenders resisted, determined to allow the attackers no farther into the city. But it was obvious to Natesha that the Rani's troops were being beaten. Slowly, the *Angrezi* soldiers were hacking, shooting, stabbing their way down the street over the bodies of the dead and wounded.

Suddenly there came a thunder of hoofbeats. "Make way! It's the Rani!" came the shouts. The weary defenders stumbled aside as the sword-swinging Rani herself, leading hundreds of her Afghan mercenaries, furiously beat at the *Angrezi* attack. Inspired with new life, the defenders screamed, "Victory to Rani Lakshmi Bai!"

The reinforcements rapidly pushed the *feringhi* rearward toward the walls.

Then the momentum slowed. Their backs now at the walls, the *Angrezi* stood firm. Gradually they began to work forward again into the city. Natesha saw that Heera Ram was fighting close by the Rani, who was tirelessly slashing with her sword, as ferocious a fighter as any man. But the British were doing their best to bring her down. Heera himself saved her at least twice from serious wounds or death.

A gun blasted near Natesha's ear. Startled, he realized that Ganga had used her musket to aid the Rani and Heera. He aimed his own musket and fired. He couldn't see if he'd hit anyone.

He heard gunshots close by, and he saw first one man near the Rani fall, then another. Instantly he realized some of the British had taken refuge in nearby houses and were shooting from cover. He moved to where he could be seen and yelled to Heera Ram, "Get the Rani to safety! They are shooting at you."

Heera saw Natesha and gave a sharp nod. "Highness!" he shouted. "You must take yourself to the fort. If we lose you to a sharpshooter, all else is lost!"

"Yes, Highness," shouted old Ram Chandra Deshmukh, also near her on horseback. "You've rallied the troops as you intended. Now you must return to the fort."

The Rani scowled. But at last, she nodded, turned her white horse, and sped down the street. Her Afghans followed. The remaining defenders, reinforced with other troops, still fought fiercely.

Heera Ram, torn between duties, decided the Rani was safe for a minute or two. He galloped to Natesha and saw Ganga nearby. "Come to the fort!" he shouted to them. "Stay close behind me." He turned and charged down the crowded street, forcing a pathway for Natesha and Ganga. All around them fighting raged. Still carrying their muskets, Natesha and Ganga ran, keeping as near to the tail of Heera's horse as possible. Although shielded in front by the bulk of the horse and rider, they felt exposed and vulnerable to the flying lead.

At last they left behind the battle itself. Heera rode rapidly through the streets and up the incline into the gateway of the fort, the panting Natesha and Ganga dashing behind.

Daylight came. The British pressed their attack foot by foot through the streets of the city toward the Rani's palace, which she herself had abandoned in favor of the fort. The buildings on both sides of the street were aflame, the screams of the wounded and dying were constant.

Natesha was in the fort's Shiva temple continually, doing his best to seek the God's aid. He kept telling himself that what was happening was part of Lord Shiva's plan. But unwanted doubts forced their way in. He was quite willing to accept that the God's desires might be ones which a mere mortal could not comprehend. However, emotionally, he was unable to fathom how the God could not be on the side of the Rani.

Ganga, too, had difficulty accepting that the God whom she had served all her life should continue to allow such a catastrophe.

Natesha wanted to visit the library to try to salvage more books, but Heera Ram, again guarding the Rani, firmly discouraged him. "Some of the worst fighting is in that area. Anyway, you'd probably be too late. Most of the buildings there are burning."

By evening, the palace and half of the city itself had been taken by the English in fierce hand to hand combat.

All the next day and into the night the fighting continued.

The British at last controlled the city. Only Jhansi Fort itself still held out. Natesha came with Heera to where Ganga stood guard duty on a section of the fort's wall. Her eyes were red from lack of sleep, and her skin shone with perspiration. There had not been sufficient water to bathe.

Heera Ram wearily told Ganga, "Her Highness has decided to escape. You should decide what to do yourselves."

"Where is the Rani going?" asked Ganga.

"Toward Kalpi Fort. She's following Tatya Tope's retreating army in the hope of joining him. When she leaves, the battle will truly be lost. It will be only a matter of hours before the British take the fortress."

"What are we to do?" Ganga asked, staring at the stones of the walkway. "We've seen how the *Angrezi* treat their victims."

Heera's eyes were dull. He looked away. "The *Angrezi* want revenge. Their sepoys will want loot. Even women may not be safe here. I must go with Her Highness to guard her. I suggest you follow. Otherwise, someone may be tempted to earn the reward the *Angrezi* offered for Panditji. You can leave at the same time as the Rani, although I doubt you can keep up with us since we will all be on horseback."

"We could try to hide," said Natesha slowly. "But I can't think of anywhere we wouldn't be found. Her Highness has encouraged me to follow her, so I can continue to counsel her. Also," he confided, "I do worry about that mad *Angrezi* captain finding me. I'm sure he hasn't given up on the treasure."

"Tonight is probably your last chance to leave," Heera said.

Natesha said, "Then we'd better go."

Ganga gave a nod. "We have little choice."

"I must go now," said Heera Ram, his eyes abruptly moist. "I wish you well. May God protect you. I'll watch for you at Kalpi."

7

Natesha and Ganga hurriedly gathered together provisions and went to the gate in the fort's north wall. Word had spread of the Rani leaving, and a small crowd had gathered to watch. Already she sat astride her white charger, her ten year old son Damodar seated behind her.

"I wonder why she doesn't have him ride his own horse," whispered Ganga.

"She must be afraid of getting separated from him in the dark," replied Natesha.

The Rani raised one hand with a sword in it, saluted, and rode through the small gate. Murmurs came from the crowd, but the people apparently realized loud cheers would only alert the British, so they restrained themselves. A lady whom Ganga recognized as the Rani's servant and a guard of several horsemen followed her, including Heera Ram on his mottled animal. Then came a large troop of more cavalry.

"They're going to split up, so the British won't know whom to follow," explained Natesha, to whom Heera had told the plans. "We should go now— maybe any *Angrezi* who see her leave will pursue her and ignore us."

Natesha carried the bundle of books from the library in his arms, including the illustrated Mangarh *Ramayana* and the *Surya-vamsham*, the epic about Shivaji. Ganga carried cooking and water pots and what little food she could scrounge. They did not carry weapons, as they wanted to appear like other refugees, and in any event they could not withstand a serious armed confrontation with British soldiers.

They slipped out the gate just as the guards were beginning to close it. No one attempted to stop them. Natesha was surprised at how dark it was; the moon was down. "Quiet," he whispered. "The *Angrezi* will have pickets posted to watch all the gates."

Any moment he expected the British to shout an alarm. But all remained silent except for the retreating hoofbeats of the Rani and her escort. The Rani was apparently riding as slowly and quietly as possible at this point.

The two hurried through the darkness along the road. Amazingly, they were not challenged.

Shortly after first light, they heard the sound of many rapid hoofbeats. "We'd better get off the road in case it's the *feringhi*," whispered Natesha.

Even as he spoke a band of *Angrezi* cavalry emerged from the nearby gardens onto the road behind them. Ganga scurried off the road, but she was too late.

"Halt!" came the command in English. "WHO COMES THERE?"

They tried to run, but the horsemen surrounded them. "Don't move, or we shoot!"

The two froze.

In English, one of the men called, "Major, sir, it can't be the Rani's party. They don't have horses."

"Then what in hell are they doing here?"

More horsemen thundered up. "What do you have, sir?" said a newcomer.

Natesha's back was to the speaker, but he stiffened. He had heard that voice before.

The reply came, "Just a man and a woman, Oliver. We'd better let them go. If the Rani's really escaping, we need to get after her." The major began to move his horse away.

Captain Oliver Hatch edged his own horse closer. Natesha remained facing away, hoping desperately he wouldn't be recognized.

"Major!" came the cry from Hatch. "This one was here in Jhansi when our people were massacred."

"Is that so! Explain it to me later. Sergeant, have two men guard these prisoners. Shoot them if they try to get away. Captain Hatch, we have to follow the Rani. We can't let her escape."

There was a moment's silence. Then came a reluctant sounding, "Yes, sir. But I want to question the prisoners later. Will you ensure they're held for me, sir? It's quite important."

"Fine. See to it, sergeant. Now let's ride!" The major spurred his horse into motion, his men following.

Hatch sat on his horse a moment, staring at Natesha. "I've waited a long time for this," he said, his eyes venomous. "I'll be back soon!" With clear reluctance he urged his horse into a trot. Then, with a last backward glance, he went into a gallop after the rest, his own troop following.

"You there!" cried the sergeant from his horse, addressing Natesha and Ganga. "Follow me. O'Reilly, stay behind them."

Natesha and Ganga reluctantly began walking after the guard. They still carried their bundles, which the British in their haste had not bothered to search.

They had gone only a short distance when, behind them, another group of horses burst across the road. "Sergeant!" shouted one of the guards. "They looked like natives. That could have been the Rani's party!"

"You're crazy! She's long gone."

"But she may have been hiding in the gardens while some of her escort decoyed our pickets."

The sergeant hesitated. "Damn! You're right. I suppose we'd better go after them."

"What about our prisoners?"

"Bloody hell! O'Reilly, you guard them. I'll try to follow that party." He galloped off.

The remaining cavalry trooper gestured with his sword, saying, "You prisoners, walk ahead of me. No tricks or I cut you down."

Natesha thought furiously. Only one guard now. But the man was on horseback, with both sword and gun.

The sound of the hooves behind them was unnerving. Natesha knew death was probable if he remained a prisoner. Hatch would try to force him to show the location of the treasure, and would most likely kill him regardless of whether or not he complied. There was still the possibility of Natesha executing the plan the priests had made, but it had serious risks. If he failed at it, Hatch would probably get the treasure *and* kill him.

Here and there among the trees and stone walls lining the road were several small shrines and temples. Natesha had played around them in his childhood, and he had worshiped at some on visits since. He suddenly thought of a plan.

He and Ganga might never again have a such a chance to escape. He whispered quickly to her in Hindustani, "I'll dodge behind that big tree. You run. I'll meet you at the tall hill south of Bhander, or else find you with the Rani or Tatya Tope—"

"—Quiet!" shouted their guard.

Out of the corner of his eye, Natesha saw Ganga nod. As they reached the huge banyan tree, he darted toward it. He debated whether he should drop his bundle of books, but he was most reluctant to part with them unless they slowed him so much he risked recapture.

"Stop!" yelled the trooper.

Natesha kept running and lunged under one of the large arched roots. In a second, he was out of sight behind the tree.

"Bloody hell!" he heard from the trooper. There were several seconds while the *feringhi* apparently tried to solve the dilemma of how to keep Ganga captive and at the same time chase Natesha.

Natesha made use of the delay; only a few steps away was a stone wall the height of a short man, surrounding much of the big grove. He dashed through an opening and ran along the wall's far side, ducking his head to keep out of sight. "Wait here!" he heard O'Reilly at last shout to Ganga.

The hoofbeats pounded rapidly as the trooper galloped around the huge cluster of tree trunks and roots. But Natesha was already at his goal: a small, stone pillared temple just inside the grove of trees. Sheltered by the domed roof was a black stone lingam of Lord Shiva, draped in fresh flowers. Heart hammering, Natesha dropped to his hands and knees behind the stone platform on which the pillars rested. At the low opening into the cavity beneath the floor, he tossed in the bundle of books and squirmed in after on the hard packed soil, scraping his bare back on the stone above. He fervently hoped there was no resident cobra, no biting spiders, no scorpions.

He heard the trooper gallop past the tiny temple, which obviously held no place for concealment in the open-walled room. The hoofbeats headed farther into the grove, where there were smaller shrines, as well as larger ones. He heard the horse race back and forth as the trooper searched. There was no way to conceal the opening to Natesha's hiding place, and he could only pray it was small enough to be overlooked.

At last, the hoofbeats returned, passed, and exited through the opening in the garden wall. There, they stopped. He heard faint swearing. Obviously, Ganga had disappeared, also.

Natesha forced himself to wait patiently, in the musty smelling space so low there was scarcely enough height for him to lie prone. He waited, and waited more. He was almost ready to work his way out, when he again heard the hoofbeats approach and race back and forth in the grove. O'Reilly was not entirely giving up.

Time passed. Eventually, there came the sound of more horses. He suspected it might be Hatch returning. Indeed, he heard the captain shout: "You bloody, stupid, fool! How could you let them escape? They weren't even armed!"

So faintly Natesha could barely make out the words, he heard O'Reilly answer, "The priest tricked me, sir. He somehow hid where I couldn't find him."

"Bloody hell! You searched the area thoroughly?"

"Yes, sir, every inch of it."

"After all this time, he gets away! Do you have any idea where he went?" The voices were coming closer; Hatch apparently wanted to see for himself where Natesha had vanished.

"No, sir," came the much quieter reply. "Why is one native so important, anyway, sir?"

"He helped kill my brother and his family, that's why!"

"I see. I'm sorry, sir."

"A lot of good that does! Bloody hell!" Hatch said again. "Bloody hell! You may have cost me a fortune, too."

"A fortune, sir?"

"Yes, dammit. He knows where there's a treasure. Enough for me to get out of this hell of a place and live like I'm entitled back in England!"

There was a moment of silence. Then: "If it's of any help, sir..."

"Yes, what?"

"Can I, uh, have a small share of the treasure, sir?"

Another moment of silence. "If you help me find it!"

"I couldn't understand most of what the nigger said, sir. But I thought I heard him whisper, 'Rani.' And maybe 'Tatya Tope.'"

Hatch cursed. After a time, he said, "I'd have expected that anyway. That's where they'll be. With the Rani. Anyway, we're ordered to keep chasing her. I'm increasing the reward on that priest. Five hundred rupees! That should tempt anyone. I'll die before I give up on finding that black bastard! Meanwhile, get busy searching a larger area. They can't have gotten very far, not a woman and a damn priest."

Natesha heard the horses again going here and there, for quite some time. Eventually, the sounds disappeared and were no more.

He waited until night fell, and with great relief, his bladder near bursting, he eased out of the low space that had successfully concealed him. Lord Shiva, he felt confident, was again providing protection. And hopefully, for Ganga, too.

At the shrine's entry, Natesha apologized to the Great God for not being able to properly purify himself by bathing. He knelt at the *lingam*, offered a lengthy prayer of gratitude, and left a rupee as an offering, with a promise of much more when he had the opportunity.

8

Gwalior, two-and-one half months later, 17 June 1858

Four miles north of the camp, the giant fortress of Gwalior was faintly visible through the shimmering, overheated air and the veil of dust raised by the movements of armies. "If only they had listened to me, Panditji," the Rani of Jhansi said to Natesha, her eyes weary and dull.

Natesha had, with great relief, met Ganga at the agreed place north of Jhansi, and they had eventually rejoined the Rani and Heera Ram and the rest of the forces of the rebels at the great fort of Kalpi on the Jumna River.

In many ways, the events at Kalpi had repeated those of Jhansi. Kalpi Fort contained the rebels' main arsenal and munitions factory, and the native army put up a strong defense when Sir Hugh Rose's army besieged it. Once again, however, after an intensive artillery bombardment the British had forced the rebels to abandon Kalpi and flee. Those who survived marched west to Gwalior.

Maharaja Scindia of Gwalior had remained an ally of the British. But Tatya Tope convinced Scindia's forces to desert the Maharaja and join the rebels. Scindia fled to Agra, abandoning his palaces and treasury, and his massive and strategic fortress. The rebels celebrated their victory with festivities crowning Nana Sahib as the Peshwa, the ruler of the Marathas and of north central India. But now, Sir Hugh Rose had surprised the rebels by appearing in the vicinity with his army.

This morning, although a broad mango tree shaded the Rani's tent, the inside was oven hot, even with three sides rolled up. Heera Ram was on guard outside, eyeing anyone who came near. The fan waved by the Rani's maid helped little against the heat. Rani Lakshmi Bai appeared on the verge of exhaustion; she had spent most of the night and much of the morning arranging the disposition of her foot soldiers, her cavalry, her artillery batteries.

The Rani took a sip of the cool *sharbat* that had been served her and Natesha. "I warned the Peshwa and Tatya Tope," she said, "that after capturing Gwalior from Scindia they should not waste their time in celebrations. Fate had smiled upon us after we lost our artillery and supplies. It was a miracle that Scindia fled from us and we were granted the opportunity to use his treasury and his army."

She shook her head sadly. "And it was all wasted. Once the Peshwa was crowned, we should have spent all our effort preparing to fight again. Now there is no time for it."

Natesha still felt disquieted when the Rani talked of military matters with him: it was an area so far removed from his own learning. But he had come to realize that precisely because he had no opinions to offer, and because she trusted him, she sometimes used him to ease some of the weight she carried upon her slim shoulders.

"Instead of feasting Brahmins," the Rani said, "we should have been organizing our food stores."

Natesha, feeling a pang of guilt, abruptly stopped sipping his sherbet. As traditional on such a momentous occasion as a coronation, the Peshwa had fed thousands of Brahmins in two weeks of banqueting. Natesha was among those feasted. Remembering the many rich meals he half consciously placed his hand on his stomach, which bulged noticeably more than when he had first arrived in Gwalior.

"I know it was because I'm a woman that they wouldn't listen to me," the Rani said with more than a trace of bitterness. "If I were a man, the Peshwa would have made me his chief general, and we would be fully prepared now." She absently took another drink of her sherbet.

Natesha straightened as he spoke at last: "But Highness, the Peshwa has given you command of the eastern defense! I've heard it's the most difficult area of all to defend."

She again shook her head. "They gave it to me only as a last resort, because they're desperate."

"And because, Highness, they know you're their best leader. In a way, they were telling you that you were right all along in urging preparations for defense."

"It's late for them to realize that, Panditji. I'm not sure even I can retrieve our cause now." She fingered a gold bracelet. "But if I don't, at least I'll die in the effort."

Jawahar Singh appeared at the entrance to the tent and cast his typically suspicious look at Natesha. Heera Ram, ever alert, stood behind him. "Highness," the general said, "The British are advancing toward us again up the southern road. They'll soon be in artillery range."

The Rani rose. "I'm just coming—I'll get on my armor."

Natesha gulped the rest of his *sharbat*. As he left, he paused by Heera Ram, who was sweaty and dust covered despite having bathed earlier. Heera's eyes followed the Rani. "She's our best hope to win," he said quietly. "I must continue to protect her at any cost."

Natesha nodded. They both moved from the shade into the blasting sun, each step stirring a puff of dust.

Throughout the hot afternoon Natesha and Ganga waited in the encampment, listening to the sounds of musket and artillery fire. It was impossible to know what was occurring in the fighting, most of which was out of sight among the low hills and ravines.

Aside from Natesha's *pujas*, there was nothing for them to do. This time it was considered impractical for non-soldiers to be fighting in the trenches or the concealed artillery batteries, any of which might be overrun at any moment.

So they waited, sweltering, hoping the Rani's leadership, Natesha's prayers, and the deadly sun would give the disparate, ill organized rebels a victory over the well disciplined, well armed *Angrezi*.

"After this," Ganga asked, "what will we do? Do you think we could go back to Jhansi?"

Natesha sat for a time. Then he said, "It doesn't seem a good idea, my love. Not after what we've heard from the people who fled after us."

Other refugees from Jhansi had also escaped to Kalpi or Gwalior. Natesha and Ganga had talked with some of them, including the priest Duleep Ram, and Rup Prasad, the assistant from the library. All had tales to tell of the massacres and looting after the British had taken the city and the fort had surrendered. Male residents, of all ages, had been the main targets of the killings, but women who got in the way trying to save their husbands had also been killed. Few hiding places had been safe. Some residents had hidden in haystacks in their courtyards, and the British had set the hay on fire, burning the people alive. Men who jumped into wells to escape were hauled out and shot. Rup Prasad and other Brahmins had hidden in a well-concealed stone niche of a house and had somehow avoided being found.

The victorious English looted houses and palaces of everything of value and destroyed the furnishings. Then the Indian soldiers who fought for the British looted anything remaining: clothes, carpets, beds, grains, even the ropes and pulleys used to haul the water from the wells. The surviving residents had been left with no food and no articles whatsoever of any use.

"The smell was horrible," Rup Prasad had said, a dazed look still in his eyes. "Houses burning. Bodies cremated in big piles in the squares. Dead animals rotting all over the city—elephants, camels, cows, horses, dogs."

Before fleeing Jhansi, he had visited the library to see what he might salvage. He told of ripped out pages from books lying scattered in the streets outside the building, fluttering in the hot winds. The soldiers had cast the pages aside to take the rich cases and silk bindings.

The British had, of course, immediately reannexed Jhansi State as their own territory.

"I think it will be a long time before Jhansi can be our home again," Natesha now said to Ganga. With a cloth he wiped the sweat from his forehead. "There's little left there for us. And Hatch *sahib* may even go again to Jhansi to hunt the treasure."

In the distance Gwalior Fort shimmered through the hot haze. Was Gwalior city a possible place to stay? Probably not. If the British won the battle today, Maharaja Scindia would return. Natesha and Ganga would risk being taken as traitors who had aided the enemy. And Captain Hatch's offer of a reward for Natesha's capture was said to still stand.

On the other hand, if the rebels won, there would no doubt be more battles ahead, for the British were unlikely to leave such an important place as Gwalior, with its strategic fortress, under the control of insurgents. Natesha and Ganga had almost no money remaining, and they knew no one at Gwalior other than a few other refugees.

"I wonder if Major Powis might help us," Natesha mused. "He'd be shocked at what was done to our temple and village. And I'm sure he'd believe me when I tell him that, since then, we've only done what we felt we had to do to survive."

"Are you certain you know where he is?" asked Ganga.

Natesha hesitated. "He was sent to Madras. But I don't know if he's still there."

"Madras is so far! And the Tamils speak an entirely different tongue."

He nodded. "We'd have a difficult time until we found the Major, even if he's still there."

Near dusk, Heera Ram suddenly galloped into view on his charger. He skidded to a stop, sending a shower of dust over them. His face was haggard from heat and exertion, and his eyes appeared moist, as if from sorrow. "Panditji!" he called, his usually powerful voice now subdued. "Come with me at once. Her Highness needs you."

Natesha cast Ganga a quick look, and hurried to Heera. Heera helped boost Natesha onto the horse behind him. They raced across fields and through ravines.

"What has happened?" asked Natesha.

They dashed into a large forested garden, and the horse bounded over a narrow ditch. Natesha was beginning to think Heera had not heard, when the reply came. Never before had Natesha heard Heera sound so anguished: "I failed to protect Her Highness. She was wounded while leading her troops."

They arrived at a group of people gathered before the doorway of a little mud building, one of several in an area shaded by large trees. A small, armor-clad figure lay on the dusty ground. Horses stood nearby. Heera reined to a stop. "We brought her here," he said tonelessly. "This is the monastery of the saint, Baba Gangadas."

Natesha slid from the horse's back, and the onlookers made room for him. Jawahar Singh approached, his penetrating gaze as suspicious-appearing as ever. "Her Highness is badly wounded," he said bluntly. "The Baba is comforting her. Come."

Natesha saw that the saint was giving the Rani a drink.

"Holy water, from the Ganges," he heard someone whisper.

It was customarily given to a dying person. Natesha moved close, in case the Rani should have some need of him.

"Damodar," she said faintly as she placed her hand on her young son. Her trusted *sardar*, old Ram Chandra Deshmukh, stood near. The Rani's dull eyes looked up at the noble. "I leave my son in your care," she gasped.

She closed her eyes and gave a small shudder.

Natesha knew she was no more in this life.

There was silence, then the sound of weeping. Jawahar Singh said in a low voice to Natesha, "Someone must perform the last rights, Panditji."

"It's never been my duty to perform them," he protested.

Those stern eyes bore into him. "But you must surely know what to do, Panditji. And Her Highness relied on you."

Natesha hesitated.

"Quickly, Panditji!" said Jawahar Singh. "The *Angrezi* could come any moment. They must not get her body."

Natesha knew that was true. He stared at her form. He had seen her only this morning: tired, even rueful, but nevertheless determined. He still had difficulty comprehending she was dead.

"There's no time to gather firewood," someone said. "We can use that haystack—it's so dry it will burn easily."

"Begin, Panditji," Jawahar Singh insisted. Natesha, tears in his eyes, took hold of himself. He hurried through the prayers and the *mantras*. It was obvious that everyone was uneasy by the manner in which they kept glancing about, as if expecting to be overrun by a troop of *Angrezi* cavalry at any moment.

At last, Natesha indicated he was finished.

Several persons gently picked up the Rani's body, carried it over, and reverently placed it on the pyre. Ram Chandra Deshmukh handed a burning torch to young Damodar. His eyes glazed as if in a daze, the boy dutifully applied it to the haystack. The straw flashed into flame.

As word spread, more and more men arrived, on horseback, on foot. All were solemn faced, many in tears. Not only had a great queen died; it was as if everyone present saw their hopes for victory over the *Angrezi* rising with the smoke.

As night fell, the haystack continued to blaze for a time, illuminating the hot sky. Sparks flew high into the darkness. Then the flames dwindled to only a glow, and finally to a smolder.

Natesha and Ganga talked into the night, wondering: how could Lord Shiva have permitted the Rani to fall? How could the Rani's own Goddess have failed to protect her?

The ways of the deities were truly difficult for mortals to comprehend.

9

Frequently the next day, artillery blasted in the distance, and musket shots could be heard. Natesha and Ganga remained in the camp, awaiting the outcome. Late in the day, word came that the British forces had regained control of Gwalior, and once again Tatya Tope was retreating.

Heera Ram appeared, and his shoulders slumped as he said, "We must decide what to do. I myself will follow Tatya Tope. He still needs experienced soldiers."

Ganga asked, "Can he hope to win against the *Angrezi* after losing so many men here?"

Heera looked at her with eyes so dull they appeared almost unseeing. "I think the war is lost. The *Angrezi* will send as many troops as it takes to defeat us. They are united in that one aim, while we are split among ourselves, with too many leaders. And none of them has the Rani's ability to plan strategies that will win against the British generals."

"Then," said Ganga, "Tatya Tope stands no chance?"

Heera slowly shook his head. "I think not. Not after today's loss. He can only retreat. And the British will pursue him until they destroy him."

"Then why should you follow him?" she asked. "You may die needlessly!"

"I have no where else to go." Heera's eyes misted. "If the Rani were still alive we might have won. She was the only one clever enough to be a match for Rose *sahib*. And she might have inspired our troops enough to fight to victory. If only I had properly protected her!"

Natesha himself was still trying to comprehend that the great lady was no longer among the living. He said gently, "You did your best. The Rani's fate was to die here in battle." He dabbed at his eyes. "I've heard the bards are already composing songs about her."

After a time, Heera wiped his own eyes and nodded.

Natesha resumed, "The gods decided that this time the *Angrezi* would win. Maybe next time it will be different. And maybe some day the Rani's memory will inspire others to defeat them."

Eventually, Heera asked, "What will you yourselves do now?"

Despair creeping into his voice, Natesha replied, "We've been wondering that also. Without Her Highness, I no longer have a patron. We have little to return to in Jhansi. And nothing at Gwalior."

Heera said, looking at the ground, "You should also know that the 14th Light Dragoons are at Gwalior. Hatch *sahib* is with that unit. And it's said the reward on you has been increased."

Ganga's eyes widened with fear. She looked at Natesha and said, "If he finds you, he'll try again to force you to show him where the treasure is hidden."

Natesha gave a grim nod.

Heera Ram said, "Then you may want to flee again with Tatya Tope, also. We'll be moving fast, and there may be occasional battles. But I doubt the *feringhi* can keep up. Tatya Tope travels lighter."

"Where is he headed?" asked Ganga.

"Only he knows," replied Heera. "But it's rumored he'll go toward Rajputana. The Jaipur Maharaja and some other lords are said to be sympathetic to our cause."

Natesha said slowly, in a tone of hopelessness, "There's little left for us in Jhansi."

"Then come," said Heera Ram.

Natesha hesitated, turning his gaze toward the south. "I hid some valuable books at the temple," he said. "They're with the treasure."

Ganga told him firmly, "We can return later. When the war is over. When Hatch *sahib* has given up."

After a time, Natesha nodded.

Whatever his failings that contributed to the earlier defeat near Jhansi and to the lack of preparedness at Gwalior, Tatya Tope was a master at keeping his troops moving rapidly and evading the pursuing British.

After two weeks' travel the monsoon came, bringing cooler weather, but also muddying the roads and swelling the streams and making them difficult to cross. Since the most ancient of times, no Indian generals had willingly campaigned in the rains. But Tatya Tope had no choice.

Day after day Natesha and Ganga sloshed through the mud, their clothes soaked and soiled. Natesha struggled to keep his bundle of books dry, and he succeeded only by double-wrapping them in layers of canvas Heera had scrounged.

Natesha quickly lost the added weight from the feasting at Gwalior. Heera Ram had the advantage of his mottled horse to keep his boots above the mud, but nothing could adequately shield him from the drenching rains. At a village, he negotiated with a Rajput landlord and procured a gentle white horse, on which Natesha and Ganga then rode double. Heera led them for a time until Natesha acquired the feel of how to command the animal. After that, they found it much easier to keep pace with the troops.

Still hounded by British troops even in monsoon weather, Tatya's army wound its way through Rajputana, always trying to keep the enemy uncertain as to the rebels' intentions. They traveled through Tonk and Bundi and Neemuch and Mandalgarh.

At Bhilwara, they fought a battle in which Tatya was again forced to retreat. By now, after such long, unpleasant marches, Natesha and Ganga were looking for an opportunity to leave the fleeing rebels, and they even seriously considered risking a return to Jhansi.

But in the cavalry skirmishes outside Bhilwara, Heera Ram glimpsed a red mustached *Angrezi* officer aggressively fighting the native troops. Captain Oliver Hatch was still a threat.

Tatya Tope had lost all his big guns, so there was no longer a need for an artilleryman, and even Heera Ram concluded it was indeed time to leave the rebellion. Thinking to avoid the British as much as possible, especially Hatch, he and Natesha and Ganga decided to travel northerly.

10

Mangarh, 16 August 1858

At an undefined point the three refugees rode across the border into Mangarh state. Still in hilly territory occupied primarily by Bhil tribals, they kept moving until they neared Mangarh city itself. There they camped for the night at the base of a hill near a small river, the water level high now from the monsoons. In the distance, perhaps a *kos* away over the farmland, they could see the huge fortress of Mangarh on its ridge, and the walled town nestling below.

Both Natesha and Ganga were despairing over what to do. Did they dare return to Jhansi? But neither of them now had a temple there, and their home was burned. And what if Hatch returned for the treasure?

Heera Ram, too, faced uncertainty. If he were taken by the British, he would be hanged as a rebel or blown apart by a cannon. Probably, he told his two companions, he would visit the fortresses of Rajput nobles until he found a thakur who would hire him as an officer for the household troops.

Ganga gestured toward the fort visible in the distance. "We're so close. You could try there first."

She realized, as she spoke the words, that there was something about this place that appealed to her. Although the hills were higher, the fortress larger, the walled town smaller, it felt in some ways like the area around her old village in Jhansi. Most of all, it was peaceful. They had seen no soldiers for days.

Heera looked for a time at the fortress. Then he turned away and said slowly, "I've heard the Mangarh Maharaja is an ally of the *Angrezi*. He may be reluctant to employ a mutineer. I think I better move on soon."

"Then we'll continue with you," said Natesha. Although he was tired of the traveling, he had no desire to part from Heera. The big soldier inspired a feeling of safety no matter how wild the territory they traversed.

Ganga felt a vague regret that they would be leaving this lovely place so soon.

That night, she fell into a deep sleep. As she slumbered, she gradually grew aware that a brilliant light approached. Slowly she opened her eyes.

Lord Shiva himself stood before her.

He was just as she had always imagined him, handsome, muscular, glowing bright as the sun. He smiled at her. With one of his four arms, he beckoned her to follow.

She rose from her bed and hurried after, seeming to flow above the ground. The Great God led her down the slope toward the stream near their camping spot.

And then he turned, smiled at her, and vanished.

Ganga abruptly realized she was back on her bedding. Agitated, the vision of her God fresh in her mind, she marveled at what had occurred. A visit by Mahadeva himself! And he had appeared to her, Ganga. He had not abandoned her after all.

She remembered no words spoken. So why had the God appeared? It seemed as if he had led her nowhere in particular. He had disappeared near the river, which was in the direction of Mangarh city. Did that mean she should go to the town itself?

The visit was so vivid in her mind, it simply must be significant. She had served Lord Shiva all her life; it made sense that he might still have plans for her. She lay in her blanket in the darkness, trying to make sense of the God's appearance.

Just before sunrise, Ganga rose for her ablutions in the river. She completed her bathing, and then she climbed from the water to return to where her companions waited. Suddenly, she stopped.

Before her, rising from the rocks above the river bank, was a *lingam* of Lord Shiva. It was perhaps waist high, smoothly rounded, and of a color darker than the surrounding stones.

Suddenly she knew: this was what the Great God had wanted her to find.

She fell prostrate on the ground. It was there that Natesha and Heera Ram discovered her.

It was wondrous, Natesha thought, that Ganga had been the person to find the *lingam*, and at this particular moment. Had it been recently exposed by the eroding effect of the heavy rains during the monsoons? Or had the Great God actually deposited the stone at that spot just before leading Ganga to it?

Either way, it was a remarkable manifestation of Lord Shiva's will. A *swayambhu*, or self-created *lingam*, was the most sacred of all objects of worship.

Even though Natesha was not a *pujari*, in view of such a momentous occasion he made an offering of food to the God, and he anointed the *lingam* with *ghee*. In a stall at the bazaar in Mangarh, Heera Ram purchased a garland of marigolds, and he returned and draped it over the *lingam.*

"Who'll tend the image?" asked Ganga. She looked at Natesha.

Natesha considered. Becoming a mere *pujari*, an officiant at a shrine, would be a significant fall in status. It was not that the worship itself was degrading; rather, it was the fact that priests took money for their work from all castes and therefore tended to have a reputation for greed. Also, although the rituals were important, they were routine, and they could be learned by anyone with a good memory.

Several villagers appeared, curious about the travelers who had come on two horses. They saw the *lingam*, and they too, made offerings.

Word spread quickly, for worshiping a *swayambhu lingam* would liberate the soul of even the lowest outcaste. Before the day's end, a group of local men had built a rough thatched roof to shelter the *lingam.*

Natesha and Ganga and Heera Ram remained camped there the next day, and the next. And the next.

Natesha still did not quite know what to think of the manifestation. Certainly it showed that Lord Shiva was still with him and Ganga, in spite of the traumatic events of the past several months. While Natesha performed his own *pujas* before the *lingam* he would wonder about the God's purpose, and he would hope for some sign or some revelation.

He frequently thought about whether there might be a possibility of finding a patron to support his scholarship. With the revolt apparently nearing an end, conditions might become more settled, and hence it might be more likely that he could find a position.

For the time being, he served as *pujari* at the new shrine, although he was careful to appear humble and used only so much of the offerings as he needed to purchase enough food to survive. In many ways it was an honor to be the first to serve a newly revealed *lingam.*

In a few days, word of the shrine reached the Maharaja of Mangarh, who decided to visit. An advance party erected a *shamiana* and spread carpets and cushions beneath the canopy. Then the Maharaja arrived, in procession on an elephant in order to show suitable honor to the *lingam* that had chosen to manifest itself in his territory.

Maharaja Sangram Singh, a short man in his early fifties, descended slowly from his elephant. He and his ministers and courtiers removed their footwear before approaching the shrine and kneeling in worship.

Natesha accepted their offerings on behalf of the God. After completing the *puja*, His Highness sat in court beneath the *shamiana*, and the ruler invited Natesha and Ganga to meet with him.

"This is an extraordinary occasion, Panditji," said Sangram Singh. "I expect a great many pilgrims will be coming to Mangarh to worship the *lingam.*"

"If Lord Shiva so wishes, Your Highness," said Natesha modestly.

The Maharaja looked to where Ganga sat. He said, "I'm told you are a *devadasi.*"

"Yes, Highness."

Natesha said, "Indeed she is, Highness. A wonderful dancer."

"Interesting," said the Maharaja. "I've never seen a dance performed in a temple. No one has danced in temples in Mangarh for ages. I'm told the same is true almost everywhere except in the south. However, I myself enjoy the dance. I often sponsor performances in my palace. Perhaps you could dance there for me and my guests."

Ganga wore an expression of uncertainty. But she said, "I'd be honored, Highness."

The Maharaja looked at the improvised shrine. "You should have a much larger temple here, Panditji," he said. "And accommodations for the pilgrims who will come."

Natesha inclined his head. "I'm sure the Great God would be pleased with that, Highness. Priests are also needed to serve the *lingam*. I myself am a scholar rather than a *pujari*."

The Chief Minister, a pudgy man with a smiling mouth and cool eyes, said, "I'm told you had a high position at the temple of Lord Mahadeva at Jhansi."

Natesha modestly inclined his head.

"Unfortunately," the Maharaja said, "I don't have the funds for building new temples. But I will grant the revenues from a village for the temple's support."

Natesha brightened. "That's most generous, Highness. Lord Shiva will be pleased."

"See to it, then," the Maharaja directed his minister. "The revenues will maintain the temple, but I doubt they will be enough to build a new one. Perhaps we can solicit donations from some of the wealthier traders."

Natesha considered. Should he mention the treasure hidden at the other temple near Jhansi? For certain, he would need help to recover it. The Maharaja was in a position to provide that type of assistance. Natesha looked about. He hesitated to mention the matter before so many onlookers. Some of them might be greedy enough to want the wealth for themselves if they knew of it. But he was reluctant to pass up the chance. Who knew when he would have another opportunity to talk with the ruler?

He said cautiously, "My previous temple has funds which could be used for construction. I'm sure Lord Shiva would not mind transferring funds from one of his temples to another, Your Highness. But I have no way to transport more than the small amount I could carry myself."

Sangram Singh raised an eyebrow and shrugged as if the matter were of no consequence. "I would be glad to provide you an escort, Panditji. And whatever transport you need."

The Chief Minister said in a quiet voice, "That temple is now in an area controlled by the *Angrezi*, Highness."

Sangram Singh frowned. He looked at the minister.

"This poses a problem," said the minister, looking about, as if for spies. "Perhaps we'd best talk privately." He spoke loudly to the assembly: "His Highness wishes to discuss a personal matter with Panditji. Please prepare to go back to the city."

Most of the courtiers and attendants rose and moved toward the waiting elephants and horses and carts. The Chief Minister said in a low voice to Natesha, "The British Political Agent at Mangarh may learn of the expedition. The *Angrezi* consider His Highness an ally. But the agent would be quite upset if he should discover that His Highness sent a party to take treasure from territory the British claim. The *Angrezi* could even use it as an excuse to remove His Highness from the throne if His Highness' enemies publicized it. So, we will have to have a legitimate purpose to conceal the real reason for the journey. Do you have any land holdings in Jhansi, Panditji?"

"Only my house, Highness. It's been burned and is no longer of much value."

"Hmm....Perhaps you have personal property there to recover? Any gold, jewelry, furnishings?"

"Only some books, Highness."

"Books. Are they of any value?"

"Some are rare, your honor."

"Then our problem is solved, Panditji. I'll see the British agent learns that His Highness is helping you to recover your rare manuscripts, which you have generously volunteered to donate to the palace library. Of course, in fact they will remain your own property."

Natesha took a deep breath and said, "It would require more wagons to carry the treasure than could be justified by my books."

The Maharaja eyed him closely. "How *many* wagons, Panditji? Just how much treasure is there?"

Natesha was still reluctant to reveal his secrets. However, he realized he had few options. The treasure could be lost forever if he did not obtain some assistance in recovering it and restoring it to the God. While the hiding place was good, it was not inconceivable that Pindaris or other looters (maybe even Hatch!) could locate it with enough effort, or by accident.

"I should think maybe five or six bullock carts, Highness. The gold is quite heavy. The bags of silver are bulky. So are the idols, the weapons, the silk robes. And even though the jewels are small and light, there are many chests of them."

The ruler was looking at Natesha, his eyes fixed in surprise. He and the Chief Minister exchanged glances.

The minister said, "Transport by cart is too slow, Panditji. I'll send camels. And a large escort by horse. In these troubled times a big escort is needed to ensure safety."

Natesha hesitated, then said, "After we get the wealth to Mangarh, it would have to be stored somewhere for safekeeping."

The minister and the Maharaja looked at each other. Then, the minister said, "If you wish, Panditji, we could store the temple's items in the state treasury at the fortress."

Natesha said carefully, "They must remain the property of the temple, however."

"Of course," said the minister. "And you could request them as needed to pay for its construction or upkeep."

Natesha was most reluctant to let the treasure out of his control. But he saw little choice. He had no other way to guard it.

He nodded. "Very well. I'm sure Mahadeva will be pleased with your assistance."

"I'll order the arrangements," said the minister. "It will take a week or two to gather the camels and guards."

Relieved, Natesha gave a nod. "Lord Shiva will be grateful." It would be a relief to get the treasure to a safe place, where that *Angrezi* Hatch could have no further designs on it.

The Chief Minister said, "His Highness can arrange for an architect to plan the temple and arrange the construction. However, since you have experience administering a temple, I assume you are willing to assist in the project?"

Natesha hesitated. "I had hoped to be able to continue my scholarship."

"Yes, well, I see no reason why you could not do that also."

Natesha realized it was a momentous opportunity, to help supervise the building of a new temple for a *swayambhu lingam*. He gave a nod. "Very well, then."

The Maharaja rose, and his party followed him to the waiting animals and other conveyances. Heera Ram approached Natesha and said in a low voice, "I spoke with one of the officers of His Highness' private guard. He invited me to the palace to discuss whether a position might be made available for me."

After the Maharaja's procession had gone, with Heera accompanying it, Natesha excitedly said to Ganga, "We'll have sufficient funds now. We can build a dance hall as part of the new temple!"

Her eyes did not light up as he had hoped.

"I think not," she said. "No temples are built with dance halls any more. The *Angrezi* have discouraged it, you know. They think it is immoral."

"This isn't British territory."

"No, but won't His Highness be afraid to offend them?"

Natesha thought for a time. "Probably," he reluctantly acknowledged. "He seems quite cautious about them. The British guarantee the safety of his state. And his place on his throne."

Ganga looked down, then up at him again. "I'm also out of practice. And I'm growing older. Where could I find other dancers to share the duties? And whom would I train to follow me? It takes many years of training."

"You could adopt a girl from a village and teach her."

Ganga looked away. "Maybe. But I think the time of dancers in temples is past. I think now people will see dances only in the palaces or at weddings."

Natesha wished such were not the case, but he sensed she was right. "Will you dance for His Highness, then, in the palace?"

Ganga looked down. "I need to think about it. For certain, I would like to dance again, even if only one more time." She looked at him. "You must have a son, my love," she said. "Maybe rather than my adopting a daughter, it would be better if you adopted a boy."

Natesha thought. For some reason the gods had not granted him a son of his own. Yet, a son was essential to perform the rites at his funeral one day. And it would be good to have some one whom he could teach to carry on his own work. He replied, "Maybe so. When the temple is finished."

11

Captain Oliver Hatch had been transferred to the British cantonment at Nasirabad, to the northeast of Mangarh. He still had not given up hope of locating Natesha and thereby finding the treasure. Although he had paid a return visit to the site of the now deserted temple south of Jhansi, after considerable destruction of the building he still had not been successful in his search.

He now had no idea where the priest and the woman had gone, but he let it be known that the reward was still in effect for information successfully leading to finding the Brahmin.

Thus, word came to him about the *devadasi* who had found a new *lingam*, and about the Brahmin priest who served it. So Hatch rode into Mangarh territories one day, accompanied by two men from his cavalry troop who had been at the raid of the Jhansi temple, and whom he considered sufficiently self interested and despising of natives. Leading an extra horse, they arrived at the small new Shiva shrine on the banks of the river the second day after the Maharaja's visit

Natesha was performing a *puja* for three local villagers, a man and two women. He looked up, and froze. His mind went numb with shock. While trying to think of what to do, he attempted resuming the ritual, but he stumbled over the words.

The villagers, too, were distracted and puzzled by the arrival of the three *Angrezi* soldiers.

The English officer watched for a few minutes. Then he said in Hindustani, "Enough! You'll come with us, Brahmin." He gave a jerk of his head and called to his men: "Travis! Vickery!" The two soldiers moved toward Natesha.

Natesha had seen Travis before. The tall, thin man with fierce blue eyes and bad teeth was the *Angrezi* who had defiled the temple by smearing raw beef about. Natesha stood and faced Oliver Hatch. "You have no right to take me," he said, as the men seized his arms. Heera Ram and Ganga were both in the town. What would they think when they returned to find him gone?

"You fought with the rebels," said Hatch, his eyes cold and full of hate. "We can hang you for that."

"You must hold a trial first," said Natesha, knowing such an argument was unlikely to carry any weight with this particular officer. The soldiers were binding his hands together with rope. He could smell Travis' foul breath and the two men's sweat. He glanced toward the villagers and saw they were running off as fast as they could move.

Hatch gave a harsh laugh. "Maybe later. Or maybe we'll let you go, if you show us where that treasure is." He gave Natesha a shrewd look. "Your treasure, or your life. How's that, Brahmin?"

Natesha said, "You're in Mangarh state now. You have no right to take me without the Maharaja's permission."

Hatch laughed harshly again. "What will he do about it?"

"This temple and I are under his personal protection."

"Then we'd better get you away from here quickly. By the time he hears, it will be too late."

The soldiers roughly pushed him toward the waiting horses. "My friends will come after us!" said Natesha.

"Good—I'd love to kill more of you black bastards!" said Hatch. "Anyway, we'll be in British territory before they can catch us."

The two soldiers boosted him onto the spare horse. The party set out, riding swiftly, with Travis leading Natesha's horse by a rope.

They rode all day, with only brief stops to rest the horses and urinate. It was highly uncomfortable for Natesha, bouncing on the hard saddle, his hands bound.

He felt fairly certain his life would be safe until they reached Jhansi, but he worried about what would happen then. Hatch would likely keep him alive until the treasure was found. But the officer was obviously not a patient man, and if Natesha didn't lead them to the wealth promptly, the British might well torture him.

The priests had formulated a plan in case the hiding spot were revealed. Natesha had no idea if it would work. But the more he thought about it, the more he realized he had to try.

They halted that night, and the British built a cooking fire. Natesha, of course, could not accept water or cooked food from *feringhi*—even had the food been something less nauseating.

The odor of their roasting cow flesh sickened him. But he listened as the British spoke in English. "That nigger thinks he's too good to eat our food," said Travis.

"Then he can go hungry," said Hatch as he carved a hunk of beef, thrust it in his mouth, and chewed.

"It's not us, it's their caste system," said Vickery, the short man with a wide nose. "We're no worse than their own Untouchables. Those Brahmins can't take food or water from them, either."

"Think he'll lead us to the treasure?" asked Travis.

"He bloody well better," said Hatch. "Or he'll end up losing his fingers one by one." He licked grease from his own fingertips.

Natesha could tell the *Angrezi* wasn't joking. Hungry and thirsty, he worried.

Before the British slept, they bound Natesha's feet as well as his hands. He himself could sleep little.

The English, anxious to get to Jhansi, rose before dawn, ate a quick meal, and hoisted Natesha back onto the horse.

They approached the Jhansi area from the south to avoid the British cantonment near the city. Natesha had continued to let the *Angrezi* think he spoke no English. Consequently, they talked freely. It became clear Hatch intended to kill him as soon as he led them to the treasure.

The village that had served the temple still lay deserted, the burned out houses crumbling back into the soil. The party rode past the site of Natesha's house, which Ganga had shared with him so many years. Only parts of the ruined walls remained.

As Natesha had expected, the temple stood abandoned. Debris left by looters and campers littered its grounds. Hatch and the two British troopers escorted Natesha into the *mandap*. It appeared that someone had pried up much of the floor paving in the dancing hall and the tower, probably searching for something hidden. The odor of bats permeated the sanctuary, where pieces of the *lingam* still lay.

"Where is the treasure, Brahmin?" asked Hatch in a low voice.

"If I lead you to it," said Natesha, "will you give me your word that you'll only take half, and leave the rest for Lord Shiva?"

Hatch stared incredulously at Natesha. But he said, "Fair enough. We'll take only half." His glance flicked to his men, who were obviously having difficulty stifling smiles.

"And if I lead you to it, will you spare me?" asked Natesha.

"Of course," said Hatch, his eyes bright, lusting for the riches.

Natesha didn't believe him for a second, but he asked, "You'll let me go immediately?"

"Naturally," said Hatch, the corners of his mouth twitching. "We'd have no further need for you. Why should we keep you longer?"

"Very well, then," said Natesha. "This way." He led them out into the temple courtyard, across to the kitchens, and into a shed with a roof half-fallen in.

Hatch left Travis on guard nearby to warn if anyone approached. Natesha showed Hatch and Vickery how to shove a brick oven to one side, revealing a metal door.

An iron bar from the smithy lay in a corner of the shed. With it, Vickery pried up the door and moved it away, revealing a large rectangular hole with a bamboo ladder leaning against one side at a steep angle.

"It leads to underground vaults," said Natesha, his voice gone hoarse.

Vickery said in English, "I'd never have guessed niggers could be so clever."

Hatch replied, "That's what's so dangerous about them. Always trying to outwit us. And you can never believe what they say, they lie so convincingly. Keep a close watch on this one."

Natesha still pretended not to understand. Now that he was so close to implementing the priests' plan, and hopefully terminating the long period of menace from Hatch, his heart was pounding so loud it seemed the *Angrezi* should be able to hear it. His stomach was queasy, and he felt about to faint.

He took hold of himself and prayed silently to Lord Shiva for strength, and to keep his wits. He reached down, grasped the ladder, and pulled it into a more upright position. He turned and stepped onto a rung. His knees were shaking so much he worried he would slip. One step at a time, he managed to descend.

Vickery held a torch, watching him. When Natesha reached the uneven stone floor, he called up, "I must have a torch to see."

"Captain?" asked Vickery.

"Give him one. Just so we keep a torch ourselves. But watch him closely."

Vickery stepped down the ladder a couple of rungs. He reached downward and handed his torch to Natesha. Then he descended until he stood on the floor.

Captain Hatch climbed down next, torch in hand. He looked about. Seeing the huge coin jars and the chests, he hurried over to them. He shook at one of the padlocks, then turned to Natesha. "You have keys?"

"No, sahib. They were up in the treasury."

"Damn," said Hatch. "It's too much bother to go try to find them. We'll just break these open.

Vickery went back up and got the iron bar. When he returned, he pried the lock off of a chest. He and Hatch raised the lid.

"Damn!" said the captain. He turned and shouted at Natesha, "There are only rocks in here, you black bastard!"

Natesha had already stepped out of the way, into the niche behind the ladder. He was trembling so hard he could barely hold the torch. Could the plan possibly work against someone as determined as Hatch?

But he was acting for Lord Shiva. The Great God would help.

Hatch was moving toward him. "What kind of trick is this?!"

No more time. Natesha yanked on the lever that hung from the ceiling. Nothing happened.

Sweat poured from Natesha's armpits and his breath came in gasps. He again felt faint. Just as he'd feared, the plan hadn't worked. He had lost.

"What are you doing?" Hatch demanded, approaching Natesha.

Another step and the *Angrezi* would be out of danger. Desperate, Natesha threw the torch at him. Hatch leaped backward to avoid it. "What in hell!"

Unencumbered now by the torch, Natesha grabbed the lever with both hands, braced his foot against the wall, and pulled with all his strength. The lever jerked free, and Natesha lost his balance and fell.

But at last the ceiling collapsed, dumping the huge load of rock onto Hatch and Vickery.

Natesha sat trembling on the earth floor in the niche, not quite believing he'd succeeded. The torches had gone out and the chamber was totally dark.

"Captain Hatch, sir—what was that noise? Is anything wrong?" came the call from outside the opening above.

Natesha waited, listening for pile of rubble to stir, expecting Hatch to shove it aside and come furiously after him. The rocks remained motionless.

Natesha still had trouble comprehending that he could have brought about such a result. But other temple priests and a clever carpenter had planned the trap and overseen its construction. And the revenge was really Lord Shiva's. Natesha was merely the God's instrument. The real treasure trove was through a concealed doorway, in the adjacent room, along with the manuscripts.

The lever still in his hand, Natesha slowly climbed to his feet and moved as far back as he could in the niche. Torchlight shone from above, and he saw that the ladder stood in place undisturbed, although the fresh pile of rubble reached its foot, and dust still hung in the air.

"Captain? Vickery?" Travis lowered the torch and saw the big mound of rubble on the floor. A boot protruded from the pile of rocks. "Good God!" Natesha heard Travis mutter. The soldier scrambled down the ladder, awkward with the torch in one hand.

Natesha hesitated. He hated to try again to kill anyone, even Travis, who had defiled the temple. And Travis was much taller than Natesha, so he would be hard to hit on the head. Should he let the *Angrezi* go?

Travis would no doubt kill *him*. And the Englishman would still want the treasure.

Intent on the rubble and what it covered, Travis did not see Natesha, who stepped from the shadows and swung the handle, hard.

The soldier was bending down and the blow bounced off his shoulder. He grunted with surprise and pain, half fell. He caught himself and whirled about.

Natesha stood facing him. It was just as he'd feared. He'd failed after all. "Brahmin!" said Travis. "What—?!"

Desperate, Natesha swung again, hard, sideways and slightly upward. This time he connected with Travis' skull, but the blow glanced off.

"Damn!" yelled Travis. He put his free hand to his head, and with his other hand he thrust his torch toward Natesha.

Bending to avoid the torch, Natesha again swung at the *Angrezi's* head, but the man's free hand was in the way. The fingers broke with a cracking sound.

Travis screamed. He held out his hand limply, face contorted with pain, staring wide-eyed at Natesha, clearly uncertain what to do, unable to draw his sword while still holding the torch.

Natesha hesitated, trying to think of some way out. He could think of none. He grasped the end of the bar with both hands and swung again with all his might. He heard a crunch as Travis' skull caved in. The soldier collapsed to the floor, releasing the torch.

Natesha, sickened, bent over and retched. He felt weak. His pulse pounded.

The torch still burned as it lay on the floor, but barely. Natesha bent and grabbed it before it could go out. Upright again, it burned brighter.

He dropped the handle so he could more easily climb the ladder. Almost too feeble for the effort, he slowly ascended, rung by rung. Out of the hole at last, he stood, doubled over, breathing hard and fast.

Finally, he recovered enough to look about.

The opening. He must cover it again. The bar from the smithy was below, buried in rubble. He doubted the handle he'd dropped was long enough. He held the torch before him and looked about. A section of slender wood pole, one of the cross-supports for the collapsed kitchen roof, lay among the debris. He tugged it out, and using it as a lever, he slowly worked the iron door back into position. Then, little by little, he levered the oven on top of it. With his foot, he smoothed the evidence from the ground as best he could. He examined the area in torchlight and decided he was satisfied.

He must leave before dawn, and he must lead the Englishmen's horses away so no one would examine this area too closely. He would return with the help of the Maharaja of Mangarh's camels and guards to get the treasure. But by then, he realized, the chamber below would be far too odorous to come in again through this entrance. He would use the alternate entry from the temple basement.

Holding the torch high, he looked toward the main temple building, where the big pine cone-shaped towers blotted out the stars. His and Ganga's existence in this place seemed as if in a previous incarnation, another lifetime.

He hoped the new temple he built would be as worthy of Lord Shiva as this prior one, even though Ganga would never dance in it.

Abruptly, a voice whispered near his ear, startling him. "Can I be of help, Panditji?"

Natesha jumped, then he relaxed just a little. He took a deep breath and spoke in normal loudness, though his voice quavered. "I think not, Heera Ram. There's no more to do until we come back with more transport. How did you find me?"

Heera Ram stood peering at him a moment in the torchlight. "After we realized you were gone, some villagers reported you'd been seized by British soldiers. It was not hard to guess who had taken you and where they would go. But where are Captain Hatch and his men now?"

Natesha swallowed. "They're...they're no more."

Heera stared at him. "They're dead? All of them?"

Natesha replied quietly, his voice now more steady, "I would have preferred to reach agreement with them. But they would not have kept their word. They were driven by their greed and hate. They saw me only as a 'nigger,' a 'black.' As little more than a monkey who wore some clothes. They would have killed me afterwards, with no more thought than they would give to butchering a cow."

Heera examined him for several moments. "I confess, you amaze me, Panditji. You managed to kill three armed British soldiers? By yourself?"

"Oh, no. I could never have done it alone. I was merely helping Lord Shiva."

"Well, soon you must tell me how it happened. I agree, there was no other way to deal with such men, but fortunately, most British are not like them."

Natesha thought fleetingly of Major Powis, the Britisher he had known and respected so long ago. He said, "That's true. We should try to remember that fact." He looked about. "Meanwhile, we should lead these horses away, Heera Ram, so they don't draw attention to this spot. Then, I think we'd best leave for Mangarh."

***

The British, of course, were finally able to suppress the Revolt of 1857. But the East India Company having managed matters so poorly, its governmental structure in India was taken over by direct rule in the name of Queen Victoria, who now held the added title of Empress of India. The struggle for Indian independence took almost another century to succeed.

Any attempt at objectively evaluating the history of British rule in the subcontinent has to conclude that there were both minuses and pluses, and huge books have been written on that topic. The discussion is beyond the scope of this brief note, except to say that whatever excuses and justifications are made, the British were foreign occupiers without the consent of those they ruled, and they held onto their power too long.

Part Five
The Treasure of Mangarh

12

Mangarh, 1976

Ghosali turned to Vijay. "I told you nothing would come of visiting this temple."

Annoyed, Vijay replied, "I said that same thing myself, if you remember. I'm merely being thorough." To the head priest of the temple of Mahadeo, he said, "I assume you don't object to our looking around more, now that we're here?"

The priest gave Vijay a slight smile, and said, "I won't try to prevent you from doing your duty. You have no objection if I accompany you and your party while you search?"

"We'd be glad of it. Would you care to lead the way?"

Having already removed their shoes near the entrance gate, Vijay and Ghosali and the witnesses followed the priest up the steps into the porch-like entry. A couple of worshipers were ringing the bell hanging from the top of the doorway to alert the god of their presence.

Vijay's heart pounded. For Ghosali, as a Brahmin, visiting a temple such as this was routine. But it was quite another matter for Vijay.

Ghosali said to him, almost as if sensing his agitation, "You must be quite familiar with this temple, having come from the area."

Vijay tried to think quickly of an appropriate reply. In spite of spending his childhood nearby, it was the first time he had ever entered this temple to Shiva. "My family preferred its own temple," he said, trying to sound casual. "I never came here myself after I was old enough to remember much."

In fact, none of his family had ever so much as passed through the gateway. Except for his father—and that had caused considerable trouble at the time. Vijay, too, would have been denied entry at this moment if the priest had known he was an Untouchable.

Reformers in Mangarh

We Indians are all imprisoned. This is true for the people in the territories directly ruled by the British. It is true for the people in the states ruled by princes and other lords. It is merely more obvious in the case of persons such as myself, who have lost their independence, ironically, for working for freedom.

—Ashok Chand, *Jail Diary of a Reform Worker*

1

Mangarh, September 1938

From a balcony of the fortress high above, the sound of the timekeeper's gong rang across the town and drifted in the open window. Ashok Chand glanced at his wristwatch. It read twelve minutes after two in the afternoon; Mangarh obviously kept its own time. He heard a motor car approach and stop in the street below. The vehicle was the only evidence since his arrival that the city was not frozen in the medieval period.

Footsteps sounded on the stone stairs, and loud raps came on the door. Ashok rose, padded over and pushed the halves open. He faced two policemen in khaki uniforms and dark green turbans. "Come with us to headquarters," said one of the officers. A thin faced man with icy eyes, he spoke in the local dialect of Rajasthani, which Ashok could understand well enough to get the gist.

Ashok took a couple of deep breaths to try to calm himself. He raised his eyebrows. "Am I arrested?" He had expected the police would want to talk with him sometime, but not this soon.

"If you fail to cooperate, we will indeed arrest you."

"On what charge?" Despite his pounding heart, he strained to keep his voice level.

The policeman, who apparently had no difficulty understanding Ashok's Hindi, puffed on a hand-rolled cigarette. He stared at Ashok. "There is no charge yet. But your hat would be enough."

"My hat?"

"Gandhi caps are now illegal in Mangarh. You were seen wearing one when you arrived."

Ashok glance at the hook on the wall where the cap hung in plain sight.

He hesitated momentarily, then asked, "May I write a note first?" The only person he knew in Mangarh was due back at any moment; what would Sundip think when he found Ashok gone?

The policeman drew on the *bidi*, blew smoke, and scowled. "Be fast."

Ashok took his fountain pen and, with a trembling hand, scribbled a hurried explanation and stuck the note in the door frame. Habitually, he reached for his cap. He remembered just in time. The policemen watched him stonily but made no comment.

Ashok slipped his feet into his *chappals*, and the policemen escorted him down the stairs. In the street an old black motor car waited, its coating of dust patterned with little splatters from the few drops of a recent, too-short, rain shower.

Ashok reluctantly climbed onto the worn cushions of the rear seat. The senior policeman slid in beside him, and the other officer sat in front next to the driver. When the car was moving down the street, Ashok took a deep breath and asked the policeman next to him, "Can you tell me why I'm going to headquarters, sir?"

The officer did not look at him. "No."

Ashok opened his mouth to insist on more information, but he realized he was unlikely to get anything further. The car's horn honked as it moved slowly through the bazaar. Despite his apprehensiveness, he tried to absorb his first views of this part of Mangarh: narrow, winding streets with the awnings of tiny, wall-to-wall shops crowding in. The scent of spices hung in the air. Graceful, barefoot women wearing the local costumes of bright red and orange and yellow full skirts, with long veil-like scarfs, moved aside for the car.

Abruptly, the vehicle was forced to stop by a humpbacked white cow sitting like a mountain in the middle of the street. The driver leaned on the horn button. More privileged than a human being in this situation, the cow stared at the police car, uncaring.

While the vehicle waited, the senior policeman lit another *bidi*. Ashok looked up at a section of the old fortress which could be seen between the roofs of two buildings. He had not expected to be so strongly impressed by it. It was surrounded by massive, crenelated walls with numerous towers. On the lower levels, the facades of the big, blocky structures were blank, but on the uppermost levels of the palaces, beauty took over. The buildings sprouted cupolas and balconies and finely sculpted, arched pavilions, all in a warm, honey colored stone.

Sprawling over the hillside so high above, the fort gave the impression, to him, that it was meant to symbolize power over the people and the city over

Mangarh

which it looked. This feeling was partly due, Ashok realized, to his having grown up in the West Punjab where the land was flat. To his mind, only the sky should look down upon the earth, or maybe the pleasant dark greenery of his father's mango trees.

But there was more. The fort was built for military purposes, in times when war was epidemic. And despite the undeniable beauty of the palace facades, when Ashok gazed up at the fortress, he could not help but think of its fantastic cost, paid for by the taxes on thousands upon thousands of peasants over hundreds of years. In states such as Mangarh, ruled by maharajas and thakurs, generations and generations of farmers had labored in the searing sun so that their lords could build those luxurious palaces—and so that the princes could wage war upon each other, over matters so trifling as an insult to one's honor or the rights to the taxes on a stretch of rocky ground.

The cow lurched to its feet and ambled off with an air of self-possession. The car jerked into motion and sped along the crowded lane as if to make up for the lost time.

Ashok grew increasingly uneasy as he wondered what to expect upon his imminent arrival at the police station. An interrogation? Maybe even a beating to discourage him from remaining in the state?

He considered a different approach to try to gauge the reactions of the police. He hesitated, then decided he probably had little to lose. He concentrated on using a casual, friendly tone, and said, "I understand the rains are late this year, sir. Do you think they'll come soon?"

The policeman reached out the window and knocked the ashes from his *bidi*. He slowly turned to Ashok with a glare. "No questions!"

Ashok hoped he hadn't annoyed the man so much as to make the situation worse. The car exited the narrow archway in the city wall and entered the newer section of town. Here the street was wider and straighter and less crowded. Soon the vehicle stopped before a one story brick building. The two policemen escorted him from the car into the structure. Their footsteps echoed on polished concrete as they strode down the hallway. The narrow faced officer stopped at a curtained doorway and knocked on a door marked, "Karam Singh—Inspector General." The highest police official in the state.

Ashok's escort held back the drape and gestured him in. A husky, middle-aged Sikh in the now familiar khaki uniform and green turban sat stiffly behind a large wooden desk. He looked up from the folder of papers before him and waved Ashok to a chair. Beneath bushy eyebrows, the most piercing eyes Ashok had ever seen fixed on him. The man said in perfect English, "Sit down, Mr. Chand." He told the senior policeman, "You may go, Jhakhar."

"Yes, sir." The officer turned and left.

Ashok sat in the hard wooden chair and waited, making a deliberate effort to keep a pleasant expression on his face. He knew his good looks and sincere friendliness usually made a favorable impression. But whether or not that would matter here remained to be seen.

Most of the population of his home village in the Punjab was Sikh. Although his own family was Hindu, Ashok had grown up with a fondness for the hard working, straightforward, Sikh neighbors whose men wore beards and neatly tied turbans. Still, he was uneasy with this particular Sikh scrutinizing him with those penetrating eyes.

The breeze from the big ceiling fan rustled papers on the desk. After what must have been half a minute, the inspector general spoke: "We know you work for the Congress Party, Mr. Chand. And we have a good idea why you're here."

Ashok knew the success of his assignment in Mangarh might well depend upon how he handled himself with this man. He opened his mouth to reply, but the police official glanced down at the open file and said, "You are from the Punjab, Lyallpur District. I'm quite familiar with Lyallpur, Mr. Chand."

Ashok was astonished that the police official should already have records on him. But he asked in a friendly manner, "You must be from the Punjab yourself, then, sir?" It was a reasonable guess, given that the man was a Sikh.

The officer stared at him. He gave a grunt, and said, "Montgomery District." Karam Singh returned his focus to the file and continued, "You're twenty-four years old, of the Arora caste. Your family are farmers, mainly mangoes and wheat, in village Kapani. Also they lend money on occasion. I see your brother is active in the RSS. After you graduated from law school in Lahore you worked with the Congress Party in Poona and Delhi before coming to Mangarh. You seem to have attracted favorable attention from Mr. Nehru. And Mr. Gandhi in particular apparently has a liking for you." The man looked up at him with the piercing stare. "You seem a talented and dedicated young man, Mr. Chand. Why would a lawyer such as yourself come to an out of the way place like Mangarh?"

Ashok was so stunned by the amount of information in the dossier that he had to struggle to formulate his thoughts. How much detail should he give the police official? How much more might be in the file itself? He replied, "I came here at Gandhiji's request to work for better conditions for the rural poor in Mangarh, sir. I assure you, I have no wish to cause any trouble."

Karam Singh said, spearing Ashok with the intense look, "Mr. Chand, His Highness the Maharaja does not wish to have any kind of disturbances in his state. He—and I—will take whatever steps seem necessary to avoid them. I want to make that clear, before you get too far along in your activities." He stopped. His stern gaze had never wavered from Ashok.

Ashok said, striving to keep his voice calm, "I understand, sir. But I would think His Highness should have no objections to my work, since he himself must surely be concerned about the welfare of his people."

Karam Singh said, without changing expression or tone, "His Highness feels quite capable of looking out for the welfare of his people without interference. From anyone." Ashok was trying to think of an appropriate response when Singh concluded: "I'll be watching you closely, Mr. Chand. I hope it won't be necessary to intervene."

Ashok hesitated, then nodded. "I hope so too, sir."

Singh said, "My funds are limited, and jails have not been the highest priority. You might find them unpleasant to stay in. You're free to go, Mr. Chand. This time." The inspector general rang a bell. A peon appeared at the door, and Singh said, "Get sub-inspector Jhakhar to return Mr. Chand to his lodging."

The encounter was so brief, Ashok could hardly believe it was over. He nodded as he rose. He managed a smile, hoping his strain didn't show. "It's been timely meeting you, sir. I hope we can talk on future occasions, so that there are no misunderstandings."

Singh stared at him, then gave a grunt.

Once out the door, Ashok let out his breath in relief. Even a British-run jail would be unpleasant. One in a feudal state like Mangarh would likely be a horror.

Sub-inspector Jhakhar and the other policeman drove him back to his room. Not a word was exchanged, even when Ashok stepped from the car and nodded at the two officers.

The note was gone from his door; apparently Sundip had returned and left again. Now that Ashok's fears of imminent arrest and jailing had receded, he sat cross-legged on his bed and thought.

A government should exist to serve its people. It should never treat citizens, even those from another state, in this manner, just because they might question its policies.

A knock came on the door, and the short, broad form of Sundip Saxena, a school teacher in his late twenties, appeared. Relief flooded his wide, plain face. "You're back! I was worried. The police wouldn't tell me anything—I was afraid they'd thrown you in jail."

Ashok realized he might look unnerved, and he tried to force himself to smile. "Not yet, as you can see. Hopefully, I'll be finished in Mangarh before I have that honor."

Sundip furrowed his brow and peered at him. "I hope they didn't change your mind about helping us."

Ashok again managed to smile. "Just the opposite. The police are more aggressive than I'd expected, but they convinced me this government does indeed need reforming."

Sundip's frowned deepened. "Even though we can definitely use your help, I'd hate to see you put away in prison."

Ashok sobered and nodded. "Jail time may be a mark of honor for freedom fighters and reformers, but personally, I wouldn't like it. Aside from the health threats, I couldn't do any meaningful work." He again smiled. "I also enjoy fresh air, and coming and going when I wish."

"Well," said Sundip, "if it gets too dangerous and you want to leave, we'll certainly understand."

Ashok took a deep breath and straightened. He shook his head. "I'll face the consequences of whatever we do here. If I'm in danger, you probably will be, too. It's only right that I share the risk."

2

Wardha, August 1938

It had started a month ago when the Mahatma summoned Ashok. The weather was hot at Wardha, virtually the geographic center of the subcontinent. As usual, Ashok hired a tonga to travel the few miles across the plain to Gandhi's ashram at the outskirts of Segaon village.

The dusty road was bordered by fields, and the two-wheeled, horse-drawn carriage frequently encountered farmers in their bullock carts. He met a throng of poorly dressed young men, apparently villagers. As the party passed, two at the forefront were arguing heatedly, and the others trudged along with slumped shoulders and downcast eyes. Ashok wondered what occasion might have brought such a group together. Clearly, it was nothing joyful.

When he arrived at the mud buildings of Sevagram Ashram, he saw immediately that something unusual had occurred. Instead of being at their usual chores, the residents were standing in small clusters in the graveled central courtyard.

Gandhi's secretary, Mahadev Desai, a tall, handsome man with a neat mustache, recognized Ashok and greeted him. "You've missed the excitement," he said. "But maybe it's better that way."

"Whatever happened?"

"We've been the target of civil disobedience, rather than instigating it ourselves." Amused at Ashok's look of surprise, Desai asked, "Did you meet a large group of villagers on the road?"

Ashok nodded. "Yes."

"They're Harijans. A few days ago, they suddenly appeared and said they'd stay at the ashram until Gandhiji met their demands. They wanted him to appoint an Untouchable to the government's cabinet."

"Bapu doesn't have the authority to do that!" Like most others who knew Gandhi well and felt affection toward him, Ashok typically called him Bapu, Father.

"Exactly." Desai looked both amused and annoyed. "But they told Bapu that he'd always gotten whatever he wanted by saying he'd go without food until he either starved to death or won his demands. So they said they'd refuse to eat until a Harijan got a cabinet post."

"They actually tried it here?"

"Yes, all of them refused to eat. But they took whatever rooms or other things they wanted. Today, they finally gave up and left. It was very difficult for Bapu. For all of us. The entire routine was upset."

Ashok nodded. Gandhi believed in the discipline of following the same schedule every day; unlike most Indians, he was a clock-watcher. "I can well imagine. How is Bapu now?"

Desai, who usually knew best of anyone what Gandhi was thinking at a given moment, turned to look toward the Mahatma's hut. He said, "It's shaken him considerably. He's resting."

"I'd like to see him when he's able."

"Of course. I'll let you know."

The next day, Mahatma Gandhi was recovered enough from the ordeal to see Ashok. Gandhi was almost seventy years old, and he looked even smaller and thinner than when Ashok had visited a few months back. But his face was joyful as ever as he sat on his cushion doing his daily spinning. Gandhi recognized Ashok, smiled his toothless grin, and nodded his shiny brown head. "Welcome, my son," he said in his singsong voice. "Please sit. You had a good journey?"

"Fine, Bapu," said Ashok. He sat on one of the thick bamboo-and-*khadi* mats. "But these past few days must have been difficult for you."

Gandhi smiled, raised a hand to adjust his wire rimmed spectacles, and shrugged his bare shoulders. "It was a trying time. However, difficulties give us an opportunity to grow spiritually. It was new for me to be on the receiving end of nonviolent coercion. I now understand how much anxiety must have been felt by my own targets. Hopefully, though, I use better judgment than those Harijans in choosing my issues. They simply did not understand that for *satyagraha* to achieve its goal, it must be aimed at a result that is possible to achieve. How could they expect me to appoint a government minister when I am not in the government myself?"

"Maybe it's a danger, Bapu, when people come to feel you can work miracles."

Gandhi nodded. The spinning wheel made a light buzzing sound, and his hands, with years of practice at the task, worked quickly. "People expect too much of me, as if I were claiming to be some sort of God. I wish they could understand that I am as mortal and as fallible as any of them. But now, my son, let's talk of the reason I asked you here. I've been thinking recently about the need to reform the dictatorial governments in the princely states. You know of Mangarh?"

"A rather backward state in Rajputana, isn't it?"

Gandhi smiled, his eyes gentle. "You refer to Mangarh as 'backward.' Some would say the same of my spinning wheel, or of wearing *khadi*. I doubt backward is a term we should use merely because a state hasn't embraced the industrial revolution. But in terms of political and social reforms, yes—I am sure backward is a most appropriate word for Mangarh." Gandhi now frowned. "Have you ever spent any time in a princely state?"

"No, Bapu."

The pile of cotton thread on Gandhi's lap steadily grew. "I was raised in one. They have a character all their own. In this case, I've received a request from leaders of the newly formed Mangarh Praja Mandal, the Mangarh People's Association. They hope to convince the Maharaja to create a legislative assembly, but so far the government has ignored them. Still, the Maharaja is new, and fairly young, so he might yet be convinced to adopt a few democratic reforms."

Ashok gave nod, anticipating where the Mahatma was likely headed.

Gandhi sat silently for a few moments as the wheel whirred. He resumed, "A famine is also expected as a result of the continuing drought, and the Maharaja's government shows no sign of plans to alleviate the crisis." He gave Ashok a meaningful look. "Hundreds, maybe thousands, could die, and thousands more would suffer. The villagers' cows, too, will die if there's no fodder due to lack of water."

Ashok nodded. "It sounds like the Maharaja somehow needs to be convinced of the urgency."

"I want you to go there, my son. Help these reformers get better organized. See if you can influence His Highness to do better for his people."

Ashok hesitated, and said, "I'm honored at your trust in me, Bapu. But mightn't it be better to send someone more experienced with princely states, who knows better how they operate? Maybe even try to recruit someone who knows Mangarh well—someone who already has the confidence of people there?"

Gandhi smiled. "You have someone in mind?"

Ashok smiled back. "No, Bapu. But someone like that must be available, somewhere."

Gandhi looked down at his work and said, "This assignment requires someone who can evaluate the situation and act independently, with good judgment. Someone who can quickly win trust and respect. Despite your youth, you've proven both in Poona and Delhi that you have those qualities."

Ashok took a deep breath. "I'm flattered, Bapu. But I know Pandit Nehru has been hoping to use me in organizing the United Provinces. Failing that, I'd hoped to work closer to my family's home in the Punjab."

Gandhi looked closely at his whirring wheel. "I've been in correspondence with Panditji. He is not expected back until November."

"Yes, Bapu." Ashok knew Jawaharlal Nehru was on an extended trip to Europe.

Gandhi's eyes turned upon him, peering through the spectacles. "Panditji is in full agreement with me that something must be done about these princely states. You may remember the Congress passed a resolution on the matter last year. Someone has actually counted the states and came up with a total of 565. They include a third of our people, and two-fifths of our land area, far too important to ignore. Most of theses states have rulers with almost absolute powers over their subjects."

Ashok nodded. He knew much of the Congress leadership considers the prince-run governments to be corrupt anachronisms.

"Of course," said Gandhi, "we have workers in other princely states besides Mangarh. But our activists face considerable resistance to change. To an extent, your going to Mangarh is an experiment. If you achieve some success, it could help show the way to reforms in other places ruled by princes."

Ashok took a deep breath. "That means a lot will be riding on me. Not just what happens in Mangarh, but the implications for elsewhere."

"Quite so, my son. But if we did not think you could handle the challenges, Panditji and I would not have asked you."

Ashok knew he could not refuse. Along with Nehru, Gandhi knew better than anyone the overall picture of what was happening in India. If they said the most important use of his time and talents was throwing himself into a medium sized princely state, then that ended the matter.

Ashok discussed the assignment more with Gandhiji, including possible approaches he might take, and the likely response of the Maharaja's government. "You may well be seen as an agitator," Gandhi said. "You could be beaten, or you could end up in jail. Possibly both."

Ashok smiled tightly. "That can also happen in British India, as you've experienced yourself, Bapu."

Gandhi laughed. "So it can."

While they talked, staff members came and went, many of them young women quietly checking to see if the Mahatma had any tasks for them to do. But Gandhi's attention remained fully on Ashok. The mound of thread piled ever higher on the white *dhoti*.

As their conversation drew to an end, the Mahatma said, "I feel I must also point out something for you to keep in mind. You are a hard worker, my son. You bring enthusiasm to whatever you do. You have a gift for inspiring those who work with you. But I will be frank. You haven't yet been in jail, and you have not truly had to feel direct consequences of your actions. You must always keep one fact in mind. You, yourself, can leave Mangarh, but the people you are trying to help will have to suffer whatever response you provoke from the authorities."

Ashok nodded, sober faced. "I understand, Bapu. I'll do my best to be careful."

Gandhi smiled. "But not *too* careful. Taking calculated chances is inherent in our work. Unless we risk ourselves, even our very lives, we will never achieve our aims."

"I've come to realize that, Bapu."

Gandhi glanced at the pocket watch he kept lying nearby. The spinning wheel came to a stop; it was time to move to the next item of his busy daily program. He gave a quick nod. "Very well, my son. See what you can accomplish in Mangarh."

3

Mangarh, September 1938

Ashok's first meeting with the Working Committee of the Mangarh People's Association was the night of the same day he had been taken to the police station. The joint household of the clan of prosperous traders occupied a tall *haveli* in the old part of Mangarh, squeezed on both sides by other houses and by small shops. The Jain family was wealthy and progressive enough to have installed electric lighting, and the inside seemed bright compared with the dark night outdoors.

Kishore Lodha, the Praja Mandal's president, puffed on his cigarette and said, "No insult intended to our guest or the Mahatma, but I still don't see why we need someone from outside to tell us what to do." The broadly built, good looking lawyer in his late twenties spoke in English rather than Rajasthani, as did the others, a fact which said volumes about the people guiding the organization.

Ashok said calmly, "I certainly didn't come to tell you what to do. It's your state, and you decide what's needed. I'm merely available if you want suggestions or help."

Sundip Saxena said, "Remember, most of us agreed we could use some aid. Since none of us has experience with what we're trying to do, what harm is there in having additional advice?"

"I still think it's an excellent idea," said Mrs. Arora, a pleasant faced, matronly woman. She and her attractive daughter wore saris, unlike most women in Mangarh who wore the local skirt and veil. She shoved her spectacles up on her nose and added, "A liaison with Gandhiji can provide moral support, if nothing else."

"And we can definitely use some practical advice," said the daughter. She eyed Ashok with a smile he found quite charming. "So far, we've been using mostly guesswork." Ashok glanced at Kishore and saw that the president's eyes had abruptly gone cold. Did he see her reference to "guesswork" as implied criticism, or was there something else involved, like his fancying the girl?

Their host Manohar Jain, a round faced, chubby young merchant, was sitting cross-legged on a bed. He peered through thick-lensed eyeglasses and said, "Anyway, now that our guest has come so far to help us, we must welcome him as the emissary of Gandhiji that he is." He smiled broadly and looked at Ashok. "I think you can be of considerable help. We're all casting about in the dark."

Kishore was frowning. "Well. On to our main item of business. It's been four months since I drafted the petition to His Highness asking for a legislative assembly. We've yet to hear a single word from the palace in response."

Manohar Jain, eyes large behind the heavy glasses, said, "His Highness' government can continue to ignore us so long as we have no power. That's precisely why we need the legislature."

"A follow up letter seems in order, at the very least," said Mrs. Arora.

"Why not request a personal audience with His Highness?" asked Manohar.

The young woman said, "Maybe we should do both. A combination of another letter and a visit to the Maharaja."

The discussion continued, with Kishore preferring yet another petition. Ashok remained silent and listened. His eyes frequently lingered on the lovely young woman. He realized he wasn't the only one noticing her; Kishore was watching her more than he looked at anyone else.

Eventually, after what Ashok felt was an unnecessary amount of debate for such a simple matter, agreement was reached that Kishore would draft and send a letter of inquiry about the status of the petition, and the letter would also include a request for an audience with the Maharaja.

Later, when they were out on the street, Sundip glanced about and whispered, "Whenever I go to these meeting, I wonder if we're being followed by the police or a spy for the government. But I don't see any evidence of that tonight."

"Let's hope it stays that way." The street was dark, with only the glow of an occasional lamp spilling from a doorway or window, and as they walked, Ashok examined the street carefully, trying to avoid stepping into gutters or other holes.

Sundip said in a quiet voice, "Kishore shouldn't have been so unwelcoming to you at the beginning. I apologize for that."

"No matter," Ashok said. "I'll do my best not to cause problems."

"You should know, he wants to advance himself socially, but it's difficult so long as Mangarh is ruled by the old circle of Rajput noblemen and their advisors. His best hope is reforms such as the legislative assembly. He might get elected to it, or maybe even become a minister if the government opens up."

"I see."

"At the same time," said Sundip, "he doesn't want to jeopardize his law practice in Mangarh courts. And he doesn't want to chance going to jail. So he tries to balance on a fine line."

Ashok glanced up to the black bulk of the fortress outlined against the stars. A lamp shone dimly in a tower on the wall, and another in a distant window of the palace area. He returned his attention to the street and asked, "What's the background of the women?"

"Outspoken, aren't they?"

"But in a pleasant way," said Ashok.

Sundip said, "Mrs. Arora's originally from Delhi. Her family's been involved with the Congress Party a long time. Her husband's a medical doctor here now. He often holds weekly free clinics for the rural poor."

Sundip seemed to have finished, leaving Ashok not yet satisfied. He tried to act casual as he asked, "And the daughter?"

"Jaya? She goes to Delhi University, but she's taking a long break from it. Pretty, isn't she?"

"That's an understatement." Ashok tried to think of a cautious way to ask more about her.

"She's smart, too," said Sundip. "Sometimes she asks the best questions of any of us."

Ashok smiled to himself, her image still vivid in his mind. Maybe working with the Mangarh Praja Mandal would have some added attractions.

Sundip added, "Kishore has obviously been interested in her. I'd guess the only thing holding him back is that he's not the same caste. But I think her parents probably wouldn't mind that as much as most, especially as both castes are roughly the same level."

Ashok sighed to himself and conceded he probably shouldn't be thinking about young women anyway, not when he was so completely committed to reform work—even though his own family were Aroras like hers, just with a different surname.

Early the next morning, birds were chirping loudly in the trees and smoke from cooking fires hung in the air as he and Sundip left on bicycles to introduce Ashok to the countryside. They wove through the narrow, twisting streets and exited through the big arch of the city gate. Then they rode over a bridge across the channel of the mostly dry river. *Dhobis* were beating clothes on the rocks at small pools.

They approached the beginning of a long masonry wall, on the other side of which rose a grove of mango trees. "The Bhim Bhawan, where His Highness lives," Sundip said. Ashok slowed at the big ironwork gate hanging open at the entrance and peered through, but he could see nothing of the palace itself except the central dome and the clock tower poking above the tops of the trees. Three turbaned guards at the gatehouse glanced momentarily at Ashok and Sundip but went back to conversing among themselves.

Just beyond the parklike grounds, they overtook a couple of shabbily dressed women, bent under big baskets on their backs. Eyes averted, the women stepped off the roadway as the bicyclists approached. After they had passed, Sundip said, "Untouchable Bhangis. They're carrying off night soil from the chamber pots in the city mansions. Maybe from the palace, too."

They steadily pedaled along the graveled road following the course of the river. They met a bullock cart carrying a farming family, the men wearing bright colored turbans. Then came several women with bundles of firewood on their backs, and another young man on a bicycle. On both sides of the narrow valley floor rose arid, rocky ridges. In a walled area stood the chimneys of a small brickwork, with the stacked rectangular blocks of clay covering much of a field. A cartload of bricks, pulled by a camel, left the yard and headed toward the town. To Ashok, raised in fertile plains well watered by irrigation canals, this seemed a parched landscape, especially after this year's lack of monsoon rains.

The road passed the gold-capped temple of Mahadeo Shiva, in a large compound enclosed by a whitewashed wall. The road became a narrow lane, where the dust lay deep. They met a line of camels, heavily laden with large bags. The caravan raised a cloud that choked throats and irritated eyes.

A short distance farther, an old, domed Muslim tomb sat beneath a big mango tree. Several villagers had gathered before the structure, apparently to pray to the saint buried there.

Ashok was hot and sweaty, as well as dirty, by the time they approached the village. "This is Gamri," said Sundip. It was a typical aggregation of tile roofed, mud plastered houses, surrounded by thorn fences for protection from bandits and wild animals. They met a couple of women carrying large brass water pots on their heads, silver anklets flashing on bare feet as they walked. Like most village women encountering strange males, these two pulled their long, scarf-like *odnis* over their faces to shield themselves from view.

A little farther along, Sundip abruptly halted his bicycle, and so did Ashok. In the distance, they saw two turbaned young men beating on another young man, who was hunched on the ground, trying to shield his head with his arms. Yet another man stood watching. One of the attackers was striking about the victim's shoulders with a stick, while the other was kicking at his sides.

"Shouldn't we stop them?" asked Ashok.

Sundip hesitated, then replied, "Better not get involved. I can guess what might be happening, but I'm not sure."

"We should help anyway!"

Sundip held out a hand to block him. "Only if you want to risk your entire effort in Mangarh. Notice that no one from the village is interfering. There are powerful interests here, and we have to be careful not to overly offend them."

Ashok felt he had to stop the assault, come what may. He asked, "Why am I here then, if I have to be so afraid to do anything?" He applied his foot to the bike's pedal. But at that moment, the two attackers and the third man moved off in the opposite direction, leaving their victim.

"Now," said Sundip, "let's see if we can help."

They rode to where the downed man was sitting up, holding his head in his hands. Sundip said in the local dialect, "Ram! I didn't realize it was you. Are you hurt badly?"

The young man straightened, dropped one hand, and looked at him. "Masterji," he said. Ashok saw that he was nineteen or twenty years old. Except for his face being heavily pockmarked from smallpox scars, he was handsome, dressed in a worn-looking but clean *dhoti* and turban.

"Are you going to be all right?" asked Sundip.

The young man drew himself to his feet, cringing from pain. "They don't know how to administer a real beating. I'll be fine. In a few days, anyway."

Sundip said quietly to Ashok, in Hindi, "He's a Bhangi. And a student of mine. The attackers were Rajputs." He turned to the young man, who was wiping blood from his forearm. "What was it about, Ram? The temple again?"

"No, they said I looked at one of their women. As if I don't have a wife of my own now!"

Sundip shook his head and told Ashok. "He got beat up a few months ago because he was seen at a shrine. The upper castes say Untouchables can't worship at it." He turned back to Ram. "Come, I'll go with you to your home, so I can make sure you aren't injured too badly."

"There's no need."

"I'll come anyway." Sundip beckoned toward Ashok, and told Ram, "Chandji was sent from the Mahatma himself, to try to help us. I'm just showing him around."

Ram bowed his head and pressed his palms together in greeting. It was obvious from his slight grimace that he was in pain.

Accompanying him, Ashok and Sundip walked their bicycles to the Untouchable area on the outskirts, and to a mud hut with thatched roof. Ram's wife let out a cry and hurried to him. Ashok saw that, though shabbily dressed, she was quite attractive, and quite young.

She helped Ram inside the hut to a pallet on the floor. Ashok followed Sundip in, ducking his head at the low doorway. The interior was dark; there were no windows and the only illumination came from the open door. The rafters were blackened from smoke from the cooking fire. But the floor was clean and smooth from an application of cow dung, long since dried.

Ram and his wife had few possessions. Ashok saw a tiny oven of bricks, a couple of pots, a grain storage container made of mud, an oil lamp, a couple of hand tools for harvesting crops, and a wooden chest, likely for storing clothes. There were three books in a neat stack on the chest: a *Ramayana* and a *Gita* in Hindi, and a mathematics text.

He had difficulty following Sundip's rapid, murmured conversation in the local dialect. But soon Sundip turned to him and said, "We should go and let him rest."

As they left the area, Ashok said, "He didn't defend himself against the Rajputs. I suppose that could have made the situation worse."

"Yes, he knows it might have escalated into a battle between castes. If he'd injured any of them, Rajputs would have retaliated in larger numbers to teach Bhangis a lesson. And the Bhangis would have lost, since Rajputs outnumber them and have all the weapons."

"I noticed the books in his home."

"Ram's my best student. He's also the oldest one now. He walks all the way to the school, three villages away. I give him free tuition and books, since he couldn't afford to come otherwise."

"That's kind of you."

Sundip shrugged. "It's the least I can do, when he applies himself so hard. It's sad—if he hadn't been born a Bhangi, he'd probably be the head of this village some day."

"I spent quite a bit of time with Gandhiji, traveling around trying to help Untouchables gain access to temples. He had a fair amount of success, though it's hard to know if the upper castes will revert back to their own ways after we left their areas."

"Personally," said Sundip, "I'd like to try to help the Untouchables. But I haven't been able to interest the Praja Mandal as a whole. Maybe because the others don't actually know any Bhangis."

4

Mangarh, October 1938

From the rooftop of the Jain family's *haveli,* Ashok had his first look at the man whose government he had come to help reform. Musicians were beating drums and blowing horns in the grand procession on the last day of the Dussehra festivities. The line of heavily decorated elephants extended up the street and around the corner. In the howdah of the largest bull elephant rode Lakshman Singh, tall, young, handsome, and adorned in jeweled necklaces and a bejeweled turban. People screamed, *"Maharaja ki jai!"* "Victory to the Great King!"

Manohar Jain gestured at the Maharaja and shouted above the noise, "The people adore him." Ashok nodded, but he didn't try to shout a reply.

The city had been packed the last ten days with villagers from the countryside. Rajput lords from outlying areas were obligated to attend the Maharaja's court, bringing their required numbers of troops. So the clatter of hoofbeats was frequently heard as bands of horsemen, armed with rifles and swords, rode through the streets. In Mangarh, as in general over northern India, the main thrust of the festival was to celebrate the victory of Lord Rama, hero of the epic *Ramayana*, over the demon king Ravana. Ram-Lilas, amateur theatrical performances of scenes from the *Ramayana*, were enthusiastically put on in the city and in the villages.

But in Rajput-controlled states such as this, the festival was much more. This was the time when the rulers reviewed their troops, inspected their army's weapons, and announced their upcoming wars, which had traditionally been fought during the fine weather of the winter months. The British had stopped almost all the warring between the princes, but the festivities remained.

The procession slowly continued. The Maharaja never glanced up at the rooftop as he swayed along in his howdah, and eventually he disappeared down the street. Still more elephants followed. Ashok counted the majestic animals and came up with fifteen. The crowd was still noisy, but Manohar no longer had to shout so loud as he said, "Now His Highness will go to the grounds outside the city wall to set fire to Ravana."

Ashok nodded. In Mangarh, as in numerous cities and towns, Dussehra culminated in the burning of a huge paper effigy of Ravana, the demon king of Lanka, in honor of his defeat by Lord Rama. Manohar led Ashok indoors. "You can see," Manohar said, "that we have a long way to go. Almost everyone worships the Maharaja. They love the show he puts on, even though all his elephants and jewels cost them dearly. If we're to have any chance at democratic reforms, we have to remember the people's feelings. We can only get an elected assembly with His Highness' approval. And the Maharaja must clearly remain the head of the government."

"A challenging task." Ashok knew a main focus of Manohar's interest in reforms was giving merchants more influence on state policies, as well as bringing improvements to help trade: better roads, a rail line closer to the city, a modern telephone system. Yet, Manohar also was genuinely concerned about the downtrodden. "It sounds like we need to speak to His Highness in person," Ashok added.

Manohar smiled. "There's no point in thinking about it until Divali's over. The entire state will be preoccupied until then."

Divali, the festival of lights and the traditional beginning of the Hindu New Year, was similar in Mangarh to what Ashok had experienced back home and elsewhere. He took care in the narrow streets to avoid ladders and dripping whitewash as people painted their houses with fresh coats. The sounds of firecrackers, lit off mostly by young boys, frequently blasted the air.

On the night of Divali itself, everyone in Mangarh set out as many little clay oil lamps as they could afford, lining the edges of their roofs and window sills and doorsteps, so the town was like a starlit fairyland.

The Aroras invited him for dinner, and he brought a box of sweets he'd purchased in the bazaar. On the outskirts of Mangarh, the home was a two story structure with front rooms on the ground floor housing the medical clinic.

Dr. Arora's warm welcome was obviously sincere, as was his interest in Ashok's earlier life in the Punjab. The short man with a neatly clipped mustache had studied medicine in London, and the family ate at a European style table with chairs. Mrs. Arora took her meal with the rest of them, rather than remaining in the kitchen to supervise the cook. Ashok found it difficult to keep his eyes from lingering on Jaya, who sat diagonally across from him.

As the sound of firecrackers came from nearby in the neighborhood, Mrs. Arora said, "Please tell us how you got started working for Gandhiji."

"I hadn't planned on it when I went to Law College in Lahore," said Ashok. "But Gandhiji came there to speak, and when I heard him, he was so compelling in his speech, so obviously loving and selfless, I knew I wanted to put my efforts into helping him. I managed to talk with him afterwards, and he was quite encouraging."

"How did your family react?" asked Dr. Arora, with raised eyebrows.

Ashok smiled at the thought. "They were surprised at first. My parents had made some sacrifices so I could go to college. They originally thought I'd set up a law practice nearby. But they adjusted quickly and have been supportive—though they do wish I'd find work closer to home."

Jaya asked, her eyes warm and full of interest, "And I heard that you know Pandit Nehru also?"

Ashok had to make an effort to concentrate on what he was saying, rather than on her. "Yes, one of my first jobs was to help build membership in the Congress. I got to know Panditji then."

"What's he like, in person?" Jaya asked.

Ashok thought for a moment, deciding what to emphasize about such an impressive leader. "He's extremely intelligent, with a good grasp of issues. I greatly admire all the sacrifices he and his family have made for the freedom cause. They could have had comfortable lives of great wealth, but instead they chose to work for the common good, even when it's meant long periods in jail."

"But what is it like to be around him? To talk with him?" she asked.

Ashok hesitated before saying, "He's a forceful personality." He smiled. "His moods can change quite quickly, and I know some people find him a bit impatient, but he's been very supportive to me personally."

There was silence for some time, and Ashok hoped he hadn't cast the great man, who had been so good to him and whom he venerated, in a negative light. At last, Dr. Arora asked, "Do you see parallels between working to get the British to leave India and working for reforms in a princely state?"

"I do, sir. In both cases, we're trying to deliver power into the hands of the people who are native to the area, so they can control their own lives, not have someone else dictate to them. And the nonviolent methods Gandhiji uses to put pressure on the British government can also be used against a Maharaja's government."

"We also should be doing more directly in the villages," said Dr. Arora. "I go on a tour once a week and try to help with medical problems. But sanitation is so bad, and the people so poor, it's a losing battle."

"And the way the Untouchables are treated is so disgraceful," said Mrs. Arora.

Ashok thought back to Ram, the Bhangi, who had been given a beating. "I've been interested in the Untouchables' situation," Ashok said, "ever since spending time with Gandhiji a few years ago when he was on his ten month tour to work for their rights. Temples were often opened to Harijans when he arrived, but I've heard they were sometimes closed again after he left."

Jaya's eyes were intent on him. "I think I remember that his opponents were sometimes violent."

Ashok nodded. "I was in Bihar when upper caste people surrounded Gandhiji's car and smashed the rear window. Later, in Poona, after I was done traveling with him, a bomb was thrown at his car and several people were injured. Gandhiji wasn't hurt, as they'd targeted the wrong car."

"I wonder if we could be successful helping Untouchables here," mused Mrs. Arora.

Her husband said, "In the villages, I make a point of trying to give them medical treatment, just like everyone else. But I suppose it's possible some of them are afraid to come to me, since the higher castes I treat might not want them so near."

"Well," said Jaya, "I'm in favor of trying to help, if the Praja Mandal can be convinced to do something."

"Unfortunately, hardly any Praja Mandal members even know any Harijans," said her mother. "So they're less likely to want to risk their lives for that particular cause."

It was now dark outside, and soon they all went up to the flat rooftop to watch the fireworks. Ashok was very aware of Jaya standing nearby, her face gently illuminated by the row of tiny oil lamps along the edge of the parapet and by the occasional starburst high in the sky.

He felt himself so drawn to her that he had to consciously keep an appropriate space separating them. Although her parents were liberal in their political outlook, he wasn't sure just how far such a view of life extended to more personal matters, such as the relationship between their unmarried daughter and young men.

5

Mangarh, November 1938

It took two more requests before the Maharaja granted an audience to the Praja Mandal leadership. Ashok, Sundip, and Kishore rode with Manohar in the Jain family's motor car to the Bhim Bhawan Palace. The grove of big mango trees, through which the driveway wound, reminded Ashok of his father's orchard. Several peacocks strutted across the area, pecking at the ground.

The trees ended, and a vast expanse of lawn appeared. Even though Ashok had seen the clock tower and glimpsed the domes from a distance, he was awed at the scale of the palace itself. Of a buff colored stone, it seemed to extend forever on either side of the pillared main entrance. The Maharaja's green flag hung from the pole atop the building, showing the ruler was personally present.

Sundip observed, "A lot of farmers worked very hard so His Highness could afford this place." It expressed Ashok's sentiments exactly.

At the informal audience, they all sat on uncomfortable velvet-upholstered straight back chairs in the council chamber, while the Maharaja leaned against bolsters on a small platform throne. Various aides sat to both sides of him. The stained glass windows spread multihued light over the room.

It was the only time Ashok had seen Lakshman Singh other than in the Dussehra procession. Today, the mustached Maharaja wore a tan colored silk *achkan*, white breeches, and a white turban with a single emerald and diamond ornament on it.

The ruler listened impassively, staring out into space, as Kishore read the petition. Then, Lakshman Singh looked at Kishore and said in a deep voice, "I already have a council. Why should I need this 'legislative assembly' you speak of?"

For once without a cigarette in his hand, Kishore said, "Highness, your council is composed only of a small number of high nobles in the state. And the members are all appointed by yourself—"

"—Based on long tradition," interrupted Lakshman Singh. "Between them, they represent all the major *thikanas* of my state."

"I understand that, of course, Your Highness. But we feel the people themselves should be able to vote on who represents them. That's the best way to ensure their interests are addressed."

Still gazing at Kishore, Lakshman Singh slowly shook his head. "I frankly don't understand your reasoning. Does a father let his children vote on how to run his family?"

Kishore said, "Of course not, Your Highness. But the people—they want—" He stopped, apparently unable to complete the train of thought.

An awkward silence resulted, and at last Ashok intervened: "But Highness, when the children grow up and become educated, it seems reasonable to give them some voice in running the family. That's the trend in modern times."

Lakshman Singh turned to stare at him. "You're not from my state. I don't understand why you've come here to criticize my government. Will you explain that to me?"

Ashok sensed that Lakshman Singh was angry, and that only traditional Rajput courtesy kept the Maharaja from a hostile outburst. Ashok put on his most pleasant smile and replied, "Highness, I'm here only because some of your people would like Mangarh to keep pace with what is occurring in other areas of India. We mean no criticism of you or your government. But letting the people have a say in their affairs is the goal almost everywhere now. That makes sense, as the people are becoming better educated, better able to take part in making the decisions that affect them."

Lakshman Singh was still staring at him. The Maharaja did not reply, but went on to the next request in the petition: "You also ask for public works projects for relief from the drought by employing rural workers. Do you really think I'm not aware of the need to help my people in such a time of trouble?"

Kishore, obviously taken aback, said, "We understand that, Your Highness. However, we uh...wanted to be sure...We have no desire to embarrass you or your government...."

Lakshman Singh scowled, and said, "If you have any criticisms to make, please make them. But I hope you're not implying that my government isn't doing its best for its people."

"We...we didn't intend to imply such a thing at all, Your Highness," said Kishore, clearly rattled.

"Good. I'll take your petition under advisement." Lakshman Singh motioned to an aide, signaling that the interview was over.

Afterwards, when they were back in the motor car, Ashok asked his companions, "Is he always that difficult?"

"I don't think so," said Manohar Jain. "I'm told he's usually charming. Most Rajput lords are, even with their enemies. But I think he really isn't able to grasp why we want changes. So he considers us to be dangerous, subversive elements."

Kishore, drawing on a cigarette with obvious relief, said, "I can predict his decision."

"He won't bother to make one," said Manohar. "Why should he? He can just forget about it."

"We mustn't let him," said Ashok. "We must keep reminding him. It's too important to his people."

"Of course, it's important," said Manohar, looking away out the window. "But when it's obvious we don't stand a chance of getting anywhere with him, shouldn't we put our efforts elsewhere?"

Ashok said, "Think of how many decades Gandhiji has been pressuring the British to free India. Yet, I've never seen him discouraged. He knows the cause is just, and that one day we will indeed succeed. We must take the same attitude with His Highness."

Manohar was silent for some time. Then, he brightened and turned to Ashok. "You're right. I'm glad you came here to inspire us. Otherwise, I might be giving up now."

The next morning, sub-inspector Jhakhar and another policeman came to Ashok's door. Jhakhar said, "Chand, you are under arrest. Put your hands behind your back."

"On what charge, inspector?" asked the startled Ashok.

"Membership in an illegal organization. Hands behind your back."

Ashok did as ordered. "What organization?"

"The Mangarh Praja Mandal."

He felt the other policeman roughly putting handcuffs on him. He raised his eyebrows. "Membership is illegal?"

"As of last evening. His Highness signed a new decree."

A hand tightly grabbed his upper arm, and they led Ashok out.

"I want to see a lawyer."

Jhakhar didn't bother to answer.

"I must insist on a lawyer," Ashok repeated.

The other policeman gave Ashok a shove, and he stumbled, barely managing to remain upright. "When you see the magistrate, you can ask him," Jhakhar said. They put Ashok in the rear of a black van. It was uncomfortable with his hands secured behind his back, and awkward to stay balanced as the van jarred over bumps and turned corners. This time, they did not take him to the police station; they took him to the Mangarh Central Jail.

With resignation, he followed the police through the iron-barred entrance in the blank brick wall. Behind him, the gate clanked shut. A jailer joined them, and they took Ashok into a low building, removed the handcuffs, thrust him into a cell. "When do I see the magistrate?"

"When you're called," said sub-inspector Jhakhar, not looking at him.

"There must be a time limit. How many days?"

The policemen and the jailer laughed. They swung the heavy metal door closed. The metallic clunk reverberated about the stone walls. The key turned in the lock.

Frustrated, Ashok looked around the cell. It was both small and dark, with a low ceiling. On the far wall, just above eye level, was a small barred window. Through it he could see sky. Half-dazed, he moved over to stand at it, and he looked up through the opening at the brightness.

He rubbed his fingers over the roughness of the stone and mortar wall. Then, he examined the remainder of the room. The only openings were the small window in the wall and a smaller one in the door. The floor was of the same uneven stone as the walls. A battered metal bucket lay in a corner, with a dented brass *lota*, or water pot, near it. There was neither cot nor bedding.

A movement in a corner startled him as a rat scurried into a narrow, dark gap where an irregularly shaped rock did not quite meet the uneven floor.

He heard voices down the hall; more men had entered the building. He peered out the tiny window in the door and saw Kishore being led down the corridor and put into a cell. The jailers locked the door and left.

A short time later, men came again and put Manohar Jain in another cell.

When Ashok heard and saw no sign that the jailers were near, he called to the others through the window in his door. Both came to peer through the openings in their own doors. "So this is His Highness' reply to our petition!" said Manohar.

"I never thought he'd do this," said Kishore, his voice flat.

"I think we have lots of work ahead of us," said Manohar.

"I think we may have a long *rest* ahead of us," said Ashok. He felt pleased with himself that he could actually joke about it, feeble though the jest might be. He called to Kishore, "How long before they have to take us before the magistrate?"

The lawyer said weakly, "Two days at the most. I doubt they'll follow the rule. I'm not sure it matters much. The magistrate does what he's told."

"Should we get an outside lawyer and fight the case?"

"I'm not sure there's any point," replied Kishore after several moments. "We'll be found guilty anyway."

"Well," said Ashok, "as a matter of principle we should not be too aggressive in defending ourselves. That backs up our contention that the law itself is illegal and the system unjust."

Later that day, after the timekeeper's gong announced two o'clock in the afternoon, the jailers took away Kishore. When Ashok called out to ask where they were taking the lawyer, the jailers told him to shut up.

In the evening, the jailers brought food on a metal plate: cold, half-baked *rotis* and thin, runny *dal*. And more water. They tossed a bedroll onto the floor, but they laughed at Ashok's request for a cot.

The bedroll stank of sweat and hair oil. Obviously, it had been much used since its last laundering. But as expected for this time of year, the night was growing chilly. And Ashok needed padding on the cold stone floor. So he used the bedroll. Unaccustomed to lying on a surface so hard, even with the bedding, he found it difficult to fall asleep. He was just drifting out of consciousness when he heard a scurrying, and tiny feet hit his face. He bolted upright.

The rats.

He squirmed further down into the bedding so his face was covered by the end. But he still found it difficult to sleep, wondering if the rats would try to get inside his covering.

Three days passed, and three nights shared with the rats. And with bedbugs. He itched all over from their bites. Always the food was the same. Each time it was brought, Ashok demanded to see a lawyer or a magistrate. The jailers ignored him.

He tried to keep his spirits up by imagining he was outside, in a garden. He thought of his family's mango orchards. He was out walking among the mango trees, looking up through the dark, glossy leaves at the bright fragments of the sky. He had always enjoyed meandering through the orchards, the foliage shading him from the sun, the soil crunching underfoot, the scent of grass and earth and trees.

Each morning, an Untouchable sweeper came, escorted by a jailer, to empty the latrine bucket. The jailers let Ashok into the courtyard an hour a day for exercise. All the other prisoners were in the courtyard at the same time. Kishore had apparently been released, but Ashok could talk with Manohar while they walked a circuit of the yard.

Early on the fourth day, jailers came and took Manohar away. Later they came for Ashok and escorted him to a room in another building, where a small, black robed, white haired man sat at a table.

Sub-inspector Jhakhar appeared and testified that he had seen Ashok in close association with other known Praja Mandal members.

Ashok requested to cross-examine Jhakhar, but the magistrate abruptly refused. When Ashok insisted, the magistrate conferred with a police official seated next to him, and then changed his mind. "You may examine the witness."

The thin faced policeman stared belligerently at Ashok.

"On what dates did you see me with these alleged Praja Mandal members?" asked Ashok.

"I don't recall," said Jhakhar.

"Was it within the past month."

"Yes."

"The past week?"

"Yes."

"But I have been in jail most of the past week!"

"Exactly. You were with other Praja Mandal members in jail. You've been seen and heard talking with them."

"Does that mean if I spoke to a murderer in jail I'd be guilty of murder?"

Jhakhar glared at him.

Ashok asked, "How do you know they are Praja Mandal members?"

"We have our sources."

"May I have the names of these sources?"

"Of course not," Jhakhar said in a tone indicating he considered Ashok an idiot. "They'd be of no more use to us."

Hoping to discover who the police informers were, Ashok turned to the magistrate. "Your Honor, I insist that the police produce these so-called sources in court. I have the right to cross-examine them."

The magistrate's eyes flicked away, and Ashok had the impression the little man was actually frightened as he conferred with a police official. Then the magistrate said, "I must deny the request. The police sources are confidential."

Ashok asked to see a copy of the law making membership in the Mangarh Praja Mandal illegal. "One will be made available when it is located," said the magistrate.

It was never produced.

The trial dragged on over parts of four days. As a lawyer himself, Ashok found the proceedings unbelievably ill organized. The magistrate appeared to know little about the law or about what was expected of him. He would look with a puzzled expression at the papers the police handed him, but he did not seem to read the documents. He frequently recessed the hearing, as if needing to consult with higher authority for instructions.

Ashok saw no point in hiring a lawyer to defend himself, both because of his own legal training and because of the farcical nature of the proceedings. He had never before seen the witness who swore to seeing Ashok at meetings of the Praja Mandal.

Ashok argued that he had never formally joined the Mangarh Praja Mandal, and that in fact he was not even eligible for membership, as he was not a citizen of Mangarh.

At the end, the magistrate found Ashok guilty and sentenced him to one year in prison.

Except for the daily hour in the exercise yard, Ashok never saw anyone other than the jailers, the sweeper, and the rats. During the exercise times he got to know a few of the other prisoners. One was a handsome young Muslim man jailed for stealing some tins of milk. "My little son was going hungry," he told Ashok. "Was I to let him starve to death? But now"—he looked around at the tall walls—"I haven't seen him for three years, or my wife. Maybe they've starved to death anyway."

"How long do you have to serve?" asked Ashok.

The young man shrugged. "I've no idea."

"Didn't the judge tell you after your trial?"

With a grin of irony, the man again shrugged. "I haven't seen a judge yet. I think the police have forgotten I'm here."

"Have you complained?"

"I complained every day for months. It didn't do any good. The jailers wanted bribes, and I don't have anything to give them. So now I don't complain any more. When God wills, I'll get out."

Ashok sadly shook his head. "When the people can vote for their leaders, this shouldn't happen any more."

The inmate gave him a look of incomprehension.

Over the coming weeks, he got to know the young father, Ajeej Husain, quite well.

On the twenty-third day, a jailer escorted Ashok to a room with two wooden benches. Waiting were Dr. and Mrs. Arora, and their daughter. Jaya looked lovely in a bright blue, *khadi* sari. Ashok was conscious of his own filthy clothes, and of the fact it had been four days since he had been allowed to bathe.

"How have they been treating you?" asked Dr. Arora, his eyebrows raised in concern.

Ashok shrugged. "Not bad, sir." He managed a stiff smile. "Not especially good, either."

"Your health is holding up all right?"

"I think so." He again made himself smile. "The rats haven't bitten me yet."

Jaya and her mother exchanged looks of outrage. Then Jaya said, "I've decided when I finally go back to college, I'll study to be a lawyer. Then I can find more ways to change how we administer so-called 'justice.'"

"There are other ways besides practicing law," said Ashok. "I've never really used my own law degree. Except for defending myself here, which wasn't very effective."

"Still, I've decided that's what I want," Jaya said firmly. "I'm in no hurry. There's a lot of work to do here first. But some day...." Her eyes abruptly showed worry as she changed the subject. "We tried and tried to get in to see you. Finally we were able to bribe enough officials and the jailers. Here—we brought you a box of sweets, and some fruit."

Ashok gratefully took a banana from her. He was very aware of her closeness when she handed it to him, of the slenderness of her hand, how well manicured her fingernails were. He felt an odd sensation, a tingling warmth, as if some sort of electrical field radiated from her to him. He concentrated on peeling the banana in the hope her parents wouldn't notice how disconcerted she made him feel. "How are the others in the leadership?" he asked, trying to keep his voice neutral.

Jaya's mother said, "Kishore and Manohar were released a week ago. They seem to have survived with no real problems."

Jaya said, her eyes flashing, annoyance in her voice, "I was insulted that they didn't arrest me, like the others."

"Probably because we're women!" said her mother. "What nonsense."

"Now, now," said Dr. Arora with a frown. "I wish you two wouldn't go looking so hard for trouble. You make life difficult enough for me as it is."

"Poor Papa," Jaya said comfortingly, though it was clear she intended no apology. She said to Ashok, "We went to see the inspector general of police and demanded he arrest us, too. He said it wasn't in his orders, so he couldn't do it."

Her mother said, "He's a frightening man, with that stare of his." She pushed up on her eyeglasses to adjust them. "Actually, it did seem to us that we could help more by being on the outside."

Jaya asked, "Have you gotten the food we've sent?"

Ashok was finishing the banana; it was just the right degree of ripeness. He felt warmed by the thought that she had been so concerned about him. He thought of the unpalatable mess that had been his regular meals. He sighed. "No, I'm sure someone else has been enjoying anything you sent."

"I could strangle them!" said Jaya.

"We've all been trying to get you free," said Mrs. Arora. "The Mahatma and Pandit Nehru have even sent telegrams to His Highness. But so far we have gotten nowhere."

Ashok smiled in gratitude. Then he said, "I have a favor to ask. There's a young father who has been here three years without a trial. If you could make sure the magistrate is reminded of the case it might help."

"Three years!" said Jaya. "Whatever for?"

"Taking tins of milk for his starving child."

Mrs. Aurora shook her head. "What a place! We'll see to it, of course."

Ashok said, "I also know he'd feel better if he knew how his family is doing. His name's Ajeej Husain, and he's from Ludva village."

"I'll make sure to stop by there and make some inquiries," said Dr. Arora. "I know there aren't many Muslims in that village, so it should be easy to locate his people."

Jaya and her mother and father continued to be his only visitors. By bribing the jailers, they were allowed to see him every week, although the other Praja Mandal members were forbidden access.

They told him Ajeej Husain's wife was surviving, but barely. His son had died from malnutrition, only weeks ago. The magistrate had agreed to review the prisoner's case.

Ashok gently told Ajeej Husain the news of his family. Tears came to the young man eyes, and then he went off by himself to sob.

Ashok looked forward all week to seeing the Aroras. Normally, he would rarely have the opportunity to be in the company of a pretty and vivacious young woman. That was the only good side of being confined in jail. The family repeatedly assured Ashok they were keeping pressure on the government to release him, and that they were urging the Congress leadership and the press to keep publicizing his plight.

He tried to make good use of his daily exercise hour in the courtyard, walking briskly and running and doing a few calisthenics and yoga exercises, and talking to Ajeej Husain and some of the other prisoners.

Aside from that, he was always locked in the cell. Between the Aroras' weekly visits, the days, the hours, and often even the minutes dragged. The idea of spending an entire year in the tiny stone room was so appalling that Ashok could not bear to think about it.

He sat in meditation morning and evening, gradually increasing the length of each time. He also frequently thought about Gandhiji, about the Mahatma's teachings, and how they might be applied to Mangarh.

Or, he reviewed his own life, everything from his earliest memories onward. How idyllic it now seemed, living in Kapani village. Even sitting in school, when he would rather have been running in the wheat fields, wandering in the mango orchards, or playing field hockey with Joginder Singh and the other boys. He thought about the many nights spent on the roof of his family's house, looking at stars and memorizing constellations, and seeing how planets changed position from week to week. In the daytime, he had sometimes enjoyed watching the changing cloud formations. He now wished he could see more than a tiny patch of sky through his jail window.

Almost three months after Ashok had first been confined, two policemen came and retrieved him from his cell. They gave no explanation, but they set him free.

Outside the jail, he found no one had been notified of his release. Fortunately, a jailer did return the small amount of money and the room key that had been on his person when he was arrested. He hired a tonga back to the room, still vacant but now quite dusty, and he thoroughly bathed and shaved himself.

He knew Sundip was no doubt off at his village school. Ashok's bicycle was still in the courtyard, and he rode it to the Arora home, where he was warmly welcomed.

"I'm delighted to be out," he said. "But can anyone tell me why they let me go?"

"We've been trying hard to get you freed, of course," said Mrs. Arora. "But I think it was the outside pressure from Pandit Nehru and Gandhiji that did it. They managed to get a reporter from a London newspaper to make inquiries."

"I see."

Jaya asked, "And is Ajeej Husain still locked up?"

"I'm afraid so."

She pressed her lips together and shook her head in disapproval. "So-called justice moves slowly here."

"I think I'll visit the inspector general about the matter."

"Afterwards," said Mrs. Arora, "I hope you're ready to take up your work again?"

Ashok took a deep breath. "Yes. But I need to go home to visit my family first."

Jaya smiled. "Just so you come back to us."

He felt his face grow warm. He grinned and said, "I'll be back."

He went to Karam Singh's office. He wasn't sure the inspector general would see him, but he was shown in promptly.

Singh waved him to a chair and stared blandly at him, waiting.

"I believe you must know, sir, that I've recently spent some time in your jail."

Singh nodded. "You have some complaint?"

"It wasn't the highlight of my life, sir. But my concern today isn't about myself." Ashok informed Singh of the problem of Ajeej Husain, who was still being held after three years with no trial, and whose little son had died.

Karam Singh's face was impassive as he gave a curt nod. "I try to avoid such things. But they happen. I'll see to it."

Feeling he'd done the best he could at the moment for the young prisoner, Ashok left for the Punjab.

6

Kapani Village, West Punjab, February 1939

The older Punjab villages often rose on mounds created by the accumulated rubble of earlier towns. But the canal colony villages, such as Kapani, had been built in totally new locations, flat as the surrounding fields. And since Kapani had been planned by the government at the time of settlement of the newly irrigated area, unlike the haphazard maze of the typical Indian village, the streets of this one formed a rectangular grid with the two main avenues intersecting at right angles in the center.

After Ashok's absence of almost two years, the village looked the same, the dome and the four slender towers of the Sikh *gurdwara* visible above the mango trees for miles across the fields. The irrigation canal, and hard work, had made Kapani prosperous like so many of the canal settlements. At 182 acres, the holdings of Ashok's family made up one of the larger farms of Kapani. The family was also among the few Hindus in a village whose population of three thousand was mostly Sikhs, with a hundred or so Muslims mixed in.

Mangos were Yogesh Chand's passion, and he had planted almost half his land in various varieties. Being of the Arora caste, traditionally merchants and moneylenders, the Chands did not till the soil with their own hands, but they meticulously supervised the work of their hired laborers. Besides the farming income, Ashok's father had added the interest from a number of loans to Muslim farmers in neighboring villages.

As Ashok had anticipated, his short, energetic mother examined him with a critical eye and commented about his loss in weight from the time in jail. Then she said with a slight smile to show she was only half serious, "You used to look so handsome in your English suit when you were studying law. I don't think I like this *khadi* nearly so well."

"You should be wearing it yourself, Mother," said Ashok with a grin. "Show everyone you want the British to leave."

Radha Chand was dressed as usual in the typical Punjabi woman's *shalwar kameez*, the tunic-like long shirt and scarf over baggy trousers. She appeared taken aback. Then, she said, "Well, maybe I will!"

"Oh, no," groaned his father, rolling his eyes upward. "Not you, too. We were embarrassed enough when our son failed to open his law practice after we'd bragged about it to everyone. And now he's even been in jail!"

Ashok smiled broadly at his father's jesting.

"Tell us what it was like in jail," pleaded Ashok's slender, pretty sister Savitri, age fifteen.

She was toying with the end of her *dupatta*, the long filmy scarf worn with her *shalwar kameez*. She was bright and capable, and Ashok was sure she would someday be an excellent medical doctor. He had been pleased that both his father and his uneducated mother should have such progressive ideas as to encourage their daughter to become a professional. No doubt it would break the heart of every young man in the village to send away its loveliest maiden. He shrugged. "I didn't enjoy it. But I managed. The hardest thing was having no one to talk to most of the time. The time dragged."

"You weren't mistreated? They didn't beat you?" asked his mother.

"No, the handling was a little rough when I was arrested. That's all."

His younger brother Prabhu, age twenty, said bitterly, "I bet if it had been the British, they'd have beaten you plenty. They're glad to have the chance to teach us natives a lesson."

"Now, son," said their father, "I don't think that's always true."

"It's true enough," said Prabhu.

Yogesh Chand looked annoyed at being contradicted, but he said nothing. He counted on Prabhu, who had remained at home rather than go to college, to eventually take over management of the farm and orchards.

Ashok's mother said, "We'd have come to visit you if we'd known. Why didn't you tell us?"

"I didn't want to worry any of you. The jail only allows visitors once a week, anyway, and it's a long way to travel, Mother."

"Did anyone else visit you?"

Ashok smiled at the thought of the Aroras, particularly of Jaya. "A doctor and his family who are in the Praja Mandal. They came as often as they could." He grinned more broadly at his mother. "You'll be glad to know they took quite good care of me."

Yogesh said, "Son, you wrote us when you first went to Mangarh that you expected to be there only a few months. Now you say you'll return to stay longer. Why so?"

The tall, broad, solemn-faced figure of Mubarak Khan appeared in the doorway. "I'd like to know that also." Mubarak Khan had grown up with Ashok's father and been like a member of the family. One of the few Muslims in this particular village, he was also prosperous, and he had built his house next door to be close to the Chands. He asked, "Am I interrupting anything? I just wanted a chance to visit with my boy."

"*Assalaam aleicum.* Come right in," said Yogesh Chand. "This is your home, too."

Ashok rose quickly and started to touch the feet of the neighbor he considered almost a second father, but Mubarak Khan held a hand up and said, "No, no, you're too big a man for that now." They instead embraced, hard and long.

Mubarak Khan seated himself. His forehead furrowed as usual, as if he were perpetually worrying about the world's troubles, he asked, "Why are you working all this time in Mangarh? And getting jailed there, no less! I thought the Congress wanted to get rid of the British, not the princes."

Ashok resumed his own seat and replied, "Certainly the British are our first priority, Uncle. But most of the princes are slow to bring progress to their people. If we can't convince them to reform, they may well have to go the same way as the British."

"You're talking as if you expect the British to leave any day," said Mubarak Khan.

"It's inevitable," said Ashok. "I can't predict just when it will happen, of course, Uncle. But I know it will."

Ashok's mother said, "I wish *I* could work for the Congress. If they ever decide to demonstrate in Kapani or Lyallpur, I'll join the marchers myself."

"You wouldn't!" said her husband.

Her face smug, she replied, "Oh, yes. I would. Women have joined the marches in other places."

"We have women working in Mangarh, even," said Ashok. "Including the family who visited me so much in jail. The mother and her daughter are both quite active." He realized he was again smiling broadly at mentioning Jaya, and he quickly sobered his face.

Mubarak Khan said in one of his rare efforts at making a joke, "Just don't let my wife hear you talk like that, please."

Yogesh Chand said to his wife, "You could be jailed for that, you know."

"I'd be in good company—Nehru, Gandhiji....And now my own boy."

Yogesh Chand slowly shook his head and said to Mubarak Khan, "My son was supposed to be a lawyer. Now he's gone to prison instead." But Ashok was pleased to hear pride in his father's voice, in spite of the mock horror. Yogesh added, "You still haven't told us why you want to return, when they seem so intent on throwing you in jail."

Ashok frowned as he formulated his thoughts. "My work isn't done, Father. I haven't accomplished a thing, other than giving encouragement and recruiting some members. And so far, I don't see any one else able to provide effective leadership for the Mangarh Praja Mandal."

"What do you hope to accomplish this time when you go back?" asked Mubarak Khan.

Ashok turned to him. "The Maharaja still hasn't acted on our petition for a legislative assembly. And the harvest has been bad. My friend Sundip Saxena says the Jats in the villages need a push to help them organize to get their taxes lowered. If I have time, I'd still like to see if I can help improve the condition of the Untouchables."

Mubarak Khan rose. "Well! It sounds as if you have enough to keep you busy for a long time. I think I'll go check on my fields now." With his customary serious expression he looked at Ashok. "You've been a son to me, too, you know, especially since I have none of my own. Come see us later."

"I will, of course, Uncle."

Later, Ashok talked alone with his brother and sister. Savitri served the three of them tea, and he was pleased to see how competent, how adult-like, his sister was at the ritual.

Prabhu, who like Savitri had remained mostly silent during the time with the adults, now asked, "Why do you want to work against the Mangarh Maharaja? He isn't even Muslim, he's Hindu."

"I don't care what faith the rulers are. If they oppress their people, they need to change."

Prabhu shook his head. "It's the British who are our enemies first. Then the Muslims. I'm all for throwing those British bastards out. But it will take more than Gandhi's prayers and boycotts to do it."

"How do you mean?" asked Ashok.

Prabhu said, "It's guns and bombs that will drive them out, not spinning wheels or burning foreign clothes."

For a moment, Ashok did not know how to respond. He sipped at his tea. Prabhu had always had a wild and impatient streak, but apparently his thinking had turned more extreme than Ashok realized. Trying to establish at least a minimal rapport with his brother, Ashok asked, "I know you're involved with the RSS. What exactly drew you to it?" The Rashtriya Swayamsevak Sangh was a fundamentalist Hindu revival organization.

Prabhu replied, his eyes cool, "I never liked much about the orchards or farming, even though father wants me to work with him here the rest of my life. Last year some friends invited me to an RSS meeting. What we do there is far more interesting than talking about irrigation ditches or some new type of mango."

"What are your meetings like?"

Prabhu straightened and his eyes brightened. He smiled slightly and replied, "We do physical training to make us strong and disciplined. Then we sing songs and read from the *Mahabharat* or the *Ramayan*. Or we hear lectures about Hindu heroes, like Prithviraj Chauhan, Maharana Pratap, Shivaji, the Rani of Jhansi. Even Guru Gobind Singh, though he was Sikh."

"Those are good heroes to follow," said Ashok with a nod.

Prabhu set down his tea cup. "You think so? They were all warriors! They weren't afraid to take up arms to fight to the death for their beliefs. How does your 'Mahatma' feel about that?"

Ashok slowly drained his own cup, giving himself a chance to consider. "I wasn't thinking of their fighting, so much as that they spoke out for what they thought was right. They were willing to sacrifice everything for their ideals. Gandhiji would very much agree with that."

Prabhu snorted. "Without their weapons to back them up, they'd all have been killed immediately. We'd never even hear of them today."

Savitri broke in, extending the tea pot toward Ashok. "Have some more *chai.*" In spite of her lovely smile, her large dark eyes looked upset. She was one of the kindest persons Ashok knew, and the disagreement between her brothers obviously bothered her. "Might you get sent to jail again?" she asked, changing the subject, but clearly concerned about the possibility.

"It could happen," Ashok acknowledged. "I'd rather avoid it. But if I worried about it all the time, the fear would keep me from doing what I need to do."

She nodded quietly, seeming to understand. "Anyway, please be careful!"

He grinned. "I'll try."

Prabhu gave one of his rare smiles, though a thin one. "I have to admit, brother, you do have some courage, even if I don't agree with how you use it."

One of the boys on Ashok's team sent the ball his way. Ashok swung with his stick, missed, and chased after. His Sikh childhood friend Joginder Singh, on the opposing team, challenged him for it. The two collided and fell just as Joginder struck the ball, sending it flying across the goal line.

They sat in the dust laughing. "It's been a while since I played this," Joginder said.

"Me, too," said Ashok. He handed his stick to one of the village youths. "Time for a break. Maybe I'm getting too old for something this vigorous."

Ashok and Joginder had played with each other constantly when they were small children, including this village version of field hockey. They had attended school together until Ashok went off to college in Lahore. Joginder remained in the village, farming with his father and brothers. He married a girl from a nearby village and already had a one year old daughter.

They walked off toward the fields, talking of acquaintances, of the price of crops, of the weather.

"How do you like being married?" Ashok asked casually.

Joginder shrugged and smiled. "She's a good wife. We're well suited. I have fun playing with my little girl. Hopefully, I'll have a son one day, too." He glanced at Ashok. "You're the same age as I am. When are you going to get married and come back here to live?"

Ashok gave a slight smile as he thought of Jaya. "Maybe some day." He hesitated, then added, "There's a girl in Mangarh." He grinned. "I don't know if she or her family would have me. And I'm not the only one who might be interested in her. But I do think about her."

"Same caste?"

"They're Aroras, too. But even though her family's involved in the Praja Mandal, they're much more settled than I am. After all, I don't even have what most people would consider a job. But I know they like me. They were my only regular visitors in jail."

Joginder shook his head. "I can't imagine being locked up all the time. How could you stand it?"

Ashok shrugged and grinned modestly. "I exercised as much as I could. Did yoga and meditation. I imagined myself outdoors, back here. I tried to keep my mind occupied. I thought about Gandhiji and Panditji and all the others who've spent so many years in prison. They survived it, so I knew I could, too."

"You still must have hated it."

"Yes, but I had no choice, so I did everything I could to make it tolerable."

Joginder shook his head, as if unable to understand. "I assume you could be put in jail again when you go back?"

"It's possible." He took a deep breath. "Maybe even likely."

"But you're still going there again next week."

"Yes."

Joginder raised his eyebrows. "Why? What's so important to risk that?"

"Gandhiji wants some examples of how reforms might work in princely states. But there's more than that. He helped me see how terrible conditions are for the Untouchables. They're the most oppressed of anyone in India. And the drought in Rajputana is much worse than here. The poor people in the villages are already close to starving. It will turn into a real famine, and the Maharaja's government gives no indication it's going to do much to help."

Joginder was examining him with a frown, clearly trying to understand. "It's important work. But Gandhi must be quite an inspiration, to convince you to give up so much."

"He is. He's so selfless himself, so loving and giving toward everyone, it seems like the least I can do is try to help him. But I don't really feel I'm giving up so much. I like the work, even when it's slow to succeed."

Joginder grinned. "Does that girl have anything to do with going back to Mangarh?"

Ashok smiled back. "A little."

7

Mangarh, February 1939

A few days after his return to Mangarh, Ashok bicycled to Gamri village to talk with Ram, after being assured by Sundip that the young Untouchable would be available. At the approach to the Untouchable community on the outskirts, a dead rat lay among deposits of human excrement. Thin children, playing in the dusty lane, stopped to stare. A naked little boy, maybe three years old, appeared to have a severe eye infection, with flies crawling over the oozing area. Ashok made a mental note to suggest to Dr. Arora that this might be a likely place to hold one of the free weekly medical clinics.

Several men sat in the shade of a hut, warily watching his approach. These early encounters with villagers were often awkward. As Ashok neared, everyone rose and moved well away from him. "No, no—you must all stay seated," he said. He parked his bicycle, stood a moment, then lowered himself to the ground.

The Untouchables remained standing, at a distance. "But *sahib*, we can't sit in your presence. It wouldn't be fitting," said a old man, bent over with age.

"Then I'll stand, too," said Ashok, slowly rising to his feet. "But I'd prefer we all sit."

The others, clearly uncomfortable, remained standing. Their eyes lowered slightly when he tried to meet their gaze. Ashok said, "Ram is expecting me."

"I'll get him, *sahib*," said one of the men, possibly in his early thirties, who seemed eager to get away. He hurried off.

Ashok and the others stood in an awkward silence. Deliberately, he said, "I'm quite thirsty from my bicycle ride. May I have a drink of water?" As he had expected, there were looks of astonishment.

"*Sahib!*" said one of the men. "You can't take water from our hands. We're Bhangis, and Chamars."

Ashok shrugged. "Gandhiji takes water from everyone. He even cleans his own latrine. How could I do any differently?"

Eyes widened at the mention of latrine cleaning, the job of a Bhangi, the lowest group even among the various Untouchable classes.

Ram approached at a casual and deliberate pace. The good looking, pock-marked young man folded his palms in greeting. "Masterji said you would be coming again," he said, referring to Sundip.

Ashok gave a nod as he returned the greeting. "Masterji has spoken highly of you."

One of the men spoke rapidly to Ram, mentioning the request for a drink. "I'll get water for you, sir," said Ram.

The others murmured uneasily. Ram left at his deliberate pace and every-one waited in quiet until the young man returned. Solemnly, he approached Ashok. He hesitated only a second before dramatically handing Ashok the brass cup.

Ashok took the container and casually raised it. As was customary, he did not touch it to his lips, but he poured the entire contents into his mouth, gulp-ing thirstily. He smiled, and returned the cup to the young man. He looked around at the group. "Now," he said, "won't you join me in sitting?"

He lowered himself again to the ground. Ram sat, too. Slowly, another man did also. Then another. A couple of old men on the outer fringe of the group remained standing. Ram said quietly, "They're afraid of high caste men seeing them sitting with you and punishing them later."

Ashok swallowed. "Would it be better if I leave?"

"No, go ahead and talk with them if you like. But we should probably go to my own home soon."

Ashok looked around at the group. Normally, the first thing one asked about in a village was the crops. But these men weren't landowners or farm-ers themselves; at best, they would be laborers who were hired to work in the fields as needed. And everyone knew the crops were poor this year. He de-cided to try a different approach. "I come," he said, "from Gandhiji." He hoped the magic of the name would help break down their reserve. "The Ma-hatma sent me to you because he is concerned about all his people. He is especially concerned about people like yourselves, whom he calls Harijans, the Children of God—members of castes many others consider inferior. Gan-dhiji feels it is essential to the new India we want to build that all of Mother India's people are treated the same."

He looked around at them and said pointedly, "No one should have to remain standing in the presence of another man, merely because that person is of another caste. *Any* other caste. And no one of any caste should hesitate to take water from the hand of any man here."

He could see they were unconvinced, their eyes shifting away or looking at the ground. Such talk probably seemed so far removed from the realities of daily life in the village as to be incomprehensible.

Most of the Harijans appeared fearful to look at him, much less speak. Ram said, "Sir, no one has ever wanted to help us before, except Masterji. These men don't understand why you should be different. Everyone is afraid you've been sent by the police to make trouble, even though I've told them Masterji recommended you to us."

Ashok slowly nodded. He'd known it would likely take time to overcome suspicions. "We should go to my own home," Ram asked. "When no harm comes from your visit this time, they'll accept you better if you ever come again."

Ashok rose and followed him. They sat in the shade of the hut outside the door, and Ashok took a sip of the milk, warm and thick with cream, that Ram offered him in a gesture typical of the hospitality even the poorest villagers showed their guests. He felt sure Ram's family could not afford their own cow, and the milk was probably a luxury they had bought just for him.

"I spent time with Gandhiji when he was touring from village to village trying to help the Harijans, as he calls them," said Ashok. "But I'd like to know more about your specific problems here, in this village."

Ram's eyes met his. "That may take a while."

"I have the time, if you do. What work do the Bhangis do, besides sweeping and carrying away night soil?"

Ram's eyes turned cool. "We're at the bottom, even among the Untouchables." Ram's young wife returned, her shawl hiding most of her attractive face. She glanced quickly at them, then entered the hut. Ram gestured toward her. "In the villages, the women sweep the courtyards of the higher castes and carry out the dung. They also clean latrines, in the houses of the Rajputs and those Banias or merchants whose women keep *purdah*. And they work as midwives."

Ashok took another drink of milk. "What of the men?"

"In the town, some of us clean latrines in the jails and army barracks or work as low paid laborers. In the villages, some, like myself, work for farmers or whoever can pay us. Others are scavengers, cleaning the roads and picking up any carcasses of dead animals."

"What do you see as the main problems, the most important ways the Harijans are at a disadvantage compared to the other castes?"

Ram snorted as if at a good joke. "We're at a disadvantage in every way. The worst jobs, the worst houses, the least food, no education, being treated as less than a dog by the other castes. Do you know, we have to call out a warning when we go into the high caste areas so none of them will accidentally be polluted by coming near us?"

Ashok nodded sympathetically. "You've been to school yourself. Would more education help the other Harijans?"

Ram looked away for a moment, then back to Ashok. "It may be the best answer in the long term. But I don't have the connections needed for a better job, so the schooling hasn't helped me in that way yet."

As they talked, other shabbily dressed village men occasionally passed, eyeing Ashok curiously, but none stopped. A growing number of children were appearing and standing to watch, but none came close, as they would have if he'd been at a higher caste household. Ashok finished the milk and set the brass cup beside him. "Still, you've set an example for the others, I would think."

Ram again snorted. "Maybe. I had to put up with a lot, though. I had my share of beatings by upper caste boys. As you saw some months ago, it still goes on. It would have been worse at school if Masterji hadn't stood up for me." He looked at Ashok, and a slight smile came to his lips. "I got even, although my tormentors don't know it."

Ashok raised his eyebrows. "You got even?"

Ram glanced about to make sure none of the children were close enough to overhear. His wife, her shawl half hiding her face, moved closer to the door to be able to hear more clearly. He said in little more than a whisper, "No one else knows. I wouldn't be telling you, except you're not from this village and Masterji vouched for you. If word got around, I'd probably be beaten to death. But every chance I get, I even the score with upper caste people who've given me a hard time."

"How?" asked Ashok, curious.

Ram grinned. "When I was in school, if a boy beat up on me, I might make sure he accidentally lost his writing slate. They're expensive, and his parents would have been angry at him. Or I ensured that a dead animal fell into his family's well at night. Or that their cow ran away, and the boy got blamed for leaving the gate open. There are lots of ways to make things happen so no one suspects me."

"I see," said Ashok, grinning even though he didn't really approve of revenge. He noticed that Ram's wife had been listening wide-eyed, apparently fascinated and horrified at the same time. "Don't worry, your secret's safe. But if you could pick some issues to try to change first to help your people, what would they be?"

The children had been edging closer, trying to hear what Ram had just said. He now thought for a moment, furrowing his pockmarked brow, and then he said, his voice now louder, "Our own well would be a huge help. Getting water is difficult. The women have to walk all the way across the village. When they get there, the women of the other castes don't let them get close. They have to beg the other women to fill their jugs for them."

Ashok sighed and nodded. "What else?"

Ram thought some more. He looked at Ashok. "You may know that I got thrashed for going into a shrine a while back. We can't go into any major temples. The priests refuse to do rites for us. We can't even get near the temples without a Rajput threatening to beat us up for polluting the area. So we have to be content with our own shrines, like *Pir* Mahmud's."

"With the rains failing, I imagine getting enough to eat will be a problem."

Ram looked away. "It's always a problem. We usually get food as pay for our work. But if the other castes are starving, they don't have anything to give us." He looked back to Ashok. "You may have heard our saying in this region: 'Happiness is to eat two meals a day.'"

Ashok thought for a while. At last he said, "We might be able to work with you on a change or two. But it would likely be dangerous. It would require courage from all Harijans."

Ram stared at him, obviously skeptical. "What are you suggesting?"

"You must pick a particular concern, then all stand together to demand your rights. Be prepared to refuse to work if your demands aren't granted."

Ram shook his head doubtfully. "That might work for some things. Maybe it could get us better access to wells if we refused to pick up dead animals. The other castes wouldn't want to pollute themselves by handing the carcasses. But the priests at the temple of Mahadeo won't care if we refuse to work. We can't go near the temple anyway."

Ashok nodded and said, "There may be other ways. The Praja Mandal is having a meeting later today. Will you come with me?"

Ram stared at him. "Go with you to a meeting in the city?"

"Yes. I think it would be helpful for the other Praja Mandal members to meet you in person."

Ram looked away. "You're sure they wouldn't mind a Bhangi being there?"

"They wouldn't mind." Ashok hesitated before amending his statement. "Well, one or two might, but they won't say or do anything about it. I'm sure it will be a good thing on the whole."

Ram thought some more. Then, he gave shrug. "I'll come, if you want me to."

Ashok pushed his bicycle as he and Ram walked toward Mangarh city. Not far from Gamri village, they passed the Moslem tomb, a square structure

Tomb of Pir Mahmud

surmounted by a dome, under a gigantic mango tree. Several people sat before the tomb, and an old woman had prostrated herself on the ground. A white-bearded man wearing a skullcap, who appeared to be the attendant, was receiving offerings from a young man and woman. "Even Bhangis can worship here," said Ram.

"A Muslim burial place," said Ashok.

"Yes, the tomb of *Pir* Mahmud. But Hindus come here, too. And Bhils and Sikhs. It's said that the *pir*, the saint, performed many miracles. He even chose this spot for his death. Many centuries ago he and his son were traveling on a long journey from Delhi. He was an old man, and the travel was tiring. When he reached this spot, he decided it was where God had intended for him to die. So he lay down and his soul left his body, and his son built this tomb for his final resting place."

Ashok nodded. "What miracles is the *pir* said to have performed?"

Ram smiled slightly, as if he disbelieved in the miraculous himself. "He's said to have cured many illnesses. And given children to barren women. So the sick come here to pray to the saint to get well, and women come here to pray for a son."

Another five minutes brought them to the riverside Shiva temple of Mahadeo, its gold-topped tower rising above the large walled compound with several whitewashed outbuildings and a bathing tank. People were coming and going from the big open gateway.

"Have you visited this temple yet?" Ram asked, a hard edge to his voice.

"No," replied Ashok. "Gandhiji says that no one should visit a temple which bars Harijans, so I don't plan to."

Ram said, "I can't get closer than we are now. And you may know I have to call out that I'm a Bhangi, so no one will accidentally get polluted by me before they visit the God."

The members of the Praja Mandal Working Committee made a great show of welcoming Ram. Ashok was pleased that Jaya's warm smile at seeing the visitor was obviously sincere. But he also had the clear impression that the men, in particular, were nervous at the thought of risking an actual undertaking. Manohar Jain talked even more volubly than usual without committing himself to a stand. Sundip, who of course knew Ram from the school, was enthusiastic in supporting rights for Harijans, but vague on specifics.

Kishore Lodha wore a scowl and said nothing, seeming to concentrate solely on his ever-present cigarette as the others discussed ways they might help the Untouchables.

The threat of an impending famine created even more uncertainty than usual as to what might be the result of a campaign to let Untouchables use more of the village wells. If the Harijans were worried about starvation and had no way to build up a reserve of food, it seemed impractical to withhold the work for the upper castes for which payment would be made in grain. So the talk concentrated more on the possibility of forcing entry to the temples.

Jaya said firmly, her eyes flashing, "I think we should visit the priests at the temple of Mahadeo. Tell them to open their doors, or else they'll see the first major demonstration of Gandhiji's *satyagraha* in Mangarh state."

Ashok smiled, delighted at seeing her take such an assertive role.

Her mother said, "I agree with my daughter. We're long overdue on such a reform."

Manohar said, "Definitely! The sooner we act the better. However, I think we need more discussion on strategies first."

Sundip said, glancing at Ram, "I agree we should think things out carefully, but we should forge ahead." He turned to Ashok. "How would you proceed?"

"Gandhiji always says you should first talk to the people whose policies you are trying to change, and try to convince them of the errors in their thinking. Only after that has clearly failed should you try more coercive methods of peaceful action."

Heads turned toward Kishore, who had been frowning. He drew deeply on his cigarette, and slowly exhaled. "I urge caution," he said. "Other issues may be more productive."

"You don't think we should support temple rights?" asked Jaya, dismay obvious in her voice.

He glanced quickly at her, then away. "I didn't say that. But is it really our top priority?"

"It should certainly be one of the top ones," said Sundip.

"Absolutely," said Mrs. Arora.

"Then it appears we're decided to pursue the matter further, including ways to enter into discussions with the temple hierarchy," said Manohar Jain, looking about with a happy smile.

Kishore said, looking down, "We should bring today's meeting to an end. I have another obligation. Next time we can discuss the alternatives in more detail."

Which meant no action any time soon, thought Ashok.

He walked with Ram back toward Gamri village, intending to go only part way, as night was falling, and he did not want to risk not being able to get back into the city after the gates were closed. It was "cow dust time," when farm boys were herding their cattle and goats back home from the day's grazing, so there was a frequent tinkling of bells in the background.

It seemed to Ashok that Ram strode more vigorously now, after the meeting. "I never expected upper castes would be willing to help like that," the young Harijan said. "I think I might be able to convince some other Bhangis, maybe Chamars too, to stand together to demand our rights. But it will take time. And unfortunately, with a famine likely, before long no one will have energy to do much."

"We should probably contact the temple administrators as soon as we can," said Ashok. He realized, of course, that as yet the Praja Mandal leaders had committed themselves to nothing specific. It was entirely possible they might discuss the matter indefinitely. But he did not try to deflate Ram's newly found feeling of having found friends and supporters for the Harijans.

They reached the compound of the temple of Mahadeo, where pilgrims were entering for the evening *darshan*, the ceremony of viewing the God.

Ram slowed, eyeing the numerous people walking toward the entrance. "Why should I be any different from them?" he asked, anger in his voice.

Ashok nodded. "It's as if you aren't even considered a Hindu."

Ram continued walking slowly. He said, "It's almost dark. I doubt anyone would recognize me."

Ashok looked at him in surprise. "You're thinking of going in?"

Ram stopped walking. "Shouldn't I have the right to worship Lord Shiva? Just as we decided at the meeting."

Ashok halted also. "Of course. But if you're caught...."

"If I'm caught, they'll beat me. But I'm used to being beaten." He grinned. "They'll also have to purify themselves and the temple. Shouldn't I still have the right? Isn't that what Gandhiji would say?"

"Of course. Gandhiji himself helped Harijans gain access to temples in the south. But there was more preparation."

"What kind of preparation?"

"As I said in the meeting, Gandhiji or his supporters first contacted the temple managers. Sometimes they agreed right away. If they didn't, he'd try negotiations. And his visits were well publicized. If there still was no result, he'd consider organizing demonstrations. Bapu never does things on the spur of the moment. Everything he does is well planned, for maximum effect. "

"He's not here."

"No, but I'd advise against doing anything so hastily. What would you gain? If you're discovered, you'll be lucky to come out whole. If you're not found out, what does it prove? That you're clever enough to pass for a higher caste for a few minutes?"

Ram said, "If I'm discovered it will at least give publicity to my cause. If I'm not discovered, I'll announce it later." He again grinned at Ashok. "Much later. After a few thousand pilgrims have done *puja*, worshiping in a 'polluted' temple. The priests will be furious. And embarrassed. But it might make it easier in the future for my people to gain access, since a Harijan will already have worshiped there."

Ashok stared at him. "If you're caught, they'd be so angry, this time you could even be killed!"

Ram shrugged. "No matter. It would bring even more publicity."

After a time, Ashok said, "Visiting the temple might publicize your cause. But it might also make the priests and the upper castes so indignant that they would retaliate against your people in the villages."

Ram asked, his voice slightly hoarse, "Are you coming in with me?"

Ashok hesitated. He decided Gandhiji's injunction against visiting the temple wouldn't apply if he were visiting in support of a Harijan. He sighed. "Since you're determined to go in, I'll come, too."

Together, they joined the throng entering the gate. They passed the stalls where vendors were selling flowers and other items to offer to the God, as well as trinkets for souvenirs for pilgrims. Ram and Ashok removed their shoes, and crossed the courtyard. Like most of the worshipers, they rang a bell hanging from a chain under the eaves to announce their presence to Lord Shiva. Some of the worshipers were stopping to give reverence to the big image of Shiva's bull Nandi, who sat facing the entrance to the principal temple building.

With the crowd, they squeezed through the door of the main structure. It was difficult to see into the inner sanctum where the *lingam* was housed, but over the heads of the worshipers in front of them they saw oil lamps burning in the dimly lit room. "It's said," whispered Ram, his voice higher pitched than normal, and his eyes wide with excitement, "that the *lingam* is a natural one discovered at this place long ago by a temple dancer. She was guided to it by Lord Shiva in a dream."

A priest was chanting. Soon he began the *arati*, waving a lamp with multiple flames in front of the *lingam*. The crowd was ringing bells, banging on drums, making so much noise that conversation became impossible.

Some of the people began the circumambulation of the shrine, walking around it in the traditional clockwise direction. However, Ram and Ashok joined the numerous worshipers who were leaving the temple, headed toward the gate.

They were putting on their sandals when Ashok clearly heard a nearby man utter the word, "Bhangi!"

"Bhangi?" someone else asked.

Ram had been recognized.

He and Ashok walked swiftly to the outer gateway. "Bhangi *hain*! Bhangi *hain*!" ("They are Sweepers!") a voice now shouted nearby. Ram and Ashok pretended to pay no attention. They joined the crush through the gate, and were soon outside.

"Bhangi *hain*!" came the shout again. In the light of the lanterns, Ashok saw two *lathi-armed* temple guards hurry in their direction.

"We'd better run," Ram said. Ashok briefly thought of stopping to try to explain. But he saw the anger in the faces of the guards and many visitors. He raced after Ram.

A number of the male temple-goers joined the guards in the chase. Up ahead, several men turned, saw what was occurring, and hurried to block Ashok and Ram. On one side stood the temple wall, on the other side were several family groups who had stopped to watch the commotion.

"The river!" called Ram. They burst past the surprised temple visitors, and Ashok literally tumbled down the bank in darkness.

The bed of the stream held little water due to the drought. Ashok had no idea how close Ram was, and he did not dare call out, for fear of giving away his own location to their pursuers. He stumbled through gravel, mud, and shallow water to the far bank. There he climbed from the river and groped through the fields to where a dirt lane shone dimly in the starlight. He was glad the searchers bore torches and lanterns, as it was easier for him to see them while they were still far away, and to move into the fields to evade them.

Ashok had to wait until dawn when the city gates were opened before he could return to his lodgings. Dirty, cut, and bruised, he at last climbed the narrow stairway. In his exhausted state he was slow in realizing that the odor of *bidi* smoke hung in the air. Just as he noticed the smell, hands roughly grabbed him from either side. "Police!" shouted a voice.

Startled, he instinctively tried to pull away. Something hard struck the side of his skull. The blow was a strong incentive to stop struggling. Someone bent his arms behind him, and he felt cold metal snap around his wrists. He was rudely turned and shoved out the door. He managed to keep from stumbling as he was prodded down the stairs. On the street they pushed him into the same car he'd been taken in before.

At the station, sub-inspector Jhakhar and another officer took him to a darkened room. They shoved him into a hard chair and aimed a bright light into his eyes. Jhakhar sat behind the light, so that Ashok could barely see him. The other policeman moved to stand behind Ashok. A match flared as Jhakhar lit a cigarette.

"Where were you last night, Chand?" Jhakhar demanded.

"I'd rather not say, sir." Ashok's hands were still secured behind his back, and already the metal dug into his wrists.

"You have no choice," said Jhakhar bluntly. "Tell us where you were."

"Was some crime committed?" Ashok asked, hoping to get a clue as to how much they knew.

Jhakhar said, sounding angry, "We ask the questions here, not you. Where were you? Who were you with?"

Not wanting to implicate Ram, Ashok said nothing.

Jhakhar said, "We can make you tell us, Chand. I promise you."

Ashok felt sweat trickle down his side. But he said nothing. He could vaguely see Jhakhar, behind the bright light, give a nod. With an open palm, the other policeman swatted Ashok on the side of the head, hard.

Ashok's ear, his cheek, the whole side of his face stung. He was abruptly furious that he, a responsible citizen and a lawyer, on close terms with world famous leaders, could be treated this way. Still he said nothing. He fought down his anger and focused on enduring the ordeal.

Jhakhar gave the impression of growing steadily more and more infuriated as Ashok continued to refuse to answer questions. The room filled with the smoke from Jhakhar's cigarettes. The other policeman frequently cuffed Ashok on the side of the face, hard enough to make his head fly to the opposite side and to jar his brains. He could smell his own sweat.

So far, he told himself, he could stand it. Indeed, he was pleased he could resist their rough handling so well. So far. But it would be easy for one of those blows on the side of his head to injure an eardrum, maybe permanently.

Ashok took a certain amount of pride in his good looks, and he was grateful for his health. He would hate to have either of them ruined.

He knew the police could get much, much tougher. The fact that they hadn't yet done so encouraged him, reinforced his hope that they didn't intend to use serious torture.

"You must be thirsty, Chand. Would you like some water?" Jhakhar asked.

Puzzled by the sudden change in routine, Ashok thought a moment. He was indeed extremely dry; he'd had nothing to drink since the meeting at Manohar Jain's house last night. And the smoke from Jhakhar's *bidis* was irritating his throat. "Yes, sir." The other officer went out. He returned with a glass of water. He threw it in Ashok's face.

At last, after perhaps two hours, they took him to see Karam Singh. The Inspector General of Police speared Ashok with that cold stare. "Mr. Chand. You look like you didn't sleep well."

Ashok's voice was hoarse as he replied, "I've had better nights, sir." He strained to control the anger he felt when he returned Singh's gaze. "And better mornings."

Singh spoke to the sub-inspector: "You weren't too hard on him?"

Jhakhar said, "He refuses to cooperate, sir. We tried to convince him."

Singh looked at Ashok. "Why aren't you cooperating? Surely you have nothing to hide."

Ashok did not reply.

Karam Singh's expression did not change. Nor did his eyes change their focus on Ashok's face. "Mr. Chand, last night a Bhangi was discovered leaving the temple of Mahadeo. I'm sure you know Untouchables are not allowed there. The Bhangi was in the company of an unknown male. Both escaped. The unidentified man's description is quite like your own. And you've been observed in Bhangiwada—the Sweepers' section of Gamri village. Was it you last night at the temple, Mr. Chand?"

In spite of his determination to be firm, Ashok's eyes slid away from Singh's stare. "I'd rather not answer, sir. But what if it were me? I'm not an Untouchable. I have every right to be there."

"So you do, Mr. Chand. The Bhangi doesn't."

Ashok now returned the inspector general's gaze. "Sir, I always thought Sikhs did not make caste distinctions."

Ashok was mildly surprised to see the official look away for the first time. Then Singh again fixed Ashok with a stare. "Sikhism doesn't, Mr. Chand. Nor do I. But His Highness is Hindu, not Sikh. And the temple of Mahadeo is under his personal protection. So the state police must enforce the ban on Untouchables."

After a time, Ashok said, "I see." He began to relax just a little.

Singh's cold stare returned, fixed on Ashok. "Mr. Chand, I must ask you who the Bhangi was."

"I can't say."

"Can't, or won't?"

Ashok hesitated, then replied, "Both, sir."

Singh said evenly, "I can use some severe means to compel you to tell me. Much more severe, I'm sure, than anything these men could have used yet."

Ashok took a deep breath. "I still can't say, sir."

Singh continued staring at him. Eventually, the inspector general said,

"I'm sure we'll find out anyway. Be more careful, Mr. Chand. You've been lucky so far. I may not always be around, and some of my men may get carried away. You might also find yourself in jail again. I strongly suggest you stay far from the Untouchables from now on."

"I appreciate the advice, sir," Ashok said, hoping Singh heard the hint of sarcasm.

Singh still gazed at him. Finally he said, "Jhakhar, take Mr. Chand home."

8

The interrogation had not been so bad as it could have been, but it was bad enough. Late that afternoon, aching all over, his face swollen, his head still hurting, Ashok took a tonga to Gamri village.

The Bhangi section seemed almost deserted. He saw a man scurry for cover at his approach. Ram's hut was empty. A couple of old men whom he recognized sat by a nearby house. They stood when Ashok approached, eyes downcast as they joined palms to greet him. He asked, "Have you seen Ramji?"

One of the men said, "No, *sahib*. He has not been here all day. The police have taken away all the other young men they could find."

Ashok flinched. "I'm sorry to hear that. You're sure Ram is not here? I was with him, you know. I'm worried about him."

The old men looked at each other. Then one said, still without meeting Ashok's eyes, "Sir, we don't want more trouble with the police. Please tell us what you want from us. We'll give it to you if we can."

Ashok realized they mistrusted him. "No, no," he said. "I have nothing to do with the police." He gestured toward his battered face and showed them the scratches and bruises on his arms. "The police did this to me."

The men again looked at each other. Then one said, "He's hiding, *sahib*. We'll tell him to contact you when it's safe."

"I'm sympathetic, of course," said Kishore to Ashok in the meeting that night at Manohar Jain's. "But it was a risk you took when you went into the temple with an Untouchable. We all know the methods the police use."

"Look at Ashokji's face, how swollen it is!" said Jaya. "Just because the police have always tortured people doesn't make it right. We need to show them that. We should act as soon as possible to help the Harijans get into the temple."

Ashok touched his cheek. It was painfully tender. There was no mirror in the room, but he was sure he must look terrible.

Kishore said bluntly, "You'd be putting yourself at considerable risk, you realize. Women aren't necessarily immune from police mistreatment."

Jaya stared at him as if uncertain how to respond.

"It's true," Ashok said. "I don't know about Mangarh. In British jails, the women freedom fighters are often given a worse time than the men. Probably in the hope of discouraging them."

Jaya gave a shrug. "I don't say I want to be arrested. But what's the point of living if we let our fears keep us from doing what we know is right?"

Her mother's look of pride was obvious. "I couldn't have said it better.

We need to contact the Harijan Sevak Sangh in Ajmer and see what kind of support we can get from them. And someone needs to let the press in Delhi know what we're doing. I'll take care of that myself."

With the apparent exception of Kishore, the Praja Mandal leaders took it as a personal affront that Ashok had been treated so badly by the police. Sundip, Jaya, and Mrs. Arora continued to argue the most forcefully to pursue changing the temple's entry rules.

The head priest at the temple of Mahadeo, furious at the defilement of the temple and the need for lengthy cleansing rituals, refused to discuss the matter. At two further Praja Mandal meetings, the alternatives were debated, and it was eventually concluded that more direct action must to be taken, in the form of a mass demonstration. Ashok requested time to try to telegraph Gandhi for advice, but it was decided this was a matter to be decided by local people who knew the situation.

Ashok found it difficult to believe that the Mangarh Praja Mandal was truly taking a serious action barely a month after the temple incident—and despite his cautionary advice. Even Manohar seemed to feel it would be wrong to forget the matter.

The Praja Mandal and the Ajmer branch of the Untouchable's organization, the Harijan Sevak Sangh, publicized the effort as widely as possible. They met with both the Chief Minister of Mangarh and the head priest of the temple to try again to negotiate the right of entry. After the talks failed, Ashok reluctantly took the lead in organizing the temple demonstration.

Over fifty people accompanied him to the temple, among them thirty-odd Harijan men, including Ram. About half the Untouchables came from local villages and half came from the Harijan Sevak Sangh in Ajmer and other areas. Mrs. Arora headed a party of seven women, including Jaya.

As they had expected, the marchers found the temple gates closed. Two ranks of state police armed with their *lathis*, barred the entrance. Karam Singh stood by them with a couple of his inspectors. Off to one side stood three newspaper reporters. One was from the Mangarh paper, and the other two wrote for Delhi newspapers. A large group of angry-looking villagers and other onlookers stood on both sides of the entrance.

Near the reporters, Dr. Arora waited anxiously with his medical bag. He had tried hard to dissuade his wife and daughter from being present, but having failed, he volunteered his own services. A small group of women stood with parcels of bandages in case they were needed.

Ashok's stomach was queasy, and there was a numbness in his hands as he stared at the reality of the police with their heavy staffs. Those *lathis*, long and thick, with their metal-bound ends, looked as if they could break an arm or a leg right in half. He had known this moment might come, but facing it at last was terrifying.

He looked at Jaya, so pretty and so determined. Despite his caring deeply about the others involved, the thought of injury to her in particular was almost unbearable.

He took a deep breath, turned his back on the police, and beckoned the demonstrators to move close, so he could speak to them in a voice that would not carry beyond the group. He again breathed deeply before he said, "We've discussed the alternatives earlier. Are we still agreed?" He was relieved that his voice didn't betray his fear. He went on, trying to sound matter-of-fact: "As we all know, if we do try to block the entrance or to go in, we'll probably be injured. Some of us could even be killed."

He realized he was half hoping that his people would back down and give him an excuse to leave—leading everyone else to safety, too.

Ram said boldly, "We're here because we have the right to be. I think we should block the entrance so no one can get in until Harijans are allowed, too. Besides, I've already been inside before."

There were some uneasy laughs.

Jaya said, equally firmly, "We want to draw attention to our demands. I don't want to see anyone hurt, but if it did happen, we'd get more newspaper space." Ashok again tried to quell his anxiety at the imminent risk of her being injured, or worse.

"Right," said a man from the Harijan Sevak Sangh. "Many of us feel we have little to lose anyway."

Ashok had been mildly surprised when Kishore turned up to join them. "We'll never get past the police," said Kishore, his eyes darting about as if desperately seeking an alternative. "There aren't enough of us."

Jaya said, "It's the publicity, and the point we're making, that are important. We want to pressure His Highness to do what he knows is right."

"Well said," commented Ashok. He wished he felt as fearless as she sounded.

There was a general murmur of assent.

"Then we're agreed," Ashok said, concentrating on sounding resolute. "As we decided earlier, the ladies will stay in the center rear. We'll all march as close to the gate as we can get, police or no." He looked around. "I hope the newspaper men do their job to spread the word."

He turned to face the police. Karam Singh was watching the demonstrators with his piercing stare, as if trying to intimidate them by his look. Ashok stood a moment. There seemed no way out.

He began moving slowly toward the entrance and the police ranks. He was aware of Sundip and Manohar on one side. On his other side were Ram and a number of Bhangis and Chamars. Through the corner of his eye, Ashok realized Manohar looked quite different, having removed his eyeglasses to avoid the possibility of having them broken.

Bystanders began throwing stones. One struck Ashok's head, hard. He half stumbled, but he took control of himself and moved on. More rocks pelted the demonstrators. He saw Kishore fall to the ground.

Karam Singh moved forward to stand before them. He called loudly, "By order of His Highness the Maharaja, this is an unlawful assembly. I order you to disperse immediately. If you fail to do so, I'm directed to use whatever force is needed."

The marchers continued slowly toward him.

Singh took several steps to the side, and he shouted a command.

The police lifted their *lathis* and stepped forward, swinging the staffs into the marchers. Ashok heard soft crunches, gasps, moans. All around him the men were falling. Something hit him in the mouth with a cracking sound. Then he felt the side of his head explode, and all went black.

When he returned to consciousness, he was lying on his back on the ground. His head throbbed horribly, and his mouth hurt. He painfully looked about, and he saw that he had apparently been carried a few hundred feet down the road from the temple. Around him lay other wounded men, with mostly women caring for them. Nearby, Dr. Arora was bent over someone.

Jaya and a young man were with Ashok, and when she saw him rise slightly, she moved near and examined at him with anxious eyes. "I was so worried! How do you feel?"

He tasted blood and swallowed. His mouth was sore. "My ear—I hear some ringing...." He summoned his energy. "How are the others?"

The young man said, "I'll bring the doctor. You shouldn't move until he can examine you."

"It's awful!" said Jaya, moving her face close. "One of the Harijans was hurt badly. Ram has a broken arm and Sundip a broken nose. My father's with them now. Most of the men have been hurt some way or other. Kishore got off just with bad bruises. By the time the police got to the women, the inspector general called them off. He had the police help remove the wounded. You seemed to be one of the worst." Her eyes gazed intently into his. "We've had some bad moments watching you."

He tried to think of a response, but failed.

She moved away slightly and peered at his face. She frowned. "Your mouth's bleeding. It looks like you may have lost a tooth."

Ashok felt with his tongue. An upper front tooth was indeed gone; a jagged remnant of the root extended from his gum. "So I did."

Jaya took a white cloth and gently wiped at the blood on his lips. She looked as if she were about to break into tears. Despite the pain and his concern about the others, he was comforted by her caring touch, and by her worry for him. He said, his words muffled by speaking through swollen, bloody gums and lips, "It's bad enough, but I've heard of worse beatings by state police. I wonder if Karam Singh gave them orders to go easy."

"This was going easy?"

"I'd say so. None of us were killed."

Although the article in the Mangarh newspaper was heavily censored, the other reporters widely publicized the aborted temple *satyagraha* effort. Both Jawaharlal Nehru and Mahatma Gandhi mentioned it in their speeches, using it as an example of the types of wrongs that needed to be righted in the new India. Dr. Ambedkar, the famous national leader for the rights of Untouchables, also spoke in support of the Mangarh efforts.

But the temple made no change in its admission policy.

Ram gave the impression of indifference toward his broken arm, even though it would be almost impossible for him to work as a farm laborer until it healed.

The ringing in Ashok's ear diminished with time, but it did not fade altogether. He continued to be partially deaf in the ear. The gap remained in his front teeth.

The Praja Mandal members and the Untouchables were unable to agree on the next step, as further demonstrations would clearly have a similar result. So the Praja Mandal decided to resume its efforts to petition the Maharaja for governmental reforms.

9

Mangarh Junction, April 1939

Jawaharlal Nehru stepped from the train, followed by his daughter Indira and several men. The crowd of several hundred greeted him, cheering him with "*Jai* Nehru!" ("Victory to Nehru!"), "*Jai Hind*!" ("Victory to India!"), "*Bharat Mata ki jai*!" ("Victory to Mother India!"). Nehru stood a moment, smiling, his hand raised in greeting to the people. He wore his customary Gandhi cap, and below his vest the long tail of his white homespun *kurta* flared out almost like a short skirt. Manohar Jain stepped forward and welcomed him, draping a garland around Nehru's neck and another around Indira's.

For a moment Ashok wondered if there might be a danger of Nehru being arrested for wearing the cap that was illegal in Mangarh. No, he assured himself, the Mangarh police would not risk the bad publicity for something so minor. He had been surprised Karam Singh had granted the permit for a public meeting. Then he found out that the Maharaja was making a point of being away from Mangarh on the date of Nehru's visit—an obvious snub.

It was the first time Ashok had seen Nehru's daughter and only child; she was usually away at college in England. Indira was a slight, attractive young woman of around twenty years in age. Her face bore an unreadable expression. Was it unhappiness, or merely tiredness, in her eyes?

Ashok, Sundip, Kishore, Jaya, and the others began leading their guests to the waiting motor cars provided by the Aroras and the Jain family.

"We're so glad you could stop, Panditji," Ashok said, talking loudly to be heard over the noise of the onlookers. "I know how busy you are. But are you sure you can't break your journey for a night's rest?"

"I wish I could, Ashok. I'd like to talk with you at length about your work here. But I'm expected at Jodhpur, too, you know, and I'm already behind schedule."

"I understand. We're delighted you could be here at all."

Kishore, obviously eager to be noticed by the famous visitor, had opened the car door and stood waiting by it. When Indira, Nehru, and Ashok had climbed in, Kishore hurriedly slid into the front seat, ensuring that he would not be relegated to one of the other vehicles.

They motored to an open area at the outskirts of Mangarh city. A crowd of several hundred had gathered, both city and farm people. The car pulled up to a small cordoned-off area where a walled tent pavilion stood by a newly erected flagpole. The fortress rose in the distance, and not far away, the domes and clock tower of the Bhim Bhawan palace could be seen above the treetops.

The cheers came continually. The car halted, and Nehru got out and greeted the crowd with folded palms. Once again he submitted to being garlanded. Ashok said to him, "Whenever you're ready, we'll quiet the people so you can speak to them."

Kishore, who had volunteered to do the introduction to the crowd said, "We also are wondering, sir, if you'd do us the honor of raising the Congress flag for the first time in Mangarh state? Many of us consider it the same as a national flag, which we'll all hopefully have some day."

"Raise the flag for the first time? Gladly. I assume those policemen won't interfere?"

Kishore glanced quickly at the small group of state police and said, "Oh, no, Panditji!"

Ashok added smoothly, "I've been assured by the inspector general of police that they won't bother us, Panditji. They're just here to watch. Anyway, I doubt His Highness would risk the bad coverage in the national press that an incident involving you would create."

Nehru gave a slight nod. "Very well then."

Ashok noticed that Indira was standing by looking bored. He said, "Perhaps your daughter would care to honor us by being the one to raise the flag? It might symbolize the dedication of the younger generation."

Nehru smiled and glanced at her. "If you're agreeable, Indu, I think it's a fine idea."

The young woman's eyes brightened. She gave a quick nod.

Kishore held up his hands, motioning the crowd to settle down. Soon they were quiet, and after a few introductory words from him, Nehru took over.

He stood in a characteristic stance, his left hand resting on his hip, while he gestured with his right arm. "I am glad," he said into the microphone, "to see the people of Mangarh state joining us in this great struggle for responsible government and for an independent India. The objective of Congress is complete independence, for the whole of India. The states such as Mangarh are integral parts, and they must have the same measure of political, social, and economic freedom as the rest of our nation."

Nehru's style was conversational, as if he were speaking to friends in their home. The people nevertheless cheered enthusiastically at the end of virtually every concept presented. Ashok looked about at the hundreds of villagers who had come from outlying areas. He saw Ram and several of the other Harijans in a small knot at the rear of the gathering.

Nehru was saying, "The full establishment of civil liberties is an essential preliminary to any progress. It is an insult to India to ask her to tolerate, in the princely states, the suppression of organizations and the prevention of public gatherings." His voice at last rose: "Are the states to remain vast prisons, where the human spirit is sought to be extinguished, and the resources of the people are to be used for the pageantry and luxury of courts, while the masses starve and remain illiterate and backward? Are the Middle Ages to continue in India under the protection of British Imperialism?"

"No!" "Never!" came the answering shouts. "*Jai Hind!*"

Nehru apparently thought that was a good place to end his short address. He beckoned to his daughter, who slowly strode over to the flagpole. The white, red, and green tricolor had already been attached to the rope. The people cheered, and the band played, while Indira pulled on the halyard and slowly raised the flag to the top of the pole. There was no breeze, and it hung limply, but that did not matter to the exuberant crowd. Ashok saw that Ram and the other Untouchables appeared caught up in the enthusiasm and were wildly cheering.

"This way, please, Panditji," Ashok said. He led them to the *shamiana* that had been erected for the meal. As they stepped under the canopy, Indira spoke to Ashok: "Is His Highness away from Mangarh, then, that he won't be receiving us?"

Ashok was surprised to realize he was slightly embarrassed, almost as if it were his duty to apologize. "Yes, Indiraji. He's in Delhi. Maybe it's better that way. You must understand, His Highness dislikes Congress intensely, especially our activities in his state. We considered it quite a concession when the government gave us the permit to hold this gathering."

Her face displayed little emotion other than a tightness around her lips. She said with obvious scorn, "These princes. What an anachronism. It's time they were thrown out. Along with their British protectors."

Ashok tactfully did not reply. He had the definite impression she was angry that the Maharaja had snubbed her father by not greeting him. Ashok knew other princes had entertained Nehru when he visited their states. But Lakshman Singh's antipathy was too strong to appear personally, even though concern for public opinion had swayed him into allowing people to gather for the occasion.

"Are you satisfied to stay longer in Mangarh, Ashok?" asked Pandit Nehru. "We can make good use of you elsewhere, if you'd prefer. The better part of a year here by now, isn't it? And much of that time you were in jail."

"I've been here around eight months, Panditji. This is a critical time now, though. We've established the groundwork, but we've actually achieved little yet. And famine in the countryside is almost certain to come. I feel I'm still needed."

Nehru was staring at him with a skeptical look. "You're from the Punjab canal districts. We were thinking we could use some of your organizing skills there."

Ashok was being asked to go back home! To leave this place of arid, rocky hills for the fertile plains he loved. To go where he could speak the Punjabi he considered his native tongue.

He glanced toward Jaya and saw she was staring at him; he thought he saw concern in her eyes. He replied to Nehru, "You saw the size of the crowd that came to hear you, sir. I'm sure it's much smaller than you're used to. But a year ago, many of them probably would not have even known who you are. We're educating them, making them aware of what's going on outside the state. They're becoming less complacent as they learn of the freedoms they've been denied for so many centuries." He was aware that Jaya was listening intently with a slight smile as he concluded, "I think they're almost ready to bring real pressure on the government if we can organize some mass demonstrations."

Nehru examined him a moment. Then he smiled tightly. "I was in jail in a princely state myself once, you know. It was a terrible experience. I caught typhoid fever there. Thought I was going to die. If you still want to stay here after being jailed, who am I to try to convince you otherwise?"

The next day, Ashok could not resist riding his bicycle past the pole displaying the Congress flag, just to admire the fact that it was here, in Mangarh of all places.

When he arrived at the open space outside the walls, he saw people here and there, standing and watching. And around the flagstaff stood perhaps a dozen state police, while two laborers were chopping at the base of the pole with axes.

Dismayed, Ashok stopped and stood, holding his bicycle. He'd feared something such as this would happen, but he had not expected it so soon. Then he realized: the Maharaja would be passing by today or tomorrow on his return from Delhi, and Lakshman Singh would not want a Congress flag flying outside his city.

The pole fell to the ground with a resounding thud and a crack as the wood split.

Ashok stared at the sight, infuriated, but powerless to do anything. Several of the onlookers were muttering to each other, also clearly upset, though a few others wore smiles of satisfaction.

Now that the act was done, a few of the policemen left, but some remained, smoking *bidis* and talking among themselves. Soon a couple of them, too, walked away.

Ashok became aware that a *dhoti*-clad young man strode over to the pole, bent and began to unfasten the flag.

It was Ram.

Still holding the bicycle, Ashok watched tensely, fearful that someone would object.

Abruptly, one of the police called to Ram: "What are you doing? Who are you?"

Ram stood and boldly said, "The secretary *sahib* sent me. His Highness wants the flag so he can burn it."

Another of the police said, "I've seen him before. He was in the crowd watching Nehru, with a bunch of Bhangis!"

"You're mistaken," said Ram. "It must have been someone who looked like me." He bent, resumed unfastening the flag, and disengaged one of the hooks.

"Leave that alone!" shouted the policeman who had recognized him.

Ram said, "His Highness ordered it." He moved to unfasten the other hook.

One of the policemen, whose back was to Ashok, stepped forward, raised his rifle vertically, and quickly brought the butt down. Ashok heard the crack as it struck Ram's skull.

The young man sagged and fell to the ground. Again the rifle butt struck his head. And again.

Ashok dropped his bicycle, ran toward them. "No!" he shouted. A policeman moved to block his way. Ashok tried to shove his way past, but the officer seized his arm.

The other policeman had at last stopped beating on the victim who lay sprawled on the earth. Ashok was shocked to see blood flowing from the side of Ram's head, and out his nose and mouth.

Ram lay motionless. His eyes were open wide, but they held a vacant look.

Ashok stood, still gripped by the policeman, watching horrified while an older officer closely examined Ram.

"He's dead," the officer murmured. He looked up at the one who had wielded the rifle. "You didn't have to keep hitting him after he was down!"

The policeman who had done the clubbing turned, and Ashok saw his face. It was sub-inspector Jhakhar, whose lips curled in a tight smile. "He was far too cheeky for a Bhangi," said Jhakhar.

Ashok could not contain himself. "You bastard! You had no right to kill him!"

Jhakhar faced Ashok. Seeing who had yelled at him, his eyes turned icy. "Take your Congress ideas somewhere else, sister-fucker. Or you'll end up just like him."

"You can't kill people just because you're police and they're Bhangis!"

Jhakhar raised the rifle to point at Ashok's chest and glared. "Get away from here. Now!"

Ashok opened his mouth to object. He saw the look in Jhakhar's eyes and closed his lips. He took a step backward. He held his breath as he reluctantly turned. He could sense the gun still pointed at his back as he began walking away. He heard the older officer say to Jhakhar in a quiet voice, "Better put that down. You went too far. There will be questions about this."

Ashok struggled to grasp that Ram was dead.

And he wrestled with his hatred of the policeman who had reacted so violently to so minor a provocation. Gandhiji, he knew, had encountered similar situations during a lengthy life spent trying to change the world for the better. If Gandhi had been present, he would have been profoundly saddened by Ram's death. However, he would also have shown loving understanding for a policeman such as sub-inspector Jhakhar, who underneath must be an angry and frustrated man to have reacted with such brutality.

Although Ashok held the utmost admiration for Gandhi's compassion toward all beings, he himself was not able to be so noble or so saintly.

At Gamri village Ashok expressed his sympathy to Ram's grieving young wife and assured himself that arrangements were made for the burial of Ram's body; unlike the higher castes, the Untouchables did not cremate their dead. He remained in the village for perhaps an hour, but he sensed his presence was making many of the Harijans uncomfortable.

When he returned to the city in late afternoon, he was amazed to see the size of the crowd that had gathered at the spot outside the walls, even though the sun shone hotly on the large open area. And more people were arriving.

The flagpole had been removed, but worried-looking state policemen stood in a circle around the spot. Ashok saw Jaya and her mother, and Kishore and Manohar. "How terrible!" said Jaya, tears in her eyes.

Ashok felt his own eyes turning moist. He gave a nod. They stood in silence for a long time. Eventually, Manohar asked, "Whatever made him try it, with the police around?"

Ashok remembered Ram's satisfaction at telling him how he had secretly gotten even with many of his higher caste tormentors. "He was actually quite clever," Ashok said, wiping wetness from his cheek. "He'd taken a lot of risks before and succeeded at them. I think he thought he could get away with it. But he didn't expect one of the police would recognize him. Or that they'd be so ruthless."

Kishore said, "We must demand that the policeman be tried for murder. It won't happen, but it's the least we can do."

There was a murmur of agreement.

Ashok said, "It's a tragedy. But it can also be an opportunity. We can help ensure something comes from his death so it has more meaning, a purpose. He'd be glad of that."

Kishore removed the cigarette from his mouth. "How?"

"The Praja Mandal can declare a statewide day of mourning and prayer. Demand that Ram's death not be in vain. Insist that the government implement the reforms we demand."

"It's a good rallying point," said Manohar, nodding.

"It's too bad we don't have the flag," said Kishore, staring at the spot where the pole had stood. "We could use it, also, to rally the people."

Jaya glanced around, as if to ensure no one else was watching her. Then, from within a fold of her sari she cautiously pulled a flattened, dust-soiled wad of cloth, red and green and white. "When the time is right," she said, "we can show it."

"It's the same flag?" asked Ashok.

She nodded as she slid it back inside her sari. "I got it before the workmen carried away the pole. The police were worried about the crowd in front of them and didn't notice me behind. I just picked it up as if it belonged to me."

Ashok and Kishore and Manohar stood gaping at her.

Mrs. Arora said, "You can be sure my heart was in my stomach while she was doing it. I would have tried to stop her, but she didn't give me a chance."

"You took quite a risk," said Ashok to Jaya at last.

She shrugged, her expression grim. "We've all taken risks." There was a moment of silence, and then she said, "Sundip says Ram's wife is expecting a child."

Ashok stared at her in surprise. He tightened his lips and shook his head. "That brutal policeman created an orphan, as well as a young widow."

Jaya nodded. "We'll keep trying to change the government. Maybe in the future, things like that won't happen."

***

The story of Ashok Chand and the other reformers resumes after the next chapter, under the title, "Mangarh Jails."

Part Six
The Treasure of Mangarh

13

Mangarh, 1976

The search of the temple of Mahadeo had revealed nothing relevant. Its sanctum, vaults, and storerooms housed a considerable quantity of valuables, but so far as could be determined in such a short time, everything belonged to the temple itself.

Akbar Khan drove Vijay and Ghosali toward town. They were passing the Bhim Bhawan palace when Ghosali said, "We haven't yet spoken again to the one person in Mangarh who knows most about the missing gemstones."

"You mean Bharat Mahajan."

"Of course," said Ghosali. "Why have you not suggested seeing him?"

A major reason, Vijay realized, was his fear that the clerk at Mahajan's jewelry shop would recognize him as an old schoolmate—and as an Untouchable. "Because," he said, "we reached a dead end when we talked to Mahajan last time. What would be the point in going back?"

"What do we have to lose?" asked Ghosali.

Plenty, thought Vijay, fear rising in his gut. "Only a little time, I suppose," he said. "But I see no point in it."

Ghosali ordered Akbar Khan: "Take us to that gem dealer in town. The same one we visited before."

"Yes, sir," said Khan.

Although B. Mahajan and Sons was the largest gem dealer in the area, the shop front was similar to that of the other small businesses on the narrow lane. Vijay and Ghosali removed their shoes at the threshold and stepped onto the white cloth covering the floor.

Arjun Oswal sat with another clerk behind the glass-topped counters. Oswal had delighted in tormenting Vijay in school, like the time he and other boys had hid Vijay's mathematics book. The cost of another book was the equivalent of a month's worth of food, and Vijay didn't have the money. After several days the book reappeared, but not after causing him great anxiety. And they had done it just because he was a Bhangi.

Vijay thought about keeping his sunglasses on, but he decided wearing them inside would only attract attention. He put them in his sportcoat pocket. He breathed deeply, trying to stay calm. He gestured Ghosali forward to take the lead. The finding of the treasure was, of course, huge news in Mangarh. And Vijay's photo had appeared in several major newspapers, in addition to his brief appearance on television news.

Ghosali held up his identification for Oswal to see, and asked, "Is Shri Mahajan available?"

Oswal apparently remembered the tax officers from the prior visit. "Yes, sirs." He rose to his feet, barely glancing at them. "A moment please!" He hurried through the door to Bharat Mahajan's office.

The portly merchant, wearing a white *dhoti* and a black vest, came out and pressed his palms together. "This way, please, sirs."

Vijay looked away from Oswal as the clerk returned to the front of the shop. The tax officers followed Mahajan into his large office, with its row of three big safes and a massive door leading into a strongroom. Mahajan ordered tea from his peon and said, "Please be seated. What brings you here again, sirs?"

Vijay gestured to Ghosali, who said, "We still have not located the missing gems we discussed with you on our earlier visit. We are wondering if you might have since remembered anything else that could be of help to us."

Mahajan furrowed his brow. "First," he said, "please allow me to congratulate you on finding the famous treasure. After reading about the hiding place, I went to look at it myself. It was quite clever of you to locate the spot."

Ghosali nodded, tight lipped in the knowledge he had personally ridiculed the idea of looking in the location.

Mahajan said, "The fact that the major gems were not with the rest of the treasure is not surprising."

"Why do you say that?" asked Ghosali.

Mahajan thrust his hands wide. "Because they are unique! They would have been given special pride of ownership. The Star of Mangarh, in particular, is such an important, valuable diamond, it would no doubt have been kept in an even more secure place."

Vijay said, "We've looked everywhere we could think of so far. Can you suggest where such gems might be kept?"

Mahajan shrugged. "The jewelry is so small in size. I should think it would be almost impossible to look everywhere those items could be. They might not even be in Mangarh. His Highness used to go to Delhi often. Also to Bombay, I think."

Ghosali scowled. "Obviously, we already know what you've just said. We've checked deposit boxes in banks and with jewelers in those cities, and found nothing."

"How likely is it that the Star of Mangarh might have been cut into smaller gems?" asked Vijay. "If it were, that might explain why it seems to have disappeared."

Mahajan looked away, apparently thinking. "It's indeed conceivable, as I think I mentioned on your earlier visit. However, I doubt it was done. To me, it would be a travesty for anyone to break up such an important piece." He looked back at Vijay and shrugged. "But who knows?"

"I've read," said Vijay, "that the Mughals didn't cut their gems into facets, that they merely polished the stones. Is it possible we could see the diamond and not recognize it, because it hasn't been cut like diamonds in modern times?"

Mahajan shook his head. "I doubt it. I remember hearing from my father that the Star of Mangarh was cut in Bombay in the 1800s. It wouldn't have quite the fire of a diamond cut after 1900 or so when the optimum angles were determined, but it would still be most striking."

Ghosali said in a loud voice, "We're getting nowhere in this conversation. Can't you offer us any other suggestions for finding it, given your long experience and your expertise in your field?"

Mahajan frowned. "As I told you on your previous visit, many rulers sent much of their wealth out of India at the time of Independence. It's quite possible that was what was done by His Highness. However," his eyes brightened, "if you do locate any of these items, I hope you will give me the chance to appraise them for you! It would be the opportunity of a lifetime."

Ghosali again scowled. "If you could be of more help to us, we would be much more likely to retain you as the appraiser."

Vijay glanced sharply at Ghosali; the statement seemed both rude and improper. But Ghosali's attention was focused on the merchant.

Mahajan narrowed his eyes. "In that case, I, too, wish I could be of more help. But I'm unfortunately not gifted with magical powers."

"I think you know more than you're telling us," said Ghosali.

Vijay tried not to show his distaste at the effort at bullying. It was no doubt obvious to Mahajan that Ghosali was casting about at random, hoping to snare a useful piece of information by intimidation.

Mahajan stood, signifying that, as far as he was concerned, the interview was finished. "I fully realize you're capable of making life difficult for me with subpoenas and raids or whatever. But I've told you what I know. I don't think you want me to make up a false story just to tell you something."

"You're certainly correct in that, sir," said Vijay, annoyed with Ghosali. "But if you do think of anything more, please contact us."

Mahajan nodded, but said nothing.

On the way out, Vijay pretended not to notice Arjun Oswal. At the outer threshold, he bent to step into his shoes.

"Excuse me," came Oswal's voice. "I believe we used to know each other. Aren't you my old schoolmate Vijay?"

Vijay froze and stopped breathing. He was aware that Ghosali stopped putting on his own shoes and turned toward him.

He forced himself to stand and face Oswal. Should he deny recognizing the man? He doubted he could get away with that, especially since Ghosali knew he was originally from the area. It would just arouse Ghosali's suspicions. "Why, yes," he said, trying to sound pleased. His mouth had gone dry, and he strove to control his voice as he added, "I thought you looked familiar, but it's been so long! Arjun, isn't it?"

He held his breath, terrified Oswal would say something that could give Ghosali a hint of their relative caste backgrounds.

"Yes!" said Oswal. "I thought I recognized you from the newspaper photo, when the treasure was found. But it seemed unlikely it could be you! The last

I remember, you'd gone away somewhere for school."

"Yes, I went to Delhi." He was trying to think of a way to quickly terminate their talk.

There was a brief pause, and then Arjun Oswal said, "You've come far from the days when we were school boys."

Vijay swallowed. "I suppose you could say that."

"In that newspaper story, your name—"

Vijay instantly interrupted, his voice louder than he'd intended: "Those newspapers always exaggerate everything, don't they?" In the village, the Untouchables never used last names; Oswal was obviously about to question using the Rajput "Singh" surname. Vijay quickly continued, "I never realized just how much the press distorted things until I had them writing something about me." Desperate to turn the conversation away from himself, he asked, "But how did you get into the jewelry business, yourself?"

Oswal straightened himself. "Shri Mahajan is a family friend." He hesitated, then said, "Not such an interesting story as yours, I'm sure?"

Vijay shrugged modestly. "Well, regrettably we must be going. Good to see you again." He bent back to his shoes. It seemed to take forever to tie them, when all he wanted to do was flee.

As he and Ghosali at last left the shop, he glanced back, and he saw Oswal was examining him intently. Vijay gave a nod of farewell. He had to concentrate on walking casually to the jeep and climbing into it.

Ghosali told Akbar Khan to return them to the fort. As they were driving slowly through the crowded bazaar, Ghosali commented, "It is not surprising that you would run into someone you used to know, in a town so small." He was watching Vijay closely.

"Not at all surprising," said Vijay. His voice was hoarse, and he cleared his throat.

"So you were school boys together."

"Yes, for a couple of years."

"Odd you didn't recognize him when you were here earlier."

Vijay shrugged. "As I told him, he looked familiar, but I couldn't quite place him. It was a long time ago. He's changed a lot. I'm sure I have, too."

Ghosali looked thoughtful. Eventually, he said, "Yes, I'm sure you have." He was watching Vijay's face. "The clerk was asking something about your name in the newspaper article."

Vijay shrugged. Thinking quickly, he replied, "He probably remembered my name from childhood and was connecting it with the photo."

Ghosali seemed content to drop the matter at that, and Vijay surreptitiously let out his breath in relief.

It had been a close one. Too close. He might not be so lucky next time. If only the search would end quickly, before anyone else recognized him.

Back at the fortress, Vijay and Ranjit drove to the top of the ridge so Vijay could inspect the digging being done by the workmen. "They're making a hell of a mess here," Ranjit said.

"That's an understatement." Vijay shook his head in disapproval. They stopped at the *garh's* oldest section, the squarish castle-like structure with rounded corner towers which used to contain the Maharaja's treasury. Akbar Khan parked the jeep in the shade, next to the blue Bentley belonging to the royal family.

They stepped out and gazed at the many piles of dirt adjacent to holes scattered about the rocky hilltop. A dozen or so small parties of men were working here and there with picks and shovels. It was hot in the sun, and in the distance, Nimbalkar sat under a small tree, watching a group of laborers, who were digging next to a rectangular stone-lined water reservoir. Vijay glimpsed a mongoose emerge from a rock pile, flow swiftly across an open area, and disappear behind a section of wall.

The prince and the princess were walking past a large oblong pit. The tractor with its powered shovel was parked nearby. Mahendra Singh was gesturing widely, obviously agitated, as he talked with his sister. Vijay sighed and approached them.

"Mister Singh," the prince said, waving his arm about, "what is the point of all this?" Sweat glistened on his face. "We'd hardly hide anything here in the open, where anyone could come find it."

The princess, an *odhni* draped over her head for modesty, said, "I'm concerned about all this disturbance of the soil. You must know this is the oldest part of the fortress. It hasn't been explored thoroughly yet by archaeologists. Now—" she gestured at the big pit "—the layers in the ground are all being mixed up, so scientists will never be able to reconstruct any useful information. And using that tractor! How can they possibly be careful with it? It's a travesty!"

As Vijay was trying to formulate a response, she bent by a pile of dusty dirt and pulled out a pottery shard, a curved piece with a dark gray glaze. She stood and turned to him, her eyes flashing. "See? We'll never know now why this was here. Was there a kitchen on this spot in ancient times? A banquet hall? Or just a picnic spot? It looks to me like it's from the Mauryan period, but now we can't tell what layer it was in, so there's no way to know the historical context!"

"I definitely see your point," Vijay said. "I didn't order the digging, but I'll talk to Batraji and Ghosaliji tonight and see if I can get it stopped."

"It's already gone too far," muttered Mahendra Singh, looking out over the piles.

"Unfortunately, I can't undo what's done so far. But I'll do my best to try to see there's no more harm."

The prince gave an abrupt nod, and he and his sister strode off toward their car.

"Are you going to look for Ghosali now?" asked Ranjit.

Vijay was silent for a moment. "I've had enough of him for the afternoon. I'll definitely talk to him this evening, though. We'll probably have to phone Batra, too. I don't look forward to that."

Ranjit nodded. He looked about. "Well, as long as we're here, I'm wondering if we should explore the secret tunnels again. In case we missed something on the earlier raid."

Vijay hesitated at the thought of going once more in those confined passages with their total darkness. Although he knew the tunnels were probably safe, he'd had a definite feeling of discomfort in them, as if all the tons of rock overhead were poised to collapse. But they were indeed a possible place to hide wealth. "I suppose there's no harm in it," he said.

They fetched a kerosene lantern and two electric torches from the equipment in the jeep and entered the arched gateway of the old castle. Several striped squirrels were playing under the *pipal* tree in the first small courtyard. Vijay and Ranjit went across the area, through the next archway, and into the former treasury with its big, empty vaults.

In a room off the end of the hallway was the opening in the floor where the laborers had excavated. There, Ranjit lit the lantern, and they descended the narrow stairway into the solid rock.

A cobweb brushed Vijay's face. Just inside the tunnel entrance, the passages branched both right and left. Ranjit held the lantern toward the right hand passage and said in a hushed tone, "Shall we try the longest one first?"

"Fine." Their voices sounded strange in the narrow space.

The tunnel was barely high enough to walk in without bending over, and as on the previous occasion, Vijay felt uncomfortably enclosed. As he followed Ranjit, their footsteps echoed harshly from wall to wall. The cool air smelled musty. Occasionally a fragment of stone crunched underfoot on the uneven floor. A rat scurried away.

Vijay shone the flashlight on the rough walls and ceiling as he moved slowly along, but he saw no irregularities that might indicate a concealed entrance or chamber. After roughly a few hundred feet, the passage ended abruptly. A doorway to the right led to another narrow stairway.

Ranjit raised the lantern higher to illuminate the stair steps that continued to the ceiling, where an iron hook was set into the underneath surface of a rectangular stone slab. He handed the lantern to Vijay, then went up the steps and reached up and grasped the hook. He pulled on it, and the slab swung aside with a screeching of rollers, revealing daylight. They climbed through the opening and out into the tiny, open-sided temple, merely a stone roof supported by a pillar at each corner. On top of the slab which had covered the exit sat the Shiva *lingam* dabbed with red paste. Flowers had recently been draped on it.

"This almost certainly was an escape route," Vijay said. They looked out over the landscape, away from the direction of the town, which was out of sight on the far side of the ridge and the fort. A man, dressed in the *dhoti* and turban of a villager, and a boy, were approaching, maybe a hundred meters away, on the path that angled up the hillside and passed by the shrine.

"I wonder if we shouldn't slide the cover back on the opening," Vijay said. "It may not be a good idea for people to know about it and maybe casually get into the tunnel." Ranjit was already shoving the slab with the *lingam* back over the entrance. Vijay moved to help. Then they waited.

The villagers were apparently on their way to cut tree branches for fuel, as the thin, sun-darkened man carried a long axe, and the boy, perhaps twelve years old, carried a sickle. The man was watching the two tax men with a look of puzzlement. The boy was staring wide-eyed.

Vijay pressed his palms together and greeted them in the local dialect. The man rested the head end of his *kulhaadi* on the ground, and he and the boy returned the greetings. The man showed yellowed, protruding teeth as he asked, "Where did you come from, *sahibs*? We didn't see you when we started up the path."

"We, uh, arrived suddenly," said Vijay.

The villager scrunched his forehead in puzzlement and asked, "You are tax officers, sirs? Hunting for more treasure in the *garh*?"

"Yes." Presumably, everyone in the area had heard about the current search. The man looked about, then scratched his white-bristled chin. "I've heard stories of others who suddenly appear at this shrine."

"Yes, uncle," said the boy to the man, his eyes bright with excitement. "It's said to be a magical place."

Vijay glanced at Ranjit, who was watching the newcomers intently, presumably picking up enough words similar to the Hindi he knew that he could grasp the gist.

"What have you heard of these others?" Vijay asked.

The man replied, "My father said he saw our Maharaja and another lord appear here one evening long ago! First they weren't there, and then they were! His Highness greeted my father, and then asked him to return to the village and not to tell anyone about it." He smiled. "Of course, my father couldn't keep such a secret."

"Can we talk to your father?" asked Vijay.

The villager shook his head. "Sorry, *sahib*, he died long ago."

"I've heard," said the boy, "that one night in the darkness, there were many men carrying chests of treasure on this path!" He gestured down the hill in the direction the two had come.

Vijay darted a look at Ranjit, then back to the boy. "Can you tell us when this was?"

"Long ago, *sahib*. Before I was born."

"Who was telling you this?"

The boy hesitated, then said, "All the men in the village talk of it sometimes."

"Yes," the older villager said, "I've heard of it, too. Some of our elders claim to have seen it with their own eyes. But they were told to leave and say nothing."

"Where do they say the treasure went?" asked Vijay.

The man again rubbed his bristly chin. "Some say it disappeared on this hillside. Some say it was carried to the bottom of the hill and loaded on bullock carts and taken to the new palace. Others say it was taken to Ajmer or Jaipur. Some say it went to Udaipur."

Vijay turned to Ranjit and asked in English, "Are you following this?"

"Most of it. It's intriguing."

The man said, "This I can tell you—no one in our village has found that treasure, or they'd be rich!"

"I wonder if we should go to the village and question more people," said Ranjit.

Vijay thought for a moment, then shook his head no. "We'd hear a lot of stories, but none of them would agree. You know how people exaggerate and embellish. It's obvious no one really knows where the treasure went, assuming that's indeed what was being carried. Even that's probably based on wild guesses."

He again shifted to the local dialect and said to the man and the boy in dismissal, "We mustn't keep you from your business." He couldn't resist adding, though he knew it would just encourage gossip among the villagers, "Kindly don't tell anyone you've seen us here."

The boy's eyes widened. The man nodded, folded his hands and lowered his head, and the boy did also. Then the man hoisted his axe over his shoulder, and the two continued on the path, glancing backward repeatedly.

Ranjit smiled. "We may have started a new local legend."

"Quite possibly," said Vijay, returning the smile.

"It must be remarkable to have a couple of the tax officers suddenly appear on a bare hillside like magic!"

Vijay grinned more broadly. "I suppose it is at that."

"Let's look more carefully at the tunnel when we go back."

"Right."

They moved the slab with the *lingam* and descended underground. They slowly walked back the way they had come, both of them again carefully watching for signs of a concealed doorway or anything that might indicate a hiding place.

Below the old treasury, Ranjit said, "Let's try the other passage."

"Right." The two continued along the branch tunnel, in approximately the opposite direction, angling downward. Again they examined the rough hewn walls, ceiling, and floor, foot by foot. Eventually, the passage ended at a wooden doorway. The hinges creaked as Ranjit shoved open the door.

They climbed a stairway, on which a wooden ladder lay against the wall. At the top, Ranjit held the lantern while Vijay removed a bar and opened another wooden door. They stepped out onto a narrow ledge in a recess by a tower in the wall of the fortress. The town of Mangarh lay below.

They looked over the ledge to the rocky soil, perhaps a dozen feet down. "No doubt, this must have been another escape route," Vijay said, "using that ladder on the stairs."

"Or," said Ranjit, "also a way to enter the *garh* secretly."

"Well," said Vijay, "I didn't see anything questionable."

"Nor did I."

They silently returned to the exit by the old treasury.

The sun was setting when they arrived back in the main courtyard. Ghosali awaited them. "I was just on the phone with Batraji," he said. "He and the Revenue Minister decided there's no point in continuing. I tried to talk him into letting us stay longer, but he's an impatient man. We leave for Delhi first thing tomorrow."

Vijay and Ranjit exchanged surprised glances. Ghosali added, "You're no doubt pleased. But I think if we stayed longer, I would be proven right. All the evidence indicates there is more wealth here somewhere."

Vijay, relieved to be leaving Mangarh, shrugged. He thought of telling Ghosali of the conversation with the two villagers by the hillside shrine, but he quickly decided Ghosali needed no more encouragement.

In the *dak* bungalow that evening, the conversation was subdued, with everyone aware of the failure of the search. Most of the team members went to their rooms early. Ranjit and a couple of others remained in the dining room, drinking.

Vijay went out onto the veranda and peered up at the dark silhouette of the fort against the stars. Did the *garh* hold more secrets, or had they discovered everything of interest? It now seemed unlikely he would ever know.

He wondered about the effect of the failure on his prospects for promotion. Certainly, it seemed unfair to hold the lack of current results against him, given his previous outstanding success. Batra and his bosses certainly wouldn't be pleased this time, but Batra himself was unlikely to forget either Vijay's earlier feat or saving his life.

Unfortunately, Trilok Mishra, whose recommendations would carry considerable weight, seemed unimpressed by the prior accomplishments. Vijay would just have to wait it out and hope.

The next morning, as co-leader of the team, he went to see Kaushalya Kumari at the newer palace. She wore a peach colored *shalwar kameez*, and it seemed to him that in it she somehow looked even more beautiful than usual. "I know you'll be glad we've decided to end the search," he told her.

She raised her eyebrows in surprise. "You're all leaving?"

"Yes. Apparently those higher up decided more searching would be fruitless." His eyes examined hers. "I wish there was some way I could adequately apologize for the trouble we've caused you. For the torn up floor in the audience hall, among other things. And all the digging atop the ridge."

She gave a nod. After a moment, she said soberly, "You're not going to repair the hall or fill in the holes, I suppose?"

Vijay said with a sigh, "I'm afraid that's not the Income Tax Department's job. You can put in a claim to the government. I think you'll eventually get it all restored—after the government drops its claim of ownership—but it's out of my own hands."

"At least our elephant should be safe now."

Vijay looked away momentarily, then back at her. "I'm sorry about that, too. You must know most of us were furious about it."

"I know very well who did it." She smiled slightly for the first time. "I do appreciate, Mr. Singh, that you've personally tried not to make things harder for us. Including warning us to keep a watch on Airavata, and stopping the destruction of the audience hall."

Feeling awkward, he shrugged. "I have my job to do, but we need to stay within reasonable limits."

"Well, I hope those higher up in your department stay satisfied this time with not having found anything more."

"So do I, Princess."

14

New Delhi, April 1976

Whenever Kaushalya went to New Delhi to see her father in Tihar Jail, she would also visit Usha Chand, often at the Chand family home. This time, a big, new signboard on the route exhorted, Improve the Quality of Goods and Streamline Distribution.

A DTC bus roared by, the sign on its side urging her in capital letters: PRODUCE MORE FOR PROSPERITY. "Produce more of what?" she asked Gopi. "Those idiotic signs and slogans?"

She parked behind the Chands' blue Ambassador in the driveway of the modest bungalow, next to the flower bed bordering the small tree-shaded lawn. Despite the tensions outside, Kaushalya always felt a sense of security, of peace, in this house. It was due, of course, to the Chands themselves. They were people of such integrity, such concern about others as individuals, and about the welfare of the nation as a whole.

It was ironic, she thought, that many of their efforts had been directed toward reforming Lakshman Singh's government in the old Mangarh state. But that was so long ago that the past differences no longer mattered to those involved.

Usha met her at the door, and the two embraced. Ashok Chand appeared and folded his hands, saying, "Welcome, Kaushalya. So good to see you." It seemed to her that his hair had more gray than on her last visit, and despite his warm smile, he looked tired. The gap in his front teeth was a clear reminder to her of his past as a reformer; he had been struck there by a *lathi* wielded by one of her father's police.

Ashok Chand was always so pleasant and modest, she sometimes had to remind herself that he was famous: a fighter for freedom, a draftsman of the Indian Constitution, a former minister in the central government. And, of course, he was responsible for that legendary 1947 train ride from Pakistan.

Over tea, Kaushalya casually asked if they had seen Pratap Singh recently. Glances were exchanged between the Chands. Ashok took off his eyeglasses and set them on the table. He said solemnly, "Unfortunately, Pratap had to go into hiding. He was warned that he was to be arrested."

"Oh, God." Her body sagged. "Not Pratap! How could he be considered a danger to the state?" She thought of the cartoons he'd drawn lampooning the Prime Minister, and of the anti-Emergency newsletters he'd shown them. Maybe he had shown the wrong persons at some time. Or maybe he was even more involved in anti-government activities than she'd realized.

Usha said, "We never know who's next, it seems. We have it from a reliable source that the arrests now total well over ninety thousand!"

Kaushalya's jaw dropped. "That's unbelievable!"

Usha nodded. "Most people don't realize the extent because the press is so heavily censored, and the detainees are dispersed in so many different jails."

Ashok added, "Thirty-three members of Parliament alone are imprisoned now."

Kaushalya shook her head sadly. "It's hard to believe this is happening!" She thought about Pratap, and she tried to imagine how it must be to have to hide indefinitely from the police, never knowing from one hour to the next if one would be found out. "Do you have any idea how long Pratap will have to stay underground?"

Ashok shrugged. "There's no way to know. Certainly for some time. Maybe even until the Emergency is over, whenever that may be."

An odd feeling came over Kaushalya whenever she thought of Pratap Singh living the life of a fugitive. He was so close to her own age, and the same social class, and he thought so much the same way. If *he* had to go into hiding, then why not her, too?

The next time she visited Usha Chand, Kaushalya asked tentatively, "I don't suppose there's any way to know how Pratap is faring?"

Usha frowned, looked away. "Confidentially, of course, I hear he's doing fine. He just feels rather cooped up, since he can't go out and around."

"That's certainly understandable." Kaushalya wondered how Usha could have learned such details, but it would be awkward to ask, since the answer could reveal contact with someone who was engaged in activities now prohibited by the government.

There seemed little more to talk about over their tea, with the cloud of so many arrests hanging in the air. When Kaushalya left, Usha followed her to the door, stepped outside. "Kaushalya," said Usha, frown lines creasing her forehead, "You know you're always most welcome in our home. But you see that brown Ambassador down the street?"

Kaushalya looked. There appeared to be a couple of men in the car. "Yes?"

"We think they're secret police. A neighbor saw them writing down the license numbers of cars. I'm concerned for your safety. It might be better if we meet elsewhere after this. Why not at Tughluqabad again next time?"

Kaushalya stared at her, puzzled. "Why should it be risky for me to come here? I'm quite willing to take the chance."

Usha glanced at the brown Ambassador.

Kaushalya suddenly realized. Mortified, she said, "Oh! I've been so dense. You talk of the danger to me. But all this time I've been putting your whole family at risk! I've been selfish, with my father in prison and my family targeted by Dev Batra and the income tax people. If those security men report my license number it could make the government suspicious of you!"

Usha was staring at her. "No," she said quickly. "It's not that at all. Please believe me. We'd all gladly accept any risk for you. But we think we're already under suspicion, so you're endangering yourself by coming here."

"You're under suspicion? Aside from my visits? Is it due to Pratap coming here, too, before he went into hiding?"

"In part. I really shouldn't say more. I wish I could."

Kaushalya peered at her, knowing Usha was sincere, as she always was. "I'm still not sure I understand. But we'll meet somewhere else in the future."

Usha relaxed, smiled. "I truly think it's better. My father and mother will miss having you here, but they feel it's for the better, too. Hopefully it won't be for long."

Kaushalya hesitated, still uncertain. "Well, yes, I suppose."

Usha came to her, hugged her tightly. "Be careful," she whispered. "I care about you."

"You be careful, too." They slowly parted, gazing into each other's eyes to reassure each other of their friendship. Then Kaushalya hurried to the car.

Later, she thought about the incident. Something was not right. Why should *she* be endangered by going to the Chands, any more than visiting anyone else? With Ashok Chand's Congress affiliations, it should be one of the safer homes in Delhi to visit.

It was puzzling.

When the scheduled day for visiting arrived, Kaushalya went to Tihar again. Mahendra was in Bombay, so she came alone.

When her father appeared, she thought he looked more frail than on the last visit. "Have you been eating as much as you should, Daddyji?" she asked.

"I don't have much appetite these days." He straightened on the chair. "No cause for worry. Frankly, I think some of my fellow inmates eat too much out of boredom. A couple have even put on weight. But I think it's better to eat too little rather than too much." He managed a smile. "Look at those sadhus who claim they eat nothing but air and still supposedly live hundreds of years."

"I'm skeptical of that, Daddyji. I think you should wait on that type of practice until you're out and I can keep an eye on you."

"At least my cough's better."

"Thank God for that!"

"I have a pair of binoculars now," he said. "Ashok Chand somehow smuggled them in to me. I use them a lot at night to look at the sky."

"That was thoughtful of Chandji," said Kaushalya.

"Unfortunately, the jail has all those bright floodlights. It makes it hard to see anything besides the moon or the brightest stars. Not like Mangarh at all." Lakshman Singh smiled. "You should know the story of these binoculars. They date back to when Ashok Chand was a Congress agitator and I put him in prison. It must have been around 1940, or so, wasn't it? I gave Chandji those very same binoculars to watch the stars and the birds, to help pass the time in jail."

Kaushalya smiled back. "How ironic."

"Things do come in a circle, don't they?" said Lakshman Singh, sounding unusually philosophic.

Mangarh Jails

Mangarh, April 1939

Early on a hot morning in the month of May, the Mangarh police came again and took Ashok Chand. He resigned himself, most reluctantly, to going to jail once more.

As the black vehicle exited the gate of the old walled town, two large-eyed, skeletal children, dressed in minimal rags, raised outstretched arms and waiting palms toward the open windows of the car. Ashok found a couple of four-anna coins in his pocket, but by then, the car was already past.

The famine was now seriously hurting people in the countryside, and more and more beggars, desperate to feed their children, had been appearing at the gates of the city and at temples. Farmers, unable to feed their prized bullocks or cows, were herding the animals to other states, hoping to sell them at a fraction of their value rather than letting the animals starve.

To the Praja Mandal leaders, it appeared that the Mangarh government was doing little to help its rural people survive. The Chief Minister proposed road building and irrigation impoundment projects to provide employment. However, it would take months for effects to be seen by the people—assuming any funds remained after the numerous officials received their kickbacks from the contractors.

The government promised that shipments of grain would be distributed in the villages, but from past experience, most of the supplies would be diverted to rich traders and nobles, who would withhold it to drive up prices. Consequently, the Praja Mandal had decided to solicit donations to purchase grain which they would give to the poor or resell themselves at low prices.

The car stopped at the central police station, and Ashok was escorted to Karam Singh's office. The inspector general fixed him with the customary cold stare and said in his austere voice, "No prison this time, Mr. Chand. His Highness wants to see you. Come."

They left the building and got into another black motor car, driven by a police constable.

"Do you know what the Maharaja wants with me, sir?" asked Ashok.

"He wants to show you some things," said the inspector general. He tightened his lips, as if displeased, and added, "It will likely take much of the day."

Relieved though Ashok was at not going to jail, he was puzzled. What could Maharaja Lakshman Singh possibly have in mind?

He thought over events of the past couple weeks. The day of mourning in honor of Ram, the recently murdered Untouchable martyr to the cause of democracy and social reforms, had drawn almost a thousand people to Mangarh city. The Praja Mandal members ensured that the demonstrations were peaceful, and the inspector general and his police did not interfere with the marches or the public meetings.

The Maharaja issued a statement of regret regarding the killing and said that the policeman responsible had been disciplined. But the ruler had not promised any changes in his government.

The car arrived at the gateway to the grounds of the Bhim Bhawan Palace. On the long driveway in to the buildings, three young male *bhistis*, water carriers, were sprinkling water from big skin bags to lay the dust on the gravel. To Ashok, it seemed a waste of a scarce resource, given the drought, although it did provide employment.

Two automobiles waited in front of the steps at the palace's main entrance. The first was a larger car, windowless under its white canvas top. The silver paint gleamed like a mirror, and flags hung from small staffs mounted on the front fenders. The door bore a coat of arms. Behind that car sat a smaller, enclosed sedan. Singh's police vehicle stopped some distance behind the latter car. "Come," he told Ashok.

They walked to the lead car. A servant dressed in a green tunic and a white turban with flaming orange tail conversed briefly with Karam Singh. Then the servant hurried up the steps into the palace. "His Highness is coming shortly," Karam Singh said. Ashok wondered why they were waiting outdoors, rather than in an anteroom to an audience chamber, but he stood silently.

A swarm of male servants in the green tunics and white turbans suddenly poured from the door and formed a line down each side of the steps. Everyone stood, growing hot in the morning sun, for perhaps five minutes.

One of the servants abruptly announced, "*Maharaj sahib aa rahe hai*" ("His Highness is coming"). The Maharaja appeared at the door, wearing a gold turban with a jeweled ornament, and a gold and white embroidered tunic-like *achkan*. He was followed by yet two more male servants and a young man in a khaki uniform and green turban. As the ruler descended the stairs, the two rows of servants bowed low, touched the ground with their right hands, then straightened and brought their hands to the tops of their foreheads. Karam Singh snapped to attention and saluted until Maharaja Lakshman Singh returned the salute with a casual wave of his hand. At the same time Ashok courteously, but not obsequiously, bowed his head and pressed his palms together in greeting. The ruler folded his palms briefly in return.

"Your Highness," said Karam Singh, "I believe you've previously met Mr. Ashok Chand."

"Yes, of course. How are you today, Mr. Chand?"

"Quite well, Your Highness."

"Good. Shall we go, then? Mr. Chand, kindly join me in the front, along with the inspector general."

Even more perplexed, Ashok said, "I'm honored, Highness." Wide though the huge motor car was, he wondered how the three of them plus a driver would squeeze comfortably into the front seat. Karam Singh held the left door open and motioned him in, and Ashok slid across to sit next to the driver's spot. At the same time, a servant opened the door on the driver's side, and the Maharaja seated himself behind the steering wheel, to Ashok's right. Karam Singh climbed in on Ashok's other side.

So Lakshman Singh himself would drive. Ashok was aware of other men opening the rear doors and climbing in. Out of the corner of his eye he saw there were three of them, two servants in the green and white livery and the young man in the khaki uniform, no doubt an aide to the Maharaja. Lakshman Singh started the engine, engaged the clutch, and the car rolled around the arc of the broad driveway and sped out the approach road through the mango trees that reminded Ashok of his own family's orchards.

Lakshman Singh spoke loudly to be heard above the engine and the rush of the wind. "Mr. Chand, I have the impression you feel I somehow am out of touch with my people. That I don't know what's on their minds. Maybe even that I don't have their best interests at heart. Today, I hope to show you otherwise."

Ashok had difficulty thinking of an appropriate response. Eventually, he said merely, "I'm pleased for the opportunity, Your Highness." He wondered if the crowds at the meetings in honor of Ram's death might have worried the Maharaja enough to have provoked this response.

Sentries at the palace gate presented arms as Lakshman Singh sped out, turned left, and headed away from the town. Ashok glanced back, and through the corner of his eye, he saw the second car following. The Maharaja increased speed until Ashok felt uncomfortable. "You may wonder," Lakshman Singh shouted above the noise, "why I'm doing the driving myself. I was taught that a good ruler must be capable of doing anything his people can do. Otherwise, how can he understand them? How can he sympathize with their daily problems? And so, among other things, I learned to drive."

The Maharaja pressed loud and long on the horn as they overtook a bullock cart. The farmer lashed the animals with his stick, quickly driving them off the road to allow the car to pass. As he did so, he bowed and *salaamed* the ruler.

"My people see me at the wheel," Lakshman Singh said, "and they know I'm not afraid to do a little work myself. They know I could tell my drivers to take me wherever I want. But unless I'm in some kind of procession, I do the driving myself. That's one less person standing in the way, so to speak, between me and my people."

Ashok nodded. "I see, Highness. Most thoughtful." He tactfully refrained from pointing out that there was quite a difference between the "work" involved in driving a car, which scarcely anyone else in the state had access to, and the work most of the people did: plowing fields, hauling water, making shoes, cooking meals, laundering clothes.

The metaled road ended and became graveled. Trailing a dust cloud, the car passed one bullock cart after another driven by farmers who quickly turned onto the shoulders and bowed deeply to their ruler. A long line of burden-bearing camels also shuffled aside. Ashok became aware that the Maharaja would often slow down for no apparent reason, then he would accelerate swiftly and drive so fast as to seem almost reckless.

Lakshman Singh suddenly braked. Ashok had to thrust a hand against the wood paneled dashboard to keep from being thrown into the windscreen.

The car skidded to a halt, dust billowing around it. The Maharaja set the hand brake, shut off the engine, opened the door. They had stopped by the tomb of *pir* Mahmud.

"Everyone can come to this place, Muslims and Hindus alike. Even the Untouchables," Lakshman Singh said pointedly. "This is the tomb of *pir* Mahmud. I pay my respects to the gods and the saints in the same places my people do. They see me make offerings to the gods, and it comforts them. They know the gods will then smile on me. And hence on the people themselves. Come."

As Ashok stepped from the vehicle, he saw that the second car pulled up behind. He and Karam Singh followed the Maharaja. Several peasants were kneeling in front of the shrine, reciting prayers. From the rear of the Maharaja's car, one of the servants took a garland of marigolds which he handed to the ruler. Lakshman Singh approached the tomb and stepped from his shoes. An old, white-bearded man wearing a Muslim's cap appeared and *salaamed*. Lakshman Singh walked barefoot up to the structure and hung the garland on the front, along with several other floral offerings. He stood there quietly a moment, palms folded. Ashok noticed that the small group of worshipers had curiously eyed the Maharaja and his party for a few moments, but then they turned back to their prayers and appeared to concentrate on their worship.

The ruler turned and padded away, stepped back into his shoes, and strode toward the car. Abruptly, as if from nowhere, a peasant appeared and threw himself on the ground before Lakshman Singh. "Up," said the Maharaja. The peasant scrambled to his feet. "What do you want to say to me?" asked Lakshman Singh.

"Great King, Light of the World, Sun of Mangarh," said the man. "I'm a poor farmer from Gamri village. My neighbor stole my cow and left me with nothing. I humbly ask that you order him to return it."

"Did he have any reason?" demanded Lakshman Singh. "Had you pledged it to him for a loan?"

"Only a small loan, Maharaja. For food, since my family was starving. But how can I repay him, now that I don't have my cow? I can no longer sell my milk in the city."

The aide had stepped close to the Maharaja and was jotting down information in a large bound notebook. "How much do you owe your neighbor?" Lakshman Singh asked.

"Eleven rupees, Great King. I borrowed six rupees, and he asks five more for interest. But I no longer have so much as an anna to my name."

The ruler said to the ADC, "Give this man nine rupees. Follow up on the matter to see that it's properly resolved. Three rupees is more than enough profit on the loan."

The peasant fell to the ground and grabbed the Maharaja's feet. "I knew you would rescue me, Great King! You have given me a new life! May the gods shower their blessings on you. May you rule forever!"

Lakshman Singh extricated himself from the man and climbed back into the car. As Ashok reentered the vehicle himself, he saw the ADC count out some rupee coins for the man and take down the name. "This happens often," said Lakshman Singh quietly to Ashok. "I assure you I didn't arrange for this man to petition me. You'll see—it will happen again before we return. Probably several times." He started the engine. The ADC hurried into the rear seat. They sped away.

Off to the right, Gamri village lay in the sun. Ashok naturally thought of Ram, who had lived there in the outskirts. What a loss! Ashok had quietly begun bringing foodstuffs for Ram's wife whenever he visited the village. With little or no money to buy food, Harijans were among the first to feel the effects of the famine, and they remained among the worst sufferers.

Lakshman Singh drove farther into the countryside. By a plowed field, an elderly woman accosted him and said that her husband had been badly mauled by a panther, and they now had no source of income. The Maharaja directed that a small monthly pension be paid to the couple.

Before he could drive off, a thin woman came up to the car and held up a baby with skeleton-like limbs and bulging belly. "Please take my daughter, *Annadata*," the woman said, her voice little more than a whisper, so Ashok could barely hear her above the idling car engine. "I can't give her enough milk. I've sold all my jewelry and cooking pots, so I have nothing left. She will die if you don't take her."

Lakshman Singh sat staring at the woman and child. "Your daughter needs you," he said at last. "It's not right to take a child from her parent. This man," he indicated the ADC, "will arrange for you to get food."

The ADC stepped from the car, conferred for a minute with the woman, and noted down some information. Lakshman Singh said in a low voice to Ashok, "How can I take every hungry child? I couldn't find enough wet nurses in the palace." The ADC climbed back in the car, and the Maharaja drove off. The woman stood by the side of the road, holding her child, watching as the dust cloud rolled over them.

The car passed a flock of vultures feeding on the carcass of a large animal. "Probably a bullock that died of thirst," said Karam Singh, the first comment the inspector general had made since getting into the Maharaja's car.

The backup car always following, they drove past scattered trees with dry, dust-coated leaves and through villages baking in the heat. Each time Lakshman Singh stopped, peasants crowded around the car, complaining of the lack of food. Mothers would hold their crying, skinny, naked babies up to show the ruler.

"I know," the Maharaja would reply. "I'll do my level best to help. But we all must cope as we can."

At one place, the villagers led the ruler and his party down to a water hole at the bottom of a natural depression. The headman said, "See, *Bapji*, usually after the rains the water is up almost to the base of the trees."

The hole was large and deep, apparently excavated years ago by the people themselves. Now, only a few inches of water lay in the bottom. On the far side, a camel was drinking. "There's barely enough for ourselves," Ashok heard one farmer say to another. "We shouldn't allow animals here now."

At another spot a man hurried to throw himself in the dust in front of the Maharaja's motor car, forcing Lakshman Singh to brake hard. The man claimed his house had burned to the ground and he could not afford another. Several villagers verified the fact. Lakshman Singh ordered he be given the money to build a new one. The Maharaja drove away to cheers of *"Maharaja ki jai!"* ("Victory to the King!")

At yet another village, the ruler was obviously expected. The inhabitants had erected a welcome arch across the road, and they awaited him dressed in their finest clothes and with a small band playing. When he stepped from the car, they garlanded him and led him to a pavilion consisting of four wooden posts, a canopy of palm fronds, and a grass mat floor. He seated himself under the shade of the roof, and the villagers gathered round. An old man began massaging the Maharaja's feet, and two boys waved palm leaf fans over him. Other villagers offered sweetmeats and water and milk.

It quickly became apparent to Ashok that the villagers had invited the ruler to discuss their petition for assistance in constructing a new water impoundment for irrigating their crops. Lakshman Singh listened thoroughly, then he addressed them. "I hear you, and I understand your problems. I would very much like to help you. Unfortunately, the drought has affected me as well as you. Because my people's crops have been so poor and they have so little money this year, I've canceled many taxes, and lowered others. This means my own revenues are down, and the funds in my treasury are quite low. It is a bad time for me to fund projects such as this."

He stopped, and he sat in silence. The people in the crowd looked at each other, disappointment in their faces, but acceptance, too.

The headman bowed and folded his hands. "You are our father and our mother, Maharajaji. We know you would help us if you could."

Ashok realized that if it had been a politician or a bureaucrat turning down their request, there would have been a lengthy discussion, perhaps even arguments. And the result would have been the same.

Lakshman Singh resumed: "It is my duty to help my people. The tank which you want to build will provide jobs so you can earn money to help make up for losing your crops. It will also store water to lessen the disastrous effects of future droughts such as this one. I've therefore decided to cut back on other expenses in order to be able to pay for your project."

Instantly, a weight lifted from the shoulders of the crowd. They looked at each other with delighted expressions. Then the cheers came: *"Maharaja ki jai! Maharaja ki jai!"*

It took considerable time for Lakshman Singh to take leave of the jubilant villagers, who would have held him much longer, if they could, to prepare a celebration feast.

"They don't have enough to feed themselves," Lakshman Singh said quietly after they had left the village, "but they wanted to feast me." His eyes looked sad, and Ashok could tell that the ruler had been moved.

By now the Maharaja's party had penetrated far into the north of Mangarh state. Lakshman Singh turned south, back toward the city. Yet another group of men stopped the car. Ashok recognized them as Jats he had seen before at Ludva, where Sundip taught school.

After their salutations, the spokesman said, "Great King, we're from Ludva village. You know how poor our crops have been. Our children are going hungry. We've asked the *kamdar* to reduce our taxes. But he keeps them the same."

Lakshman Singh scowled. "You've petitioned your Thakur?"

"We have, Maharajaji. But he says he needs the revenues. He's even added a tax to pay for the marriage of his son, and also for a new motor car."

Lakshman Singh sat for a time. Then he said, "Your village is on lands where your Thakur is the ruler. There's little I can do."

"But you are the King!"

Lakshman Singh replied, "I'll talk to your lord. That's all I can promise."

The peasants, crestfallen, nodded and saluted him.

Lakshman Singh drove off. "Damn that Mangal Singh!" he said loudly. "He treats his people worse than *pi*-dogs! His lineage has always been at odds with mine. But he's an old man, and I must treat him with respect. Some day he'll want something from me, and then he'll have to listen to reason. Meanwhile, unfortunately his people must suffer!"

Ashok said cautiously, "Don't your own tenants have their problems, too, Your Highness? Besides the famine and poor crops, I mean. Few schools, hardly any doctors or hospitals, unmaintained roads, not enough wells, oppressing the bottom castes."

Lakshman Singh frowned at him. "Of course. But it's always been that way for the villagers. They don't know anything better. I must introduce improvements gradually, or the people will be upset. I'm working to better their lot, but it takes time. This drought doesn't help. I plan more public works projects like that irrigation impoundment to help lessen the impact."

Ashok could think of no tactful reply; this did not seem the appropriate time for a detailed discussion of the unjustness of the Mangarh government's tax system or the inefficiency and corruption of its bureaucracy.

Cenotaphs

Early in the afternoon, the Maharaja halted the car by the gate of a walled garden by the almost dry lake, the Hanuman Sagar, just outside Mangarh city. He led Ashok and Karam Singh into the big tree-shaded compound. There, Ashok saw perhaps a dozen large, octagonal shaped stone pavilions, each surmounted by a fluted dome. "The cenotaphs of your ancestors, Highness," Ashok said. He had passed the park on previous occasions.

"Yes, my ancestors' cremation ground. These are their memorials." The

Maharaja led Ashok to one of them. A frieze of exquisitely carved elephants in various poses encircled the structure below the carved rims of the floors. At the base near the ground, a plaque in *devanagari* script read, "Maharaja Hanuman Singhji," with the dates of his reign listed according to the Hindu calendar, roughly translated as 1530 to 1600 A.D. Lakshman Singh bowed his head and folded his hands in respect for a moment. Ashok and Karam Singh did likewise. "Probably the greatest of my ancestors," said Lakshman Singh. "After withstanding the siege at Chittorgarh, he made peace with the Mughal Emperor Akbar, who would otherwise have conquered Mangarh. He then guided Mangarh to its height of prosperity."

He took them to another cenotaph. "Maharaja Arjun," he said. "A great general for the Mughal armies. A great builder of temples. At another cenotaph: "Maharaja Ganesh. A great builder also."

He stopped before another and paid honor to the ancestor. He said, "Maharaja Madho Singh. Possibly somewhat of a rogue, but a great patron of the arts. Mangarh's wealth grew even more under his reign. He was quite clever at keeping in the good graces of Emperor Aurangzeb."

He gestured to another: "Maharaja Sangram Singhji." Finally, he halted at another and paid his respects. "My own father. Maharaja Bhim Singhji. He built the palace where I live. That's why it's named Bhim Bhawan, you know."

As he led them back to the car, the Maharaja said simply, "This is my heritage, my burden if you will. I must carry on my family tradition in the spirit of my ancestors. I feel my duty to my people most keenly. I have a bond with them going back many hundreds of years."

Ashok could only nod.

They returned to the palace in silence.

There, Maharaja Lakshman Singh shut off the engine. He turned to Ashok and said, "Now you've seen. I'm like a father to my people. They even call me '*Bapji*,' Respected Father.' Do you still think I'm not doing a good job for them?"

"Highness," said Ashok, "I've never doubted your sincerity, or your love for your people. And I'm impressed by their strong feelings for you in return. But—" he paused while he tried to frame his thoughts in a tactful manner.

"But you still think I need all these modern reforms you want."

"Essentially, that's correct, Your Highness." He hesitated, then resumed, "I know you are motivated only by the highest sense of duty and of love for the citizens of Mangarh. But you alone—acting through your officials in most cases, but nevertheless at your own direction—still determine what your government does. The people themselves have no say. They must rely totally on you to decide what is best for them."

Lakshman Singh frowned. "It's always been that way, Mr. Chand, for thousands of years in Mangarh. Through an unbroken chain of my ancestors. All of them have known it's their *dharma*, their life's work, their purpose in being, to serve their people. All of my youth I was trained for only that. Who else is better qualified to know what's best for the people? The politicians who would take over?"

"The people themselves," Ashok replied quietly.

Lakshman Singh raised his eyebrows. "'The people themselves,' you say. But the people are simple, uneducated. Shrewd politicians could easily manipulate them. How are the people to know what is best? The world is getting more complicated by the day."

"Exactly, Highness. That's why more schools are needed, more education. All the people should be given the chance to learn."

Lakshman Singh sat staring at him.

"And if I may, Highness—another factor to consider. You yourself are dedicated to ruling in the best interests of your people. But there have been occasional rulers in the past, have there not, who were more selfishly motivated? What is to prevent that from happening again?"

The Maharaja nodded. "Rulers must be properly trained. They must be made aware of their heritage and their duties. I intend to ensure that's the case when I have children of my own."

Ashok persisted, "Take the Thakur of Baldeogarh, for example. He's far from loved by most of his people. Shouldn't the people have the right to petition him to change his ways, and perhaps even to remove him eventually if he doesn't?"

"He's their lord," said Lakshman Singh, a look of astonishment in his eyes. "Does a son reject his father simply because they disagree?"

Ashok struggled for the words to make him understand.

But the Maharaja said, in a slight change of subject, "I must tell you I very much regret the death of that Bhangi. You know I ordered the policeman who was responsible to be disciplined. I would never have permitted the beating if I'd been there. I want you to know I've also ordered a stipend sent to the widow."

Ashok gave a nod.

Lakshman Singh peered at him. "Mr. Chand, I need a Minister of Education in my government. Given your interest in that area, I thought of you. I think that in spite of our disagreements, you could serve well in that position. It would give you a genuine opportunity to expand education in Mangarh as you wish. Naturally, an ample stipend goes with the post. If you're interested, you can work out the details with my Dewan."

At first Ashok was too taken aback to reply. Was Lakshman Singh really so worried as to try to buy him with such an offer? It was out of the question to accept, of course. He would be able to accomplish little in an administration that was so hostile to him and much of what he believed in. At last Ashok said, "I'm sincerely honored, Your Highness. But, regretfully, I think my other commitments preclude me from accepting the post at the moment."

Without another look at Ashok, the Maharaja got down from the car and mounted the steps between bowing lines of servants.

After leaving Karam Singh, Ashok went to Manohar Jain's nearby trading office. There, he found that word had been passed of his being picked up by the police, and that his Praja Mandal friends were meeting at the Arora's home to try to decide what to do to help. He hurried to the large house on the outskirts of the city.

He was warmed at seeing the relief on their faces, particularly Jaya's, when he walked in. Even Dr. Arora was there, having left his patients to fend for themselves in the front room clinic.

Ashok briefly told them where he'd been.

"We were terribly worried," said Kishore between draws on his cigarette. "No one had any idea what they'd done with you."

Jaya asked incredulously, "You actually spent most of the day with the Maharaja himself? What did he say? Did you convince him to make any changes?"

"I tried," said Ashok, still trying to assimilate what had occurred. "I don't think we can expect much to come of it, at least not soon. He's convinced that since he knows what's best for the people, there's no point in getting them involved. And he distrusts politicians."

"He may have a point there," said Dr. Arora with a chuckle. "But they're the price we will need to pay for democracy."

"Better to have politicians," said Sundip Saxena, "than lords like the Thakur of Baldeogarh."

A couple of them laughed ironically.

Jaya's mother said, "We must have His Highness worried, at least a little, if he went to so much effort with you."

"He even offered me the Education Ministry," said Ashok.

"He didn't!" said Jaya.

Kishore, cigarette in hand, stared at Ashok. "What did you say to him?"

"Naturally, I turned it down."

Kishore rubbed his chin thoughtfully. "It might have been a good opportunity for you."

Ashok gave a short laugh. "I hardly think so. His Highness merely wanted to get me under his thumb, so he could ensure I kept quiet."

"Still," said Kishore, "it could have made you quite wealthy." He snuffed out his cigarette in the ashtray.

"You wouldn't have accepted it yourself?" asked Manohar, raising his eyebrows.

Kishore shrugged. "I didn't have the chance. But it might have provided a forum to do some good for the people."

"I doubt it," said Jaya, her eyes narrowing as she stared at him. "Anyway, the cost would have been too high." She turned to look at Ashok, and he saw what he felt sure was genuine admiration.

2

Ludva Village, Baldeogarh Thikana, June 1939

It was the hottest period of the year, and Ashok was glad to be seated in the shade of the big *pipal* and *neem* trees. Kumbharam Jat, who was tall and energetic at over sixty years of age and who boasted an abundant white mustache, strode over to him and said, "You should stay behind, Ashokji. What we're about to do may be even more dangerous for an outsider than for ourselves."

Ashok indeed was apprehensive about going to petition the notorious Thakur Mangal Singh, the absolute ruler of the largest *thikana* in Mangarh state, at his fortress. Despite the drought and famine, the Thakur had refused to reduce taxes. He was unpredictable and irascible, and the Jats risked at least the possibility of eviction from their homes and their farms, most of which had been in their families for generations. They also risked physical injury if the Thakur should be angry enough to order them attacked by his police.

"No," Ashok said, "I want to stand with you. Besides, as we've said, we should be safe on a *durbar* day." The Thakur would be holding court, and the Jats had calculated that Mangal Singh would not want the decorum of his *durbar* ruined by unseemly violence. Since over a hundred Jat farmers had promised to attend in support of the petition, it was also hoped that the Thakur would be reluctant to risk an assault on such a large number of men.

Kumbharam gave a nod and marched over to where his family was assembled. Sundip Saxena taught school in Ludva, so it was the first village where Ashok and Sundip had worked to help the Jats organize themselves. The not unpleasant odor of cow dung hung in the air. Being populated predominantly by farmers of the vigorous, hard working Jat caste, Ludva was well-kept, and the residents frequently boasted to outsiders about having one of the few schools in Mangarh state. Although small, with openings on three sides, the school was one of the few brick structures in the village, and the pride of everyone.

Ashok had found the situation in the Mangarh villages such as this quite different from that of the canal colonies of the Punjab. There, most of the farmers were relatively recent settlers who had obtained their land directly from the British-administered government. But in Mangarh, the feudal system had been in place for centuries, and the peasants could be forced to work for the nobility, for little or no compensation, at any time. Taxes were heavy, and new ones could be added at the whim of the village ruler. In theory, many of the peasants held rights to the land they tilled; in practice they could be evicted almost at will by their landlords.

Ashok joined Sundip and watched as Kumbharam stopped for a moment and looked at his house, clean and whitewashed, and sheltered by an ancient *neem* tree, which looked dry now under its coating of dust. His son Taru, who stood as tall as Kumbharam but was broader in build, bent and embraced his own young son and his two little daughters in turn, then stood and gazed for a moment at his wife. Although men and women could not show affection for each other in public, it was clear the couple realized that on this day their lives might well be changed forever.

"Shall we go?" asked Kumbharam loudly.

Taru gave a nod, and they climbed aboard their bullock cart. Ashok and Sundip clambered in also. These farmers had managed to keep their bullocks in spite of the drought and famine, although the animals looked thin, with bones pressing prominently against their hides. In honor of the occasion, Kumbharam and Taru had painted their bullocks' horns in broad green, white, and red bands like the colors of the Congress flag.

They rolled out of the village, and the remaining carts pulled into line behind, stirring up a huge cloud of dust. Ashok tended to forget how uncomfortable bullock carts were to a person not accustomed to them. They traveled at roughly the same speed as a person walking, and with no springs for cushioning, the riders felt every bump, almost every pebble in the ill-kept road. There was no canopy for shade, and the sun beat down as if intent on roasting the occupants. Being in the lead vehicle at least meant the dust was minimized for Ashok and his cart mates.

The procession rolled along the lanes between fields. At the next village, other Jats joined in. And more at still the next village. Then, on the horizon, they could see the domes and battlements of Baldeogarh castle rising above its own small town. Ashok looked backward and made a rough count. "Almost a hundred men," he murmured to Sundip. "Considering the risks, it's a remarkable turnout."

"It certainly is!" Sundip said. "This should give Mangal Singh's police second thoughts about giving us a hard time."

The closer they drew to the fortress, the more subdued became the Jats. It was as if some invisible ominous cloud hung over the spot, dampening the spirits of anyone approaching.

The guards at the gateway in the town wall eyed the procession with open hostility as they motioned for the Jats to park their carts outside. There would not be room for so many vehicles in the town itself.

Inside, several citizens stared as if not knowing what to think, as the Jats strode through the narrow, twisting, cobblestoned streets toward the fortress. Too soon for Ashok, the bastions of the castle gate loomed above.

It was so silent in the *durbar* courtyard that when one of the seated Rajput nobles shifted position, the clink of his buckler startled a couple of his neighbors. Despite big awnings suspended from the adjacent buildings, the paving and the rock walls radiated heat, turning the enclosure into a gigantic oven.

To Ashok, it seemed miles across that floor between the two rows of hostile eyes to the *gadi* where the scowling Thakur Mangal Singh awaited the petitioners.

Most of the hundred-odd peasants remained some distance from the Thakur, crowding about the entry archways. But Kumbharam marched boldly up to the throne, made his obeisance, and deposited the coin that was his gift. Three younger Jat men did likewise, as did Ashok and Sundip.

Kumbharam, standing stiff and straight, tall as a tent pole, held out the petition. The seated Thakur, white-bearded and of similar age, but quite short in stature, held his head rigid as he ignored the document and glared past Kumbharam at the assembled farmers.

It was ironic, thought Ashok, that neither Kumbharam nor Thakur Mangal Singh could read the document. Both were illiterate. Ashok and Sundip had done the drafting of the peasants' demands.

Eventually, the *kamdar*, the Thakur's chief revenue official, casually took the paper. He was short and fat, and the sides of his *achkan* were darkened from sweat. He did not bother to look at the document.

Ashok had assumed there would be no opportunity to present the request verbally; it was more or less a formality to offer the petition at the Thakur's *durbar*. But he had not reckoned on Mangal Singh's temper.

"What is the meaning of this?" snarled the Thakur.

Kumbharam drew backward almost imperceptibly, but he kept his composure, even in the face of the anger of the lord who held almost total power over him and the other farmers. "Sire, *Annadata*, we who are your humble servants respectfully request that you withdraw your recent new taxes. As you know, *Bapji*, our crops have not been good. These taxes are a very heavy burden on us. We also ask that you no longer require us to work for you without pay. We feel it is not fair—"

"—How dare you question my rights!" the Thakur interrupted, his face reddening. "I have always had these rights, like my father before him, and his father before him! All the way back to Lord Baldeo, who once sat on the *gadi* of all of Mangarh!"

Kumbharam hesitated. His face was perspiring, perhaps from fear as well as from the heat. Such overt anger and harsh words were never seen in the Jat councils to which he was accustomed. Recovering, he replied, his voice quavering but still definite, "This is true, *Annadata*. But we feel it's time to change. We—"

"—Time to change! What makes it time to change? Because that idiot Nehru says so? Because that lawyer Gandhi who pretends to be so holy says so? Or because these men—" he abruptly gestured toward Ashok and Sundip "—who are not even from my *thikana* say so?"

Kumbharam opened his mouth, but the Thakur continued, "Why do you listen to them? Why do you let these city men, these agitators, turn you against your own lord, who has been a father to you for your entire lives?"

"*Bapji*, you are still a father to us. But we, your sons, have heavy burdens. We are counting on your well known love for us all, on your generosity, to lighten our loads."

The Thakur glared at the old peasant. For a time, both stared at each other, neither moving. Then Kumbharam lowered his eyes. He quickly raised them again. "*Bapji*, some of these taxes do not seem right to us. The one to buy you a new motor car...."

"What?" asked the corpulent *kamdar*. "Why shouldn't your Thakur have a new motor car? Surely you don't want him to feel ashamed in the presence of his fellow lords when he goes to Mangarh city for the Maharaja's *durbar*?"

"Your Honor," replied Kumbharam, "we are always glad for our Thakur *sahib* to have a new motor car. But perhaps he might get by with his present one for another year when times are bad for his people. Mightn't the other lords praise him for his sacrifices on behalf of his children?"

The *kamdar* glared at Kumbharam. You're too clever by far for a Jat peasant, he seemed to be thinking.

Kumbharam continued, "*Bapji*, the petition also protests the shooting last month of the Jat bridegroom who was riding a horse in his wedding procession. We see no reason why the privilege of riding a horse should be limited to Rajputs."

The Thakur was staring incredulously at him. "Leave at once," Mangal Singh growled in a voice so low those at the far edge of the crowded floor could not have heard.

The petitioners made their obeisances and backed away. The Rajputs lining the aisle were muttering to each other, eyeing the Jats.

"I think we'd better leave fast," whispered Ashok when they reached the pillars of the entry arches. He had been certain it would be safe to present the petition; surely the Thakur would not breach hospitality by harming the Jats at his own fortress. Now Ashok had doubts. Mangal Singh and his men were so clearly hostile. They might not be above punishing the peasants as a lesson to others who might want conditions changed.

The petitioners hastened down the cobblestoned ramp, out the castle gate, and through the town to their bullock carts. Kumbharam and Taru climbed into their own vehicle, and Ashok and Sundip and several Jats joined them. Taru immediately drove off, and the other Jats, many in carts, many walking, followed.

"Thakurji is like a bull elephant," said Kumbharam. "He's king of his herd, and nobody will budge him if he doesn't want to move."

"Better hope the elephant doesn't turn into a hungry man-eating tiger, Father," said Taru.

The sun beat down as if to add its own oppression to the occasion. Ideally, the Jats would have waited until dusk to begin to travel.

"What do we do next?" Sundip asked.

Ashok looked at Kumbharam and said, "That's up to the farmers. As we discussed before, a meeting of all the Jats of the *thikana* might be in order. They can decide whether they want to begin refusing to pay the taxes and resisting the forced labor."

"I know what *I* want," said Kumbharam. "If we back down now, we'll never make any progress."

"Father, we could lose everything," said Taru. "Our lands, our cattle, maybe even our house."

"So we could," said Kumbharam calmly, as if it were of no consequence to lose all he had labored for his entire life. Ashok watched the old man in admiration.

"If the Thakur's officials confiscate our land, how will we live?" asked Taru. "How will we feed our families?"

"A way will be found," said Kumbharam. "It may be difficult, but a way will be found. We can't continue to suffer these injustices. We're Jats. We're descended from the same stock as the Rajputs. Why should they look down on us? Just because we don't eat meat and we allow our widows to remarry? Just because our women work alongside us instead of hiding in *purdah*?"

"They'll never agree we're equal to them, Father."

"Of course not. But they have no right to oppress us. To keep us poor by seizing the fruits of our labor and calling it taxes."

"*Rais hain,*" ("They are the lordly ones") said one of the other Jats in the cart.

That summed up the attitude of most of peasants, thought Ashok, the attitude that kept them in bonds and in debt throughout their lives. The attitude that gave power to the upper castes. *Rais hain.* And therefore the nobles' most outrageous behavior could be excused.

Shouts came from the carts in the rear. Ashok and the others looked back.

A cloud of dust plumed about a large number of horsemen rapidly overtaking the peasants. Ashok felt a sinking in the pit of his stomach. The riders could only be Rajputs, since no one else had so many horses. And the Rajputs in Baldeogarh had been furious.

A gunshot rang out from the horsemen. And another.

Ashok looked about for concealment. In the crowded cart there was no room to crouch behind the wooden sides. The driver of the cart behind panicked, rolling full tilt off into the rough field. Several horsemen veered off to follow him. The other Rajputs surrounded the leading carts and peasants.

One of the horsemen, followed by several others, rode up to the head cart.

It was Thakur Mangal Singh. He held his rifle cradled in his arm but did not point it toward the peasants. Not so with his men; several of them aimed their guns at the Jats.

"Out of the cart!" shouted the Thakur. "It's time you learned how to behave toward your betters."

There was a moment's hesitation, then Kumbharam and the others, Ashok and Sundip included, climbed from the cart.

"On the ground!" shouted the Thakur. "Flat on the ground!"

The farmers again hesitated a moment, but the sight of the aimed guns quickly decided them. Everyone fell into the dust.

Except Kumbharam. And Ashok Chand.

"On the ground!" screamed the Thakur.

The men stood in the full blaze of the sun, which threatened them almost as much as the Rajputs. "*Bapji*," replied Kumbharam, gazing up at the mounted ruler, "it's not right that you treat us this way."

"How dare you defy me! On the ground! At once!"

Kumbharam stared at him a few moments. Then, slowly, he lowered himself to his stomach on the soil.

Ashok remained standing.

"You, too, agitator! On the ground!"

"If I may, Thakurji, I'd first like to ask a question," said Ashok. His knees were shaking, but he was surprised that his voice remained calm. "I'm puzzled by one matter."

The Thakur scowled. "On the ground!"

"But Thakurji, you're a Rajput lord, and I have a question only you can answer about Rajputs."

The Thakur drew his torso back slightly, his eyes blasting anger, but also looking puzzled. He barked, "Be quick."

"Lord, we don't have Rajputs where I'm from. But I've always been told how valorous they are. How their *dharma*, their duty, is to protect the farmers under their patronage. So I'm puzzled by how you could think of attacking unarmed men. Could you enlighten me, sir, as to how a Rajput could do this?"

The Thakur stared down at Ashok, face turning purple with rage. Mangal Singh all but screamed, "These farmers have duties to their lord—just as their Thakur has duties to them! In the old days peasants would never have dared defy their lord as these have done!"

Ashok nodded slowly. "I see. What, then, do you plan to do, Lord?"

"Teach them! When they feel our whips on their backs, they'll remember who the gods have placed on earth to rule them!"

"You'd—you'd whip them? Just for bringing a petition to you?"

The Thakur's horse shifted, its tail swishing at flies. Mangal Singh said, "Be glad we don't use them as target practice for our guns! You too, agitator—on the ground!"

Ashok opened his mouth to say, "You can't get away with this!"

But then he realized: He *can* get away with it. He has the power of life and death in his domains.

"No," said Ashok. "Shoot me."

The Thakur stared at him, forehead creasing in puzzlement.

Ashok said, "What's the difference if you whip me or shoot me? Either way, I can't fight back. What would your ancestors say if they saw you now?"

The Thakur glanced over the scene: the farmers lying flat on the ground, the Rajput horsemen with their rifles ready, the empty bullock carts, Ashok standing alone, the sun threatening to bake them all if they did not have the sense to find shade before long.

The Thakur sat still for a time in his saddle. Then he gestured toward Ashok and Kumbharam's group and shouted to his men, "Take these leaders to my jail! Seize all the carts and bullocks for the taxes these Jats owe me. Let the others walk home in the heat. That will show my mercy!"

Mangal Singh wheeled his horse about and sped back in the direction of Baldeogarh, several of his retinue trailing him.

Ashok did not see the Thakur again. But he saw all too much of the Thakur's jailers.

The captors took him and Sundip and Kumbharam and Taru in one of the bullock carts to Baldeogarh fort. There, in a basement chamber, they stripped the prisoners naked and tied them face downward to wooden frames. A jailer vigorously thrashed their buttocks with thin bamboo canes.

The captors then untied the bruised, cut, bleeding men, returned their clothes, and locked them into a single cell. The low ceilinged, stone-walled room was so hot as to be almost unbearable. It stank from the sewage pit in the corner, where flies buzzed about by the thousands.

The prisoners survived the night, but Ashok could not recall ever being so miserable, even in the Mangarh Central Jail.

The next day, the jailers tied the captives one at a time on their backs on a wood table. They thrashed the soles of the prisoners' bare feet with bamboo staffs. Ashok felt sure some of the bones of his feet must be broken. He could barely manage to hobble, in great pain, back to the cell.

There they remained for two days, sweltering in the heat and nursing their battered feet and their cut buttocks, trying to keep the flies off their wounds.

The jailers furnished the captives with buckets of water. Warm water, and of questionable cleanliness, but it was wet and it kept them alive.

Then, jailers again stripped Ashok, Sundip, Kumbharam, and Taru bare, led them to the wooden frameworks, and forced them to bend over and spread their legs. The prisoners' wrists and ankles were tied to the frames. The jailers then thrust sticks dipped in chili powder up the captives' rectums.

The pain-wracked prisoners were returned to the hot cell and left to sweat for two more days.

In addition to being in constant misery, Ashok was outraged. Though he had heard such practices existed, it was quite another matter to be a victim of them. He found it impossible to comprehend how the Thakur and his jailers could treat other human beings in such a way.

He wondered what Gandhiji would do in his place. Pray for forgiveness for the torturers, probably.

Ashok wanted to somehow take immediate action against those responsible. Not, of course, to inflict the same tortures on the jailers—that would make him no better than they. But to bring them to justice.

There was no advance notice of the prisoners' release, so no one was waiting when the *thikana* police marched Ashok and Sundip Saxena and Kumbharam Jat and Taru out the gateway of Baldeogarh fort. All four walked gingerly, their soles still tender, their anuses burning.

The police shoved Ashok hard, and he fell sprawling on the hot cobblestones. Kumbharam and his son moved to help, but Ashok painfully drew himself to his feet.

"Well," said Kumbharam, whose eyes were dull and who now looked as if he had suffered every one of his sixty-plus years, "If we didn't know before why we fought, we do now."

Ashok again wondered if having the stick dipped in chili powder shoved up his rectum had done permanent injury. And he had never been more frustrated. How could he bring punishment to those evil, ignorant monsters, so that they could understand what they inflicted on others? And so it would never happen again?

But there were immediate, practical concerns.

"We've a long walk," said Taru, "especially with no water."

Ashok took a step and winced. He cast an eye about in the hope of seeing someone who might offer them a ride, but he saw no one. They managed to limp a mile outside the town on the hot, dusty plain before a farmer gave them a lift in his cart, and water to drink. As they jarred along the rough road, Ashok wondered how long it might be before he could walk again without pain.

They soon discovered they had become heroes; word had spread of how Kumbharam and Ashok had stood up to the feared Thakur himself. Rather than being cowed by the Thakur, most of the Jat peasantry were outraged. They talked of holding a strike when the time seemed right.

Gradually, Ashok's physical pains subsided. What remained was the fear of another incarceration, and more torture, in the dungeon of Baldeogarh castle if he were to continue working in that *thikana*.

For the moment, he took a break from trying to assist the Jats. But the diversion was only temporary, he assured himself.

3

Kapani Village, West Punjab, June 1939

The Punjab, though it was Ashok's home, felt even hotter than Rajputana. The sky was a broad, featureless glare, and the soil was dry and cracked. Still, the flatness of the landscape was welcome after the arid hills of Mangarh.

"Son! You're so thin. And so pale!" was his mother's greeting.

But his father said, "You look healthy enough. A little thin, though, as your mother says. Better eat lots of my mangos. I notice you waited for the season before you came to visit."

Ashok grinned. "I did think of that."

Savitri looked even prettier than before, if that were possible. Her schooling had continued, and she was enthusiastic about her studies, and about the possibility of going to medical college in a few years.

He found, to his surprise, that his brother Prabhu had left home, and that no one knew where the young man had gone. "Probably," said Yogesh Chand in disgust, "out blowing up railroads somewhere. I hoped the RSS might help him. Instead it put a lot of no good ideas into him."

"So they're actively involved in terrorism," Ashok said, frowning. The Rashtriya Swayamsevak Sangh was a militant organization, and he'd heard occasional talk about its fanaticism, but he'd paid little attention. Its methods were far removed from the approach of Gandhiji.

"They're even more anti-Muslim than they are anti-British," his father replied. "But all that training in fighting with sticks and so on—it's clear to me that in the long run they want action, not talking. Your brother got so he wouldn't even stay in the house when Mubarak Khan comes over."

Ashok found that incredible. Mubarak Khan was like a member of the family. So what if he was a Muslim?

Yogesh Chand proudly set down a basket of his latest mango crop for sampling. "These are Dussheris."

Ashok bit off the end of one and sucked at the flesh. "It's delicious, Father."

"Yes. This stock came from the Lucknow area. I've started trying to raise some Alphonsos from near Bombay. I don't know if they'll like our climate here or not. I'm also trying Raspunias. They're juicy, supposed to be especially good for sucking."

"Tell us about your arrest," urged his mother.

"It wasn't exactly an arrest, Ma. More like an abduction." While devouring mangos Ashok related his experiences, leaving out the torture with the hot chilies.

Everyone fell silent, trying to imagine experiencing the horrors. Eventually, his mother asked with a change of subject, "How are we going to get our sons married? Prabhu never writes us, and we hardly ever see you."

Ashok thought of Jaya. Should he mention her? It was still far from certain her family would prefer him over other possible men, even over Kishore. He said, "It's best we not think of it now. Not so long as I'm in Mangarh, anyway."

"We could at least arrange a betrothal."

Ashok shook his head. "Not yet, Mother. I don't know how long I'll be tied to Mangarh, and it wouldn't be fair to keep someone waiting."

"It's not unheard of for engagements to be long, or even for husbands and wives to be separated a long time," she persisted.

Ashok struggled for words. "I, uh, well, I could be imprisoned again, you know. I hope not, but if it did happen, it could be for some time. I just don't think I'd want anyone to be worrying about me if that happened."

"Other than us, you mean," said his mother.

"Of course, that's what I meant, Ma."

When they were alone, Savitri said to him, "It almost sounds as if you have some other reason for not wanting Mother to look for a wife. You haven't already found a girl you fancy?"

Ashok hesitated. He'd never mentioned his attraction to Jaya to anyone here, other than to Joginder Singh on his previous visit. But he'd always felt close to his sister, despite their age difference. He said, "There's a young woman in Mangarh. I'm very fond of her. Her family and she were the ones who visited me in jail."

"She's our own caste?"

"Yes, she's an Arora."

Savitri smiled broadly, her large eyes lit with excitement. "I'm so glad. You need someone there who cares about you."

Ashok smiled tightly. "I have friends like Sundip Saxena, you know. I've mentioned him."

She rested her hand on his arm and smiled back at him. "That's different."

Mangarh, July 1939

Ashok had sent word to his friends in the Praja Mandal of the date of his arrival. He stepped from the train at Mangarh Junction and strode toward the waiting tongas. He was thinking of Jaya, hoping he'd have the opportunity to see her this very day.

Two men in the khaki uniforms of the Mangarh police approached. One said, "Mr. Chand, I have a copy here of an order banning you from Mangarh state. Come with us."

"Oh, no," said Ashok under his breath. Not jail again so soon. But he straightened his back and composed his face.

They put him in a car, and drove him not toward Mangarh city, but the opposite direction. In half an hour, a striped pole barred further passage along the road. By it were a small guard station and customs house. The state border.

One of the police handed Ashok five one-rupee coins. "A bus will be along soon, Mr. Chand. We'll see you get on it. You're not to come back, or you may be jailed. Is that clear?"

"Quite."

He wondered how they'd known when and where he was arriving.

Five days later, he was on a bus nearing Baldeogarh, on the way to Mangarh city. A feeling of dread grew as he came ever closer to the fortress where he had been jailed and tortured. He wished the bus would not stop at the station at Baldeogarh, but unfortunately that place was a fixed part of the route to Mangarh. What if he somehow fell into the hands of the Thakur's police again?

He told himself he was being foolish. Yet, as he watched the town draw near it seemed as if the very air were oppressive. Villagers on the road gave the impression of being sullen and unhappy. Even the peacocks in the fields appeared listless, their tails dragging.

Once again, he had sent word to the Praja Mandal to expect him. He was somewhat fearful of ending up in a Mangarh jail again, but this was more than balanced by his eagerness to resume his work and to see Jaya, not necessarily in that order of importance.

The bus pulled into the loading area of the small station at Baldeogarh. Ashok tensed as he saw a group of three uniformed men wearing the khaki of the Mangarh state police, and a couple of men in the green of the Baldeogarh *thikana* police.

The police waited while the departing passengers left the bus, then two of the khaki-clad officers of the state police climbed aboard. Ashok pretended to ignore them, but he felt sweat breaking out on his forehead and palms.

The state policemen stood a moment at the front, then they moved along the aisle toward him. They stopped, and one said, "Ashok Chand, we have orders to take you into custody. Come."

He was trembling, terrified that they would turn him over to the *thikana* police, but he did as they directed. They escorted him to a black car. He let out his breath and sagged in relief when they drove away from Baldeogarh.

Again, they took him to the border of the state and released him. One said, "By now, Chand, you know there's no point in trying to evade us. If you come again, you really are going to jail."

Ashok decided Karam Singh had one hell of a good spy system.

He spent a week in Delhi before returning. This time, a driver for the wealthy Congress supporter, Adinatha Seth, took Ashok in a private motor car.

They passed the checkpoint at the state border with no difficulty. The customs official barely glanced at Ashok before waving the car on.

It was late afternoon when the car arrived at the outer fortifications of Mangarh city. There it was stopped by police, who again took Ashok into custody. "We have an order to confine you, Mr. Chand," said the senior officer.

Somehow, they had again known of his arrival. There was an informer in the inner circles of the Praja Mandal, and Ashok was quite certain who it was.

Would he be tortured again? Hopefully, that wouldn't be permitted now that Maharaja Lakshman Singh was better acquainted with him. But the Maharaja didn't necessarily know how the police interpreted their duties.

4

Instead of delivering him to the Central Jail, the police took him in a black van through the narrow streets of the old, walled section of Mangarh city. The vehicle entered the gateway of the ancient fortress. Engine roaring, it slowly climbed the steep, rough, stone-paved road, passing the palace wings and curving up behind the lower levels. The van entered a gate near the very top of the hill. Ahead, Ashok saw a separate, low, squarish castle with rounded bastions at its corners and a couple of taller, twin towers in the center. The vehicle drove through the arched gateway in the middle of the castle wall and stopped in a courtyard with a large *pipal* tree toward one side.

The escorting police came to the back of the van, opened the doors, and beckoned for Ashok to step out. Waiting were two short, slender men in bulky white turbans and green coats who led Ashok and the police through a broad doorway. Ashok assumed these men must be Bhil tribals who guarded the fort. The party escorted him down a short hallway to where an iron door stood ajar.

"Inside," said one of the policemen.

Ashok entered. The room was of rough stone. A barred window pierced the thick wall slightly above eye level. The room contained a *charpoy*, a bedroll, a bucket, and a small wooden table. On the table sat a brass water pot. A niche in one of the walls held an oil lamp.

The escort left. One of the guards closed the door with a clanking sound that echoed about the small stone room. The key turned in the lock.

Ashok glanced about, knowing he would likely have ample time to get to know the room thoroughly. He saw little of interest other than the items first noticed.

He sat cross-legged on the cot, and he thought. Almost a year in Mangarh so far. Was it worth it having been so persistent about coming back, if this was to be his fate?

He had worked hard during the year, and much had happened. Still, he could not truly say the Praja Mandal had yet accomplished any of its aims. Maharaja Lakshman Singh had not instituted a single reform. Neither had Thakur Mangal Singh of Baldeogarh. And the Untouchables still did not have their temple entry rights or any other privileges.

Yet, Ram had been killed. Ashok and other leaders had been jailed—and tortured—by both the Maharaja and the Thakur.

The timekeeper's gong rang, announcing seven o'clock in the evening. A key turned in the lock. The door swung open, and one of the white turbaned, green coated guards entered, a young man of slight build, carrying a metal tray. "Time for food, *sahib*," he said.

Ashok had not eaten for many hours, so he was hungry, and the aroma was appealing. The guard placed the tray on the table, then stood and waited.

Ashok sat on the edge of his cot, tore off a piece of *roti*, and used it to scoop up some *dal*. He said with surprise, "The *rotis* and *dal* are still hot."

The guard gave a slight smile and said, "They're from the old palace kitchens nearby, *sahib*. The cook has instructions for you to have fresh and healthy food, though simple."

Ashok thought for a moment. Given that the guard addressed him respectfully and that care was being taken with his meals, it sounded as if he would likely be treated reasonably well, presumably with no torturing. He asked, "Do you have other prisoners to feed?"

The young guard shook his head no. "Only yourself, *sahib*."

Ashok raised his eyebrows. "So this is not a regular jail?"

The guard again shook his head. "It's used only rarely. For important prisoners. You're the first in several years."

"I see. Surely, the guards aren't here solely because of me?"

"The guards are here because of the treasury, *sahib*. Now we will guard you also."

Ashok frowned, puzzled. "You'd put a prisoner right next to the treasury?"

The guard smiled broadly. "Not any prisoner. Not a robber. He would be put in the Central Jail. But you're different."

Ashok continued his meal, deciding not to mention that he had spent his share of time in the Central Jail also. He asked, "Are you a Bhil?"

"Yes, *sahib*. All the guards are Bhils. It's been our duty to guard this place and the rest of the fort for many generations."

"I see." Ashok chewed on a piece of *roti*. "I assume I can have visitors?"

The Bhil gave a nod. "Once a week, sir, two persons at a time. A policeman must be present during the meetings and listen."

"I can send and receive mail?"

"Yes, but the police must first read it."

Ashok fell silent. Then he asked, "Is it true there's a great treasure stored here? In underground vaults?"

The young Bhil smiled and looked away. "Many men ask us that. We're sworn not to reveal what we guard. Only what many people already know—part of this building has been a treasury for His Highness for many years. There are other strong rooms, also."

Ashok asked, "Will I be allowed out to exercise?"

"Of course, sir. You may use the courtyard. Please call to us when you want to go out. One of us will come and unlock your door."

The Bhil seemed content to remain and answer questions. Ashok gestured to the bucket. "And do I empty it at that time?"

"Oh, no, sir. A Bhangi will come every morning to take care of that."

A Bhangi. Ashok thought of Ram. "I'd like to empty my own bucket, instead," he said.

The Bhil's eyes widened. "But, sir, the Bhangi would be upset at your taking his work from him. How would he earn his pay, to feed his family?"

Ashok thought for a moment, and nodded. "Of course. It was a foolish idea."

The Bhil looked away, apparently embarrassed.

Ashok asked, "Will it be possible for me to get some books to read? And something to write with?"

The Bhil looked back to him. "I don't know, sir. But I'll ask my captain."

Ashok finished his food. "May I go out into the courtyard now?"

"As you wish, sir. Please come, then."

Ashok followed the young man from the cell, down the short corridor, out the door. He couldn't help thinking of how easy it would be to knock the Bhil unconscious and maybe escape. But that wasn't Gandhiji's way, of course, nor was it Ashok's.

A tall, slender old man in a guard's uniform stood in the courtyard, outside the doorway. A rifle hung across his back.

The large entry gate into the courtyard was closed now, and so was the smaller one opposite it on the far side of the enclosure. Beyond the wall on that side rose the foliage of another *pipal* tree, so there must be yet another courtyard there. Several monkeys scampered along the edge of the wall and disappeared on the other side.

The younger guard left with the food tray, but the old man watched as Ashok walked the length of his own courtyard several times. It was exactly twenty-five paces the long direction, about seventy-five feet. The other dimension was around forty-five feet. In two corners next to the outer walls, steps led up to the top of the bastions.

Ashok gestured to one set of stairs and inquired, "May I go up?"

The old man shook his head. "I'm sorry, *sahib*. It's not permitted."

So Ashok now knew the limits of his world. He looked at the sky. In that dimension, at least, there were no boundaries. As a child living on a plain with few tall obstructions, he had grown to love the sky, which so few city people bothered to look at. He could lie on his back and watch it for hours: the changing cloud formations, the kites or the vultures circling high above, the small green parrots wheeling about in great arcs. And, of course, the stars and

Courtyard of Mangarh Fortress Jail

planets and moon at night.

Ashok could not help but compare his new cell to those he had occupied previously. The others had clearly been built to house prisoners; this one, on the other hand, gave the impression of having been a storeroom at one time. The bars in the windows and the iron door might just as well have been designed to keep potential thieves out, rather than to keep prisoners in. His bed was comfortable, quite in contrast to the hard floors in his earlier cells.

In the morning, Ashok's door opened to admit the Harijan who would empty his latrine bucket. The man who shuffled in, followed by the young Bhil guard, was old and bent, with stubble of white whiskers. He did not look in Ashok's direction.

But Ashok recognized him as being from Gamri village and said, "Uncle, it's good to see you."

The sweeper gave a start; of course, it was unusual for anyone to acknowledge his existence. "*Sahib*, I heard you were here!"

"Yes, but please don't call me *sahib*, Uncle."

"How have you come to be here? We were told you angered the Maharaja!"

Ashok gave a rueful smile. "His Highness banned me from his state. I persisted in coming back. He decided the only way to solve the problem was to confine me."

The old man stood staring at him. At last, he said as he bent to pick up the bucket, "My people are sad you're here. You've been a good friend. Few men care for us."

"Let me take the bucket myself," said Ashok, moving forward.

The man seemed shocked, backed off with the bucket. "No, no, sir! It's my work, my duty. And in your case, I'm most honored to serve you."

He hurried out. The young Bhil said, "You can bathe in the corner of the courtyard, sir. Then tea will be coming, and breakfast shortly after. Is there anything else you'd like now?"

Ashok could not help but smile. Although he was being well taken care of, he could come up with quite a lengthy list of things he would like to have here. Starting with the companionship of some people who were quite dear to him. But he said, "Not at this moment."

The Bhil left.

Although Ashok hated being confined to so limited an area, the company of the two guards helped pass the time. He talked with them at length about life in the Bhil villages, which he had seen only brief glimpses of while passing through the hills.

"The Rajputs conquered your people and turned them from hunters to farmers," said Ashok to the young Bhil, whose name was Surmal, and to the old man, Bilado, one day. "You don't resent that?"

Bilado shrugged and gave a smile. "That was long ago. Anyway, what could we do? We accept our fate, as you do. For generations we've been proud to serve our lords, the maharajas. They've been fathers to us and have cared for our needs and treated us with respect. In return, we've guarded their forts and their treasure and their prisoners. They trust us more than their own blood kin, who might be tempted to betray them for personal gain."

Ashok raised an eyebrow, impressed.

"We're raised on stories about our duty," added young Surmal. "There once was a man of our tribe whose small son stole a mango from the garden in the fort. The father killed the son. He knew that some day his son would grow up and be in charge of guarding the treasury. And if he would steal fruit as a boy, he might destroy the honor of all of us by stealing gold or jewels as a man."

Ashok gave nod and looked appropriately awed. He had heard that in some areas, including the Ajmer-Merwara territory not far to the north of Mangarh state, Bhil tribals had a reputation for being bandits. But that obviously didn't hold true for these Bhils of Mangarh. "No Bhil has ever betrayed the trust?" he asked.

Bilado stiffened his back. "Never," he replied, a stern look in his eyes.

With no idea how long he would be here, on the third day Ashok established a routine. He began after his morning ablutions with some meditation and simple yoga exercises. After breakfast, he went for a brisk walk around and around the courtyard. He then read and thought until lunch, and he wrote in the diary he was beginning to keep using the paper supplied to him. In the afternoons, more exercise, conversation with the guards, and more reading. Then contemplation, perhaps watching the pigeons or parrots fly about, or squirrels or monkeys running around in the courtyard. At night, after dinner, he would often look up at the stars or the moon. Bats would dip and swerve over the courtyard, aiding in controlling the mosquito population.

His routines helped him cope with being confined, but the activities were still far from sufficient to fill so much time. He often found himself looking up at the sky, the only part of the outer world that he could see. He envied the ability of the birds to so casually escape, to soar about wherever they pleased.

He began saving scraps of *rotis* to toss to the squirrels. They would dart close to snatch the food, but they remained leery of him.

His thoughts often turned to Jaya and the other people outside, free to go about their activities virtually unhindered. It had been so long since he had seen Jaya, he wondered if she thought of him, other than only occasionally. Picturing her lovely face, her lively eyes, her animated manner of talking, was the pleasantest topic he could dwell upon.

Still, boredom was inevitable, and for want of anything more to occupy himself, he went to bed relatively early. Seven days dragged by in this way.

Escorted by a policeman, Jaya and her father came to visit him at the end of his first week. Ashok's heart pounded, and he felt himself grinning foolishly at the sight of her. It had been far too long. She wore an orange sari and looked even prettier than he remembered.

Were her broad smile and the warm look in her eyes merely for a very good family friend, or was there more? He was almost certain it was the latter.

They brought him a box of sweets, and fruit, and a copy of Mark Twain's *Huckleberry Finn*. Sundip had sent him Rudyard Kipling's *Kim*. The policeman inspected each item thoroughly. He flipped through pages of the books with a puzzled frown. He read a short note that Sundip had stuck in *Kim*. Although the policeman spoke some English, it was clear he was unfamiliar with the books and was wondering if they were subversive. But at last he handed them and the note to Ashok.

Ashok tore his eyes away from Jaya and quickly read the note: *I've been intending to read this someday, but you now have more time than I do. Sundip*

"For a fact," Ashok said, smiling grimly.

With the officer listening to every word, conversation had to be circumspect. They inquired as to each other's health, and ensured that Ashok's food was adequate, the other comforts satisfactory.

Gazing frequently at Jaya to compensate for the long time without that pleasure, Ashok told them about his recent visit to his family. Then, he glanced at the policeman, who appeared not to be listening intently. Ashok said casually, "Word got out about the details of my arrival back here. Three times."

Jaya and her father exchanged quick looks. "It's obvious who did it," said Dr. Arora.

Jaya nodded, her face abruptly grim. "We'll be careful now. It's awkward, though, especially with no definite proof."

The policeman stared at them, apparently having sensed they had edged into a forbidden topic. So Dr. Arora began speaking of how bad the famine was affecting the villages.

The visitors stayed the two hours allowed. "I'll be back," Jaya said, her eyes holding his. "Mother insists she gets a turn next week. I know Sundip and Manohar would like to visit, too. But they've agreed to let us have first chance at you." She smiled and looked at her father.

"I think I lose out for a while," Dr. Arora said with a wry grin. "Though I strongly hope to see you on the outside quite soon."

Ashok was warmed by the clear assumption Jaya would visit next time. It was the others who would be trading off. The implications were obvious, and he wondered what kind of conversations the Aroras had been having among themselves.

"Is there anything you'd like us to bring? More books?" Jaya asked.

"More books would be good." He added with a smile, "Just be sure to bring yourself."

She grinned at him. "I won't miss it."

He saw that Dr. Arora was looking away, but a smile was twisting his lips.

When they left, his quarters were so quiet, so empty.

It was technically illegal, of course, to hold him without seeing a magistrate. But even if he did go before a judicial officer, the official would do as he was directed by higher authority, so Ashok decided there was almost certainly no point in pushing the matter.

He was not allowed to use the walkways of the outer walls of his courtyard. However, eventually they gave him permission to climb the steps to the two inner towers. There, he could walk along top of the short stretch of wall between the cupolas, the wall which divided his own yard from the adjacent inner courtyard. From the towers he was able to see most of the upper area of the fort—the portion covering the ridge top—and he could look out over the top of the parapets at the city.

He would often gaze at the parts of the town that were visible from his spot. Much of it was too far away to see details, but he thought he could just barely see a corner of the roof of the house in which Jaya and her family lived, and he would wonder what she, in particular, might be doing at the moment.

There were so many disadvantages to being confined, but the part he hated the most was being separated from other people, never so much as seeing a woman or a child.

From the towers he could also look into the other courtyard, onto which the treasury rooms opened. He could easily have descended the narrow stairway into that courtyard. It was never expressly forbidden, but he got the clear sense when they gave him permission to go into the towers that the authorization did not include going beyond them.

After the second week, the guards stopped locking him into his cell during daylight hours, except when rare visitors came to and from the treasury. However, always they kept an eye on him, usually both men, but sometimes only one.

Every week his friends came for the allotted two hours. Each time, he was especially aware of Jaya's presence. He kept wishing he had the opportunity for a conversation with her alone. Not to say anything in particular, just to have the two of them focus their attention solely on each other, without the constant nearness of others.

That was impossible, of course. Even if he were out of prison, it would have been improper for him to be alone with an unmarried young woman.

Ashok felt frustrated both at the shortness of the visits, and also at the fact that with the policeman present he could only get the barest hints of what reform activities the others might be involved in. So far as he could ascertain, they were doing little at the moment.

It was partly because they were not quite sure what to do next, and because Ashok himself was not available to lead them into action. And it was also out of fear of landing in jail. With Ashok and his allies virtually certain that the spy in the Praja Mandal leadership was its own president, the organization was handicapped until they found an appropriate way to remove him.

When Ashok had been confined a month, two policemen came and took him in a motor car to their headquarters to see Karam Singh.

"Sit down, Mr. Chand," said the inspector general. Singh looked over Ashok with a piercing examination. "We've been getting quite a few telegrams about you," he said. "From Mr. Nehru and Mr. Gandhi, among others."

"I'm pleased to hear that, sir."

Singh sat staring at him. "Are your quarters and food adequate?" he asked at last.

"Yes, quite satisfactory. For a jail."

"You're not being mistreated?"

"No, not really."

"Is there anything you'd like there?"

"I'd certainly be glad of more visitors. It's lonely there, without even any other prisoners. And I'd like more books. And newspapers. And more writing paper."

Singh stared at him, and said, "My main concern is that you not have the opportunity to encourage further reform work. You may increase the number of visitors to three at a time, but since I have to assign a trusted officer to closely monitor you during the visits, I think we must limit the visits to no more than twice a week. I'll see you get a regular newspaper. The visitors can continue to bring you books, provided my officer inspects them first to ensure they're not used as a means of sending messages. Will that be satisfactory?"

"It will do. And the writing materials?"

Singh frowned. "Our main concern is that you not correspond with other reformers."

"I won't. You have my word. I want to write to my family. And to keep a diary."

"You won't write to Gandhi or Nehru?"

"I'd like to. But if you prohibit it, I won't."

Singh thought a moment, nodded. "You'll have the writing items, so long as you don't write to those two or to other Congress leaders. Even indirectly. Is that all?"

Ashok gave a shrug. "I'd like to have visitors longer, every day. But I can get by."

Singh said, "You know you have the right to be brought before a magistrate. Do you wish a trial?"

"Is there any point in one?"

"That's for you to decide."

Ashok sighed. "I assume I'll get sentenced to whatever term you or His Highness decide."

Singh said nothing.

"And when I'm freed at the end, I'll just get arrested again and sentenced once more."

Singh inclined his head. "Quite possibly."

They sat in silence for a time. Ashok gave a wry smile. "I think it probably makes you look worse, and it gives better publicity to my cause, if you hold me without trial."

Singh stared at him, grunted. Then Singh said, "I can free you any time, you know. Even this very minute. Provided you leave the state and do not return."

Ashok thought for a time, then said, "I can't promise that."

"Then I must send you back to the cell."

Ashok returned his stare and did not reply.

Singh called to the officers to return Ashok to the fortress prison.

Week followed week, and Ashok kept to his customary routine with only minor variations.

On his forty-sixth day, some time after the timekeeper's gong announced nine o'clock, and after Ashok had been locked into the cell for the night, he heard a motor car climb the hill and enter the courtyard. He looked out the window and, in the dim lantern light, he saw Maharaja Lakshman Singh, with a servant accompanying him, step from the car and strode into the inner courtyard which the treasury rooms faced. The driver remained in the car. He backed, turned around, and drove out the gate. Ashok heard the car descend the rough stones of the hill road.

Puzzled, Ashok wondered why the Maharaja would remain in the treasury without transportation.

He watched for a time. He heard occasional muffled sounds of doors opening and of voices, drifting over the wall from the treasury courtyard. But there was no further activity within view of his window, so at last he sat on his cot. He expected at any time to hear the Maharaja leave, perhaps by foot. But no sounds came.

With little else to do, he stood for a long time again at the window. Now he heard no sounds coming even from the treasury courtyard. Was Lakshman Singh remaining there all night then, perhaps in some kind of *puja*? He had heard of wealthy people giving worship to their money, but somehow that seemed unlike the Maharaja.

At last, when the timekeeper's gong signaled midnight, Ashok tired of the wait and lay down on his cot and slept.

He awakened early in the morning, as usual. So far as he knew—and he was a light sleeper—there had been no further activity in either courtyard. Surmal came to open his door.

"May I go out?" Ashok asked?

"Oh, yes."

"I thought perhaps if His Highness was still here, you might not want me to."

"His Highness isn't here today."

Ashok peered at the young Bhil's face. Surmal smiled at him. Ashok thought of asking about the occurrences last night, but he did not. It was really none of his concern.

He made his customary circuits of his yard and the two towers. From the tower, he looked down into the treasury courtyard. The area appeared deserted.

So when, and how, had the Maharaja left?

That night, Ashok realized, sitting on his cot, that no one had locked his cell door.

How could the diligent, faithful Bhils have failed in their duty?

For at least an hour he waited, and the door remained unlocked.

Ashok hesitated. Finally, he could not resist slowly pushing it open. The hinges were well enough oiled that the door made virtually no noise.

He quietly moved down the hall to the outer door. It hung ajar by a couple inches.

He knew Bhil guards patrolled the walls at night; he had seen them often from his window. So he did not go out into the courtyard, as he saw no point in alerting them to the fact that he was free to come and go from his cell.

Eventually, he shrugged to himself, went back into his cell, closed the door, and went to sleep.

The next morning, when Surmal arrived with breakfast, the guard merely pulled open the door, greeted Ashok as usual, and deposited the food on the table.

The Bhil did not appear at all surprised that door was unlocked. Ashok thought of asking about it. But there was no need to embarrass Surmal if, indeed, the guards had made an error.

That night, the cell door was again unlocked. Ashok now knew it was intentional; the guards would not fail in their duty two nights in a row.

Were they inviting him to escape? Unlikely though it might appear at first, it was indeed possible. The Maharaja's concern was probably not so much to punish Ashok as to render him incapable of further agitation for reforms. That goal could be accomplished just as well if Ashok escaped and left the state.

Curious, he left his cell and went to the courtyard door. As with last night, it hung partly open. He quietly pushed it further ajar and slipped out.

He looked up at the wall. Where were the guards? He saw no evidence of them. Casually, keeping in the shadows, he walked through the courtyard, to the main gate. The doors were closed, and the massive wooden bar was in place. So far as he could discern in the dim light, the padlock and chain secured the bar. The smaller door, meant to allow an individual to enter and leave without having to open the entire gate, was also locked.

Ashok did not intend to try to escape at this moment; there were too many considerations involved for such a hasty decision. But he was curious. Was escape even possible, since the main gate was secured?

There was no apparent way to leave over the outer walls. Although he could easily get to the top of them by means of the stairway, they were perhaps twenty feet high at the lowest point. And while the stones were somewhat rough, they were too smooth for someone so inexperienced in rock climbing to descend without a rope. Maybe he could tear his bedding into strips and tie the pieces together until they were long enough for him to climb down them from the top of the wall. But that would be quite a job, especially when he had no knife or scissors.

He thought of the next courtyard, where the treasury was located. Was there an easy exit from it? He'd seen no gate when he'd looked at the area from the towers. Yet, Lakshman Singh had apparently left from there, somehow.

He hesitated. Surely the guards must be nearby. They would never leave the treasury unattended.

He could not see them up on the tower, even though the moon was fairly bright. He quietly climbed the steps on this side. Once on the platform, he stood against a roof pillar of the tower and looked out over the treasury courtyard. The guards, he decided, must be inside the building below.

He again hesitated. Was it a trap? If he were seen, could he be accused of trying to rob the treasury?

Possibly. But what could Lakshman Singh gain by such a charge? Ashok was already a prisoner. Maybe his reputation could be put in question, and thus the reform movement harmed. But it would be easy for the police to plant false evidence or make false accusations against anyone at any time. Ashok had the impression that was not Lakshman Singh's way.

Deciding to take the chance, he descended the steps to the treasury courtyard. He stood for perhaps ten minutes in the shadows, watching. Suddenly, a doorway opened, and the light of a lamp shone. A guard strode to a stairway across the yard and climbed it. He slowly made a circuit of the walls, looking out over the surrounding area. He descended the same stairs and went back inside the building. Never once, so far as Ashok could tell, had he examined the inside of the courtyard itself.

Ashok wondered again: How had the Maharaja left? Was there a rear doorway reachable only from inside the treasury?

He shrugged inwardly. He'd had enough excitement for one night.

He quietly returned to his own courtyard, to his bed.

The question nagged at him all the next day.

Was there any way to escape, assuming he should decide he wanted to?

That night, more out of intense curiosity than out of any intention to leave, he again went into the treasury courtyard, careful to remain in the shadows in case the guard should appear.

Gradually, he crept around the entire perimeter of the yard. He could see no way out, only doors opening into the storerooms and the treasury.

Still puzzled, he returned to his own quarters. He sat on his bed, the cell door open.

The lack of locked doors, the lack of guards, both seemed an invitation to leave. But how?

A sudden inspiration came: maybe he'd been looking too far away! What about his own building? Was there another exit? He'd never been inside any of the other rooms opening off the hallway.

Seizing his oil lamp, he went out and tried the door opposite. It was locked. He tried the next door. It swung inward.

He saw a storeroom. And another door, a small, low one. He went over to it and tried the latch.

It opened. Beyond the door, a steep, narrow stairway led down. A dank odor came from the passage, and the bat droppings littered the steps.

Carefully, he descended the stairs, holding his lamp ahead and downward to better illuminate the way. A cobweb brushed his face. At the bottom a narrow passage, carved from the solid rock, led straight ahead, and another passage branched to the left.

His lamp held ample oil. Which tunnel should he take? The left one would seem to head roughly in the direction of the main part of the fortress, overlooking the city. The other appeared to lead the opposite direction, toward the rear side of the ridge, away from the town.

He chose the one heading toward the city. The floor was dusty, seeming unused. He followed it a short distance, his head almost touching the ceiling. Small rubble crunched into the dust underfoot. The passage continued perhaps a few hundred feet, angling downward. It ended at a wooden door.

He hesitated a moment, then tried the door. It opened. Beyond, to the left, a narrow stairway led upward. A long wooden ladder lay on its side the length of the stairs, propped against the wall. He ascended the steps to another doorway, a small but heavy wooden one, secured by a sliding wooden bar.

He quietly slid the bar aside. He cautiously pushed on the door. It opened with a creak of old hinges onto a stone alcove, and he was immediately hit with the freshness of outside air. He stepped onto the floor and turned. He saw dark sky sprinkled with stars, and below lay the lights of Mangarh city.

Where was he? Shielding the flame as best he could from possible sight by guards, he examined the place. He appeared to be on a small ledge in a recess of the fortress wall, partially hidden by a bastion on one side. He extended his lamp. There was a drop of perhaps twelve feet to the rocky ground that fell away steeply toward the city.

So that was why the ladder was nearby. If he chose, he could leave his prison. Right now.

Tempting though it was, he wasn't yet ready. He must think through all the ramifications.

He stood for perhaps a quarter hour, looking out over the city, listening to the night sounds. Then he returned the way he had come.

When he came to the branch in the passage at the bottom of the stairway to his own portion of the fort, he hesitated only a moment. He was intensely curious as to where the other tunnel went. He continued walking.

Unless he had lost his bearings, he was now under the part of the castle surrounding the treasury courtyard. He came to a tall, narrow opening in the right hand wall of the passage. Another stairway led up. To the treasury?

Ahead, the main passage continued, slanting downward now at an angle, as far as he could see, until it was lost in darkness. The floor seemed cleaner here, and he saw that in the center the stone appeared smoother, polished by the passing of many feet.

Suddenly he wondered—could this be how Lakshman Singh had left the treasury? Where might the passage lead?

He resumed walking, hurrying as fast as he could go without blowing out his flame.

Much longer than the other passage, this one continued perhaps a thousand feet. Then the tunnel ended, and in the right hand wall was a door, barred from the inside, but not locked. He slid the bar aside and pushed the door open to reveal a tiny room. To the left was another door, again secured. He unlatched the bar and opened the door. Ahead, steps led upward.

He ascended the stairway. There was no door at the top; instead, the steps ended at a slab of stone overhead which formed a small square ceiling. Near one corner a large swivel hook attached to the slab extended through an iron eye affixed to the wall. A wide crack extended on all four sides where the slab met the walls.

It was obviously a trap door of sorts. Ashok set his lamp on a step. Not really expecting to succeed, he unlatched the hook. He shoved upward on the slab. It did not budge. He shoved with all his strength. Still no movement. It must be extremely heavy, or else it had a weight resting on top of it.

Holding his lamp up, he examined the slab closely. There appeared to be scrape marks forming a broad arc.

Suddenly, he had an inspiration: maybe the door was intended to pivot, not to lift.

He set down the lamp. He seized hold of the hook, and using it as a handle, tugged hard. The slab slid a short distance. He pulled again. It slid farther, pivoting on a corner, scraping slightly but apparently bearing most of its weight on some sort of rollers recessed in the top of the stairwell walls. He pulled until the handle was against the opposite wall, so that the slab could not move further.

He seized his lamp and climbed up through the opening. He stood inside a small, four-sided, stone pillared *chhatri*. The ground fell away steeply before him, and he saw stars in the sky. The landscape was dark. He turned and saw a Shiva *lingam* atop the slab which normally covered the opening. Behind the *chhatri* rose the wall of the fortress.

So this was a small shrine, a tiny temple, just beyond the outer wall on the rear side of the rocky ridge. In the dim moonlight, he could see a trail hugging the hillside, leading both directions.

Apparently, this was designed as an escape route from the fort in case of a siege. But why the recent use, perhaps even by Lakshman Singh himself? It was puzzling.

He stood for some minutes, peering into the night, enjoying the feeling of being outside the walls. Not far away, a jackal howled.

His lamp would not last forever, and someone might see it and come to investigate. He stepped back down into the stairway, slid the slab with its *lingam* back over the opening, secured the latch, and hurried back along the tunnels to his cell.

The opportunity was clearly there to leave the confinement he detested. Should he do it?

God, it was tempting. He hated not knowing how long he would be here. Without any specific sentence passed on him, he could be held for years.

He loathed the inactivity, the lack of human contact other than Surmal and Bilado for five days out of every seven. He had doubts about how much the Praja Mandal or the Jats or the Untouchables would accomplish without him there to prod them.

But if he did escape, he would have two choices: go into hiding, or leave Mangarh. If he left Mangarh, he also left his work undone. If he remained in the state, in hiding, his effectiveness would be limited, and it also would be difficult to keep his location secret so long as a government informer headed the Praja Mandal.

He thought about how Gandhiji and Panditji always served out their own terms until released.

He wrote about his decision in his diary, finalizing his determination through inscribing the words on the page:

> *My confinement serves significant purposes, including demonstrating my own commitment to changes in Mangarh, as well as showing my solidarity with the many nationalists in British India who have also been imprisoned.*
>
> *Most important of all, by the very fact of my own imprisonment, I am demonstrating how repressive the Mangarh regime truly*

is, regardless of Lakshman Singh's statements to the contrary.

The next night, the cell door remained locked, and every night thereafter. Ashok often regretted missing the opportunity to leave. He would reread the portions of his diary concerning his decision, reminding himself of why he had chosen to remain despite the almost desperate urge to rejoin the outer world.

The little striped squirrels had lost their fear of him and now came to eat from his hand. Ashok sometimes felt a twinge of guilt about feeding them when so many people were going hungry, but the scraps were tiny, and he enjoyed the company. He could now identify each of the animals, by their behavior as much as their size or by details of their fur. One of them was clearly dominant, and another frequently challenged him. Others just came close and waited for Ashok to toss them a piece of *roti*. He thought about naming each animal, but he never did. Somehow, it seemed as if it would discount their dignity as squirrels to give them mankind's tags.

His human friends informed him during a visit that the famine was worsening. And before the listening policeman cleared his throat in objection, Sundip managed to tell Ashok that the Jats were talking of organizing a boycott of the Thakur Mangal Singh's taxes.

But the main issue of conversation, one which the policeman permitted, was about war breaking out in Europe with Hitler's September invasion of Poland. Ashok and his friends all agreed that they did not want to see Nazism triumph over the democracies. At the same time, they were furious that the British Viceroy of India, Lord Linlithgow, had officially declared India on the side of England in the war without consulting any of the Congress office holders or party leadership. The precise ramifications of that remained to be seen, but Ashok and the others strongly felt that if the British wanted India's help in the war effort, then in return they should schedule India's independence as soon as possible.

On a dark, clear night in early autumn, well after the timekeeper's gong had announced ten o'clock, Ashok was in his cell when the Maharaja's motor car drove into the courtyard. Ashok looked from his window as an ADC got out and opened the door for Lakshman Singh. They talked in low voices, and from the rear of the vehicle a bearer brought a long tube which gleamed in the starlight. The ADC withdrew from the car what appeared to be a small suitcase and a bundle of rods or sticks. This time, the Maharaja did not go into the treasury. Rather, he climbed the steps to one of the towers, and the bearer and ADC followed.

Curious, Ashok watched. It was too dark to see details, but he could tell that the three men were positioning the items they carried up. When they were done, the tube, resting on a support, pointed out of one of the arched openings of the tower cupola. Ashok at first had the impression the device was a gun, perhaps a swivel cannon of the type mounted on the back of camels. But what was there to shoot at up here in the dark?

Suddenly he realized: the tube was a telescope, and Lakshman Singh was using it to look at something. What? The stars? He remembered now a casual mention that the Maharaja had a hobby of astronomy.

Stargazing with the Maharaja

The mystery solved to his satisfaction, Ashok lost interest; it was simply too dark out to discern exactly what was going on. He returned to his bed and stretched out. He had almost fallen asleep when he heard someone enter his building. Lamplight shone at his door.

"Mr. Chand?"

"Yes, what is it?"

"Please come. His Highness wishes to speak to you."

Puzzled, yet excited at the change in routine, Ashok rose and followed the ADC up to the tower.

Lakshman Singh was peering through the smaller end of the telescope. He looked at Ashok, and straightened. "Mr. Chand. How are you being treated?"

Ashok shrugged in the darkness. "Well enough, Your Highness."

"Your health is good?"

"Quite good."

"The guards treat you satisfactorily?"

"Oh, yes, Highness. They're actually most pleasant."

"Good. Please let me know if you ever have any complaints."

Ashok batted away a whining mosquito and was quiet for a moment. Then he said, "I'll do that, Highness."

Lakshman Singh turned back to the telescope. Ashok assumed the interview was over. But the Maharaja asked, "Do you have any interest in astronomy, Mr. Chand?"

Surprised, Ashok replied, "I used to watch the night sky as a child. I learned most of the constellations and the brightest stars, although I've forgotten a lot. I now often amuse myself by watching the stars and planets, or the moon."

Lakshman Singh had been peering at him in the dim light. He responded, "Excellent! I'm glad to find a kindred spirit. In this modern age, not many people notice the night sky, you know." He waved toward the instrument. "This is a three inch refractor. Back at my palace I use a twelve inch reflector on a permanent mount, but the ridge and the fortress block out much of the north sky. I come up here occasionally to see what I've been missing. Have a look."

Ashok did so.

"It's aimed at part of Ursa Major, the Big Dipper," said Lakshman Singh. "I'm using a low power lens so it shows a wider field. M81 is at one edge, and M82 at the other. M81 is the oval one. It's a spiral galaxy, though you can't really make out the arms." Ashok saw a tiny hazy oval shape.

Lakshman Singh said, "The other object, the thinner one, is M82. It's an irregularly shaped galaxy—not a spiral one."

"They're striking," Ashok said. "I wish I'd had a telescope like this when I was a child."

They looked at several more objects, and at some star filled areas, through a heavy pair of wide-field binoculars.

"Tell me, Mr. Chand," Lakshman Singh said at last. "Why didn't you escape when you had the chance? I tried to make it easy. My Bhils wouldn't have harmed you, you know."

"I wasn't sure about that, Highness. But if I'd left, I'd have needed to start pressing you for reforms again. And you'd probably have just put me back here."

"You could have left my state. The police wouldn't have interfered."

"My work is here now, Highness. I feel I'm needed. And I must have unrestricted freedom if I'm outside."

"Doesn't the Congress have work elsewhere for someone so talented as yourself?"

"I could be put to use, Highness. But I made a commitment here."

Lakshman Singh fell silent. Then he said, "You must feel strongly about me and the way I do things. I just don't understand. I've tried to show you how much I love my people. Why do you think I'm so bad?"

Ashok tried to find the words. "Maybe we have a fundamental difference in how we view the world, Highness. In my view, people should run their own government. In your view, princes should run it for them. I'm interested in compromise, in meeting you somewhere in the middle. But you seem to feel it's all or nothing."

Lakshman Singh was again silent for a time. Finally, he said, "Looking at the stars night after night gives me a long term view. The constellations have changed little since human beings have been on the earth. In my mind, democracy has existed on our planet only for seconds, relatively speaking. But kings have ruled their people since the earliest known times.

"Men seek power, Mr. Chand. I'm convinced that most politicians—not yourself, but most—want power mainly for themselves, not for the people they profess to serve. I, on the other hand, grew up knowing that I must use my power only for my people, not for myself. Time may well be on your side, Mr. Chand. But to my mind, democracy has not yet been around long enough to prove itself. If what I see happening in the future in the rest of India demonstrates to me that the people are better served under democracy, I will gladly resign my throne and run for public office. But I haven't yet been convinced."

"I think I understand, Highness. I don't agree, but I understand."

"I thought you would." Lakshman Singh continued, "Another matter—there's no such thing as 'India,' you know. It's just a term foreigners came up with. Our subcontinent has always been hundreds of separate states. Each with its own ruler. Even when Ashoka Maurya or the Guptas or the Mughals or the British conquered large areas, they still let most of the traditional kings continue ruling. They knew it would be too difficult to impose a single new government on such a vast region with so many different traditions, so many languages."

He stopped, and Ashok tried to formulate a response. However, the Maharaja resumed, "You wait and see, Mr. Chand. If the British leave and your Congress tries to impose its rule everywhere, the result will be chaos. How will you even decide what language to use? No matter which one you choose, hundreds of millions of people won't even know it."

Ashok took a breath, and replied, "Maybe so, Your Highness. But if the British have been able to unify most of India, why can't we Indians take over the framework and do the same thing? We can use English temporarily as a language until a consensus is reached to use Hindi or some other one."

Lakshman Singh was again silent for a while, before saying, "Maybe you Congress people can do that. You might be able to succeed. *If* you leave the princes alone, and you don't try to destabilize us or to tell us what to do."

Ashok thought for a few moments, formulating his reply before he said, "Highness, I don't think you, or the other princes, can continue your absolute personal rule if you're surrounded by areas where the people themselves govern. Europe is a good example. In one country after another, the people have either thrown out their kings or limited their powers severely."

Lakshman Singh did not reply immediately. Then he said, "Speaking of Europe, what do you feel we Indians should do about the war?"

"I wouldn't presume to advise you on that, Highness. There are good arguments on both sides. However, I personally feel if the British want us to help them, there should be a price. They'd better promise to leave India as soon as the war is over."

"We princes, most of us, have offered help to the British, you know. I've sent a contribution of money to their war effort and an offer of troops."

Ashok said, "You have an understandable interest in the English maintaining their power, since they support the status quo regarding the princes. Highness, I don't want to see the Germans defeat the British any more than you do. However, I can't see diverting Indian treasure or spilling Indian blood when they promise us nothing in return."

Lakshman Singh stood quietly a moment, then shook his head. "I think we'll continue to disagree, Mr. Chand. Unfortunately, I feel I have no choice but to keep you confined so you can do me no further harm."

Thinking the Maharaja was finished, Ashok turned to leave.

"Wait," said Lakshman Singh. He handed Ashok the binoculars. "Keep these. You can see much of the heavens with them. They'll help you pass the time at night. During the day, too, of course. You can see your birds better. And here, keep this star map. I have another. The names on it are all Western ones—I assume you don't mind."

Ashok gave a nod in the dark. "I'll be glad for them, Highness. The names I learned as a child were the English ones."

During the daytime, he used the binoculars to look out over the city, as well as to watch the birds. While the intervening houses and trees blocked the view of all but a corner of the Aroras' roof, he would often gaze at it anyway, as if the binoculars could somehow bring Jaya and her family physically closer.

At night, the binoculars opened up an expanded universe for Ashok to explore. With the help of the star chart, he relearned every constellation visible at that time of year. Within a month he was as familiar with the night sky as he was with the walls of his cell.

Although when the moon was up its brightness dominated the sky and washed out the dimmer stars, the moon itself became an old friend and companion. Beginning with the fourth month of imprisonment, the cycles of the moon also became another measure of the length of his confinement.

The view of the sky was much better from the top of the wall between the two towers, of course, than from his cell. So Ashok casually began to take his binoculars up there at night, as well as during the day. The guards made no objection.

One night, Ashok happened to be sitting quietly atop the wall by one of the towers, scanning the Celestial River, the Milky Way, with the binoculars. Shortly after the timekeeper's gong sounded ten o'clock, he heard a motor car ascending the road. The Bhils opened the gate, and the car entered.

Ashok's eyes had grown accustomed to the darkness, and he identified the tall form of Maharaja Lakshman Singh stepping from the car. The ruler strode through the inner gate, across the courtyard, and into the treasury.

Ashok saw no reason to leave, so he returned his attention to the sky. The iron-barred windows of the treasury abruptly began to glow as more lamps were lit within. From his perch atop the wall, Ashok could easily see across the small courtyard into one of the rooms. Lakshman Singh sat before a table, and a Bhil guard set first one, then another small box before him.

The Maharaja raised the lids. Numerous items in the boxes sparkled in the reflected flame of the lamps. Not really intending to spy, but too curious to resist, Ashok turned the binoculars to the window and adjusted the focus.

As he'd expected, the boxes contained jewelry. He saw the Maharaja lift out a necklace of gemstones and examine it. Even with the binoculars, it was impossible to be sure whether the stones were diamonds or a different type of gem, but they looked large. Lakshman Singh put it down, examined yet another necklace, with big translucent red stones, which Ashok took to be rubies. Then the Maharaja closed the lids.

The guard removed the boxes and deposited more on the table.

Ashok guiltily lowered the binoculars. So there were indeed jewels kept in the treasury. The full quantity was impossible to know, but there seemed to be a number of boxes.

He sat quietly, no longer really looking at anything, thinking of how so many peasants of Mangarh were starving while their ruler kept vaults of gems—which had been bought by the taxes paid by those same farmers.

Soon Lakshman Singh left the building, returned to the car, and was driven back down the hill.

"What continues to justify such inequities?" Ashok wrote in his diary. "Only that things have always been so. That is simply not sufficient reason anymore, now that we know better ways of governing."

5

In prison at Mangarh fortress, 1940

The seasons passed. The winter was pleasant in the daytime, the best time of the year in terms of comfort, although it sometimes grew much colder at night than Ashok preferred.

Then the weather began to grow warmer. In early spring, a storm with hot winds blew in from the desert, coating everything with gritty dust. The hot season was coming, and Ashok did not look forward to it, confined as he was in a courtyard whose stone walls would absorb and re-radiate the heat.

He had counted nine new crescent moons, beginning nine complete cycles of the moon's phases. Nine months of confinement.

Jaya and her mother continued to be his most consistent visitors; almost always Dr. Arora accompanied them. The feeling grew in Ashok that the Aroras were family to him. They were the ones in whom he found he could confide his feelings when he felt at his lowest: his loneliness, his doubts, even his despair at not knowing how long the confinement would last. Both Dr. and Mrs. Arora reassured him, encouraged him, told him of their admiration for his continued resolve.

And there was Jaya. Even with one or both of her parents present at every visit, he found his eyes would always return to meet hers, or to rest on the lovely lines of her face. Her smile, the sparkle in her eyes, somehow made him feel all was right with the world despite its problems. Between her visits, he thought almost constantly about her, and he yearned for a more normal life in which he could be with her far more than a mere twice a week.

Jaya brought him a book of the writings of the American, Henry David Thoreau. The policeman inspected the book carefully but let him keep it. Apparently the officer didn't realize that one of the essays in the book, "Civil Disobedience," had greatly influenced Mahatma Gandhi's thinking.

Ashok had never read the essay before. He found it slow going, and Thoreau was much more of an anarchist than Ashok could ever be. But some of the writing spoke to him.

"Under a government which imprisons unjustly," Thoreau wrote, "the true place for a just man is also in prison."

Regarding his own time in jail, Thoreau had written: "I could not help being struck by the foolishness of that institution which treated me as if I were mere flesh and blood and bones, to be locked up....I could not but smile to see how industriously they locked the door on my meditations, which followed them out again without let or hindrance, and *they* were really all that was dangerous."

Ashok fully agreed. Like Thoreau, Ashok was confined with his dangerous ideas. But he kept wondering if he had somehow made an error in judgment, or if he had overlooked some aspect of the matter that another person could quickly point out to him. The thought that he might be undergoing such deprivations, such frustrations, unnecessarily was almost more than he could stand. He wished he could write to Gandhiji to ask for advice, as well as comfort. However, he had given his word he would not correspond with other reform leaders.

Perhaps the most difficult aspect of it all was not knowing when the con-finement would end. Tomorrow? Next week? Another month? Or—a thought too depressing to contemplate—next year?

One morning, the cannons on the fort walls began to boom. From the palace and the city below came the sounds of drums beating, musicians play-ing. Bursts of firecrackers rent the air.

No festival was scheduled for this period, Ashok was certain. What could be happening? He watched the celebrations with his binoculars, puzzled, but he was unable to discern the nature of the festivities.

In late afternoon, Surmal came. "Good news, sir! You're free to go."

Ashok wondered if he'd heard correctly. "You mean—I can leave this place?"

"Yes! You're free! A son has been born to His Highness. Mangarh has an heir to the throne now. It's traditional to release prisoners on such an occa-sion."

Ashok frowned. "I wonder if this means I'm no longer banned from the state."

Surmal looked perplexed. "I can't say for certain, but I would think you're free to do as you wish, sir."

It did not take long for him to gather up his relatively few belongings. He took only the quickest of glances around his cell. Hopefully, it was the last time he would ever see it.

As he left, he saw two of the squirrels beneath the tree, watching him. He wondered how long they'd remember him and the treats he'd provided. He still found it hard to grasp he was leaving.

Surmal said with a smile, "We'll feed them for you, sir."

Ashok looked at him for a moment. "I'll miss them. And you, of course." He smiled broadly. "But not too much."

Knowing that Ashok would be freed, Jaya and her parents waited outside the gate with Manohar and Sundip. They greeted him with excitement, de-light, and relief. But Sundip's head was bandaged, his arm was in a sling.

"What happened to you?" Ashok asked.

Sundip grimaced. "Some Rajputs took me away and gave me a beating. But I'll be all right."

"How did it happen?"

Sundip seemed reluctant to talk, but he said, "I'm sure you know the crops were bad again. The rains were still not enough. This time the Jats were better organized. They all refused to pay the Thakur's taxes."

"That's wonderful!"

"Yes—it was remarkable. But the Rajputs seemed to think I was the one who organized it, and they decided to teach me a lesson. Several of them rode on horseback to the school and demanded I come with them. They took me away before most of the Jats realized what was happening. When word spread, the Jats came after me. By then I'd already been beaten and left by the side of the road. When the Jats found me, they were so angry they all marched toward Baldeogarh."

Sundip stopped.

"Tell him the rest," said Manohar quietly.

Sundip said, "The Rajputs returned. They attacked the Jats on the road, then they went to the village. They set the school on fire, started abusing the women, looting the houses. They said they were taking everything they could find to pay the taxes the farmers owed. They destroyed most of the houses when they were done.

"Everyone was demoralized. Then, the next day the Thakur's men served notice all the Jats who'd resisted the taxes were being evicted from their lands. Unfortunately, that's the way things stand now."

Ashok's mouth had dropped open. "What's happened to the Jats? Are Kumbharam and his family all right?"

Sundip frowned and looked away. "Their house is gutted and they've lost their land. All their savings were looted from their home. They're camping in the ruins while they try to decide what to do."

Ashok sadly shook his head.

Jaya said, her eyes narrow with anger, "Kishore has just been appointed Education Minister for the state! It proves we were right about him. And to think he was the Praja Mandal's president! I suppose you can thank him for all these months in jail."

Ashok had been worrying about what to do about Kishore, so that the organization could be more effective and function with less likelihood of betrayals. Now the matter was taken care of. "We have a saying in the Punjab," he said. "'Honor and profit were never found in the same dish.' But the police would have caught me before long anyway."

There was silence for a time. Ashok asked, "Do you know whether I'm still banned from the state? If I am, I might as well go back to jail right now."

Manohar furrowed his brow and said, "The release of prisoners on the birth of an heir to the throne is traditionally a general amnesty. So I assume the ban against you must be dissolved—although I suppose it could be reimposed again."

"The Praja Mandal is still illegal," Jaya said. "So we could all still end up in jail again. We have to be careful not to use its name. And to be cautious about how we hold our meetings."

"Being too careful means we'd be ineffective," said Ashok. He looked about at them, and then his eyes came to rest on Jaya. "I'm wondering if I should leave Mangarh. I assume if I try to do anything constructive, I'll just end up in jail again."

Jaya's eyes widened, and a stricken expression came over her face. He wished he could somehow speak to her privately; now that he was no longer imprisoned, he definitely wanted to pursue marriage. But he did not necessarily have to remain in Mangarh for the negotiations with her family.

Manohar stared at him, bug-eyed behind the thick eyeglasses. Sundip appeared at a loss for words. Mrs. Arora looked as if the idea horrified her.

At last Jaya asked, her brow distorted as if in pain, "You'd really leave? But you're one of us now! You've sacrificed more than any of us!"

Sundip said bluntly, "There's no one here who can take your place."

Manohar said, "You know how little we accomplished while you were in prison. We can talk and plan. But you're the one who gives us the courage to act."

Mrs. Arora said with a warm smile, "I can understand your thinking it might be time to leave. You've already done far more for us than we could have imagined. But I strongly hope you'll stay."

Ashok stood silently for a time. Then he grinned and said, "I think you're underrating yourselves and overstating the need for me. But I'm realizing I don't want to go. I think I can still find more to do here."

He was glad to see the looks of relief on their faces—and of joy on Jaya's.

Ludva village, Baldeogarh Thikana, April 1940

At the door of their courtyard, Kumbharam and Taru welcomed Ashok and Sundip to the fire-charred remains of the house with no obvious signs of regret. The old man said, "Out of jail at last! You must be glad to be breathing the air of the countryside after so long."

Ashok looked about. The house's flat roof, devoid of its supporting beams, had collapsed to the ground. The family was obviously living out of doors in the courtyard. "I'm sorry," he said inadequately. Again, his anger rose at the thought of the Thakur who so abused his privileged position. How to bring such a man to mend his ways? Especially when the man was in such absolute control of his fiefdom?

Kumbharam shrugged. "We'll build again. What else is there to do?"

"But your fields...."

"We'll find a way. We can work for others. At least we weren't beaten or our women raped, as were so many."

Ashok glanced at Taru, who was scowling. Obviously the son was not so accepting of the matter as the father.

"It's a good thing," Kumbharam was saying with a light in his eye, "how all the Jats stood as one. We forced Thakurji to take notice. He must have been worried, to react so strongly against us!"

Ashok was still furious that such a thing could be permitted to happen. "I wonder if the Maharaja can do anything to help," he mused.

"I think His Highness was worried also," said Sundip, "to have so many farmers defying their lords. He made it clear that this time he supported the Thakur."

Ashok gazed at the ruins. He asked, "What's your next step?"

"We'll rebuild our house," said Kumbharam.

Ashok breathed deeply. He knew he shouldn't feel such intense anger. Gandhiji wouldn't approve, and he would insist on a nonviolent approach in dealing with the perpetrators. "Could you get your fields back if you apologized to the Thakur, told him you'd pay the taxes after this?"

Even Taru looked surprised, and he said, "We would never stoop to such a thing! We're in the right. Some day we'll prevail. If not my father or me, then maybe my own sons."

Ashok stared at him, awed at the strength of such determination.

6

Mangarh, April 1940

Ashok was pleased that his old lodgings were made available to him again. A few days after his release, he was on the street walking toward his room when a familiar figure came into sight. He froze a moment in astonishment.

Then he exclaimed, "Prabhu!" He moved swiftly to embrace his younger brother.

Prabhu seemed surprised at first, and he was stiff in returning the hug.

"What brings you to Mangarh?" asked Ashok, assuming his brother must have come just to see him.

Prabhu hesitated. Then he replied, "I'm here on business."

"Business?"

Prabhu's eyes slid away. "You wouldn't be interested in the details. I'm gathering some information for the RSS."

Ashok deflated. After a moment, he said, "I see. When did you get here?"

"Only yesterday."

Yesterday! And Prabhu had not even looked his elder brother up yet. "You should be staying with me! My room's small, but we'd manage."

"I'm staying with some...friends," Prabhu replied.

"Oh? Maybe I know them."

"I doubt it," Prabhu said. "They're not from Mangarh."

"Oh," said Ashok, puzzled. "Have you seen Mother and Father recently?"

"Not for some time. You've probably been there since I have."

"It's been almost a year—I was jailed a long time. I need to go home again soon. But Savitri writes that everyone's fine, though they all worry about you. You really should write to them!"

Prabhu said nothing, but looked down the street.

"Father's concerned about when you'll return," said Ashok. "He'd like to have you take over more of the management of the farm."

Prabhu shot him a quick glance, then looked away. "I can't say just when I'll be back," he said. "It will probably be some time."

"Come with me to my room! We'll chat." As he made the invitation, Ashok suddenly realized how convenient it would now be to arrange for his brother to meet Jaya and her parents. It would be a first step toward establishing communication between the two families.

Prabhu looked at him. "I'll stop by soon, but I can't right now. I have some matters to attend to."

"So you're still doing things for the RSS?"

"Sometimes. I have a variety of projects I'm working on."

"Oh. Well, my room is in the third house, down around the corner to the right."

"I'll come by." Prabhu turned and moved rapidly down the street. Ashok stood staring after him some time, deep in thought. The gulf between the two brothers was wide. The militant RSS, with its emphasis on terrorism, was the exact opposite of Gandhi's teachings on nonviolent action.

Whatever was the RSS planning in Mangarh?

Ashok walked slowly to his lodgings.

Lord Linlithgow, Viceroy of India, was expected in Mangarh next week to hunt tigers with the Maharaja. At a meeting in Manohar Jain's house, Sundip suggested taking advantage of the upcoming visit by staging a demonstration against the fact that the British so consistently supported the status quo in Mangarh.

Manohar said, "A demonstration would make Lord Linlithgow aware of our displeasure. But it would also embarrass the Maharaja. What will that accomplish?"

"First," said Sundip, excitement in his eyes, "it will tell the Viceroy we want the British to leave. They might stop propping up regimes like Mangarh. Second, it would point out to our Maharaja that there are limits to his own rule. If he doesn't make some reforms, and the unrest grows, the British might step in, maybe even insisting on changes."

Ashok was thinking. The Viceroy of India was probably the most powerful man in the British Empire, maybe even in the world. The King of England had been reduced to little more than a figurehead; it was England's Parliament that passed the laws, and the Prime Minister and his cabinet who administered the empire. Even the American President, Franklin D. Roosevelt, had to deal with his Congress.

The Viceroy of India, however, exercised almost dictatorial powers over 400 million people, a population second only to China in numbers. And although a Maharaja like Lakshman Singh held virtually unlimited authority within his own little state, he remained in power only so long as the Viceroy saw no reason to ask him to abdicate.

Ashok now said, "I agree that having the highest representative of the Crown right here on our doorstep is too good a chance to pass up. But we need to plan our strategy carefully to make the most of it."

Sundip said, "Most of the beaters for the tiger hunt will be villagers who are forced to work for no compensation. We could demonstrate against that—it might make the Viceroy feel at least a little guilty."

"We can wave black flags in front of the Viceroy, and shout our message to him," said Jaya. "It would get press coverage all over India!"

Ashok thought some more. Black flags were a traditional way of expressing disapproval, so the significance would be unmistakable. "The issue of forced labor is a good one," said Ashok. "But—" He stopped and again fell silent, thinking.

"But *what*?" prodded Jaya.

"Security is extremely tight wherever the Viceroy travels. How will we keep the police from arresting us in advance? They're sure to find out about our plans. I can't imagine either His Highness or the inspector general letting us go through with it."

"Maybe we could distribute the flags a couple days before," said Sundip. "Then the leaders most likely to be arrested—ourselves—can go into hiding. We can suddenly reappear in time for the demonstration."

"They'll still arrest us then, won't they?" asked Jaya solemnly.

Sundip replied, "Some of us. But they'll be too late to stop the demonstration. The flags can be small enough to hide in our clothes, and we'll mix in with the crowd."

"I'm troubled by our going into hiding, and trying to keep most of the plan so secret," Ashok said. "Gandhiji always publicly announces his intentions before the event. It's part of his devotion to Truth. He treats his opponents as friends he happens to disagree with, not as enemies."

"I agree with the principle," said Jaya thoughtfully. "But in this case, wouldn't it be completely ineffective if we announced it in advance? If we're arrested before the Viceroy even comes, he won't so much as hear about our protest."

Everyone but Ashok nodded. They looked at him.

"I think I'm outvoted," he said.

After more discussion, it was agreed: they would prepare immediately for the demonstration, and they would go into hiding the day before the Viceroy's arrival.

The next day, as Ashok was returning through the city after a visit to the Jat villages to inform them of the demonstration, he again saw Prabhu. His brother was sauntering near the main gateway in the outer wall of the old fortress, looking up at the walls, as if trying to peer over them. He saw Ashok, and stiffened. He seemed to hesitate a moment, then he nodded to Ashok, formed a smile on his lips, and greeted him.

Ashok stopped his bicycle. "Looking at the sights in Mangarh?"

Prabhu said, "That's right. It's an impressive fort."

"I've seen all I want of it," said Ashok.

Prabhu's eyes narrowed as he peered at Ashok. "Oh? You've been inside?"

"I was jailed there for the greater part of a year."

Prabhu continued to stare at him. "I see." He looked at the gate a moment, then back to Ashok. He gave a lopsided smile. "I hear there's quite a treasure in the fortress. A big diamond. Lots of gold. Where is it kept?"

"One of the treasuries is in the small fort on top of the hill, near where they held me. But I've no idea how much gold or jewels are there."

"You never saw any of it during all the time you were in jail?" Prabhu spoke in a light tone, almost tauntingly.

Ashok hesitated, thinking of the boxes of jewelry he'd watched Lakshman Singh examine. He decided that since what he'd witnessed through the binoculars should have been private, he'd best not tell anyone. He said, evading a direct answer, "I was confined to my cell and exercise yard."

"Oh. Well, I must be going."

"There's, uh, there are some friends I'd like you to meet while you're here," Ashok said, thinking of Jaya and her parents.

"Fine. I'll try to visit you soon." Prabhu strode off rapidly in the direction he had been headed, leaving Ashok frustrated by the brevity of the encounter. After all, they were brothers!

Once again, he wondered what Prabhu could be planning. The casual reference to the treasure—militants had committed robberies before to finance their activities. Could Prabhu be involved in something of that sort? He had a hard time seeing his brother as a robber. But Prabhu had always been so reserved, so difficult to know.

Still thinking, Ashok remounted his bicycle. More likely, Prabhu's appearance here was somehow related to the Viceroy's visit. Was Prabhu going to cause some kind of disturbance, maybe of a more violent nature than the Praja Mandal would prefer?

When he saw his brother again, he would insist on more of an explanation. Ashok resumed his pedaling.

A crowd of thousands packed the streets before the gates of the old fortress where the Maharaja and the Viceroy were holding a *durbar*. Afterwards, the two rulers would drive from the fortress, through the old part of the city, and out to the newer palace.

Waiting were rural families in their bullock carts, farmers on their camels, even a few doctors and lawyers from town wearing European style suits. Mixed in among them were the organizers of the black flag demonstration— the men dressed in the *dhotis* and turbans of farmers, the women wearing the long, full skirts and shawls of villagers. Hopefully, with the disguises they would avoid arrest, at least until the flags had been unfurled and the slogans shouted.

Ashok felt top-heavy in the bulky turban he was unaccustomed to wearing. The *jutis*, the heavy, boat-shaped shoes worn by those farmers who could afford them, were stiff on his feet. He thought Jaya looked quite attractive, barefoot in a *ghagra*, with the *odhni* worn over her head to shield her face. It was the first time he had seen her in anything other than a sari.

The Mangarh state police and army, as well as the Viceroy's own guards, lined both sides of the street, but they made no effort to discourage onlookers from climbing on top of the walls bordering the gateway, or from sitting in the trees along the road.

Ashok saw Karam Singh drive slowly by in his car, obviously ensuring that adequate arrangements had been made for security and to keep the crowd under control.

Ashok casually looked over the assembled crowds. As he did so, he glimpsed a familiar form. Prabhu was hurrying along, two other young men behind him. He and one of the others carried satchels. They seemed to be moving away from the gateway. In the milling throng, no one paid them the slightest attention.

Maharaja Lakshman Singh and Lord Linlithgow would be entering and leaving the palace through that gate. Ashok was now sure Prabhu was going to create some kind of violent disturbance.

It was even a possibility that his brother and his companions would try to assassinate the Viceroy of India.

Ashok wondered if Karam Singh knew of Prabhu's presence. But Prabhu had been in Mangarh only a few days, and the inspector general's spies might not have realized the danger.

Ashok began to perspire. What should he do? He had his own demonstration to worry about, but he needed to try to prevent any possible violence. And if anything did happen, his people might even be blamed for it and arrested.

He eyed the widely spaced lines of soldiers along the road. There was no indication the authorities expected anything other than a peaceful assembly.

He started toward the group of police. And stopped.

To the Praja Mandal members present, he would appear to be consorting with the opposing side.

And he would be informing on his own brother! Should he try to talk

Prabhu out of it? Not much chance. Threaten to expose him? But Prabhu might only seem to agree to call off any attempted killing. What if he and his men had already planted a bomb? Even if the Viceroy were not killed or injured, innocent bystanders might be hurt. Could he trust Prabhu to tell the truth?

He saw that Karam Singh had parked his car a short distance inside the gate, an area from which the crowd was excluded, and he was talking to a couple of his officers.

Time was obviously short. Ashok forced himself to turn to Sundip. "I need a word with the inspector general," he said. "I want to try for some assurance the police won't use their *lathis* on the crowd. Innocent bystanders could be hurt."

Sundip, who appeared somewhat strange wearing a villager's turban, looked at him in surprise. "Singh might arrest you when he has you so close! Or try to question you."

"I'll take the chance."

Sundip said, "I'll join you."

"No need for both of us to risk arrest. Anyway, I think I might have a better chance of reaching an understanding with him if I'm alone. We've talked a number of times, you know."

Sundip hesitated, then shrugged. "Be careful what you tell him! And hurry—the VIPs should be along any moment."

"Right." Ashok hurried behind the line of soldiers, to where a half dozen policemen stood on either side of the gate.

Too late, he saw that the officer who appeared to be in command was sub-inspector Jhakhar, smoking his usual *bidi*. Apparently Jhakhar had been reinstated to his position, even after clubbing Ram to death.

Of all the policemen to have to deal with! Ashok took a deep breath and him. "I need to speak to the inspector general."

Jhakhar exhaled smoke and eyed him suspiciously, perhaps slow to recognize him in the peasant's outfit. "What about?"

"It's extremely urgent. For his ears alone. He'll definitely want to hear it."

The thin faced sub-inspector drew on his *bidi* and stared at Ashok, as if debating whether to arrest him on the spot. At last, Jhakhar said, "You're ridiculous, Chand, trying to look like a villager. I knew who you were right away. I think you're up to some trick."

Ashok looked intently at him. "There's no time to argue. The inspector general will be furious if he finds out you've delayed the information!"

Jhakhar stared at him a few moments more, then cast down his *bidi* and spoke to a subordinate: "Take charge. I'll be right back. Come with me, Chand."

Ashok followed the policeman through the gateway to where Karam Singh stood talking with several officers. Singh saw him, and stopped the conversation as Jhakhar approached and spoke quietly.

Karam Singh's cool eyes appraised Ashok. "Good day, Mr. Chand. What's this urgent business?"

"May I speak to you privately, sir?"

Singh shrugged and led Ashok a few steps away. "Well?"

"Sir, I think there may possibly be an effort to kill the Viceroy today. I've seen a...a man I know who favors violent methods here, along with a couple others. I could be wrong, but I doubt he'd be here unless he'd planned something."

Singh raised his eyebrows. "You've no idea how they're planning to act?"

"No. But I saw them leaving the area by the gate, carrying bags. I'm almost certain they'll do something. Maybe even a bomb."

Karam Singh turned to the sub-inspector and ordered, "Take my car—delay the Viceroy and His Highness at all costs until I send word!"

He said to Ashok, "Can you point out this man you suspect?"

Damn! thought Ashok. It was one thing to warn the police to take precautions. But to have to identify his own brother!

He grimaced. "Yes. I'd rather they didn't see me, though. This way."

As he swiftly led Singh toward the gate, the inspector general asked, "You know this man's name?"

Ashok hesitated, but he saw no realistic alternative. "Prabhu Chand. He's my younger brother."

Singh shot him a look of surprise. After a moment, he said, "I see."

They were at the gate. A short distance down the street, at the edge of the crowd, Ashok saw Prabhu and his two companions conferring with each other. Taking care not to point with his hands in case he was observed, Ashok said, "That's them. Those three young men down on the left."

Singh saw where he looked, turned back to him, and said, "All right. You're not planning anything other than waving your flags?"

"That's correct," said Ashok, not surprised that Singh knew about the planned demonstration.

"I'll see my men don't harm any of you today, assuming you keep everyone under control. But if things get out of hand I'll have no choice." He turned and began rapidly calling orders to his police.

Ashok slipped back to where Sundip and Jaya and her mother waited. He tried to be unobtrusive, but he felt as if every eye in the crowd were upon him. "How did it go?" asked Sundip.

Ashok took a deep breath. "Fine. If we don't get too carried away the police won't harm us." He hesitated, then said, "There's some sort of delay, though. I think the police have something on their minds besides us."

He noticed Jaya's eyes on him, a puzzled look on her face. But she said nothing.

Khaki-clad policemen were slowly moving among the spectators on both sides of the street. Other police appeared to be carefully inspecting the gate area.

In a couple of minutes Ashok saw, down on the other side of the road, several police suddenly converge on Prabhu and his companions, seize them firmly, and escort them into a van which had just edged through the crowd.

"I wonder what that was about," said Sundip, staring at the van.

"Maybe they spotted some known criminals," said Jaya quietly. Ashok did not look at her, but he was sure he felt her gaze burn into him.

So far as Ashok could see, the search of the gate turned up nothing. He agonizingly wondered if he had betrayed his brother for nothing.

A half hour later came the Maharaja and the Viceroy in His Highness' big open touring car, the same one Ashok had once ridden in. Onlookers began cheering the two leaders.

The Praja Mandal-led demonstrators unfurled their black flags and wildly waved them overhead, shouting, "*Swaraj!*" ("Home rule!") and "No *begar!*" ("No forced labor!").

Most of the other onlookers appeared surprised, but gradually many of them took up the call, and it spread throughout the crowd, increasing in volume, competing with the *Maharaja ki jais* and the cheers for the Viceroy and the British Raj.

His Highness and His Excellency pretended to ignore the protestors as the leaders progressed down the street, occasionally waving to the crowd.

The police watched closely but made no move to silence the demonstrators.

The people's shouts diminished and faded as the car moved out of view.

"Well!" said Jaya, dropping her *odhni* to reveal bright eyes and a dazzling smile. "I don't know if it will make a difference, but they definitely had to notice us!"

"We'll hope the press noticed, too!" said Sundip.

Ashok, in a daze over what had happened with Prabhu, said nothing as his friends debated the possible effects of the demonstration.

"It's hard to believe," Manohar said, "that none of us are being arrested for what we just did."

Sundip said, peering at Ashok, "I think Ashokji must have more influence with the inspector general than we realized."

Ashok's mind was numb as he struggled to come up with an explanation. "I convinced him that allowing us to express our opinions would be more impressive to the Viceroy than a display of government repression."

Manohar shook his head. "I wish more of us had such strong powers of persuasion."

Ashok soon left, telling his friends he wasn't feeling well. He shrugged off their expressions of concern, trying not to dampen their enthusiasm as he agonized over what he had been compelled to do. Back in his room, he shed the stiff shoes and the big turban and lay on his bed, feeling far more despair than when he himself had been taken by the police.

What was happening to Prabhu? Should he try to see him?

He did not see how he could face his brother. He could not lie, and the truth about who had informed the police would almost certainly come out in the course of conversation.

On the other hand, if he made no effort to see Prabhu, his brother would wonder about the reason. But perhaps Prabhu would simply assume Ashok didn't know about the arrest.

Ashok wondered if he should try to hire a lawyer on Prabhu's behalf. However, it would then be obvious to Prabhu that Ashok knew about the arrest. A visit by Ashok would then be expected, again almost certainly resulting in the information that he had informed the police.

Ashok kept telling himself it was Prabhu's own fault. But that argument wasn't satisfactory. He wished Gandhiji were here to advise him.

What would Gandhiji do? For Gandhi, Truth was the highest ideal. Clearly, Ashok had been right to try to prevent an assassination. But what should be done now?

Gandhiji would probably go immediately to the police headquarters, ask to see Prabhu, confess all to him, and ask forgiveness.

But, as Ashok constantly reminded himself, he wasn't Gandhi. The hours dragged on. Ashok, torn in too many directions, miserable over what he'd done, took no action.

At last, he got out his writing paper and his fountain pen, and he wrote a letter to Gandhiji, explaining what had happened and asking for advice.

Then he took his diary, and he began to write, hoping the process would help sort out his thoughts, help alleviate at least a little of his anguish.

The next day, Karam Singh appeared at Ashok's lodgings. Haggard from lack of sleep and anxiety, the surprised Ashok invited him in.

The inspector general's face was impassive as usual, but his stare somehow seemed less cold. He refused the seat Ashok offered. "I won't stay, Mr. Chand," he said. "But I wanted to tell you that all three men we apprehended had loaded pistols. They confessed to planning to assassinate the Viceroy. In fact, they boasted about it."

Ashok sat down, put his head in his hands. In a way, it was a relief to know he had not informed on his brother in vain. But he still must somehow face Prabhu. And his parents. What would he tell them?

Singh said more quietly, "I've informed his Highness privately that the information came from you. But I've told everyone else it was one of my own spies who uncovered the plot. I don't think anyone but the sub-inspector knows the information came from you. I've ordered him not to tell under any circumstances. So your brother need never know unless you inform him yourself."

Ashok said in a low voice, "But I do need to do that. I need to tell him I was responsible. May I see him?"

Singh stared at him a moment, then said, "Since the Viceroy was the intended target, your brother and the two others have been removed from the state by Lord Linlithgow's security detail. The prisoners could have been held and tried in Mangarh, but it would have been embarrassing for everyone and drawn unwanted attention here. The British can deal with the matter more quietly. I believe your brother will be taken to Calcutta, and ultimately to the Andaman Islands."

Ashok felt a wrenching in his gut. The Andamans. A prison isolated far out in the ocean, where escape was unfeasible and conditions reportedly harsh.

Singh put his hand on the door latch. "Mr. Chand, I won't forget this. Neither will His Highness. It would have been horrible, not to say extremely embarrassing to both of us, if the plot had succeeded. And His Highness realizes he himself might also have been injured or killed at the same time. He's authorized me to tell you that the ban on the Praja Mandal will be lifted immediately. But we still cannot ignore you if you go too far in your agitation for reforms."

Ashok gave a nod.

Singh left.

Ashok grappled with what to say to his parents. He'd expected to bring up the subject of Jaya with them soon. Now that must wait. The time would come, but regrettably not as soon as he'd planned.

At least there was also some good news resulting from yesterday's incidents. Ashok slipped on his *chappals* and went to tell his friends that the Mangarh People's Association was no longer illegal. For the time being, they could work without constant fear of their own arrests.

***

Beginning around 1920, reform movements were active in most of the more prominent princely states, including Jaipur, Marwar (Jodhpur), Mewar (Udaipur), Bikaner, Kota, Bundi, and Bharatpur, as well as in Bijolia and in British-controlled Ajmer. These efforts more often than not were met with hostility from the rulers and their governments, and the reformist leaders were often jailed, or worse. The movements were occasionally partly successful, usually depending upon both how active and well organized the reformers were and how receptive the individual ruler was to modernizing his government.

At Independence in 1947 and shortly after, the princely states rapidly dissolved and were absorbed into larger, democratically ruled states of the new Indian nation; that period is a subject of the later story in this book, "The Costs of Freedom." Many of the reformers—as well as some of the princes and princesses—were elected to parliamentary offices and became government ministers, both in the central government and in state governments.

15

New Delhi, April 1976

Dev Batra was on the telephone once more. "I'm back at the Ashok Hotel again, Princess. It would be quite pleasant to have you visit me here."

Kaushalya thought quickly. "Does that mean you have some good news for me about my father, Batraji?"

"I'm sure a visit from you could lead to some extremely good news. Shall we say for dinner, tonight?"

"I'm sorry, I have another engagement, Batraji. Some other time, maybe."

"Break the other engagement."

She sighed. "I can't do that. But there's still no reason to keep holding my father. Your tax raiders have given up. Clearly no one thinks there's anything more to be found. So there's nothing to be gained by keeping him hostage."

"Maybe the tax raiders have given up on finding more treasure. But I haven't. Nor have I given up on you."

The man was absolutely despicable. Expecting her to offer herself in exchange for freeing her father from jail.

"You need to think carefully, Kaushalyaji, before you refuse me again," he was saying. "Almost no one held under the Emergency is getting released. Far more are still getting arrested—even Congress members. Like your friends."

"Like my friends?"

Batra was silent. Then he said, "Maybe I spoke too soon. Anyway, Kaushalyaji, don't wait too long. Someone may find another reason to keep your father even longer." He broke the connection.

Frustrated, angry, she hung up the receiver. She hadn't truly expected to get her father freed easily, treasure or not. And Batra's attempt again to get her to his hotel suite was no surprise.

But what did he mean by Congress members who were her friends?

She didn't have many friends who were active in Congress. Acquaintances, yes, but not friends. In fact, Ashok Chand was the only one she could think of at the moment. Could Batra have accidentally let it slip that Ashok

Chand was to be arrested, along with some others?

Was she reading too much into Batra's words? Maybe he was just being sarcastic with the term "friends." Or maybe he was merely having some fun, knowing she'd worry about what he'd said.

She'd better play it safe, just in case. She dialed the Chands' number.

There was no ringing sound on the other end of the line.

She tried again. Still nothing.

She frowned as she replaced the receiver. She stood and looked out the window at the garden, not seeing the flower beds or the big trees that shaded them. It was by no means unusual for phones to be out of order. Still, could the timing be more than a coincidence? What if the authorities had directed that the Chand phone be disconnected so no one could warn them?

She realized she was probably being overly paranoid. However, these were times to make almost anyone that way.

She told Gopi where she was headed, and she hurried alone outside to the Jaguar. As usual, Amar opened the driveway gate, and he rushed to chase the resident white cow away before it could get in to eat the flowers.

She drove fast, worrying that she might already be too late. On the Chands' street, however, everything seemed normal near the house. Even the brown Ambassador with the security men watching the area was nowhere to be seen. She slowed as she cruised past, and she saw that the Chands' own blue Ambassador was parked at its usual spot in the driveway. Relieved, she continued down the street and was about to turn homeward.

Then she realized she should at least mention her concern to the Chands, in case they needed to take some sort of extra precautions. She would make it brief. She turned around at the next intersection, went back, and parked by the driveway gate.

She was relieved when Usha answered the door with a surprised look that quickly changed to a smile. The two embraced. Kaushalya said hurriedly, "I know what you said about not coming to the house. But your phone isn't working."

"I know. It's been out all morning. I'm so glad to see you!"

"Is your father here? I should probably talk with him. It won't take long."

"Yes, he's here. Come on in. I'll get him."

Ashok Chand appeared and welcomed her as usual.

"It's probably nothing," Kaushalya told him. "But I was talking with Dev Batra this morning and he mentioned arrests of my Congress friends. I had the impression he meant some *new* arrests. Then he acted as if he'd slipped up by saying anything." She glanced at Usha, then back to Ashok Chand. "You're the only persons I have much contact with who I know are actively associated with Congress. So I thought I ought to at least mention it to you...." She let her voice taper off.

Chand's face had become sober. "When was this conversation?"

"About twenty minutes ago or so. I came over straightaway."

He glanced at Usha. "We'd better play it safe."

"Right, Father."

To Kaushalya's puzzlement, without another word Usha rushed down the hallway toward the rear of the house.

"Thanks so much for coming," Ashok Chand said. "I don't mean to be inhospitable, but for your own safety, it might be wise for you to leave quickly."

"I'm just going," Kaushalya said. "I hope I wasn't being foolish."

"No, you were showing great concern for us. We definitely appreciate it."

The sound came of several vehicles approaching at high speed and coming to a halt with screeching tires. Ashok Chand hurried to the front window and looked out.

"Unfortunately," he said dryly, "I think we're all too late."

16

Kaushalya saw several khaki-clad figures hurrying past the side windows of the Chand home. Then the door shook with loud raps.

"Go tell Usha," whispered Ashok Chand. "I'll try to delay them a minute."

Confused about just what was occurring, she ran down the hall, only to meet Usha and her mother Jaya, both of whom looked worried. "The police are here!" Kaushalya said.

They all rushed back to the entry hall, where Ashok was loudly conversing with someone on the other side of the door. Usha gave a nod to him.

Ashok called through the door, "Very well—I'm opening it now!"

He did so, and admitted a middle aged, stocky man in the uniform of a police superintendent, followed by three constables. "I'm terribly sorry, Mr. Chand," said the superintendent. "I have orders to arrest you, and anyone else in your house."

"Under what charge?" asked Ashok Chand calmly.

"Harboring fugitives wanted under the Maintenance of Security Act."

Kaushalya stood numbly, stunned.

Chand gave a nod. "Very well, I'll come with you. But there's really no need to take anyone else, is there? This young lady, in particular," he gestured toward Kaushalya, "had only stopped by for a minute. You may have seen her arrive just before you, in fact."

"I'm truly sorry, sir. But I'm ordered to take in everyone found here—"

At that moment, another policeman, in an inspector's uniform, entered the house. "Sir, we've caught three persons trying to leave over the garden wall. They're all on the wanted list."

The superintendent nodded, turned to the Chands. "Sir, ladies, we intend to give you every courtesy. If you wish to pack some belongings to take with you, we'll be glad to wait."

"You're most kind," said Ashok Chand. "But we've known for some time that the police might appear here. We already have kits packed. Except, of course, for our visitor. May she be allowed to go, since she has no idea of what this is about?"

"Yes," put in Jaya Chand. "She's totally innocent, we assure you."

The superintendent frowned. "If I could, sir and madam, I'd gladly release her on the strength of your word." He turned to Ashok. "I've always admired you, and I know you would speak only the truth. But I've no choice at all." He lowered his voice. "If I had an option, I would not be arresting any of you. Especially a famous freedom fighter and former government minister, and," he turned to Jaya Chand, "a prominent and respected lawyer. It's definitely the low point of my police career."

Ashok Chand actually smiled. "You're forgiven, superintendent. You must do your duty. If it weren't you arresting us, it would be someone else. But, really, this young lady here is the daughter of a royal house. It would be scandalous to take her in. Can you simply ignore her presence, pretend she wasn't here?"

The superintendent hesitated. For the first time he spoke to Kaushalya. "Who might you be, then, Miss?"

"My name is Kaushalya Kumari, of Mangarh."

"She is the daughter of His Highness the Maharaja," said Jaya Chand.

The superintendent's eyes narrowed. "Your father himself is imprisoned, is he not?"

"Yes," said Kaushalya, hoarsely.

"It's truly a shame, then, to have to take you into custody also, Princess. But again, I unfortunately have no choice."

While the Chands were gathering up their baggage in the rear of the house, the superintendent said to Kaushalya, "This is a dark day. I'm not only arresting you, Princess, but also a living legend. Every school child knows how Ashok Chand drove that train full of refugees halfway across Pakistan to safety."

"There have been a number of dark days recently," said Kaushalya tartly.

"And I'm ashamed of my part. I often think of resigning. But is there any point to it? I have all these years invested in my career, and also a family to support."

Kaushalya eyed him for a time. Then she said, "I guess each person must answer such a question himself."

"Yes. I think I have found my own conscience to be deficient." The superintendent gestured toward the inspector and constables outside the door. "If we were alone, I'd let you go and take the consequences. But those men have the same orders, too."

The Chands appeared, and, along with Kaushalya, were escorted to the waiting jeeps. "I'm so sorry you were dragged into this," murmured Usha. "It's what I tried to warn you about before. And it's ironic that you were only trying to help us."

Kaushalya strained enough to manage a tight grin. "I'm in excellent company."

She saw the other three detainees, who had been hiding in the Chand house. One of them was quite familiar. "Pratap!" she gasped. Then she realized she should be more careful of what she said, due to the danger of the police overhearing something that might be used to incriminate either Pratap Singh or herself.

He saw her and gave a wry grin, but apparently thought it best to say nothing also.

Pratap had been hiding with the Chands! Now, so much fell into place about their behavior. Kaushalya felt like a prize fool. All these months the house had been a refuge for Pratap and other fugitives.

Usha's concern about her coming to their home made sense now. If government agents were watching Kaushalya because of the income tax investigation, they might have followed her to the Chand home and become suspicious of why she had gone there so many times. But somehow they had found out anyway.

Although she well knew the harsh discomforts to be faced in jail, she found she was relieved to at last be involved in openly taking a stand for principles that were important and just. She and Pratap and the Chands were being arrested for the cause of freedom and democracy for India's people, just like her father, and just like Gandhiji, Nehru, and so many others in the earlier struggles.

When they were all in the jeeps, she heard the inspector radio to someone, "The tigers are caged."

She couldn't resist whispering to Usha, "*Tigers* indeed! Don't we wish."

At the station, the detainees were treated almost as honored guests. Additional chairs were brought into the front room so all could be seated, and a constable brought them tea. The superintendent and the inspector disappeared into an office. Pratap was sitting next to Kaushalya, and he leaned toward her. "I'm so sorry you got scooped up along with us," he whispered.

She managed a tight smile, surprised at how calm she was. "It's an honor. Who are the others?"

Pratap gestured toward another young man and said in a low voice, "Dilip's a student at Delhi University. He's wanted for leading protests." He inclined his head toward the other detainee, a gray haired man. "Mr. Parikh is wanted for sheltering fugitives in Bombay."

The police superintendent reappeared, sober faced. "Minister Chand, ladies, I thought we were to hold you here for some lengthy time. But I'm directed to take you all straightaway to Tihar Jail and to turn you over to the superintendent. There's a van waiting outside. However, I have no intention of using handcuffs or shackles on Mr. or Mrs. Chand. I'll forgo restraints on the rest of you also—but you're all on your honor not to try to escape."

"We accept with gratitude," said Ashok Chand.

"Yes, indeed," said Jaya Chand with a pained expression.

They sat on the hard benches along each side in the back of the police wagon. Again, Usha said to Kaushalya, "I wish there were some way to get you out of this. We were prepared to accept the risk ourselves, but we had no right to drag you into it. I'm sure you'll eventually be released, though it could take a long time."

"Really," said Kaushalya, "don't worry about me so much. I'll manage. I'm in the best of company. I only wish I'd done more to deserve it!" She gestured toward Pratap and the other two fugitives. "You were helping out these people and others, while I was doing nothing."

"That's not true!" said Usha. "If anything, you probably hate the Emergency even more than we do. You were just fighting it in a different way, trying hard to get your father out of jail."

Kaushalya looked down. "And now I'm joining him there."

"There are the other women from royal houses there, too," said Jaya. "The Rajmata of Jaipur, the Rajmata of Gwalior...."

"Yes, I know."

The gate of Tihar was only too familiar to Kaushalya.

One by one they were passed through the small steel door.

Inside, the jail superintendent appeared, also too well known to her, and solemnly took custody of the new detainees.

Except for Kaushalya. "Princess," he told her, "it appears you have a friend in a high place. You're free to go."

She stared at him. "What? You're sure?"

"Quite."

She glanced at her fellow detainees. It didn't seem right to just abandon them. She turned back to the superintendent. "What if I don't want to leave?"

"Kaushalya!" said Usha. "We know you mean well, but please don't be foolish."

"Yes, definitely!" said Pratap, moving between her and the interior of the jail, as if to block her entrance. He said gently but firmly, "You'll be much safer if you're free."

She met his eyes, and she was both unsettled and warmed by the concern she saw. "I don't think I want to be free if you aren't." She glanced at the Chands. "Or you, also."

Ashok Chand said, "Kaushalya, we all appreciate what you want to do, but there's absolutely no purpose in your staying here."

"My father is here, too!"

"You can help him more from the outside," said Ashok Chand.

The jail superintendent said with a frown and a tone of annoyance, "I couldn't hold you anyway, Princess. Not after I've been specifically directed to release you."

"Who directed it?" asked Kaushalya, although she was almost certain.

The superintendent turned away. "I'm not sure I'm permitted to say, Princess. But he's a big man in the government."

It had to be Batra. "May I at least see my father while I'm here?" she asked.

The superintendent glanced back to her, his eyes cool. "Princess, you know it's not the day for visiting."

Feeling like a traitor, she bid farewell to the Chands, Pratap, and the others. "Is there anything I can do for you?" she asked as she turned to leave.

Ashok Chand smiled. "Just keep the faith. This too will pass. I know—I've been through it a few times."

Back at her own house, tears came as she thought about her friends in jail. She hated feeling so helpless.

And Dev Batra probably expected her—at the very least—to contact him to thank him for her release. But she was in no mood to talk with him. He had steadfastly refused to arrange the same release for her father, who was in much worse need of it. And he undoubtedly would want repayment.

For now, she postponed the call.

17

Mangarh

Upon returning to Mangarh, Kaushalya had Bhajan Lal drive her, with Gopi, to Savitri Chand's house.

"Auntie, I'm so sorry about your brother and the family," Kaushalya told Dr. Chand. "Is there anything I can do?"

Savitri Chand smiled in gratitude, but shook her head no. "Our lawyer is working on it, and some of my brother's friends in the government. I think the rest of us must be patient."

"I feel like such an idiot," Kaushalya said. "I had no idea what they were doing. They were probably sheltering Pratap and other fugitives in the house at the very times I was visiting and I never had an inkling. Usha warned me off, but I never understood why."

Dr. Chand nodded. "She was just trying to protect you, I'm sure."

"I only hope nothing I did led the police to them."

"Oh, no. There was probably some informer involved. I'm sure the arrest had nothing to do with you."

Kaushalya sat silently for a time, looking at the floor. Then she looked at Savitri Chand. "I feel so frustrated! It seems like I should be able to do something to help, but I can't think of anything."

Savitri Chand smiled gently. "My brother's used to jail."

"I know," said Kaushalya morosely. "My father put him there often enough. But Usha and her mother, too! I feel if they're in jail, I should be also."

"I can't help but feel the same. But I'm sure they would tell you to stay away if at all possible."

Kaushalya shook her head. "Maybe I should be in one of the anti-government demonstrations in Delhi. Then I'd be arrested again for sure."

"Or have your head bashed in a *lathi* charge. No, better to stay here."

"I hope I'm not using it as a convenient excuse, but I think my father does still need me free to help him. He's not at all well."

Dr. Chand gave a solemn nod. "There are other ways to help resist the government, besides doing something to end up in jail."

18

New Delhi, April 1976

Now that Vijay was back in Delhi, he began a routine for the meditation practices suggested by Guru Dharmananda. In his small but pleasant flat in Nizamuddin East, he would meditate for a time in the mornings before leaving for the office, and again at night. Although he was unable to resolve the dilemmas inherent in his masquerade as a Rajput, he acquired more of an acceptance of his state, as well as more of a faith that eventually matters would somehow work out.

When he walked or rode his motor scooter the five kilometers to work and back, he sometimes thought about the items of jewelry and the gold that hadn't been found. With his promotion still so much in doubt, it could help him considerably if he came up with an idea that would lead to locating them. But the search had been so thorough. It seemed most likely the missing riches were no longer in Mangarh. If so, where had they gone?

New signboards continued to appear. One day, as he was riding his scooter, he saw a sign that urged: Defeat the Design of Sabotage by Reactionary Forces.

He increased his speed to quickly leave such utter nonsense behind.

On another day, as he was walking, he saw a large, new sign above the ground floor on a building: The only magic way to remove poverty: HARD WORK - CLEAR VISION - IRON WILL - STRICTEST DISCIPLINE. Indira Gandhi.

He shook his head, and he resumed thinking about the missing jewelry and gold. And about Shanta. But he resolved neither one.

On yet another day, he had just parked his scooter near the entrance to the Chandni Chowk bazaar when he saw a small crowd. A tall, attractive woman was being photographed by a couple of camera-bearing young men. She was standing next to a new sign, which she was gesturing toward. In red letters it said: YOU HAVE TWO, THAT WILL DO. Sanjay Gandhi.

He recognized Urvashi, whom he had met at Dev Batra's farmhouse. He thought for a moment, and he decided the slogan was probably the best he'd seen yet in Delhi in terms of the catchiness of the wording, and maybe even in its likely effectiveness. Urvashi's gaze drifted toward him and paused for a moment, then moved on with no sign of recognition.

He was concentrating on a file on his desk when Akbar Khan, the driver, appeared and diffidently asked if he might speak to the *sahib*.

"Of course. Please sit down." Vijay indicated a chair.

Akbar Khan looked at it uneasily, obviously unaccustomed to being seated in the presence of a superior. Vijay saw frown lines in the small man's forehead, a worried look in his eyes.

"Can I help you with something, Akbar Khan?"

"*Sahib*, I didn't want to trouble you...." He stopped, staring at the floor.

"Please go on," urged Vijay, careful to sound unhurried. "I'm glad to help any way I can."

"Sir, I wouldn't have come to you. But you have always treated me kindly. Not like some of the other officers. So I thought maybe...."

"I'm glad you came to me. What's the problem?"

"Sir, it's my home! A bulldozer is nearby, pushing down houses. Our whole neighborhood is to be destroyed!"

"A bulldozer? Who is doing this?"

"The government, sir! The police are there to stop anyone from interfering. I tried to talk with them, but they said they'd arrest me. I'm afraid to do anything now. But my house was built by my father's father! Where will I live if they pull it down?"

Vijay stared at him, surprised, uneasy, yet doubtful. "There must be some reason. Why would they do this?"

"They say our *mohalla* is a slum. That Sanjay wants to make the city beautiful by getting rid of slums, to open up views. *Sahib*, our neighborhood isn't rich. But it's not a slum. Most of the houses have been there many years. The neighbors have known each other for generations!"

Sanjay again. Vijay shook his head, frustrated. "I truly wish I could help. But I don't know what I could do."

"Sir, if you would just come see! Maybe the police would listen to you. They said they'd arrest me if I didn't go away. But you...."

Vijay again shook his head. "I have little influence. Very little." He saw Akbar Khan's look of disappointment, and felt as if he were somehow betraying the long-time driver, who had always been so loyal and dedicated. He took a deep breath. "If you want, I'll come—maybe I can think of something if I see what's happening."

Or, he thought, seeing Akbar Khan's spirits lift, maybe the incident's over already.

They went out into the late morning heat. They took an autorickshaw toward the predominantly Muslim area near the southern wall of the old Mughal Delhi, only a couple kilometers from the office. As they drew near, a police jeep, lights flashing, passed them.

A crowd had gathered where Akbar Khan told the driver to stop. As Vijay paid the driver, two van loads of police arrived.

A bulldozer roared, and Vijay turned toward the sound in time to see the wall of a house collapse with a tumbling crash. A cloud of dust rose, millions of tiny particles glistening in the sunlight.

Vijay strode over to a gray-bearded Sikh policeman who appeared to be one of those in charge. "Can you tell me what's going on, *sardarji?*"

The man, sweating from standing unshaded in the noontime sun, shot him an annoyed look and said, "You'd best leave if you want to avoid trouble." He returned his attention to the gathering crowd.

Vijay took out his Income Tax Officer's identification, showed it. The policeman spared it a quick glance, then said, "DDA's targeted these houses for clearance. The people who live here obviously don't like the idea."

So the Delhi Development Authority was involved. "Can you tell me who's in charge for the DDA?"

The policeman inclined his head. "Chap's over that way."

Vijay went in the direction indicated. He saw a small knot of men in civilian clothes engaged in animated discussion with several uniformed police. He approached one of the civilians, a smallish, middle-aged man who seemed not to be actively engaged in the conversation. "Excuse me, sir, can you tell me why those houses are being torn down?"

The man turned tired eyes toward him. "Redevelopment. More bulldozers are coming soon."

"On whose orders?"

"Delhi Development Authority. Look, we're just following directives."

"Whose directives?"

The man turned away. "They came straight from the top."

"The top—you mean the head of the DDA?"

"That's right."

"But why?"

He shrugged and waved a hand to gesture helplessly. "I'm the wrong one to ask—I just handle resettlement. We've told these people the government will give them new houses in the suburbs, bigger houses than they have here. But some of them don't like the sterilization requirements."

"What? Did you say *sterilization*? Before they can get new houses?"

The man again gestured helplessness. "Right. It's required to get most anything from the government now, you know—" Abruptly, a stone struck his shoulder. "Bloody—!" His eyes darted about.

A volley of bricks now sailed through the air. Other men yelled as they were hit.

The crack of a gunshot echoed over the excited murmuring of the crowd. A woman shrieked. Suddenly people were running in all directions.

A can-like object flew overhead, struck a wall and fell, an acrid smelling mist rising from it. Tear gas! "We'd better leave!" Vijay shouted to Akbar Khan.

"But, sir—my house is only two streets away! I should go to my family."

Vijay glanced at a line of policemen advancing with bamboo *lathis*. He wondered if his Income Tax Officer's ID could get him and Khan safely out. The police appeared to be giving no one an opportunity to explain or plead. Vijay seized Khan's arm. "Your family's probably safer than we are right now. We need to leave!"

More gunshots.

Reluctantly, Akbar Khan nodded.

They ran, only to encounter a cordon of policemen with cane riot shields and iron-tipped staffs, who faced a wave of panicked women, children, men, all trying desperately to escape the area. Apparently the police were allowing no one to leave.

More shots. A young man near Vijay clutched at his chest and fell. An old woman bent over the victim, shrieking.

Vijay looked about, trying to see where the firing came from. He saw men in police uniforms on nearby roofs, taking aim with rifles. He crouched, trying to make himself inconspicuous in the crowd. He tugged at Akbar Khan, pulling the man into a hunkered-down position also.

"This way, sir!" Akbar Khan said in Vijay's ear. "I might get us out."

Still half bent, he shoved through the crowd, Vijay close behind. People were pressing in on all sides as Khan reached a small doorway. He pushed urgently on the latch, but nothing happened. "It's locked!" a man shouted to him. "We've already tried."

Suddenly, the screaming increased. Vijay glanced outward, saw the row of police advancing, bashing at people with the *lathis*. They now were only several meters away, smashing shoulders, skulls, whatever was in their path.

Akbar Khan desperately worked the latch, tugged on the side of it. Abruptly it gave, and the door swung inward. Vijay hurled himself after Khan. He entered a tiny opening between two buildings, barely wide enough to squeeze through. He followed Akbar Khan, and behind him, he was aware of others forcing their way in, and the screaming receding to the rear.

The narrow space led to an alley, and the alley to a street, where the sounds of the gunfire and screams were far enough away to be muted.

They stopped. Other people poured past, but no police.

Drenched in sweat from the exertion in the heat, and from fear, with a trembling hand Vijay took his handkerchief and wiped his brow. Never before had he been in a situation where his life was in such obvious, immediate physical danger. Unsure of directions, he asked Khan hoarsely, "Can you lead us away from here?"

Although they now seemed safe, Khan looked dazed. After a few moments, he gave a nod and mumbled, "This way, *sahib*. I'm sorry. I didn't think the police would shoot at people!"

Although still weak from the fright, at the same time Vijay felt almost as if he had another chance at life. He never, ever, wanted to get into another situation so full of peril.

As they walked, Akbar Khan's eyes kept returning to him. "There's nothing I can do to help," Vijay said. "I'm sorry."

"Yes, sir."

"You'd better get your family away before the machines get to your house."

"Yes, *sahib.*"

"You know I'd help you if I could."

"Of course, *sahib.*"

Vijay thought about the destruction, the shooting. He thought about how dependable Akbar Khan had always been, about the countless hours of work to keep the jeep gleaming and clean, when it was not really even a requirement of being a driver. He wished he had influence with anyone at a level high enough to matter.

He wanted to reject the thought that came.

He knew one person who might, possibly, have that kind of influence. However, he detested the thought of having to pay court, to beg a special favor on the basis of a personal connection.

But Akbar Khan's peril would not allow him to do nothing.

They flagged down a passing autorickshaw and returned to the office. On the telephone, Vijay located Dev Batra at the Ashok Hotel, and he took Akbar Khan there.

In the outer room of the suite were an assortment of petitioners and hangers-on, seated on a couch and chairs grouped around a coffee table. The ever-smiling Gulab appeared from the room beyond, nodded to Vijay, and ushered him and Khan in to where Dev Batra, scowling, was seated in a large armchair. Batra took a puff on a cigarette and laid it in an ashtray. "Sit, Singhji. What can I do for you?"

Vijay gestured Akbar Khan to the couch beside him. Speaking in Hindi so Khan could understand he said, "Sir, this man is my driver. He's about to lose his house near Turkman Gate. I thought you might be able to prevent it. A riot is going on there this very minute. People are even getting shot! I think we were quite lucky to escape without being hurt, maybe even killed."

Batra tightened his lips and shrugged. "Naturally, I know about the riot. But what do I have to do with such things?"

"You have influence. Can you get the police recalled, give people time to cool down?"

Batra snorted. "It's obviously gone too far for that. You need to talk to the head of the Delhi Development Authority. But I think you'd find him far too busy right now."

"So you can do nothing to stop people from getting hurt and killed?"

"Who do you think I am? God himself? I don't have *that* much power!"

Vijay sat for a moment. Then he gestured toward Khan. "The bulldozers are pushing down houses in his neighborhood, and he's been told his house will be among them. Batraji, these aren't shacks in a slum, they've been there for generations. It's simply not right."

Batra took a draw on his cigarette. He gave a wave of his hand and said gruffly, "The land's gotten too valuable. The DDA plans some office buildings, I think. They'll make a lot of money off the scheme."

"The government would throw people out of their houses just to get money?"

Batra gave a harsh laugh. "It's been done before. Where have you been? Look—this is one of Sanjay's pet projects. I don't know if he really cares about the office buildings. But he wants to beautify the city, you know. Open up views to the big mosque. I'm sure he won't stop at this point."

"But Batraji, you know him so well. He might listen to you."

Batra stared sharply at Vijay. "Sanjay is busy. He hates to have people question him. Why should I annoy him over this matter? I don't even know this man of yours."

"He's been my driver for many years. He's very loyal."

Dev Batra frowned.

Vijay sat, his gaze locked with that of Batra. It seemed indelicate to remind the man that Vijay had saved his life, as well as salvaging a failed raid Batra had ordered.

The two men stared at each other for what seemed forever to Vijay. Then a slight grimace twisted Batra's lips. "What street is this man's house on?"

Vijay looked to Khan, who replied, "Numbers 2245 to 2256, Gali Dakotan, Turkman Gate, *sahib*."

"Gulab, write that down," ordered Batra.

Vijay saw that Gulab was scribbling on a pad.

Batra said, "I'll see what I can do. But after this if you want favors from me, try to make them easier ones."

Vijay nodded, stood. "I'm grateful, Batraji."

Batra gave a regal wave of his hand. Gulab smiled them out.

In the hallway, Akbar Khan asked, his eyes tired but hopeful, "Is that *sahib* really going to help, sir?"

Vijay hesitated. He couldn't be sure if Batra would actually act. "Don't expect too much. He may not be able to get the orders stopped at this point."

Akbar Khan gave a nod and said calmly, apparently resigned to whatever Fate might bring, "I understand, sir. It's in Allah's hands, praise be to him. My entire family will be grateful that you've tried."

"Get your family to safety. Take as much time away from the office as you need."

He looked down. After a time, he replied, "Yes, sir. I'll do that."

"And be careful, Akbar Khan."

Khan looked up at him and nodded. "Yes, sir. I'll definitely try"

It was difficult to get work done the remainder of the day. He kept wondering what the bulldozers were doing, what was happening with the rioting. He drank cup after cup of tea as he shifted the files around on his desk, trying to find one that would capture his attention. But his thoughts would return to the situation at Akbar Khan's neighborhood.

On the way home from the office, he had the autorickshaw head toward the Turkman Gate area, but the streets were closed off, and no one he asked seemed to know much more than he did.

After a thorough bathing, he had dinner at Ranjit's flat that night, and he went over the main events with Ranjit and his wife Vimala Kaur.

"I've never been so afraid in my life," he said. "It's the first time I've actually heard a bullet going through the air! I hope I never do again."

"You were lucky to get away unharmed," said Vimala.

"Yes, I think we were."

Although he knew the government was censoring the news, he found it incredible that nothing, absolutely nothing, was on the radio or television about the Turkman Gate troubles.

There was no mention in the newspapers the next morning about the incident. However, Akbar Khan waited at the office, looking exhausted, but smiling. "It's a miracle, sir! The bulldozers have moved away. Everyone says no houses will come down on my street!"

"Is the rioting over?"

"Yes, sir. There's a curfew." He frowned. "The police are breaking into some of the homes nearby and stealing things. But no one is being shot now."

Vijay relaxed a bit, nodded.

"Allah, praise be to him, was merciful to us. But others have lost their homes. The bulldozers are still working in other areas."

Vijay nodded. After a time, he said, "I think not much can be done about the others. Probably not about the looting, either."

"No, sir. But my family and neighbors are most grateful to you."

"I didn't do much. It was Batraji."

"He didn't want to help, sir. It was you who got him to."

Vijay waved the thanks away. "I'm glad it worked. Frankly, I didn't think it would."

He soon found that Akbar Khan had told everyone who would listen about the matter, and that once again he was a hero of sorts, at least among the office staff.

19

New Delhi, May 1976

Mahendra repeatedly assured Kaushalya that he was working on a plan to get their father out of jail.

"You have to tell me what you're working on!" she insisted one evening when they were seated in the living room of their Delhi house. Now that they were in the midst of the hot season, the ceiling fans were beating the air, but the room remained stifling.

Mahendra took a drink of his Scotch and shook his head no. "It might not work out."

"I'm going crazy trying to think of something myself. If it's this hot for us, Daddyji must be absolutely sweltering in Tihar. Can't you give me a clue?"

He hesitated, then shook his head again. "It involves politics."

"I assumed that! But how? Are you making some sort of deal with Congress leaders?"

He looked away. "Something like that."

"But what are you offering them?"

"I can't tell you." He drained his glass, poured some more.

"I can't imagine why they'd need more votes for anything from the Opposition. They've got control, anyway."

Mahendra slammed the glass down. "Kaushi, I can't tell you yet!" He stood, grabbed the bottle, and strode out to the veranda.

She held her head in her hands.

The next night, she returned to Mangarh. With Usha Chand in jail,

Kaushalya's main confidante was Dr. Savitri Chand. On a visit to Dr. Chand's house on the outskirts of town, Kaushalya mentioned Dev Batra's demands. She gave an twisted grin of irony. "He wants me to spend time with him," she said. "And more. I'd never do it, of course."

"Your father would rather die than have you even *think* of it," Savitri Chand said firmly.

"I know. But it's hard to think that I hold the key to getting Daddyji out of jail and that I can't use it. I find myself feeling guilty over it!"

"Don't. It's Batra who bears the responsibility, not you."

"But I just don't know what else to do!" Kaushalya burst into tears, a rare event indeed. Sobbing, she let Savitri Chand hold her.

"There must be hundreds of thousands of people detained all over India now," said Savitri Chand. "Thousands of lawyers are working on getting them freed. The Emergency can't go on forever, you know."

"I suppose. It just seems like it."

Kaushalya received a telephone call from Mahendra, who was still in New Delhi. His voice sounded odd as he said, "Father's freed. I'm leaving to pick him up in a few minutes."

"Oh, at last! How did it happen?"

He did not answer at first. Then, he said, "I've been talking with Congress leaders. At the very top. I convinced them to free father. There was a price for it."

"A price?"

"I've switched parties. I tried to get them to agree to my merely dropping from active politics and resigning from the Swatantra Party. That wasn't enough. They said I had to actually join Congress."

"Mahendra! You didn't!"

"I had to." He sounded defensive. "You said yourself we had to get Father out. And we had to get those tax people off our backs *somehow*."

"But Mahendra, Father wouldn't have wanted you to join Congress! It's against everything he stands for! It always has been, even since before Independence!"

There was silence on the phone for a moment. Then he said, "Dammit, Kaushi, I had to! They'd have tried him as a criminal eventually, assuming he lived that long."

"Selling yourself out can't be the only way!"

"You saw how Father looked in jail last time. It would be a wonder if he survived another month there!"

She said in anguish, "I'll never forget how he looked for the rest of my life. But, Mahendra, he wouldn't have wanted to get out this way!"

There was a pause, then: "There were other reasons, too, Kaushi. I'm tired of being in the Opposition all the time. It's impossible to get anything accomplished."

"I can't believe you're saying that."

Mahendra spoke with a harsh edge in his voice, "Kaushalya, it's done. I've got him out. I'm taking him to the Chitale Hospital. You'd better come here." The line went dead.

Lakshman Singh was asleep when Kaushalya arrived late at night at the small hospital that catered to people able to pay a substantial amount for pleasant surroundings and private rooms. She had a cot moved in near her father, so she could stay with him all hours. At least the room was air conditioned, so as long as the electricity remained on, the temperature was comfortable.

She had brought books along to keep occupied, and in the morning, she was rereading her personal copy of Ashok Chand's *Jail Diary of a Reform Worker* when her father awoke, coughing. A smile spread across his face when he saw her. "Kaushi!"

She dropped the book and hurried to him and they embraced. He had lost so much weight, she clearly felt his shoulder bones though the hospital gown. Then he had to turn his head away as his body was seized by more coughing.

"Now that you're out, we'll get you over that, Daddyji," she said.

He grinned weakly. "Just get me back to Mangarh, and I'll be fine."

"We'll do that as soon as we can, Daddyji."

Mahendra arrived with a servant boy from their Delhi house, carrying a breakfast prepared by their cook. Lakshman Singh fed himself, eating slowly. "I'd almost forgotten how much better this could be," he said, "than what we were able to cook in jail."

Later, when Kaushalya had eaten an orange and some toast herself, Mahendra said, "Kaushi, I need to talk with you."

"All right."

They sat in the hospital's pleasantly furnished lobby. "Kaushi, the Emergency won't last forever, I know that. But even when it's over, Congress will still be in power. The only way I can have any effect on its policies is to be part of it."

He tried to catch her eyes, but she avoided looking at him. She looked away, trying to come up with something to say.

"Kaushi, I'm not betraying my principles! Congress isn't all bad. Sure, I disagree with a lot of their methods. Especially during the Emergency. Too many of the leadership are corrupt and self-serving. But most of them *are* concerned about the best interests of India. And they promised me a ministry sometime in the next few months. I can do so much more with that, than as a mere backseat member of the Opposition!"

She looked at him and said dully, "I hope you didn't sell out mainly for a ministry."

"Of course not, Kaushalya! How could you think such a thing? You aren't trying to understand."

She took a deep breath. "I thank god that Father's freed. But I still think your approach was wrong. Especially after what they're doing to our country. There are thousands of others still in jail, you remember. A lot of them are our good friends."

After three days, Kaushalya and Mahendra brought their father to their bungalow in Delhi, where he began taking walks in the gardens in the relative cool of the early mornings. One or the other of them always went with him, but he was able to saunter without any help. Four days later, at his insistence, they drove him to Mangarh.

Back at home, Lakshman Singh improved more quickly. Despite the unpleasant heat, former subjects immediately resumed coming to the Bhim Bhawan palace in the mornings to welcome him back and to seek their ex-ruler's advice on problems or his help in settling disputes. In the afternoons, he had Bhajan Lal drive him through the city and the surrounding countryside. People would stop whatever they were doing, bow and bring their hands to their foreheads to salute him as he passed in the familiar blue Bentley.

One evening, Kaushalya joined her father for a picnic at the small, white, domed summer palace on the Hanuman Sagar. It was hot, but two big, portable, stand-mounted electric fans made the temperature tolerable. Before eating, they sat with cool drinks in the cane chairs, enjoying the bougainvillea-draped veranda overlooking the lake. The delightful scent of jasmine hung in the air.

"I remember," Lakshman Singh said, "sitting at this very spot thirty years ago with Stanley Powis, discussing what it would mean to join my state with India. I was right about some things, like how bad the politicians would be at running the country. But I was wrong about the people demanding a return to my rule."

Kaushalya smiled gently at him. "Ways of thinking do change over time, Daddyji. Even though the people still respect you, the idea of being governed by a Maharaja seems old fashioned to many of them now."

"I know." The sun was setting behind the hills when he said, "I do want to be in politics again, whenever this so-called 'Emergency' is over."

"What would you do, now that Mahendra represents Mangarh in Parliament?"

He was quiet for a time. He had never criticized Mahendra for the switch in allegiance, but to Kaushalya his complete silence on the subject was enough to indicate his views. "I need to work that out," he said. "But I have to do everything I can to make sure Madam recognizes India isn't her personal empire to do with as she wishes."

Kaushalya tensed. "You aren't going to do anything to land yourself back in jail, are you?"

"Oh, no. I'll wait until the Emergency is over, when people who disagree with the government can speak freely again." He looked off into the distance. "You know, Kaushi, I really shouldn't have locked up Ashok Chand and those other agitators. I thought I knew what was best for my state, but I was wrong about that. So long as they weren't using violent means, I should have tolerated them."

She smiled at him. "Chandji knows you meant to do the right thing."

His own smile was a wry one. "Yes, well, there's nothing like being in jail yourself for a long period to make one realize that you don't send people there if there's any reasonable alternative."

She thought of Pratap in jail at this very moment, and of Usha with her mother and father. It seemed so unreal that she, herself, could be enjoying such a pleasant, quiet place, while her friends were enduring the crowded, rank-smelling, noisy confinement of Tihar jail.

After dinner, the two sat watching the stars come out over the lake until the mosquitoes became too much of a nuisance.

Kaushalya found her father looking at her more and more, at times when he didn't think she would notice. It gave her an odd feeling, as if he were trying to fix her in his memory in case he had to leave again.

"What are you thinking about, Daddyji?" she asked him one day in the dining room of the Bhim Bhawan palace, when he'd been watching her as they had coffee after their evening meal.

The servants had disappeared into the kitchen, so there was no one to overhear as he answered, "You, Kaushi. How beautiful you look. How fortunate I've been to have you."

She felt tears come to her eyes and quickly turned her head away.

"I have a lot of regrets," Lakshman Singh said. "One of them is that I've never seen you wear our finest jewels. You'd look so dazzling with the Mangarh Pearls around your neck. Or the Mangarh Emerald pinned on your sari. And I'd like to see you just once with the Star of Mangarh, to see you outshine it, as I expect you would...."

Her mouth had dropped open. She stared at him. "Daddyji! You still have them!"

He smiled at her for a time. Then he shrugged and shook his head slowly from side to side. "I shouldn't have mentioned them. It wasn't fair to you."

"I don't understand."

"There's no need for you to, Kaushi. Better forget the matter."

Kaushalya said in as stern a voice as she could muster, "Daddyji, do you have those jewels, or don't you?"

Lakshman Singh refused to say more.

20

New Delhi, September 1976

Finally, the monsoon rains brought relief from the months of intense heat smothering northern India. And at last, despite the failure to find the missing gems and gold, Vijay received official notice of his promotion to Assistant Director for Inspection.

Trilok Mishra summoned him to congratulate him, even offering him tea after Vijay was seated. Seemingly, the old accusation about taking gifts had been forgotten. "You will probably be assigned to head an office in a smaller city somewhere," said Mishra. "Udaipur seems likely. There's an opening there."

"I think I'd like that, sir. It's a pleasant town. Full of history." He added belatedly, "Of course, I'll miss this office and everyone here."

Mishra gave a nod. "You'll do well. I imagine the salary increase will be welcome, also."

"Yes, sir."

The tea came, and Vijay took a sip.

"You're not married," Mishra observed, with disapproval in his tone. "No one but yourself to spend the added income on, then."

Vijay hesitated, preferring not to discuss such personal matters. But a response seemed warranted this time. "I do send some money to my family in my home village, sir." Should he say more? There seemed no harm in it. "I'm also building a school in my home village. The added salary should be enough to subsidize a teacher."

Mishra stared at him in obvious surprise. "Quite impressive, Singh. More people should take matters into their own hands as you're doing. Not demand so much of the government."

Embarrassed now, Vijay almost wished he hadn't said anything. "I suppose so, sir."

"Yes, it's true," said Mishra. "People are always wanting more." He gestured toward his huge portrait of the Prime Minister. "Indiraji does a magnificent job. But people don't understand that government resources are limited. Especially with so much money being diverted by corruption. That's why the mission of our department is so vital. We can at least try to ensure the government receives the tax moneys it is entitled to."

"I certainly agree, sir."

"Well, I know you still have work to attend to, Singh."

"Yes, sir." Vijay finished the last of his tea and rose.

"You're a good man, Singh. Let me know if I can ever be of any help."

Surprised, Vijay replied, "Thank you, sir. I appreciate that."

Back in his own office, he thought about the likely upcoming transfer. He would definitely miss Ranjit. And some of his other colleagues. He realized he most regretted leaving Shanta.

Was there any way, without it seeming inappropriate or causing embarrassment, that he could ask her if she'd apply for a transfer to his new posting? Shanta could be invaluable with her quick mind, her good judgment. And every day her smile would brighten the office.

But of course, such a request was out of the question. Everyone would no doubt assume he had some ulterior motives, and both their reputations would be adversely affected.

After congratulating him, Ranjit said, "Be glad you work for the Income Tax Department and not for the Delhi Administration. You've heard about their new requirements for anyone appointed to a post?"

"What are you referring to?"

"Family planning is the first part of Sanjay's 'Five Point Programme,' you know. Under the Delhi Administration, preference for posts is now given to candidates with two or fewer children." He grinned and looked pointedly at Vijay. "And especially bachelors who are willing to be sterilized."

Vijay blanched. "If that's true, it's not funny."

Ranjit sobered. "Unfortunately it *is* true. And I know it isn't funny. There's a woman who's becoming quite notorious for her zeal in rounding up, uh, candidates."

"Sounds like the woman I met at Batra's farmhouse quite a while ago. Urvashi something or other?"

"That's her! If you see her again, you'd better run the other way."

When Vijay entered the office the following Monday morning, he saw, seated on a floor in the outer room, a small man wearing a turban in the style like the peasants of his own village, conversing with two of the peons and a male stenographer.

Uncle Surja! How could his uncle have found him *here*?

Panicked, Vijay stared at the small gathering. His uncle appeared uncomfortable in the office surroundings. The way the staff looked at Vijay with an odd combination of unease mixed with barely repressed amusement, he could tell they had learned something. The mere fact of his uncle sitting on the floor to avoid being on the same level as higher castes was telling.

Vijay had often wondered what he would do if a relative somehow located him. He'd tentatively decided he would brazen it out and hope no one realized just how low caste the relative was. After all, many people had poor relations who could be somewhat of an embarrassment at times.

But now that he faced the predicament, his mind went numb and his hands shook. He took hold of himself and tried to look pleased rather than stricken. He said, "Well! What a surprise! Welcome, Uncle. He moved forward and bent to embrace Surja. "I'm so glad you were able to find me at a time when I'm in Delhi!"

They separated, and his uncle pushed himself to his feet. Vijay said, "Come into my office, Uncle." He tried not to show how desperately anxious he was to get his uncle away from the staff in case nothing too revealing had yet been said. "How's your health?" he asked absently as they walked.

Vijay was too preoccupied to listen carefully as his uncle replied, "What you'd expect for an old man. I had the same fever from the rains I get every year. Malaria, you know. And the operation—" They stepped through the drapes into the small office, and his uncle said, "You must be a very big man, Nephew—a room all to yourself!"

Vijay shrugged, tensely forcing a smile of modesty. "Many other men have offices like these. Some are much larger rooms. A lot fancier, too." He stood stiffly, then dragged a chair closer to the desk. "Please sit, Uncle."

His uncle looked at the chair a moment, as if he'd never been offered one before, then awkwardly seated himself in it. He sat rigidly, a strained look on his pockmarked face. Vijay glanced quickly around, trying to see the office as his uncle must: the wooden desk, its top covered with papers weighted down against breeze from the ceiling fan; stacks of files with papers half spilling out, tied by heavy strings; black telephone; bell on the desk to summon peons; the obligatory framed photo of Indira Gandhi on the wall, beside an advertising calendar from Nirula Engineering. Not luxurious by New Delhi standards, but certainly not what a poor villager would see every day.

"What brought you all the way to Delhi?" Vijay asked, fearful of the answer, which was so likely to have something to do with a request for aid of some sort.

"We need your help," his uncle said. "To do something about the government. No one in the village has your influence. But after we saw your picture in a newspaper from Delhi and read about you, we knew you must be a big man here!"

"What brings you here, Uncle?" prompted Vijay again. It seemed to him that the man was upset and worried even beyond what could be expected from the disorientation of coming from a quiet village to a government office in New Delhi. "You said you wanted to do something about the government?"

His uncle shook his head sadly. "It was horrible. We've never seen anything like it before, even from the police! To...to...force us to do that...."

"To do what?"

"*Nasbandhi*! Even young men! Even men who haven't had children. My own younger son! How will he have sons of his own now?"

Vijay had gone rigid. "What? They forced Govinda to get *sterilized*?"

"Yes! That's what I've been telling you! The Family Planning men—they came with the Block Development Officer and the police. They said we had to offer fifty people to be sterilized. We refused, so the police just grabbed some of us! They took me and my son! Many ran away, but the police caught some of them. They even searched our houses! They said they were searching for people who'd hidden, but if they found any money or jewels, they took those, too."

Vijay stared at him, appalled.

"How can they do such a thing?" his uncle asked. "How can the government do this to us? We're used to the police taking gifts to leave us alone, to paying them to protect us. That doesn't bother us. But this is different. How can they do this?"

Vijay let out his breath. "I don't know," he said, his anger growing. "Things are different now. The Emergency, you know." Govinda sterilized! At only eighteen years old. Never to have a son or a daughter! If only he'd brought his cousin to Delhi to live with him as asked, it would never have happened.

"Can you help us?" his uncle asked. "We've heard doctors can sometimes change men back the way they were before. Can you make them send us doctors to do that?"

Vijay looked away. He gave his head a shake. "I doubt it," he said hoarsely. "That's an entirely different department, you know. Family planning has nothing to do with taxes. I wish I could help, Uncle. But I'm not so big a man as you seem to think."

"Your men said you saved the houses for your driver and his family."

Vijay frowned. Could he get Dev Batra's help again? It might not be totally impossible, but it would certainly be awkward. "That was different," he said as he mulled the matter over. "I was able to ask a big favor as repayment, about something that was happening right then. I don't think I could do it again, especially not so soon."

"Shouldn't the government at least pay us money? We can't afford to hire a lawyer to sue in court. But sometimes the government pays, what do you call it—compensation? Maybe we could use that to pay the doctors to help us."

Vijay looked away as he thought. Could Dev Batra in fact do anything? Batra had warned him not to ask for anything big or difficult again. He thought of Urvashi, who was so stridently involved in the sterilization project. Giving compensation of any kind would mean the government admitted it was wrong on a major program. It might set a precedent for hundreds, even thousands, of other claims. It was hard enough to get reimbursed when the validity of a claim was unquestioned. He sighed and looked back to his uncle. "I don't want to promise you anything, to get your hopes up, when it's not likely to happen. Not under *this* government."

His uncle lowered his eyes. "I thought you would know other men. Maybe even bigger ones. Maybe even Indiraji. Anyone who could help."

Vijay again looked away. "I wish I did, Uncle. I truly do." Seldom had he felt so inadequate. He wondered if he should ask if the *nasbandhi* procedure had been painful, if the wound was still sore. Probably the psychological pain was the worst. Especially for Govinda! He shuddered to think of what it must have been like to be seized, forced to submit to an operation like that. And in a country that was supposed to be democratic! How did the government ever expect to get people to go along with birth control if it terrified them, made them distrust the very idea? This type of approach had to be counterproductive.

His uncle again looked around. "Nice office." In the context, the statement seemed more an accusation than a compliment: if you're important enough to have such a nice office, why can't you do anything?

"I've saved some money, Uncle," Vijay said. "We'll definitely pay a doctor ourselves to try to reverse the operations."

His uncle brightened, slightly. "That's most kind of you, Nephew."

Vijay tried to bring his churning feelings under control. "It's the least I can do. I only hope it will work. And when the Emergency's over, we'll do our best to bring charges against those bastards who did it."

There was silence, and eventually, he asked, "Where are you staying, Uncle? You must stay with me, of course."

"Oh, I would never want to trouble you. I'll just find somewhere. My needs are simple, you know." They went through the ritual of Vijay insisting and his uncle objecting, knowing full well that his uncle would stay with him.

His uncle then said, "I talked with the other government men while I waited for you. They say you are a very important tax man. Especially after finding the treasure."

"I was just lucky," Vijay replied. He'd been worried about that chat his uncle had with the peons and the stenographer. "Don't believe everything you hear in the city, Uncle."

"They were very interested in you, Nephew. They asked all about our village, what work we do. I thought you would have told them by now."

Vijay felt the room begin to tilt.

"One of them actually thought you were a Rajput!" his uncle said, and guffawed. "I told them if you were a Rajput, then so was I. They all thought it was quite a joke. They had a good laugh."

They knew!

Vijay gripped the arms on his chair to steady himself.

His uncle was eyeing him with a puzzled look. "You seem pale, Nephew. Are you feeling all right? You don't have a touch of malaria fever, too?"

Vijay took out his handkerchief and wiped his moist forehead. In a few moments he said weakly, "Actually, Uncle, I *don't* feel so good. I think I may leave for the day."

"Don't let me keep you from your work. I can just wait here until you're done."

Vijay stood. "No, let's go to my home."

21

It was a trial having Uncle Surja come to the small two-room flat, to have to fix meals and arrange the bedding. His uncle then asked him to read from the *Ramayan*. Vijay complied for ten minutes or so; as he concluded the passage he realized he couldn't remember a word of what he'd read.

Somehow Vijay survived to the next morning, but he slept not a second the entire night. The impact at the office of the revelations would be devastating.

And his uncle would no doubt want to stay at least a few days, maybe longer, to see the sights of Delhi.

In the morning, Vijay hinted that he had a great deal of work to do in order to leave Delhi soon, while at the same time going through the ritual of encouraging his uncle to stay a while. To his relief, his uncle insisted on returning to Mangarh right away to report to the rest of the family, and Vijay saw him safely onto a bus.

When Vijay entered the outer office, he felt certain the peons and stenographers looked strangely at him, gave each other odd glances.

They knew.

Even aside from the joke about being a Rajput, everything about his uncle's appearance and demeanor and conversation shouted "Untouchable!" The information would have spread to everyone within minutes. Vijay strode through the doorway curtains into his own office and took his seat behind the desk. He sat, holding his head in his hands.

What would it mean?

He doubted it would affect his promotion, not at this late date. Withdrawing his Assistant Directorship after it had already been approved would amount to saying that the department was prejudiced against Scheduled Caste people.

But the humiliation of being found out was agonizing. By pretending to be high caste, he had demonstrated that he, himself, considered one's caste important. He had shown he felt himself so inferior by his own birth that he had to hide his origins. And in being found out, he made himself look to be a liar, a fraud.

"May I come in, Vijay?" It was Ranjit Singh's voice.

Vijay straightened himself, tried to make his voice sound even. "Of course."

Ranjit sat down. "I just wanted to let you know I don't believe it. Even if it were true, it wouldn't matter to me. Not one bit. But I know it's ridiculous. I've told everyone that."

Vijay was looking down at the desk top. He said weakly, "I'm grateful. But it's true."

Ranjit stared at him. "It's true?"

Vijay looked up, but he couldn't meet his friend's eyes. "Yes."

"You're joking!"

"No. It's true."

Ranjit still stared. "I don't believe it."

Vijay's eyes met his briefly, then darted away. After a time: "It's true." He glanced back to Ranjit and saw his confusion.

"You're serious."

Eventually, "Yes."

"Well." Ranjit sat frozen. He at last looked away. "As I said, it doesn't matter. Only..."

"What?"

Ranjit again stared at him. "Why the hell didn't you ever tell me? I feel like a fool! Assuring everyone you were Rajput, when...."

"I'm sorry, I really am. I didn't think anyone other than myself would be hurt if it were found out. I should have known better."

They sat there in silence, both looking down. Then Vijay said, "I'm grateful for your standing by me."

Ranjit hesitated, then shrugged. "You'd do the same for me." He examined Vijay. "I'll make out all right. People may even admire my loyalty, once they're done laughing at me. But how are *you* doing?"

Vijay sighed, again held his face in his hands a moment, then looked up. "I'll be OK. It's hard, but I'll brazen it out."

"It won't change much of anything, you know" said Ranjit. "You've helped out a lot of the staff, and they haven't forgotten. Everyone here respects you for your work, not your caste. That won't change."

Vijay gave a slight nod. "I'm glad." His voice sounded like a croak to him. There was an awkward silence. Then he said, "The tongues must really be wagging. I suppose Ghosali is floating through the air with joy."

Ranjit shook his head. "Actually, he seems furious that he allowed himself to be fooled by you. He doesn't dare say it, of course, but I think he may even be outraged at the thought that such close contact with an 'Untouchable' might have polluted him." He looked closely at Vijay. "I'm still not sure I believe it. You're really not joking? This isn't some kind of a test for us, to see if we're prejudiced?"

Vijay managed a stiff, crooked smile. "It's not a joke. Or a test. I wish it were."

Ranjit again looked away for a time, then back. "Why did you do it, *yaar?*"

Vijay told him about what it was like growing up as an outcaste. About all the years of humiliations, of beatings, inflicted by the other schoolboys. About his father being killed for working for better conditions for the Untouchables. "I decided I was never going to suffer those types of insults again. I wanted to help my people, but not to get killed for it like my father. It seemed like I could help more by joining the same class as the oppressors, getting some influence, being in a position to send money for improvements."

Ranjit nodded. "I see. Like the well and your school. Maybe I don't blame you. Maybe I'd have done the same, if I'd gone through what you did. Still, it's hard for me to get used to the idea."

"I understand."

"Well." Ranjit stood. He looked at Vijay, and shook his head. "As I said, it doesn't matter so much in the long run. Let me know if I can help. Anything."

"You've already helped. I'm grateful. And sorry."

Ranjit gave a quick nod, and he left.

Files lay open on Vijay's desk. Although he stared at them, he had no idea what they contained. The morning dragged. Thoughts, feelings churned within him. Ranjit would not spread the word, but by the very fact he stopped denying the rumors, everyone would be certain—

"May I come in?" Shanta stood in the doorway. Her usual smile was there, but subdued.

"Please."

She came forward, stood, glanced at him, and at the chair before his desk. Awkwardly he gestured toward it. "Please sit if you'd like."

Shanta sat, and looked at him with troubled eyes. "I've talked with Ranjit. If I'm saying anything that's out of line, just let me know. I wanted to tell you it doesn't matter to me, personally. I understand completely why you wanted to hide your background—a lot of Scheduled Caste people do. You just decide that you don't want to tolerate any more humiliation. And that you could help your people more if you were higher caste."

Vijay nodded, his lips fixed grimly.

She continued, smiling warmly at him, "I wanted to assure you that you can go on being just as effective in your job. I know from experience. Being Scheduled Caste, at least in government offices, causes difficulties mainly if you *let* it cause difficulties. Some people avoid you. Some talk about you behind your back. I've always considered that to be their problem. I don't let it become mine. Most people treat you the way you expect to be treated. If you show them that you respect yourself, they'll respect you, too."

Vijay again nodded. "That makes sense."

She gave him one of her dazzling smiles. "End of lecture. You'll do fine." She rose. "Let me know if I can help any. Even if it's just talking about it."

He managed a tight smile in return. "Thanks, Shanta. You've already been a help. A big help."

She left, a luminous figure in a bright blue sari, an oasis of comfort in his desert. Suddenly he realized: I no longer have to pretend I'm above her socially. Abruptly, his entire reality rearranged itself, as if the earth had shifted on its axis and down had become up. The implications were enormous. Marriage was now feasible for him. A family.

It took some minutes for him to adjust to the idea, to confirm that there was no fault in his thinking.

It was true. And he knew the woman who had just visited him was the one he wanted. Was Shanta a realistic possibility? Two days ago, any such relationship with her would have caused so many complications as to be out of the question. But no longer—now that he was openly a Dalit, too.

There were still barriers. The Chamar shoemakers of Agra might be "Scheduled Caste," but that didn't necessarily mean they'd look kindly on a marriage with a Bhangi sweeper, whom even the Untouchables considered the lowest of the low.

Still, it was quite feasible. If she would have him, of course. If he was acceptable to her family. The more he pondered the idea, the more it excited him. The idea of having Shanta share his life, beside him always, was like encountering a refreshing breeze after months of unbearably hot days.

Unable to sit still, he stood and rapidly paced about his office as he began to plan. What would his own family think about it? His mother might have a moment of initial disappointment at not being the one to initiate the search for a wife for him, but her next feeling would be pure delight that he would be married *at last*. And when she met Shanta, there would be no doubts whatsoever.

He'd better get moving on it right away, before Shanta and her family decided to get involved with arrangements with some other possible husband.

Shanta. How right for him she was. He fervently hoped she'd agree. Somehow, based on a lot of little signs over the past months, he felt she would.

22

Mangarh, January 1977

As abruptly as she had imposed the "Emergency," after a year and a half of virtual dictatorship, Indira Gandhi lifted the ban on political parties. She released her leading opponents and called for elections in March. The move took her opposition by surprise, but they rallied quickly, as the elections were only two months away.

Kaushalya telephoned Delhi and learned, to her relief, that the Chands and Pratap Singh were among those released. They had been in jail for eight months. She made plans to go to Delhi for a visit, as soon as they had a few days to recover and get accustomed again to their freedom.

At dinner the evening after the elections were announced, Mahendra asked, "Did you hear Swami Surya's prediction? He consulted his astrological tables and says the voters will give Indiraji and her Congress a huge victory."

"I certainly hope not!" said Kaushalya. Then she realized: "Oh!" She looked to her brother. "I forgot for a moment that if Congress loses, you won't be in the ruling party."

Their father said, "I'm going to run for Parliament again. Against Congress, I'm afraid, son."

Speechless, Kaushalya stared at him. He'd hinted at getting involved in politics again, but she'd assumed he'd adopt some other approach.

Mahendra said, "But Father! *I* represent this constituency! Do you mean you'd try to run in another district?"

"No. I'd run from Mangarh, naturally. Now that you've switched, you're the Congress Party candidate. I don't want Congress representing Mangarh. So I'll be running against you. Unless you choose to withdraw."

Mahendra, too, was now speechless. At last he managed, "Father, you know I did it largely for you! And they've promised me a ministry!"

Lakshman Singh shrugged and said, "We do what we have to do. I know I must run. Somehow we must eliminate this scourge on our land. If you feel you must run, too, then of course we must be against each other."

"Daddyji," said Kaushalya, "it's your health I'm concerned about. Are you really sure you're up to it?"

"We do what we have to do, Kaushi."

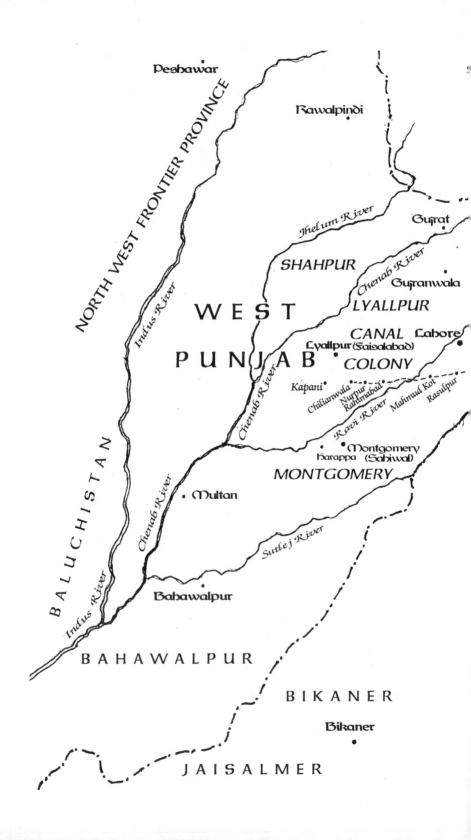

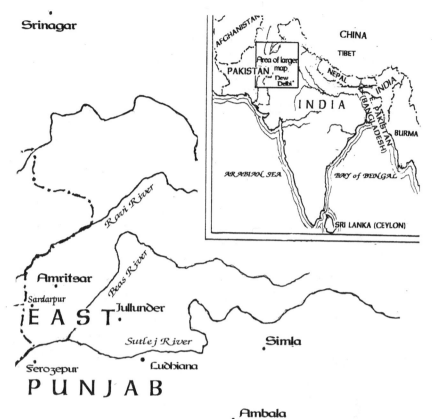

Srinagar

Ravi River

PAKISTAN

Amritsar
Sardarpur

E A S T

Jullunder

Beas River

Sutlej River

Ferozepur · Ludhiana

P U N J A B

Simla

· Ambala

Patiala

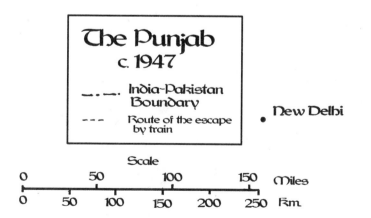

The Punjab
c. 1947

— · — India-Pakistan
Boundary

- - - Route of the escape
by train

· New Delhi

Scale

0   50   100   150   Miles

0   50   100   150   200   250   Km.

The Costs of Freedom

1

Western Mangarh State, early June 1947

The big Buick convertible leaped into the air and returned to the sands with a spine-jarring landing. Not slowing, it sped across the desert. A terrified herd of antelope scattered before it. Still it sped on. In the front passenger seat, Stanley Powis, British Political Agent at Mangarh, thrust his solar topee back onto his head with one hand while he gripped the hand-hold with the other.

What didn't he do in the name of duty! He hated the way the Maharaja of Mangarh drove. But he'd had an unusually good relationship otherwise with the thirty-six year old ruler, and he did not want to risk jeopardizing it. He knew Lakshman Singh was fully aware of his discomfort. That was probably one reason the ruler insisted on these drives from time to time: to show that even though the British may be paramount in India, the Maharaja of Mangarh could put the Viceroy's representative in fear for his life, and get away with it.

In the back was a young Rajput aide-de-camp, who had even less choice than Powis about the ride. The backup car somehow managed to remain in sight, but it was well behind.

Powis having to put his life at risk was even more ironic, given the announcement on All India Radio three days ago. After roughly two centuries of dominance, the British were completely withdrawing from India—*and in the incredibly short time of two months.*

The car shot straight toward a small conical rock hill of the type often found in the desert bordering the western slopes of the Aravalli range. As they neared, the top of the hill resolved into a tiny whitewashed temple. From the earliest times, these hilltops, like so many other natural features, had been sacred to gods.

Lakshman Singh stabbed hard on the brake pedal. The heavy car whipped from side to side in the sand. A broad grin on his face, the Maharaja spun the steering wheel first one way, then the other, slowly regaining control. After what seemed like forever to Stanley Powis, the big vehicle skidded to a halt.

Lakshman Singh turned to smile broadly at his British Political Agent. "Pretty good driving, Stanley?"

Powis took a clean handkerchief from his pocket, unfolded it, and wiped his brow. He looked at the Maharaja. "Any chance I could drive on the way back, Highness?"

Lakshman Singh laughed heartily. "Very good, Stanley! You think I'm a crazy daredevil driver, but you're too polite to say so. Come. Let's walk."

The ADC in the back seat remained with the car. Lakshman Singh strode briskly to the base of the hill. Powis kept pace at his side until they started up the path that wound up to the temple. Then he let the Maharaja lead.

It was beastly hot in the June sun. Why had Lakshman Singh come *here*? Normally this type of place intrigued Powis; all the ancient places of Rajputana fascinated him. For years he had been captivated by the region where so much of the past survived: the palaces, the walled cities, the temples, the mountaintop forts, the desert villages, the jungle-clad Aravalli Mountains. He also felt a curious affinity for the colorfully clad people, the peasants as well as the aristocracy.

Sometimes, indeed, he felt he believed in the Hindu concept of reincarnation—perhaps in a prior life he had been a Rajput himself, or at least associated with them. He had virtually memorized the classic book on the region, Colonel James Tod's mammoth *Annals and Antiquities of Rajasthan*. He felt privileged to be associated in person with a Maharaja who was a direct descendant of rulers such as those Tod had written about over a century ago.

At last they reached the top of the hill. Lakshman Singh slipped off his shoes and folded his hands before the image of the deity, a crudely formed man on a horse. Stanley Powis wasn't sure which god this was, although it looked like a form of Bheru or Bhairava. Sometimes to his bemusement, he found that the worshipers even gave conflicting names for a god.

Lakshman Singh removed some rupee notes from his pocket and placed them at the base of the image. Powis was surprised that the Maharaja would be carrying cash. Usually a prince would think it beneath his dignity and would have his servants handle it.

Lakshman Singh lit a cigarette. Then, he sat down on the masonry plinth. His forehead glistened with perspiration. He said, "It's too hot now to come here. But this is one of the few places where we can talk undisturbed for a while before the villagers find me."

Powis smiled in sympathy. No matter where a person drove, the minute you stopped the car, people started appearing as if they had materialized from the earth itself. It was especially true when the Maharaja went out driving. People always wanted his *darshan*, or else to petition him for some favor or another. That was one reason Lakshman Singh liked to drive fast across the scrub lands away from the roads; fewer persons bothered him then.

"So you people are leaving us at last," Lakshman Singh said. "August fifteenth. A little over two months away."

"So it appears." Powis had expected the announcement, but not the date. So soon! He still got numb when he thought about it.

"And that bastard Jinnah gets his Pakistan, carving a big chunk out of India forever."

"I suppose Muslims have some legitimate worries about being dominated by Hindus once we British leave," said Stanley Powis.

Lakshman Singh looked out over the plain, in the direction of Jodhpur, which of course was much too far away to see. "Any advice for me?"

Powis said, "I agree with Sir Conrad that you should continue to hold out for independent status." Like Powis, over the course of a long career in India, the Viceroy's Political Advisor, Sir Conrad Corfield, had grown sympathetic to the rulers of the princely states. "When the British Paramountcy lapses, so do all its treaties with you. The new Indian government will have to completely renegotiate with you and the other princes."

Lakshman Singh grinned at him. "That means I can do whatever I please, at long last."

Powis grinned back. "You usually do anyway, Highness."

"But if I'd ever gotten too far out of line, you'd have made sure I was deposed. Like Alwar."

"His Highness of Alwar was an extreme sadist, Highness."

"And I'm not, even when I inflict my driving on you?" Lakshman Singh again smiled. Then he turned sober. "I think the Congress may give me trouble. Even the changes I've made don't seem to satisfy them."

Powis sighed. His main failure as British Political Agent at Mangarh had been to make Lakshman Singh really understand the need for reform. Major reforms, not just window dressing. He said, "Highness, you can't exist forever as an island of one-man rule in the center of an ocean of democratically governed people. Even the King-Emperor has to go along with the will of his people as expressed in Parliament. We've discussed this before."

"I've got a legislative council, Stanley."

"Which you appoint by yourself." Lakshman Singh looked away. "Another matter, Highness. It might defuse the Congress complaints at least a little if you let Ashok Chand out of jail again."

The Maharaja shook his head no. "That agitator's caused me a lot of problems. And that bloody diary of his! I wish I'd known he was going to publish it as a book. He makes me seem ignorant of any modern ideas, as well as incompetent at running my government."

"It's not quite so bad as all that, Highness. In a way you come out looking quite humane, the way you tried not to make it too hard for him in prison."

"Humph! I've made my share of mistakes. That may have been one."

"He's been detained over a year this time, Highness. And I understand his father's quite ill."

The Maharaja replied, "Yes, his wife has been constantly after me to let him out."

"Jaya Chand is a lovely lady," observed Powis. "It's hard not to feel some sympathy for her, even though you know I don't care for her husband's political views."

"She may be pretty, but she's too outspoken and persistent for my taste."

"Maybe that's understandable if she wants her husband freed."

"Maybe. She can't give me a guarantee he'll behave, though. You know she's been involved in her share of agitation herself. I should probably have locked her up, too. Even her mother has been rather vocal about so-called 'reforms.'"

"Yes, Mrs. Arora has become somewhat notorious."

The Maharaja turned to a different subject. "You'll be leaving here in a couple of months, Stanley. What will you do? Go back to England?"

The thought disturbed Powis greatly. "Sooner or later I'll have to. Sooner is better, I think. There's really no place in India for me now. Even though I've spent almost all of my forty-one years here. Even though my grandfather and my great uncle and my father all died here."

"You must have family in England?"

"Some cousins. No one close. And no position waiting."

Damn, Powis thought—it would be a comedown to "return" to England. Probably no job, and only a marginal pension. No more bungalow (meaning mansion). No more servants. No title. Little more respect than that due the laborer next door.

"If I were to offer you a place as a minister in my government, would you be tempted?"

Powis looked at the Maharaja with real affection. "I'm flattered, Highness. Yes, I'd indeed be tempted. But I'd probably have to say no. I think it's better if we British get out. I'd just be a reminder of times most Indians would probably rather forget."

Lakshman Singh did not argue. He said merely, "The offer remains open."

"Again, thank you, Highness. I'm grateful." Powis had enjoyed his time in Mangarh. He'd been fortunate in discovering an unexpected friend in the ruler he was supposed to keep an eye on.

Powis had another major regret. He'd never been able to think of a good excuse for insisting on seeing the legendary treasure that was said to be guarded by the Bhil tribals in Mangarh's huge fort. But he realized this yearning of his was a trivial one, in the big picture.

Down on the plain, two small parties of people were converging on the hill from separate directions. If Powis and Lakshman Singh remained here, soon the ruler would be probably caught up in listening to complaints or petitions of one kind or another. Normally, he would patiently listen to his subjects, viewing it as an important obligation of his privileged position. But today, he had larger issues to concern himself with, matters affecting his entire state and its future.

"Stanley," the Maharaja said, "why don't you drive back."

2

New Delhi, 25 July 1947

The wood paneled, semicircular meeting room of the Chamber of Princes had been uncomfortably hot despite the whirring of the fans mounted atop columns throughout the room. The temperature was well over a hundred degrees outside as Lakshman Singh left the building with Vikram Singh, Raja of the small southeastern Rajputana state of Shantipur. Although Shantipur was entitled only to a nine-gun salute compared to Mangarh's fifteen guns, the two rulers had been good friends ever since they were princes attending Mayo College in Ajmer.

They stood in the shade by the entrance to the gigantic, round sandstone structure that would soon become the Parliament Building for the new government of India. "Have you decided yet what you're going to do?" asked the slight, mustached Shantipur Raja.

Lakshman Singh shook his head. "Not yet. And there's so little time to decide something so important."

The two and many of their brother rulers had just heard an address by the new Viceroy, Lord Mountbatten. Impressive in his white admiral's uniform, his chest half covered in medals, Mountbatten had strongly urged them all to immediately sign an Instrument of Accession announcing their alignment with either India or Pakistan, whose central governments would be paramount over the states *only* in three important areas: defense, foreign affairs, and communications.

Mountbatten had insisted that the central government would not have any authority to encroach on the sovereignty or the internal autonomy of the prince-ruled states in any other matter. Since the Viceroy was an aristocrat himself, even a cousin of King George, many princes assumed he would not urge them to do anything contrary to their best interests.

Lakshman Singh said, "I've assumed I'll opt for total independence for Mangarh after August fifteenth. But the Viceroy's damned persuasive. I think he could talk a tiger into parting with its fur coat. I have some serious reservations, though. I'm not at all convinced the Congress Party will keep its word."

"I have doubts, too," said Vikram Singh. "But I have no real choice. Shantipur's small enough we have no chance of being viable alone. I'll accede to India. You have more options, both because of your size and your location."

"I take it you haven't considered Pakistan."

Vikram Singh raised his eyebrows in surprise. "Oh, no. We're almost all Hindu, and we're so far from the Pakistan border. Don't tell me you're thinking of it?"

Lakshman Singh frowned. "Well, it's an option. I'm trying to consider all the possibilities."

Three days later, Lakshman Singh attended a reception held by Lord Mountbatten in the Viceregal Palace. The 340 room sandstone and marble edifice, capped by a giant central dome, was built by the British on a scale that far surpassed Lakshman Singh's own Bhim Bhawan palace in Mangarh.

Some fifty other rulers were also present, and around a hundred or so chief ministers and other representatives. A legion of servants in white tunics and gold and scarlet turbans awaited the needs of the distinguished guests. It soon became obvious to Lakshman Singh that the main purpose of the reception was to persuade the rulers to promptly align themselves with one or the other of the new nations. One by one, ADCs led the princes to one side of the huge reception hall to speak to the Viceroy.

It was the first chance Lakshman Singh had to talk with Mountbatten personally. The tall, handsome Mountbatten, again in his white uniform, was at his charming best. "I know of the long history of your family and of Mangarh, of course, Highness. You have a heavy burden to fulfill in order to preserve that great heritage. Have you made a decision yet?"

Lakshman Singh was warmed by the Viceroy's seeming understanding of the difficulty of the issue. But he said, "I'm still considering the matter, Excellency. I don't wish to be hasty on such an important question."

"Yes, well, you have a point. But if I may speak frankly, don't wait too long." Mountbatten lowered his voice. "I have it on good authority that a certain Jain millionaire has just donated considerable funds to the Congress to start an insurrection in Mangarh after 15 August. Not that you should be swayed by threats into doing something you feel isn't in your best interests, of course. But I felt you'd like to know."

Lakshman Singh stiffened. He tried not to let his face betray his dismay.

"If you're planning on acceding to India anyway," Mountbatten went on, "it's almost certainly better to do it sooner than later. You might avoid some unpleasantness that way. But now I see Mr. Menon is waiting for you."

A somewhat portly, bespectacled Indian stepped forward. Lakshman Singh scarcely heard the last words. An insurrection! He managed to thank the Viceroy for the information and turned to acknowledge Menon, while at the same time he briefly considered the status of his state army. Could it defend Mangarh if need be? It all depended, of course, on how large the insurrection was. "If you'll just come this way please, Your Highness," V.P. Menon said.

Lakshman Singh focused on him. Menon was a competent career civil servant who had been the primary draftsman of the plan to create Pakistan, although he was not actually drawing the boundary line. He was currently Vallabhbhai Patel's chief lieutenant in the newly formed States Ministry, which would handle relations between the central government and the separate, individual kingdoms still ruled by princes.

Menon led him across the room to where Patel was taking leave of another Rajput ruler. Universally referred to as "Sardar," an honorific title of leadership, Patel was widely considered the most important native Indian statesman after Jawaharlal Nehru and Mahatma Gandhi. Although Nehru would be Prime Minister, many, in fact, thought Patel a likely rival to Nehru for leadership of the new India.

"Your Highness! So good to finally meet you," said Sardar Patel, bowing his head in respect with palms pressed together. Newspaper writers often compared Patel with a Roman senator in appearance. Patel's white *khadi* robe was indeed draped in a manner somewhat reminiscent of a Roman toga, and his large bald head glistened. Patel confidently met the Maharaja's eyes and continued, "Your state is so important historically. How fortunate you are to be guiding it at such a critical time."

Lakshman Singh wondered to what extent Patel was pouring on the flattery. It was hard to tell—Mangarh *was* significant historically, despite its relatively small size. "So nice of you to say so," he replied.

"Yes, I look forward to the possibility of working with you on matters of common interest, Highness. Naturally, we have no desire whatsoever in interfering in your internal affairs, but we stand ready to help in whatever way we can, and to cooperate with your own officials regarding the railway and telegraph lines crossing your state and so on. I assume you have no problem with this?"

Lakshman Singh stared at him, wondering to what degree he should be suspicious. Certainly the type of cooperation Patel suggested was reasonable, indeed essential. But could it merely be the opening wedge for Congress interference in other areas? "No problem at all, sir," Lakshman Singh replied.

"Then I take it you're inclining favorably toward signing the Declaration of Accession to India," Patel said smoothly.

"I'm giving it serious consideration, of course," replied Lakshman Singh. "As soon as my ministers have studied the matter thoroughly, I'll be in touch with you."

"Fine!" said Patel, although Lakshman Singh sensed from a cloud that had abruptly veiled the man's eyes that he was unhappy with such a noncommittal response. Patel continued, "I know you realize the urgency of the matter and will expedite it. It seems to me you have nothing whatever to lose, since the areas of authority you'd be granting to the central government are ones you've never exercised and must have no interest in anyway."

Lakshman Singh deliberately remained vague. "As you said, I'm expediting the matter as quickly as possible."

"I'm pleased, Your Highness. If we can do anything at all to answer any concerns, please let me know. It's been so good to talk with you at last. A real pleasure! But I see His Highness of Palampur is waiting to speak to me. I hope we can talk again, quite soon."

"That's my wish also, sir."

An insurrection in Mangarh! Was it even possible? A year or two ago, even, he would have said the idea was absurd. Now he wasn't so sure. Ashok Chand, perhaps the principal leader of the so-called "reformers," was still in jail. Lakshman Singh felt certain Chand was unlikely to instigate a revolt himself; he professed to be a follower of Mahatma Gandhi, and hence to avoid violent methods. However, there were other agitators in Mangarh now, some of whom were not so scrupulous.

Lakshman Singh decided it was time to return to his state. But first, there was one more meeting.

The green and white Muslim League flag hung outside the mansion at 10 Aurangzeb Road. Inside the front door, Muhammad Ali Jinnah, the man almost solely responsible for the creation of Pakistan, greeted Lakshman Singh with a thin lipped smile that was probably as close as the taciturn leader came to turning on charm.

A wealthy lawyer educated in England, Jinnah wore his usual immaculate Western style suit of light colored linen. At age 71, so thin as to be almost skeletal, he stood almost six feet tall, but he was shorter than Lakshman Singh by three inches. Jinnah escorted the Maharaja to an armchair, then seated himself by a table bearing a stack of newspapers, which Jinnah was said to read obsessively. Nearby, on his mantelpiece, stood an oak plaque bearing a silver map of India, with Pakistan shaded green, the traditional Muslim color.

"Would you care for a cigar?" asked Jinnah, extending an elaborately decorated box.

"Thank you, no. I'm partial to these." The Maharaja drew out one of his own cigarettes and lit it.

"I think it quite likely," Jinnah said casually, after lighting his cigar and taking the first puff, "that Jodhpur, and possibly even Jaisalmer, will accede to Pakistan. If they do, then no one can seriously argue that Mangarh should not accede also, since there will be no Indian territories intervening between us."

Lakshman Singh was watching Jinnah's face intently. "And what if Jodhpur and Jaisalmer don't align themselves with Pakistan?"

Jinnah drew on his cigar and smiled thinly. "Mangarh would not be contiguous, but does that really matter? Look at the distance that will separate West Pakistan from East Pakistan. Two thousand miles!"

"Is there anything you can offer me that Patel and Nehru won't?"

Jinnah said, with a sly smile, "I'll offer you precisely what I offered Jodhpur." He puffed on the cigar and waited dramatically.

"And what is that?" asked Lakshman Singh at last, his own cigarette forgotten.

Wordlessly Jinnah fitted his monocle to his eyes, removed a piece of paper from the table beside him, unscrewed his fountain pen, and signed his name at the bottom of the sheet. He removed the monocle, and his deep sunk eyes glittered as he handed the paper to Lakshman Singh. "You may name your own terms. Anything you want. You fill in the page above my name."

Lakshman Singh looked at the paper, blank save for Jinnah's signature. Why was Jinnah willing to pay almost any price to have a Hindu state affiliated with Pakistan, a land created purely for Muslims? No doubt, a large part of the reason was that Jinnah realized his neighbor, India, would be far more powerful both militarily and economically. Whatever he could do to increase Pakistan's prestige and influence at the expense of India's was worth almost any cost.

And Jinnah was known to have an immense ego. Lakshman Singh had heard that the Congress leaders had snubbed Jinnah on occasion, sometimes deliberately, and sometimes through carelessness. Jinnah would no doubt consider any gain for Pakistan as a loss to the Congress leadership, and as convincing proof that he had outmaneuvered them.

Lakshman Singh looked over at him. "I'd like to freely import weapons into my state."

"Of course. You have every right to defend any threats to yourself or your government."

"Assuming Jodhpur joins with Pakistan, I want railway access to a port."

"Jodhpur must agree. But I've told him he can use Karachi as a free port. He'll also have control over the railway to Sind. I see no reason you couldn't use the same route."

"The famines are often bad in some parts of Mangarh. I may need aid occasionally."

Jinnah waved a hand in the air. "It is yours. Just ask. I'll see you get all the grain you need."

Lakshman Singh nodded. He snuffed out his cigarette in the ashtray. He rose and carefully folded the piece of paper. "I'll have to think on it."

Jinnah stood also. "Naturally, Highness. My offer remains open until you decide. However, please do keep in mind that you may find it more difficult to accede to Pakistan after 15 August. There will be no British to help keep the Congress in line, and they may try to prevent you."

Lakshman Singh eyed him. Did Jinnah know, then, about the threatened insurrection in Mangarh? He asked, "If, ah, I am aligned with Pakistan and I should run into any difficulties with pressure from the Indian central government, what assistance could I expect?"

Jinnah said, his face solemn, "If you are aligned with Pakistan, naturally I would guarantee your defense against external threats." He gave his thin smile and added, "You may insert that on the page you are carrying also."

Lakshman Singh nodded, and took his leave.

Delhi's Imperial Hotel always seemed overcrowded, and it smelled of floor polish and a spice Lakshman Singh could never quite identify. In spite of the numbers of newspaper correspondents, Western businessmen, and British officials constantly milling about the public areas, it was the most prestigious hotel in the city, and consequently the one where all the princes stayed. As the Maharaja was crossing the lobby on the way to his suite, with his ADC, a secretary, and two bearers close behind, a distinguished looking man moved into his path.

"Your Highness, I'm Henry Seldon, *Times* of London. May I have a word with you?"

Lakshman Singh, still thinking about the meeting with Jinnah, replied, "Perhaps later, Mr. Seldon."

"It will only take a moment, sir. What are your plans regarding your state? Will you accede to India?"

"Later, please."

Fortunately the reporter wasn't as pushy as some, and Lakshman Singh escaped without his ADC having to intervene.

When he arrived at his suite with the intention of getting ready to leave for Mangarh, he was surprised to see V.P. Menon waiting, already seated in the living area. Menon rose, but Lakshman Singh waved him back to the chair. Menon quickly apologized for the interruption, then came straight to the point. "Highness, we know certain states are seriously considering alignment with Pakistan instead of India. It's natural that you may be one of them."

Menon already knew! Obviously, someone was watching him, or Jinnah, or both. It made sense. Lakshman Singh replied, "Naturally, that is an option, Mr. Menon."

"Highness, have you considered that this might bring on violence between Hindus and Muslims in your state? Your huge Hindu majority would not take kindly to withdrawing from association with India in favor of a Muslim nation. Even if you, their ruler, say it is for the best."

"Mr. Menon, I'm trying to consider everything. Frankly, however, Mr. Jinnah has offered me some extremely good terms."

"We will match them. Within reason, of course."

"Food for famine relief, if needed?"

"Naturally, Highness. We'd be poor allies if we didn't help in such a case."

"Railway access to a port."

"You have it. We'll see that a line is built connecting Mangarh with the Gulf of Kutch."

"Free import of arms."

"That goes without saying. After all, it's *your* state. But we'll put it in writing."

Lakshman Singh sighed. "I'm returning to Mangarh at once. I hope to give you your answer soon."

V.P. Menon rose. He hesitated, then said, "Highness, I must be quite frank. We would consider it very undesirable from the standpoint of strategic defense to have a peninsula—or an island—of Pakistani influence reaching such a long way into India. I sincerely hope you will see that your interests are far better served by aligning yourself with India. Historically, geographically, politically—and by reason of religion—that makes the most sense."

Lakshman Singh said bluntly, "Mr. Menon, I understand your point." He also saw the not so subtle threat.

But if he did agree to accession to India, could he trust these leaders to keep their word about no additional interference in his state?

Mangarh, one day later

Lakshman Singh summoned his Dewan to the office in the Bhim Bhawan Palace and waved him to a chair. The big ceiling fans were whirring at full speed, and servants kept the reed mats over the windows wetted down, but the room was still hot.

"Care for something cold, Dewan?" asked the Maharaja. "Mango *sharbat*? Ice tea?"

"The *sharbat* would be good, Highness," said Ahmad Hasan Aruzi.

The manservant who had been standing near backed away, then hurried off. "Dewan," said Lakshman Singh, "what have you heard about any agitators who might be trying to incite a revolt in Mangarh?"

The prime minister said in surprise, "Why, only today I got wind of a possible plot from one of our informers, Highness. Someone's offered a great deal of money."

"Adinatha Seth," said Lakshman Singh.

Ahmad Hasan Aruzi knew the Maharaja had his own sources of information, but he was surprised that the ruler could have learned this while not even in the state.

The Maharaja continued, "Do you have the names of any others who might be involved?"

"A few, Highness. Some are well known to you, like Sundip Saxena. The Congress Party has also sent in a couple of new men. We're having difficulty locating their whereabouts, but we know they're here. It's said as a first step they're going to instigate a big demonstration calling for Ashok Chand's release. The Mangarh Praja Mandal leaders have already sent another petition asking that you let him go."

"I've outlawed the Praja Mandal again. So how can they request anything?"

"Through sympathetic persons who feel Chand's been held long enough, Highness."

"I've had no one see me personally about it recently, other than Ashok Chand's wife." He gave a wry smile. "She tries to see me every day."

"Highness, they may be afraid you'll put them in jail, also. We receive a continuing stream of telegrams and letters. That *Jail Diary* book of his has made him quite well known, it seems."

"And me, too. That bloody book!"

Ahmad Hasan Aruzi looked away.

The Maharaja asked, "How long has Chand been in jail now?"

The prime minister looked back to him, frowning. "Over a year, this time, Your Highness."

"That long!" The Maharaja appeared to be thinking. Then, he said, "Prime Minister, do you think Chand could be involved in organizing any of this pressure for me to accede to India?"

"It seems unlikely, Highness. A policeman is always present whenever anyone visits. Even if Chand somehow slipped out occasional messages, it would be a cumbersome way to arrange anything. Anyway, as a Gandhian, I doubt he'd encourage violent actions. Peaceful protests are as far as he'd go."

The Maharaja was silent for a time. Then, abruptly, he said, "You're a Muslim. What would you think if I aligned Mangarh with Pakistan, instead of India?"

Ahmad Hasan Aruzi stared at the ruler in disbelief. Ahmad had been Dewan of Mangarh for less than two months, and he wondered if he would ever get used to Lakshman Singh's ways. The Maharaja seemed to take delight in confounding him.

The servant returned with the *sharbat*, and Ahmad sipped at it. "I take it you're serious, Highness?" he said at last. The cool glass felt good, and he cupped both hands around it to the extent he could.

Lakshman Singh wore the slightly amused smile that Ahmad had become accustomed to seeing; it frequently made him wonder whether the Maharaja was having a private joke at his expense, or whether it was merely that Lakshman Singh habitually viewed the world as a stage meant for amusement.

The Maharaja said, "I'm quite serious. You need only look at a map. I have it on good authority that Jodhpur and Jaisalmer are both negotiating with Jinnah to see if he'll give them better terms than they could get from India. If either one joins, we'll then have a common boundary with Pakistan, or at least with states that have granted certain of their powers to Pakistan. But you haven't answered my question."

Ahmad said cautiously, for it wouldn't do to have his employer become suspicious of his loyalties, "Highness, even as a Muslim, I find it difficult to see Mangarh as part of Pakistan. Aside from the fact that you're Hindu yourself, so are over eighty per cent of your subjects. If you count Sikhs, it goes up to ninety per cent. You have less than ten percent Muslims. Culturally, as well as geographically, it makes much more sense to align Mangarh with India."

"Then you still don't think Mangarh could remain a totally independent nation, in a treaty relationship with India and Great Britain?"

Ahmad sighed inwardly and repeated what he had advised the ruler on previous occasions: "Highness, Mangarh is of too marginal a size to be a viable independent nation. It has no industrial base. Vital rail and telephone lines cross it, as well as roads, so the new Indian nation will insist on your complete cooperation in keeping those links open, and will want your customs barriers abolished. Your state army is small and not particularly well-equipped, so India will be able to dictate almost any terms to you it wishes."

"What if my army were not so small and ill-equipped?"

Ahmad examined the ruler's face, trying to read his thoughts. Sometimes Lakshman Singh seemed phenomenally perceptive and intelligent; other times, such as the present moment, he seemed incredibly dense or naive. "Highness, a state the size of Mangarh can't possibly hope to stand up to the Indian army. India will inherit all the troops and the equipment the British have built up, except for the twenty percent or so that will go to Pakistan."

Lakshman Singh was silent a while. Then he said, "Maybe you're right, Dewan. But we will pursue every possible means of keeping Mangarh independent. And we'll at least explore the possibilities of loosely aligning with Pakistan. If nothing else, the fear that we'll do just that may convince India to give us better terms in order to keep us on their side."

Ahmad nodded. "As you wish, Your Highness. Naturally, I'll do my utmost to follow your desires."

The Maharaja smiled. "And you'd like to know more about what I'm thinking."

Ahmad allowed himself to smile tightly. "That would indeed be helpful, Highness."

"I frankly don't trust most of those politicians to keep their word. I don't trust Jinnah, and I don't trust Patel. I'm not sure about Nehru. Gandhi's probably truthful, but I just can't understand his thinking. I'm afraid that once I give up any of my powers to these politicians, once they get a toehold in my state, they'll figure out ways to take more. Maybe they'll just seize my government by force of arms, or maybe they'll send more agents to stir up the people against me."

Ahmad frowned. He thought for several moments. "I'm not sure about the politicians myself, Highness. I think to some extent you'll have to take a chance without knowing the exact outcome." He stopped, and saw that the ruler was listening intently. Ahmad continued, "I do know you can not remain completely independent. You'll have to choose between Pakistan and India. And it would be highly awkward, and highly provocative to the leaders of India, if you chose Pakistan."

Lakshman Singh sighed. "You make your points well." He rose and walked to the wall, where a big map of Mangarh State hung. "So much to lose," he said quietly. "After almost a thousand years of my ancestors' rule, and so many battles to keep independent, I'm the one who's likely to have it taken from me."

"You haven't lost it yet, Highness. With some careful planning and luck, you won't. But you'll need to negotiate with the Congress leaders, and you really will need to make some reforms." He drained the last of the *sharbat*.

The Maharaja turned to him and said, "I realize that now. And that being the case, I think maybe it's time to release Ashok Chand."

Ahmad let out his breath. The move was long overdue. "That seems appropriate, Highness. It might also defuse any demonstrations, at least to an extent."

"Free him today."

Ahmad nodded. "At once, Your Highness." He handed the empty glass to the servant, stood, and *salaamed*.

"But expel him from the state. We have enough worries about agitators." The Maharaja waved a hand. "You may go."

3

New Delhi, early August 1947

Several days after his release, Ashok Chand still savored the feel of freedom, of being able to walk through the streets in the lovely dawn time, when the sky grew light and the birds in the trees chattered raucously.

Fortunately, his health had not been adversely affected by the past year in the Mangarh fortress prison. While he had often been uncomfortable in the dampness of the monsoon, the cold of winter, and the heat of spring and summer, Karam Singh, the longtime Inspector General of Police, had ensured he did not suffer unduly. Unlike many prisoners, Ashok had a roof that did not leak and blankets enough to ward off the chill.

Jaya had been able to visit him twice a week, as had her parents. Of course, that was not nearly often enough for those involved. Sundip Saxena and Manohar Jain and other friends from the Mangarh Praja Mandal had been allowed less frequent visits. Since Ashok was required to leave the state immediately upon his release, he and Jaya went to Delhi, where one of her uncles made a couple of rooms in his large bungalow available.

Only the intense heat marred their joy at being together. "The monsoon is so late," Jaya said their first afternoon there. "Delhi seems even hotter than Mangarh."

They lay on the bed in their quarters, directly under the rapidly spinning ceiling fan. Everything in the room was so hot that after only the briefest interval of lovemaking, they soon separated their sticky bodies, joining only their fingers.

Ashok, said, smiling broadly at her, "Compared to the fortress jail, this is paradise."

She closed her eyes and grinned. "And it's like being a new bride all over again."

They lay close together for a time, eyes shut. Then, he said, "I have to go to the Punjab soon, you know." He hadn't been able to see his parents and sister the entire time he was jailed. Savitri had written that their father, with heart problems and weakened by this year's recurrence of malaria, had also contracted pneumonia. While he was over the worst of it, he was still weak and coughed a lot.

"Of course," said Jaya. "I'll come, too, even though I saw them a couple of months ago. I want to be with you."

"And I wouldn't want to be separated from you again. Especially so soon." He thought for a time. "That editorial in today's *Statesman*, though, recommended people not travel by train right now unless it's essential. And there are so many troubling rumors. I'd better try to get more information."

Before deciding on a date to leave, Ashok requested a meeting with Sardar Patel and V.P. Menon to inquire about further plans for work in Mangarh. He was given an appointment at Patel's home—for five o'clock in the morning.

When he arrived, a few minutes early, large number of people were already waiting by the round pillars of Sardar Patel's porch. Soon Patel emerged, followed by his middle-aged daughter Maniben, who served as his assistant. Patel, reminiscent as always of a toga-clad Roman senator, had a patrician's confident air as he glanced at the waiting visitors, pressed his palms together briefly in acknowledgment of their greetings, and then struck out on his rapid walk. The legion of persons hoping for a word with him followed in his wake. Patel's daughter, in a *khadi* sari, led each one in his turn up to speak with her father.

Patel turned into the Lodi Gardens and strode through the park past the various domed tombs. The number of followers dwindled as Patel dealt with each. By the time Patel left the park and headed back to his house, only a few persons remained. Maniben dropped back and told Ashok, "My father would like Mr. Menon to be present when he talks with you. So your turn must wait until we're back at the house."

Ashok nodded. He had not minded either the wait or the walk, quite the contrary. He was relishing the pure joy of being out in the fresh air of morning, unconfined by walls.

More people were waiting on the porch when the walkers returned to Patel's home. But Maniben beckoned Ashok into the house itself. V.P. Menon was already there, and Maniben introduced Ashok. It was the first time Ashok had met the capable civil servant who, as the highest ranking Indian member of the Viceroy's staff, had drafted the partitioning plan for Lord Mountbatten.

Now, Menon was assisting Sardar Patel in the newly formed Ministry of States. "So good to meet you at last, Chandji. I'm familiar with your excellent work in Mangarh, as of course is Mr. Patel. And I've read your book. I greatly regret that we were not able to spring you from jail sooner." Menon removed his eyeglasses and briefly polished them with a handkerchief.

Ashok smiled. "Many people have been spending time in jail. Including Sardar Patel."

"Yes, but not recently. I understand you have just gotten out."

Patel reappeared and ushered them to comfortable chairs. He said in English, "It's so good to see you again, Ashok. Please be seated. I'm expecting Jawaharlal shortly."

Ashok assumed his own time would likely be cut short when Nehru arrived. So he tried to quickly outline his concerns to Patel. "Sir, I've been somewhat out of touch, of course, while in jail. I'm uncertain as to how I can continue to help at the moment. I'm expelled from Mangarh state and would risk imprisonment if I return, but I'm willing to go back there if you think it desirable. I was also hoping you might tell me how negotiations are going with His Highness of Mangarh regarding accession to India."

Patel's heavy-lidded eyes had been fixed on Ashok. He now replied briskly, "As far as the negotiations go, the Maharaja of Mangarh hasn't yet agreed to accede, but we're reasonably confident he will. Consequently, there's no need for you to risk jail again at this time. It's only if the Maharaja balks at accession, or if he seems ready to align himself with Pakistan, that we'll need the Praja Mandal to put some pressure on him through disturbances or such." Patel leaned forward and lowered his voice. "I'll tell you, confidentially, that we've been offered a very large sum of money by Adinatha Seth to fund whatever activities might be needed to convince the Maharaja to accede to India." He leaned back in the chair and swept the air with a hand. "At the moment, I suggest you enjoy your freedom. Take a well earned rest, get to know your family again."

"I will, sir. Could you also tell me how you view the role of states such as Mangarh after India is free?"

Patel frowned, almost as if annoyed, but he replied, "That's a difficult question. At the moment, we're most concerned to prevent the obvious chaos that could result if even a few rulers insist on conducting their own foreign affairs or not cooperating with us on keeping communications and transportation links open. Once we have all the princely states aligned either with us or with Pakistan, we will have to turn our attention to the extent to which we will encourage democratic reforms by the rulers, consolidate administration in certain regions, and so on. But right now, we must proceed cautiously, take first things first."

"I understand. Sir, do you see any likelihood of actually integrating the princely states with India, as opposed to merely aligning them with India for certain purposes?"

Patel's lips formed a tight grin. His eyes met V.P. Menon's, then returned to Ashok. He again leaned forward and spoke more quietly. "Naturally, we have that hope. I'll tell you, again in confidence, that Mr. Menon and I have had certain discussions regarding that possibility. But we can't predict even the near future with certainty. We will have to take one step at a time, hoping that events will make possible further unification at a later date." He straightened and looked beyond Ashok. "Ah, here's Jawaharlal. I'm glad he was able to come while you're still here."

Nehru strode in and greeted them. Ashok rose to his feet and folded his palms in greeting. He thought there was a tenseness in the air when the soon-to-be Prime Minister of the new India entered the presence of his rival Patel; both of their smiles appeared frozen on their lips, not involving their eyes. But Nehru's gaze warmed when he addressed Ashok. "A true pleasure to see you free again. I hope you're in good health, after all that time locked up?"

"Quite good, thank you, Panditji."

Nehru appeared older, with a few more lines in his face than Ashok remembered from the last occasion they had met a few years ago. Nehru smiled wryly as he seated himself. "One never knows in these *state* prisons. I much prefer the British as my jailers. I got quite ill, you know, the only time I was ever imprisoned by a Maharaja. And Mangarh is such an antiquated state. Picturesque, but archaic. How is your lovely wife, by the way?"

"She's fine, sir. We're delighted to be together again, of course."

"Naturally. And she's a fine worker for our cause. It must have been extremely difficult to be parted for so long."

Ashok smiled and nodded. "Seeing her only twice a week wasn't nearly enough. But you know all about that type of thing."

Nehru gave him a mischievous look. "Your *Jail Diary* is becoming almost as popular as my own book. You aren't trying to displace me and take over the Congress, are you."

Ashok laughed. "Hardly, Panditji. You've had too many years' head start on me."

Patel said, not smiling at the exchange, "Panditji, Ashok was just asking what work is next for him. He's spent so much time in Mangarh, and that experience with a princely state can continue to be quite useful in the States Ministry."

Nehru pressed his lips together and frowned. But he said to Patel, "Dealing with the princes and convincing them to incorporate their states into the new nation, without using force of arms, will continue to be one of our biggest challenges. And my own ancestral Kashmir will likely be a major problem. It's awkward having a Hindu ruling a Muslim majority area that might opt for Pakistan if given a choice. I hate to leave someone as capable as Ashok to you and V.P., but given all his recent years of experience, the States Ministry may be the most valuable place for him at the moment."

Patel gave a smug smile, obviously pleased at getting what he wanted.

"I'm glad you're not going to try to take him away." He looked at Ashok. "So we'll keep you working for us. Why don't you have a few words with V.P.—and arrange to stay in touch."

"Thank you, sir. I will." He took leave of the two leaders and went out with Menon.

In the hall, V.P. made a note of how to contact him. Ashok looked about, ensured there was no danger of being overheard, and said to Menon, "I don't like asking a question for my personal benefit. But I know you drafted the plan for the partitioning of Pakistan. My own family's holdings are in the Lyallpur colony. Can you give me any idea of whether or not I should be worried for them?"

Menon stared at him through the spectacles. "The Boundary Commission is working in complete secrecy. The exact path of the dividing line through the Punjab may not even be announced until after August fifteenth."

"I see. Well, sorry to trouble you with it. You must have thousands of matters on your mind at this time."

"Quite all right." V.P. Menon glanced about, confirmed they were still alone, and said, "You've earned the right to know everything possible about the situation. What I'm telling you is in strictest confidence." He waited for an acknowledgment.

Ashok nodded. "I understand."

"You may have heard that some of the less moderate Sikh leaders are calling for Sikhs to take up arms if they think the dividing line gives too many of their people or their sacred sites to Pakistan. We have intelligence that Sikh extremists have linked up with the RSS and are planning terrorist actions to disrupt trains. And we know Sikhs plan widespread attacks on Muslims in revenge for the violence in West Punjab last spring and in Lahore. All this will give Muslims excuses for even more attacks on Sikhs and Hindus."

Ashok sadly shook his head. "What a mess."

"And going by the distribution of religions, the most logical place for dividing the Punjab may be between Lahore and Amritsar." Menon looked significantly at Ashok. "I wouldn't go so far as to advise Hindus and Sikhs to flee the canal colonies. But if my family had all its assets there, I'd certainly take some precautions, just in case."

Ashok now realized there could be no delay—he must go to the Punjab immediately. "I appreciate your frankness. I better visit my family in Lyallpur District. So I'll be out of touch for a week or so. But I'll contact you as soon as I'm back."

Menon gave an understanding nod. "I wish you well. I'd like to hear your impressions when you return." He hesitated, and added, "I heard the mentions of your wife. Are you thinking of taking her with you?"

"Yes. We've been apart for so long already, I hate to think of being separated again so soon."

Menon pressed his lips tight, then said, "It's certainly not my place to tell you to leave her here. But we don't know exactly when the violence will break out, or where. You don't want her to be caught in it."

Ashok stood rigid for a moment. Then he nodded. "Again, I appreciate your being candid."

Menon looked intently at Ashok. "Do be careful."

4

New Delhi, early August 1947

The train began to roll out of the New Delhi station. Vendors ran along the platform trying to retrieve soft drink bottles or tea glasses through the open windows. From his seat in the crowded second class carriage, Ashok looked back at Jaya and they waved at each other. He saw the tears in her eyes, and he blinked at the moistness in his own. In moments, she was out of view.

It had taken him most of the two days before he left to talk her out of coming with him. He knew he was probably being overly cautious in insisting that she stay behind. But he simply could not stand the idea of risking her, when it really wasn't necessary. And she had, after all, been to Kapani only two months previously.

The train's oven-like cars were even more crowded than usual. The overhead electric fans made little impact on the air temperature in the packed carriages.

The majority of travelers were Muslims, identifiable by the squat, tapering, cylindrical caps worn by many of the men, and by the *burkhas* of some women. The families were obviously emigrating with all the belongings they could manage. But a small minority were Hindus or Sikhs, probably going to the Punjab on family business like himself.

He would be going through Lahore, since that city provided the best connections to Lyallpur. Even though Lahore had been the principal center of the recent massacres and of widespread arson, he would never personally leave the confines of the railway station, and the wait there for the train to Lyallpur should be short.

He kept wondering where the partition line would fall. India without Lahore, that center of culture and education, that famous old Mughal capital, seemed unthinkable. But certainly Muslims had significant claims to it. He kept telling himself, however, that with so many prosperous Sikhs in his own family's area, it simply would not make sense to include the Lyallpur district as part of Pakistan.

A silence fell over the many Muslim passengers when the train pulled into the red brick station at Amritsar, thirty-five miles before Lahore. Not one of the Muslims stepped down to the platform to stretch their legs or to buy food or drink. He was glad, himself, not to be a Muslim in this particular place, a principal center of Sikhism and the site of the Sikh's famous Golden Temple. With so many Muslims being targeted in the city, the potential danger to them was arguably more extreme here than anywhere else in India.

An elderly Muslim man came into the carriage, leading a younger man by the arm. The young man's entire face was wrapped in white bandages through which brownish stains had soaked. They were followed by a woman in a head-to-foot *burkha* who carried a child. They had no baggage.

Ashok slid over to make some room for them. The old man gave a nod of acknowledgment. When they were seated, the elderly Muslim inquired where Ashok was going, After receiving the reply, the man responded, "We are going to Lahore where we have family." He shook his head sadly. "What you see is all we have with us. We had to give up everything we carried, to buy our way to the station platform. But it was God's will that we get to the train safely."

"I'm truly sorry for your troubles," said Ashok. "It's terrible for men to treat you that way."

"Yes," said the man. "But what was done to my son's face was worse."

"May I ask what happened?"

The old man shook his head sadly. "My son went through a Hindu neighborhood while coming back from his work. I'd told him to stay home, but he insisted, as he didn't know when he'd be able to earn more money. A couple of young Hindu men threw acid in his face." He again shook his head. "I've heard it's happening to many others in Amritsar."

The hour or so from Amritsar to Lahore passed uneventfully, and the family prepared to leave, along with most others in the carriage. "You should not leave the station," said the old man. "The city is not safe for Hindus."

"Fortunately," Ashok said, "I can make my next connection without leaving the platform."

As he stepped down, he smelled the smoke from the fires burning in Lahore. The station was strangely silent, in contrast to the usual bustle and the calls of vendors and porters and the noisy conversations. The waiting passengers moved cautiously, talking in low voices, as if using care to avoid any unintentional insult or offense which might incite violence. Hindus and Sikhs congregated in some areas of the platform, Muslims in others. Members of each religious group uneasily eyed the other.

The caution was forgotten when the westbound train rolled in and passengers, mostly Muslims, rushed to get aboard, pushing and shoving, frantic to ensure they would not be left behind. Ashok managed to squeeze on amongst Muslims with their big loads of belongings.

This carriage, like the earlier one, was hot and crowded. It seemed to Ashok that an uneasiness, an apprehension, hung in the air. Part of it was surely due to the emigrants' uncertainties about relocating and starting a new life. But much of it must also be due to the growing violence.

When they had been traveling for close to an hour across the flat Punjab plain they saw the other train. Their own car came to a halt. On the adjacent track, another passenger train blocked the sun's glare as it slowly passed, mere feet away, headed eastward toward Lahore.

First Ashok noticed bullet holes in the side of a carriage, and then the broken and blood-spattered windows. "Sind Express," someone muttered, identifying the train.

Utter silence fell over Ashok's car. He saw the body of a Sikh man, head lolling at an angle against a window, turban almost fallen off, blood covering the bearded face. Then the body of a woman, a red gash at her throat, sprawled against another window. A headless baby lay on her lap.

In his own carriage, a woman began sobbing. Car after car drifted past, each full of death. The horror of seeing, so close, hundreds of mutilated and dismembered corpses stunned him. When the last car was gone and the sun's glare again blasted him, he was lightheaded and nauseous.

The atrocities in the Punjab had seemed abstract and vague, until now.

Now the violence was far too real.

Eventually, his train resumed its travel. Nobody spoke. He tried not to think of what he had just seen.

At last the train arrived in Lyallpur. The city, with its logical layout and wide streets, a product of British planning, seemed peaceful. Indeed, everything appeared quite normal; the troubles elsewhere in the Punjab that had led to the massacre on the Sind Express and to the destruction of much of Lahore appeared to have passed over this prosperous place.

The bus ride to Kapani village was also without unusual incident. First, through the shimmering heat the mango and orange orchards appeared, and rising above them were the white dome and towers of the Sikh *gurdwara*, their temple and community center. Then Ashok could see the tops of the two storied *pukka* brick houses of the most affluent, including his own family's home, and finally the mud plastered walls of the more numerous single story houses. The village seemed little changed, except that the recent prosperity from the wartime increase in agricultural prices was evident in the new construction.

Starting in the 1890s, the area had been settled largely by hard working Sikhs from other parts of the Punjab who were allocated grants of acreage near the new lower Chenab Canal by British administrators. As in the other West Punjab canal colonies, much of the area had been inaccessible by roads, and the settlers worked in the scorching sun to clear brush and scrub and level the fields, as well as dig channels to their holdings from the main channels. They also had to build their homes, plant, tend, and harvest their crops, and transport the crops to market when roads were rudimentary or nonexistent. The sites for the villages or *chaks* were identified on the survey maps by numbers, which in many cases continued to be used in place of names. As time went on, the villages and towns grew, and railroads and roads connected them. Now, after four decades of development, the Lyallpur colony was perhaps the richest agricultural area in Asia.

It looked so peaceful here, the horrors Ashok had seen on the train seemed of a totally different world. He tried to shove the images from his mind for the time being.

His parents and Savitri had received the telegram alerting them of his coming, and they greeted him with long, hard embraces. "It's been so long!" said his mother when they separated. "I kept writing to that Maharaja, but he only answered the first letter. After that, he just ignored me." She appeared more aged, her forehead lined from worry, no doubt over her husband's health, as well as over both of her sons being in jail.

Ashok managed to smile thinly. "He thought he was doing the best thing for his state, Mother." He was surprised at how much weight his father had lost from the bouts with malarial fever. And he wondered how much the worry over his brother Prabhu, still imprisoned in the Andaman Islands after seven years, had affected the health of both of them. Shortly after Prabhu's arrest, Ashok had visited them and reluctantly told them of his own part in the matter. He had been gratified that, although they were extremely upset, they had assured Ashok he'd had no other choice, given that the alternative was allowing Prabhu to try to assassinate the Viceroy of India.

Savitri, at least, appeared in good health and, at age twenty-two, was stunningly pretty. Ashok was relieved that she had returned to the village at the end of the Medical College term and had therefore missed the wave of communal violence in Lahore.

"How was your trip, son?" asked Yogesh Chand, his voice both thinner and raspier now. "We've heard about all the troubles in Lahore and Amritsar. Other places, too, of course."

Ashok hesitated, wondering how to describe what he'd witnessed. He shifted his eyes away. "I saw a train that had been attacked by Muslims. It was the worst thing I've ever seen. And I met some Muslims who had been assaulted by Hindus and Sikhs." He swallowed and looked back to them. "It's all utter madness. Fortunately, I didn't face any real problems myself."

"Well," said his mother, "thank God you had a safe journey. And there aren't any problems here, so you can relax now. But tell me, son, why didn't your wife come with you?"

Ashok glanced away, then back to her. "She wanted to, Mother. I didn't let her. I was too unsure about whether the train would be safe or not. It's one thing for a man to travel through troubled areas, quite another a woman."

His father coughed several times. "Especially such a pretty one." He managed a grin. "And you managed to snare her without any help from us."

Ashok smiled back. He had waited until the end of that long visit seven years ago to bring up the possibility of his marriage to Jaya. As he'd hoped, his mother was thrilled that at last one of her sons was interested in taking a wife. His father had been equally enthusiastic. It had taken a few months of long distance negotiations, but Jaya, too, had been determined nothing would stand in the way, and her parents had been enthused, seemingly unconcerned over Ashok's current lack of a profitable profession.

"Everyone at school is talking about your book!" Savitri told him. "I get a lot of attention when they find out you're my brother."

"That's not the reason you get the attention," he said, grinning. He was pleased to see she could still blush.

Although dismayed at the widespread savagery, his father and mother were excited that the British were truly leaving. Savitri was more interested than they in the additional events outside the village, pumping Ashok eagerly for more news.

The family sat on the roof in the evening, where they also slept in the hot season, hoping to take advantage of any cooling breeze that might appear. "I still think you should all leave, just as a precaution," Ashok told them as they sampled the recent mango harvest. "A little time in Delhi might even be enjoyable. And the doctors there might be some help to you, Father."

"You know I hate cities," said Yogesh Chand in his hoarse voice. "Almost everything we have is tied up in our lands. And we need to be here to watch over my mango trees." He fell into a fit of coughing. When it was over, he said, "Anyway, we might not even be included in Pakistan."

"I wish they'd announce the boundaries, just so we'd know," said Ashok's mother.

"The men I've talked with in Delhi all assume Lahore will be part of Pakistan," said Ashok. "You know what that means for us here, since we're even further west." He sliced open into a Dussheri mango and bit into it. "Delicious."

"Pakistan. 'Land of the Pure,'" said his mother. "It just doesn't make sense to me."

"I'd rather not be governed solely by Muslims," said his father. "There's always the danger they might decide to pass laws putting us at a disadvantage." He sucked the flesh from a Raspunia. "Still, we've always gotten along fine with them." He again lapsed into a coughing spell. Then he said, "I've loaned a fair amount of money to Muslims. If Kapani does turn out to be in Pakistan, I'd hope the new government won't do anything to hurt our getting repayment. Both governments have guaranteed the safety of all citizens and told us to stay where we are. Still, I confess those attacks on Hindus and Sikhs by Muslim mobs have me a bit worried."

Ashok said, "The Sikhs and Hindus have been doing their share of attacking Muslims, especially in the Amritsar area. Violence breeds anger and revenge, which in turn just brings more violence."

"It's all so pointless," his mother said. "I only wish they could see that. Or that the authorities would stand firm against it. Why don't they stop it?"

Savitri said softly, "I think it's too widespread, Mother. And sometimes the police think they can benefit from the loot, just like the mobs."

Their mother shook her head. "The British should do more to stop it. They still have control of the army, even if they are in the process of leaving."

"I'm sure they're trying," said Yogesh. "But after we've kicked them out we can't expect them to keep on solving our problems."

Their good friend and neighbor, Mubarak Khan, appeared at the head of the stairway. After the exchange of greetings, he began on a mango and said, "There's no reason at all to worry about it here. My brother Muslims know the local Sikhs and Hindus had nothing to do with the violence elsewhere."

"It's all those other districts," Ashok's mother said, shaking her head. "I don't understand why people there do such things, but I'm glad everyone here is more sensible."

Indeed, there did seem to be little cause for concern in Kapani. When one of the Muslim farmers from the nearby village of Chak Number 109 came with a loan payment, he expressed dismay at all the violence elsewhere. "But here," he assured them, "Hindu and Sikh and Muslim are all brothers."

Ashok had a private conversation with his mother, trying to encourage her to leave for a time just to be cautious. She replied, "I'd gladly go to Delhi. But you can see your father shouldn't travel. He needs rest. Besides, he loves it here with his mangoes. Even when he was feeling well he never wanted to leave the village."

"I don't suppose you'd leave without him? Even for a short visit to see your daughter-in-law and her family?"

"I'm tempted. But it's a long way to Delhi. I'd worry about your father the whole time."

Ashok sat for a time, then asked, "Do you have any objection if Savitri comes with me when I leave?"

Radha Chand smiled. "She's been so much help to us. I'm afraid I'm a bit spoiled by her. But I couldn't stand in her way if she wants to go."

Ashok ventured, "If you won't come, I could at least take some money to deposit for you in New Delhi. Just in case. Or some of your jewelry, Mother."

She sighed. "It seems so pointless to have me here and my jewelry there. Still, maybe it makes sense."

"And can you send some cash with me to Delhi for safe keeping?"

"I'll be candid with you, son. We don't have much cash left after building the house. Almost everything else is loaned out. Mostly to Muslims, in fact. That's one reason we haven't bought a motor car." She smiled again. "Your father's too soft-hearted. He's always giving the borrowers more time to pay, or else lowering interest rates when he sees they're having difficulties. I think he's especially sympathetic because so many Muslims find it so shameful to be in the position of having to borrow at all." She watched Ashok a moment, then said, "When must you leave?"

"I can stay a few days. But you know I must get back soon. I have a family there now, too."

The heat continued, with no rain in sight. Ashok stopped by the house of his childhood friend Joginder Singh for a visit. He entered the family compound to find the Sikh reinforcing the boards in the side of an old bullock cart. New wheels had already been added to the vehicle. Two other carts sat in line by the wall.

"Going into the transport business?" Ashok asked jokingly.

It seemed to Ashok that for some reason Joginder was embarrassed. He looked away from Ashok and shrugged. "We just decided it was time to get our equipment in order." He glanced about, then returned his gaze to Ashok. "I don't expect we'll have to leave Kapani. But we might as well be prepared just in case."

Ashok frowned. "The government says there's no need to think about moving. Everyone will be protected."

"You trust the government that much?"

"Not necessarily. But I have a lot of faith in the people. We've been friends with Muslims here our entire lives. I can't imagine they'd suddenly turn on us, regardless of the madness in other areas."

Joginder said, "I've heard a lot of rumors. Some from Muslims themselves. There's talk of gangs being organized in some of the other villages to attack Sikhs and Hindus as soon as the border is finalized."

Ashok said, "I get the impression that the talk is always about somewhere else. No one's seen Muslims arming themselves here, have they?"

After a moment's hesitation, Joginder said, "Actually, yes. I was in Chak Number 12 last week. That village is mostly Muslims, you know. I happened to stop by a blacksmith's shop. He was making swords by the dozen. When he saw me there, he tried to pretend they were scythe blades."

"Maybe they *were* scythes! The shape can be about the same."

Joginder snorted. "I'm Sikh. I know a sword blade when I see one."

5

Mangarh, early August 1947

"What do you suggest I do, Stanley?" asked Maharaja Lakshman Singh. They had come in early morning to the Moti Mahal, the small, white marble summer palace on the edge of the Hanuman Sagar. The air smelled of jasmine, and the red bougainvillaea vines were brilliant against the white walls of the pavilion-like structure. Though the two men sat in the shade of the arched balcony with servants waving huge fans, already the day felt hot.

Powis took a sip of Scotch and frowned, looking across the lake to where the domed cenotaphs of the Maharaja's ancestors were reflected on the calm waters. He hated to be put in this situation. If it wasn't a direct conflict with the duties of his job as Political Agent, it should be. However, he was leaving in a few days. He owed it to his friend to give the best possible advice.

He turned back to the Maharaja. "Highness, Jinnah's terms are good. But they're worthless if they cause the Congress to foment an insurrection against you. Or furious Hindus in Mangarh to rise against their Muslim neighbors. Or the Indian Army to invade and take over Mangarh. All those are likely possibilities if you align yourself with Pakistan."

"Jinnah has said he'd help defend me."

Powis looked down. "Jinnah may even mean it, in a general sense. But if it means war with India, especially so soon, he'd probably find an excuse to avoid it." He fixed his gaze on the Maharaja. "Highness, I don't mean to offend, but the way I see it, he's probably using you to gain more bargaining power in his negotiations with the Congress. He'd be delighted to have you say you'll join Pakistan for that reason. But surely you don't think he's really enthusiastic about a Hindu majority state with a Hindu ruler as part of the Muslims' 'Land of the Pure!'"

Lakshman Singh let out a long sigh. He looked across the lake and was quiet for a very long time. Then he said, "I knew I could count on you for good advice, Stanley. My Dewan said almost exactly the same things, even though he's Muslim. I've also come to those conclusions myself." He looked intently at the Britisher. "And now, I have another request. There are some items I need from abroad. You'll be traveling to England. Could I engage you to make some purchases for me?"

Powis smiled and eased back in his chair, now that the subject was less monumental. "I'd be pleased to help you however I can. What do you have in mind?"

Lakshman Singh looked away. "I'll tell you in a minute." He returned his gaze to Powis. "First, I have some questions for you. Can I trust the Congress to keep its word about not interfering in Mangarh? Will they really limit their interest to *only* those three matters—defense, foreign relations, and communications?"

Powis tensed and straightened himself again; he had thought he was getting off these awkward matters. He took a deep breath and replied, "I doubt it, Highness. I think they are getting the best deal they can at this moment, so the princes don't give them problems by cutting communications lines or embarrassing them abroad. But I don't think they'd be satisfied with islands of princely-ruled states right beside Congress-ruled territory. Regardless of what they say, they don't like princes. They're democrats, social reformers. Like Nehru, many of them are even socialists. They'll want to run it all. It may take years, but I think they'll try to gradually chip away at your powers."

Lakshman Singh pursed his lips. "That's my fear, too. Another question, Stanley. Do you agree that the Congress is going to make a mess of running the new India?"

Powis frowned. "I agree it's quite possible they'll botch it up. It's not entirely their fault, but they haven't had much experience running a country, and this is a hell of a complex one. Plus, there's all the infighting among themselves. They have trouble agreeing on anything."

"When people get dissatisfied with the Congress, do you think they might insist on a return to rule by the princes?"

Powis stared at him, then shrugged. "Highness, I've no idea. It's possible. Anything's possible. At the very least, they might be glad to have limited constitutional monarchies, like in England."

Lakshman Singh leaned back and smiled. He said, "Rule by princes is all the people have ever known, except for some areas the British took over. You've seen how my people feel about me. I'm their *Ma-Baap*, their *Anna-data*. They know nothing about democracy. Or socialism. It's only a few agitators causing all these problems. Personal rule is the Indian way, not democracy. The people need to know whom to go to for help with their problems. They know they'll get help from *me*. It's the same way in the other states. I'm positive the people will demand a return to princely rule soon, when they find out just how much they've lost."

Powis furrowed his brow and replied, "Power is addictive, and I'd guess once the politicians have tasted it, they won't give it up. *They'll* be the new princes. *They'll* be the ones who drive the big cars, live in big houses, give government jobs to their relatives and friends. For someone to try to reverse the clock, so to speak, to change the form of governments again might cause real disruptions. Even bloodshed!"

Lakshman Singh nodded. "I couldn't agree more." He took a piece of paper from the table beside him, unfolded it, and handed it to Powis. "That's why I want you to buy these for me." While Powis read it with increasing surprise, Lakshman Singh said, "Naturally, you'll have a commission on the purchases, Stanley. I was thinking of ten percent."

Stanley Powis looked up. His eyes were wide behind his spectacles. "I have to be frank, Highness. I don't know anything about these matters!"

"You can ask questions. You know people who could steer you to the proper sources."

Powis blinked. Ten per cent! On such a large order, that could certainly help change the dismal picture of his retirement. "I'm strongly tempted, Highness. I do need to think about it, for a short time. I'll let you know before I leave, of course."

"That will be fine. However, if you decide not to do it, I hope you'll at least make some inquiries in Britain and send me the names of some alternative agents."

Powis took a deep breath. "Certainly, Highness."

He shouldn't do it, he knew. But Great God in Heaven—ten per cent! It was at least worth serious consideration.

The Maharaja ordered the many lights illuminating the driveway and the gardens of the Bhim Bhawan Palace turned off. Ahmad Hasan Aruzi joined him on the roof terrace. The Maharaja's manservant, Shiv, stood by holding a small wooden box. Lakshman Singh indicated the big tubular instrument on its oddly shaped pedestal. "Twelve inch Newtonian reflector," he informed his Dewan. "On an equatorial mount, just like the big observatory telescopes.

The axis of the mount is pointed at the north star, making it easier to compensate for the earth's rotation. That way you can follow the motions of the object you're watching by moving the telescope in only one direction."

"I see, Highness." Ahmad was not sure he did understand, but it probably didn't matter.

"I'll let you look through it in a moment," Lakshman Singh said. He seemed to be trying to locate something halfway up in the sky by looking first through the smaller telescope mounted like a rifle sight on the barrel, then looking through the eyepiece on the side.

While Ahmad waited, he looked up at the heavens. The August night was warm. Since the monsoon was so late, the sky was also clear, except for a few wisps of clouds low on the horizon, and the stars shone in abundance. As his eyes adjusted to the darkness, he could see the ghostly outline of the old fortress on the hill. Below, the town sparkled with occasional electric lights and the tiny glows of kerosene lanterns and oil lamps. Once in a while a sound carried from the town—dogs barking, a cart creaking, a voice raised in argument. In the hills a jackal howled. The manservant Shiv stood nearby like a tall, dark statue, waiting silently until the Maharaja again asked for his services.

Lakshman Singh said, still looking through the eyepiece, "That date for independence from the British—Friday, August 15th. It's all wrong, you know. Every astrologer agrees."

Ahmad had heard that the choice of the date, made by Lord Mountbatten without consulting astrologers, was causing consternation among many people. Being dubious himself about the scientific merits of astrology, Ahmad was not overly concerned. But millions of others, who wouldn't make any decision other than the most routine without the help of their astrologers, were distraught. "Because Fridays are inauspicious days, Highness?"

"That's only part of it. I've talked with my own *jyotishi*, who's been in contact with others. He says it's one of the worst conceivable times." The Maharaja looked over at Ahmad. "The day will be under the influence of Saturn, the most malignant of planets. Saturn, Jupiter, and Venus will all lie in the worst house possible. I can't imagine a more unfavorable day for independence. But not only that, it's a bad day to partition the country, to tear Pakistan away. We will be under the sign of Makara, which is hostile to all centrifugal forces."

"I see," said Ahmad tactfully, glad it was dark so he didn't have to be concerned about his facial expression.

"Mountbatten doesn't understand," said Lakshman Singh, turning his attention back to the telescope. "He insists it's too late to change the date. Even if it means drought, famine, floods, massacres. We're *already* having massacres. And the monsoon is long overdue."

"We simply have to do our best to forestall those disasters we can," said Ahmad. "Like protecting the Muslim residents of Mangarh in case of violence by the Hindus."

"This isn't Alwar," said Lakshman Singh. "I'll personally see nothing happens of that sort."

"I know all the Muslims appreciate your concern, Highness."

Lakshman Singh said, still looking through the eyepiece, "Your own family has been in India many generations. Were they converts to Islam? Or Muslim immigrants?"

Somewhat surprised at the personal nature of the question, Ahmad replied, "My ancestors have been Muslims for as long as we know our history, Highness. They came to Delhi with the first Sultans. They moved to Daulatabad when Muhammad bin Tughluq tried to establish another capital there. I've mentioned before that one of my ancestors is said to be *Pir* Mahmud, the saint buried in the tomb by the highway east of town. He died on the journey to Daulatabad, and his son had the tomb built. Later my ancestors moved north again."

The Maharaja seemed to be concentrating on what he was observing through the eyepiece. Eventually he said, "As a Muslim, do you mind telling me what you really think of this idea of Pakistan?"

Ahmad thought a moment, then said, "Not at all, Highness. I consider myself Indian, of course. Like my father before me, and my grandfather, I feel I've done well here. I have no need to live in a land populated mostly by Muslims. I dislike the idea of creating two nations out of what should be one."

"Mmmm. You feel your religious brothers would have enough protection as a minority in India?"

"Probably. Naturally there would be occasional disagreements between Hindus and Muslims, Highness. Like whether a mosque is really on the site of a temple, or over Hindus wanting to protect cows and Muslims wanting to eat them. But nothing that couldn't be resolved."

"So emigrating to Pakistan has no appeal for you, personally."

Ahmad hesitated, then said, "Not as such, Highness. I've never even been to the Punjab. However, I am concerned because of my family. My two brothers are moving to Pakistan. My own son, even though he's only twenty, is talking of going. I'd hate for my wife and I to be the only family members left in India."

"So you *are* thinking of going?"

"It's a difficult decision, Highness. Maybe sometime. Certainly not right away."

Soon Lakshman Singh said, "Come look at this."

Ahmad stepped closer, peered through the eyepiece. It took a few moments for him to position his eye properly. Then, he saw a sprinkling of what seemed to be thousands of glittering stars against the blackness. They formed a ball-like formation, farther apart toward the outer edge, crowding ever closer together in the center until they blended together in a glow. "It's beautiful, Highness. What is it?"

"M 13," said Lakshman Singh. "The Great Globular Cluster in the constellation Hercules. *Lakhs* of stars clustered together like a big ball. So far away it took 35,000 years for its light to reach us. The bigger the telescope, the more individual stars you can see. I plan to order a larger one myself. I've seen about everything I can with this one."

"Astonishing," said Ahmad. "So many stars in one spot!"

"Yes. It helps put our own problems in perspective. Just think—*lakhs* of stars like our sun. Without the telescope it's all one tiny little point of haze in the sky. And there are thousands more of those clusters. *Crores* of stars. Maybe even millions of them with planets like our own."

"It's truly amazing. Beyond comprehension by us mortals," said Ahmad, trying to fathom how the Maharaja could be so taken with traditional astrology on the one hand and with modern scientific astronomy on the other.

"It makes one humble," said Lakshman Singh, "to be in the sight of a God who could make all that." He pulled out the eyepiece, placed it carefully in the box which Shiv held open for him. Then he fit a small fabric cover over the hole left by the removal of the eyepiece. He attached larger covers, tightened by laces, over the open ends of the main telescope tube. "Come," he told his Dewan.

Ahmad Hasan Aruzi followed the Maharaja downstairs to the ruler's office. With the surprised Dewan looking on, Lakshman Singh signed the Instrument of Accession to India. He sent Shiv to get the royal seal so they could affix the impression to the document.

Considering the tremendous significance of the signing, Ahmad thought it odd that there was no public ceremony whatsoever. "Should I make an announcement, Highness?" he asked.

Lakshman Singh shrugged. "I suppose that's necessary. Just spread the word quietly, though. I don't want to give those agitators any more cause to celebrate than I have to. This way, they may be a little uncertain as to whether or not I've really done it. By the time they find out for sure, the impact will be diminished. They may even decide it's too late for any big festivities."

Ahmad Hasan Aruzi smiled at the ruler's cleverness. He asked, "Highness, should I dispatch the document to New Delhi by messenger?"

Lakshman Singh grinned. "Of course not. Just drop it in the mail tomorrow. That way I'll keep those chaps in Delhi wondering a little longer."

Once outside the Maharaja's door, the Dewan sighed and shook his head.

Stanley Powis sat in his bedroom in the upper floor of the British Agency, burning papers. A previous political agent had installed a fireplace, complete with marble mantle, undoubtedly to make the room seem like home. Powis had never used it until now.

Sir Conrad Corfield had directed the political agents in the various states to destroy those records which might prove embarrassing to the princes when the Ministry of States took over the residency buildings and their contents. Powis had held off until tonight. These records had been compiled over a century of hard, dedicated work by his predecessors and himself. In many ways, they were all that remained in Mangarh as evidence of lives spent here in difficult toil under often adverse conditions of climate and isolation.

But some of the records must go. He had burned the detailed reports of the sexual preferences of Maharajas Sangram Singh and Bhim Singh, as well as of a couple other, lower ranking, members of the ruling family. The practices included sex with two or more women at once, orgies in which close male friends participated, sex with girls so young as to obviously be prepuberty, and sex with a girl and a young man at the same time.

What he was looking at now were reports, some from eye witnesses, some from mere rumors, of the financial status of the Maharaja. Powis' predecessor, James Oakley, had been quite meticulous about recording every rumor concerning the "Mangarh Treasure," a subject that fascinated Stanley Powis as well.

Oakley had apparently been convinced that a huge trove of wealth existed. And that much of it was stored in the State Treasury and much in the old fortress—probably in the wing that had been the former Maharaja's living quarters, since the Bhil guards seemed most protective of that portion of the palace. Stanley Powis had reached a similar conclusion.

Should these papers be burned? He was reluctant to preserve anything that might give the new Ministry of States information that could be used against Lakshman Singh. A socialist government was not likely to be sympathetic to large concentrations of wealth in private hands, especially in the hands of a person they might view as an undemocratic despot. The new politicians might very well wage a propaganda campaign against the remaining members of the old order, to attempt to make the populace envious and distrustful of them. In Powis's view, therefore, the less actual information they had, the better.

Stanley Powis fed the papers to the flames. But with every rumor, every statement consumed by the fire, his curiosity grew. He would dearly love to see such a treasure with his own eyes before leaving Mangarh for the last time.

Would Lakshman Singh allow him to view it? Probably not. The rumors generally said that only the Maharaja and the Bhil guards had access to the wealth.

But he and Lakshman Singh were friends, were they not? If he promised the Maharaja he would protect the secret, would Lakshman Singh let him see the treasure?

Almost certainly not. It was foolish to even think of it. He shoved the idea from his mind, and he dumped the last of the papers on the fire.

Then an inspiration came. He smiled.

6

Kapani Village, West Punjab, 14 August 1947

August fourteenth arrived. Pakistan became an independent, separate nation, one day before the date set for its neighbor India to be free.

But the boundary between Pakistan and India still had not been announced. At least Mangarh was one of the many princely states which had decided to accede to India. Ashok heard that fact on the radio.

"You must be pleased about it!" said Savitri, who had been listening with him and the rest of the family.

"I am. I wasn't at all sure what the Maharaja would do. He's been so slow about making changes, it wouldn't have surprised me at all if he'd held out and tried to stay totally unaligned."

Ashok's mother said, "Does that mean he'll lose his powers? It would serve him right after putting you in jail so many times!"

"Unfortunately," said Ashok, "it won't make much difference in Mangarh right away. The accession is mainly symbolic. But many of us in the Congress Party are hoping that's only a first step. We'll just have to see what happens now."

There were frequent reports of the most horrible violence in Lahore, including massacres at the railroad station. And more trains carrying refugees were attacked elsewhere.

August fifteenth came, the day for the independence of India itself. The family sat around the radio, listening to All India Radio's coverage of the celebrations in Delhi. They listened to Nehru's speech about a "Tryst with Destiny."

Part of Ashok wanted to celebrate. India was free, except for the princely states like Mangarh, anyway. Pakistan was free, too.

But too many factors soured what should otherwise be a joyous day. Foremost was the horrible violence in so many areas. And Ashok could not help but think of Mangarh state, which, in spite of having a new Dewan and aligning itself with the new nation of India, was essentially still its old feudal self.

He also missed Jaya; she should be with him on such an occasion.

Plus, here in the canal colonies everyone was in the odd position of not knowing which of the two new nations they were now part of. Should they celebrate the independence of India, or of Pakistan? Many chose one or the other in the hope that their personal preference would soon be borne out. Many chose to celebrate both. In any case, the uncertainty was worrisome.

Ashok began thinking seriously about returning to Delhi.

And then a trickle of Muslim refugees began arriving, with tales of barely surviving terrible attacks, and of the losses of wives, sons, daughters to rampaging Sikhs and Hindus.

Mangarh, 14 August 1947

The Dewan found the Maharaja standing on a balcony, staring out at the hills.

"Highness," said Ahmad Hasan Aruzi, "many of your Muslim subjects are getting ready to leave for Pakistan. They're afraid for their lives after hearing what's happening in places like Alwar and Amritsar. They apparently think there's no longer any place for them in a country dominated by Hindus."

Lakshman Singh turned to him, and shook his head in disbelief. "Damn! How can they think that? Don't they know I'll protect them?" He pounded his fist on the railing.

It was a rare event when the Maharaja became truly angry. The Prime Minister said, "Highness, they're afraid of things getting out of hand. For whatever reason, apparently the British and the rulers in several other states have stood by and just let people get killed. The police are either afraid to intervene or they don't want to."

"Well, I won't tolerate that in Mangarh! Order my car. If I have to, I'll visit every Muslim family in the state!"

"It shouldn't be necessary to go quite that far, Highness. But it would be good for you to go about and reassure people."

"I want my army and police ready to act if they need to. Colonel Husain's the highest ranking Muslim officer, isn't he? Tell him to come with me. Forget the car, we'll use a couple army jeeps. That should help convince people. And when we get back, I want Karam Singh here, so I can tell him I expect the police to fully cooperate."

In an hour's time—unusually fast for events to move in Mangarh—the jeeps bearing Lakshman Singh, the colonel, and several soldiers were edging through the crowds in the Muslim quarter of Mangarh city. *Burkha* clad women watched as the small cavalcade stopped, and resident men salaamed and greeted the visitors.

Lakshman Singh called from his jeep: "*Assalaam aleicum.* What is this nonsense about some of my family leaving to go to Pakistan?"

The men looked at each other, silently consented to a spokesman, who replied, "Maharaja, everyone's heard of thousands of Muslims being killed in Amritsar, in Delhi, many places. Of our women being raped, houses looted."

"But no such things have happened in Mangarh! So why would people leave?"

"They're afraid, Annadata. They don't want to be killed, or to have their daughters taken and used for pleasure. Or to have their houses and lands stolen."

"How can that happen here? You must know I would not tolerate it!"

The men glanced at each other. The spokesman said, "We know you mean well, Your Highness. But you can't be in every street, night and day, or in every village. And you can't be sure that every policeman is as eager to protect us as you are yourself."

Lakshman Singh gestured toward the soldiers. "I give you my word—I'll send hundreds of these men out at the first hint of trouble." He lowered his voice. "Colonel, may I please have your pistol?"

The puzzled officer removed his revolver from its holster and handed the weapon to the ruler.

Lakshman Singh said, "See this gun? I'm a very good shot. I promise you I will *personally* shoot any man—Hindu, Sikh, anyone—who tries to harm my people just because they are Muslims. And I will shoot any policeman or soldier who fails to take action to protect my Muslim subjects in such a situation. See that my promise is known to everyone!"

Clearly impressed, the men looked at each other, nodded. The spokesman said, "We believe and trust you, Maharaja. We're grateful. We'll pass the word."

The jeeps moved on, and Lakshman Singh repeated his promises, both in the city and in several key villages with large Muslim populations.

The next morning, in accordance with instructions from the Political Department, Stanley Powis ordered that for the first time in over a century the Union Jack would not be raised over the British Agency in Mangarh. He was overseeing his final packing when a delegation from the Mangarh Praja Mandal arrived and began attaching the Congress tricolor to the flagpole line.

Powis hurried out. "What's the meaning of this?"

"We're here to assume control of the Agency, sir," said the leader. Powis recognized Sundip Saxena from the earlier demonstrations. He said sternly, "Control of this agency goes to the new Ministry of States. And this is a princely state, not part of Congress-administered territories. So until someone from the ministry comes, you've no right to fly any flag other than Mangarh's!"

Sundip Saxena shrugged. "I'm sure if I were to call New Delhi, they'd agree with me. It's only a matter of a few days at the most before someone from the States Ministry comes here to take over the building."

Powis glared at the flag. Damned Congress. The idea of *their* flag flying on *his* building! He thought briefly of sawing the flagstaff off at the base. But they'd just put up another pole. "What's that round thing in the center of the flag?" he asked. "It doesn't look like Gandhi's spinning wheel any more."

"It's been changed to Emperor Ashoka's *dharma chakra*. The wheel of the law. This is the new national flag of India. Some leaders thought a spinning wheel was too old fashioned for a modern nation."

Powis mulled this over. So they'd given up the spinning wheel, but for another symbol dating back thousands of years. "Oh, hell," he muttered, shaking his head. "Put up your bloody flag."

He made a point of not looking at it when he left the Agency to say farewell to Lakshman Singh.

Both friends were subdued, knowing they might never again see each other. At best, any future meeting would likely be years away.

"Highness," said Powis, "I've been thinking about your request."

Lakshman Singh raised an eyebrow, and waited.

"I don't deny that I would benefit considerably financially by the commission. But it's so far removed from anything I've done before. If I did it, it would be mainly as a favor for you, in honor of our friendship."

Lakshman Singh nodded. "I'd be grateful, of course, Stanley."

"You'd be reposing considerable trust in me."

Lakshman Singh smiled. "So I would. I know you wouldn't let me down."

"Then I have your confidence, in general? You feel I would be discreet and not reveal your private affairs to anyone?"

"Of course. Do you doubt that?"

"I merely wanted to hear it from you. Because I have a request to make, myself. Before making it, I'll tell you that I agree to taking on the purchase of the arms on the terms you suggested. My own request is entirely separate from it."

Lakshman Singh said, "I'm grateful for your help. And I'm quite interested in hearing your request. I think highly of you, and I'm glad to aid you in any way I can."

"Highness, I'd like to see the Mangarh Treasure. It's a personal desire of mine—I swear to you that I'll never reveal anything about it to anyone under any circumstances without your own specific permission."

For the first time since Powis had known him, Lakshman Singh appeared dumbfounded. The ruler stared at him. Then a smile grew on his face. "That's quite a request, Stanley. You seem certain that there *is* a 'Treasure,' as you call it."

"I'm certain, Highness." Actually, Powis was not absolutely sure, in spite of all the reports and rumors. The Treasure almost certainly existed at one time. But it might well have been dissipated to nothing over the years.

"You've seen it? Or know someone who has?"

"No, Highness. But I'm sure it exists. I can't give you all my reasons."

Lakshman Singh pressed his lips together. "You must know the tradition that only I, and my eldest son, are authorized to see it—if it exists."

"So I've heard. But I assume that what one ruler has ordered, his successors can change."

"We are discussing family tradition. As head of the family, I'm bound to preserve its customs. This is a land of traditions, of customs, as you yourself well know."

"Only too well. But traditions are changing, Highness, even in Mangarh. I thought maybe...." Powis paused only an instant, then he continued, in a definite tone: "I've presumed too much on our friendship, Highness. I apologize. I shouldn't have done it, but the temptation was too great, knowing there's a chance I might never return here. Please forgive me. I was unsure how strongly you felt about the matter. Now that I know, of course I wouldn't dream of persisting. Naturally, I'll still undertake your commission. I hope our friendship isn't undermined by my presumption and my lack of tact."

Lakshman Singh smiled. "Don't be so quick to withdraw your request. You're doing me a favor. A *big* favor. One involving a large sum of money. It's only reasonable before you embark on the mission that you know that I have the financial resources to make good on the purchase."

"I never doubted that, of course."

"Let me finish, Stanley. Under my authority as head of my family, I'm waiving the rule that prevents anyone else from access to our strongrooms, for the reason that you must have definite assurances that our assets will cover the large purchases I'm asking you to make. Now please don't give me any argument that would undermine my reasoning. Or give me time to change my mind."

Powis stared at him, and a broad grin broke out on his face. Then he sobered. "I'm honored, Highness. More than I can say."

Lakshman Singh smiled back. "You should be, my friend. And I'm holding you to your oath. I could be quite embarrassed if you ever revealed to anyone what I'm about to show you."

When they had finished the viewing, the stunned Powis had not had the time to actually examine at length even a hundredth part of the fabulous store.

As they were returning to the Bhim Bhawan Palace, Powis, still overwhelmed, took hold of himself enough to say to the Maharaja, "Highness, I've heard a number of rulers are transferring some of their assets out of India. To England, Switzerland, and so on. Just in case the Congress government someday decides to pass taxes that are too high. Or decides your wealth really belongs to their government instead of yours. Have you considered that?"

Lakshman Singh nodded. "I appreciate your concern. Yes, I've thought of it. I've decided not to send any assets abroad. For one thing, unlike many of my brother princes, I don't travel to Europe regularly. But I also think the treasure could be useful, under the same conditions in which I might need your purchases. Like my ancestors, I consider this wealth a sacred trust. To be used for the good of Mangarh, not myself. If I sent it to London or Zurich or wherever, it would be as if I had decided to convert it to my own personal use."

"Still, Highness, aren't you putting all your eggs in one basket now?"

The Maharaja shrugged. "Maybe. But it's a basket in Mangarh. It's convenient to have it here where I can watch over it. You've touched on a point that concerns me, though. I'd all but decided to move part of the treasure to another location here. Talking with you has firmed up my decision. Then even if part of it is somehow stolen or otherwise lost to me, the remainder should still be safe."

"That seems wise, Highness. Conditions are changing so quickly. Who knows what the future holds?"

Eight months later, the shipments arranged by Stanley Powis began arriving in Mangarh.

Lakshman Singh's trusted Bhil guards stowed the armaments securely, and secretly, in the old fortress. The Maharaja was sure that the Congress politicians would make every effort to take over his state, and with the overwhelming resources of the central Indian Government, they would likely succeed.

But he was also certain the day would eventually come when the people of India, or of Mangarh at least, would tire of so-called "reforms" and demand a return to Princely Rule. He would be prepared to back them with whatever was needed, whether money or military force.

7

Kapani Village, Pakistan, 17 August 1947

On August 17, two days after independence, the boundary award was at last announced. The Punjab was split along a dividing line between Lahore and Amritsar. Lahore was in Pakistan. So was all of Lyallpur District, and indeed even districts farther to the east. Kapani village was in Pakistan, by a considerable distance.

"I just can't believe anyone could do this to us," said Ashok's father. "Since two days ago we're citizens of Pakistan. No longer Indians!"

"And no one even asked us," said Ashok's mother.

"*Pakistanis*," said Savitri. "The word sounds so strange."

"But it's what we are now," said Yogesh Chand. He went into a coughing fit, as if choking on the idea.

The family was silent for the most part, trying to comprehend what it would be like to live in the same village, but in a new country, with a new government overwhelmingly dominated by Muslims.

Already, two new families had come to the village, Muslims from the east, drawn to Kapani because they had relatives. A young father named Abdul Rasool, a nephew of Mubarak Khan's wife, abruptly appeared, carrying his year old son. The man was dirty, exhausted, and obviously still in shock from his ordeal.

Ashok and Savitri went over to ask Mubarak Khan if there was any way they could help. The young man was resting inside, but Mubarak said, "He comes from a Muslim village east of Amritsar. A mob of Sikhs attacked in the night last week and killed everyone they could find, including his wife and his other son. He managed to grab the baby and hide in the millet fields. It's amazing he was able to get here, and with the baby still alive."

"It's terrible!" said Savitri. "How can human beings do such things to each other?"

Ashok shook his head sadly. "What can one say under the circumstances? I know the Sikhs are furious at having their people divided by the boundary line. But this isn't an answer."

"We must be careful to make sure such things can't happen here," said Mubarak Khan.

Over the radio came reports of violence even more widespread, new atrocities. In the eastern part of the Punjab, which had remained part of India, Sikhs were attacking trains and killing Muslim refugees.

And in Lahore and many of those rural parts of the Punjab that were now Pakistani, Muslims were attacking trains and villages, slaughtering Sikhs and Hindus. Worrisome rumors spread that all non-Muslim police in Pakistan had been ordered to give up their guns, and that in some districts the officials of the new government had actually adopted a policy of encouraging non-Muslims to leave.

Then mail delivery ceased in Kapani, clear evidence all was not well in their own district. Ashok wavered about returning to Delhi. If trouble did come, his parents might need help here.

A quiet exodus began of some residents who slipped away, or else left on a long visit to family in India. First to leave was Dwarka Tandon, one of the Hindu schoolteachers, who had no real ties to the village other than his job. Next was the family of Bhupinder Singh, one of the wealthiest Sikhs, who owned a trucking business and hence had vehicles to transport belongings across the new border to Jullunder, where there were relatives. Next was the prosperous Sikh family of Chattar Singh, with their own motorcar, a rarity in this region.

These defections were unnerving to the remaining residents, who naturally wondered if perhaps they should be leaving also. But like the Chands, most families had almost all of their assets tied up in their land or in local loans. They could not simply abandon everything they had worked for to start anew from nothing in India.

The fourth day after announcement of the boundaries, a convoy of bullock carts approached Kapani, heading east toward the new Indian border. Ashok's family joined the other residents to see what was occurring. Wheels creaked and the bells around the bullocks' necks jingled as the lead carts rolled down the main street and stopped at the square in the center of the village. Most of the carts carried Sikhs, young men and women, old people, children, riding on piles of hay obviously intended as fodder for animals, or on heaps of household goods.

Many of the travelers carried buckets to the well for water. Directly in front of Ashok and Savitri stood a cart which was transporting a handsome young Sikh man with an attractive wife and two small boys. The cart was brightly painted and well kept, the pair of bullocks healthy looking. The man returned with two full buckets of water, and set one down for each of the bullocks. The animals began noisily drinking.

Ashok asked, "Where are you from?"

"Chak Number 92," replied the Sikh. "We left there three days ago. We're on our way to the refugee camp at Chilianwala, then we'll go to India." He watched his wife fill a couple of large rectangular metal cans with water and said, "We're relieved to be able to replenish our supply. Can you believe it— we've gone since yesterday morning with what little we had left from the day before. The villages we passed through were Muslim, and they wouldn't let us use their wells or canals!"

Ashok shook his head. "That's hard to imagine."

"That's awful!" Savitri whispered, her eyes large.

The Sikh gazed at Savitri. He stood straighter and smiled in spite of the topic of conversation; Ashok had long ago noticed Savitri had a warming effect on men, regardless of age. "I swear it's true," the Sikh said. "I wouldn't have believed it myself if it didn't happen to us."

Soon the convoy began to move out, and the Sikh family climbed back aboard their cart. "We wish you well," Savitri called. Ashok and the other villagers also gave their good wishes. "*Sat Sri Akal*, God is Truth!" came the shouts from the emigrants.

As the last cart passed, Ashok estimated over a hundred of them. He watched the other inhabitants of his own village for a time. Most looked worried. He could guess what they were thinking: Should we be leaving, too?

Ashok and Savitri lagged behind as their parents returned to the house. He said to her, "I'm wondering if maybe I shouldn't stay longer. Just in case there's trouble. What if you all have to leave?"

She drew her *dupatta* closer around her shoulders and did not reply at first. He saw the drawn look on her face. But then she brightened, looked at him, and said, "I know we'll manage. I just can't believe anything so bad will happen. Not here. You know we'd be glad to have you. But your wife needs you more than we do. Especially after you've been in jail so long. I'm just glad you were able to come for as long as you have."

Ashok thought for a moment. He stopped and looked at their family's tall brick house, so imposing, so solid looking. Savitri stopped and waited with him. He said, "I appreciate the fact that you're staying home to help."

She smiled at him and shrugged. "With things so unsettled in Lahore, I can't see medical school starting up again for a while, anyway. So I'm glad to do whatever I can here." Her smile left. "My main worry is Father. First the malaria, then his heart, then the pneumonia. He seems better right now, but I'm just not sure. I don't have the experience yet or the equipment to examine him properly. And I'm not sure about the doctors in Lyallpur. I wish he would go to Lahore—no, even better, to Delhi, to be certain he gets the best treatment."

"He won't go."

She frowned. "I know. But," her warm smile returned and those large eyes met his, "don't let it stop you from leaving. Right now your wife is thinking how much she misses you."

Ashok forced a grin. "I wish there were some way for me to be both places."

"I'll send for you if we really need you."

"Be sure you do. And I hope you won't let your worries about Father and Mother keep you from returning to school."

She shrugged. "I'll definitely go back as soon as I can. Mother really supports my being a doctor, you know, just as she favored your own work, even though it took you far away."

Ashok grimly nodded. He wasn't pleased with the situation, but there seemed little he could do, given the alternatives.

That evening, shortly after dinner, they were seated on the roof, waiting for night to come, hopefully with a cooling breeze. Mubarak Khan suddenly appeared from the stairway, his eyes worried. "I just don't understand it. I've heard our village will be attacked tonight!"

"An attack *here*?" said Ashok's mother. "I don't believe it! How do rumors like that get started, anyway?"

Ashok's father raised his eyebrows. "How can that be? An attack by whom?" He went into a coughing spell.

Mubarak Khan replied, "Nobody we even know!" He remained standing, where usually he would have seated himself. He shook his head. "Muslims from other villages. They're saying they want revenge for Sikhs killing our brothers. They've heard Kapani is mostly Sikhs, and that they own a lot of property." He looked intently at Yogesh Chand. "Even though you're Hindu, you may be in danger, too. You must all come to my house. If anyone looks for you there, I'll say you're under my protection. God willing, that should stop them."

Yogesh said, staring at him, "We're grateful for your offer. But I can't believe there's serious danger. And if there were, mightn't having us there endanger your own family?"

Mubarak Khan looked about at them. "You are my family, too! How could I not help if you're in need? You'd do the same for me—you know you would."

Ashok was thinking furiously, trying to evaluate options. "Do you know what the others in the village are doing?"

"I've heard the Sikhs are gathering in the *gurdwara*," Mubarak Khan said. "Beyond that, I don't know."

Yogesh had another coughing spell. Then he managed to say, "The *gurdwara* is a solid building. It has its own well, besides the wall around it. If we do leave our house, maybe we should go there, rather than endanger our brother."

"I still don't believe it," said Ashok's mother, shaking her head.

"I insist—you must come to my house!" said Mubarak Khan. "So does my wife. My house is as solid as the *gurdwara*. And the *gurdwara* will be overcrowded. It's also the first place that will be attacked."

"There's something to that," agreed Yogesh.

"Then it's settled," said Mubarak Khan. "Come. Bring whatever valuables you want, in case they should loot your house."

"This all seems so silly!" said Radha Chand, shaking her head. "We'll all be laughing at ourselves tomorrow."

"We better not take a chance, Mother," said Savitri, her large eyes filled with distress.

"That's right," said Mubarak Khan. "If we're wrong—and I pray to God we are—we'll at least know we were all foolish together."

"Come," said Savitri. She took her mother by the arm and herded her toward the stairway. The others also descended from the roof. Ashok felt as if he were playing a part in some incredible theatrical production as he helped the family gather up bedding, the more valuable household utensils, prized possessions, and jewelry and cash. Then they trooped next door.

8

The women of the Khan household had not taken up *purdah*, as had some of the more pretentious of the newly prosperous Muslims. Consequently, everyone mixed together in the main room and on the roof, where they could see over much of the village since the house was two storied.

As darkness fell, the fireflies came out. The mosquitoes increased in number, and bats swooped overhead. The conversations among the Chands and Mubarak Khan's family were subdued; given the unprecedented situation, no one quite knew what to say. Normally, there would have been gossip about other people in the village, or about relatives or aspects of daily life: clothing, food, weather, farming. Now, everything except the impending danger receded into irrelevance.

"What's that sound?" asked Ashok's mother, abruptly. "Besides the dogs, I mean."

The sound was faint and far-off, but unmistakable. "Drums," said Ashok.

"That's not good at all," murmured Yogesh Chand.

No one responded.

Dogs began barking at the outskirts of the village, as the drumbeats grew increasingly louder.

The families stood by the edge of the roof, silently peering into the growing darkness. After a time, a line of flaming torches appeared across the fields and drew closer.

Sooner than Ashok would have expected, gun shots shattered the night in the direction of the *gurdwara*. From across the village, came shouting and screams. Flames licked from the roof of a distant house. Ashok watched in horror, finding it difficult to believe what was happening.

Mubarak Khan's wife began sobbing. Mubarak himself and Yogesh Chand occasionally conversed in low tones, trying to think of some action they could take.

Ashok felt so helpless, so ineffective. What would Gandhiji do? Probably, Gandhi would go out to meet the attackers and try to talk reason back into them. Given the Mahatma's immense reputation for saintliness and for showing no favoritism to any religion, he might possibly succeed.

Ashok debated briefly with himself over whether or not to go out and try. But he was not Gandhiji. Although Ashok had once dared that despotic feudal lord, the Thakur of Baldeogarh, to shoot him, he was far more afraid to face this Punjab mob.

He had seen the Sind Express. And he had heard enough to know that when people were caught up in religious fanaticism and the excitement of a mob, a single, ordinary man could do nothing against them. If he confronted the rabble, they would not listen. They would almost certainly kill him, possibly a vicious and painful way. And he also had a duty to remain with his family, to try to help them as best he could.

However, he was uncomfortable with this reasoning. There must be something more he could do. Only he couldn't think what it might be.

Abdul Rasool, his tiny son in his arms, joined them. The refugee was a large boned, broad faced man with a hurt look in his eyes. "Muslims should not be doing this!" he said. "Of all people, *I* should be the one to want revenge.

But would that bring back my wife and my elder son? By killing someone else's women and children?"

Everyone was silent, not knowing how to reply.

He raised his voice and said, "Maybe I could go talk to the leaders, and tell them why they are wrong."

Mubarak Khan shook his head no in the darkness. "It's good of you to say that. But it wouldn't work. They're too eager for blood and loot."

Abdul Rasool said, his voice steady, "I could at least try."

More gun shots were sounding, more houses bursting into flames.

"Your forgiveness does you credit," Ashok told him. "But I think it's too late. And you might well get hurt yourself. Your son needs you."

The shooting near the *gurdwara* intensified. From time to time came shouts and screams. But it was impossible to know exactly what was occurring.

Soon a crowd of shadowy men ran down the street. Ashok heard them batter on doors here and there, breaking in. Half a block away, flames began to flicker in the windows of a house. Ashok was aware that their own home was conspicuous for its size and *pukka* construction.

It was next in line. As part of the mob converged on it, Mubarak Khan said in a loud, urgent whisper to Yogesh Chand and Ashok, "You should go downstairs! Even though it's dark, they might see you with their torches if they look up here."

"Yes, come, Mother, Savitri!" said Ashok. He rushed them down the stairs, into the small inner courtyard. Mubarak Khan remained up on the roof to watch. The sounds came of hammering, battering, then a cracking of wood.

"They've broken in," Mubarak Khan called down in a loud whisper. Loud thumps and crashes drifted over the courtyard wall.

"It sounds like they're ransacking everything," murmured Ashok. He hoped his parents had good hiding places for any money and jewels they hadn't brought along.

"I just don't believe it," said his mother, shaking her head, her eyes dull. "How can this happen *here*?"

A pounding came on the front door of the house. "What do you want?" Mubarak Khan shouted down from the roof. "We are Muslims. Leave us alone. *Pakistan Zindabad*!"

Ashok and his family hurried from the courtyard into the house, to be out of sight in case someone climbed the section of exterior wall to look in. "Open up! Prove your faith!" came a shout from outside. The pounding on the door grew louder.

Another voice said, "It's true, they're Muslim—everyone knows it."

"Do you have any Sikhs or Hindus with you?" shouted someone else.

"Only my family!" said Mubarak Khan.

Just then, Yogesh went into an uncontrollable fit of coughing. His wife did her best to muffle the sound with her hands. Ashok was fairly sure the noise couldn't be heard outside the house.

A voice shouted, "We know you're friendly with Yogesh Chand. Where is he?"

"I think they've left their house," called back Mubarak Khan.

A rumble of voices. Then someone shouted, "They have profited from loans to our Muslim brothers. We need them to cancel the loan papers."

"You'll have to look somewhere else!" shouted Mubarak. "Anyway, he charged you far less for your loans than anyone else would have. You should be grateful!"

They heard the raiders talking among themselves. Then the same voice called, "If you have nothing to hide, why don't you let us in?"

"Because you have no business in my home! My wife is ill, and your shouting upsets her. Go away!"

Now they heard Abdul Rasool's voice shouting from the roof: "Why are you after innocent people? I'm the one who should be wanting revenge, not you! My wife and my eldest son were killed by Sikhs near Amritsar. But the killers are there, not here!"

"You don't want them avenged?" shouted a puzzled voice.

"Not this way! Not against people who had no part in it. And neither would Allah want innocent blood spilled!"

"What kind of a man are you?" shouted another voice. "Sikhs have killed our brothers and sisters, so Sikhs must die."

"Yes! Yes!" came the shouts.

"You're insane!" shouted Abdul Rasool. "No one in this area has done anything to harm us Muslims! God will hold you accountable, each one of you!"

"You sound like a Hindu!" screamed a man.

"Yes! Yes!" shouted others.

"No!" came another voice. "It's what he says. Sikhs killed his family at Amritsar. Come, we're wasting time here!"

A few moments later, Abdul Rasool slowly descended the stairs, shaking his head. "They've gone totally mad."

More muffled talk outside. Then a voice came again: "We have other business. But if we don't find the Chands, we will be back. And we will search your house!"

The sounds of the mob moved on down the street.

A crackling noise came from nearby, and a bright, wavering glow illuminated the area. "It's our house!" said Ashok's mother. She buried her head in her hands and broke into sobs. Savitri tried to comfort her, but her own eyes were wet, also. Yogesh sagged back in despair. Ashok sat staring at the floor.

Mubarak Khan came down to them, looking saddened and tense.

"We owe you our lives," said Ashok.

"It was God's will that you be spared. I was merely His instrument."

"We have to go now," said Yogesh. "We can't put you in danger when they come back."

"That's right," said Radha Chand, straightening and wiping her eyes. "You've risked your family enough."

"Bah," said Mubarak Khan. "They wouldn't harm us."

"They might, if they're angry enough at you for misleading them," said Ashok.

"No, you still must stay here! This is your home, too," said Mubarak Khan. "Especially now. God willing, this madness will go away soon."

Ashok's father went into a fit of coughing. When he could speak, he said, "There can be no argument. We'll leave."

"Where would you go, with your own house burning?"

"To the *gurdwara*," said Yogesh Chand.

"But," said Mubarak Khan, "that's where the fighting will be the worst!"

"I haven't heard any shooting over there for a while," said Abdul Rasool.

Yogesh said, his voice hoarse, "Maybe the raiders have given up. Even if they come back, the *gurdwara* will be defended by a lot of men. Some of the Sikhs have guns. And maybe we can help. Here, we're only a hindrance."

Ashok had been frowning. "I don't like the idea of the *gurdwara*, Father. It must already be overcrowded. The raiders will concentrate their attack on it, since they know most Sikhs will be there."

"You have a better suggestion?"

"Maybe hide in the fields, like Abdul Rasool did when he escaped," Ashok said weakly, knowing it wasn't much of an alternative.

Yogesh shook his head. "There must be Muslims all over. They might see us before we found cover. They could also hear my coughing. But the *gurdwara's* close. We can get into it through the back gate."

"Savitri, what do you think?" asked Ashok.

Her large eyes looked dazed. "I don't know. I just don't! Nothing seems right!"

"I say the *gurdwara*," said their father. "It's our best chance, with so many defenders. I haven't heard shots over there in a while, so if we hurry we might be able to slip in while the attackers are gone."

"Do you want to take your jewelry and other valuables?" asked Mubarak Khan.

"No, we'll come back afterwards," said Yogesh. "And," he looked away, "if we don't come back, it's yours."

"I'd save it for your relatives," said Mubarak Khan, shaking his head. "But you'll be back."

The Chands tearfully embraced him and his family, but briefly, as they did not know how much time they had before the raiders returned. They left from the back entrance. Ashok was fearful they would be spotted, but most of the raiders appeared to be looting houses on the far side of the village.

The Chands had to first pass their own burning house. Yogesh Chand moved swiftly, his head down, and did not look at his home being destroyed. Radha Chand stopped and, still unbelieving, stared at the smoke and flames. Ashok took her arm and firmly urged her to continue. Savitri took one glance and then averted her moist eyes.

They hurried down a lane to the back gate of the *gurdwara*, where they announced themselves to the defenders. They were well known, of course, and were quickly admitted.

The *gurdwara*, as Ashok had expected, was jammed with Sikh families and their belongings. The normal dividing line separating women from men was ignored tonight. The defense was organized by headman Daljit Singh, in his sixties and sporting a luxuriant white beard, and retired jemadar Buta Singh, his shorter beard peppered with gray. Ashok saw at least a dozen rifles and a couple of revolvers held ready. All the other men appeared armed with at least a sword. Maybe, he decided, coming here hadn't been such a bad idea after all, given the alternatives.

Inside the building, Savitri immediately began tending the injured, examining wounds and bandaging them with strips torn from garments. Ashok and his father and mother squeezed in between two Sikh families near the center of the floor.

Then they heard a murmuring of many voices outside. The raiders had returned. Through the windows, Ashok saw the flickerings of torches. Dozens of voices began shouting, "*Pakistan zindabad*! *Pakistan zindabad*!"

A leader called to the Sikhs, "Give yourselves up and convert to Islam! Then everyone will be spared!"

Daljit Singh yelled back, "Never! Guru Gobind Singh did not surrender. Neither will we!"

The other Sikhs roared their approval, "*Sat Shri Akal*!"

There was a short silence. Then came a gunshot from outside. And another. Then a volley of shots.

The Sikhs' guns replied. Ashok saw Joginder Singh returning from the roof, sword in hand. He stood and edged over to Joginder, who gave a negative shake of his head. "They have reinforcements. There must be thousands of them! Where could they have gotten so many guns?"

"I bet some of them are from Pathan or Baluch army units," said a nearby Sikh man.

Joginder said to Ashok, "You may regret joining us here. We've only a few hundred rounds of ammunition left. When it's gone..."

Ashok did not reply. What was there to say?

The shooting continued. Ashok heard a commotion from in front. Shots rang out close by. A couple of screams. One of the lookouts at a window called, "They tried to set fire to the *gurdwara*. Our men in the yard stopped them."

Ashok sat down by his father. From time to time Yogesh Chand went into a coughing fit.

Hour after hour through the night the exchanges of gunfire continued. At last, Ashok approached the patriarch, Daljit Singh, and said quietly, "I can try to negotiate with them, maybe agree we'll all leave Pakistan right away. It doesn't look encouraging, but we have nothing to lose."

The old man, his perspiring face lined with weariness and worry above the bushy white beard, looked at Ashok with bloodshot eyes and shook his head no. "They'd just kill you. Or they'd make false promises, then ambush us while we were trying to leave. Like Guru Gobind Singh's attackers did."

Ashok remembered that particular story about the founder of the Sikh Khalsa. But he persisted. "Isn't it at least worth trying? Otherwise..."

Daljit Singh pressed his lips tightly together, again shaking his head. "They'd see it as evidence we're weak, and they might launch an all-out assault. This way, they're uncertain of our strength."

Ashok reluctantly returned to his parents, and he tried again to think of something he could do.

The attackers did seem to be refraining from a rush on the *gurdwara*, which, while costly, might have overwhelmed the defenders.

Then word was passed in whispers: "Only a few bullets left." Some of the leading Sikhs conferred with Daljit Singh and Jemadar Buta Singh.

Daljit Singh stood by the door and addressed the refugees packed inside, his voice strong despite his advanced age and his worries: "Fellow Sikhs, we are nearly out of ammunition. The fighting will then be our swords against their guns. We have choices. We can agree to convert to Islam—"

There were loud shouts of "No!" "Never!"

He continued, "We can wait—maybe they will decide we are not worth the effort and will go away. Or maybe the army will yet come and save us. If we wait and they rush the *gurdwara*, our women may be dishonored and our children killed. Or," he paused for effect, "we can do as the valiant Sikhs did when they defended Guru Gobind Singh at Chamkaur—we can rush out and die fighting, but send many of the Muslims to their paradise."

"Yes! Yes!" came the shouts.

"But what about our women? Our children?" asked one of the men.

Daljit Singh replied solemnly, "If we leave them, we must make certain they can not be injured or dishonored."

Oh, my god! thought Ashok. He looked quickly at his mother. And toward Savitri, who was in the back bathing a wound. Did they realize what that meant?

A heavy silence filled the *gurdwara*. Men and women glanced at each other. At their children.

One man said in a voice weak with emotion, "I think we should have a choice. Those who want, can convert to Islam. Maybe we can save our families that way. Those who want to—to die fighting, may do so."

There were a few murmurs of agreement.

One man said, "That's cowardly! Sikhs don't give up their faith, even if it does mean death."

A loud chorus of agreement.

"I say, let everyone choose!" said another voice.

Joginder Singh spoke up. "We have some non-Sikhs, too. They must be free to make a choice."

Eyes turned toward the Chand family.

"That's right," said someone. "They don't have to defend our faith. They can choose to go if they want. Those Sikhs who wish to can join them."

Voices rose in agreement.

Jemadar Buta Singh went to the door and called out to the attackers beyond the courtyard wall: "A few here want to leave. Is the offer still open to convert to Islam in exchange for their lives?"

"Yes, yes. We swear on the Qur'an!" came a shout. "All who come out can convert to the Faith. They will be our brothers and sisters. We will not harm them!"

Savitri now joined the rest of her family. She had been off tending the wounded and had not heard the entire discussion.

Ashok's father shook his head sadly. "Let's go out. We must do it, or we'll all die."

"Give up our own gods? How can we do such a thing?" asked Ashok's mother.

"It's only temporary," said Yogesh. "We can renounce the conversion later." He coughed hard.

Ashok thought of Daljit Singh's doubts that the attackers' promises could be trusted. But there appeared to be no other option if his family were to be saved.

Still, leaving seemed so cowardly, like he would be a traitor. He had known most of these people throughout his childhood. They were his neighbors and friends, like Joginder Singh. On the other hand, his parents and sister needed his help. And he had a duty to his wife now.

Savitri shook her head. "I can't leave. There are wounded men here who can use my help. I'll join you later."

Ashok whispered urgently, "You don't understand. There won't *be* any later."

"What—what do you mean?"

"They all intend to die. Women and children first."

The realization hit her like a slap across the face. "No!"

No one replied.

Savitri straightened her shoulders. "I'll still stay. There are wounded I can help right to the end."

Ashok shook his head and tried to keep the panic from his voice. "I admire you for that, but you'd only be able to help a few, for a very short time."

Tears glistened in her eyes. "It will still be a comfort to them in their—their last moments."

Ashok wiped at his own eyes. "Others need you, too." He gestured toward his father and mother. "Our own parents. And *me*. I couldn't stand losing you!"

Savitri wiped at her tears with the end of her *dupatta* and stared at him.

He could see her doubt growing. He said firmly, "If you come with us, there will be *thousands* you can help in future years as a doctor."

She looked at her mother and father, who were gaping at her with eyes wide with dismay. At last, she whispered, "I'll come with you. But do I have to change my faith?"

Ashok, remembering his law school training, said, "Legally, a choice made under duress can be retracted later." He was anguished at the thought of claiming to be a convert when he had no intention of retaining the faith, and of having to deliberately lie. But he saw no good alternative.

Savitri, her face wet and sad, said, "All right. I'll do it. May God forgive me."

"They've left us no choice," said Radha Chand, shaking her head.

Feeling conspicuous and more than a little ashamed, Ashok rose. He approached Joginder Singh, and embraced him, hard. He swallowed, and said in a hoarse voice, "We had good times. I'll always remember you."

His childhood friend was rigid as a wood beam, his eyes distracted. "And I, you," said Joginder at last. His distress was obvious in his eyes. He would likely still be alive when his wife and daughter died. As Ashok separated from him, Joginder glanced at Savitri, and whispered to Ashok, "Cover her head as much as you can."

Ashok looked at her, and nodded. It was good advice. Such beauty might be too tempting to the men outside. Joginder moved off, and Ashok whispered to Savitri. Fear glazed her moist eyes momentarily, then she drew her *dupatta* over her head, so it concealed most of her face.

But with her erect, lissome figure, he knew covering her head would fool no man. "Try to act old. Hunch over a little," he whispered.

She looked momentarily puzzled, then nodded, and bent over slightly.

The Chands said other farewells. The men at the door opened it, and Ashok and his family filed out. A few Sikhs, including two men, quietly followed. Ashok did not look to see who they were.

They crossed the small courtyard, where a dozen or so Sikh defenders stood guard. "Move through fast, in case they rush the gate," said one of the men as others slid the bar from the door.

Ashok went out the gate first, half expecting to be shot.

But there was no gunfire. Quickly the small group of Hindus and Sikhs moved into the street. Ashok heard the gate slam shut behind them. Feeling exposed and vulnerable, he said to his family, "Let's get out of the way, in case the shooting starts again."

Already, forms were moving toward them from the shadows.

9

There were those who wanted to kill them right away. But some of the leaders insisted on keeping the promise of letting them convert to Islam.

Ashok tried hard not to think of what was happening in the *gurdwara*. He heard occasional muffled screams from inside, and puzzled shouts from the attackers outside.

The Muslims led their captives to the small mosque on the far side of the village. Ashok, close to exhaustion from lack of sleep, virtually in shock from the attacks and from the mass suicide occurring at the *gurdwara*, dreaded the upcoming conversion ceremonies.

To be a Muslim male meant to be circumcised.

But if he had stayed in the *gurdwara*, right now he would be witnessing every woman and child put to the sword.

By the doorway he removed his footwear, as did the others. He washed his hands and feet at the basin. He entered the dim, bare room. An *imam* began reading from the Qur'an.

Ashok, dazed, paid no attention to the words. He kept asking himself: What would Gandhiji do? What would Bapu do, if he were here now? Would Gandhiji perform the equivalent of a miracle, shaming these men by eloquently and forcefully making them see the horrible wrongs they were committing?

Ashok knew he could speak out himself. He could boldly tell the *imam* that what these men were doing was an affront to the very God they supposedly followed. But he also knew he did not have the tremendous prestige and moral persuasiveness of Mahatma Gandhi. Rather than convincing the Muslim tormentors, he would likely get himself killed. And his family needed his help.

The reading continued for what seemed a long time. Near the end, the sounds of much shooting and screaming and the clashing of steel came from the direction of the *gurdwara*.

The *imam* concluded his reading. Just then a Muslim man rushed in and hurriedly whispered to the *imam* and several others. Stunned surprise spread over their faces. "All are dead? Every one?" asked the *imam*.

"Yes! They killed them all! Every woman and child!"

Savitri began sobbing, and shaking, her head buried in her hands. Ashok felt numb, lightheaded, sick to his stomach. His parents sat frozen.

A barber had been summoned, and he cut the hair and beards from the two Sikh men to be converted, who appeared even more dazed than Ashok.

Eventually the sounds of fighting from across the village diminished, to be replaced by occasional yelling, the sounds of windows breaking, miscellaneous other noises of looting and celebration.

Ashok kept expecting the circumcision knife to appear. A man carried in a platter. On it were several small pieces of meat which smelled as if they had just come from roasting over a fire.

The *imam* said, "You must now seal your conversion by eating the flesh of a cow."

Ashok's father and sister gasped. His mother let out a small shriek of dismay. For strict vegetarians such as the Chands, eating any meat was unthinkable. And this wasn't just any meat. It was beef, from the most sacred of animals. The Sikhs, too, were muttering to each other in annoyance.

Radha Chand said, "No. Even if I'm a Muslim, it's not right for you to make me eat anything I don't want."

"*Beguma sahib*, you must!" said the *imam*. "It is part of the ceremony."

"Does it say so in the Qur'an?"

The *imam* consulted with one of the other Muslims. At last, he said to her, "*Beguma sahib*, do as you wish. But the others must eat the flesh of the cow to prove their sincerity."

"Wait," said Ashok. "If my mother doesn't have to eat it, neither do the rest of us."

Some of the Muslim men muttered to each other. One of them shouted, "I knew we couldn't trust them! Let's kill them!"

"Yes!" shouted others. "Yes!"

The *imam* held up his hand, and said loudly, "*Kafirs* have always had the right to convert, to become our brothers and sisters. I have made an exception for the lady out of respect for her. But if the others will eat, you must spare them."

There was grumbling among the men, but they said no more. Ashok opened his mouth to insist that as a woman Savitri was entitled to abstain also, but then he cut off the words. It would call dangerous attention to her, and anyway these men were no longer thinking with logic or reason.

Afterwards, as the vile lump sat in his stomach, Ashok was sure he would vomit. He looked for an opportunity to disgorge it outside of the seeing of his captors. From the pale faces of the other family members it was obvious they wanted to do the same.

Suddenly, Savitri did. She bent over and the contents of her stomach poured out. She retched and retched, and she pulled her *dupatta* slightly back from her face to prevent its being soiled.

Ashok glanced around. Men were watching her and glancing at each other with smiles. Some murmured to each other.

Ashok held his breath. His heart was pounding. If they realized her beauty, they might be too tempted. Hoping to distract them, he doubled over also. His stomach needed no further invitation. The meat expelled itself from his mouth, along with a large quantity of burning digestive juices. Out of the corner of his eye, he saw Savitri pull her scarf back over her face. He hoped the harm had not already been done.

The *imam* directed the converts to sit and wait outside the mosque. A couple of armed guards stood by. Occasionally other men came, looked over the new Muslims, then left.

Despite their own predicament, Ashok's thoughts kept returning to the deaths of so many Sikhs at the *gurdwara*. Almost certainly, Joginder was no longer alive, nor his family, nor any of the others the Chands knew so well. He kept thinking there must have been some way that such senseless slaughtering could have been avoided.

From time to time, he glanced at the guards and at the various other men who came and went. Was he imagining it, or did they frequently gesture toward Savitri as they whispered to themselves? A sense of foreboding rose in him. What could he do if they tried to molest her?

Mubarak Khan approached from the direction of his house. Ashok felt slightly less worried now that a true Muslim friend was present. Mubarak glanced at the two guards and said loudly to them, "Don't you know the others are dividing up property over on the other side of the village? Why don't you go get your share—I'll keep an eye on these people."

One of the men shifted uneasily and said, "I don't know why we're guarding them anyway, when they've converted to our faith."

The other said in a voice so low Ashok wasn't sure he heard correctly, "I think it's because of her—the pretty one."

The first guard replied, slightly more loudly, "She can wait. Maybe we were told to stay here so someone else could get our share of the property! Let's go before we're too late." He said to Mubarak Khan, "Watch them carefully. We'll be back soon."

The two men hurried away. Mubarak came closer to the family and said, "You must all leave! You're not safe, even though you've converted—especially the women. God willing, you should be able to get to the refugee camp at Chilianwala. Come quickly. I've brought food and water for you to take. And your jewelry." He bent and whispered to Ashok, "I heard some men talking. They intend to grab your sister."

Ashok nodded and urged his family, "Come! It's our best chance."

He took his mother's arm and urged her forward.

The Sikh converts were watching them. "You'll come, too?" Ashok asked.

They looked at each other; a couple shook their heads no. "We'll take our chances here," said one of the men. "We have too much property to leave."

The Chands moved quickly to follow Mubarak Khan around a corner and down a lane. At the edge of the village Mubarak led them to a shed where three fabric-wrapped bundles were stowed, along with a long knife and a makeshift spear, and a pile of dark clothing. "Food and water," Mubarak Khan told Ashok and his father, indicating the bundles. "Even some of the mangoes you gave me. And these *burkhas* were sent by my wife and daughters in case you wish to disguise yourselves as Muslim women. They are black, so you won't show up so much at night. I can accompany you and pretend I am escorting my wife and her sisters or daughters."

A day or two ago, the idea of masquerading as a Muslim woman would have seemed ludicrous to Ashok. Now it made extremely good sense.

But his father protested, "Why not just have the women wear them? We men can act as if we're Muslims without putting on these!"

"As you like," said Mubarak Khan. "However, you realize"—he glanced at the women and lowered his voice—"if there's any doubt, you may be asked to show you're circumcised."

Yogesh stood still a moment. Then he swore under his breath and, in another coughing fit, began struggling to get one of the tent-like garments on over his head. Mubarak Khan assisted him.

Ashok managed to get into one without help. He was surprised he could see quite well through the cloth mesh covering the face.

"Ready?" asked Mubarak Khan.

"Yes, let's go," came Yogesh's voice, sounding grumpy under the *burkha*.

"Ready," said Ashok.

"Be sure to cover your feet and hands if we're stopped," Mubarak Khan told the men. He looked at Ashok, and said quietly, "You're too tall for the *burkha*. Roll up the legs of your trousers. If we see anyone, try to hunch down—maybe pretend you're an old woman."

Ashok quickly rolled up the legs, and Mubarak Khan led the family quickly down the lane. After him came Ashok's father, then mother, then Savitri, and finally Ashok. The lane rapidly narrowed, eventually becoming not much more than a path. "My mangoes," Ashok heard his father mutter, footsteps faltering as he looked at the lush, dark orchard across the fields.

Even with the protection of the *burkhas*, Ashok was glad when the tall sugar cane hid them from the sight of anyone on the outskirts of the village.

Almost immediately they encountered a party of a half-dozen Muslim men armed with scythes and swords. Mubarak Khan greeted them, and kept walking. Ashok did his best to walk like an old woman and to shorten himself so his feet weren't exposed.

He could see the Muslims quite clearly through the mesh, and he was terrified they would be able to see him. But they passed, instinctively avoiding close visual examination of a brother Muslim's women. When the danger was over, Mubarak Khan stopped.

He wiped sweat from his forehead and said, "Allah was with us that time. But maybe we shouldn't push our fates too far. I suggest you hide until nightfall. There should be enough moonlight to see your way. There's a thicket there by the canal bank. I'll return after sunset to go with you again. You can pass more easily for Muslim women in the darkness."

Yogesh Chand said, "There's no need for you to endanger yourself any further. We should be safe, dressed as we are."

"There's no danger to *me*. I can prove I'm Muslim."

Ashok said, "They may be angry at you for helping us, and attack you, too."

Mubarak Khan waved a hand in dismissal. "Not likely. Let's not argue. I'll be here right after sunset. But—" he hesitated "—in case I'm not, don't wait more than an hour for me. You must move as quickly as possible toward Chilianwala. If something should happen so I can't find you again—But I'm sure I'll be back. You're welcome to my bullock cart, if you'd prefer it to walking."

Ashok said, "It would be easier, Uncle, but it would make it almost impossible for us to hide if we need to."

Yogesh Chand coughed. He cleared his throat, and said, "That's true. We'd also have to stay on the roads, which would be more dangerous. No, we'd best walk."

Mubarak Khan quickly embraced Yogesh and Ashok. "We owe you so much," said Ashok.

"Nonsense. How could I not help my own brother's family?" Mubarak turned and hurried toward the village. The Chands edged into the thicket of trees and brush by the canal bank. When they had settled on a location and were seated they watched the smoke rising above their village. Occasionally, they heard parties of men going back and forth along the nearby path, shouting, laughing. More than once they heard gunshots in the distance.

The sun crept across the sky, slowly, very slowly, lowering to meet the horizon. They shared some of the food. Yogesh Chand took a long time eating one of the mangoes. All the while he was gazing far over the fields at the tops of his own orchard trees. Periodically, he went into a spell of coughing.

Ashok worried about the sound being heard by people using the path. And he frequently thought about Joginder and the other Sikhs of the village.

Savitri sat staring at the ground most of the time. At times, she would wipe away the tears that appeared on her cheeks.

Radha Chand's eyes were dazed. Occasionally, she closed them for a long while. In late afternoon, when it had been quiet for some hours, she said, "This seems so foolish, sitting here like animals. At the edge of our own village."

"Everything that's been happening is foolish," said Ashok.

"Why don't you go and see if it's all right to return now, son?" she said.

"Return to what, Mother? Our house is burned, and we're probably still in danger there."

"Why did we ever bother to convert if it didn't make us safe?" asked Radha Chand.

"Some men won't respect the conversion, Mother. Many will, but some won't."

She shook her head. "Why did we bother, then? Especially the rest of you, who even had to eat that—that cow meat?"

Ashok sighed. "I think we might not be alive now if we hadn't."

Mubarak Khan was an hour and a half late in coming. When he finally appeared, he was hurrying, glancing back over his shoulder, and Abdul Rasool was with him. Mubarak said in relief upon seeing them, "I was sure you would be gone by now. Some of them accused me of helping you get away. I finally convinced them I had no part in it. But I was afraid they'd follow me. I had to wait for a good chance to sneak off. Unfortunately, I think I'd better return before they miss me, but Abdul said he'd be glad to go with you. If anyone questions you, he'll say he's escorting his aunt and cousins."

Yogesh Chand said to Abdul Rasool, "We're grateful. But what about your baby?"

Mubarak Khan answered for his nephew: "My wife will look after the little one."

Ashok said to the young man, "You're courageous to risk helping us. If we're discovered, you could be killed, too."

Abdul Rasool shrugged, his face sober. "What's happening to you isn't right."

Mubarak Khan looked at the Chands, tears in his eyes, and said, "God go with you. When this madness passes, we'll meet again." He again swiftly embraced first Yogesh, then Ashok. They all had moist eyes.

"We're grateful," said Ashok.

Mubarak Khan shook his head. "I should do more. But what? You are still welcome to take my bullocks and cart."

"That's kind of you. It's safer if we don't, though," said Ashok, regretting the need for his parents, especially, to go so far on foot.

"You'll look after my mangoes?" asked Yogesh weakly.

"Of course! As if they were my own. And,—" Mubarak hesitated— "if for some reason you can't come back, I'll do everything in my power to help see you get paid fairly for what you've left."

Yogesh tried to cover a sob.

"You know you'd do the same for me," said Mubarak. "Anyway, we'll see each other again. Hopefully, quite soon." After another round of farewells, he headed toward the village, glanced quickly backwards, then walked more swiftly.

The Chands and Abdul Rasool set out, moving quietly along the paths between the fields, eastward toward Chilianwala. The moon had risen, and it shed enough light for walking.

Ashok knew it would probably take the better part of two days to cover the eighteen miles. Much could happen in that time.

When they passed the nearby village of Chak 121, there was the strong odor of smoke. Assuming that it might have been burned, they skirted the village through the fields. Through the mesh of the *burkha*, Ashok saw Abdul Rasool had tears in his eyes. Ashok whispered to him, "This must remind you of what happened in your own village. I'm very sorry."

Abdul nodded. "No one should have to experience such a thing. I think every time I smell smoke, I'll remember."

"It's kind of you not to look for revenge, like so many are doing."

Abdul shook his head and said quietly, "That would be pointless. Why cause more suffering? If I were to meet one of the men face-to-face who I knew for certain had killed those I loved, then I might not be able to control myself. But it makes no sense to take vengeance on those who had nothing to do with it. I think the men in the mobs can't be true Muslims—they must just enjoy having an excuse to kill, and to take someone else's property or women."

A dog barked not far away, so they fell silent as they walked.

Providentially, only a few hours later they encountered a foot convoy of Sikhs and Hindus from neighboring Chaks 128 and 122 who were heading east to the refugee camp which had just been established at Chilianwala. Abdul Rasool then bid farewell, and after embraces, he left.

10

A day later, exhausted and filthy, they arrived safely at the camp. Refugees, thousands of them, packed the grounds of Government High School, near the railway station. The day was hot, and a stench rose from the mass of unwashed people, and from the latrines.

The camp administration had created a crisscross grid of pathways through the grounds in order to bring some sort of order to the confusion, and refugees with the same village of origin were placed together in the same spot. Since no others had yet arrived from Kapani, Ashok's family was assigned at random to a place near the main school building. Some persons had rigged shelters from bed sheets or tarps attached to poles or to bullock carts, but most refugees lived fully exposed to the elements. Due to Yogesh Chand's ill health and age, and the fact that they had no bullock cart for protection, the camp commander took pity and managed to find a canvas tarp and some poles for a shield from the sun.

There were clearly too many refugees for the school yard, but they were prevented from spilling across the camp's boundaries by the railroad line on the north, a branch irrigation canal on the east, a road on the south, and a low brick wall on the west. And by the fierce looking khaki clad soldiers wearing green berets, who patrolled the entire perimeter, ostensibly to prevent attacks by Muslim mobs. The Frontier Force Rifles were made up mostly of Baluch and Pathan Muslims. To Ashok, it was too much like putting foxes in charge of guarding chickens.

Shortly after arriving, as he made his way through the seated and standing masses of people to cross the camp, Ashok recognized a face he had seen before, the young Sikh man whom he had talked with when the cart convoy passed through Kapani. The man, carrying one of his little sons, started to walk past Ashok with a dazed, abstracted look, apparently not remembering him. Ashok greeted the Sikh and reminded him where they had met. "How is the rest of your family?" Ashok asked.

The man did not look at him after the first glance. Tears formed in his eyes. "Our convoy was attacked before we reached here. They took my wife. My other son was killed. I...we...tried to fight them. But there were too many." He started to say something else, but then shook his head. He wandered on.

Ashok, trying to think of an appropriate response, stood staring after him, mouth partly open. Then he looked about at the thousands of other refugees, each living their own tragedies. And who knew how many entire communities, like the Sikhs of Kapani, had died in their own villages?

He returned to where his parents and Savitri were resting after their traumatic escape. "Can you stay with Mother and Father for a while?" Savitra asked. "I'm told the two doctors are overwhelmed with work. I thought I might go see if I can help."

"Of course," Ashok said. He squatted on his haunches. Savitra rose, gave him a wan smile, and began moving away through the milling and seated people.

Hours passed. When the time came for distributing food rations and she hadn't returned, he went to search for her. One end of the school building served as the makeshift hospital for the camp. It was obviously inadequate, as wounded and ill refugees were lying about outside, shaded by blankets and tarps strung on ropes. Family members were seated with many of them.

A couple dozen men and children were standing in a semicircle, watching something occurring next to the building. A girl hurried up with a bucket of water and forced her way through. As the onlookers parted, Ashok glimpsed Savitri gesturing to the girl to set the bucket down by a woman who was lying on the ground.

"What's happening?" he quietly asked one of the men, a stocky Sikh whose leathery skin was evidence of many years of laboring in the sun.

"A woman's having a baby," the man said. "I've never seen it before! Men are always kept away. This may be your only chance. Have a look!"

Ashok stared at him. "Don't you think she wants some privacy?"

"Here? Are you mad? Nobody gets any privacy with so many people around."

"But you don't have to stand and watch."

The Sikh scowled at him and returned his attention to the birth.

Savitri, who had been bending over her patient, stood. It was the first time Ashok could remember seeing her truly angry. "Go away!" she said loudly to the onlookers. "Don't you have any shame?"

Ashok took the arm of a boy who was watching. "Go somewhere else," he said, gently but firmly shoving the boy away. He raised his voice. "Everyone get away!"

Some of the people edged away a step or two. A couple of men didn't budge. One boy left, but two more took his place.

Savitri's tired eyes met Ashok's, and her face softened slightly. She gave a quick nod of gratitude, then knelt by her patient.

Ashok opened his mouth to scold the onlookers again and insist they leave. But he realized it was hopeless. Even if he were successful at getting some to leave, others would crowd in. Clearly, this was yet another situation in which the normal standards of society were suspended.

Ashok began helping the medical staff whenever he felt he didn't need to be with his parents. Balding, middle aged Dr. Krishnan, who had assumed leadership of the medical staff, seemed knowledgeable and competent. The other doctor was a small, withdrawn, harried looking man who seldom spoke, and typically gave his orders to his patients and staff by means of impatient gestures. Three or four nurses and a dozen volunteers, mostly young male students, also worked in the dispensary.

Even though Savitri still had two more years of medical school to complete, she assisted Dr. Krishnan in much the same capacity as an intern. Overseeing the deliveries of babies, of which at least one was born in the camp virtually every day, became part of her regular duties. Ashok helped her rig a screen of tarps so there was considerably more privacy, though fascinated children still peeked through the gaps.

Savitri also assisted with the women who needed treatment for multiple rapes, cut off hands, and hacked-off breasts. The latter cases generally soon died.

There were no medical instruments, so Dr. Krishnan was forced to perform surgery with razor blades. Medicines were also nonexistent. The camp commander's pleas to the local authorities for medical supplies went unanswered.

More refugees arrived every day, many of them wounded, many of them sick. Men came to the camp with hands and arms chopped off, stab wounds, concussions, burns, cut throats. Many of the injuries proved fatal.

Then there were the circumcisions resulting from forced conversions to Islam. All of the wounds were red and sore; most were infected. Whenever Dr. Krishnan attempted to treat one with no medication, Ashok felt immensely grateful he had avoided that particular trauma in his own "conversion."

Ashok also acted as the overworked doctors' liaison with the camp commander, a tall, lean Sikh in his forties named Sant Singh, who had been a public works officer before Partition.

Many people became ill, and eventually it was discovered that lime had been mixed in with the flour provided to the camp. The camp commander protested vigorously to the civil authorities in town, who promised an investigation.

With her competence, her beauty, her quiet cheerfulness, Savitri became as well known in the camp as Dr. Krishnan, and even more popular. Many of the people began to look upon her almost as a goddess of healing. Young men, in particular, began finding sprains and other injuries as an excuse to have her tend to them. She took it all good naturedly and matter of factly, efficiently dealing with each case before moving to the next.

It was not only in the villages and on journeys that the West Punjab had grown dangerous for non-Muslims. The camp itself had its perils, even aside from disease and poisoned food. The railway line bordered the camp, and occasionally Baluch or Pathan soldiers on a passing train would actually shoot into the crowded refugees, killing some, and giving the doctor and his helpers more wounded to tend.

The Baluch guards, provided supposedly to protect the camp, instead frequently abducted girls at night and raped them. The camp commander protested every incident to both the police and the military, but neither seemed willing to act decisively to end the incidents. Ashok worried over Savitri, but she insisted she'd take care to avoid the so-called guards. "Anyway," she told Ashok, "At twenty-two years I'm probably too old. Most of the unfortunate girls are at least five years younger than I."

"You're not at all too old," he said gravely. "Please be careful."

Latrines had been dug in the far corner of the camp, by the wall bordering the neighboring fields. But they were not convenient for many, and the stench was unbelievable. So the refugees either stepped through a gap in the wall and used the edge of the field, where they were subjected to harassment from the military guards, or they used buckets which they carried out to the edge of the camp and dumped in a ditch alongside the railroad tracks. Baluch guards stationed at the edge of the camp would laugh and make joking comments at the women whenever they went to dump their buckets.

The toilet facilities attached to the hospital building were totally inadequate and the clogged plumbing seldom functioned, so the medical staff was forced to use the same methods as the other camp inmates. Ashok insisted on taking Savitri's bucket so she could avoid coming near to the guards. At first she adamantly refused, insisting no one should have to do such a thing for her. But Ashok persisted. He took hospital pans to empty at the same time, and he reminded her about how even Gandhiji took his turn at cleaning latrines. Finally, she agreed, mainly to get him to be quiet.

A refugee train stopped and took aboard over two thousand of the inmates, most of whom had priority over the Chands either because they had been in the camp longer or were in more urgent need of proper medical attention.

The one telephone in the camp commander's office was totally inadequate for the needs of the thousands of refugees. Ashok wrote a number of times to Jaya, but he did not receive a reply and had no way of knowing if she had received his letters.

Cholera struck, brought in by a recent group of arrivals. At Dr. Krishnan's direction, an effort was made to isolate the sick in one part of the camp, but under the crowded, unhygienic conditions the disease quickly spread. Vaccine was requested through the military's radio, but it did not come.

Ashok knew he would never, ever, forget the foul odor of people lying in pools of their own pale yellowish excrement, too weak from loss of fluids to move or to clean themselves. Some of the stricken recovered. But many died in spite of the valiant efforts of the medical staff and volunteers.

There was no fuel to cremate so many dead, so contrary to Hindu and Sikh religious practices, burial was the only alternative. Ashok and other volunteers, many of them students, dug the graves and carried the bodies on makeshift stretchers to the site.

The Chands were careful to drink only boiled water and to keep themselves clean. But still, no one knew whom the disease would strike next. Savitri and Ashok were especially at risk due to their daily contact with the sick.

The cholera appeared to pass them by, but Yogesh's cough grew worse. Savitri and Ashok and their mother worried about him. "He should be some place where there's shelter," Savitri told Ashok. "If the dispensary wasn't already overflowing I'd put him in there. All these nights out in the cold can't possibly be good for him."

Ashok talked to the camp commander, who promised to try to get the family on the next available train to India.

On a cloudy, grim day, some of the refugees who possessed bullock carts left in a large convoy. But Ashok's family lacked a cart, and his father did not have the strength to walk the seventy miles to the border.

That night, Savitri was working late assisting the doctor. She took a break to use her bucket; as usual the plumbing in the toilet room was clogged. Ashok had gone back to tend their parents, and rather than leave the bucket sitting until morning, she decided to take it out herself to empty. It was dark, after all, so the guards should not be able to see her face or even guess her age.

"I'll be back soon," she told Dr. Krishnan, who was finishing his daily report.

"No hurry," he said. "I'm tired. I'm turning in as soon as I'm done. The volunteers can wake me if there's an emergency."

Savitri put her *dupatta* over her head, grabbed the bucket, and went out. The night was clear and cool. The camp was mostly dark. With the shortage of kerosene, only a few lanterns burned in strategic locations. She made her way along one of the narrow straight paths toward the perimeter. Already, many of the refugees were curled up for the night, their blankets over their heads. Others sat close to their cooking fires, talking. Few paid any attention to her in the darkness.

She could have found the latrine area in the darkness by its stench, even if she were not able to dimly see the ditches. There, she stopped to peer into the night, wondering where the Baluch guards might be. Seeing and hearing nothing, she continued to a trench, dumped her pail, then went to the water tap.

Suddenly, rough fingers clamped over her mouth. At the same moment, strong, hard hands seized her arms from behind. She struggled desperately with no effect. Nothing was said as they dragged her toward the wall, like she were a child's doll. She kept trying to scream, but the rough hand over her mouth pressed tight. She tried to drag her feet, but the hands that held her merely pulled harder.

When they forced her through a gap in the wall, one captor went ahead to pull her. In the dimness she discerned a beret above a mustached face on a tall uniformed figure.

They dragged her far out into the field. Then they forced her onto her back on the hard soil. She still strained to get away as she felt her waistband ripped open. A hand still clamped her mouth. They tore off her clothes and forced apart her legs. She screamed and sobbed and shrieked as they violated her, but the muffled sounds did not carry far enough to alarm anyone who might help.

By the time the third man thrust into her, she was no longer conscious.

Ashok, exhausted, slept through the night. In the morning, when he awoke, he found Savitri had not returned to the family's spot to sleep. He hurried to the dispensary and saw she was not there.

He rushed to where Dr. Krishnan, assisted by a nurse, was examining a chest cut. Ashok tried to remain calm as he asked, "Do you know where my sister is?"

The doctor glanced at him, then returned to examining the wound. "I haven't seen her yet this morning."

"She didn't come back to our spot to sleep."

Krishnan's head jerked around to stare at Ashok. "When I saw her late last night, she was heading for the latrines. Just before I left to go to bed." He called out to the rest of the staff: "Anyone seen Miss Chand this morning?"

There were no replies; a couple of the student volunteers shook their heads no.

Ashok said, trying to keep calm, "I'll look around."

He passed by the latrines, made a quick check of the camp and asked a number of people who knew Savitri if they'd seen her. Nothing.

He went and informed the camp commander.

Sant Singh stared with widening eyes as Ashok told him. Singh pounded on his desk and shook his head. "Damn! Not *her!*"

"You think it was the guards again?"

Sant Singh looked past Ashok, out the door. In a low voice, he replied, "Let's hope not. But based on past experience, I suspect they know something about it."

"Can you ask them?"

Singh gave him a troubled look. "I will. But I don't think they'll tell me anything. By god, Ashok, I hope I'm wrong. You know we aren't allowed to go outside and search. I'll protest to the authorities. But it's hard to be optimistic."

"Why won't the officials do anything? And can't the army commander order his men to return her?"

Sant Singh again looked past Ashok. He sighed. "Many of the officials don't care. They just want to be rid of us all, dead or alive. I think Major Turnbow would like to help us, but he insists he can only go so far with his men right now."

"I want to talk with him. As soon as possible."

Sant Singh examined Ashok, clearly reluctant. Ashok said, "I won't say anything to hurt the camp's relationship with him. But maybe if he sees that my sister—all these girls who are being taken—are persons, someone's loved ones, not just more statistics, he'll do something."

Singh stared at him a moment. Then he looked away and nodded. "The major should pass by before long on his morning tour. I'll take you with me when I report this to him."

Ashok left. He tried to conceal Savitri's disappearance from his parents in the hope she would turn up, but word quickly spread throughout the camp that the beautiful "lady doctor" had vanished, and soon his father and mother knew, also.

Ashok's mother said, "*Anything* can be happening to her, right now! How can the commander permit this? And why doesn't the army do something? Are they all cowards?"

"They're in an awkward situation, Mother," Ashok said, though for the most part, he agreed with her.

She began crying continually, oblivious to efforts to comfort her. His father sobbed quietly in between coughing spells, appeared to grow weaker, more withdrawn.

Ashok spent considerable time tending his mother. Eventually, some neighboring women took over the task, allowing him to escape for a while.

Wherever he went, refugees would approach him to commiserate. Shortly before his meeting with the major, two of the students who had worked with Savitri approached him. One handed him a heavy paper bag. It was full of coins and rupee notes. "The refugees took up a collection," the young man said. "It's a reward to try to get the lady doctor back."

The tears Ashok had been holding back now came. Other girls, other women, had been abducted also. But never had there been such a collection taken throughout the camp.

Major Turnbow was an India-born Englishman who had decided to stay on with the Pakistani Army for a time. From his dark features and complexion, he appeared to have some native Indian blood. He listened impassively to Sant Singh's plea for aid, and the offer of the reward of over two hundred rupees, his eyes staring past. When Singh had finished, the major spread his hands. "Sardarji, we've been over this type of problem many times. I understand your situation. I hoped you understood mine."

The camp commander said, "Major, it's been bad enough when the very men who are assigned to safeguard us have instead done us harm. But in this case they've kidnaped one of our medical staff! How can you, as their superior officer, tolerate such behavior?"

The major grew rigid, and his eyes narrowed at the implication that he was unable to control his men. He replied, "We have no proof the guards were even involved. Anyone could have crept close in the dark—" He stopped as if realizing what he could be interpreted as disparaging his men's competence at preventing unauthorized access to the camp.

Ashok spoke: "Sir, as Mr. Singh has said, the woman who's missing is my own sister. I understand your difficulties in maintaining order among your troops in an unsettled time such as this. However, if you mention the reward, maybe you can at least get some information. Maybe some of your men might remember seeing something that could give you or the police a lead as to where she's been taken."

The major was staring at him. He said, obviously hesitant, "I'll make some inquiries, of course. I always do. But I wouldn't count on results. We've had no luck in the past."

"Sir," said Ashok, "do you have a sister of your own?"

The officer looked away. "Yes," he answered hoarsely. "I have two."

"Then if you imagine how you'd feel if they were abducted, you have some idea how I feel. How my family feels."

The major was silent for a time. Then he looked at Ashok. He said quietly, "I'll try. That's all I can promise."

Frequently throughout the day, Ashok went to stand near the edge of the camp, looking outward, hoping for some sign of Savitri. He watched the Baluch guards, wondering which of them had taken her, trying to think of some way to compel them to bring her back. He hoped the reward, an appeal to their greed, might work.

What would Gandhiji do? He tried to imagine. Gandhiji would probably go talk to the guards themselves and make a personal appeal.

Maybe Ashok was selling the guards short, but he doubted even an appeal by Mahatma Gandhi would have much effect.

Late that afternoon, Sant Singh sought him out. "The major stopped by, Ashok. So far, no luck. His men say they know nothing."

Ashok clenched his fists.

"Give them more time to think about the reward," said the camp commander. Ashok nodded. The camp commander left.

Ashok tried not to hate the Baluchis, but he failed. Again he wondered what Gandhiji would do. Try to love these men who had abducted her? Maybe. Probably. But Ashok realized he was not so much of a saint as Gandhi.

Abruptly, he heard angry shouts from the direction of the far edge of the camp, and several shots rang out.

He cautiously hurried to where he could see what was happening. Several male refugees were carrying a couple of wounded men toward the dispensary. A young Sikh man saw Ashok, came to him and said, "It was about your sister, Ashokji. These men screamed at the guards to bring her back, calling them cowards and cursing them. The guards ignored them. Then someone threw a rock at one, and the Baluchis started shooting."

Ashok shook his head and muttered, "Oh, god. Look," he said weakly, "she wouldn't want anyone injured on her behalf. Try to keep everyone calm, so no one else gets hurt."

The Sikh nodded. "I'll try to pass the word."

Ashok stared helplessly toward the guards, still standing with their rifles ready.

Throughout the camp's brief existence, refugees had been fired upon, wounded, abducted, and killed. But none of the incidents had resulted in such a voicing of outrage as this.

A day passed.

Word came from the major: one of the Baluchis had informed his officer that he had seen four of the other guards seize a young woman near the latrines that night and take her from the camp. They had all raped her. Then they had taken her into town and sold her to a Muslim who was passing through with a mob.

The four guards denied all knowledge of the incident. There was no information available regarding where the unknown Muslim had taken her.

Another day passed. The major said he had ordered disciplinary action for the men involved and transferred them from the camp.

Another day passed, and another.

There was no further information about Savitri. Ashok tried and tried to think of some way to find her. Though he knew it was absurd, he fantasized about organizing some men to form a search party. The idea, of course, was out of the question. Savitri could be fifty miles away by now, even farther, in almost any direction, and well hidden. Outside the boundaries of the camp (some would say even *inside*) it was the equivalent of enemy territory.

And then word flashed through the camp that another refugee train was expected. Ashok visited the commander. "Is it true there's a train coming? Today?"

"We expect it around noon," Sant Singh replied quietly.

Ashok shook his head. "We're supposed to be on it this time. But I can't leave with my sister missing."

Sant Singh sighed and looked at him. "There are your parents to think of. No one can guarantee when another train will come. Or even if there will be another. Maybe there will, maybe there won't."

Ashok considered his father and mother. And Jaya. "I'll think about it. There's danger on the train, too."

Sant Singh said, "This train's supposed to be guarded by Gurkhas and Hindu soldiers, not Muslims. Let me know if you decide you don't want to go, so I can assign your spots to someone else. I think you'd be wise to leave while you can, though. I'd go myself if I didn't feel responsible for the camp."

"We should probably go because of my father's health," Ashok said.

Singh raised an eyebrow. "I don't suppose you'd want to send them ahead alone."

Ashok took a deep breath. "I don't think so. My father's so ill. My mother hasn't traveled for years. With conditions so unsettled, I'd feel a lot better if I was along to help."

Sant Singh said, "A lot of refugees have had to leave family members behind. It's said an agency is going to be set up by each country to locate missing persons and reunite them with their relatives."

Ashok tightened his lips. "That could take months. Maybe years."

Sant Singh said nothing.

Ashok stood in thought.

Singh said, "You know how fond everyone here is of your sister. Maybe I shouldn't say it, but her loss bothered me, personally, more than most of the others put together. I promise you—if she turns up, we'll do everything we can for her. We'll send her after you as soon as possible."

Ashok nodded. "I appreciate that. Especially when there are so many others with problems."

Singh said, "Your sister was special. We all feel that."

Ashok went to the dispensary and talked with Dr. Krishnan. "Your father needs better treatment," the doctor said. "Better shelter. Medications we don't have here. If I were you, I'd get him out of here. If your sister returns before I leave for India myself, I'll see she understands you had no choice but to go. I'll tell her I insisted you leave because of your father's health."

At last Ashok nodded. "I'll go. May I leave a note with you, to give to her?"

"Of course."

11

The station platform was crowded solid with the waiting refugees. Despite efforts of police and guards to keep them away from the track, the mass of people surged toward the train as it rolled into the station. Ashok had to summon all his strength to keep himself and his mother from being pushed into the path of the giant locomotive. He was aware of the closeness of the huge rolling mass of black metal, of the high steel wheels grinding by only inches away, of the hot, wet steam whooshing from the cylinder. Then the engine and the tender were past, and he had to concentrate on not being shoved into the sides of the carriages before they stopped moving.

Even before the train came to a complete halt, small-statured soldiers with oriental features were dropping from the cars, forcing the packed refugees to give way slightly.

"Gurkhas! Gurkhas!" people shouted jubilantly.

"It's about time we got decent guards," said Ashok's mother, her voice scarcely audible above the noise.

Thank god, Ashok thought. The Gurkhas, who came from the Himalayan foothills, were widely considered to be among the best soldiers in the world, and their loyalty was legendary. With them as guards, the chances of getting safely to the border were vastly increased.

The refugees rushed like passengers on a sinking ship racing for a lifeboat. The crush of people pushed Ashok into the steps of the nearest car, and he concentrated on pulling his father and mother aboard.

The car was already mostly full with people from earlier stops, mostly Sikhs, easily identifiable by the men's turbans and beards, but also a few who appeared to be Hindus. Ashok hurried his parents to the rear of the carriage. There his father and mother managed to squeeze onto the end of a hard wooden seat next to a Sikh couple with two children, a boy of around twelve and a girl perhaps half that age. Ashok stood leaning against the wall next to his mother.

The train sat for some time after it was fully packed with people, both in the cars and on the roofs. Even in this season, the Punjab plain was hot at midday, and the air inside the carriage was stifling. The odor of so many sweating bodies without recent opportunities to bathe was almost overwhelming. There must be three thousand or so persons on the train, Ashok guessed. The refugees inside the car were mostly quiet except for shifting positions, occasional whispers or mutters, the crying of babies.

The Sikh man on the far side of Ashok's father, seated where he could see out the window, suddenly said, "The army guard's leaving!"

"No, not leaving," said another man who was peering out. "Other solders are taking the Gurkhas' place. The new ones look like Baluchis."

Ashok's mother looked at her son. "It can't be," she said. "How can they do this to us?"

Ashok's father grumbled weakly in resignation, "Why not? They've done everything else."

Gloom settled over the car, based on previous sad experience with Baluchi "guards." The dangers were still real; few trains made it to the border without being attacked. And Chilianwala was roughly seventy miles from

Sardarpur, the first town across the border in India. Seventy miles of now-hostile territory.

At the front of this car stood a Sikh man in a khaki army or police uniform. The man turned to look toward the rear, and Ashok recognized a familiar face.

Karam Singh! What was the Inspector General of the Mangarh state police doing on the train? Singh saw Ashok, stared a moment, then gave a brief nod and looked away.

Ashok's first thought was that Karam Singh had followed him to the Punjab to keep an eye on his activities. He quickly realized the idea was absurd. No one in Mangarh could care what Ashok did outside that state. One good thing about being in Pakistan—probably the *only* good thing now—was that Ashok was out of Mangarh jurisdiction and hence could not again be imprisoned there. Karam Singh must have some totally unrelated reason for being on the train. Indeed, Ashok saw that the police official seemed to be in charge of a white haired old Sikh gentleman and an old woman—quite possibly Singh's own parents.

At last the train began to move, so smoothly Ashok found it mildly surprising to see the station buildings gliding past. The train continued to roll relatively slowly, never picking up much speed even when Chilianwala was left far behind.

The slowness made the ride seem to drag interminably. Ashok worked his way forward in the car and greeted Karam Singh. He saw that the police chief wore a revolver in a holster.

After introducing Ashok to his parents, Singh said, "I'm not missing the irony, Mr. Chand, that we've both found ourselves in the same predicament."

Ashok grinned tightly. It was indeed ironic that the man who had imprisoned him three times in Mangarh was now something of a fellow refugee. "I've heard nothing from Mangarh," Ashok said. "Has it escaped most of the troubles?"

"It's been remarkable, really," said Karam Singh. "No problems whatsoever. And it's all due to His Highness. The Maharaja said he'd personally shoot anyone who laid a hand on his Muslims. And he made it clear he'd shoot *me* if my police didn't act immediately in case of any need to protect them!"

Ashok nodded. "Apparently that's what it takes. A decisive statement from those in power that any incidents won't be tolerated, and the willingness to fully back it up."

"That may be oversimplifying matters, but so it would seem. If everyone in authority in West Punjab had done their jobs, our families wouldn't be fleeing for their lives." He looked intently at Ashok. "So you see, that Maharaja you were always agitating against has turned out to be the savior of many of his people. If Congress had been in power in Mangarh, do you really think there would have been no violence whatsoever?"

Ashok could not answer. The question was worth pondering.

Abruptly, the train stopped. People began murmuring, as they worried about the cause of the halt.

Singh shook his head, his lips grim. "Every stop is another opportunity for someone to attack us."

Ashok nodded. "My parents will be worried. I'd better get back to them." He edged through the crowded aisle to his seat.

After twenty minutes or so, the train again began to move. Only to stop again after a mile or so.

The Baluch soldiers stepped to the ground, and they could be seen strolling toward the rear of the train. Again the passengers worried aloud about what was going on. Were the guards leaving? Did that mean no protection at all now?

No one in authority came to give an explanation. The train eventually began rolling again.

The loss of Savitri, leaving their lands and orchards, leaving behind the life they'd known—all cast a dismal pall over Ashok's family. Of course he himself had Jaya waiting in Delhi. She had seemed so far away these past weeks, so far removed from his own life. Almost as if she were on the other side of the world.

She must be frantic with worry. He wondered if she had gotten any of his letters. It was similar, in a way, Ashok thought, to being in jail, this lack of any control over the course of one's life. The frustration over not being able to rescue Savitri was maddening, almost paralyzing. The extent to which Fate ruled the destinies of men was only too obvious. The destinies of thousands of human beings on the train were now in hands other than their own—the hands of the train driver and crew and the unreliable guards, as well as the hands of whatever Muslims might be waiting to attack.

Ashok kept telling himself there was nothing more he, personally, could do. He must resign himself to whatever was in store, whatever fortune held for himself and his family and the others on the train. But he did not want to accept that fact. His impotence to help his sister tormented him. He did not want to have to passively accept, in a similar way, whatever perils might still face the passengers on the train.

Then Fate stepped up and touched him on the shoulder, in the form of Karam Singh. "Mr. Chand, I must have a word with you."

Ashok had not seen him coming, so he looked up in surprise. Karam Singh glanced about, apparently to see if there was anywhere they could go to speak privately. There wasn't.

He bent down by Ashok's ear and whispered, "I've been told by a railway employee that he saw the driver take a bribe to stop the train this side of Nurpur Road. A mob of armed Muslims will then attack. I'm going to the locomotive. Will you come help?"

Ashok looked at him in astonishment. Karam Singh, who had jailed him in Mangarh, was asking *him* for help? But maybe Singh didn't know anyone else on the train well. And indeed they now shared a concern in getting safely across the border. "What about the soldiers?" Ashok asked. "Even if they're Muslims, can't any of the officers help?"

"They're no longer on the train," Singh said quietly. "They didn't get on again after they jumped off at the last stop."

Ashok shivered despite the heat. No army protection at all. It looked suspiciously like the trainload of refugees had been set up for an ambush: switching from Gurkha to Baluch army units as the guards, then the Baluchis leaving.

He glanced at his parents. Who would watch over them if an attack came while he was absent from the car?

But he could not refuse. Helping the entire trainload of refugees was a higher duty even than that to his family. "I'll be back as soon as I can," he told his parents. His mother looked as if she wanted to object, but she didn't. His father simply gave an almost imperceptible nod.

Karam Singh hurriedly led the way, squeezing through the crowded car. Time was short, so he rudely bulldozed his way between people. Nurpur Road could not be far away. They reached the end of the carriage and pushed through the clot of standing men in front of doorway. Singh called back to Ashok, "This is hopeless! Let's try the roof."

The roof. The only thing Ashok hated worse than confinement in a small space was heights.

Already Karam Singh was outside, boosting himself onto the horizontal iron bars of a window. "Help me up!" he called to the nearest men on the roof. Two reached down and grabbed his arm. Soon he had scrambled onto the top.

It was Ashok's turn. He tried to ignore the roadbed rushing by, the swaying of the car. First he grabbed the window bars. He managed to get a foot up onto the lower one. Then Karam Singh had hold of his arm and was pulling. A Sikh man on the roof grabbed the other arm.

Ashok's foot slipped. Terrified, he hung free over the rushing roadbed. It felt as if the men on the roof were pulling his arms off. His toe found a window bar again. He used the foot to help push himself up. His belly scraped over the grit-encrusted, rounded metal of the roof edge. At last he was on top, flat on his stomach, feet hanging out into the wind. He scrambled to his knees, and slowly, shakily stood, his feet planted far apart for balance.

Although the tops of the cars, too, were crowded with young and middle aged male refugees, mostly Sikhs, it didn't seem quite so packed as the interiors below. Karam Singh ran ahead, agilely stepping between the seated men.

Concentrating on where to place his feet to keep from stepping on people or tripping over the low ventilators, pointedly avoiding looking to either side, Ashok tried to keep up. Warm air blew at his face and tugged at his clothing.

He hated the jumps from one carriage roof to the next, when through the gaps he could see the ground rushing by below. He fully expected to lose his balance each time he leaped to a swaying, curved, grimy surface. Somehow, each time he succeeded in landing on the next car.

What would they do when they reached the engine? Karam Singh had his revolver. Ashok wondered what, if any, contribution he could make himself. He wasn't armed, and anyway he'd never held a gun in his life.

Singh glanced back at him. "We're slowing! Hurry!" Ashok could sense the deceleration. The smoke and soot from the chimney flew into his eyes now. Singh practically threw himself through the narrow gaps between the seated people. Ashok half ran, half staggered the length of each roof, trying to keep up.

They jumped onto the lead car and raced to the front, not caring any more whether they stepped on a leg, a foot, a hand, so long as they did not lose their balance.

Far down the track the minarets and the temple towers of Nurpur Road peeked above the surrounding trees and houses.

The oblong black box of the tender stretched before them, and ahead of it the engine. Karam Singh dropped over the side, onto the coal. Ashok followed.

In spite of worry over what he might face up ahead, he was vastly relieved to be off those treacherous roofs. It seemed incredible he had done what he had, much less survived the experience.

Stumbling and slipping on the gritty black lumps, he scrambled after Karam Singh to the head of the tender. The steel bottom of the compartment sloped into a flat-bottomed "V" like the inside of a boat's hull. At the center front was an open door through which the firemen shoveled coal.

Singh drew his revolver. He stepped from the tender to the footplate of the locomotive.

12

The railroad was wide gauge, so the engine was monstrous in size, with a broad open-backed room enclosing the footplate. Even with the driver and two stokers, there was ample space, so Ashok stepped on also. Coal dust gritted underfoot, and heat radiated from the metal front wall.

The firemen saw them instantly and froze, their mouths agape, eyes wide. The driver had his back to them and was looking through one of the small windows that faced ahead along the side of the boiler. He turned and saw Karam Singh and the pointed revolver. "Keep the train moving. Speed up again!" Singh shouted.

The driver stared at the police officer. "Faster!" Singh barked.

The driver froze a moment. Then he said, "Inspector *sahib*, the signal is against us!"

"I don't give a bloody damn about the signal. You keep this train moving!"

"Inspector, sir! Another train may be coming! We must wait!"

"It's Inspector *General*!" said Singh, not bothering to say that he had no real legal authority in Pakistan. "We'll take our chances on another train! You speed up, or I'll shoot you!" Singh's eyes, fierce even under normal circumstances, flashed terrible fire.

The driver, anxiety in his own eyes, moved a lever. The slowing ceased, and in a few moments the heavy train gradually began to accelerate. The driver turned back to Karam Singh. "Why are you doing this, sir?" he asked loudly. "Why are you putting our lives in danger?"

"Empty your pockets," ordered Karam Singh.

"Sir, this is an outrage!"

"Empty them, or I'll kill you!"

The driver's eyes bulged in fear. After a moment he tugged on his pants. From one pocket he pulled forth a gigantic wad of bills.

"Give that to me!" said Singh.

The driver hesitated, then handed it over. His look turned to one of anger. Singh handed the wad to Ashok. Dazed, Ashok opened his mouth to object. But he realized this was no time to argue. He took the money, and for want of anything better to do with it, he stuck it in his pocket.

"Now," said Karam Singh to the driver, "you no longer have any reason to stop the train."

The driver looked out the window. The outlying buildings of Nurpur Road were near. Suddenly, he yanked another lever.

Steel wheels shrieked on rails, the engine jerked and shuddered. Ashok barely kept his balance. Karam Singh fell to the floor but almost instantly regained his feet, his pistol again pointed at the driver.

At the same moment, the sound of gunfire and shouting came from outside the train. Ashok glanced ahead and saw hundreds of men running toward the tracks, brandishing swords, rifles, spears.

Before Ashok realized what was happening, Singh had struck the driver on the side of the forehead with the revolver butt. The driver dropped to the footplate, releasing the brakes.   Karam Singh grabbed the long regulator lever and applied pressure. The huge engine hesitated, then started regaining speed.

"Can you drive this?" Singh shouted to Ashok.

Astonished, Ashok glanced at the maze of tubing on the bulkhead, the many levers, wheels, dials.... He shook his head. "No!"

"Do it anyway—I'll defend us! This is the regulator. It's like a throttle."

The driver was stirring, climbing to his feet.

Numbly Ashok grasped the lever. The warm, rounded metal felt smooth and polished. He applied more pressure to the bar, desperately hoping he was doing the right thing.

He glanced at the driver, who appeared dazed and was holding his head with a hand. Ashok thought about asking one of the firemen for help, but the two men were cowering in a corner of the tender, clearly terrified.

A bullet struck a steel wall, ricocheted off. The *whoosh-whoosh-whoosh* of the steam increased in tempo as the train slowly gained speed.

A loud report came from just behind Ashok. He looked backward just in time to see a man, shot by Karam Singh, fall from the side of the engine. Two more were trying to climb aboard.

Karam Singh shot again, then once more. Both men dropped to the roadbed.

The train was still accelerating. On both sides men raced to keep pace. Slowly the attackers began to drop back.

Apparently seeing it was hopeless, a couple of men slowed, raised rifles to their shoulders, and fired. A bullet *thwanged* off the side of the cab. Then another. A window shattered on the left front.

The reports of the gunfire were falling farther behind. No more bullets found the engine. But there were thousands of passengers in the carriages behind.

Ashok maintained pressure on the regulator. The Nurpur Road station platform flashed alongside, with people standing on it. A uniformed official frantically waved a red flag, which even Ashok knew meant "stop!"

What if a train were ahead? Or a vehicle were on a crossing? Looking out the small window on the right front of the forward wall, along the curve of the boiler, he saw nothing. But he reached up for the loop of cord he assumed must operate the whistle and tugged.

The whistle shrieked in warning. The railway station buildings zipped by. More people waited on the platform.

A signal arm appeared on its gantry. The signal was in the lowered position. Ashok thought that meant it was safe to proceed. But he wasn't certain.

The train swayed and rattled over switch points. Ashok tensed for several seconds, then let out a big breath. Obviously the points were in the proper position, and the engine was safely beyond them.

Karam Singh looked down at the driver, who now sat up, holding his head. Singh looked at Ashok. "I'd throw him off, but we may need his help."

Ashok nodded. Sweat from the intense heat ran into his eyes, and he wiped his forehead with the back of a hand.

The driver grasped a polished handrail by the open doorway, apparently to support himself. But suddenly, using his hold on the rail as an aid, he thrust himself out the door and jumped clear of the tender. Ashok looked just in time to see him hit the ground. Then the corner of the tender blocked the view.

Karam Singh looked worried. Then he glanced at Ashok, and shrugged.

The stokers, meantime, were still crouching in the corner of the tender. Singh waved the pistol at them. "Doesn't it need coal?"

One of the firemen, a tall, mustached man, his forehead covered with sweat-streaked coal dust, opened the firebox door. Heat shot out. The other stoker, a short, clean-shaven man with a terrified look in his eyes, grabbed his shovel and began tossing coal from the tender into the round, hotly glowing, hungry mouth.

The taller man clanged the firebox door shut. He turned a valve.

"What's that?" asked Karam Singh gruffly, as if he suspected the man might be trying to sabotage the engine.

"Injector, *sardar* s*ahib*! It shoots in steam and replaces the water the boiler uses."

Singh stared at him, finally nodded. He took some bullets from a pocket, cracked open his revolver, and replaced the spent cartridges.

Still the train accelerated. Telegraph poles shot past the windows. The *whooshes* of the engine came too close together now to differentiate. To Ashok, it seemed as if he was going as fast as any train he'd ever ridden on. He looked at the dials, but none of them appeared to indicate speed. Fifty miles an hour? Sixty? He wasn't sure.

"You'd better ease off," Karam Singh said. "We don't want to derail going around a bend."   Ashok nodded. The insanity of what he was doing made his heart pound. Men must need twenty years experience to qualify for driving an engine like this. And he had three thousand or so lives, not to mention all the equipment, riding on his actions!

What if, up ahead, there was a similar, but oncoming, train carrying thousands of persons?

The thought terrified him. He moved the regulator lever so the engine slowed slightly.

Ashok now saw the sign on the wall in front of him, near the small forward-facing window:

CAUTION

—IS YOUR SIGNAL CLEAR?
—HAVE YOU THE CORRECT AUTHORITY TO PROCEED?

On the right hand side of the sign was a drawing of a signal with the semaphore arm in the lowered position.

Authority to proceed.... Ashok's agitation grew. Although he knew almost nothing about railroad operations, he did know that single line tracks were divided into sections. To proceed from one section to the next, at the stations the driver had to take physical possession of a key or token which constituted the permission to continue.

Lacking such authority, there was serious danger of a collision with another train. Or of derailment, if the switching points were not in the necessary position.

He caught Karam Singh's attention and pointed to the sign.

Singh read it, scowled, and shrugged. "We're our own authority!"

Ashok looked at the two large round gauges. The numbers, the positions of the needles, were meaningless to him. But the engine was running furiously fast.

How far to the border? He remembered it was at least fifty miles beyond Nurpur Road. An entire hour!

The engine seemed to be running smoothly. The two firemen appeared to have accepted the change of command. Frequently, one opened the firebox and tossed in a few shovels of coal, distributing it to various spots on the grate.

At least on the flatness of the Punjab plain there were no steep grades to contend with, and no sharp turns. Only the possibility of oncoming trains. Or improperly set switch points. Or ambushes.

Despite the other dangers, the thought of the oncoming train worried him the most. He tried to remember the schedules of the westbound trains. Surely there must be at least one per hour normally, even if only a goods train. But timetables had gotten irregular with the troubles at Partition, the diverting of trains to carry refugees.

A signal arm flashed by. In the up position.

The tall, mustached, stoker said, "The signal is against us, sir!"

Ashok said to Karam Singh, "This must be Rahimabad—I think I remember it has a siding. What if we're supposed to go onto the siding to let an oncoming train past?"

Singh's face glistened with sweat. He pressed his lips together tight. Then he said, "Maybe you'd better slow down. Fewer people killed that way if we collide or jump the track."

Ashok adjusted the regulator arm. The engine began to decelerate.

The same fireman said to him, "Water, *sahib?*"

Thinking the man was offering a drink, Ashok nodded yes.

"Rahimabad is a watering station, *sahib*. You must stop, take on water." He pointed to a glass tube which apparently showed the water level in the boiler.

Water for the engine.

But how could Ashok stop at that *exact spot* for the water spout to fill the tank in the tender? This was pure insanity! He asked the stoker, "Can we get to the new border without stopping?"

The fireman frowned. He wiped his mustache with the back of a coal dust blackened wrist. "I've never done it, *sahib*! It's twenty miles beyond the border to Amritsar. I don't think we can last so long."

"We don't have to get to Amritsar," Singh said. "We just have to get over the border to India. We should be safe anywhere there."

The fireman shrugged. "Maybe we can get that far, God willing."

Singh frowned, and said to Ashok, "We'd better stop for the water."

"I don't know how long it takes to stop the train."

Singh scowled. "Neither to I." He asked the stoker, "Can you stop the train at the right place?"

The fireman eased backward. "*Sahib*, I have never driven it before!"

"What if we overshoot?" Ashok asked. "How do we back up?"

Singh asked the fireman, "Do you know how to reverse?"

"That wheel, *sardar sahib*." The man pointed.

The train was still slowing.

But not, Ashok saw, nearly slow enough. The Rahimabad station was coming up fast. And he saw the front end of another train. It appeared to be on a line alongside the main track, but what if it should try to move onto the main line?

Tensing, not sure what the result would be, he gently applied the brakes. Then he saw the crowd on the nearer end of the platform. All men, many of them waving the green Pakistani flag. Waving rifles, swords, spears...

"Keep going!" shouted Karam Singh. "Don't stop!"

Ashok released the brakes and closed the regulator. He blew the whistle hard and long. The shorter fireman opened the door and frantically shoveled in coal. The *whoosh-whoosh* increased rapidly in tempo.

They rumbled past the train on the siding, almost close enough to reach out and touch it. On the other side came shouts from the station platform. Bullets whanged off the cab. The station buildings flashed by. Then the engine was beyond.

But Ashok wondered what was happening back in the carriages, where his parents and all the others were. There was no way to know.

The mustached stoker shouted, "Sir! Get down!" He pointed. Ashok looked out the open window on his side. Only a few yards away, a man on horseback, riding parallel to the locomotive, was aiming a rifle directly at him.

Before Ashok could duck, Karam Singh's pistol fired and a red spot blossomed on the rider's forehead. The man pitched from the horse.

Shaken, his ear ringing from the gunshot little more than a foot away, Ashok continued to accelerate until he judged they must be doing well over fifty miles per hour again. He adjusted the regulator to a steady speed.

Another signal appeared ahead. In the up position.

What if that meant the track was already in use? The sweat poured from his armpits, from his forehead. The train started into a long curve to the right. It was impossible to see anything around it. He grabbed the whistle cord and tugged, gave a series of long warning blasts. Loud though it was, he doubted any oncoming train could hear it in time. He looked for the smoke of any train that might be ahead but saw none. Instead, a long framework of girders came to view.

The short, clean-shaven fireman spoke for the first time. "Bridge, *sahib*. Ravi River."

Gods! What if they had a head-on collision on a bridge? Should he slow just in case? Or speed up to get across as fast as possible?

He maintained speed. The ground fell away. Then the steel girders of the tall framework began zipping past. The wheels drummed on the elevated rails. One section of bridge. Another. Another. Another. The swollen, metallic-gray river seemed a mile wide.

Finally the girder framework ended. The ground rose to meet the level of the track. At least if the train hit another head-on, the cars wouldn't fall into a river.

On they went. Another signal, in the down position. Ashok relaxed just a little.

A small station flashed by. Ashok caught the name: Mahmud Kot.

As he had done from time to time, the taller fireman again opened the injector valve.

Another signal. Up position. Ashok began to sweat harder. On and on, speeding down the track, the long nose of the boiler like some racing animal's snout.

As far ahead as he could see, which wasn't nearly far enough, the track was still clear.

Another station coming up fast, a larger one. He read the sign: Rasulpur.

He tugged on the whistle, kept it shrieking as they tore through the station, rattling on the switch points on both ends. Then into the open, shooting straight between the fields of sugar cane and wheat.

How much farther to the border? He couldn't remember any towns beyond Rasulpur, but he wasn't sure.

On and on, thundering down the track, with potential death waiting just out of sight up ahead.

Was it his imagination, or was the engine slowing? He looked at the gauges. If he was reading them right, pressure seemed to be falling off. He realized he hadn't seen the firemen filling the firebox recently.

He looked at them and gestured toward it.

"Coal is almost gone, *sahib*," said the mustached stoker.

"Almost gone!" Karam Singh shouted. He stepped into the tender. At the bottom of the "V" the floor was virtually empty. "How could this happen!" he screamed at the fireman.

The man said, "We made it last as long as we could, Inspector *sahib*. But the engine is going so fast! And the load is heavy. So it burns more coal. We didn't stop at sheds to take on more."

"You didn't say we needed to!"

The fireman frowned, but shrugged. "Going too fast to stop, *sardar sahib*! By the time I realized it, there was nothing we could do."

Singh appeared as if his face were going to burst a blood vessel. At last he said to Ashok, "Better slow down. Stretch out the fuel as long as we can."

Ashok felt ready to collapse.

He'd known this was insane. When they ran out of fuel, they'd be stranded, defenseless, miles inside the Pakistan border. And there would not only be the threat of oncoming trains; if they were standing still they might also be struck in the rear!

The engine continued to slow. "Heavy train, *sahib*!" said the mustached fireman. "Not enough pressure left." He began turning valves.

The train coasted slower and slower.

It gradually came to a halt. The stoker set the brakes.

The quiet was unearthly after the noise of the huge locomotive and of the wheels on the tracks.

"We need to get everyone off," said Karam Singh.

"In case it's hit by another train?" asked Ashok. He was surprised at how loud his voice sounded in the stillness.

"There's that. But we still need to get to the border. Now we'll have to walk."

Walk! "Any idea how far?"

"Not far," said the taller fireman, pulling his sweat and coal dust laden mustache into shape. "Only a few miles. And no trains have been attacked on this part of the track—yet."

"You're coming?" Ashok asked both firemen, assuming that since they too, must want to leave Pakistan.

"We have to stay to warn oncoming trains" said the shorter, clean shaven man. "We'll go a short distance both directions." He added, grinning tightly, "You did well driving, *sahib*."

"Yes, good work, Chandji," said Karam Singh, with a nod.

Ashok grabbed a hand hold to brace himself, feeling too drained to move for a time. He wiped his sweaty forehead. His voice was hoarse as he said, "I certainly couldn't have done it without all of you. And I think some higher power kept us away from collisions." He thought about the fact that he would likely be dead now if Singh had been only a second or two slower in shooting the man on the horse. He wanted to say something about it to the inspector general, but at the moment, he couldn't think of appropriate words.

They all descended to the roadbed, Ashok climbing down stiffly. Then, he looked up at the locomotive. Its blackness towered above and seemed to stretch ahead for a hundred feet. The three drive wheels on this side were almost as tall as he was. Had he, who had never so much as driven an automobile, actually guided such a huge, complex piece of machinery?

It had been oven-hot in the cab, and it was blistering here, under the blaze of the unshaded sun. The engine gave off clanking and hissing sounds as metal contracted and remnants of steam escaped.

He felt a wad in his pocket and wondered what it was. He extracted it and looked in surprise at the roll of money. Sheepishly, he handed it toward Karam Singh.

Singh shrugged. "Keep it. You earned it."

Ashok looked down at the currency. He wouldn't retain any of it, of course. He would give it to someone who needed it worse. To some of the refugees, or to the family of the martyred Harijan, Ram, in Mangarh. He shook his head "no" at Karam Singh, but for now, he put the roll back in his pocket.

He looked back to where the refugees were disembarking from the carriages. He should go find his parents and Savi—

Suddenly, he realized he hadn't thought of Savitri for the entire time he'd been driving the locomotive.

Now, he had left her even farther behind. He could not avoid the feeling he had abandoned her. His sister had been defiled—and not by only one man. Then sold to a stranger, and taken to some unknown place.

Ashok wondered what had come over himself back at the camp. How could he have left her like that, no matter what the reason?

Angered, frustrated, still feeling weak, he began trudging back to look for his father and mother.

Word quickly passed among the refugees about what had occurred, and about the roles of Karam Singh and Ashok Chand. As the people stepped from the cars, they whispered wonderingly, gazing with admiration at the two men who had delivered them so close to India. Ashok's parents appeared in the distance, walking slowly, slumped with their defeats. When his mother saw him, she straightened. Her face took on a look of amazement and she hurried toward him, his father struggling to keep up. Ashok heard her saying to everyone within hearing, "That's my son! He drove the train here!"

The refugees, all three thousand or so of them, began walking toward the border. A few wore bloodstained bandages; a couple wounded persons were carried by other refugees. Clearly the passengers had not escaped the attacks on the train entirely unharmed. But at least, thought Ashok, there had been no mass slaughter as on other trains.

Underfoot, the roadbed ballast and the steel rails radiated heat as if emphasizing that these people were no longer wanted on this soil.

In a mile or so, the head of the column, with Ashok near the lead with his parents, reached the spot where the mustached stoker waited. The man pointed up the track toward a small building with a set of tents in two different spots near it. His face broke into a wide grin. "Border posts, *sahib*!"

The close-by refugees heard, and the cry traveled down the line. "Border post! Border post!"

Many refugees began running ahead, shouting, "*Jai Hind! Jai Hind!*" Victory to India. As they passed Ashok, they looked at him with jubilant expressions. Almost at once, the shouts changed: "*Jai Ashokji! Jai Ashokji!*"

Ashok looked away, embarrassed. Some hero. With luck and with some help, he'd driven a train. But he'd deserted his own sister.

He looked back, toward the train, as if Savitri would miraculously appear among the other refugees who were flowing past. He took hold of himself. He was still responsible for getting his parents to safety. He turned and stared down the track toward the border.

He thought of how, such a short time ago, there had been no imaginary line dividing the earth at that point. In an act virtually as violent as the chaos it encouraged, men had partitioned the surface of the world on the basis of some feelings about how some human beings differed from other human beings. Feelings so strong that many men—who after all came from the same source, the same maker as their fellows—decided they could no longer so much as tolerate living in the same villages as some of their brother and sister humans.

What a difference an invisible, invented, line could make! Where before, all was one, now all was separate. Instantaneously, Ashok's homelands in the Punjab had become alien territory where he and his family were no longer even tolerated, no longer even allowed the basic right to remain alive.

He shook his head at the stupidity, the insanity, of it all. In a big sigh, he let out a lungful of air. *Pakistani* air, he reminded himself with an inward smile of irony.

"Son! Aren't you coming?" his mother demanded.

Ashok gave her a nod. He turned to the fireman and said, "We're most grateful for your help. You saved my life when you warned of that man who was going to shoot me. When will you join us in India?"

The man frowned, and he looked off toward the west. In a moment, he said, "I doubt I'll have that opportunity, sir. I will remain in Pakistan. The other fireman is Hindu, but I'm Muslim."

After a time, Ashok took a deep breath and nodded. He looked away, blinked at the sudden tears in his eyes, and began walking with his father and mother slowly toward the so-called border.

***

An Afternote: When he reached Delhi, and his reunion with Jaya, Ashok Chand was embarrassed to find he had become a national hero. Somehow, despite his protests, Karam Singh's role in the escape was given second billing. It was Ashok Chand, the often-imprisoned, freedom-fighting Congress leader, author of *Jail Diary of a Reformer*, who had risen to the occasion and taken the controls of the giant locomotive, delivering thousands of refugees to safety.

But many thousands of others were less fortunate. Mahatma Gandhi, who had maintained a saintly equanimity throughout a half century of struggle and imprisonment, was finding the brutality and unprecedented scale of the communal violence to be the greatest test of all of his faith in humanity and in a higher justice.

Within a week, Ashok was summoned by V.P. Menon in the Ministry of States. They joked about perhaps appointing Ashok as Minister of Railways, due to his recent intimate experience with the workings of trains.

Ashok said that if experience was the criteria, "Minister of Prisons" might be more appropriate. Menon replied dryly that, unfortunately, there were thousands of people with similar experience in that category.

Eventually, Ashok Chand did indeed become a cabinet minister. But before that, he served as Regional Commissioner, Central Rajputana States, assisting in wrapping up the affairs of several princely kingdoms, including Mangarh. It was Ashok who worked with Lakshman Singh compiling the lists determining which properties belong to the Maharaja personally, and which belonged to the new Rajasthan state government.

Over a year after her disappearance, Savitri Chand was located by a search commission and brought to India. She eventually recovered from the horror of her experiences enough to resume her medical training and become a physician. But she chose never to marry.

There were an estimated seventy-five thousand other women abducted and raped, Muslims as well as Hindus and Sikhs, on both sides of the new border. Both India and Pakistan set up agencies to find and recover these women. Thousands were located and returned to their families, occasionally against the preferences of either the woman or her relatives.

After extensive volunteer work with refugees, Jaya Chand finished her legal training and eventually became a highly regarded lawyer in New Delhi.

Upon completing his duties as Regional Commissioner, Ashok Chand became Deputy Secretary in the Ministry of Refugee Rehabilitation, organizing resettlement.

It was a huge undertaking. There were an estimated *six million* Hindus and Sikhs in India, who, like his own family, had been displaced at Partition. And, similarly, Pakistan had millions of Muslim refugees to resettle. The exchange of populations was the largest in the history of the world.

As at the Sikh temple in Kapani, during the conflicts hundreds, and probably thousands, of women and children were killed by their male relatives to protect the honor of the victims, their families, or their particular faith. No one aside from those directly involved can know the extent to which these "martyrs" agreed with the decisions resulting in their own deaths.

What is certain is that all these violent events were a shameful beginning for both new nations. Over half a century later, the horrors still affect not only the psychological health of millions of individual survivors, but also the collective psyches of each country.

* * *

One of the most surprising stories in the history of India, indeed of the world, is that of how the rule by princes—the traditional form of government in the subcontinent for at least three thousand years—disappeared in roughly a three year period at Independence.

The tale you have just read depicts the first phase of this, the "accession" or alignment of most of those native states with either India or Pakistan after Partition. At that time, the rulers of the larger kingdoms ceded to the new national governments only their control of military defense, foreign relations, and communications. Otherwise, those princes retained full powers within their territories.

Yet, within two more years, the princes were pressured and persuaded into signing agreements giving up their remaining sovereignty and completely merging their states with the new Indian nation. This included turning over the assets of their state governments, among which were buildings and their furnishings, huge sums of cash, state jewels, military equipment, and 12,000 miles of railways. One estimate is that the total value of cash and investments alone surrendered by the rulers was 95 crores, around 745 million pounds. The rulers kept their private, personal assets, including family heirloom jewelry and their residential palaces.

In exchange for their huge sacrifices in helping launch the new nation, the princes retained their honorific titles and certain personal privileges, and the Indian government committed itself to paying them pensions called "privy purses," which would be greatly reduced with each succeeding generation. A huge portion of the stipends were used by the princes to pay salaries and pensions to their dependents and current and retired employees, as well as traditional obligations of supporting numerous temples and charities.

In the beginning, the cost of the privy purses paid by the Indian government was around 580 lakhs per year, or 4 million pounds. V.P. Menon himself, who handled most of the negotiations, wrote that "if the assets we received...are weighed against the total amount of the privy purses, the latter would seem insignificant."

The basics of the agreements were written into the Indian Constitution to assure the princes that the commitments were sacrosanct. Nevertheless, beginning with Nehru, efforts were made to curtail the Indian government's obligations. In 1970, under Prime Minister Indira Gandhi's Congress government, the agreements were abrogated, and the surviving princes and their heirs were left with broken promises in exchange for their families' immense donations to the nation.

Part Eight
The Treasure of Mangarh

23

Mangarh, February 1977

Later, Mahendra sought out Kaushalya when she was seated with Gopi outdoors on a terrace, sketching the patterns made by the old fortification walls as they snaked up and down the surrounding hills.

"I don't know what to do," he said, pulling up a cane chair. "I can't imagine running against my own father in the elections."

She put down her sketch pad and peered at him over the top of her reading glasses. "You can't take it personally, you know. It's Congress he's against, especially Madam."

"Of course. But it's damn awkward for me. I feel I owe it to Congress to follow through in campaigning."

A servant arrived with a tray bearing a Scotch and water Mahendra had ordered. "I know how you must feel," Kaushalya replied. "But Father said himself, 'We do what we must do.' If you think you have to try to keep your seat, then do so. He'll understand."

Mahendra took a long sip of his drink. "But *father against son*! Everyone will think I'm disloyal to him. It will get national attention. I can see the headlines already: 'Royal House Divides Against Itself.'"

Kaushalya frowned. "Unfortunately, I suppose that would be likely." She took off her glasses.

Mahendra sighed. "I realize I don't really have a choice. I'll have to withdraw my candidacy. But I hate being forced to do it."

She smiled sympathetically. "I can understand that. It's certainly to your credit if you withdraw. You'll have chances to run again in other years, though."

Mahendra slowly shook his head. "I'm not sure Congress will forgive me. They'll think I've switched loyalties yet again. Or that I joined them only to free Father. They might even think he and I prearranged it."

"If that's true, look at what it says about them. Do you really want to stay involved with people who think you should put party loyalty above your duty to your father?"

After a time, Mahendra set down his glass and slowly stood. "I know I'll end up having to withdraw, but you can't blame me for not hurrying into it."

She nodded. "I don't." He turned and, eyes downcast and shoulders bent as if carrying a burden, walked slowly toward the palace entrance.

Time was short for campaigning, with the elections only two months away. After announcing his candidacy, Lakshman Singh had Bhajan Lal drive him to the fortress. He instructed Harlal, the mahout, to have one of the howdahs cleaned and placed on the elephant Airavata the next morning. He said nothing to Kaushalya or Mahendra about his actions.

The next day, preceded by three marching musicians and by Naresh Singh the ADC on horseback, a lavishly decorated elephant walked majestically down the road from the old fort, with the ex-Maharaja of Mangarh in its howdah. Behind, walking, came Shiv and a half dozen retainers.

The sky was overcast, threatening a winter rain, as the procession went slowly past the *havelis*, then through the crowded, narrow streets of the bazaar. The onlookers were at first surprised to see the elephant, the only one remaining in Mangarh. Then they were astonished to see their former ruler in the howdah.

Every last person, of course, knew of the imprisonment, and of the income tax raids. And regardless of what they felt about the old days of autocratic rule, hardly anyone in Mangarh other than a few strong Congress supporters liked the Emergency, which they saw as taking away their democratic rights.

At first only a few old people saluted and cheered. But then the younger ones joined in. The crowd grew, and many joined the procession. The cheers grew until all of central Mangarh reverberated with the traditional cry: *"Maharaja ki jai! Maharaja ki jai!"* "Victory to the King!"

Lakshman Singh smiled and returned the greetings. It was not as if he was renewed by the cheers, exactly. He was quite aware now that the days of his rule as Maharaja were never to return. But he also felt instinctively that the people needed a way to protest the misuses of office by those to whom they had entrusted their destiny as a nation.

After he and his procession returned to the fortress, the rain began to fall.

When Kaushalya learned of his approach to running for office, she smiled broadly. The procession was an appropriate one for an ex-ruler's campaign, and just what the people of Mangarh would like.

"I wish I could join you," she told him. "I'd love to march with the others along behind you."

He chuckled. "I don't think Mangarh is quite ready yet for that. Too many older people still think you should be in *purdah*."

"What about Gayatri Devi of Jaipur? It's been at least ten years since she campaigned herself all over her constituency. The Maharani of Gwalior did the same thing. And they've won huge victories!"

Lakshman Singh frowned, but he was smiling slightly at the same time. "I suppose times are changing. But I fear I can't change quite fast enough myself to keep up with them. Maybe in the *next* election you can campaign with me."

Kaushalya left for a brief trip to Delhi for a joyful reunion with the Chands. She was disappointed to find that Pratap had left to visit his family in Shantipur, but then, that was to be expected after he had been locked away for so long.

The day after her return to Mangarh, Lakshman Singh again went on his procession through town. He had complained to Kaushalya about not feeling well, but he insisted on campaigning anyway.

This time, the sky was sunny and clear. Naresh Singh again rode his horse before the elephant. The ADC found he rather enjoyed this harking back to the old days of royal processions, the last of which he could barely remember from when he was a child.

As on the first occasion, as soon as the entourage entered the walled city from the gateway to the fort, the crowds grew, and so did the volume of the cheers: *"Maharaja ki jai! Maharaja ki jai!"* People of all ages rapidly gathered. Uniformed school boys in blue sweaters and girls in blue skirts joined the rear of the procession. An elderly, turbaned man limped along behind. Women on their way to the temples and farmers visiting the bazaar stood to watch. Naresh even noticed an ancient man on a balcony waving a green flag from the old Mangarh state, probably hauled out after a quarter century in a storage chest.

He glanced back occasionally at Lakshman Singh, who was turning from side to side, acknowledging the cheers with folded palms and smiles. The procession reached the town wall on the far side and turned, rather than going out the gate into the newer residential areas.

Suddenly, Naresh was aware of a wave of alarm sweeping through the crowd, of the exuberant expressions changing to consternation. The cheers abruptly stopped.

He turned to look. Lakshman Singh lay slumped over the side of his howdah seat.

Harlal the mahout halted Airavata and scrambled around to look closely at the Maharaja. Naresh turned his horse and urged it quickly alongside the elephant. He bent to examine the ex-ruler's face, which was slack-jawed, the eyes closed.

Dr. Savitri Chand had been watching with the crowd, and she shoved her way near as the ADC and several of the escort lowered Lakshman Singh to the street, placing him on a blanket someone produced.

The street was utterly silent as Dr. Chand swiftly examined him.

She decided against efforts at revival. It was quite obvious to her that the ex-ruler's soul had already departed. She shook her head. "He's gone," she whispered to the ADC.

The news swept the crowd. Men began to sob and women wailed.

Naresh Singh sent a senior retainer to the palace to notify Mahendra Singh and Kaushalya Kumari, while the others of the entourage formed a circle guarding the body until a vehicle could arrive.

Kaushalya dipped her finger in the red paste and dabbed it on the center of Mahendra's forehead.

He looked vacantly at her, obviously numb over his father's death. "Why did you do that?"

She blinked at the moistness in her eyes. "Don't you remember? As soon as a Maharaja dies, the nearest family member has to mark the heir-apparent as the new ruler. The *gadi* isn't supposed to be vacant, even for a few minutes." The reason for the tradition was to avoid giving any potential usurper time to organize and seize the throne. Even though the rationale no longer applied, Kaushalya felt it was important to follow the custom.

Mahendra shook his head. "I'm not sure I should go through with the ceremonies. It all seems so hollow, with no powers anymore. Even the title of Maharaja has been legally abolished."

Kaushalya wiped at her tears and stared at him. "You'd let the *gadi* fall vacant? After a thousand years?"

Mahendra gave a slight shrug. "Parliament officially abolished it. It's vacant anyway."

"That's just a law passed in Delhi. Our people here have their own ways. It has to do with tradition, not with laws."

Mahendra again shook his head. "Times have changed. Now that the people themselves choose their government, I doubt they want carryovers from the days when they had no rights. Except for maybe a few old men who are still living in the past."

Kaushalya took her handkerchief and dabbed at her eyes. "I think you're wrong. I think most people like having some old traditions coexisting with the new."

Mahendra asked, "You expect a popular outpouring? *Lakhs* of people like in the old days? We'll be lucky to have a thousand turn out for the funeral, most of them elderly. Any others will just be curious."

She shook her head and left, too caught up in her grief to argue.

Word spread quickly, as it always does in India. All night a continuous line of people filed past the bier in the audience hall of the Bhim Bhawan palace where Lakshman Singh's body lay in state. Mahendra, who stood guard beside his father, was coming to realize that perhaps Kaushalya was right.

At dawn, a small group of the top nobles of Mangarh, wearing their finest turbans and jewels and silk *achkans*, waited when he came out to receive them. All gave their condolences. Then the Thakur of Amargarh spoke for them: "Mahendra Singhji Pariyatra, in accordance with custom, we invite you to become the next Maharaja of Mangarh."

Mahendra gave a nod of acknowledgment and said soberly, "I'm honored at your invitation. I'll take it under serious consideration. I want to be sure I can be worthy of living up to the great legacy left by my father and all the other holders of our *gadi* before him."

The nobles exchanged puzzled looks, obviously expecting immediate acceptance. Narayan Singh, Thakur of Baldeogarh, said, "I assume we can begin planning your installation ceremony for the thirteenth day, as our tradition requires."

"We'll naturally do what's appropriate," said Mahendra. He saw two of the *thakurs* glance at each other, perplexed at his vagueness. But he preferred not to voice his doubts at the moment, in public, and so close to his father's body.

The crowds began to gather even before dawn. By bullock cart, by bicycle, by bus, by camel, by foot, the people came to the city and claimed their vantage points along the route. Many of them first filed past the bier in the palace. Ministers of the Rajasthan state government came in their cars, paid their respects in the palace, and then awaited the procession with its long walk to the cremation grounds five kilometers away at the cenotaphs on the shore of the Hanuman Sagar.

As customary in Mangarh, Mahendra would accompany his father and light the funeral pyre. Kaushalya, however, must remain at the palace, away from public view.

The old gun carriage had been extracted from the stables and hurriedly cleaned. Kaushalya watched, wet-eyed and weary, from an upper floor window in mid-morning as Lakshman Singh's body was placed on the carriage, and the Rajput horsemen fired a thirteen-rifle salute. In the old days, the cannons of Mangarh fort would have fired.

Lakshman Singh's Bhil guards walked first to clear the way. Then came the elephant Airavata, wearing his finest trappings and jewels. Next were Rajput horsemen and camel riders, followed by Naresh Singh and other palace workers, dressed in white, the color of mourning, and the family priest, his head shaved. A truck heaped high with the many floral tributes followed. Then came the carriage with the Maharaja, his head raised slightly so that everyone might see him. Mahendra, dressed all in white, marched immediately behind. Next came the other family members, the nobles, and the state government ministers.

Kaushalya and Gopi went to the roof of the palace to observe. The procession itself, she thought with satisfaction, must be nearly a kilometer long. Maybe longer. Even more impressive were the throngs of onlookers lining the route. Thousands and thousands of them. Despite the distance, she could hear the same shouts that had greeted her father whenever he passed throughout his reign: *Maharaja ki jai! Maharaja ki jai!*

He was pleased, she knew, from wherever he was watching.

She sat for a time and let the tears come.

Afterwards, Mahendra told her, "You were right. I can't let everyone down, even if I do think the installation ceremony's probably an anachronism. It was amazing to see all those people with tears in their eyes. Rajputs, of course. But also farmers, shopkeepers, craftsmen. I had no idea so much feeling remained for Father."

Red-eyed, Kaushalya gave him a smug smile. "I knew you'd come around."

He shrugged. Then he said, "Will you go with me to Father's office?"

"It's..." She swallowed and blinked away more tears. "It's your office now."

"I suppose. But it will be a while before I think of it that way."

He sat at the desk, and she sat in one of the chairs. "You realize," he said, "that you share equal ownership with me in all the family property. As the closest relatives, we're the heirs."

"I wasn't sure about myself," said Kaushalya. "I thought maybe as the only son and successor to the throne you'd get most of it yourself."

"That might have been true in the old days. But not now, especially after the Hindu Succession Act was passed. And after royal titles were abolished. Now you share equally with me in all the joint family property. At most I'd be the *karta*—the manager of the family property still held jointly. But naturally I'll consult you on major decisions. And any time you want, you can ask to partition the joint property to give you full control over your own share."

"I see." Right now, the matter seemed of little importance.

Mahendra continued, "I understand Father's written will also divides his own separate holdings evenly between us." He smiled grimly. "We're both extremely wealthy."

"I suppose."

He handed her a letter. "You should read this. Father intended it for both of us."

She put on her glasses and immediately recognized their father's handwriting; the letter was dated shortly after his release from the hospital.

She read quickly. Their father talked in general terms about the disposition of his property, mostly just as Mahendra had stated. Then, he wrote:

> As you know, during my lifetime I chose not to reveal to either of you the location or quantity of our family's wealth. I consider most of that wealth not to be personal, but rather to be held in trust for the people of Mangarh. While I have confidence in your ability to keep any information secret, tradition has held that only the ruler have the knowledge. I made only one exception to this during my lifetime, for reasons I considered sufficient.

> You are well aware that a considerable quantity of treasure has been found by the tax authorities. The issue may arise as to whether or not any remaining undeclared wealth exists. Because the tax authorities are still interested in our affairs, I would not feel comfortable in answering this question of additional wealth in writing.

> I have confidence that if a serious need arises, adequate funds will be available. God provides. Put your trust in Ekadantji. While we have had difficult times, he has never failed us. And remember that this material world is a transient one for us, where all is illusion and any wealth is temporary at best. The true reality is hidden. It is where we quest for the eternal that we find the true extent of our wealth. So I hope you will visit our Guru and trust in him as I have.

> Another matter. Kaushalya, my dear daughter, I know you have not been receptive to my efforts to find a husband for you.

She stiffened at this, but she nevertheless continued reading: *I think I understand your reluctance since you feel you are not quite ready, due to wanting to complete your schooling. Still, it was my duty as your father to try. Now it will be Mahendra's as head of the family.*

> I have been reluctant to propose one certain name because I know that you instinctively reject any person I propose. I was waiting in the hope that you would decide upon him yourself, in which case I would have raised a number of objections just to ensure that you decided more firmly in his favor. However, now that I am no longer around to do so, I feel compelled to mention a possible choice, solely so that there is no danger of his being overlooked.

> Pratap Singh is a fine young man. I have always liked him, and I grew even fonder of him when we shared our quarters in prison. I won't try to enumerate all his fine qualities, as you already know them. It is fortuitous that he happens to be a Rajput of

*suitable princely status. I would probably approve of him for you
even if he were not.*

Kaushalya's hands shook, and she held her breath as she finished reading:

*Since Pratap Singh's father and I are old friends, naturally
the subject of a family marital alliance has come up. I have been
receptive but have made it clear to him that you have your own
mind. I expect that his father will approach our family before long
with an offer of Pratap in marriage. The choice is of course yours,
but it would please me greatly if on your own you should happen to
decide he is the one for you.*

> *Your Loving Father,*
> Lakshman Ajay Singh,
> *Maharaja of Mangarh*

Not wanting to meet Mahendra's eyes, not trusting herself to speak, Kaushalya continued to pretend to study the letter.

Pratap Singh. One part of her rebelled against anyone trying to influence her on such a crucial matter.

Another part knew Pratap was an excellent choice. She had already thought about him so much and so favorably. She would consider the matter more later.

Mahendra said, "I won't try to affect your choice of husband unless you decide you want me to. I know quite well you've a mind of your own. But I'm here to help if you wish."

"Thanks," she said hoarsely. "Maybe some other time."

"What do you think of this business about the possibility of more treasure?" Mahendra asked, obviously anxious to shift to a less emotion-laden topic. "In a lot of ways you were closer to Father than I was. You probably understand his mind better."

"Haven't you done the obvious? Asked the Bhil guards?"

He seemed embarrassed. "Yes, I did. They were very respectful. But they told me they no longer guarded any treasure, so such matters were beyond their knowledge. I had the feeling they weren't telling me all they knew, but I thought it better not to press them on it. Not yet, anyway. They must have their reasons."

Kaushalya reread the portion of the letter in which her father mentioned the wealth. She looked up at her brother and shrugged. "There's no way to be sure from this. You know his sense of humor—he'd like nothing better than to try to confound us even after he's gone. But...." She again read the letter.

"But?" prompted Mahendra.

"I think there's more wealth. Otherwise he wouldn't have mentioned it."

"That's what I thought. But I wanted your opinion, too."

"And not long ago he spoke of some of the state jewels, just as if he still had them."

"So if there's more, where is it?"

24

March 1977

The Indian voters decisively told Indira Gandhi and her government what they thought about the "Emergency" by overwhelmingly defeating her and her Congress Party at the polls.

The twelve days of formal mourning for Lakshman Singh were over, and Mahendra had been installed as the new Maharaja of Mangarh, although with no formal powers and no title either, legally. By a narrow margin, Mahendra had been an exception to the defeat of Congress candidates; the voters had returned him to office, in part out of respect for his position in succeeding his father as Maharaja. Ironically, he was again a member of a party that was in the Opposition.

Kaushalya felt tremendous relief at the result of the elections. Finally, the politicians should realize the wisdom of the people. Not only did Indira and Sanjay have their wings clipped, but Dev Batra must be having a humbling experience also—the very same people he had helped put in jail were now in power.

After a late night celebrating with the Chands in New Delhi, Kaushalya, wearing a blue silk sari for the occasion, drove the old Jaguar back to Mangarh House where she and Gopi were staying before returning home. A white Mercedes like the one Dev Batra used was parked around the nearby corner, but she paid no attention. Many wealthy people lived in the neighborhood, and a number of high government officials had the use of similar cars.

She was puzzled to find that the driveway gate hung open, and Amar the *chowkidar* was not in sight. This was a matter of concern, especially at night. But there could be many explanations, so she thought little of it as she parked in the driveway. A few lights were still on in the house, but that was typical.

Then she saw the white cow in the flower beds. It raised its head to peer through the dimness at her. Now she knew something wasn't right. Amar would never let the cow onto the grounds if he were able to prevent it. She started toward the animal to chase it out, then decided it was more urgent to find out what had gone wrong.

When she entered the front hall, she immediately saw that pictures on the wall were askew, furniture out of place. There was an odor of cigarette smoke. Abruptly, she became alarmed.

"Welcome back, Princess," came the familiar voice of Dev Batra.

Her breath caught; she whirled toward him.

She heard rapid footsteps behind her, and before she could see who it was, her arms were seized.

She struggled to free herself but could not break the powerful grip. She was able to turn her head enough to glimpse that it was Batra's man Sen who held her. "How dare you!" she shouted.

Gulab also appeared, grabbed her hands and, despite her struggles, began to quickly bind them tightly together with a length of heavy cord.

"This is an outrage!" she shouted to Batra as she strained to squirm free.

"Save your protests, Princess. I am in a hurry." Batra lit another cigarette.

"Where are our *chowkidar* and my maid? And our cook?"

"Tied up in the kitchen. They're quite safe, so long as you cooperate."

"What do you want?!" She feared she knew the answer, given Batra's
desire to seduce her.

She was wrong.

"Those big gems that were not found with the rest of the treasure," said
Dev Batra, watching her face closely. "I need to know where they are."

"Whatever do you mean? Your tax raiders searched for weeks for those.
I've no idea where they are! They may not even exist anymore. But why are
you involved yourself? Shouldn't the tax officers be the ones?"

Batra blew out a cloud of smoke and scowled. "If they find anything, it
would be like the rest of the treasure. You'd get most of it back after the taxes
were paid. Which could take a while. I need these gems for myself."

"You'd...*steal* them from us?"

He laughed harshly. "I suppose you'd call it that. Princess, I need to get
out of India for a while. I've heard the new government's going to investigate
me, along with Sanjay and Indiraji and others. I also owe a lot of money. With
Sanjay and Indiraji out of power I've lost my income. I can't finish my farmhouse. The Ashok Hotel will no longer let me stay there unless I pay what I
owe. The government even wants my car back!"

"Maybe it serves you right."

He glared at her. "This time, I won't let you refuse me, Princess. I think
you know where those gems are. I'll do whatever is necessary to find out. You
understand?"

"I...think so."

"Are they here at this house?"

"I told you I don't know anything about them. I doubt very much they're
here."

"We searched the house well, but one never knows—they could be too
cleverly hidden. Still, it's more likely they'd be in Mangarh. Is that right?"

"I suppose—if they still exist. But I truly don't know!"

His tiny eyes were fixed on her while he took another draw on his cigarette. "I don't believe you, Princess. You need to cooperate more. Sen! Bring
in that old woman."

The big man hurried out of the room.

"Leave her alone! She doesn't know anything about them."

"Maybe not. But you do. And you don't want to see her hurt."

Sen pushed Gopi in from the kitchen. A piece of white cloth was wound
tightly over her mouth as a gag. Her eyes were defiant, but her forehead was
creased with worry.

"How dare you treat her like that!" shouted Kaushalya.

Batra said, "Gulab—your knife."

Gulab moved behind Gopi and, smiling at Kaushalya, tested the blade of
his knife with a thumb. Then he roughly seized Gopi's head and bent it back,
applied the knife blade to her throat.

Kaushalya's mouth had gone dry. "No!" she screamed hoarsely.

"Gulab keeps his knife extremely sharp," said Batra. "The slightest pressure will draw blood. A little more pressure, and her throat is cut. She'll die.

Now where, exactly, are the gems?"

Kaushalya again strained to get a hand free of the bonds, but it was impossible. "I'll do everything I can to help. Just don't hurt her!" She thought furiously. "I assume the gems would still be in Mangarh. But my Father was the only one who knew for sure."

"He would have told your brother, or left some instructions before he died. Neither one of them are available. I have only you. And you must have a good idea—I'm sure you've seen those jewels, probably even worn them."

"You're wrong!" She thought of her father's comment that he wished he'd seen her wearing them. If only he'd confided in her, she could probably put an end to this before they injured Gopi.

"They have to be in your Mangarh palace, right? So they're close to where you live."

"I suppose—I don't know! But don't hurt her!"

Batra scowled, still watching her face intently. "It seems obvious they're at your palace. But you have a lot of servants there. They'll get upset if they see us dragging you in, maybe they'd call the police. We'd have a hard time rounding so many up. So when we go there, you can send your maid in to get the gems. Gulab will have his knife at *your* throat then. Your woman must know that if she betrays me, you die. But first you must tell me exactly where they are."

She struggled to come up with something to satisfy him, something that might give her a chance to free herself and Gopi. She said, "They're not in the Bhim Bhawan. They're at the fortress. Or at least they were." She was thinking of the Bhil guards—hopefully, she could summon them for aid. She didn't know exactly how she'd manage, but they seemed her best hope. They were armed, and they were almost the same as having her own personal security force.

"That doesn't make sense," said Batra, his eyes narrow. "You'd want to keep the jewels closer to you, where you live."

Her heart was beating fast, and she could feel herself perspiring, as she tried to lie convincingly: "That's what everyone thought. But the tax raiders searched the Bhim Bhawan so thoroughly. We decided the gems would be safer at the fort—it's a larger area to hide them in."

"What about the guards?"

Her mouth was dry, and voice was hoarse as she said, "I'll tell them it's all OK, that they should stay away from us."

Batra snorted. "I'll bet. But you and your woman don't want to get hurt, so I don't think you'll do anything to make them suspicious. Anyway, we can deal with them if we have to. And we can stay in the car if they threaten us— my Mercedes has armor plating and bulletproof glass. What about anyone else who sees us?"

She thought, then she cleared her throat and said, "If we go late in the day, there shouldn't be anyone there. The sweepers and other workers will be gone then. If someone is still around, I'll tell them not to bother us."

Batra considered this. Then: "Tell me exactly where the gems are."

She hesitated. Once she'd lied about the location, she would have to stay committed to the deception. "They're in one of the palace wings. Well disguised in a ceiling. It's difficult to describe exactly."

Batra grinned. "I know you'll be glad to show us personally."

She again hesitated. Despite trying to keep her voice calm, there was a quaver in it as she asked, "What will you do with us afterwards?"

Batra smiled tightly. "I'll turn you free, of course, Princess. I'll be leaving India for a while, so you wouldn't be able to harm me. The Congress will be back in power again in a year or two. I'll come back then, and if you tried to bring charges against me, I'd just deny everything. My friends will protect me."

Despite her situation, she couldn't resist saying, "I doubt Congress will be in control again so soon. I think the people have had enough of them."

Batra laughed. "The leaders in the new government will be too busy arguing among themselves to accomplish anything. Congress is the only party that can bring stability. The people will soon be glad to go back to Indiraji's decisive leadership."

"I certainly hope you're wrong!"

And she wished she could believe him about turning them loose.

She was made to sit next to Batra in the back seat of the Mercedes, with Gopi on the other side of her. She hated being so near the man, and she wasn't surprised when he placed a plump hand on her upper leg, and moved his foot so it was against hers.

"Don't touch me," she hissed.

He laughed, and left his hand and foot in place. Through the silk of her sari, his hand felt sweaty, despite the air conditioning. She squirmed away, but there was little room to move before she was pressing into Gopi.

With her own bound hands, she tried to shove his hand off of her. He again laughed. Eventually, to her surprise, he removed it, and he didn't place it on her again. He apparently had other matters to preoccupy him.

There was little traffic at this time of the night, still well before dawn. The Mercedes sped out of Delhi, its headlights briefly illuminating an occasional bullock cart or bicyclist, or a car or truck running without lights to save batteries.

Kaushalya was tired, not having any sleep yet that night. On the drive into Rajasthan she had considerable time to think, in between dozing. Gopi's gag had been removed, but there seemed little they could say to each other in this company.

It seemed unlikely Batra would turn her and Gopi free, knowing they would immediately go to the police. And the incident would be in the newspaper headlines within a day. Assuming he was able to get out of India, he might still be arrested and extradited. And if he ever returned to India, they could indeed bring charges against him and Sen and Gulab, especially in Mangarh, where Batra had less influence: assault and kidnaping. And robbery, or at least attempted robbery. Even in Delhi, if the Congress came back to power, she doubted Batra would be able to get the same degree of high level protection he'd enjoyed in the past, not with the Emergency over.

So it seemed more likely than not that he'd feel he had to kill them to keep them quiet.

She wondered briefly if he and his men were truly capable of that. They almost certainly were—especially if they felt they had to in order to protect themselves.

Her wrists hurt from the bindings, and she grew stiff from having to sit in the same position for so long. Only the occasional headlights of another vehicle penetrated the darkness outside. She thought of and discarded numerous plans, in between waves of tiredness that came and went.

At last, hoping that in her exhaustion and worry she hadn't overlooked anything important, she settled on a number of options, depending on what happened.

The Bhils were her first hope. Even if they couldn't intervene for fear of injury to her or Gopi, they might be able to summon the police. That might be tricky, as she and Gopi could be used as hostages by Batra, so their lives would still be in danger.

If she were unable to get help from the Bhils, she could try to lose Batra and his men in the labyrinthian old palaces, which she knew so well. She wasn't exactly sure how she would do it, especially without leaving Gopi in danger, but she could be alert for a chance.

Soon after daybreak, they stopped at Batra's uncompleted farmhouse. There, she and Gopi were allowed to use the one bathroom that was functioning, with a guard outside the door. Then the captives' hands were untied so they could eat a breakfast of *rotis* and bananas. While they ate, Batra talked with Gulab and Sen about the house, obviously upset at the delays in finishing it due to running out of funds.

"You like my farmhouse, Princess?" Batra asked as Sen and Gulab were rebinding her hands.

Annoyed at the question in such inappropriate circumstances, she said tersely, "I always like houses in the country."

He frowned, clearly not satisfied. "This house makes up for the one my family lost in the Punjab in 1947."

"You had a swimming pool and disco room there, too?"

"Of course not—" His eyes hardened as her sarcasm registered.

She said, "You came within a hair's breadth of losing your life at Mangarh. Do you think Mr. Singh would have saved you if he knew you'd do this to me and my maid?"

Doubt entered Batra's eyes for a moment. Then he straightened himself. "Yes. I think he's what you would call a moral man, Princess. He'd have saved me or anyone else without hesitating an instant. And I've told him I owe him. In fact, he's already called on me for part repayment."

"And what would he say if he could see you now?"

Batra's eyes hardened further. "I know you think I'm not a good man, Princess. But I will tell you what evil is. It was in '47 when our neighbors, people we'd known all our lives, people we'd shared Divali and Ramadan with, came and killed my father and raped my sister. Because we weren't the same religion, and because they wanted to steal our farm and decided they could get away with driving us off." His voice grew louder. "I worked hard to get this farm to replace the one we lost to Pakistan. To have one even better! I don't intend to lose it again!"

"Even if you have to steal from me, from *my* family."

He shrugged, and said less loudly, "You still have most of that treasure, as soon as the government releases it. And where did it come from? You know it was all looted in the first place! That big diamond—stolen in a raid in the south, wasn't it? And I heard that ruby was looted in Shivaji's time, too."

"That's....different. They were taken during war—"

He laughed. "All stolen! And I bet your ancestors killed the owners in the process. So you can hardly complain if I take what shouldn't have been yours anyway, or if I keep you captive for a little while."

She knew his arguments had flaws, but exhausted and distraught as she was, she had trouble at the moment seeing just what they were.

25

They continued to Mangarh, arriving in mid-afternoon. There, they drove straight to the fortress, avoiding going through the center of town so fewer people would see them. Reflexively, without even thinking, Kaushalya pulled the tail of her sari over her head. This was Mangarh, and there were customs to be followed. It was bad enough she was wearing the sari, which was not traditional for Rajput women in this region.

At this time of day, Surmal and the first shift of guards would still be on duty, Kaushalya thought. And the night watch would come on in a couple of hours. So there should be at least some chance to call on the Bhils for help.

"What are we going to do about those guards, boss?" asked Sen as the car neared the gate.

"Her Highness will tell them not to bother us," Batra said. "Right, Princess?"

"That's right," she said hoarsely.

"If you try to warn them," Batra said, "you'll only get people hurt. We'll have to take one as a hostage, and Gulab can cut off his fingers one-by-one until the rest surrender. Then we'll carve up the other guards if you don't cooperate."

She felt nauseous at the thought. Would he really try that? He might, if he were truly desperate. He might even kill the Bhils afterwards. Otherwise, they'd be witnesses against him.

What to do? She'd counted on the guards in the upper levels of the *garh* to see what was happening, and either to help her themselves or go to the police. That now seemed less likely.

As usual, the outermost gate at the bottom of the hill was open. The Mercedes drove through the arch and around the sharp turn, then roared up the rough, cobblestoned approach road. When they arrived at the gateway to the main courtyard, Kaushalya was puzzled to see the big doors closed; only the smaller aperture in one side was open. Normally the entrance would not have been closed until the sun had set.

The young, broad faced Bhil guard named Nagario stepped out and walked over to the driver's side of the car.

Sen rolled down the window, stuck his pistol in the Bhil's face, and said in Hindi, "Don't move."

The surprised guard took a step backward. His hands moved halfway up, as if reaching for the rifle slung across his back, then he reconsidered and froze.

Kaushalya called to Nagario in the local dialect, "You must do as he says, so no one gets hurt."

The Bhil looked more closely at her and realized who she was. After a moment, he gave a nod.

"Drop your rifle to the ground," Sen ordered.

Nagario, understanding the Hindi well enough, slowly did so.

Sen and Gulab got out of the car.

"Where are the other guards?" Batra asked the Bhil, while Gulab picked up the rifle.

Nagario looked to Kaushalya.

"You must answer him," she said.

The Bhil said slowly, "I am alone on this day. All the others are in their villages, for the festival of Bheru."

"What luck!" said Batra. "Maybe my star is starting to rise again already! Swami Surya told me things would get better for me soon."

Kaushalya's hopes sank as she realized she'd totally forgotten that the local Bhil's most important festival was at this time. And with the treasure no longer in the fortress, Surmal probably had seen no harm in leaving only one man on duty so all the others could join their families to celebrate.

Gulab produced another piece of the heavy cord, and they securely bound Nagario's wrists together behind his back.

Sen and Gulab unbarred the huge doors, and straining, managed to swing them open. They took the keys from the Bhil and dragged him inside, to the adjacent guard office.

Then Sen drove the Mercedes into the courtyard.

Airavata stood chained in his usual spot. Except for the elephant, the *garh* appeared deserted.

Kaushalya felt desolated at the Bhils' absence. Now, losing her captors in the maze of the palaces appeared to be her only remaining chance. Unless....

She glanced at Airavata. She looked quickly around the courtyard. Seeing no one but the elephant, she could only hope.

"There's that bloody animal," Batra said. "I have a score to settle with him. I should have killed him long ago. Now I have another chance."

"My pistol's a little small for an elephant," Sen said.

"We'll use the guard's rifle, of course," said Batra.

"You wouldn't!" Kaushalya gasped.

"No one does what that elephant did to me and gets away with it!"

"But—he's an elephant, not a man! And you provoked him."

"He made me look like a fool. I can't forgive that."

"Elephants are sacred, the same as Lord Ganesh!"

Batra's brow furrowed, and he stood still for a moment. At last he said, "Maybe in general. But not this elephant." He gave an impatient wave. "I won't shoot him quite yet. Someone might hear the shots and come investigate. I'll do it when we're ready to leave." He ordered Sen, "Drive up across the next courtyard, to the palace wings. I want the car close by in case we have to leave in a hurry."

When the Mercedes was parked, not far from the entrance to the Madho Mahal, Sen and Gulab pulled Gopi from the car and again put the cloth gag in her mouth. "You be careful with her!" Kaushalya said. "Don't you dare hurt her!" She strained yet again at her bonds, but her hands were still secured tightly together.

Batra laughed. "Just what are you going to do about it? But we won't hurt her unless you're lying about the jewels. If you are, we'll hurt her plenty." He got out, holding the guard's rifle, and directed Sen and Gulab, "Take the old woman into that stable and tie her to one of the posts, out of sight."

"Gopi!" Kaushalya called. "Be strong! We'll get out of this."

Gopi started to look back, but the men jerked her forward and she stumbled. Gulab and Sen supported her and dragged her swiftly away.

"You've no cause to treat her that way!" Kaushalya told Batra.

He shot her a hard look. "That all depends on you, Princess. Get out of the car."

Leaving the air conditioned Mercedes, Kaushalya felt the heat of the blazing sun, especially strong in the masonry courtyard. She tried not to show her fear. Would they really harm Gopi when they realized she couldn't produce the gems?

She drew the tail of her sari more tightly about her face; it felt so improper, being in Mangarh in the company of only men. But at the moment that was an extremely minor concern.

Sen returned and asked, "Should I lock the car, boss?"

"Just take the keys with you. Now, then, Princess—show us where these jewels are."

Kaushalya led them into the Madho Mahal. It was considerably cooler out of the sun and away from the hot stones. They went down a corridor and up a stairway. Through a series of pillared rooms. Across a small courtyard. She was delaying, hoping to be able to find herself separated far enough from her captors that she could quickly duck around a corner and flee out of the maze of rooms and hallways, leaving her pursuers lost and confused. They would find their way out, but she hoped to have reached help by then.

It would be hard to get out of sight before Sen could use his pistol. And Batra still carried the guard's rifle. She hoped they'd realize they couldn't find the jewels if she were killed. But she couldn't count on them thinking that quickly.

Gulab stuck to her like a raptor to its captured prey, and Sen wasn't much farther away. She took them into the *zenana*, and then wove her way to the Hanuman Mahal.

There, Batra said, "You're leading us nowhere. Don't think you can confuse us or get away. I spent enough time here I have some sense of the layout. If the gems are here, take us to them!"

She was a little concerned that they would damage the sculptured plaster holding the glass fragments in place, but she decided to take a chance. She led them, by a different route, back the general direction they had come, until she reached the entrance to the Sheesh Mahal, the Hall of Mirrors.

After trying several keys, Gulab unlocked the door. They entered the room, long, with its high vaulted ceiling. She pointed upward, where thousands of tiny pieces of glass sparkled in the light from the small windows and the open door. "They're up there."

"Up there? It looks like just a lot of pieces of mirrors and colored glass," Batra said.

"That's what it's supposed to look like. Some of them aren't."

"Which ones?"

"In the very center."

"It's too dim to see it well."

"Then I guess you have to believe me."

"So that's why the tax men didn't find the gems—they saw them, but thought they were just colored glass! Very clever."

"We thought so, too," she said dryly.

"But we need a ladder to get up there."

"In the storerooms."

Sen said to Batra, "There are so many pieces of glass, it could take a long time to figure out which ones are real jewels."

Batra said gruffly to Kaushalya. "You know which are real?"

"I...think so."

Batra cursed. "You'd better be telling the truth, Princess. I'll be very angry if you're lying. I might go back to see your old woman."

"Just get the ladder and see."

"Show us where it is."

The more delays the better, she thought again. She led them down to a room in a basement level. She decided they didn't need to know there was another ladder stored a lot closer.

Sen handed his pistol to Batra, and he and Gulab each took one end of the long wooden stepladder. It was a struggle for them to negotiate the tight turns.

They were trying to get the ladder around a corner and up a steep, narrow stairway when the ends became jammed against the walls. Batra impatiently thrust the pistol in his pocket and grabbed at the stepladder with his free hand to help jerk it loose.

Gulab and Sen were on the far side of the ladder. In effect, it formed a temporary barrier between them and Kaushalya at about waist height. She realized there would probably never be a better time. She bolted around the corner, through a doorway.

A shot echoed behind her. She was already out of sight, but it was so loud, so frightening. She hoped someone would hear and call for help. But that seemed unlikely.

She ran down a hallway. With her hands tied, it was awkward to keep her balance and yet move quickly in the sari, with its hem threatening to catch on her the tiny heels of her sandals. The heels were also clacking noisily on the stones, despite her efforts to move quietly. What if Batra and his men were able to follow her by the sound?

She slipped the shoes off. It would be cumbersome to carry them with her hands bound, so she kicked the sandals into a dark corner, hoping they wouldn't be conspicuous evidence of the way she had come.

She listened a moment, heard nothing.

More quietly now, she padded down a stairway, around a bend, down a ramp, the masonry floor smooth and cool on the bottoms of her feet.

She deliberately took a circuitous route through the *zenana* so they'd have more difficulty following her. She hurried across a courtyard where the sunbaked stones burned her tender soles. Down a hallway. Around a corner and down a long balcony.

She considered. It was still quite a distance to the main courtyard and to anyone who might be able to help her. There was the risk of running into one of her captors on the way.

If only she could get her hands untied, she could protect herself better.

She thought of the display of weapons on the wall of the private audience hall. Unfortunately, it was directly below the Sheesh Mahal, and both opened onto the same courtyard. What if Batra and his men had returned there to try to get the jewels?

Since it was almost on the route out to the main courtyard, she decided to take the risk. She quietly went down a stairway and through a screened arcade to the court which the small audience hall faced. She listened a minute for sounds coming from the Sheesh Mahal on the upper floor, but she heard nothing.

She hurried into the arched porch of the private audience hall. The weapons displays were higher on the wall than she had remembered, but she went over to the mandala-like arrangement of daggers. Although they were securely held by iron stables embedded in the wall, she was able, with some straining, to apply her wrists so that the binding cord could be rubbed against the blade of one of the bottom knives. The angle was awkward, and she quickly realized that the dagger was no longer sharp. Still, she had worn away the outer strands of the cord, and continuing to rub at it seemed her best hope, so she persisted.

She stopped to listen. No sounds. Where had her abductors gone?

She resumed rubbing. At last the cord separated, and she drew it off. Her wrists ached from the effort, and were raw and numb from the tightness.

She looked to see if she could take one of the weapons from the wall. The daggers were tightly secured. But maybe one of the spears, if she could reach them.

She stood on the tips of her toes, and was able to coax a spear free of the two staples that held either end of the shaft.

It felt heavy, and she hefted it awkwardly. It was designed, she knew, to be wielded by a warrior on horseback. Never had she herself expected to use such a lance as a weapon. Still, now that her hands were unbound and she had at least one means of defense, she did not feel quite so helpless.

Where to go? It was a relatively short distance across this court to the indoor ramps leading to the next courtyard, where the Mercedes had been parked. But she remembered that the door was normally locked on that route, and she had no keys.

She started toward the more roundabout way, into the Madho Mahal.

"Don't move, Princess."

She jumped.

Batra's voice had come from a columned room as she padded by.

He stepped out, holding the rifle pointed at her chest.

He grinned nastily. "I see you managed to arm yourself. And freed your hands. Congratulations. But don't try to use that spear on me. My bullet will be much faster."

She tried to suppress her panic, and debated whether to try anything with her lance. Such a move seemed foolhardy.

"Drop the spear."

She wanted to obey. But she could not stand to give up her best means of defense, which she had struggled to acquire.

"No."

"No?! Are you crazy, or what?"

"If you want it, take it from me."

"I'll just shoot you instead."

"Go ahead. That will get you the jewels in a hurry."

Batra thought a moment, then bellowed: "Gulab! Sen! Come here!"

She knew that as soon as one of the others arrived, they could easily overpower her.

Would Batra shoot if she ran?

He had before, but he hadn't hit her. Maybe he'd been too startled to think clearly.

She heard footsteps coming down a nearby stair.

She ran.

"Damn you!" screamed Batra. She heard him pounding after her.

But he didn't shoot—not yet, anyway.

She could run fast barefoot, though the low hem of her sari was hindering her somewhat. On the other hand, Batra was heavy, obviously in no condition for a long chase.

She abruptly realized she was headed into a dead end, where he could trap her until his helpers arrived.

She ducked through a narrow door, stepped off to one side, and instinctively thrust the spear as he lunged through.

He screamed as it pierced his upper arm. The rifle fired, then clattered to the floor as he dropped it. He turned and his little, glittering eyes met hers.

She drew back the spear, now glistening scarlet on the blade, and started to thrust it into his chest.

Seeing his pained, startled look, she hesitated. She had never before tried to kill anyone.

She knew her Rajput ancestors would not have backed down. But she couldn't do it.

Sen and Gulab would arrive any moment. Still holding the spear, she ran, into the Madho Mahal. Through rooms and corridors, down a ramp and a stairway.

And out the exit into the heat of the courtyard, where the car sat gleaming in the sun.

Sen stepped into view, the pistol leveled at her. "I knew you'd end up here, Princess. Drop the spear."

She fought back tears.

"Drop it! I'm a good aim—I'll ruin your hand with my first shot."

She hesitated, then let the lance fall clattering to the paving stones.

Gulab appeared, now carrying the rifle. Then came Batra, holding his hand to an arm where blood soaked a large part of the white sleeve. His face tight with pain, he said, "Let's get back and finish our job. Gulab, tie her again. Then knock her about a bit. And watch her closer this time!"

Gulab leaned the rifle against the wall by Batra. Roughly, he retied Kaushalya's hands, tightly enough that the cord cut deeply into her wrists.

Then he slapped her on the side of her face, so hard her head bounced.

He slapped her again, on the other side.

Her head and neck hurt and her ears rang, and her cheeks stung. However, she had expected Batra to take even worse revenge on her.

When it came, it was not quite what she expected.

"I think we need to hurt your old woman first," said Batra, grimacing from his wound. "To show you we're serious. So you don't try something stupid again."

"No! I won't run off again. I promise!"

"I wish I believed you. Sit down."

"What?"

"Sit down, so we can watch you better."

Kaushalya awkwardly lowered herself to the pavement, which was still quite warm, although now in the shade.

"Gulab, go cut the old woman's throat."

"No!" screamed Kaushalya.

Gulab, with a pleased smile, drew his knife and strode toward the stable where Gopi had been tied.

"No!" Kaushalya started to rise.

Sen shoved her back down.

"There's no need!" she shouted.

"You're taking too long," Batra told her. "And you're too uncooperative. You need to know we're serious."

"I believe you. Don't hurt her! If you do, I won't tell you anything. You'll have no hope of getting the gems then."

"Nice try," said Batra. "But we'll make you talk. You've no idea how eager you'll be, when we take turns cutting on you. It would be a shame to ruin such a beautiful face and body, but if we have to...." He bent his head toward his bloody arm. "And I owe you for this."

She tried desperately to think of a way to stop them, before Gulab did anything to Gopi.

Batra was looking into the distance. "What in hell—"

Several persons had entered the main gate of the lower courtyard and were looking about. And still more were entering—apparently townspeople, men and women of all ages.

"Bloody hell!" said Batra. "They must have heard the shots!"

"They couldn't have got here that fast," said Sen. "Something else..."

Batra looked at the turbaned figure in the balcony above the big gate, who was gesturing and talking loudly to the arrivals. "The timekeeper! I forgot the bloody timekeeper!"

Just as I'd hoped, thought Kaushalya.

Batra called loudly, "Gulab—come back!" He shot Kaushalya a look of fury. "The timekeeper must have gone for help."

"He didn't need to," she said, hoping her mysterious reply would distract them; the arriving people were puzzled at why the gong—for the first time in any living person's memory—had not rung on the half hour.

She could barely see Airavata through the opening into the lower courtyard. Dusk had arrived, and she wasn't sure, but she thought there was no longer a chain on the elephant's rear leg. And she was sure she saw the top of a turban sticking up beyond Airavata's back. She was almost sure that, as she'd hoped, Harlal the mahout had come to feed and bathe the elephant, and had realized what was going on. She held her breath.

"Hell!" said Batra. "The gong hasn't rung the whole time we've been here. Everyone's coming to find out why!"

"We can't kill them all," Sen muttered. "But we can scare them off with our guns."

"They're still witnesses," said Batra. "And they can have the police after us before we can leave the country. We'd better get out of here right now, before they get a good look at us."

They hurried toward the Mercedes, Sen dragging Kaushalya.

The arriving townspeople were still too far away to interfere, even if Kaushalya's captors hadn't been armed.

But the mahout gave a command, and Airavata ran towards Batra's group.

Gulab saw the animal first. "The elephant's loose!"

"Bloody hell!" said Batra. "Get in the car!"

Sen reached the Mercedes first, released Kaushalya, and opened the driver's door. Airavata was thundering across the courtyard, the old, white mustached mahout now fully in sight astride the elephant's neck.

"Shoot him, dammit, shoot him!" screamed Batra.

Sen aimed his pistol at Harlal, who, although a smaller target, was far more vulnerable than the huge elephant.

Kaushalya threw herself into Sen as he shot. The report of the gun, so close to her head, was deafening. But she saw that Harlal was apparently unhurt, and Airavata was almost upon them.

"Bitch!" Sen swung hard at her head with the side of the pistol barrel. She ducked, and the gun grazed her hair. She lost her balance and fell on a knee to the stones.

Sen frantically moved to point the gun at Airavata's forehead, but the elephant was upon him. With his trunk Airavata seized Sen around the chest and jerked him into the air. Sen screamed as the elephant threw him.

Sen's upper back hit the courtyard paving stones with a cracking thud, and he lay, screaming in pain.

Gulab had grabbed the rifle and was trying to aim at Airavata. Kaushalya struggled to her feet. Just as she had with Sen, she threw herself into Gulab. He stumbled, and the shot rent the sky.

Batra had leaped into the rear seat of the car and slammed the door.

Airavata's trunk struck the rifle from Gulab. No longer smiling, Gulab seized Kaushalya, holding her tight to him as a shield. He desperately tried to pull her into the front seat of the Mercedes. Kaushalya resisted with all her will, scraping her heels on the edges of the paving stones.

Airavata waved his trunk about, trying to find a way to pull Kaushalya free without injuring her, or else to pull Gulab from her. At last he grabbed Gulab's upper arm and pulled, hard. Gulab screamed and released Kaushalya. She darted away.

Gulab found his knife with his other hand and drove it into Airavata's trunk.

The elephant shrieked, but he still held Gulab's arm and began dragging the man off. Kaushalya tried to think of what to do, but she was stymied by her hands being bound.

Batra, in the back seat of the car, was shouting something. Airavata saw his old nemesis through the window. Changing the focus of his anger, he loosened his trunk slightly. Gulab tore the arm free.

Airavata stepped toward Batra and drove a giant tusk at him. The bullet-proof glass buckled and a network of cracks appeared, and the metal around the edges bent inward. The window somehow held, probably because the elephant hadn't put his full weight behind the thrust.

"Get us out of here!" Batra screamed at Gulab.

Gulab jumped behind the steering wheel and slammed the door closed.

At Harlal's command, the elephant slipped his tusks under the Mercedes' rear bumper just as the engine started. The elephant lifted the back end of the heavy vehicle as if it were a toy.

Gulab stomped on the accelerator. The rear wheels whined, spinning furiously in the air.

The elephant moved sideways a few steps, pivoting the car on the front wheels, then dropped it at Harlal's order.

The tires screeched and smoked on the paving stones. Then they found purchase and the Mercedes leaped forward.

Gulab frantically turned the car to avoid hitting the courtyard wall head on. The Mercedes skidded and slammed sideways into the masonry.

Airavata ran close and reared up. He thrust his front feet onto the car's roof, buckling it and shoving the vehicle downward on its springs.

Gulab again hit the accelerator. Sheet metal tore and sparks flew as the car shrieked along the wall. The car turned and sped down to the main courtyard, then across it, the townspeople scrambling out of the way.

The Mercedes shot out the gate and disappeared down the hill, the wheels battering on the cobblestones.

"Are you all right, Highness?" called Harlal, dismounting from Airavata's neck.

She was shaking, but managed to say in a trembling voice, "I'm fine." She awkwardly wiped away a tear. She added bitterly, as Harlal began to untie her hands, "If only they hadn't gotten away."

A tremendous crashing sound came from down the hill, followed by the clangings of pieces of metal coming to rest on stone.

Then silence.

"I had the lower gate closed, except for the little door," Harlal said quietly. When he had pulled the cord free from her wrists and tossed it aside, he stood, looked toward the bottom of the hill, and thoughtfully twisted his mustache. "Those *goondas* must not have seen it in time. The gate can withstand big battering rams and charging elephants, you know."

26

Kaushalya had finally regained most of her normal composure after her ordeal. Gopi was still furious, but not seriously injured.

Sometimes Kaushalya found herself anguishing over what might have happened if events had turned out worse.

Airavata was recovering well from the knife wound to his trunk. Dev Batra, Gulab, and Sen were in varying states of critical condition in a room guarded by police in a hospital at Jaipur. The wreckage of the Mercedes remained at the bottom of the hill, the object of much bemused sightseeing.

In her suite at the Bhim Bhawan Palace, Kaushalya thought about the gems Batra was so anxious to get. If they were still somewhere in Mangarh, they must be in a location that, while safe from theft, was one she or her brother would eventually think of. Could she be missing the hiding spot merely because she knew it well and therefore took it for granted? She looked out through the windows toward the hillside, but she was reviewing in her mind the places she was so familiar with and saw so often. She thought of the rooms in the palace: the reception room, the audience hall, the dining room, the drawing rooms, the office, the prayer room, the long corridors, the porches, her own quarters, even the strong room. She could easily visualize each place, and none stood out as worthy of further inspection, especially after being so thoroughly searched by the income tax officers.

She thought about the old fortress: the gateways, the big courtyard, the stables, the audience halls, the men's and women's living quarters, the hall of mirrors, the armory, the old treasury. Most of it was almost as familiar as her own suite, and again, all of it had been extensively examined by the tax people.

She remembered Guru Dharmananda's lecture about how the answers to most questions were within one's own self. Could that apply to a problem such as this?

She had done so much thinking on the matter in recent weeks, maybe her subconscious mind had already developed the answers and was waiting to be called upon. She stepped out to her veranda and sat in a comfortable cane chair.

She closed her eyes, breathed deeply several times to relax, and began repeating her mantra.

After several minutes, when she felt calm and receptive, she asked herself the question: where is the Star of Mangarh? And where are the other major gems?

Her mind casually roamed over the possibilities again. Somewhere in the old fortress? If so, in what part?

In this very palace? If so, where?

She thought some more. Were there other possibilities, outside the properties owned by her family?

She thought about her father's letter to Mahendra and herself. If he had provided any clues, the letter was a likely possibility. She remembered what he had said. He had mentioned finding a husband for her, of course, and he had mentioned Pratap. But she would think about that aspect of the letter some other time.

A major emphasis of what he'd written had concerned spiritual matters: trusting in the family's God, Ekadantji. And trusting in Guru Dharmananda. Could there be clues in that?

Soon, some intuitions came. Excitement grew within her. The ideas had a feel about them that was right.

She stood and hurried through the corridors to the office, where she found Mahendra seated at the desk. Still standing, she said, "I've been thinking about those gems. Father would not only have wanted to hide them where they weren't likely to be found by someone outside the family, he'd have wanted to ensure we never sold or lost control over the hiding place."

Mahendra peered at her. "So the gems should be here in this palace? Or in the fortress?"

"Maybe." Her eyes narrowed. "What can you think of that we'd never part with, no matter what happened? Even if we were forced to sell this palace or give it to the government?"

Mahendra frowned. "Oh, there are a number of things. The throne. The Bhavani Sword, assuming we still have it somewhere. Paintings."

She stared at him intently. "But what would we hold on to at all costs?

The very last item we'd give up?"

Mahendra furrowed his brow and thought for a time. "Ekadantji, I suppose. We could hardly part with our family God."

She smiled. "Exactly. Let's go visit him."

"You think Father mentioned him in the letter for a reason?"

She shrugged. "Maybe. Vijay Singh looked there and couldn't find anything. I was with him at the time. But still, maybe we overlooked something."

They went down the hall and slipped off their sandals. The priest was not present, so they were alone. Both stood a few minutes in an attitude of prayer. Eventually, Mahendra looked at her. "Well?"

She examined the room, trying to see it afresh. It was bare, except for the stone pedestal on which the God sat, and the draped table with the more minor objects of worship. The room was lit only by the small flames of the oil lamps, but her eyes had adjusted enough to see everything clearly.

She said in a whisper, "We looked at quite him closely when tax officer Singh was here. I'd like to do it again."

Mahendra gazed at Ekadantji. "Just so we do it respectfully."

They padded up to the image. "I'd like to lift him," said Kaushalya. She folded her hands and bowed her head.

Mahendra did likewise. "Great God," he murmured, "we mean no offense to you. We ask your help and forgiveness." After several seconds silence, Mahendra said, "I'll lift him, while you look."

He bent, took firm hold of the base, and raised the foot-high statue.

Underneath lay the finely woven cloth covering the pedestal. Kaushalya tugged it off. The stone surface showed no seams. Frowning, she examined the sides of the pedestal. "I don't see anything," she said. She replaced the cloth.

"Should I put him back down?"

"Can you hold him a while longer?"

"Yes, he's not so heavy."

She examined the base of the pedestal, then the floor. Nothing obvious. "Can we move the pedestal?"

"We can try. I'll set Ekadantji on the floor for now."

They slid the stone aside. As she had seen previously, there was only the smooth surface of the floor beneath it.

"Inside the pedestal?" asked Mahendra.

"Let's look at the bottom."

Carefully, they tipped it up. The hollowed-out inside appeared smooth and bare. Silently they maneuvered it back into place.

Kaushalya let out a sigh. "Oh, well. Daddyji fooled us again."

Mahendra lifted Ekadantji and moved him to the pedestal.

"Wait," said Kaushalya. "Is he hollow?"

"Probably. He'd be much heavier if he weren't."

She took hold of the base of the image and tilted it so she could see the bottom. The lower surface was slightly recessed, and a crack showed around where the bottom met the sides of the base. There appeared to be no way to remove the bottom panel. She gently, respectfully, probed at it with her fingers. It seemed to her that it gave slightly under the pressure.

She pressed harder. Suddenly the panel popped out, almost dropping before she caught it. She saw a small spring latch on each end of its upper surface.

"Well, I'll be...." said Mahendra in a half whisper.

"Something's inside. It looks like a wad of cloth."

Gently, hoping Ekadantji didn't mind, Kaushalya pulled at the fabric. It came out.

Mahendra set Ekadantji down on the pedestal.

Kaushalya knelt, placed the wad carefully on the floor, and slowly unfolded it. Inside was yet another cloth, red, wrapped around a roundish object. She unfolded it.

A huge, clear gem sparkled in the light of the oil lamp flames.

"A diamond?" asked Mahendra wonderingly. "But it's so big!"

They stared at it a moment, then Mahendra cautiously took it between his fingers and raised it. The facets sparked and flared as he turned it.

"The Star of Mangarh," whispered Kaushalya.

He set it down gently. He looked at her, grinning with embarrassment as well as excitement. "My hand's trembling so much I was afraid I'd drop it."

She smiled widely. "It's so—so clear, aside from being so large!"

He laughed, nervously. "Your eyes look almost as big as it does."

They stood for a time, gazing at it. "Found at last," Mahendra said. He shook his head. "I was beginning to believe it didn't even exist any more."

Bharat Mahajan was at the palace only minutes after Mahendra phoned.

The gem trader leaned forward at the desk in the palace office, his eyes ravenous as Mahendra unwrapped the diamond. Kaushalya stood near, watching, half afraid he'd tell them it was a fake, but almost certain it wasn't.

The gemstone lay on the cloth as if it contained its own light, overwhelming all else in the room.

Mahajan put a magnifier in his eye and bent over. After a few moments he sat upright long enough to say, obviously struggling to stay calm, "There is no question whatsoever. It is the Star of Mangarh." He immediately lowered his head again, examining the diamond minutely.

Mahendra and Kaushalya exchanged looks, both smiling broadly.

Eventually, Mahajan sat upright and took the loupe from his eye. He turned to them. "What an honor! It's a privilege for me to see such a stone as this. It's probably the highlight of my life."

Mahendra, still smiling, asked, "Can you give us any idea of its value?"

Mahajan sobered. "You realize it's the seventh largest diamond in the world?"

Mahendra and Kaushalya again looked at each other, wide-eyed. He turned back to Mahajan. "We knew it was a major gem, but we didn't know exactly how important."

"I shouldn't attempt to estimate its worth yet. I'll have to do some research." He looked to Mahendra. "I'm quite intrigued—do you mind telling me where it has been all this time?"

Kaushalya and Mahendra again exchanged glances. "I, uh, apologize," said Mahendra. "I think not quite yet. It's possible we might want to return it there. If we feel we can reveal the information later, you'll be first to know."

Mahajan nodded. "I do hope you have a highly secure place to keep it? I'll be totally discreet myself, of course, but once word does get out, there will be a huge amount of interest in the stone. Including by those who might steal it and hide their theft by replacing it with a replica."

"I think we'll manage," Mahendra said. He gestured toward the massive door of the strong room.

"You might also consider insurance. Of course, the premium would be quite high."

Scarcely able to stand still, Kaushalya said with a wry smile, "It seems we have a lot to think about."

"And if you should ever decide to sell the diamond, please do keep me in mind. Not—" he smiled fleetingly "—that I could begin to afford it myself. But I would be honored to negotiate the sale with those who do have the necessary wealth, or to make arrangements with a major auction house. I've had experience doing both. Even though my base is in Mangarh, I do travel abroad, and I'm better known in those circles than many here might expect. I can provide you with references, if necessary."

"Oh, definitely we would call on you," said Mahendra. "You and your family have served our own family well over the years."

When the gem trader had gone, Mahendra took a deep breath. "Well! I suppose we'd better lock it up. We can't stay here watching it forever."

Kaushalya was gazing at the diamond, feeling the sudden responsibility of safeguarding it, and of overseeing its custody wisely. She dragged her eyes away to look at him. She glanced at the strong room and gestured toward it. "Do you think that's a safe enough place?"

"Where else would you put a rare diamond? It would be quite a job to break into that room."

"Maybe we should return it to where it's been all this time. It seems to have been safe there."

Mahendra frowned. "That's true. But somehow—the *puja* room isn't even locked, usually. People have to be able to get in and out to worship."

"But if no one else knows the diamond is there?"

Mahendra thought, then he gave a lopsided grin. "I'm sorry, I just can't put it in an unlocked room."

Kaushalya shrugged. "All right. I suppose the strong room's safe enough for the moment."

When it was secured behind the heavy steel door and the three giant padlocks, Mahendra let his breath. "I feel I can relax a bit now."

"Me, too. Though I could have looked at it all night! Especially since I won't be able to sleep, anyway."

He smiled at that, and said, "There's a big question remaining. Is there still more, somewhere?"

She frowned. "Not that we don't have enough! But I think there may well be more. The ruby, the emerald, the Mangarh Pearls, among other things."

He looked down at the desk top. "If there's more, I feel we have a duty to try to find it and see that it's all properly cared for. I don't know where to look, though."

"Have you asked the Bhil guards again? Now that you're installed, they might be more candid."

Mahendra lifted his head. "I talked with Surmal. He says Father instructed them not to discuss it, even with me. He told them if I ever needed to know more, I could figure it out on my own. But right now I haven't a clue. Oh, I suppose I could try ordering them to tell me. If there's ever a major crisis that requires more funds, that's what I'll do. But short of that, I hesitate to make them disobey Father. They still revere him."

Kaushalya looked away. "I've been thinking about another idea. I'll let you know if it leads anywhere."

27

In the hills, near Mangarh city

Gopi accompanied Kaushalya while Lal waited with the car. Guru Dharmananda was seated on the veranda of his cottage. Kaushalya slipped off her sandals, mounted the low step, and bent to touch his feet.

He smiled at them. "What brings you to see me today, Kaushalyaji, Gopiji?

"Guruji," asked Kaushalya, "do you know where the rest of my father's treasure is?"

"I was wondering when you were going to ask. I promised him I wouldn't volunteer the information, but that I'd tell you or your brother whenever one of you made a direct request."

Kaushalya felt herself let go of some of the tension that had built up over the past months. She smiled slightly, and exchanged glances with Gopi.

The guru rose, went into the cottage, and then returned. He handed her two large metal rings; one with three large keys on it, the other with a couple dozen smaller ones.

"So you've had it all the time?"

"I suppose you could say that. I've never thought of myself as keeping it, though. I merely gave your father permission to store some valuables on part of the ashram grounds. The rest was all his doing. He and his Bhil guards brought it here at night in bullock carts. I'm told it took them more than one night. I was off on a trip myself when they were unloading it." The guru again smiled. "Your father told me he trusted me because he knew I had no interest in worldly wealth."

"He didn't visit you much in recent years. I can't help but wonder why."

"Actually, he visited me a number of times, but usually at night or early in the morning—before dawn—when he was less likely to be seen. I think he wanted it to appear to others that he no longer had much association with me, for fear someone might think of searching here."

Kaushalya gave a nod. "I suppose that could explain it."

"You realize, it didn't occur to me for a long time that he might be concealing something from the government. I assumed he just wanted to hide some valuables in a safe place. But much later, when I thought about it, I told him if anyone from the government ever asked me directly, I would have to tell the truth. He said he didn't mind. We both agreed it wasn't likely I'd be asked. He never did tell me whether or not he was doing anything illegal. I think he probably thought he wasn't. I got the impression he thought this particular wealth belonged to his old state, and that under the agreements he'd signed, the new Indian government didn't have any rights to it."

Kaushalya was turning the keys over in her fingers. "I assume it's in the caves?"

He grinned, obviously enjoying himself. "Very clever of you."

She laughed. "It took me long enough." It was so obvious, now. The caverns were reputed to be dangerous because of the chance of cave-ins, so for many years they had been kept boarded up and locked.

The guru said, "I'll call my current visitors together for an extra discussion. You should then be undisturbed for quite some time."

She examined the keys. She had assumed a disciple or even Guruji himself would go with her. Apparently, he thought she and Gopi should be alone, and he needed to ensure they weren't bothered by curious ashram inmates.

"You'll need a lantern," he said. "I'll get you one."

He returned with it, and lit it for her. She nodded, and rose.

"When you're finished," said Guruji, "please come and wait for me here."

She nodded absently, stepped from the veranda, slipped her sandals back on. The ground was rocky and dusty underfoot as she trudged up the slope, followed by Gopi.

The rectangular openings were in a row, cut into the cliff. Rough wooden doors covered each hole. She set down the lantern, tried the keys on the ring of three in the padlock on the first door. The second one worked. She removed the lock.

The heavy door dragged on the ground when she pulled, and she stubbed a toe on a rock, but with Gopi's help she managed to swing the door open. Even without the lantern she could see all the chests inside, some wooden, some steel. The boxes all had handles on the end for ease in carrying, some of rope, some of wood, some metal. Most of the chests were considerably larger than those the tax people had discovered in the fortress.

Within the cave it was much cooler than outdoors. She put on her glasses and inspected the wax seals on several of the containers; they bore the imprint of her family's coat of arms. She tried the keys in the padlock of one of the large chests until she found one that opened the lock. She broke the wax on the seal, pulled off the string, and lifted the heavy lid.

The chest was full almost to the top. Even in the indirect sunlight, the gold bars gleamed.

"So much!" Gopi exclaimed.

"Yes." Kaushalya stood looking at them for a time. At last, she slipped her fingers into a gap between two of the bars and lifted one out. She was momentarily startled at how heavy the gold was for its size.

She set the bar on the ground. Speaking in a whisper, as if still trying to keep a secret, she said, "I think I'll take this one now, to show my brother." She closed the lid and relocked the chest. She retrieved the gold bar and handed it to Gopi, saying, "This is awkward to carry because it's so heavy."

They left the vault. With some effort, she and Gopi shoved the door closed. She slid the bolt home, replaced the padlock and used the key to lock the shackle tight. She moved on to the next cavern. Again, the door was difficult to open, but she managed. More chests were stacked inside. She opened one at random. It was full of gold coins. She removed a few, stuffed them in her other pocket, closed the chest and relocked it.

She and Gopi shut the door of the cavern. She replaced the lock, and moved on to the next door.

Inside were still more chests. She opened one. It was packed with swords, daggers, knives, all wrapped in cloth. She examined several and noted their blades were well oiled to prevent rust. Most of them had gold or jeweled handles, intricately worked.

She closed and relocked the chest.

She opened another, with a lid that fit more tightly than those on the other chests. In the chest were stacked large, thick, cloth-wrapped rectangles. The scent of old, dried *neem* leaves met her nostrils: the leaves were used to deter insects from attacking paper or other potentially edible substances. The gold, the jewelry, the weapons had failed to excite her. She felt only the burden of the immense wealth. But now her pulse raced as she broke the seal on one of the bundles and quickly unwrapped it.

Within, between wooden covers, was a stack of thick paper pages. She lifted the top sheet. On one side was writing, in the *devanagari* script. On the other side was a miniature painting. She recognized a scene from the life of Krishna. "One of the sets of paintings missing so long from the palace library!" she said to Gopi.

She unwrapped another. A *Ramayana*, exquisitely illustrated! She was eager to unwrap the others, to see what lost treasures awaited her. But she had already taken quite some time, and the guru might be tiring of keeping the inhabitants of the ashram occupied so they would not notice the open cave doors. Maybe it was better, anyway, to save some of the painting bundles for later. The anticipation of opening them would be delicious.

She set aside the two opened sets, but resolutely closed and locked the lid on the remainder. She stood, raised the lantern, and looked around. The light revealed another doorway, unblocked, in the rear of the chamber. Cautious of where she stepped on the rough floor, she slowly walked through.

Another chamber, much larger, was piled floor to ceiling with the chests. One of them, on the top of a shorter stack, drew her notice. The box was slightly smaller and much more finely worked than the others, appearing to be of sandalwood with silver reinforcing and ivory inlays. There were two locks on it, where most of the others had one. She tried the keys until she found first one, then another that worked.

The chest was filled to the brim with shallow cloth-lined wooden trays, each laden with jewelry glittering in the light of the lantern. She removed a huge, green stone. "That's the one my grandfather wore in the portrait in the palace! The 'Mangarh Emerald!'" She admired it for a moment, then gently deposited it in her pocket, careful to make sure it was secure in the bottom.

She closed the lid and relocked the chest.

She took a deep breath of the stale air, but made no effort to open the others. It was all too much. She stood a while, looking at them, thinking of her father, and then she gathered up the books and left.

They waited perhaps ten minutes on the veranda before Guruji returned. He approached with a smile twisting his lips. He was carrying a long, cloth wrapped bundle.

"I take it you weren't disappointed, Kaushalya?"

"No! It's more than I ever imagined!"

"What will you do with it all?"

"I've been wondering about that. It's up to my brother, too—not only me."

"But you found it. It's your burden at this moment.' He grinned more broadly.

She shook her head. "My brother and I have to decide together. I trust him, even if we sometimes disagree." She looked at Guruji. "I suppose you'll want us to take it away now?"

"As you wish. It's been there quite a while. A few months more, even longer, won't matter." He smiled at her again. "Will you tell the government?"

She flinched. Slowly she said, "We'll have to, won't we? More taxes and penalties. But there should still be a lot left over."

"One more thing," said the guru. With both hand, he slowly extended the oblong bundle to her.

She handed the objects from the cave to Gopi. She grasped the long package, and said, "It feels like a sword."

"It is." His eyes were unusually solemn.

A thought was coming, infusing her with fresh excitement.

"I'll help you unwrap it," said the guru.

When the sword was revealed, she saw the small hilt was inlaid with an intricate network of gold filigree. It was instantly apparent that the weapon was of the finest craftsmanship.

But there was something more. The sword had presence, an aura of gravity, that made it more than just a superbly crafted weapon.

She admiringly took hold of the handle, and she immediately felt an energy. It was as if the object radiated a field of well being, waiting to be summoned. As if whoever held it would have all doubts dissolved, as if all insecurities would fade into insignificance.

She looked at the guru, not knowing what to say.

He was eyeing her, smiling. "It's a powerful weapon," he said.

She lay the emerald, the gold bar, the illustrated manuscripts, the coins on the table in front of her brother.

He stared at them a moment, then grinned. "You found more? Where?"

She told him.

He laughed. "I have a clever sister." He lifted the huge green gem and held it up to the light. "The Mangarh Emerald, isn't it?"

"Yes. And there's more of everything where it was." She shook her head and grinned. "A *lot* more."

He shook his head. "So much! And I wouldn't have thought to look there. Father never ceases to surprise me."

"That's not all." She took the long, slim bundle. Even through the cloth, she again sensed the magic of the finely crafted weapon. She wondered if she were only imagining that it felt as if it were both lighter than it should be, and at the same time, heavier.

She slowly, reverently, unwrapped the weapon, given to their ancestor Madho Singh by the legendary Maratha King three hundred years before. The sword was bared now except for its scabbard, and she held it horizontally in both hands. She had the odd feeling that if she were to let loose of it, the weapon would suspend itself in the air.

"Look," she said to Mahendra, her voice a whisper. She withdrew the blade enough to reveal the inscription: *Shri Bhavani.*

"My God," he said, his own voice hoarse. "Is this really *it?*"

She held it out to him, and he carefully took it. She watched his expression turn to one of awe as he felt the presence in his hands.

"I think Father had good reason to keep it hidden," she said. "We should probably keep it secret, too. It's too important to let word of it get to those who might exploit it as a symbol in advancing one religion or group at the expense of another."

He was staring at it as if mesmerized. Eventually, he looked up at her. "You're absolutely right."

28

Vijay's last task before taking up his new position as Assistant Director of Income Tax at Udaipur was to complete the inventory of the items in the caverns. It took him, Shanta, Ranjit, and the others brought in from Delhi the better part of a week to count and record the objects.

Included in the treasure were the huge ruby, "the Blood of Shivaji," and the five-string necklace, "the Mangarh Pearls." He had not yet attempted to value them or the other items. The newly revealed trove was in the *crores* of rupees, but he wouldn't even attempt to guess at the total. A hundred *crore*? Five hundred? Whatever the final figure, it would be too much for the mind to grasp.

At first there had been the question as to whether part or all of the find should belong to the government. But the lawyers had examined the instruments governing the merger of Mangarh with the Rajasthan Union. It had tentatively been determined that with the possible exception of the gold, the wealth was in fact listed in the covenants as the Maharaja's ancestral family and personal property, although it was described collectively rather than naming individual items. Wealth tax and penalties would have to be paid, but still there would be *crores* left to Mahendra Singh and Kaushalya Kumari.

Shanta had left the night before on the train from Mangarh junction, headed to Agra to help her family finalize arrangements for her and Vijay's fast-approaching wedding, and Ranjit had taken the jeep into Mangarh city to check on the security of the vaults.

Two weeks previously, Vijay had visited Udaipur to get a feel for the office he would be heading, which was housed in a large bungalow in a pleasant neighborhood north of the center of the city. Since his predecessor had left some time before, Vijay took custody of the official brass seal. He now used it to imprint the wax sealing the string on the last box of the treasure with "ADI UDAIPUR".

The chest was taken by the armed guards escorting the Bhils, who were in charge of transporting the items to the strong rooms. Surmal, the guard captain, was there, and Vijay could not resist asking, "You knew where the treasure was all along, didn't you?"

The man smiled as if embarrassed. "Yes, sir. I supervised moving it from the fortress."

Vijay sighed, and nodded. "I thought so."

"I apologize, sir, for not being able to speak to you about it while you were searching. I had my orders from His Highness. It was my duty to follow them."

"Of course. I understand."

A.S. Nimbalkar was standing near, and Vijay said to him, "It appears the Shivaji sword wasn't among the items we inventoried."

"No, sir." Nimbalkar looked away. "I think I'll give up my search. Everything leads to a dead end. We must find other ways to rally fellow Hindus. I think we must focus on educating everyone of the dangers to Hinduism posed by followers of other religions."

"Since Hindus have something like an eighty-five percent majority, the dangers can't be so great," Vijay said.

"Oh, yes, sir! Most of India's troubles are due to these other people and their influences trying to undermine our society. Those Muslims who are trying to steal Kashmir from us are only the most obvious example."

The jeep was arriving, bringing Ranjit back from Mangarh city, and Vijay edged away. Nimbalkar went to get into the Matador van that would take him and several others back to Delhi.

Ranjit approached and handed Vijay a newspaper. It was a day old copy of the *Times of India*, and the headline on the front page said, "Celebrity Swami Charged with Smuggling." Vijay read the first few paragraphs:

> *Swami Surya, spiritual and astrological advisor to many of India's most prominent politicians, industrialists, and film stars, was arrested today after a lengthy probe by the Central Bureau of Investigation. The swami is charged with smuggling gold, diamonds, and other high value items, making use of his many international contacts. It is alleged in the charge sheet that he often brought the smuggled items in by air to a landing strip on a farm in Rajasthan owned by former political operative Dev Batra. Batra faces numerous criminal charges himself for kidnapping, assault, and attempted robbery. Unavailable for questions by reporters, he is currently hospitalized in serious condition after a motor vehicle accident while fleeing.*
>
> *"I am totally innocent," said the swami. "If I am named in connection with anything illegal, it is only by unfortunate association. Like Jesus Christ, I accept all persons who come to me as friends and followers. I am deeply disappointed that some of my acquaintances have apparently made improper use of their friendship with me without my knowing."*
>
> *When asked by a reporter if his advanced spiritual knowledge didn't give him some intuition that the illegal activities were occurring, the swami replied, "We all know this is a dark age. Evil is rampant. These powerful forces can sometimes cast spells that obscure the truth, until one becomes aware of their actions and takes steps to counter them."*
>
> *The swami was asked about his earlier astrological prediction that Indira Gandhi would win the recent elections with a huge victory. "The planets have been in confusing configurations these past several months, making it extremely difficult to get unambiguous readings," he replied, before being taken off to await his bail hearing.*

Vijay shook his head and handed back the newspaper. Kaushalya Kumari had returned from the ashram buildings, and she was exchanging a few words with the guard captain. She wore the Rajput long skirt and veil in shades of bright orange, and Vijay was reminded of how attracted to her he had been. He still was, in a way—certainly there was good cause.

But the strength of the infatuation was no longer there; his upcoming marriage to Shanta was foremost in his mind. He found himself grinning at the thought of his bride-to-be's warm smile.

He composed his face, walked over to the princess, and asked, "What will you do with all the wealth?"

Kaushalya Kumari turned her attention to him. "There are so many needs," she said. "We feel we hold the treasure in trust for the people, you know. Fortunately, my brother and I mostly agree. We'll set up charitable organizations to provide seed money for self-help projects and family planning and education among the poorer rural people. And we'll work with the villagers on reforestation."

Vijay nodded. "All that's badly needed."

She smiled. "We have to be careful to spend money wisely, though. Too often, the government or outsiders think they know what's best for the villagers and end up wasting funds. The people themselves can usually tell us what will work best. We should listen to them."

He again nodded. "I certainly agree, coming from a village myself."

Her eyes lit with enthusiasm. "I also have some personal pet projects. I want to make outsiders aware of Rajasthan's heritage. Now that we have the funds, my brother agrees with converting parts of the fortress and the Bhim Bhawan Palace into small hotels. We'll encourage tourism in Mangarh by renovating much of the fort and turning it into a museum. And we'll offer tours and treks into the Aravallis and the villages. It will provide jobs for many of the local people."

He grew excited himself as he thought of the implications. "Those are wonderful ideas. They'll not only help preserve the buildings and the natural areas, they'll help people at the same time."

"Maybe you'd like to work with us," she said, her gaze resting on him. "Much of what we do in the villages will be with the Scheduled Castes. We'll need volunteers who are well known to the people. Preferably someone of their own."

Vijay stared at her. "So you must know about me. Where I came from."

She again smiled. "My father realized who you were from the very start. He would have apologized to you about his prank involving the tunnel if he hadn't been arrested first. It didn't occur to him that you'd be so upset until it was too late."

Vijay frowned and turned his gaze away as he absorbed this. Then he looked back to her and said, "That doesn't matter now. But...he must have been quite angry when I found part of the treasure, after he had financed the very education that got me my position."

Kaushalya Kumari shrugged. "Only he would know. It wasn't his nature to complain about such things. I'm sure he didn't feel you owed him a thing. After all, your father was killed by his police. And you were doing your duty as you saw it. Fulfilling one's *dharma* was the highest of virtues to him."

Vijay had suddenly grown hoarse, and he cleared his throat before saying, "Still, I might well not have been able to escape my condition, or help out my people, if I'd had to do it without financial aid. I hoped to tell him how grateful I am for my education, but he died before I was able to."

She smiled. "It wasn't necessary to tell him. I think he got some pleasure from watching you in action, even though you were working against him. It showed him his efforts to help you had been fruitful."

Vijay thought for a time and then nodded. He returned the smile as he said, "I'd definitely like to help in your work. And I've saved money to start a school in my own village. Maybe your father would think he made a good investment in me after all."

She smiled once more. "I'm sure of it."

Vijay pressed his hands together in farewell. She did likewise and nodded.

Vijay stepped into the jeep and gestured to Akbar Khan to leave.

Kaushalya watched them drive away, and then she headed down the hill toward her guru's ashram.

***

The harsh excesses of the sterilization program during the Emergency resulted in a backlash among the people and a distrust of government family planning policies that set back population control efforts in India for decades. The unfortunate consequence is that India's huge population continues to grow at an extremely fast rate, magnifying the already serious social, environmental, and economic problems.

Voters returned Indira Gandhi to Parliament a year after her defeat. The Janata government brought charges against her for the excesses during the Emergency and, ironically, sent her to Tihar Jail for a week.

In 1980 she again became Prime Minister when her Congress (I) Party regained its majority. In June of that year, her son Sanjay died in the crash of a stunt airplane he was piloting.

Indira Gandhi was assassinated in October, 1984, by her own Sikh bodyguards, primarily in retribution for an attack on the Sikhs' Golden Temple at Amritsar to dislodge separatist terrorists.

Her other son, Rajiv Gandhi, succeeded her as Prime Minister. He later lost the position when Congress was voted out of power. In May, 1991, South Indian Tamils assassinated him when he was campaigning to return himself and the Congress Party to power; the killing was in retaliation for his sending the Indian Army to help suppress Tamil insurgents in Sri Lanka.

Sanjay's widow Menaka Gandhi, who left the Congress Party, has been active in politics, including serving as Minister of Culture and crusading for causes such as environmental protection and animal welfare.

In recent years, the Congress Party has not been in control of the country, but it is still an extremely strong force. Rajiv's Italian-born widow Sonia Gandhi has become the principal leader of the party, and many Congress supporters hope that she and her children by Rajiv—daughter Priyanka and son Rahul—will revive the "Nehru-Gandhi Dynasty."

Notes

General Notes

Cartographers have not placed the Mangarh of these novels on maps other than those in this book and its predecessor. For travelers who wish to search for the town in Rajasthan, it might be wiser to be satisfied with experiencing other Rajasthani cities and villages similar in spirit to Mangarh. Likewise, historians and other chroniclers have not written of the Pariyatra Rajput clan or the other inhabitants of the former princely state of Mangarh. However, many other residents of the Rajasthan region and their ancestors have lived much as described in this book.

When portraying characters and incidents based on recorded history, I tried to be as accurate as possible. I often created fictional events to illustrate a historical occurrence or time period, and in those cases I went to considerable effort to be true to the spirit of the actual times and places involved. When portraying actual historical personages taking part in incidents created by my own imagination, I tried to be true to their personalities to the extent those can be revealed by research. In the following notes, I specify for each story which were actual historical characters and events, and to what degree I used my imagination.

My interviews with actual persons for background information are covered in my Acknowledgments. I personally visited almost all the sites I have written about in India, some more than once. I consulted literally thousands of references over two decades.

Notes on the Particular Stories

THE TREASURE of MANGARH: The Time of the Emergency

A number of people named in my separate Acknowledgments section contributed significantly to my ability to write this story. I am deeply grateful to each of them.

The events taking place during the Emergency are fictionalized in this book, but most are based on similar actual occurrences. Of course, Indira

Gandhi and Sanjay Gandhi actually lived, and they reportedly acted on occasion in that time period similarly to how I depict them. All other characters are fictional. No other characters are based on any real persons, living or dead, although some fictional characters were inspired in general by a combination of two or more actual persons. I don't follow sports and had never heard of the golfer Vijay Singh until long after the story was completed. My Swami Surya, despite the similarity of name to some other living gurus, is not based upon them, and indeed I wasn't aware of a prominent swami who goes by that name until this book was ready to go to press.

With regard to written sources, I'm especially indebted to the following four books for inspiration regarding royal treasures during the Emergency, and regarding the Indian Income Tax Department:

1. Crewe, Quentin, *The Last Maharaja: A Biography of Sawai Man Singh II, Maharaja of Jaipur*. London: Michael Joseph, 1985. Part of the book describes income tax raids on the Jaipur royal family, including the lengthy, and unsuccessful, search at the Jaigarh Fort for the legendary Jaipur treasure protected by guards of the Mina tribe. Both the current Maharaja and the previous Maharaja's wife, the well-known Gayatri Devi, were jailed at Tihar for a long period during the Emergency.

2. Kasbekar, Sushama, and Palekar, Balachandra, *The Tax Dodgers*. Bombay: Popular Prakashan, 1985. A novel about the Income Tax Department and its raids. As mentioned in my Acknowledgments, coauthor B.B. Palekar, a former Deputy Director of the Directorate of Inspection (Investigation), was extremely generous with his time in writing detailed answers to my many questions.

3. Malgonkar, Manohar, *The Princes*. New York: Viking, 1963. An outstanding novel about the last days of a royal family before Indian Independence, partly involving the family's legendary hidden treasure protected by a tribe of Bhils.

4. Scindia, Vijaya Raje, with Malgonkar, Manohar, *The Last Maharani of Gwalior: An Autobiography*. Albany: State University of New York, 1987. Extensive details about the Maharani's tribulations during the Emergency when she and her family endured a lengthy raid by tax officers searching for hidden wealth. Like the previously mentioned Jaipur royal family members, the Maharani was jailed during the Emergency, part of the time at Tihar.

MASTER BUILDER: The Mughal Emperor Shah Jahan and the Building of the Taj Mahal

Mohan Lal and Chandra and their family and employees are fictional, as are the priest Soma and the Mangarh rajas. All other characters actually lived and are mentioned in records.

The identity of the real architect of the Taj Mahal, if indeed there was only one primary designer, is not known for certain. In *Taj Mahal: The Illumined Tomb*, W.E. Begley and Z.A. Desai make a circumstantial case that the architect was one Ustad Ahmad Lahori. Some think Shah Jahan himself may have been the principal designer; certainly he possessed knowledge and talent regarding the design of building and gardens.

Maybe it is indeed more probable that the architect was Muslim rather than Hindu. Still, R. Nath, in his books on Mughal architecture and the Taj Mahal, has presented fascinating suggestions that much of the design of the Taj had its origins in the rules laid down in the Hindu *shastras*. In my story I have assumed that in addition to the obvious Persian and Indian Muslim origins, the Taj Mahal does have strong Hindu architectural influences.

The quotations from the eulogy by Shah Jahan are excerpted with grateful appreciation from Nath, R., *The Taj Mahal and Its Incarnation (Original Persian Data on its Builders, Materials, Costs, Measurements etc.)*. Jaipur: The Historical Research Documentation Programme, 1985.

SHIVAJI'S FORTUNES: The Maratha King Shivaji and the Mughal Emperor Aurangzeb

All major events involving Shivaji and Emperor Aurangzeb and his officials occurred much as depicted in the story, and all major characters actually existed. Only Madho Singh and the characters from Mangarh are fictional. There are several theories about the current location of Shivaji's legendary Bhavani Sword, and scholars are unsure of the authenticity of the claimants to the title.

The drawing of Shivaji on horseback is from a statue at Poona.

LOYALTY: The Founding of the Sikh Khalsa by Guru Gobind Singh

Almost all the events depicted involving Guru Gobind Singh, including the more minor incidents, actually occurred, although with persons other than Sant, Kesar, and Bir. Among the actual martyrs at Chamkaur were Sikhs named Sant Singh, Bir Singh, and Kesar Singh, although apparently no details are known about them. Sant Singh, who resembled Guru Gobind, did take the Guru's place, including wearing his clothing and fighting to the death, to help enable the Guru's successful escape from Chamkaur.

Sources for quotations:

The translations of the Japji (the Sikh morning prayer), of the poem with images from farming, and of the poem about battle, with the last two poems slightly modified by myself, are all from: Singh, Khushwant, *A History of the Sikhs, Vol. 1: 1469-1839*. Delhi: Oxford University Press, 1977.

The translation of the hymn about the brotherhood of Hindus and Muslims is from Singh, Gopal, *Guru Gobind Singh*. New Delhi: National Book Trust, India, 1966.

The translation of the hymn to the sword is from Gupta, Hari Ram, *History of the Sikhs, Vol. 1: The Sikh Gurus, 1469-1708*. New Delhi: Munshiram Manoharlal, 2d. ed. 1984.

TEMPLES TO SHIVA: The Rani of Jhansi and the Mutiny of 1857

The Rani of Jhansi, her officers and ministers, Tatya Tope, the other leaders of the rebellion, and the British General Sir Hugh Rose all lived and fought much as depicted in the story, and the main events involving them occurred in the locations described. All other characters are fictional, as are the Shiva temples at the beginning and end of the story and the garden and shrines depicted near Jhansi. Most readers probably find the term "nigger" offensive, as do I, but it was in common use by foreigners in India during this period.

Usually a Brahmin such as Natesha would not have functioned both as a scholar *and* as a priest officiating regularly at temple rituals; he would have been either one or the other. However, it is not impossible for the same person to fill both roles, and occasionally a Brahmin did so.

By the time of the events depicted, *devadasis*, or temple dancers, had mostly disappeared from north India, but they were still common in some major temples in Orissa and southern India until well into the twentieth century. Dancers in north India, commonly referred to as "nautch girls," were usually entertainers attached to the courts of rulers, or else they were prostitutes who performed at private parties.

REFORMERS IN MANGARH and MANGARH JAILS: The Reform Movements in the Princely States

Although Mahatma Gandhi, Jawaharlal Nehru, and his daughter Indira, as well as the Viceroy, Lord Linlithgow were actual persons, the incidents involving them with Ashok Chand in "Reformers in Mangarh" and in "Mangarh Jails" are fictional. None of the other characters existed in reality, but the major happenings in the story are based on true events involving reform workers in various princely states. Sadly, the details of torture such as those inflicted by the orders of the fictional Thakur of Baldeogarh are based on numerous actual incidents.

I took considerable liberties with the depiction of Ashok thwarting the attempted assassination of the Viceroy, but indeed terrorists acts were supported by the Hindu RSS organization, which functioned much as described.

THE COSTS OF FREEDOM: *Independence and the Accession of the Princely States; the Partition of India and Pakistan*

The scenes involving the fictional Maharaja Lakshman Singh and real historical figures such as Nehru, Menon, Patel, Jinnah, and Mountbatten are based on actual incidents and negotiations involving those personages and other princes.

The events depicted at Partition involving the fictional Chand family, including the forced conversion to another religion, are, sadly, based on numerous historical accounts involving countless victims—Hindus, Muslims, and Sikhs alike.

The railroad line between Chilianwala and Amritsar is fictional, as are the towns along it, but the tale of Ashok Chand and Karam Singh driving the trainload of refugees to safety was inspired by an actual incident in which a locomotive driver had been bribed to stop his train at Amritsar so the passengers could be massacred. A British lieutenant and two of his men ran over the roofs of the carriages to the locomotive, took over the train at gunpoint, and the Britisher drove it across the border. In this real life case, the passengers were all Muslim refugees, delivered safely into Pakistan.

Character Lists

*The names of the characters of most importance in the stories are in **bold** type. Pronunciations, when shown, are very approximate; many sounds in Indian languages do not have a corresponding sound in English.*

THE TREASURE of MANGARH: The Time of the Emergency

The Mangarh (MAHN gar) royal family:

Kaushalya Kumari (Koh SHAL ya Ku MA ree), the Maharaja's daughter, Rajput.
Lakshman Singh (LUX mun Singh), ex-Maharaja of Mangarh, Rajput caste.
Mahendra Singh (Mah HEN dra Singh), the Maharaja's son, Rajput.

The income tax raiders:

Vijay Singh (VEE jay Singh), male senior income tax officer, Untouchable claiming to be Rajput, from village near Mangarh.
Shanta Das (SHAAN ta Daas), young woman income tax officer, Buddhist, from Untouchable background in Agra.
Anil Ghosali (A NEEL Go SHA lee), male income tax officer, Brahmin caste from Calcutta area of West Bengal, Vijay's rival.
Ranjit Singh (Ran JEET Singh), income tax officer, Sikh religion, Vijay's friend, from Delhi. Ranjit's wife: Vimala Kaur.
A.S. Nimbalkar (Nim BAL kar), new male income tax officer, member of fundamentalist Hindu RSS organziation.
Krishnaswamy (KRISH na SWA mee), young income tax officer, Tamil from South India.
Mrs. Janaki Desai (JAAN a kee De SAI), woman income tax officer from Delhi.
Akbar Khan (AAK bar KHAN), male jeep driver, Muslim from old area of Delhi.

Other characters associated with the royal family in Mangarh:

Gopi (GO pee), Kaushalya's maid/companion.
Shiv, Maharaja's elderly retainer.
Naresh Singh (NAR esh Singh), Maharaja's aide de camp (ADC)/personal secretary, a Rajput; his father ruled Vijay's village.
Bhajan Lal (BHA jan LAAL), driver for royal family.
Surmal (Sur MAAL), Captain of Maharaja's Bhil (tribal) guards at old fortress.
Nagario, a Bhil guard at the fortress.
Airavata (Air a VAT a), the elephant.
Harlal (Har LAAL) Airavata's mahout (elephant driver/keeper).

Characters in Gamri village:

Manju (MAN ju), Vijay's mother, a Bhangi (Untouchable sweeper outcaste).
Surja (SURJ), Vijay's uncle, a Bhangi.
Govinda (Go VIND), Vijay's cousin, a Bhangi.
Yogesh (Yo GESH), Vijay's cousin, a Bhangi.
Roop, Yogesh's wife, a Bhangi.
Hanwant (HAN want), Bhanwar (BHAN war), young village boys, Bhangis.

Other Mangarh area characters:

Guru Dharmananda (GOO roo Dhar ma NAND a), guru of Kaushalya and her father; a Brahmin from Himalayan foothills, former medical doctor.
Peter Willis, Guru's American assistant.
Dr. Savitri Chand (SAA vi tree Chand), lady medical doctor, Kaushalya's confidante and aunt of Kaushalya's best friend Usha Chand, Arora caste from the Punjab.
Arjun Oswal (AR jun OS waal) , former schoolmate of Vijay's, clerk in gem showroom.
Bharat Mahajan (Bhar AT Ma HA jan), gem dealer, Jain religion.

Delhi area characters:

Dev Batra (Dev BAAT ra), unscrupulous high level political worker, crony of Sanjay Gandhi, originally from Punjab area.
Gulab (Gu LAAB), one of Dev Batra's assistants/henchmen.
Sen, one of Dev Batra's assistants/henchmen.
Dilip Prasad (De LEEP Pra SAAD), Deputy Director of Inspection.
Trilok Mishra (Tree LOK MISH ra), successor Deputy Director of Inspection.
Usha Chand (OO shuh Chand), Kaushalya's best girlfriend, university student, Arora caste.

Ashok Chand (a SHOK Chand), former cabinet member and Congress Party politician, famous worker for India's freedom from British rule, originally from village in Punjab, Usha's father; Arora caste.

Jaya Chand (JAY a Chand), prominent lady lawyer, Ashok's wife/Usha's mother, Arora caste.

Pratap Singh (Pra TAAP Singh), graduate student, son of ex-Maharaja of Shantipur, a Rajput, friend of Chand family and of Kaushalya Kumari.

Amar (AH mar), *chowkidar* (watchman/gate-keeper) of Mangarh royal family's Delhi house.

Indira Gandhi (In DEER a GAAN dhee), Prime Minister of India; daughter of Jawaharlal Nehru, India's first Prime Minister; no relation to Mahatma Gandhi.

Sanjay Gandhi (SAAN jay GAAN dhee), Indira Gandhi's son.

THE MASTER BUILDER: The Mughal Emperor Shah Jahan and the Building of the Taj Mahal

Mohan Lal (MO han LAAL) the Master Builder, Hindu.

Chandra (CHUN drah), Mohan Lal's son.

Ram Das (Raam DAAS), Mohan Lal's servant and cook, Hindu.

Bhagwan Das (Bhag waan DAAS), a master stone carver, friend of Mohan Lal, Hindu

Dungar Shah (DOON gar Shaah), Chief Minister of the Maharana of Udaipur.

Raja Arjuna (RA ja AR jun), ruler of Mangarh.

Soma, a Hindu Brahman priest.

Shah Jahan (Shaah Ja HAAN), son of Mughal Emperor Jahangir, later Emperor himself, Muslim.

Mumtaz Mahal (MOOM taaz Maa HALL), the Emperor's beloved deceased wife.

Mukarrimat Khan (Mu KAR ri mat Khaan), head of the Emperor's building department, Muslim.

Qadir Zaman Khan (KAA dir Za MAAN Khaan), master builder from Arabia, Muslim.

Utad Isa (Us TAAD Ee saah), Turkish master draftsman/artist in Agra, Muslim.

Ram Lal (Rahm LAHL), garden designer.

Ismail Afandi (Is mail Ef fen dee), expert designer of domes, from Persia, Muslim.

SHIVAJI'S FORTUNES: The Maratha King Shivaji and the Mughal Emperor Aurangzeb

With Madho Singh in the Deccan and Agra, and in Mangarh:

Madho Singh, Rajput prince, second son of the Raja of Mangarh, Hindu.
Gopal Singh (Go PAAL Singh), Madho's cousin and chief lieutenant, Rajput, Hindu.
Prem Chand, Madho's manservant, Hindu.
Nathu Singh (Na too Singh), Madho's most experienced Rajput warrior, Hindu.
Devi Singh, experienced Rajput warrior with Madho, Hindu.
Puran Singh, young Rajput warrior with Madho, Hindu.
Ajay Singh, the youngest Rajput warrior with Madho, Hindu.
Chiranji Lal, master swordsmith in Mangarh, Hindu.

In the Deccan:

Shaista Khan (SHAI staa Khaan), Mughal viceroy of the Deccan, under Emperor Aurangzeb, Muslim.
Maharaja Jaswant Singh, Rajput ruler of Jodhpur, serving with the Mughal army.
Himmat Singh, Rajput officer from Jodhpur under Jaswant Singh.
Mirza Raja Jai Singh, Rajput ruler of Amber, general of Emperor Aurangzeb's Mughal army in the Deccan, defeated Shivaji.

Raja Shivaji (SHEE vaa jee), warrior King of the Marathas, people of the hilly regions in the Deccan Plateau, Hindu.

In Agra, protecting Shivaji:

Kumar Ram Singh (Raam Singh), son of Raja Jai Singh of Amber, charged with Shivaji's safety in Agra, Hindu.
Tej Singh (Taij Singh), Rajput officer under Ram Singh, Hindu.

In Agra, accompanying Shivaji:

Shambuji (Sham bhoo jee), Shivaji's son, Hindu.
Hirozi Farzand (Hi row zee Far zand), Shivaji's brother-in-law.
Paramanand (Parm a nand), Shivaji's court poet.

In Agra, hostile to Shivaji:

Aurangzeb, Mughal Emperor or Padshah, Muslim.
Falud Khan, also called Siddhi Falud, commandant of the Emperor's police, Muslim.
Mirza Muazzam, assistant to commandant of police, Muslim.
Rand Andaz Khan, commandant of Agra Fort, Muslim.

LOYALTY: The Founding of the Sikh Khalsa by Guru Gobind Singh

In Mangarh and/or on the journey:

Sant, young man of Jat farming caste.
Kesar, young Jat man, Sant's friend.
Bir (Beer), artist and traveler.
Hukum (Hoo kum) Sant's elder brother.
Rukmini, Hukum's young wife.
Ravana (RAA vaa na), Sant's horse.

In Anandpur and/or at Chamkaur:

Guru Gobind Rai, later Guru Gobind Singh, spiritual and military leader of the Sikhs.
Parsadi (Par SAA dee), Guru Gobind's trained elephant.
Sundari (SOON da ree), Sant's wife.
Anand (AA nand), Sant's little son through marriage.
Padmini, Kesar's wife.
Ajit Singh (A JEET Singh), the Guru's eldest son
Zorawar Singh (Zo RAA war Singh), the Guru's second son.
Daya Singh (Da YAA Singh), the first of the Five Beloved Ones, the first Sikh man initiated into the Khalsa.
Dharam Singh, the second Sikh man `of the Five Beloved Ones.
Wazir Khan (Wa ZEER Khaan), Muslim Mughal general leading the army against the Sikhs on belhalf of Emperor Aurangzeb.
Kanaiya Singh, Sikh warrior accused of aiding the enemy.
Sangat Singh, Sikh warrior.

TEMPLES TO SHIVA: The Rani of Jhansi and the Mutiny of 1857

Natesha (Na TESH a), Brahmin priest and scholar, follower of Lord Shiva.
Ganga, Natesha's longtime lover, a temple dancer and follower of Lord Shiva.
Maricha (Ma REECH), Brahmin priest, friend of Natesha.
Major Powis, British officer, friend of Natesha's.
Jemadar Heera Ram (Hee ra Raam), native cavalry lieutenant and artillery expert, a Bramin, friend of Natesha and Ganga.
Captain Oliver Hatch, British officer seeking loot, Natesha's pursuer.
Travis, British soldier serving under Captain Hatch.
Vickery, British soldier serving under Hatch.
Shankar, Brahmin servant at Jhansi.
Rani Lakshmi Bai, queen of Jhansi, Hindu, Natesha's patroness and a leader of native forces rebelling against the British.
Lakshman Rao, the Rani's Prime Minister, Hindu.
Jawahar Singh, Rajput, the Rani's army commander.
Gulam Ghaus Khan, the Rani's Afghan chiefl gunner.
Ram Chandra Deshmukh, elderly nobleman advising the Rani.
Damodar Rao, the Rani's young son.
Duleep Ram (Da LEEP Raam), Brahmin priest at Jhansi.
Rup Prasad, librarian at Jhansi, a Hindu.
Sir Hugh Rose, British general leading the army against the Rani and the other rebels.
Tatya Tope, commander of the Peshwa's native rebel army, a childhood friend of the Rani. The Peshwa, Nana Sahib, was the chief ruler of the Marathas in the revolt against the British.
Munsa Lal, commander of the gun crew Ganga joins.
Raghuvir, spongeman on the gun crew Ganga joins.
Baba Gangadas, a Hindu saint near Gwalior.
Maharaja Sangram Singh, ruler of Mangarh.

REFORMERS IN MANGARH: The Reform Movements in the Princely States

In the Mangarh area:

Ashok Chand (A SHOK Chand), male follower of Mahatma Gandhi, age 24, Hindu Arora caste of merchants and landowners from the Punjab.

Sundip Saxena (Sun DEEP), male school teacher, age 26, active in Mangarh Praja Mandal (Mangarh People's Association).

Jaya Arora (Jay a A ror aa), age 20, female college student, active in Praja Mandal, from Arora caste.

Mrs. Arora, Jaya's mother, active in Praja Mandal.

Dr. Arora, Jaya's father, medical doctor.

Manohar Jain, age 26, male from wealthy family of traders, active in Praja Mandal.

Kishore Lodha, male lawyer, age 28, president of Praja Mandal.

Karam Singh, Inspector General of Mangarh State Police, Sikh from the Punjab.

Jhakhar, sub-inspector in Mangarh State Police.

Lakshman Singh (LAX man Singh), Maharaja of Mangarh, age 28, Rajput caste.

Ram (Rahm), Untouchable Bhangi (Sweeper), age 18. Eventually father of Vijay Singh.

Manju, Ram's wife, age 16, Bhangi. Eventually Vijay Singh's mother.

Jawaharlal Nehru (Ja wa har LAAL), leader of Indian National Congress and of freedom and reform movements, age 50, later to be first Prime Minister of India.

Indira Nehru, Nehru's daughter, age 21, eventually to be Indira Gandhi after marrying Feroze Gandhi (unrelated to Mahatma Gandhi). Also eventually to become Prime Minister of India.

At Wardha:

Mohandas K. Gandhi, age 69, also respectfully called **Mahatma ("Great Soul") Gandhi**, leader of independence and reform movements.

Mahadev Desai (Ma haa dev), Mahatma Gandhi's male secretary and assistant.

In the Punjab:

Yogesh Chand, Ashok Chand's father, age 49, owner of orchards and farmland, moneylender, Arora caste.

Radha Chand, Ashok's mother, age 46.

Prabhu Chand, Ashok's brother, age 20, active in RSS, militant fundamentalist Hindu organization.

Savitri Chand (SAV ih tree Chand), Ashok's sister, age 15.

Mubarak Khan, Muslim neighbor and friend of Chand family.

Joginder Singh, Ashok's childhood Sikh friend.

MANGARH JAILS: The Reform Movements in the Princely States

Most of the characters in this story are listed in the section above for Reformers in Mangarh."
Additional characters in "Mangarh Jails" are:

In Mangarh:

Surmal (Sur MAAL), guard at Mangarh fortress jail, age 20, from Bhil tribe.
Bilado, guard at Mangarh fortress jail, age 51, from Bhil tribe.
Adinatha Seth (Aa dee naath Seth), wealthy Congress supporter from Delhi.

In Ludva Village:

Kumbharam Jat (KUM bha raam Jaat), farmer of Jat caste, age 65.
Taru Jat, farmer son of Kumbharam Jat, age 35.

At Baldeogarh:

Mangal Singh, Thakur of Baldeogarh, ruler of the largest estate in Mangarh, Rajput, age 64.

THE COSTS OF FREEDOM: Independence and the Accession of the Princely States; the Partition of India and Pakistan

Many of the characters in this story are listed in the section above for "Reformers in Mangarh," although they are all around eight years older by the time of "The Costs of Freedom."
Additional characters in this story are:

In Mangarh:

Stanley Powis, British Political Agent at Mangarh, age 42.
Ahmad Hasan Aruzi (AH mad Ha SAAN), new Dewan or Chief Minister of Mangarh State, Muslim, age 39.
Shiv, the Maharaja's manservant.

In Delhi:

Vikram Singh, Raja of Shantipur, friend of Lakshman Singh; Hindu.
Lord Louis Mountbatten, last British Viceroy of India.
Muhammad Ali Jinnah, Muslim lawyer, age 71, leader of movement to create Pakistan, first Governor General of Pakistan.
Vallabhbhai "Sardar" Patel (VAL lab bhai Pa TEL), leader of Indian National Congress, head of new Ministry of States, handling relations between the new Government of India and the princely states; Hindu.
Maniben Patel, Sardar Patel's daughter and aide.
V.P. Menon, senior civil servant, draftsman of plan to create Pakistan and Sardar Patel's chief lieutenant in the States Ministry; Hindu.

In the Punjab:

Abdul Rasool (Ab dul Ra SOOL), a Muslim refugee, young father, and nephew of Chand's neighbor Mubarak Khan.
Daljit Singh (Dal jeet Singh), elderly leader of Sikhs in Kapani village.
Jemadar Buta Singh, retired army officer, Sikh.
Dr. Krishnan, medical doctor at refugee camp.
Sant Singh, commander of refugee camp, a Sikh.
Major Turnbow, English officer serving with new Pakistani Army.

Glossary

A note on spellings:

For place names, I generally used the modern form, although sometimes I used an earlier name when it seemed appropriate in a particular story. Since even the latest events in the book take place before the adoption of "Mumbai" for Bombay, I've used "Bombay" throughout.

Many words and names from earlier historical times end in a short "a" sound. This final "a" has been dropped in modern Hindi and its dialects. Thus, for example, Rama becomes Ram, and Ashoka becomes Ashok. In each story I have usually tried to adopt the form in use during that particular historical period, although occasionally I departed from the practice for consistency and simplicity.

Also, transliteration from the Indian languages into English is only very approximate, so the same word often has two or more commonly used spellings in English. For example: *sati* and *suttee*; Shiva and Siva; Ashoka and Asoka; and Mughal, Moghul, and Mogul. In writing this book I have usually adopted the form I felt to be most common in recent writings for general audiences.

Pronunciations (when shown) are very approximate; many sounds in Indian languages do not have a corresponding sound in English. Since the book is intended mainly for a general public readership, I haven't attempted to use any of the diacritical marks that are standard in scholarly works.

accha: All right, okay.

achkan: A knee-length, high collared, tunic-like coat.

ADC: Aide-de-camp, a military officer (usually relatively young) acting as an assistant to a ruler.

Adi Granth, or *Granth Sahib*: The book containing the holy writings of the Sikhs.

Akbar: Probably the greatest of the Mughal Emperors; ruled from 1556 to 1605 C.E.

Amber: Fortress and city, the capital of the Kachhwaha Rajput clan before the capital shifted to Jaipur.

ankus (an kush): Elephant goad, usually a stick with a curved metal point on one end.

anna: Former coin worth one-sixteenth of a rupee.

Annadata: "Giver of grain"; honorific form of address for certain rulers.

amir (a MEER): A Muslim chief or nobleman ranking below a *malik* during the Sultanate. Later used for nobles in general.

Angrezi: The English people.

apsara (AAP suh rah): A nymph of Indra's heaven.

Aravallis: Range of low mountains stretching diagonally across Rajasthan.

Arora: A merchant and trader caste of the Punjab.

arti (AR tee): Worship of a god, especially by waving lights in front of the image.

Aryan: Literally "noble." Relatively light-skinned nomads—horsemen and cattle herders—who have been believed by most scholars to have invaded and conquered the Indian subcontinent c.1500-1000 B.C.E. (the theory has been increasingly questioned in recent years).

ascetic: A holy man who practices self-denial as a spiritual discipline.

Ashoka (A SHOH ka): Famous Emperor of the Mauryan dynasty; ruled almost all of the Indian subcontinent from 269 to 232 B.C.E.; credited with making Buddhism a world religion.

ashram (AASH raam): A guru's place of retreat for meditation and instructing disciples; an abode of ascetics and *sadhus*.

assalaam aleicum (uh suh LAHM oh uh LEH koom): Muslim greeting.

Aurangzeb: Mughal Emperor who ruled 1658 to 1707 C.E. An orthodox and often-intolerant Muslim, he was responsible for persecution of the Sikhs as well as Hindus.

babul: A hardwood tree, often scrubby in nature.

bagh: A garden. Used as a suffix, as in Golbagh, or "Rose Garden."

Bai: Lady; title added to women's names.

baksheesh: Largesse, a tip or bribe.

bajra: Cereal grain, a type of millet.

Bania: A small merchant, shopkeeper, or moneylender.

banyan tree: A type of fig tree; it can grow quite large, with numerous air roots and multiple trunks, which often cover a wide area.

baoli: A well.

Bapu (BAA poo): Father. Often used as a term of respect for Mahatma Gandhi by his followers.

Bapji (BAAP jee): Respected Father.

bazaar: A shopping area.

begar: Obligatory labor without pay.

B.C.E.: Before Common Era; an increasingly preferred alternative abbreviation to "B.C." (which has obvious Christianity-related connotations), even though the years are counted exactly the same way. Also see the entry for "C.E."

Benares: Banaras (Kashi in ancient times), city on the Ganges River.

betel (BEET el): The leaf used in *paan* for chewing.

Bhagavad Gita (BHA ga vad GEE ta): "Song of God," a section of the great epic *Mahabharata*, containing a long dialogue between Krishna and Arjuna, the "Bible" of Hindus.

Bhai: Brother.

Bhairava: An aspect or form of the Hindu god Shiva.

Bhangi (BHAN gee): Member of the sweeper caste; traditionally "Untouchable" scavengers and disposers of human body wastes.

Bharat: India.

Bharat Mata: Mother India.

Bharat Mata ki jai: Victory to Mother India.

bhawan: Building or house.

bhikkhu (bhik KHU): A Buddhist or Hindu monk, a mendicant.

Bhils, Bheels (Beels): Race inhabiting the hills and forests of much of western India; the aboriginal tribal people of Rajasthan.

bhisti: A water carrier.

bidi (BEE dee): Handrolled cigarette.

bigha: A measure of land area, about five-eighths of an acre or one-fourth of a hectare.

big man: A man with considerable influence or prestige or wealth.

bindi: A dot or other mark worn on the forehead by many Hindu women; it has no particular religious significance; often a matter of fashion. Sometimes erroneously called a "caste mark."

Brahma: Great god of creation; a member of the Hindu trinity.

Brahmin: Member of the highest caste, traditionally priests and scholars.

budmash (BUD mash): A criminal or bad person.

burkha (BUR kha): Head-to-toe robe worn by orthodox Muslim women; because it covers the face, it has a mesh area or eye holes to see through. Also called a chadr or chador.

Campa Cola: A popular cola soft drink.

caravanserai: An inn for caravans or travelers.

caste: A hereditary group in Hindu society, ranked in status in comparison to other castes. Traditionally, members of a caste usually marry only within the same caste, and members follow the same or similar occupations (this is increasingly changing in modern times).

C.E.: Common Era (Christian Era according to some); an increasingly preferred alternative abbreviation to A.D., which is from the Latin *anno Domini* ("in the year of our Lord") and hence connotes a reference to Jesus Christ. However, the years are counted in exactly the same way.

chai: Tea.

chaitya: A Buddhist place of worship.

Chamar (cha MAR): An Untouchable caste whose duties traditionally include working with leather.

chandalas: Untouchables who cremated dead bodies.

chappals: Heavy leather sandals.

chappati (cha PAA tee): Round, flat, thin, unleavened bread.

charan (CHAA run): Member of a particular caste of bards or poets.

char: Four.

char bagh: A formal Mughal garden with four quarters radiating from a center.

charpoy (CHAR poy): A simple cot or bedstead, usually with stringed webbing on a wood frame.

Chauhan (CHOW han): A major Rajput clan.

chhatri: A dome supported on columns (literally umbrella); often used for memorials to rulers or chiefs.

chital: A deer.

chitra shali: A picture gallery in a palace.

chowkidar (CHOWK ee daar): A watchman.

Congress: The Indian National Congress, the principal organization working to free India from British rule, and later the major political party governing the country from Independence until recent years.

crore (kror): Ten million; 100 *lakhs*.

dacoit (da COIT): Bandit, robber.

dak **bungalow**: Resthouse maintained by the government for traveling officials. "*Dak*" means "mail."

dal: Lentils.

Dalit (DAL it): Literally "Broken People," a relatively recent term for Harijans, Untouchables, or Scheduled Castes.

darshan (DAR shan): The sight of a saint, deity, ruler, or holy place.

dasas, *dasi* (DA see): A slave or black person.

Deccan: Hilly plateau region of south-central India.

devanagari (de va NAA ga ree): The script used to write Sanskrit and Hindi.

dewan (DE wan): Chief minister.

dharma: Hindu duty or divine law; a person's *dharma* is determined by his caste, sex, position in the family, etc. Also refers to the teachings of the Buddha.

dhobi (DHO bee): Washerman.

dhoti (DHO tee): A wide length of cloth, usually white, wrapped around the lower body of Hindu men; commonly worn in rural areas of northern India, and traditionally worn at home and for worship.

Divali (dih VAA lee): Hindu festival of lights in October/November.

Diwan-i-Am: Public Audience Hall in a ruler's palace.

Diwan-i-Khas: Private Audience Hall in a ruler's palace.

doab (do AB): An alluvial plain, often between two rivers.

dupatta (du PAA taa): A head scarf, often long and diaphanous.

durbar (DUR bar): A royal audience, court, or assembly.

durry: A small cotton rug.

Dussehra (Duh SAY ra): Hindu festival in October/November when the battle between Rama and Ravana from the *Ramayana* is acted out (the *Ram-lila*).

farman: An official written proclamation by a ruler.

feringhi (fer IN gee): Former term for outsiders, including Europeans or foreigners.

gadi (GAA dee): Cushion or bolster used as a ruler's throne.

Ganesha: Elephant-headed Hindu god of wisdom and good fortune. As the Remover of Obstacles, he is prayed to before major undertakings.

Ganga (GAAN gah): The Ganges River as a goddess.

garh: Fort, as in Mangarh.

gecko: A small, harmless lizard; commonly found indoors on walls in the tropics.

ghagra (GHAA gra): Full skirt commonly worn by village women of various castes in Rajasthan.

ghat (ghaat): Wide steps leading down to water for bathing; also the slopes of a range of hills.

ghee: Clarified butter, often used in a liquid form in cooking, also used in rituals.

gur: Raw brown sugar.

gurdwara: Sikh temple.

guru: Spiritual teacher or master; also a founder of the Sikh religion.

halva (HAL va): Sweet dish made from flour, sugar, and *ghee*.

Hanuman (HAA nu man): The monkey who helped Rama in the great epic *Ramayana*; later considered a god.

Hara, **Hada**: Rajput clan of Bundi and Kota in Rajasthan, a branch of the Chauhan clan.

harem: Women's quarters in a house or palace.

Harijan: Literally "child of god," Mahatma Gandhi's term for an Untouchable.

Harijan Sevak Sangh:

Hathi Pol (HAA tee pole): Elephant Gate.

haveli (ha VE lee): Large urban house or mansion.

Hawa Mahal (ha WAH ma HALL): Hall or palace of "winds," with latticed windows to catch the breeze.

Hindi: The general language of much of northern and central India.

Holi (HO lee): Major Hindu festival marking the coming of spring; people throw colored powders and water on each other.

hookah (HOOK uh): Type of pipe with a large bowl and hose, in which the tobacco or marijuana smoke is drawn through water. Also called a hubble-bubble.

howdah (HOW daa): Seat or cabin carried on the back of an elephant.

huzoor: Literally "the Presence;" "sir;" an honorific form of address.

imam (ih MAAM): Leader of prayers in a Muslim mosque.

inshallah (in sh aal LAH): "God willing."

jai: "Victory."

Jains: Religious sect founded in the 6th century B.C.E. by Mahavira. One of its emphases is on *ahimsa* or noninjury to living beings. Because this is interpreted to prevent Jains from engaging in agriculture and many other occupations, traditionally numerous Jains have been traders and (later) industrialists. Consequently, Jains as a whole are wealthy and influential out of proportion to their actual percentage of the population.

jelabi (juh LAA bee): Syrup-filled sweetmeat.

jati (JAA tee): Indigenous term for a caste.

jagir: A hereditary assignment of land granted by a ruler.

jagirdir: The holder of a *jagir*.

Jats: An agricultural caste of northern India.

jemadar (jem ma dah): A native officer in one of the British native military units; the equivalent of a second lieutenant.

ji (jee): Suffix added to a name to show respect; also used separately as "yes."

jouhar (jou HAR): Mass suicide by women, usually by fire, to avoid capture in war after a defeat.

jowar (jo WAR): A millet grain.

kanchli kurti (KANCH lee KUR tee): Traditional outfit worn by Rajput women in Rajasthan; *kanchli* refers to a bra-like piece, and *kurti* to a blouse; worn with an ankle length skirt and a long head scarf.

Kachhwaha: A Rajput clan, it ruled the former Jaipur state and Sikar. Amber was the capital before Jaipur.

kafir: An unbeliever, often a foreigner.

Kailasa (kai LASH a): Himalayan mountain, home of Lord Shiva.

kamdar: Manager or revenue agent of an estate.

kameez (ka MEEZ): A fitted tunic worn over baggy trousers by both men and women (also see *shalwar-kameez*).

karma (KAR ma): In Hinduism, Buddhism, and Jainism, the law of cause and effect in which every act results in consequences in this life or in future lives.

Kashi: Ancient name for the city of Benares or Varanasi.

khadi (KHA dee): Rough textured, hand woven cloth. Wearing it became a symbol first of opposition to British rule, and then of adherence to the Congress Party.

khan: During the Sultanate period, a nobleman of the highest rank. During the Mughal Empire, a title of distinction awarded by the Emperor. Later, many nobles began using the title as a hereditary privilege.

kharif (kha REEF): Crop of the monsoon or rainy season.

khejri (KHEJ ree): A tree common in Rajasthan's desert regions, prized for its sparse shade and its many uses, including fodder from the leaves.

kite: Hawk-like bird of prey.

kohl : Eye make-up made from charcoal.

Koran, Qur'an (Kuh RAHN): The Muslim holy book, written in Arabic.

kos: A variable unit of measure for long distances, assumed to equal approximately two miles for the purposes of this book.

Krishna: Popular Hindu god, an incarnation of Vishnu.

Kshatriya (k SHA tree ya): Member of the warrior and princely caste, ranking just below the Brahmin caste.

Kumar, Kunwar, Kumara (koo MAR): Heir of a *raja*; term used for a son during a father's lifetime.

Kumari (koo MAA ree): A princess; often a surname for a Rajput ruler's daughter.

kurta (KUR ta): Long, loose, collarless sleeved tunic or shirt.

lac: A red dye made from insect shells.

lakh: One hundred thousand.

Lakshmana: Rama's loyal half brother in the great epic the *Ramayana*. The fictional Pariyatra Rajput clan of Mangarh consider themselves descendents of Lakshmana.

lassi (LAA see): A cool drink made from yogurt, sweetened or salted.

lathi (LAA tee): Long bamboo staff with iron on the tips, used as a weapon by police.

Limca: A popular soft drink.

lingam, linga: An image of the erect male reproductive organ, often simplified and stylized, the symbol of the god Shiva.

lota: A small, round metal pot for carrying water.

Maa-Baap: "Mother and Father;" honorific term of address for certain rulers.

maha (MA ha): Prefix meaning "great."

Mahabharata (ma ha BHAA ra ta): One of the two great Hindu epics (the other is the *Ramayana).*

Mahadeva (ma ha DAYV a): "Great God," another name for Lord Shiva.

mahal (ma HALL): A palace, or an apartment within a palace.

Maharaja (ma ha RAA ja): "Great King," highest ranking of a hereditary ruler of a Hindu princely state.

Maharajkumar: Son of a Maharaja.

Maharana (ma ha RAA na): Ruler of the princely state of Mewar or Udaipur.

mahatma: "Great soul," a person revered for wisdom and selflessness. The term can be used before a name as an honorary title, as with Mohandas K. Gandhi being called Mahatma Gandhi.

Mahadeva: the Great God, a term applied to Shiva.

Mahavira: Founder of the Jain religion, a contemporary of the Buddha.

mahout (ma HOOT): An elephant driver.

maidan (my darn): An open park, field, or plain.

maithuna: A sculpture on a temple depicting a sexual union.

mali (MAA lee): A gardener.

malik (MAA lik): During the Sultanate of Delhi, a nobleman ranking above an *amir* and below a *khan*. During Mughal times, it often meant a *zemindar* or large landlord. Later broadened to mean a "master" or landowner-employer.

mandapa (MAN da pa): Hall of a Hindu temple, usually pillared.

mandir (MAN deer): Temple or palace.

Mangarh (MAAN gar): In this book, a city and state in the Rajasthan region. "Man" means "respect" or "prestige;" "garh" means "fort."

mansab: A rank of an officer in the Mughal army, described by the number of horses or cavalrymen the person was entitled to command.

mantra (MAAN tra): A repetitious prayer or incantation or a verse. The words have mystical or magical powers.

Maratha (ma RAA ta: Native of the Deccan.

Marwar: "Land of the Dead," desert region that was the kingdom of the Rathore Rajput clan of Jodhpur.

Masterji: A respectful title for a school teacher.

Mauryan: The dynasty and empire founded c. 323 B.C.E. by Chandragupta Maurya, at its height in his grandson Ashoka Maurya's rule, 269 to 232 B.C.E.

mekhala (mek HA la): A girdle worn around the waist in earlier eras.

mela (ME la): A festival or fair.

Mewar: Formerly the kingdom of the Sisodia Rajput clan of Udaipur.

minaret: Tower in a mosque from with the Muslim faithful are called to prayer.

mleccha (mlech a): Foreigner, impure or unclean. Sometimes formerly used by

Hindus referring to a foreigner such as a Muslim invader.

mohur (MO hur): Obsolete gold coin.

moti (MO tee): Pearl.

mudra (MOO dra): A hand gesture with meaning or symbolism, as in worship or dancing or drama.

muezzin (moo EZ in): Person who calls Muslims to prayer five times a day from a mosque.

mugger (MUG ger): A crocodile.

Mughal (MOH gul): Also Moghul, Mogul. Term for the Muslim dynasty which ruled most of India from the 1500s to the 1700s.

mullah (MOO lah): Muslim priest.

mujra (MOOJ ra): A formal salutation.

munshi (MOON shee): A clerk.

nagar (NA gar): Town.

namaste, namaskar: The traditional Hindu greeting, meaning "I bow to you in respect." The palms of the hands are pressed together and the head bowed as if in prayer.

Nandi: The bull on which Lord Shiva rides. A statue of Nandi is common in Shiva temples.

nazar (NA zar): Gifts or coins offered to a ruler on ceremonial occasions as tribute or tokens of respect or allegiance.

neem: An aromatic tree with a fine, comb-like foliage. Its leaves are a natural insecticide; twigs are used for brushing teeth.

nimbu pani (nim boo PAA nee): A popular cold drink made with lime juice or lemon juice, water, and a syrup or honey.

Nirvana: Buddhist term for Enlightenment.

niwas (NEE was): An abode, small palace, or apartment in a palace.

obeisance (English word): A body posture such as bowing and touching the ground or stretching oneself out on the floor to show honor or submission to a ruler or other person of high rank or respect. The exact requirements varied with the particular situations and time periods.

odhni (ODH nee): Also *orhni;* the shawl or long veil worn by Rajasthani women over the head.

paan: Also *pan*; a chew of betel leaf wrapped around slaked lime, areca nut, and spices.

Padshah (PAD shaah): Emperor.

pallav (PAL lav): The portion of a sari that is left over after wrapping the body. Usually draped over the shoulder, sometimes it is first pleated and then pinned into position.

palanquin: A covered litter for conveying wealthy or prestigious persons, usually carried by four or more men. Also called a *palki*.

panch: Five.

panchayat (PAN cha yat): A committee which decides or governs village or caste affairs, traditionally with five members.

panch **witnesses**: Citizens recruited to act as impartial observers of a government raid.

pandit (PUN dit): A Hindu scholar, wise man, teacher. The term is often used before a name as an honorary title, as in Pandit Nehru.

Panditji (Pun dit jee): Honorific form of *pandit*. Often used as a term of respectful address to Jawaharlal Nehru.

pani (PAA nee): Water.

Pariyatra (pa ree YAA tra): Early name for the Aravalli mountains; in this book, the Rajput clan, with its home territory of Mangarh state.

peon: An office boy or messenger.

Peshwa: Head ruler of the Marathas.

pi (pee) dog: Abbreviation of *pariah* for common mongrel dogs.

pindaris: Roving bands of raiders.

pipal (PEE pal): A sacred fig tree; the Bo tree of the Buddhists.

pir: Muslim saint or religious teacher.

pol: A gate.

Praja Mandal: People's Association.

prasad: Food blessed by a priest in a temple.

puja (POO jaa): Hindu worship or ritual to a deity.

pukka PUK ka): Proper or strong, so a *pukka* road is a paved one, and a *pukka* house is one of brick rather than mud.

pundit: See *pandit*.

punkah PUN ka): A ceiling fan; in earlier times, it was often a large, hanging flap of cloth operated by hand or foot by pulling a rope.

pur (pour): A city, as in Jaipur, Udaipur, Jodhpur.

Puranas: Ancient Hindu sacred texts of historical myths and legends, dealing with the lives and exploits of gods and goddesses.

purdah: The veiling of women and/or their seclusion in homes.

qazi (KA zee): A judge.

Qur'an, Quran, Qu'ran (Kuh RAHN): Alternate, more currently preferred, transliteration for Koran.

rabi: Crop of the winter or dry season.

raga (RAa ga): An instrumental music piece.

Raj (RAAJ): Reign; British rule in India.

Raja (RAA ja): A king or ruler inferior in rank to a Maharaja, which means lit. "great king."

Rajasthan (RAJ as tahn): "The land of kings," the name for the modern state which encompasses the former princely states of the Rajputana region of northwestern India.

Rajasthani: Language spoken in the Rajputana or Rajasthan region; its many local dialects are considered to be variations of Hindi.

rajkumari (raj ku MA ree): A daughter of a Raja; a princess.

Rajput (RAAJ poot): Literally the son of a king; a Hindu of certain clans of the Kshatriya or warrior caste in northern, western, and central India.

Rajputana: Name given by the British to a region ruled mostly by Rajputs in northwestern India, west of Delhi. Most of it later became the state of Rajasthan.

Rama (RAA ma): Hero of the *Ramayana*, a prince who is an incarnation of the god Vishnu, idealized by Hindus as the embodiment of a dutiful, selfless, dedicated ruler.

Ramayana (Raa MAA ya na): Great epic poem; its hero is Rama and its heroine is his wife Sita. In the epic, the demon Ravana kidnaps Sita, and Rama must recover her from Ravana's palace on the island of Lanka.

Ram Rajya: The reign of Rama as King, a legendary ancient golden age. Often said to be the ideal toward which a ruler should aim.

ram, ram (raam raam): A form of Hindu greeting, saying the name of Lord Rama.

rani (RAA nee): A queen, wife of a raja. Maharani is the wife of a Maharaja.

Rana (RA na): Title of the ruler of Rajput state of Mewar or Udaipur.

rasa (RA sa): Flavor or sentiment, a particular emotion that a piece of art arouses in the viewer.

Rathor or Rathore: Rajput clan ruling Jodhpur and Bikaner.

Rig-Veda: See Vedas.

rissaldar: An native Indian officer commanding a cavalry troop.

roti (RO tee): Round, flat, thin, unleavened bread; commonly made from *bajra* grain in the Mangarh region.

RSS or **RSSS**: The Rashtriya Swayamsevak Sangh, or National Service Society, a militant Hindu revival organization.

rupee (ROO pee): Abbreviated Rs.; the standard unit of Indian currency. In the mid-1970s, worth roughly fourteen U.S. cents (seven rupees to one U.S. dollar).

sabha (SAA bha): An assembly.

sacred thread: The cord worn over the shoulder and across the chest by males of the three upper Hindu classes, awarded to them as boys in initiation ceremonies.

sadhu (SAA dhu): A Hindu ascetic, often a wandering holy man.

sagar (SA gar): A lake.

sahib: Also *saheb* (Approximately pronounced suh HIHB or SA'ab). A term of respectful address to a superior, similar to the English "sir." Applied to European men in India, but also to natives of higher status, in which case when used in Hindi after a person's name it roughly means "Mister."

salaam (sa LAAM): A respectful greeting.

sama: Music and dancing of the *sufis*.

samand: A reservoir.

sambhar (SAM bhar): A large deer.

samosa (sa MO sa): A pastry filled with vegetables or meat.

sannyasin (sann YA sin): An ascetic who has renounced worldly life to follow a spiritual discipline.

Sanskrit: The classical ancient language of India (except for the south); studied in schools and used in rituals; otherwise no longer spoken.

Sarasvati: The Hindu goddess of the arts and learning.

sardar: Rajput chief, nobleman or lord; a form of address for a Sikh man ("*sardarji*"), roughly equivalent to Mr. or Esquire; an honorary title of leadership applied to Villabhbhai Patel.

sari (SAA ree): Also *saree*; draped traditional women's garment, it consists of six or more yards of a single length of fabric. The style of wrapping varies from region to region.

sarpanch: Elected head of a village.

sati (SA tee): Also *suttee*; the self-sacrifice of a woman on her husband's funeral pyre. Also refers to a woman who has done so.

Sat Shri Akal: Sikh greeting and rallying cry: "God is Truth!"

satyagraha: Mahatma Gandhi's form of civil disobediance or noncooperation.

sepoy: A native infantry soldier. Also used generically to cover all native soldiers. A corruption of the Hindustani *sipahi*.

serai (se RAI): An inn for travelers.

Shah Jahan: Mughal Emperor who ruled from 1628 to 1658 C.E. He ordered the Taj Mahal built as a tomb for his deceased wife Mumtaz Mahal. In his final years he was imprisoned by his son Aurangzeb, who usurped the throne.

shaikh (sheek): A Muslim mystic spiritual teacher.

shalwar (shahl WAHR): Baggy trousers.

shalwar kameez (shahl WAHR kuh MEEZ): Also *kamiz-salvar*; women's outfit of baggy trousers and long shirt or tunic; originally from the Punjab, it has spread to much of India; commonly worn by Muslim village women in Rajasthan.

shamiana: An open-sided tent pavilion.

sharbat: A syrupy fruit drink, frequently served cool or mixed with crushed ice. Often translated as "sherbet."

sharia (sha ree YAA): Muslim religious law.

shastra: A sacred text or treatise on a subject.

sheesh mahal: Lit. "hall of mirrors," a hall with its walls and ceiling covered with thousands of tiny mirror pieces.

shikar: Hunting.

shikhara (shi KHAR ra): The tower of a Hindu temple in northern India.

shilpa shastra: Sacred text on architecture.

Shiva (SHEE va): Great god of destruction and re-creation, a member of the Hindu trinity. He is usually symbolized in temples by a stone *lingam*. He is also often represented as Nataraja, the Lord of the Dance, with the dance representing creative energy. He rides on the bull Nandi. His wife is called by various names in her different aspects, including Parvati, Kali, and Durga. Shiva is often called by other names, such as Mahadeva, "Great God."

Shivaji: Deccan ruler who unified the Marathas and resisted conquest by Mughal Emperor Aurangzeb; lived 1627 to 1680 C.E.

shraddha (shraad): Ceremonies in honor of the dead.

Shudra: The lowest of the four Hindu broad classes, traditionally servants and manual laborers.

Sikh religion, Sikhism: The faith established in the 15th century by Guru Nanak and continued by his nine successor Gurus, ending with Guru Gobind Singh. Sikhs believe in one God, and a sacred text, the *Granth Sahib*. Their temples are called *gurdwaras*. Most men wear beards and turbans and use the surname "Singh" ("Lion"); women use the surname "Kaur" ("Princess"). Sikhs are concentrated in their homeland of the Punjab region of northwest India, but many have migrated elsewhere.

Singh, Sinha, Simha: "Lion," a last name adopted by Rajputs and by male Sikhs, as well as by others.

Sisodia (shi sho dee a): The Rajput clan ruling the former state of Mewar, including its capitals of Udaipur and Chittor.

Sita (SEE ta): Hindu goddess; Rama's wife and the heroine of the *Ramayana*. Considered as an example of the ideal wife because of her selflessness and loyal devotion to her husband.

sitar (SI tahr): Stringed musical instrument.

sowar: A trooper of Indian cavalry.

stambha: A pillar or tower.

stupa: A masonry-covered hemispherical mound of earth, tumulus-like, containing Buddhist relics.

Swaraj: Home Rule or Self Rule.

swayambhu lingam: A naturally occurring, self-generated *lingam*, considered to be part of the pattern of the universe and thus most holy as an object of worship.

sufi: Muslim mystic and ascetic.

Sultan: Originally the equivalent of a Muslim king or emperor. The title later degenerated until rulers of even very small territories called themselves sultans.

sura (SU ra): An alcoholic drink in Vedic times.

svayamvara (svay YAM va ra): "Self-choosing," in which a princess would choose a husband from a gathering of suitors after a contest.

swami: A holy man or spiritual teacher, an advanced member of a religious order.

tabla (TAA bla): A small drum.

tank: An artificially constructed pond or lake.

tanka: A unit of currency during the Sultanate.

tapas (TA pas): Literally, "heat." Ascetic practices, hardships and austerities designed to conserve one's energies to be focused in desired channels.

taslim (tas LEEM): A form of obeisance to a ruler in which one touches the ground and then places the palm of the hand on one's head.

thali (TA lee): A circular metal plate used to serve food.

Thakur (TAAK er): Local ruler or village lord.

thikana (ti KAN a): A hereditary estate, sometimes quite large, headed by a Thakur.

thug (tug): Member of a religious fraternity of professional assassins who garroted their victims, usually travelers, as offerings to the goddess Bhavani. The practice (*thugee*) is said to have been eliminated by the British in the 19th century.

tilak (TIL ak): Mark of blessing or caste made on the forehead with a colored paste. Applied to the forehead of a ruler at the time of coronation, sometimes with blood.

tonga (TAAN guh): A horse-drawn, two-wheeled carriage.

torana (tor RAN a): A gate or archway.

tulsi (TUL see): A basil plant, sacred to the god Vishnu.

turban: Traditional men's headwear; a long length of cloth wrapped many times around the head. Worn now mainly in villages, and by Sikhs. The styles of wrapping traditionally varied from area to area and with the wearer's status.

Untouchables: Persons so low in social ranking as to be traditionally considered outside the caste system. Close contact with them is said to "pollute" persons of many higher castes. Although the practice is now illegal, it continues in many rural areas.

ulema: The experts in Muslim religious law.

Upanishads (oo pa NISH shads): Books of Hindu philosophy and metaphysical speculation, probably composed c. 800 to 300 B.C.E.

urs: Festival at the anniversary of the death of a Muslim saint.

ustad (us TAD): The master of a craft.

vaidya: Physician.

Vaishya: The third in status of the four broad Hindu classes, below the Brahmins and Kshatriyas, but above the Shudras; traditionally traders, businessmen, and artisans.

Varanasi (va ra NA see): Alternate name for the city of Kashi, the great Hindu pilgrimage center, Anglicized as "Benares."

varna: One of the four traditional major class divisions; the four *varnas*—Brahmins, Kshatriyas, Vaishyas, and Shudras—were each subdivided into many castes (*jatis*) and subcastes.

vastu shastra: A text on architecture.

Vedas: Lit. "revealed wisdom." The earliest and most sacred scriptures of the Hindus, probably composed c. 1500-900 B.C. The ***Rig Veda*** consist of religous poetry; the ***Sama Veda*** of hymns; the ***Yajur Veda*** is a priests' manual of ceremonies; and the ***Atharva Veda*** consists of magical spells.

vihara (vi HA ra): A Buddhist monastery, with living quarters.

vina (VEE na): A popular stringed instrument.

Vishnu: A great god, the preserver of the universe, member of the Hindu trinity. To set things right on earth, he is said to have incarnated as an avatar in a material body nine times—including as the Buddha, Krishna, Rama, and Jesus Christ. He rides on Garuda, a huge bird.

yaar: "Friend."

yogi: A Hindu ascetic; practitioner of yoga.

yoga: A system of exercises or meditation with the goal of gaining control of the mind and body. There are many different variations.

yuvraja (YUV ra ja): An heir apparent, crown prince (of a Hindu state).

zamindar, zemindar (ZAA min daar): Landlord of a large estate.

zenana (ze NAA na): Women's living quarters or harem; usually entry was forbidden to males except children and close relatives.

zindabad: "Long live."

Acknowledgments

In America

My wife Sandra has been incredibly supportive, patient, accepting, and tolerant of me and my work over the years as this book grew into a much longer and more demanding project than either of us anticipated. My family and friends in general have shown interest throughout. Our son Shaun has been encouraging about my writing projects, despite my often being so busy with them. My sister Gale has been an enthusiastic promoter of sales of my books, and her husband Marcel has also been a strong supporter. My sister-in-law and brother-in-law, Karen and Asko Hamalainen, have loyally attended my slide show and reading events.

I was highly fortunate in having the entire manuscript of this book read by Dr. Adil Godrej, who grew up in India and attended college in Rajasthan, and who generously gave me numerous detailed and valuable insights.

Dr. Louis E. Fenech of the University of Northern Iowa kindly reviewed and provided valuable feedback on the story "Loyalty" about the Sikhs, his area of historical expertise.

Johnny Douglass, wonderful long time friend, good neighbor, and astute reader, gave helpful comments on "The Master Buiilder." Catherine Bennett, Elisabeth Green Streeter, Paige Seaborg, and Carla Phillips, all of whom I met through on online group interested in Indian books and films, have given me useful feedback on various stories.

The book is also far better because of encouragement and editorial help, on early drafts, from a number of local writer friends. Melinda Bell Howard, Janet Fisk, and Rudy Martin gave regular, insightful advice as well as much needed moral support over the years. Other accomplished local book authors who commented on various parts and provided encouragement include Thom Jones, Judy Olmstead, Tom Maddox, Claire Davis, and Dennis Held. Gene Barker, Ruth Ann Lonardelli, Beth Fern, Keith Eisner, and Tom Grissom also provided useful feedback.

Our long time friend Yagya Sharma gave me the benefit of his Hindi and Sanskrit knowledge, as well as relating his experiences at Partition when he was stranded at college in Lahore during the troubles. Our good friend Zahid Shariff helped with the Muslim perspective, especially on "Master Builder," and with relating some of the troubles he and his family underwent at Partition. Friends Umesh and Veena Vasisth have shared with me their experiences growing up in India and their own difficulties in Lahore at Partition.

I greatly appreciated proofreading help for typographical errors from Pam Davidson, Miriam Foster, Carol Horner, Karl and Leslie Johnson, Fred Kellogg, Scott and Pam Mullins, Debby Porter, Emily Ray, Rita Robison, Glen

Scroggins, Peter and Ginny Taylor, and Wim and Rae Verhoef. Considerable and generous additional help on proofreading earlier work came from the late and dearly missed Surain af Sandeburg, from Rain (Robert) af Sandeburg, and from Frederick Su.

Our good Sikh friend Charanjit Singh Sodhi has long been helpful, and his father, H.K.S. Sodhi, was a thoughtful and hospitable host on a recent stay in Delhi. Friends Har K."Kris" and Suman Gupta helped in many ways, including contacts both in India and locally. Jagdish and Shanti Rohila greatly helped with contacts in India. Raj Laksmi Phoha gave me useful background information about her life in India. Purshotham Singh Mokha provided useful information about Sikhs. Many other persons originally from India, including friends involved with People for Progress in India of Seattle, have also helped.

I could not have written nearly as detailed a book without convenient access to the extensive collection of books related to India in the Suzzallo Library at the University of Washington in Seattle. Many of those books were provided by the Library of Congress Special Foreign Currency Program. Irene Joshi, formerly the South Asian Librarian at the University of Washington, was helpful on a number of occasions. Locally, I made extensive use of the Olympia Timberland Library; the Washington State Library; and The Evergreen State College Library.

Through Dr. Ann Godzins Gold of Syracuse University, author of the wonderfully insightful *Fruitful Journeys: The Ways of Rajasthani Pilgrims*, I became associated with the Rajathan Studies Group, several members of which have given me useful help. Dr. Lloyd I. Rudolph of the University of Chicago provided valuable advice related to names of Rajput royalty. Dr. Lindsey B. Harlan of Connecticut College, author of another book I found helpful, *Religion and Rajput Women*, gave advice on clothing of young Rajput noble women.

I am indebted to the late James A. Michener's historical novels, especially *The Source*, for the concept of the organizing format for the book.

In India

Col. K. Fateh Singh and his wonderful wife Indu have been incredibly helpful hosts during a number of stays at their Megh Niwas Hotel in Jaipur. Colonel Singh has been responsible for many of my best contacts in Rajasthan and much of my knowledge about Rajput life. He has been an excellent guide on excursions to villages and other sites in the Jaipur region. Indu Singh provided useful information from her own childhood as the daughter of a major Rajput thakur. Their sons Udai and Ajay have also been helpful.

Jaivir Singh and his delightful wife Ila have hosted me in their impressive family fortress at Palaitha in the Kota area. Jaivir's father, Lt. Gen. K. Bahadur Singh, and mother, and many other family members welcomed us in Kota. Jaivir is a concerned citizen, knowledgeable about wildlife, and he has been a good friend, a valuable source of contacts and of information about Rajput life and farming, and an excellent guide during excursions around Kota and Bundi and at Ranthambhor Wildlife Refuge.

Jagdish Parikh of Mumbai, a good friend and a philosopher with a social conscience, has been the source of many stimulating conversations. He and his family were excellent and helpful hosts in Mumbai. Our good friends Kamal and Mita Parekh and family, including daughter Radhi Parekh, have been extremely generous and helpful hosts in the Mumbai area.

Our longtime friend Arya Bhushan ("A.B.") Bhardwaj, founder of Gandhi-in-Action, has been helpful and inspiring in talking of Gandhian work and modern politics, including background information about the period of Emergency when he was jailed for his own activities. He and his wife Rani and son Kapil have been most hospitable during our visits with them in New Delhi.

In the Jodhpur area, L.C. Tyagi and wife Shashi Tyagi, the inspiring founders of Gramin Vikas Vigyan Samiti or Gravis, have taken us on tours of the organization's impressive projects to help the rural poor in the deserts. Their Dr. Prakash Tyagi and his wife Dr. Vasundhara welcomed us on a tour of the organization's new hospital at Tinwari. Dr. R. P. Dhir and wife Usha were helpful and hospitable both on a desert tour of Gravis projects and in Jodhpur.

Balwant Singh Mehta of Udaipur, an energetic worker in the freedom and reform movements from the 1920s onward, and later a draftsman of the Indian Constitution and holder of high government posts, gave me both useful background information and inspiration. His son Bhagwant Singh Mehta assisted us in many ways, including escorting us on a visit to a Bhil village and arranging for Surmal, a Bhil student, as a helpful guide. Grandson Sandeep Mehta, yoga and meditation teacher, took us on an interested and enjoyable visit to Tapovan Ashram, where we were also welcomed and hosted by managing trustee Dr. R. C. Mehta.

Brigadier Jagmal Singh Rathore, proprietor of the fine Hotel Shri Ram in Bikaner, was generous with his time and knowledge in showing us around that area and answering many questions, and his son Yogendra and the rest of the family were very hospitable.

In Udaipur, the late R.S. Ashia, Curator of the Bhartiya Lok Kala Mandal (Folk Museum) in Udaipur, was a helpful and generous friend, and he and his wife and family were very hospitable. I miss him greatly.

Thakur Sajjan Singh of Ghanerao, another charming host, provided much useful information about life in the headquarters of an important *thikana* on our we stays in his interesting Ghanerao Royal Castle hotel.

Mr. B.B. Palekar of Mumbai, who became a friend through correspondence, was extremely generous and helpful in providing me with details of the organization and operation of the Income Tax Department. Any errors in interpreting those details are of course my own, and he bears no responsibility whatsoever for the subject matter or the plot of the story or the characters depicted. Mr. Palekar also introduced me by mail to Mr. Ramdas Bhatkal, former Managing Director of the Mumbai publishing house Popular Prakashan Pvt. Ltd., who was helpful with information about the Emergency period.

An Income Tax Department official in a Rajasthan city was extremely generous in providing background information about the workings of the department and about the organization of tax raids. He preferred to remain anonymous, but I nevertheless greatly appreciated his detailed and valuable assistance.

Long before I thought of depicting income tax officials in my novel, we visited both the office and the home of Ballwant Singh, an Income Tax Commissioner (now retired) in New Delhi, and his wife and family. Although he was a direct source for income tax information, the background details from visits with him were most helpful, as were other useful contacts through him at that time.

I have had interesting conversations with Rawat Nahar Singh and wife and family while staying at their excellent Deogarh Mahal palace hotel in Deogarh; with Rao Sahib Narendra Singh at his interesting Castle Bijaipur hotel in Bijaipur; and with Dr. Onkar Singh Rathore and son Jitendra Rathore at the excellent Hotel Rampratap Palace in Udaipur.

Mr. Verma, Chief Instructor of the Western Railway Training School in Udaipur, gave a helpful demonstration of the railway switching systems, using a fascinating model railroad.

Amrendra Singh, proprietor of the well-run Chandralok Hotel near Saheli Bagh in Udaipur, was a helpful host during our stays at the hotel.

Ashwani Singh Chauhan was a helpful and cooperative driver on our most recent tour of Rajasthan.

Darshan Singh Bhinder has been a helpful source of information about Sikhs, as well as a good friend, guide, and host. He and his family have entertained us on many visits in Delhi and Agra.

Bhagwan Singh Sodha was a very helpful and genial guide in Jaisalmer. His brother Tane Singh Sodha, their mother, and other residents were most hospitable in their desert village of Khuri. Kr. Teej Singh spent considerable time showing me around his family's manor house and the village of Mundota near Jaipur.

The following people have been hosts in whose homes we stayed. Most of them went far above the call of duty in treating both myself and members of my family royally, and I learned much from them which I have used as background in the book: Dharam Veer Parihar and family in Jodhpur; Gyan and Madhu Narula and their children Manju, Alok, and Vivek in Navin Shahdara, Delhi; and their neighbor Gopal Krishna Arora, his daughter Deepti, and family; Dr. Shakuntala Deshpande and her husband and family, and Dr. Subi Chitale and Ashok Chitale and family, all in Indore; Dr. S.N. Mehrotra and wife and family in Gwalior; Mrs. Shankarkumar Sanyal and family at the headquarters of the Harijan Sevak Sangh in Calcutta; Y.D. Sharma and family in Ajmer, his son Desh Bandhu Sharma in particular, and their tenant, P.R. Chaturvedi.

The late Yaduendra Sahai, Director of the Maharaja Sawai Man Singh II Museum in Jaipur, was quite helpful, especially in teaching me some characteristics of old manuscripts.

A large number of other people kindly hosted us in their homes for meals and/or significantly helped us in other ways; I have learned something from each of them.

A Note on the Type

The text is Times New Roman, for readability and compactness. Subheadings and running heads are Zapf Chancery Bold BT and Demi BT, copyright 1990-93 by Bitstream Inc. Main titles and illustration captions are Rebound ttnorm, copyright 1994 by ImageLine, Inc. The wording of signs is denoted by Arial. The use of these fonts is gratefully acknowledged.

About the Author

Gary Worthington has done extensive research over a period of two decades on major historical periods of South Asia. He and his wife Sandra have traveled extensively in India and elsewhere.

His wide range of interests include personal spiritual growth, graphic arts, and the night sky, as well as numerous social and environmental issues and vegetarianism. He designed the home he and his wife live in, on a forested site near Olympia, Washington. An adult son, Shaun, lives elsewhere.

In his legal career, he has been a lawyer in private practice, for the Washington State House of Representatives, as an officer in the U.S. Navy, and more recently helping develop the unique new Cama Beach State Park on a historic waterfront resort site formerly operated by his wife's family on Camano Island, Washington.

He strongly encourages your comments regarding this book. Please write to him in care of the publisher, or else by e-mail through his Web site: www.GaryWorthington.com.

His Web site includes personal tips on traveling and other information related to India.

For some suggestions regarding organizations working in India, please see the next page.

Some Organizations Working in India
Recommended by Gary Worthington

Many fine non-governmental organizations (NGOs) are working to help improve societal and environmental conditions in India. A given amount of money usually stretches much farther in India, helping far more people, than the same amount of funds would if it were spent in the Western world.

Unfortunately, some NGOs in India do not use their funds well or are scams, so it's wise to carefully evaluate an organization before sending it money.

The following NGOs are ones I have had personal contact with and that I feel are effective. All have information about themselves on their Web sites. Many, many other organizations do good work but are not listed because I don't have sufficient personal experience with them.

People for Progress in India (PPI) is a Seattle, Washington based organization funding relatively small-scale projects in India that help people become economically self-reliant. PPI is run entirely by volunteers, so almost all funds go directly to the projects in India. Address: P.O. Box 51231, Seattle, WA 98114. Web site, with a list of current projects: www.ppi-usa.org

Gramin Vikas Vigyan Samiti (GRAVIS) is an organization based in Jodhpur, Rajasthan, working to assist the rural poor of Rajasthan's Thar Desert region. It has a wide range of programs, including schools and a hospital, but most of the work is in the farming villages themselves. Address: 458, Street No. 3, Milk Man Colony, Pal Road, Jodhpur, Rajasthan 342 008, India. Web site: www.gravis.org.in

ASHA for Education has many chapters in both America and India. It funds mainly educational projects. Web site: www.ashanet.org

SERVAS is a worldwide organization promoting peace and international understanding through stays in the homes of volunteer hosts. India has around 650 hosts who are interested in having foreign visitors stay with them at no charge, in order to get to know them and to introduce them to Indian culture. The normal stay is two nights, but guests may be invited to stay longer. Travelers and hosts join through the branch of SERVAS in their own country after an application and a screening interview and paying a membership fee. Upon paying a refundable deposit, travelers receive a directory of hosts in the country they plan to visit, with background information on the hosts and their families. SERVAS also has hosts in around 130 other countries. Contact information is on the SERVAS International Web site: www.servas.org
The United States SERVAS Web site is at: www.usservas.org

Centre for Science and Environment (CSE), based in New Delhi (Web site: www.cseindia.org) has an online magazine called **Down to Earth** with good articles and editorials on current India-related social and environmental issues. Web site: www.downtoearth.org.in

Quick Order Form
India Fortunes and India Treasures

Orders are shipped within 24 hours from New Hampshire. For expedited shipping or international orders, request additional information.

Order toll free: 800-345-6665. Have your Visa or MasterCard ready.
Secure online orders: www.TimeBridgesPublishers.com
Mail orders: Pathway Book Service, 4 White Brook Road, Gilsum NH 03448
Fax orders: 603-357-2073. Fax this filled-out form if you wish.
International phone orders: 603-357-0236

Ordered by:
Name _____
Address _____ .
_____ Zip _____
Phone number: _____ - _____ - _____
Email address: _____ (in case of questions)

Ship to: (Only if different from above)
Name _____
Address _____
_____ Zip _____

Please send the following copies of :
India Fortunes:

_____copies	**Paperback**	**$15.95 each**	$ _____
_____copies	**Hardcover**	**$26.95 each**	$ _____

India Treasures:

_____copies	**Paperback**	**$15.95 each**	$ _____

Add shipping: $3.95 for first book
($1.50 each additional book) $ _____
WA State residents: add 8% sales tax _____

TOTAL $ _____

Payment:
____**Cheque enclosed**   **Credit Card:** ____Visa ____MasterCard
Card number: _____ Expir. date _____
Name on card: _____

Your signature _____

To contact **TimeBridges Publishers** direct, for information only:
1001 Cooper Pt. Rd. SW, Ste. 140-#176, Olympia, WA 98502
Phone: 360-867-1883; Fax: 360-867-1221
info@timebridgespublishers.com